# Fade Into You

*The Complete Series*

Dakota Willink

Dragonfly Ink Publishing

# Praise for the Fade Into You Series

"A beautifully written novel about first love and heartbreak."
**— Tamara Lush, RITA Finalist**

"A breathtaking blend of passion, heartbreak, and healing, where every page pulses with raw emotion and unforgettable chemistry. It's a gripping journey of love and redemption that lingers long after the final chapter." **— Mia's Book Blog**

"Dakota Willink gives you all the feels and stolen moments you crave!"
**— Crystal's Book World**

"Dakota brought me back to that feeling of finding my soulmate. Every glance, every touch, and every heartbreak felt achingly real." **— Not Your Moms Romance**

"A soul-stirring journey of love, longing, and deeply relatable characters. Dakota's powerful storytelling is emotional and irresistibly addictive." **— Once Upon a Romance Blog**

"This is a book that will stick with me for years to come."
**— Magic Beyond The Covers Book Blog**

# Also By Dakota Willink

**SHAMELESS BILLIONAIRE CLUB**

(Billionaire Dark Romance)

**THE STONE SAGA**

Heart of Stone

Stepping Stone

Set In Stone

Wishing Stone

Breaking Stone

**TRUSTFALL TRILOGY**

Take Me Under

Take Me Darkly

Take Me Forever

---

**FADE INO YOU SERIES**

Untouched (New Adult Romance)

Defined (Second Chance Romance)

Endurance (Sports Romance)

---

**STAND ALONE BOOKS**

The Sound of Silence (Dark Romantic Thriller)

Untouched

Dakota Willink, LLC

*This book is an original publication of Dakota Willink, LLC*



Library of Congress Cataloging-in-Publication Data
Untouched | Copyright © 2019 by Dakota Willink
Defined | Copyright © 2019 by Dakota Willink
Endurance | Copyright © 2021 by Dakota Willink



Cover design by Dragonfly Ink Publishing
Copyright © 2022

# Untouched

## Fade Into You Book 1

**He was a gorgeous troublemaker with a cocky attitude.**
**She was the girl he shouldn't want.**
**They only had one summer—and a promise to have no regrets.**

I wasn't prepared to meet a girl like Cadence.
She was shy and innocent, and nothing like the girls who usually flocked my doorstep.
But how could I resist her mile-long blond hair and emerald eyes?
I knew I shouldn't want her.
The rest of my life had already been decided for me.
A summer fling shouldn't have happened.
But it did.
Now the clock is counting down until I have to return home to hell that awaits me.
As September draws near, I get closer and closer to losing everything I never thought I wanted—her.

*Dedicated to the strong women who have dared to be powerful, brave, confident, and fearless. You'll never have today again, so keep making it count!*

"Not even the brightest future can make up for the fact that no roads lead back to what came before–to the innocence of childhood or the first time we fell in love."

—Jo Nesbo

# Prologue

*Washington D.C.*
*16 Years Ago*

Rain slashed through the night sky, the fierce wind causing water droplets to pelt against the windows in angry torment. The storm was a force of nature, one strong enough to match the pain that raged through my body. In agony, I screamed, my cry louder than the thunder that boomed outside.

Voices called out around me, the sound a distant echo in my mind. I didn't know if it was because I couldn't hear them, or if it was simply, I didn't want to hear them. The scent of antiseptic was pungent in the air, but I barely smelled it. I could only focus on the pain. The pain in my heart. In my body. I couldn't decide where it hurt the most. I only knew I ached all over from the fire that lashed through me.

I whimpered in misery as more molten heat erupted inside me, the pain so severe, I thought I might rip in two. An unexplainable urge to escape came over me. I knew this day would come, but I didn't know if I could endure it for much longer. Tears clouded my vision, blurring the shapes throughout the bright white room as a barrage of questions ran through my mind.

*When would it end? What about when it was all over? Could I go through each day facing the reminder of something I could never have?*

The questions terrified me, and they were ones that played in my mind for the better part of a year. I didn't know if I wanted to do this. I didn't know if I *could* do this. I wanted to believe I could survive, but I wasn't sure if I had the strength to get through it. Somewhere in my mind, I knew the physical agony was only temporary. But I also knew the torment in my heart would never fade.

The knives tearing at my back and abdomen seemed to subside, allowing me a moment to remember the day I discovered my fate. I had tried to run. That night was similar to the current one with pouring rain, flashes of lightning peppering the blackened night sky.

I had come home and packed my things in a fury, not paying much attention to what I was doing. I recalled how I struggled to muffle the sound of my sobs as I dumped the contents of my dresser into a suitcase, praying I remembered to pack the essentials in my distraught state. There had been a creak in the floorboards of the old Victorian house that I lived in. The sound had caused me to startle.

Glancing up from my suitcase, I had spotted my mother standing in the wood door frame of my bedroom. I recollected how kind and sympathetic her eyes were. When she spoke to me, I had nearly crumpled from the sound, her voice soothing me in my darkest moment.

"I know why you're trying to leave, Cadence," she had said. "You don't have to run. We will get through this together and as a family. Come now. Wipe those tears. There's a good thunderstorm outside. From the sounds of it, St. Peter is having a good game of bowling with the angels. How about we go sit on the back porch and enjoy the show?"

I forced my mind to focus on the present day and stared up at the woman who stood next to my weakened body. My mother. My one constant and always my rock. Tears swam in her eyes and I felt my sadness swell. I was consumed with loss and regret. I never wanted to disappoint her. Although she assured me I didn't, I was never able to shed the cloak of shame I wore day in and day out.

Thunder boomed again outside, causing the windows to rattle. My heart constricted. St. Peter wasn't bowling with angels today. No. This storm was a display of God's wrath. Despite my mother's strong front, I knew I had destroyed her. This pain was my punishment.

I dropped my head between my shoulders and tensed as a new kind of burn ripped through me. The searing flames were back, alive and stronger than before. My body racked with sobs, quivering and shaking until I felt I couldn't take it any longer. I looked up again at the woman who meant everything to me. Her eyes, a vibrant green that matched mine, were filled with worry. But they were also full of strength. I tried to call on every whisper of encouragement she ever gave me, needing to hear her words to get through this suffering. Perhaps it was selfish. I didn't deserve to draw on her strength, but I didn't know if I could continue on without it.

My mother's hand stroked the top of my head, over and over again, quieting my tears. It was then, in the quiet, I heard it. The sound was like the most beautiful calliope music, a powerful melody that made all the pain and torture disappear.

And suddenly… I was free.

# Chapter One

*Abingdon, Virginia*
*17 YEARS AGO*

**FITZ**

I stared out the window at the passing scenery. Field after field. Barn after barn. It seemed like hours had passed since we got off the interstate. The last store front was at least ten miles back–if one would even call it a store. It was more like a rundown mini-mart with a couple of old-fashioned gas pumps out front. Any sign of civilization seemed to fade more and more with every mile the big cheese burned. And yeah, that's what I was on. A big yellow cheese bus.

I scowled to myself, still pissed at my father for choosing this hunk of junk as my means of transportation out to no-man's-land. It was hotter than the flames in hell on this godforsaken thing, too. According to the bus driver, the a/c was busted.

My father was treating me as if I were back in grade school, not like someone who just completed his fourth year at Georgetown University. I wasn't allowed to take my own car here nor could I arrange for a car service. Those were his rules. It was always about his rules–and have mercy on any soul who tried to defy him. That included me.

"Hey, Fitz! Check it out, man!"

I turned to look in the direction of my friend, Devon Wilkshire, my partner in crime who got into this mess with me. He'd been slouched in the seat across from me for most of the ride. Now he was standing and peering out the grimy bus window.

"What? More cows?" I snapped irritably.

Devon laughed and jabbed his finger against the glass.

"Seriously, look," he insisted.

I glanced over his shoulder just as the big cheese rolled to a stop. The sign for Camp Riley came into view, a large wooden slab with painted gold lettering. Symbols for varying performing and creative arts decorated the sign–music notes, paint brushes, ballet shoes, theater masks.

*Just fucking great.*

I rolled my eyes and a knot of dread formed in my gut. Hand me a basketball, and I'd be in my element. I wouldn't call myself a jock. In fact, I hadn't played much at all since high school, but I could understand any sport better than this artsy crap. I detested it and my father knew it; however, he currently held me by the balls. The next three months were going to royally suck.

"No shit, Sherlock. The camp is our intended destination after all," I shot off sarcastically.

"No, dumb ass," Devon fired back. "Not the camp. The girls. They're everywhere."

Raising an eyebrow, I let curiosity get the best of me and stood to cross the aisle in order to get a closer look. Sure enough, there were girls. And a lot of them too. From the looks of it, they just departed from a different bus that was parked in front of ours.

I glanced around at the passengers on my bus. A bunch of nerdy and sweaty looking high school boys lounged about. Some were clutching bulky instrument cases, their expressions full of excitement when they noticed our arrival. Others were lost in their Game Boy Advance systems, a handheld game console I never really got into, and they didn't seem to notice the bus had stopped moving. There were a few guys sitting in the back who appeared to be college-aged. They were most likely here to work at the camp, just like Devon and me.

Either way, looking at the pathetic sausage party around me, I couldn't help wishing I had hitched a ride to camp on that *other* bus.

Turning to look out the window again, I shook my head and let out a low whistle. If I was going to be stuck here, I might as well make the best of it. I might be able to have a bit of fun at this hellhole after all, but I'd have to be cautious. I was fairly certain my father would be getting regular reports. That was just his style. It would be in my best interest to stay off the radar of the camp officials.

"They look a little young," I observed.

"Not all of them. Look over there," Devon said and pointed to the right of the growing crowd. Sure enough, another group of females had gathered, clearly old enough for Devon and me.

"There are quite a few of them. I bet they're here to teach or some other bullshit like that. Maybe this punishment won't be so bad after all," I joked.

"That's for sure! I think I'm going to try to find myself a flute player," Devon announced.

"A flute player? Why?"

Devon grinned and tapped a light punch to my shoulder.

"Because this place is part band camp. I want to see if music chicks are really like they are in that movie we saw last year. You know the line. *That one time, at band camp...*"

I snorted a laugh at his reference to *American Pie* although I highly doubted any girl here would be like the one from the movie. Even from my position on the bus, the girls who looked to be our age seemed a little too uptight with their high-end clothing and regal stances. Still, I returned his smile and thought about the possibilities as my gaze continued to scan the crowd of females. Most of them were decent looking, some prettier than others. We'd have to be careful. Separating the instructors from the students might be tricky until we got a better feel for the place. The last thing Devon and I needed was to get in trouble for shagging a minor on accident. We already had enough heat on us.

"Look, man. Whatever you do, just make sure she's legal," I told Devon.

"Yeah, no joke. I won't mess around with that shit."

My attention landed on one girl in particular in the crowd. She didn't appear to be a new arrival. She stood with a clipboard in one hand and a pencil in the other, pointing in various directions in an attempt to organize the mass of giggling teenage girls.

She was pretty. Very pretty, but not in a made-up way like I was used to seeing. This girl seemed natural. Real.

My eyes traveled up the length of her petite body. She wasn't tall, appearing to be just a few inches over five feet. Normally, I liked the tall and leggy type, but there was something about the way her shapely legs disappeared under the cut-off jean shorts. Her white t-shirt was fitted, accentuating small, perky breasts, and knotted at the waist to reveal the smallest area of skin just below her navel. Her blond hair, the reason she caught my attention in the first place, fell in soft waves over her shoulders. The color could only be described as golden–as if her natural color was a light brown that had turned to spun gold by the kiss of sunlight.

"That one," I said to Devon and pointed.

"Which one?"

"The blond with the clipboard. I call dibs."

Devon looked to where I was pointing. He gave a slow nod in appreciation.

"Nice find! I'd say it's time we get off this stinking cheese, Fitz. The ladies are waiting."

"Yep, they sure are," I chuckled and grabbed my navy duffel bag. Slinging the strap over my shoulder, I headed toward the front of the bus.

"Enjoy your stay at Camp Riley," the bus driver said cheerfully.

*Yeah, right.*

The driver obviously thought I was here by choice. I mumbled some sort of half-hearted thanks and climbed down the steps. As soon as my feet hit the gravel driveway, heat and humidity slammed into me. There was a subtle breeze in the air, but even that was hot. If I thought it was scorching on the bus, I was sadly mistaken. The summer air in the remote countryside of Abingdon, Virginia was suffocating.

I blinked from the sudden wash of sunlight and pulled the sunglasses off the top of my head to shield my eyes. I turned around to wait for Devon, but he was already off chatting it up with one of the girls who we had assumed to be among the instructors. I smirked when I saw she was holding what could only be described as a flute case.

Leaving him to it, I turned and began navigating through the sea of people waiting for instruction. My sight was set on my blond with the clipboard. Well, technically she wasn't mine–yet–but she would be. She just didn't know it.

As I approached, I realized that she was shouting out names in a rollcall fashion, checking off those who answered, directing them to different areas of the camp. Her voice was sweet, yet still held an air of command. She didn't seem to notice me when I walked up to her. She was too engrossed in her list.

My original estimation of her height was accurate. Now that I was standing directly in front of her, I guessed her to be no more than five feet two inches tall–tiny, petite, and perfect. I took a step closer and peered down at her clipboard. As I leaned in, her scent wafted toward me. She smelled like sweet vanilla, and I nearly groaned.

*Hell, yeah.*

Before the week was over, this girl would definitely be all mine.

"What about me? You haven't called my name yet," I drawled out, sounding just as cocksure as I felt.

She glanced up at the sound of my voice, quirking one of her eyebrows up in surprise. Bright green eyes met mine, and I sucked in a sharp breath. They were shaped like almonds–exotic, vibrant, and unexpectedly disarming. Her lips pursed into what could only be described as a perfect heart. They were lush and full, with a thin coat of gloss giving them a subtle sheen.

God help me, I didn't even know this girl's name, but I wanted nothing more than to lean down and bite that pouty lower lip.

Her eyes were concentrated as she stared back at me, and an unfamiliar sort of energy passed between us. Something flashed in those deep pools of green, but I wasn't given a chance to figure out what it was. Much to my disappointment, she looked away too quickly and glanced behind me.

"Damn it. That bus wasn't supposed to show up for another twenty minutes," she said irritably and shook her head. Not skipping a beat, she flipped a page on her clipboard. "Name please."

Devon came up beside me, and I glanced his way. He was grinning ear to ear. My guess was he already scored plans with the flute player. I shifted my bag to my other shoulder and rocked back on my heels.

"Fitzgerald Quinn," I told the pretty blond. "But you, sweetheart, can call me Fitz."

"Everyone calls you Fitz," Devon said in a snarky tone. I jabbed him in the ribs with my elbow.

She ignored us and ran her pencil down the length of the list. Coming to a stop near the bottom, she glanced up in surprise. Her eyes darted back and forth between me and Devon.

"Fitzgerald Quinn. And you must be Devon Wilkshire," she said with a frown.

"The one and only," he replied, then bent at the waist in an exaggerated bow. When he returned to a standing position, his mouth tilted up into a crooked smile and he tossed her a wink.

*Asshole.*

He was flirting, and it was pissing me off. I'd already staked my claim on this girl.

"Yeah, I know who you two are. Both of you can have a seat over there," she said and pointed to a wooden bench that sat between two large oak trees.

"Why don't you let me stay here and help you? The sooner we get these kids organized, the sooner you can give me a private tour of this place," I offered, winking suggestively. I tried to sound self-assured, but surprisingly, my words actually came out shaky. Lame. Nervous almost.

*What the hell?*

At twenty-two years old, it wasn't like this was my first attempt with a pick-up line. Piling on the charm always came naturally. Yet this girl made me feel like I was back in junior high school. Trying to shake off my nerves, I placed a hand on her forearm, just below her elbow, and allowed my fingers to dance lightly over her smooth skin.

She glanced down at my hand, her beautiful face pinching into a grimace. She looked downright irritated. A slight breeze came up to ruffle her hair, causing it to wisp across her face and cover her eyes. I didn't like the obstruction. I wanted to stare into those bright eyes, get lost in the sea of green that matched the forest behind her. It took all my restraint to keep myself from reaching up to brush away the strands of hair.

*What has gotten into me?*

I snapped out of whatever reverie I was having when she tugged her arm free with obvious disdain. She shook her head, then placed her pencil between her teeth. Bending slightly at the waist, she lowered her clipboard to secure it between her knees. Reaching into her back pocket, she produced a rubber band and pulled her hair into a messy bun of sorts on top of her head.

And damn. That simple act just may have been the sexiest thing I'd ever seen.

After she seemed satisfied her hair was secure, she took hold of the clipboard and pencil once more, her eyes narrowing at me.

"I've got this. I don't need your help, but I do have a lot of work to do," she told me, her voice dripping with contempt. "I'll get to you later after I sort out the rest. Guys from USC get special instructions."

*USC?*

It took me a second or two to figure out what she meant.

"University of Southern California? We're not from Calif–" I began in confusion, but she cut me off.

"I know where you're from. For right now, you need to have patience. Take a seat. Both of you," she ordered sternly, her eyes shifting between Devon and me.

I was taken aback.

*Who did this girl think she was? And why did she think Devon and I were from California?*

Sure, she knew my name. But it was obvious she didn't know *who* I was. If she did, she wouldn't be speaking to me in such a patronizing way. I was used to girls falling all over me. Devon said it had nothing to do with my good looks, but everything to do with my name and status. Whether he was right or not didn't really matter. I'd never experienced discernable rejection such as this. Yet her snappy tone and take-charge attitude stirred something in me. I wanted her–like *really* wanted her–even though I should be annoyed with the way she brushed me off.

"I'm sorry, sweetheart. I didn't catch your name," I said, suddenly feeling an overwhelming obsession to get to know this girl.

"That's because I didn't give it. And for the record, my name isn't sweetheart," she pointed out matter-of-factly.

Her glare was icy. This girl was a spitfire for sure. I was kind of digging it too. Devon sniggered beside me, and I had to fight the urge to slam my elbow into his ribs again.

"So, what is it then?" I asked impatiently.

She angled her chin up and narrowed her eyes. She seemed to be contemplating her words before she finally spoke.

"It's Cadence. Cadence Riley."

I glanced up at the sign above her head.

*Camp fucking Riley.*

I closed my eyes as the realization of who she probably was dawned. She was obviously too young to be the owner of a camp that was established decades ago. More than likely, she was the owner's daughter or granddaughter. I turned to look at Devon. His eyes were full of dread, an expression I was sure matched my own. Of all the girls here, I decided to set my sights on this one.

So much for staying off the radar.

# Chapter Two

**CADENCE**

The last of the new arrivals had finally dispersed, and the road was now free of buses and crowds of people. Each camp member had been given their housing assignments and was sent to unpack their belongings. Now, all that I had left to do was to give direction to the twenty housing leaders, all of who stood in front of me, staring expectantly.

Wiping the slight sheen of sweat off my brow with the back of my hand, I took a minute to appreciate the view of the valley offered from the roadside. Abingdon was a truly beautiful place and it was full of some of my best childhood memories. The valley below was a vast stretch of green, flush with abundant pines and age-old trees. However, despite its beauty, it was too hot to stand in the blazing sun and give the leaders their instructions. I motioned for them to follow me instead.

"As you know, you've all been chosen to be housing leaders to the students at Camp Riley," I began. "I have instructions for you, but I think we could all use a break from this heat. Let's head over to Creator Hall where it's air-conditioned."

I turned toward the gravel pathway that led into the camp and started to walk. Once I hit the shaded canopy of the tall oaks and pine trees, the relief from the scorching sun was instant. It wasn't unusual for Virginia to experience intense heat waves during the summer months, but ninety-four degrees was a bit extreme for mid-June.

"Excuse me, but does that include us? I'm not sure if we were assigned to be housing leaders," said a low voice off to the side.

I slowly turned to my head to the left. Fitz, frat boy number one, was addressing me. Frat boy number two, Devon, just sat there with a stupid grin on his face. I shook my head, not knowing what to make of the pair. Fitz's question was polite and well-spoken, and it was a fair one. There was no way for them to know what their job assignments would be because I hadn't decided yet. My parents just told me to use them as needed.

I looked back to Fitz and tried to be indifferent to the way the muscles in his shoulders bunched as he stood up from the bench where he had been seated. His t-shirt hugged him in a way that said there were hard, rippling muscles and taut skin beneath. I tried to disregard that chiseled jaw line–yes, freaking chiseled–like he was sculpted marble. His prominent cheekbones belonged on the cover of a fashion magazine.

Nevertheless, my attempt at ignoring all six feet of that rugged gorgeousness was futile. For the second time since meeting Fitzgerald Quinn, butterflies danced in my stomach.

The first arrival of those unwelcomed flutters came when he softly brushed his fingers over the skin of my forearm. His grin had been wide with an excess of both cuteness and suggestiveness. The combination caused a jolt of electricity to zap me, sparking what could only be described as fire all over my body. I had been terrified if he lowered his hand closer to my wrist, he'd be able to feel the rapid beat of my pulse.

I didn't know why he got to me so much. The feelings he sparked were unfamiliar and foreign. He was just another dumb boy after all. Okay… an extremely attractive dumb boy, but I found myself taking a page out of my mother's acting playbook in order to hide my body's reaction to him. It was better to keep all that bad boy charm far away from me.

This was the first time my parents had put me in charge of Welcome Day at the camp, and I didn't want to mess it up. When they told me there were going to be troublemakers headed my way, I did my research. Fitzgerald Quinn was the son of a successful and very rich politician. Devon Wilkshire was heir to a Fortune 500 company. From private grade schools to an Ivy League College, both were born with silver spoons in their mouths. It wasn't unusual for the students and instructors at Camp Riley to come from money and prestige. Nevertheless, these two boys recently found themselves in trouble for something or other–I just wasn't sure. I only knew I didn't need that kind of distraction right now.

Keeping that in mind, I decided on the perfect job for them. I would assign them to a place where they would seldom cross paths with me–but more importantly, to a place where I wouldn't cross paths with Fitz.

Ignoring the fact I could still feel the sizzle from where his hand had touched me, I adorned a poker face and answered his question.

"You're not housing leaders, but I do have assignments for you. After I give the leaders their instructions, I'll give you yours."

I was sure neither one of these rich boys had ever waited for anything before in their lives. I figured it would be good for them to have to wait a bit longer. They needed to know who was in charge around here. Besides, if they learned their place early on, perhaps I could avoid any further touching from Fitz.

I turned toward the ancient oaks that lined the long gravel drive. Their moss-covered limbs arched over us as we walked, giving shelter from the sweltering sun. We completed the short walk and entered Creator Hall. Approaching one of the long cafeteria tables, I rubbed the sweat from the nape of my neck. I breathed deep, taking a minute to appreciate the cool a/c. I knew I wouldn't be in here for very long. Turning to face the individuals who would help inspire the creative young minds this summer, I motioned to the room around me.

"Welcome to the twenty-fifth summer at Camp Riley. Some of you are returning instructors, some are new to the camp. For those of you who don't know me, my name is Cadence Riley. My parents are the founders of the camp." I paused when I heard a snort. I looked at the back of the group. Fitz's sidekick obviously thought something was funny. "Do you have a question, Mr. Wilkshire?"

Devon actually had the decency to look embarrassed, before muttering something that sounded like, "No, ma'am."

Turning my attention back to the rest of the group, I tried not to let my irritation show and continued on.

"Creator Hall is central to all housing on the grounds. This area of the hall is the cafeteria where all meals are served to both students and staff. In the event someone needs medical attention, a small infirmary is also located in this building. The grounds are divided into four sections–Music, Visual Arts, Dance, and Theatre. Each section has five cottages that serve as the summer living quarters for our students. These cottages will have between eight and ten students. From sun up to lights out, they are your responsibility. You've each been assigned as leaders to a cottage that matches your area of expertise. As some of you may already know, Camp Riley used to be a small mining village, but it was abandoned during The Great Depression. While the cottages have since been restored to include modern plumbing, there aren't enough showers to go around. Instead, everyone will share a central bathhouse which is separated into male and female facilities."

A pretty girl with dark hair raised her hand to ask a question, and I nodded at her to go ahead.

"I applied for both dance and performing arts. Do you know which housing section I was assigned to?"

"What's your name?"

"Sophia Stanton."

I picked up my clipboard, riffled through the papers, and searched for her resume.

"Sophia. You're a drama major at Juilliard, have taught ballet at Steps on Broadway, and you're looking to gain more experience with choreography. Is that correct?" When she nodded, I smiled brightly at her. "You have an impressive resume. You've been assigned to Demi-pointe, one of the dance cottages. Welcome aboard!"

"Thank you!" she beamed.

I went on to explain other buildings in the camp, such as The Flourish. It was the only store on the grounds where students could buy things like extra art supplies, replacement strings for instruments, or dance footwear. The store also sold essentials such as toiletries, water, and snacks. When I told the group stamps, envelopes, and postcards were also available for purchase to those who wanted to write home during the summer, I was interrupted.

"Stamps? Who uses snail mail anymore? Don't you have email?" Devon asked incredulously.

I nearly rolled my eyes, but somehow managed to refrain. I was beginning to think Fitz had all the brains in that operation. I had half a mind to dub them Batman and Robin. While Fitz seemed calm, cool, and collected, Devon seemed to have more foolish impulses. He was like a toddler who had yet to learn manners.

"We don't have internet on site, nor do we have computers available for student or staff use," I told him. He pinched his face up as if he were dumbfounded by the idea. I wasn't about to explain the astronomical cost of computers to someone who clearly didn't understand the value of a dollar. Instead, I said, "This is a camp for the arts. The students here don't care about keeping up with their America Online accounts. Many don't even have one. Besides, there's something to be said about handwritten letters. Pen and ink add personality that cannot be achieved with a keyboard."

Devon shrugged and slouched against the back wall.

"I guess I'm just used to Georgetown. When we're there, they make it seem like–"

"Dude! Does this place look like Georgetown? Stop being a tool and let the lady talk," Fitz snapped at Devon, then turned to me. "I apologize for my friend. Please continue."

A sizzle of intrigue with a shot of terror raced down my spine. As much as I admired Fitz for standing up to his friend, I found myself eyeing him warily. I still didn't trust him. I had a feeling he was just trying to get into my good graces. I watched the terrifyingly beautiful boy carefully, only to find a third wave of butterflies hit my stomach when he casually ran a hand across the back of his cropped dark hair. His eyes met mine–gorgeous pools of gray, hooded with thick dark lashes. There was mischief swirling amidst those slate grays, and I could only imagine the thoughts that were running through his mind. Naughty things–of that I was sure.

When the corner of his mouth tilted up in a crooked smile, it was a real struggle to suppress the sigh that wanted to escape my lips. My pulse quickened again, and I had to fight the flush that threatened to flood my cheeks.

*Jesus take the wheel. I have officially gone off the road.*

"Thank you, Fitz," I acknowledged, trying desperately to maintain my composure. "Now, where was I?"

I continued on, giving each cabin leader their instructions for the evening and told them where to report with their students in the morning. After answering a few questions, the leaders began to leave one-by-one and head toward their assigned cabins. Once they all left, I was alone with Batman and Robin.

*This should be fun.*

I gave them both an overly sweet smile and beckoned the two troublemakers with my finger to follow me. Fitz–as arrogant as he seemed–actually looked nervous about what lied ahead. I walked ahead of them, out of the cool air of Creator Hall, and into the humid air outside. I didn't look back to see if they were following, but I could hear them whispering behind me. I couldn't make out what they were saying. I only heard the occasional hiss from Fitz telling his friend to shut his mouth.

I stopped when we came to the barn that stood a little less than an eighth of a mile from the main hall. I opened the expansive red barn doors and gestured them inside. As expected, my father was inside, surrounded by his collection of tools, mops, and brooms. He appeared to be trying to fix a large metal wheel of some sort. His hands were filthy, and I noticed a black grease smudge on his left cheek.

"Hey, Daddy," I called out cheerfully as I made my way toward him. He smiled when he saw me, causing the age lines on his tanned face to deepen.

"Cadence! How are you, kid? Survive the first day okay?"

"Ask me tomorrow. It still isn't over," I joked.

"Tell me about it. It's only day one, and already an axle for one of the stage curtain pulleys broke free. Your momma was fit to be tied."

"I'm sure I'll hear all about it later," I laughed. "I heard you saying at dinner the other night you were a little short staffed this summer. I came to offer you some help. I'd like you to meet Fitzgerald Quinn and

Devon Wilkshire. I thought janitorial duties would be a great fit for them. I'm sure you'll have plenty of work to keep them busy."

And that was something I was certain of. My father was nothing short of amazing, and I loved him dearly, but he was no-nonsense. After all, he was the master carpenter for every building in the camp. It was his sweat and blood that brought my mother's vision to life. There was no doubt he'd make sure these boys ended the summer with more than a few hard calluses. If I was a betting girl, I'd wager Fitz and Devon knew it too. I could feel their glares without even having to look at them.

"I'm sure I'll have more than enough work to keep these boys busy!" my father laughed. Turning to Fitz and Devon, he wiped the grease from his hands on a rag before reaching out to shake theirs. "Pleasure to meet you. I'm Jameson Riley, but the people around here call me Mr. Jimmy. What cabin will you boys be staying in?"

Both Devon and Fitz turned to me questioningly.

"Oh, didn't I tell you?" I asked with fake innocence. "We're booked solid this year, so you'll be staying here, in the loft of the barn."

I smiled and turned on my heel, leaving both to stare wide-eyed in my wake.

# Chapter Three

**FITZ**

Pissed as all hell, I threw my duffle bag down on the mattress in the barn loft. Calling it a mattress was a stretch. It was actually just a large pad spread over a couple of bales of hay. Yes, hay. I was going to be sleeping like the goddamn hired farm help. I guessed, in a way, I was. Only I wasn't getting paid to be here.

"This is your fault," I snapped at Devon. "You could have just kept your mouth shut, but no. You had to be a dick, and now, that chick is gunning for us. I mean, she made us fucking janitors!"

He waved me off as he unpacked a few things from his bag.

"Me? I believe you pissed her off first when you called her sweetheart. Seriously, man. Did you see her face?"

"Yeah, I probably shouldn't have done that," I admitted.

"Relax. Tonight wasn't that bad. All Mr. Jimmy made us do was sweep some shit up in the main hall. Where else could Miss Bossy-Pants-Cadence have assigned us? Did you think you'd be assigned to teach dance?"

"Yeah, sure." I scoffed. The idea was laughable. "Honestly, you're probably right. You heard that girl Sophie's resume. They wouldn't have assigned us to any of the students in this place. We don't know anything about any of this artsy crap. Only the cream of the crop teaches here."

"Oh, yeah. Sophie was definitely the cream of the crop alright. Kind of makes me wish I was assigned to be a dance teacher. I wouldn't mind that one dancing around my dick."

I raised a curious brow.

"What happened to the flute player? Not old enough?"

"Oh, hell no. I told you I wouldn't make that mistake. Didn't you see her at the camp leader meeting? Her name is Jessica, and she's twenty. It's her second summer teaching here. She's with the music protégés," he told me. He flashed a sly smile and added, "I'm leaving to meet up with her in just a few minutes."

I grinned.

"Is she bringing the flute?"

"I hope so," Devon said with a waggle of his eyebrows.

I shook my head and laughed.

"You move fast, man. Have fun."

"Why don't you come with me? Maybe she has a friend."

"Nah, you go on ahead. I think I'm going to head over to the bathhouse and grab a shower."

"Don't be a pussy. Come out," Devon pushed. I briefly considered going with him. If his flute player had a friend, a bit of female company might distract me from the miserable situation I was in. The problem was, I didn't want just any female to keep me company. I only wanted one.

Cadence.

I had no idea why I wanted her. She was a pain in the ass, a prissy know-it-all. If her rigid posture was any sort of insight, I'd say she was a prude too.

She was also off limits. The forbidden fruit.

Yet I couldn't stop thinking about her. It didn't make sense, she wasn't even my type.

I glanced over at Devon who was slipping on a pair of leather dock shoes. I wanted to tell him what I was thinking about Cadence–the girl whose vanilla smell was like an addicting drug I never wanted to stop sniffing–but when I spoke, I couldn't find the words to describe what I was thinking.

"From what Mr. Jimmy said, he expects us to report by six tomorrow morning," I replied instead. "I want to hit the hay early tonight."

Devon burst out laughing.

"Hit the hay! I never understood that expression until now!"

My brow furrowed in confusion until I saw where Devon was pointing. I followed his finger to the bale of hay that would be my bed for the next three months. Realization dawned, and I smirked.

*Fucking ridiculous.*

Despite Devon's hysteria, I wasn't finding any of this remotely funny. I felt like I was living in a present-day version of Little House on the goddamned Prairie.

"Don't be too late, man," I warned. "I'm not going to be responsible for dragging your ass out of bed in the morning."

"Yeah, yeah. Don't be jealous because I'm getting action on day one while you sit here like a shmuck," he said as he swung himself over the top rung of the ladder. "I'll catch you later."

I watched Devon's head disappear down the ladder and sighed. Today had been one long ass day. I was hot, sweaty, and miserable. The idea of a shower never sounded so good. Unzipping my duffle bag, I grabbed my toiletries and a fresh pair of gym shorts, tossed it all into a smaller drawstring bag, and followed Devon's path down the ladder.

After exiting the barn, I glanced around at the camp. It was heavy and quiet. So quiet. Bugs hummed in the massive trees that hugged the still night, and the sound of crickets was the only noise that could be heard. It was a sharp contrast to all the ruckus during the dinner hour. Overeager students had piled into Creator Hall, acting like they hadn't eaten in a week, swarming the place like vultures. By the time Devon and I got there to grab our dinner, it was slim pickings. We learned right then and there, we'd have to get to the hall early if we had any hopes of getting anything decent to eat.

Now, it appeared the students were tucked in for the night, yet it was barely ten o'clock. I didn't mind. Hopefully, that meant I'd have a peaceful shower.

When I entered the bathhouse, it wasn't anything like I would have expected. Perhaps I assumed I'd find something reminiscent of my sleeping arrangements, but it was more in line with the modern look of Creator Hall. Ceramic tile lined the floors and walls, the silver bath fixtures looked like they had recently been polished to a sparkling clean. The wall to my right had shelves lined with multi-colored towels while the adjacent wall held a long horizontal mirror and countertop with at least twenty individual sinks. Straight ahead, there was a separate room, I assumed where the showers were located. After grabbing a towel from one of the shelves, I headed in that direction.

Twenty minutes later, I was showered and dressed in a pair of gym shorts, not bothering with a t-shirt. It would most likely just become drenched in sweat once I stepped outside. It didn't matter that the sun had set, the night was still hotter than hell. The slight breeze from earlier in the day had died, causing the stagnant air to be even more humid and sticky.

As I approached the doors to the barn, I slowed my steps. I didn't feel like going to bed just yet. I felt restless for some reason. Perhaps it was the quiet of the dark night. I wasn't used to it. Having spent the last four years at Georgetown University, the campus was often bustling with something or another, especially in the dorms. I began to regret not going with Devon. At the very least, it would have given me something to do.

On impulse, I dumped my drawstring bag inside the main doors to the barn. I wanted to explore this place and see what I was *really* in for this summer. The camp was surrounded by woods. There had to be hiking trails of some sort. Holding onto that hope, I headed toward the outskirts of the camp.

As I walked, I passed numerous cottages. All of them had artsy names like Clarinet Chalet and Harmony Hearth. Even the path I walked on was called Watercolor Way. I supposed some would call it charming. To me, it just screamed boredom. It wasn't like I didn't appreciate those with talent. Hell, step-mother number three used to drag me to the Kennedy Center in D.C. to watch performances more times than I could count. Although I never admitted it to her, I actually enjoyed the plays and musicals I saw. It was an escape from reality–even if it was only for a few hours. However, watching was one thing. Being in the thick of a production was something entirely different, and it definitely was not my thing.

Once I reached the edge of the camp, a thrill of excitement shot through me when I saw a dirt path leading into the woods. It wasn't very wide, narrowing in areas where the brush had become overgrown. Still, it looked like it was in use. I could see where plants had recently been trampled. Taking that as a good sign, I continued on.

The path was winding and downhill but relatively short. Thankfully, there was a full moon, allowing enough light to seep through the trees so I could see where I was going. After about ten minutes of walking, I reached the bottom of the hill. The trees parted to reveal a wide span of flat earth with a decent sized lake in the middle of it. The moon reflected off the glass surface, creating a mirror for the tall oaks and pines that surrounded it. I glanced around, expecting to find more artsy named buildings, but there were none. The only structure was a small dock straight ahead of where I stood.

*Jackpot.*

The location was nothing short of amazing. Assuming I was allowed free time, I'd be spending much of it here. I could make it my own retreat, a respite of sorts before I needed to go back to the reality that was my life in September.

A pang of dread hit me when I thought about the future my father had already decided for me. The last time I saw him, the conversation had been grim. I was out of options. He officially owned my ass. His parting words to me rang in my mind.

*"We'll go public with the news once you complete your sentence. Thankfully, we managed to keep your screw up out of the papers. Your absence will be a simple explanation. We'll tell everyone you were away on a volunteer mission working with*

*kids. The press will eat it up. Then we'll say, now that you've returned, you can't wait to begin the next phase of your life. The date has already been set. Plans will be finalized while you're gone. You have three months. Don't fuck it up between now and then.*"

I closed my eyes and shook my head. Trying to push the thoughts away, I took a few steps toward the dock.

I stopped short when I heard a rustling to my left. A golden streak darted from the edge of the woods about five hundred yards away. It bounded onto the dock before coming to a stop at the edge. It was a dog, a golden retriever to be exact. It was looking back at the spot where it had come from, wagging its tail expectantly. My eyes trailed over to where the dog was looking.

And that's when I heard her.

"Dahlia, wait for me, girl!"

Cadence emerged from the woods at a slight jog, her golden hair glowing under the light of the moon. Her hand was wrapped around the handle of a rectangular box of some sort, but I couldn't make out exactly what it was.

I don't know why, but I panicked. It was like I was afraid of being caught even though I hadn't done anything wrong. I retreated backward a few steps until I reached the dirt path. Concealing myself in the dark cover of the forest, I squatted down behind a tree and peered around it.

When Cadence reached the dock, the dog circled impatiently around her legs as she set the box on the wooden planks beneath her feet. She reached down and scratched the dog behind her ears, then pulled a stick from the back pocket of her jean shorts. She teased the dog with it for a moment or two, making the dog bark and jump. I heard her laugh, a throaty and melodious sound before she threw the stick in the lake. The dog was off like a shot, bounding off the dock and into the lake with a loud splash, disturbing the calmness of the night.

I watched the dog amidst the rippling water for a moment before turning my attention back to Cadence. She was bent down over the box at her feet. A second later, music began to play. It was then that I realized that the box she had been carrying was a Boombox. I didn't think people actually used those anymore. From the size of it, it had to be an older model. The sound of U2 poured through the speakers, the music carrying effortlessly in the still air.

The dog returned, and the pair continued to play fetch. My eyes stayed glued to Cadence. I couldn't stop watching her. Just looking at her knocked the air from my lungs. I was mesmerized.

Her hair was still piled on the top of her head in that haphazard knot. With the way the moonlight shone behind her, I could see a few wavy pieces falling around her face, creating a halo effect. Her white t-shirt clung to her body, tucked tightly into the waistband of her jean shorts. She was stunning. Gorgeous. And so incredibly sexy. The whole package sent a shiver of lust through my veins, prodding at my dick. No girl had ever incited such a reaction from me.

Unexpectedly, she reached for the hem of her shirt and pulled it over her head. A rush of air filled my lungs and my balls tightened. When she bent to remove her shorts, I swore under my breath.

"Shit!"

The last thing I needed was to be caught being a peeping tom. I needed to get the hell out of there; however, I paused when I realized she was wearing a bikini underneath her clothing. Unable to tear my eyes away, my gaze traveled the shape of her curves, completely entranced as I watched her move to the edge of the dock. Raising her arms above her head, she dove into the water and disappeared from sight.

A few moments later, she resurfaced and swam toward the water's edge. Once she reached it, she climbed out and made her way back onto the dock. The dog trailed behind her, tail wagging and stick in her mouth, anxiously waiting for another toss.

I heard Cadence laugh.

"No, Dahlia. That's enough for tonight."

It seemed as if their brief visit to the lake was coming to an end, and I knew that was my cue to leave. I didn't want her to accidentally find me. She'd probably think I was a deranged lurker.

I stepped away from my hiding spot behind the tree and made my way back onto the path. Just as I was about to leave, I heard a faint cry. The cry was quickly followed by a splash, and the dog began to bark. I turned back, but I didn't see Cadence anywhere. The only thing I saw was the ripples of water rolling in the moonlight.

*Did she fall in the lake? Or did she just jump in again?*

I waited for her to resurface. Seconds ticked by, but it seemed like minutes.

No Cadence. The dog continued to bark.

*Shit.*

Without thinking, I ran toward the water. I hastily kicked off my leather sandals and rushed into the shallow edge of the lake. The dog spotted me, her bark becoming mad and protective. She began to chase me into the water, but I ignored her. Once I was waist deep, I dove under and began to swim toward the area where I saw the water rippling.

I began a futile search. I couldn't see a thing. Only blackness. Shadows danced as moonbeams were interrupted from the current I made with each stroke. I tried to feel my way around the bottom of the lake. My hands weaved through the thick bed of underwater grass and rock. It wasn't long before I began to get confused, as old images tangled with the present, dotting my vision and causing me to become disoriented.

*A swimming pool.*

*A pair of panicked wide eyes and bloated limbs.*

*The screams.*

*The police.*

It all came at me in a rush, the memories haunting me until I completely lost my bearings. I wasn't even sure if I was in the right place anymore, I only knew I had to find her. My lungs began to sting–I needed to get air soon.

I quickly resurfaced to gulp in a breath of air and looked around. I was near the edge of the dock and close to where I saw the splash. Sucking in another deep breath, I plunged back into the water. It was all I could do to keep the panic from overtaking me.

I pushed through the water for what seemed like eons before coming to the surface once more. My heart was pounding, and I was becoming increasingly short of breath as I tried to push back my fears. I treaded in place for a second or two before deciding to swim to a shallower area. Once I felt my feet touch the muddy bottom, I called out through hoarse lungs, "Cadence! Cadence!"

I heard a sharp intake of air above me, and I looked up.

"What are *you* doing here?" Cadence demanded. She was on the dock above me, her face aghast and full of accusation.

Relief flooded through me before it was quickly replaced by embarrassment. To her–with my arms flailing about in the lake and the way I screamed her name with obvious alarm–I must have looked like a complete idiot. I should have just waited a little longer for her to resurface. Instead, I had acted on impulse, foolishly allowing my fear of the past to take over any sort of rational thought.

Yet there she stood. She was perfectly fine, on the dry dock, and not drowning at the bottom of the lake.

*I'm a fucking moron.*

Trying to regain some sense of dignity, I looked at her pointedly and tried to come off as nonchalant as possible.

"I went for a walk and ended up here. I thought you fell in," I told her with a shrug. For added effect, I tossed her a cocky grin even though I felt anything but. When my eyes traveled down to her bare midriff, she gasped again. Crossing her arms over her body, she backed up until she disappeared from my view.

*Dammit.*

I tried to hurry out of the lake, but the press of the water against my thighs slowed my progress. By the time I made it out, Cadence already had her shorts and t-shirt on and was slipping on her shoes. Her dog, Dahlia, was laying calmly at her heels. They both looked up when I stepped onto the dock.

"It's not polite to spy on people," Cadence muttered tersely when I walked up to her.

"I wasn't spying. Like I said, I was going for a walk and came upon this place," I told her. She didn't respond. Instead she bent down to silence the radio that had still been playing. "Wait, that's a good song. Don't turn it off."

Her stiff posture seemed to soften a little as she glanced up at me with curious eyes.

"You like U2?" she asked.

"Who doesn't?"

She smiled slightly, seeming to relax a bit more before stiffening once again.

"True, but it's getting late. I should go," she said.

I didn't want her to leave. I wanted her to turn the music back on. I wanted to stay on the dock with her, listening together in the quiet night as we stared up at the stars that dotted the sky. And if one thing led to another, I wouldn't complain.

As much as I wanted to convince her to do just that, I thought better of it. Another day maybe. My pride had just taken a pretty big blow after the foolish search for her potentially drowned body. It needed more time to recover before I made another pass at her. Plus, she was obviously uncomfortable in my presence. I just wasn't sure if it was from the cheap line I used on her earlier in the day or the fact I was intruding on her privacy here at the lake.

She bent to pick up her Boombox, then signaled a quiet whistle to Dahlia. The dog sprung to her feet. I wasn't sure what compelled me to do it, but I reached out and wrapped my fingers around her slender arm. Electricity seemed to sizzle under my palm, shocking me so much, I nearly pulled away. Yet I somehow held my grip firm.

"Cadence," I said, her name coming out more like a question.

"Yes?"

"I'm sorry for spying on you. I didn't mean to."

In the light of the moon, I was able to see her face flush at my words, and her skin grew warm under my hand.

"It's okay," she said somewhat shyly, taking me by surprise. "Thank you for trying to…um, save me."

My hand lingered on her arm for a moment longer before she slowly backed away and was out of my reach. Left alone on the dock, I watched as Cadence and Dahlia disappear into the cover of the forest.

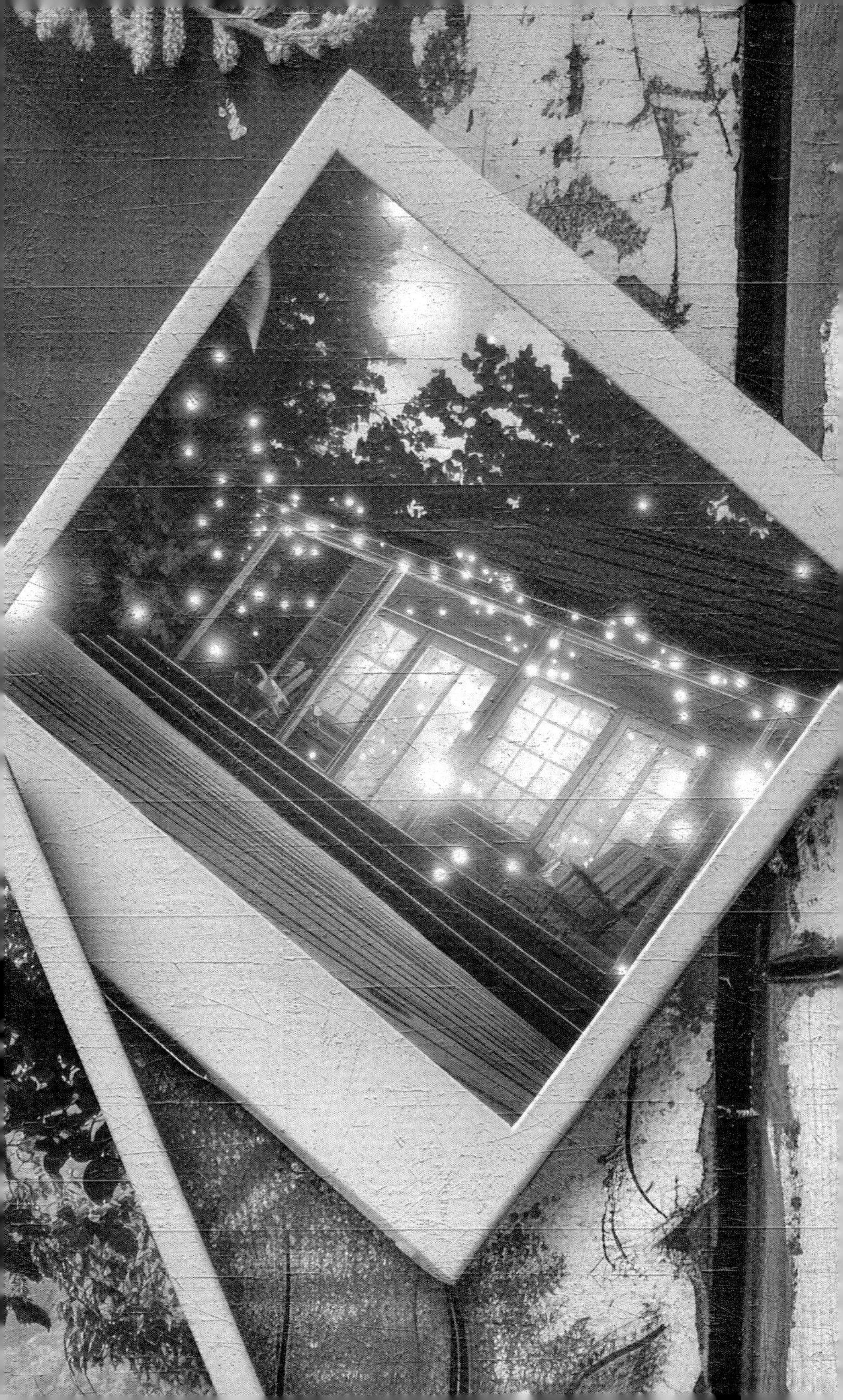

# Chapter Four

**CADENCE**

I climbed the front steps to the cottage I shared with my parents with Dahlia at my heels. Dumping my knapsack and radio at my feet, I lowered myself onto the porch swing and sat back to stare out at the campground.

It was quiet now, all the new students probably already asleep. Opening day at Camp Riley was always exciting. I looked forward to it every year, but it was exhausting. Combine that with the abnormally hot temperatures Virginia was experiencing, it was also physically draining. I understood why my parents handed me the responsibility of organizing the students on arrival day this year. At their age, they never would have been able to stand out there in this heat, waiting to greet the busloads of students.

Pulling a water bottle from my knapsack, I opened it and took a swig. The water was tepid since it hadn't been on ice since that morning, but at least it was hydrating. Despite my recent swim, the relief of the cool lake had been short-lived. My body was already overheated from the walk back to the cottage. On impulse, I cupped one of my hands, poured a bit of water into it, and then splashed it over my face in an attempt to cool off. Dahlia looked up at me curiously, then licked the droplets that rained down in front of her paws.

I could hear the voices of my parents coming through the open windows of the cottage. My mother was chatting on excitedly about the plans she had for the students the following day. My father, always so encouraging, agreed with her plans and made a few more suggestions.

"Come on, girl. Let's go inside and hear all about what Momma's planning," I said and reached down to ruffle one of Dahlia's ears. Her tail wagged as she sprang to her feet. Following her lead, I walked up to the wood-framed screen door, and we went inside.

I found my father sitting at the age-worn oak kitchen table with a bourbon nightcap, listening to my mother with rapt attention. He was the epitome of everything good–a faithful and hardworking husband, and an ever-present father. My mother, always steadfast and energetic, was pacing and waving her arms about in excitement. Her graying hair was swept up into the usual tight knot on top of her head, and her tiny figure seemed lost under the long nightshirt she wore. My father nodded his head in agreement to whatever she had just said, both of them turning to look in my direction when I came in.

"Oh, Cadence! You're finally back! How did things go today?" my mother asked enthusiastically.

"Pretty good, especially considering this was my first time running solo. A few glitches, but I handled it."

"Oh? Such as?" She raised a brow curiously.

"I didn't know what to do with the new boys who were added to the camp roster at the last minute. I decided to set them up to work camp maintenance with daddy."

"I put them right to task tonight too," my father chimed in. "They seem like good, hardworking boys. They did as I asked them to, no questions asked. I think they'll work out just fine this summer."

"Yeah, right. I think they're going to be trouble," I muttered. "I doubt boys from USC are capable of being hardworking."

"USC?" my parents said in unison.

"University of Spoiled Children," I clarified.

My mother laughed, a long melodious sound, and I couldn't help but smile.

"Oh, Cadence, give them time. How many times have I told you not to judge a book by its cover?"

"Trust me, Momma, they're a couple of jokesters. These boys are no good."

"Well, try to keep an open mind. If you have any problems, make sure to let us know."

"I will," I promised. "So, tell me about your meeting with the camp leaders. Were you able to finalize your plans for the summer? Have you decided on a production?"

My mother clapped her hands together, her excitement evident.

"The meeting was wonderful! It was probably the most productive one I've had to date! We have some creative geniuses with us this year, and I can't wait to start! I was just telling your father about it. Sit down, and I'll fill you in."

Pulling out a chair at the kitchen table, I settled in to listen to my mother explain the musical production for the current year. She had given the leaders a choice between *West Side Story* and *Singin' in the Rain*, and they decided on the latter for its comedic attributes. While one of the leaders was ecstatic about who they would choose to play the roles of Don Lockwood, Kathy Sheldon, and Cosmo Brown, another one of the leaders couldn't wait to start teaching the *Academy Award*-nominated musical score.

Enraptured by her excitement, I couldn't help but be in awe over her many accomplishments. It wasn't just the music camp. My mother was successful at everything she set out to do. My parents were originally from New York. My mother had been an actress on Broadway and a fairly famous one too. My father wasn't one for acting, but he was good with his hands. He had worked his way up the ladder at Imperial Theatre and managed the stage crew for the production of *Minnie's Boys*. My mother starred as Minnie and the rest, as they say, was history.

Their engagement was short by modern standards–they were married within three months of their first meeting. With young, romantic ideas, they took a road trip to Virginia, wanting their honeymoon to be far away from the fast life of New York. I smiled wistfully as I recalled the many times they spoke about the long walks they would take amongst the vast green trees, watching the beautiful sunsets. They had been on one of their walks when they stumbled across an abandoned mining town. My mother fell in love with its quaintness and was saddened to see it had been left to ruin.

Years later, after struggling to get pregnant, my mother decided she was done with her stage career. She blamed her many miscarriages on the rigorousness of the theatre. Leaving everything behind, they went back to Virginia and purchased the old town they fell in love with so many years before. Nevertheless, theatre was still in their blood, so they converted the town into a summer camp for creatively gifted youth. With my mother's notoriety, students poured in every summer, itching for their chance to learn from the great Claudine Benton-Riley. The impression she left on many was great. While I didn't share her musical or stage talents, I did hope one day I would be able to impact as many as she did.

After listening to my mother carry on for close to an hour, I glanced at the wall clock in the kitchen. It was nearing eleven. My father had already gone to bed thirty minutes ago. As much as my mother's enthusiasm was contagious, six-thirty was going to come very early. She seemed to notice I was running out of steam when I surrendered myself over to a yawn.

"I think it's time for you to head on to bed, Cadence. You seem tired, and I've talked enough for one night." She smiled softly at me.

"I'm sorry, Momma. You know I love to listen to you chatter on about the happenings at the camp, but I was up really early this morning."

"Don't worry about it," she waved off with a flip of her small hand. "I know you've had a long day."

I stood up and walked over to where my mother was sitting. Wrapping my arms around her, I gave her a brief hug and kissed her on the forehead.

"Night, Momma."

"Good night, sweetie."

Entering my bedroom, cold air from the window a/c unit assaulted me. As I began to strip out of my clothes, I realized how slimy my skin felt. Between sweat and the lake water, I definitely needed a shower before I could climb under the clean sheets on my bed. I looked at the comfortable twin mattress with longing, knowing I wouldn't have time to launder the sheets tomorrow. With a sigh, I grabbed a towel and my pajamas and headed to the bathroom in our cottage. At that moment, I didn't think I'd ever been so grateful to my father for adding a shower to our private residence. Just the thought of walking to the bathhouse made me feel even sweatier.

Fatigue seemed to make my bones physically ache, but I felt more like a human being again after the shower. I towel dried my hair and then quickly secured it back into a loose French braid. Slipping into a pair of cotton shorts and a tank top, I shuffled back to the kitchen to turn off the lights. Just as I was about to go back to my bedroom, I noticed Dahlia standing by the front door. Normally she would be curled up on her pile of blankets in the corner of my room at this time of night.

"Do you need to go out, girl? Drink too much lake water?" Her tail wagged and she nudged her nose at the door. "Alright, let's go. But be quick about it."

I unlatched the lock for the front door, opened it, and Dahlia pranced around to the back of the cottage. Knowing she would take a few minutes to find the perfect place to do her business, I sat on the top step of the front porch and waited.

After a few moments, I heard a rustle near the side of the porch and looked to see what it was. Dahlia must have heard it too because she came bounding from the back of the cottage and was off like a shot.

"Dahlia!" I called out in a loud whisper. Then I saw what caused the rustle. A rabbit.

*Damn!*

I chased after her, afraid to call her name too loudly because I didn't want to wake my parents or anyone else.

It was useless.

In and out of the brush she went, sniffing around at a rapid pace, determined to catch her prey. I loved her, but as the sweat began to run down my back, I wanted to strangle her.

"So much for the shower," I muttered to myself.

When I finally caught up to her, I grabbed her by the collar and scolded her. Her head drooped, and her tail went between her legs. I instantly felt guilty for chastising her even though I shouldn't have. After all, she was the one who ran from me.

I shook my head.

"Pup, when will you ever learn. Rabbits are way faster than you!"

Her tail wagged. Clearly, all was forgiven. I chuckled and motioned for her to follow me back toward home–to my bed. Sleep was calling my name.

A flicker of light caught the corner of my eye, and I turned to see where it was coming from. Someone had turned the light on in the barn. It would be odd if it was Fitz just getting in. He should have returned from his little spy adventure some time ago.

*Where would he have gone after leaving the lake?*

I had seen Devon chatting it up with one of the camps music instructors, so perhaps it wasn't Fitz at all. Maybe it was his sidekick returning late.

*Or, what if there was something wrong? Like, seriously wrong.*

A twinge of guilt hit me for making them sleep in the barn. The night air was like a sauna, and unlike all the cottages, there were no window air-conditioning units in the barn to cool them down.

*What if one of them had a heat stroke? Or worse. What if one of them fell faint from the heat and stumbled off the ladder to the loft?*

The barn wasn't that far of a walk from my cottage.

*I'll just go make sure everything is okay, then I'll go to bed.*

At least–that's what I told myself.

Drawn like a moth to a flame, I slowly turned away from the bed that had been beckoning to me just seconds before and headed toward the light. The curiosity I felt was almost a compulsion. In a matter of a few minutes, I found myself just outside the barn, peering up at the window where I had seen the light come on. I wasn't sure if I felt guilty for spying or if checking on a guest was somehow my duty. I only knew I was unable to look away.

I saw Fitz move into view, his back was to me, the bulk of him filling almost the entire frame of the window. His short hair was in complete disarray, the top sticking up wildly as if he had been violently running his hands through it. Suddenly, he turned to face out the window. Panicked, I skirted behind a nearby tree.

I couldn't make out his expression, but I didn't think he saw me. He stared out the window for a time before walking closer to it and pressing his palms to the window ledge. He dropped his head between his shoulders. He almost appeared sad, and I couldn't help but wonder what this privileged boy had to be sad about.

After a time, Fitz stepped away from the window, and the light was extinguished. I wasn't sure what compelled me to head toward the barn in the first place. My worries were silly. Everything was fine. Feeling guilty, I stepped away from the shadows and turned toward home. Dahlia followed alongside me, prancing happily when she found a stick on the pathway.

"No, girl. No more fetch. It's time for bed." She whined for a moment, but she knew the rules. As I took the stick from her mouth, she began to growl. "Dahlia! Don't you dare growl at me!"

Then I heard the snapping of a twig to my left, and I realized she wasn't growling at me at all. A warning flapped through my insides, as if it were carried on wings. The hair on the back of my neck stood up and goosebumps prickled down my arms.

*It's probably just another rabbit.*

Another twig snapped, and I knew I wasn't alone. Someone was within the thick trees that lined the pathway. I tried to peer through the darkness, but the lush canopy of the overhead leaves blocked the moonlight and made it difficult to see.

"Hello? Is anyone there?" I called out. No one responded. Dahlia continued to growl in a low rumble while images of every horror film I'd ever seen came to mind. I was currently playing the role of the stupid person in the movie–the one who went out into the dark all alone, only to be captured and eaten by a team of zombies.

"It's not polite to spy on people, sweetheart," said a voice from behind me. I nearly jumped out of my skin, the words making my pulse pound violently in my ears. I knew the voice repeating my words from a few hours ago. It wasn't a flesh-eating zombie at all. Zombies didn't call people 'sweetheart'.

It was Fitz.

# Chapter Five

**CADENCE**

With my heart racing from a mixture of paranoia and embarrassment, I slowly turned to face Fitz.

"Don't call me that. And I wasn't spying. Dahlia went after a rabbit. I had to chase after her." It was true. Sort of. I just didn't add that instead of heading home after I caught her, I continued to walk toward the light in the barn, concerned he might have befallen some sort of tragic accident. I'd be damned if I'd admit that to him though. Instead, I tilted my chin up and retorted with a question. "What are you doing out and about this time of night? You should be in bed."

My tone sounded more accusatory and mother hen-ish than I had intended, but he didn't seem ruffled. Nor did he answer me. He just took a step closer, then another. I willed my feet to back away from him, but I couldn't move. As much as I didn't understand it, he affected me. From the very first time I looked into his gray eyes, the attraction was instant. It was like the kind you see in movies or read about in books, and it made me feel all sorts of strange things.

But I knew better. He was a boy, and boys were a distraction I didn't need. Still, I couldn't deny the mysterious magnetic pull I felt toward him. I saw the arrogant and possessive way he looked at me. It wasn't my imagination. I could tell Fitzgerald Quinn was used to having his way with every girl who crossed his path. That just gave me more of a reason to stay away.

"It's not safe to wander around alone at night," Fitz warned.

"I'm not wandering," I said a little too quickly. My voice sounded breathy and slightly high pitched. I cleared my throat and tried to sound more confident. "I know my way around here. It's my second home. I've spent every summer here since I was born. Besides, I'm not alone. Dahlia is with me."

He looked down at Dahlia. She was no longer growling and held another stick in her mouth. I had no idea when she picked *that* one up. With her tail wagging expectantly, she was forever relentless in the pursuit to play fetch.

"For some reason, I don't think she's much of a guard dog," he chuckled. It was a low, throaty sound that made me a little weak in the knees.

When his eyes moved from Dahlia to me, he trailed the line of my body and stopped on my chest. I followed his gaze. I was dressed for bed, wearing nothing but a pair of white short-shorts and a pink tank that didn't leave much to the imagination. Now, with him standing mere inches from me, I found my breath becoming shallower with every moment that passed. I felt my nipples pebble under his scrutiny, poking visibly through the thin cotton material.

Mortified, I crossed my arms over my chest and found the strength to take a step back. Fitz at least had the decency to look embarrassed over being caught. He averted his eyes, cleared his throat, and mumbled an apology. I took another step back, very conscious of the way my traitorous breasts pressed through my shirt. Fitz reached out a hand to me.

"Cadence, wait."

"I need to get home and go to bed, Fitz. You should do the same."

"No, I…." he trailed off, seeming confused. "I meant it when I said you shouldn't be out here alone. Let me walk you home."

*Walk me home? What's with this guy and his savior complex?*

At the lake, he seemed genuinely worried for my safety. Just like he was now.

"I'm fine, really. I know these woods. I don't live far," I insisted.

"Cadence, I am going to walk you home." His tone was assertive, not giving me a choice.

Cocking my head to the side curiously, I stared at him. Both his words and actions made me pause. Perhaps I judged him too harshly. My mother's words of advice about not judging a book by its cover came to mind. Still, the way Fitz had come on to me after he disembarked from the bus, no one could blame me for assuming he was nothing but arrogance and trouble. But maybe–just maybe–there was more to him than I originally thought.

I looked around. The cottage I shared with my parents was off the beaten path, placed between Creator Hall and the barn. I always felt safe at the camp despite the fact that it was full of newly arrived strangers. For all I knew, one of them was an axe murderer in disguise. I doubted it, but still. Perhaps I shouldn't be so naïve and heed a bit of caution.

"Alright, Fitz. My cottage just up and around the bend."

He nodded, and we began to walk in awkward silence.

"So," he said after a few minutes, interrupting the weird quiet that settled between us. "That lake spot is pretty amazing."

"Yeah, it is," I agreed.

"Do you go there often?"

"I usually go in the evenings with Dahlia. Sometimes, I just want to go for a quick swim or to listen to music. It's the one place I can crank up the volume without my momma telling me to turn it down. Other times, it's a quiet place for me to study."

"Study? Didn't you just say you only spend summers here?" he asked, sounding surprised.

"I'm taking a few homeschool college courses through American University over the summer to get a jump on things. I'd like to get my master's in social work within five years if I can."

"That's ambitious. Social work, huh? Not a lot of money to be made there."

"Money isn't everything, and I want to help people," I responded with a shrug.

"Ambitious and noble," he mused.

I frowned. Fitz was saying the same things my parents had said to me. My mother would have loved to see me follow in her footsteps and pursue the arts, but it wasn't for me. My father just wanted me to be happy but was concerned about the student loan debt I'd be strapped with. While they were supportive of my choices, they worried. I understood why, but they didn't understand my drive. I wanted to go out and make a difference in the world. I could stress about the loans later.

I almost voiced my thoughts but thought better of it. Fitz came from a wealthy family. He couldn't possibly understand the meaning of financial burden. I pursed my lips tightly together, feeling mildly annoyed. A change of subject, one that wasn't about me, was in order. I was normally a very private person, yet in just a few short minutes, this boy had me revealing way too much about myself.

"What about you? What's your major?" I asked.

"I had a double major in political science and public relations. I graduated this past May with dual bachelor's degrees."

"Are you going on for your master's?"

"Me? Yeah, right," he stated dismissively. Then he laughed like he found the idea of continuing education absolutely absurd. "More school isn't in the cards for me."

"Why are you making it sound like a joke? There's nothing funny with trying to better yourself, Fitz."

He slowed his pace and I glanced over at him. The look he gave me was grim. When he spoke again, his voice was hesitant.

"It's not about trying to better myself. It's just that, even if I wanted to continue with my education, I can't. I don't really have a choice in the matter. My father…." He trailed off, and I waited expectantly for him to finish. "Let's just say he has other plans for me."

I wanted to ask what those plans were, but there was something in his tone that stopped my questions. He seemed bitter almost, and I thought it best not to pry. We just met twelve hours ago after all. It wasn't any of my business.

"So, what do you think about Camp Riley so far?" I asked, deliberately changing the topic to something a little less awkward. We were almost to my cottage, and I was grateful to only have to keep up the small talk for another minute or two.

"It's not bad. It's a little too quaint and village-like to be called a camp in my opinion. When I found I out I was coming here, I was picturing tents and shit like that. The lake spot is cool though," he said nonchalantly. "If you don't mind, I may pop over there in the evening once in a while. I like it there."

I thought about his statement and what it could mean–what it could possibly *lead* to. The thought of him coming to my spot, intruding on *my* space, immediately upset me, and I responded without thinking.

"Actually, I do mind. That place is private to me, Fitz. If you start showing up, students or camp leaders could find it and think it's okay for them to go there too."

"Okay, okay. No need to snap," he said, holding his hands up in mock surrender.

*Had I snapped?*

If I did, I didn't mean to. I smiled sheepishly.

"I'm sorry. It's just…okay, I'll think about it," I conceded. "But if I give you the go ahead, you can't tell anyone else about it.

*Did I really just agree to think about it? Have I gone mad?*

I glanced in his direction only to see a slow smile spread across his face. There was no denying he was celebrating a small victory as a result of my concession.

*Jerk.*

Still, I didn't take back what I said. I stayed silent, not sure what to make of this mysterious boy who had tried to be my knight in shining armor twice in one night. I could feel his eyes on me as we walked. Something strange shot between the two of us that I couldn't quite explain. It was as if he were hooking me with something unseen with every glance he stole. My heart fluttered, and my skin coated with a sticky sheen of sweat – only this time, it wasn't from the humid air.

When we came upon my cottage, Dahlia pranced up the steps.

"This must be your place," Fitz observed.

"Yeah, this is it."

"Okay, well…um." He hesitated. "I guess this is where I tell you to have a good night."

It was strange. It almost felt like he had just walked me home from a first date, and this was that weird moment where you weren't sure if the boy was going to kiss you. I studied his face–he was most definitely looking at my mouth.

*Oh, hell no. No kissing allowed, buddy!*

I quickly sidestepped away, just in case.

"Thanks, Fitz. Same to you. And thank you for walking me back."

"Sure. No problem. I'll see you around."

"Yeah, maybe." I shrugged in a noncommittal way. Unable to make actual sustained eye contact, I turned away and tossed a wave over my shoulder. "Goodnight, Fitz."

Once I was safely inside the cottage, I closed the front door a little too quickly, the wood making a loud bang against the frame. Another day, I may have worried about the noise waking my parents–today was not that day. I was too busy relishing in the relief I felt from being able to put some space between Fitz and me. The run-in at the lake, the unexpected walk, and those piercing gray eyes… Fitz and his bad boy charm were just too hard to resist. I leaned against the back of the door and exhaled with a sigh. I needed to put up a barrier to stop that magnetic pull. No good would come out of seeing more of Fitzgerald Quinn, of that I was sure.

# Chapter Six

**FITZ**

The first week at Camp Riley had gone by surprisingly fast. Mr. Jimmy was a slave driver, but there was something about him that made the work easy to endure. He had an easy-going way, yet still commanded sweat and blood from the laborious tasks he doled out to Devon and me. Today, our job was to split wood for the fire pits scattered all over the camp. Even though I thought it was too damn hot to sit around a campfire, the younger kids seemed immune. They spent their evenings roasting marshmallows, singing, and playing tunes for each other on their shiny instruments.

I, on the other hand, spent the evenings alone in the loft, patiently waiting for Cadence to invite me to her secret place by the lake. I tried to get her out of my head, but it was damn near impossible. That blond was now buried under my skin and she unknowingly had my head going to all kinds of places it shouldn't.

The problem was, I barely saw her. I wondered if she was deliberately staying away from me or if she was just too busy with her own camp duties. If I saw her, it was usually in the cafeteria during the dinner hour, looking like she just stepped off the pages of *For Him Magazine*. The crazy thing about it was I knew she didn't even try to look that damn good, it was just natural. However, the minute I spotted her, she seemed to vanish in the crowd of ravenous campers all vying to get their meals.

Tonight, I laid on the thin mattress that covered my bale of hay, staring absently at the wood rafters of the ceiling. I was bored out of my fucking mind. Devon had taken off more than an hour ago, having made plans with yet another chick working the camp. Of course, he gave me hell for not joining him. He said I was pussy-whipped for sitting here, pining over a girl who wanted nothing to do with me. If I heard him say one more time I needed to go out, find a random chick, and get laid, I thought I would knock his teeth out.

I told him to fuck off instead.

Seven nights here, and I think he'd shacked up with seven different girls. He was the one who was the fool. The minute they all started talking to one another, the shit was bound to blow up in his face. I was tired of that sort of drama.

My stomach growled. Lugging the chopped wood to all the cottages had taken longer than expected and caused Devon and me to get to Creator Hall late. By the time we arrived, there wasn't much food left. I needed more to eat than just the small bowl of cold pasta salad I managed to scrape up. I glanced at my watch and saw it was nearing eight. The students should have cleared out from the cafeteria by now.

My insides rumbled again. Sitting up, I swung my legs over the side of the makeshift bed and slipped into my leather Birkenstocks. There had to be something else in the kitchen I could grab. If not, I would grab a bag of chips from The Flourish. It wasn't a very nutritious option, but it was better than nothing. Climbing down the ladder, I headed out to search for food.

Once I reached Creator Hall, I pulled open the heavy wood door. I halted in my tracks when I saw a familiar head of long blond waves. I'd recognize those golden strands that I itched to run my fingers through anywhere.

Cadence was seated at a table with her back to me. I smiled to myself as I proceeded forward in her direction. I forgot all about the food I came here in search of. Just seeing her again made me completely numb to any hunger pains I had been experiencing. She was wearing a tank top again tonight. It was a light purple one this time. But much to my disappointment, I could see white bra straps peeking out at her shoulders and knew I wouldn't be getting the same show I received on the night I arrived.

*Such a shame.*

On closer inspection, I also noticed a tattoo on the back of her right shoulder. It was strange I hadn't seen it before, but then again, she normally wore a short-sleeved t-shirt with the Camp Riley logo during the day. Seeing the ink on her was surprising. She didn't seem like the type to have a tattoo. She was just too…reserved.

*Maybe there's a little rebel hiding in there somewhere after all.*

I slowly walked a few steps toward her so I could get a closer look at her ink. It was a tattoo of a flower and a stark contrast against the creamy color of her skin. The petals were filled in with a pale blue. Leaves shaded in muted green, gray, and black poked out from behind the flower, flowing down into an intricate scroll that disappeared under the seam of her tank. The overall design was small and feminine–just like her.

She was hunched over and appeared to be writing in a notebook. She had headphones on with the cord extending to a Walkman that was resting on the table in front of her. The music in her ears must have muffled any sound I made when I came in. So intently focused on what she was doing, she also hadn't seen me. I took another step closer and peered over her shoulder.

She wasn't writing in a notebook like I originally thought. She was drawing on a sketchpad, creating an image of a flower, similar to the tat on her shoulder. I watched the tip of her pencil shade the edges of the petals, creating highlights where necessary to bring the drawing to life.

"That's really good," I observed.

Cadence jumped and quickly flipped over the sketchpad to hide the drawing. When she turned around, her eyes narrowed into a sharp glare when she saw I was the one standing behind her. She ripped the headphones from her head and tossed them on the table.

"Why are you always spying on me?" she accused.

I felt the right corner of my mouth tip up in amusement.

"Relax, sweet–" I stopped, nearly calling her 'sweetheart' again and watched as her glare darkened. "I was hungry. I just came in to see if the kitchen had saved any of the leftovers from today. I didn't even know you were in here."

Her eyes flashed with accusation.

"You were about to call me sweetheart again, weren't you?"

"Maybe," I admitted with a wink.

"Well, don't do it."

"Why not? It's a fitting nickname for you, Cadence."

"Oh, really?" she admonished sarcastically.

I inched forward. Her face was tilted up to look at me. There wasn't anything sweet about her sassy attitude–not at all–but I was lucky enough to catch a glimpse of what was underneath all that sass the night I walked her home. There was a sweet innocence about her, a shyness that was endearing. Then there were those lips of hers. They were lush and full, her upper lip outlining a perfect heart shape.

As if my arm had a mind of its own, I reached up and traced the line of her lip with the tip of my finger. Her eyes widened, and I felt the sudden intake of her breath, but she didn't push my hand away.

"Your mouth. It's shaped like a heart," I told her, surprised by the brutal honesty of my words. "I imagine it tasting sweet. I can't help but call you sweetheart."

She flushed a violent shade of red before pulling her head away from my touch. The sizzling connection broke, leaving me stunned over the intimate moment.

I shouldn't have touched her like that. It wasn't sexual–it was so much more than that. And it was extremely unnerving. Still, I ached to touch her again, to feel her warm skin against my fingertips.

She turned back to her drawing pad and picked up her pencil.

"Go away, Fitz," she muttered.

I eyed up the sketchpad that still sat face down on the laminate surface. I knew she was waiting for me to leave before she flipped it back over. On impulse, I snatched it up.

"Hey, give that to me!" Cadence shrieked. She stood and tried to pull it from my hands, but I was too fast. I sidestepped her effortlessly and began to retreat backward.

"I'm still waiting for my invitation to the lake. But…" I drawled out. "I think someone's been avoiding me. Invite me to the lake, and I'll give your drawing book back."

"Fitz, that's mine," she warned as she advanced toward me.

Turning on my heel, I quickly dashed toward the cafeteria doors. Pushing through them, the humid night air assaulted me.

I could hear Cadence yelling at my back, and I laughed. Pausing in my retreat, I turned and tilted my lips up into a mischievous grin. She was standing inside the door to Creator Hall, her hands on her hips.

"If you want it, come get it," I teased.

"Damn it, Fitz! Don't be a jerk! I told you to give it back!"

Instead of heeding her demands, I took off running. I knew it was juvenile, but there was something about the way she constantly avoided me that had driven me to insanity. I wanted to break down the barriers she tried to put up. I didn't know why. I only knew, during the lonely nights in the loft over the past week, she was all I could think about. My need to get to know her had become an obsession.

I ran with no destination in mind and was surprised when I reached the outskirts of the camp, the path to the lake just up ahead. An idea struck. If she wouldn't invite me to the lake, it was time to take matters into my own hands.

# Chapter Seven

**FITZ**

I could hear Cadence behind me, trying to catch up, but I was faster. I ran down the path, not stopping until the trees opened up to the vast lake. I slowed my pace and turned around, falling into a backward jog. Cadence burst through the trees, her face livid. She stopped running and planted her feet in a wide stance, her jaw set tight and fists clenched at her hips. She looked murderous, but it just might have been the sexiest thing I'd ever seen.

I grinned, and then turned to step onto the dock. Once I reached the end, I laid down, placed the sketchpad on my chest, and extended my arms to rest my hands under my head. Then I closed my eyes… and waited.

It took her a few minutes, but I eventually heard the wood dock creak when she stepped onto it. I opened one eye to peer at her.

"You really are a jerk, Fitz. You know that, right?"

"Maybe. But you're selfish for wanting to keep this place all to yourself," I retorted with a wink.

"I am not selfish!"

I sat up and shrugged, flipping through the sketchbook as I did so. It was full of various colored pencil drawings. There were people and animals, but most of the sketches were of flowers. More often than not, a sunset was always the backdrop. Overall, I was impressed by what I saw. The girl had some serious talent.

"Calm down, sweetheart. I'm only teasing you." She scowled but didn't scold me for using the pet name. I couldn't help chuckling at her expression. I reached out and patted the dock. "Come sit down next to me. There's a great sunset tonight. We can watch it together, and you can tell me about why you include a sunset in so many of your drawings."

She eyed me warily before looking out over the water. She seemed to soften a bit as she stared out at the orange, pink, and purple sky. When she looked back at me, she smirked.

"If this is some lame attempt to get in my pants, it's not going to work."

It wasn't a lame attempt at anything. Sure, I absolutely wanted to get into her pants–any hot-blooded male who laid eyes on her would want the same–but I wanted to get into her mind more, to get to know the person behind her beautiful shell; however, I didn't say any of those things to her, but put my hands up in surrender.

"Don't worry, I'll keep my charm at bay. Perhaps I should place a bag over my head too," I added. "That way you won't have to worry about succumbing to my good looks."

"Good looks, huh? You're not just a jerk, you're an *arrogant* jerk!"

I saw the corner of her mouth twitch. She was fighting a smile.

"Are you going to stand there pretending to be all mad at me? Or are you going to sit down?"

She pursed those gorgeous lips of hers and seemed to consider her options. When she eventually lowered herself to sit next to me, I grinned with satisfaction.

"Don't think you've won this round, mister. I'm only sitting because it would be a shame to miss such a beautiful sunset," she stated somewhat petulantly. She looked out over the lake again. "The colors are so vibrant tonight. It's hard not to appreciate it."

"Right. You're sticking around for the vibrant colors. It has nothing to do with my charming good looks at all," I joked. She swatted at my arm playfully. The light slap was almost flirtatious, and I took it as a good sign. Feeling more confident with the situation, I leaned back on one elbow and placed her sketchpad on the dock. I opened it up to the drawing she had been working on in the cafeteria. "So, you like to draw sunsets and flowers?"

She glanced down at the drawing I was studying.

"Sometimes. The colors of the sunsets are hard to ignore. Plus, I kind of have a thing for dahlia's."

"Is that why you named your dog that and why you have a tattoo of one on your shoulder?" I asked with genuine curiosity.

She subconsciously reached around to touch the ink on her shoulder.

"Sort of. I mean, I've always loved the flowers. I've been coming to this lake for as long as I can remember just to sketch them." She pointed out past the shoreline. "They grow wild along the edge of the woods that surround the water. After I turned eighteen, I had a tattoo artist ink one of my drawings onto my shoulder."

"I like it," I told her. Impulsively, I reached up to trace the lines of the design with my finger. She glanced back at the finger that touched her but didn't jerk away like I thought she might. Another good sign. "So, what about your dog's name?"

Cadence laughed. It was a beautiful, lyrical sound I wanted to hear a lot more of.

"Now that's a different story. My father named her Dalilah, but then she became obsessed with eating dahlia flowers when she was a puppy. I would bring her here when I was drawing. While I drew, she would make herself sick off the flowers. Her name just sort of morphed into Dahlia over time. What about you? Do you have any pets?"

"I used to when I was a kid. My mom…" The words died on my lips as a stab of grief hit me. It was like the sentence got stuck in my throat, and I was unable to continue. I hadn't talked about my mother in so long. The last thing I wanted to do was dredge up a painful past. I didn't need to go back to that dark period of my life. Choosing not to respond, I just continued to flip through the sketchpad instead.

"What about your mom, Fitz?" she asked after a time.

She stared down at me and our gazes locked. I thought I might drown in the green sea of her eyes. There was something building between us, a slow burn I could feel in my bones. I didn't know if it was friendship or something more. I only knew it was there, and I didn't want to ruin it. But for some reason, I spilled the story anyway.

"I had a dog, but I was forced to give him up after my mother died."

"Oh, no! That's when you would have needed your furry companion the most! Who on earth made you give him up?"

I tossed her a rueful smile. Her astonished innocence, the disbelieving way she perceived giving up a pet as such an atrocity made me feel a little jealous. She came from a *normal* family, not one fucked up and broken like mine.

"My father." I shrugged and tried to act indifferent. "After my mom died, I had to go live with him. He had remarried. Wife number two–or maybe it was number three? I can't remember because number two didn't last long. Anyway, she claimed she was allergic to dogs. I was told they gave him away to a good family but later found out otherwise. The real truth was my father had him put down."

Her eyes widened in horror.

*Yeah, believe it, sweetheart.*

"What was your dog's name?" she asked softly.

"Boomer. He was a Siberian Husky with one gray eye and one blue.

That was why I picked him out of the litter. My mom had blue eyes and I have gray."

If she knew the rest of the story about how I found out Boomer had been put down, she'd be traumatized. I couldn't tell her that my father had caught me crying over the loss of my mother a year after she died. I was just a kid, but he told me I had to get over it. He said she was never coming back, and crying was for wimps. That was when he told me Boomer had been euthanized. He said the dog made me soft, and it was time for me to start acting like a man.

To this day, I hadn't forgiven him for that. He could have just let me believe that my childhood pet had been sent to a good home, but no. Cruelty was his specialty.

"That's so sad. I can't even imagine losing Dahlia. I'm sorry that happened to you, Fitz."

"Nah, don't worry about it. It was a long time ago," I tried to shrug off. I looked out across the water. Only faint lines of purple and dark pink could be seen, the sun having completely disappeared behind the vast hills. "I'm talking too much. We ended up missing most of the sunset."

She glanced in the direction of the sunset but didn't seem to see it. She appeared lost in thought. Eventually, she turned to me with pensive eyes.

"I feel like I misjudged you. I thought you were just some spoiled rich kid. I'm sorry about that. It may be none of my business, but I am curious. Why did your mom die?"

I returned her stare for a moment, hesitating with my response. Our conversation had turned very deep, very fast. I didn't want to spend any more of the night talking about my past. It was a total downer. Besides, it was what it was. I couldn't change it.

"Breast cancer," was my only reply, then I jumped to my feet. I reached for her and pulled her up to stand next to me. "Come on. We've had enough sad talk for one night. Let's go for a swim."

"A swim? But I don't have my bathing suit!"

"So, what? Go in your clothes… unless you're up for skinny dipping," I teased with a wink.

"I will *not* go skinning dipping!"

I grinned and tore off my t-shirt.

"That's what I figured."

I stepped to the edge of the dock, poised to jump in. At the last minute, I turned and grabbed her forearm. There was no time for Cadence to react. Pulling her to me, I hurled us off the dock and into the water.

"Fitz!" she squealed after we resurfaced. "I can't believe you did that! Do you know how freaking uncomfortable it is to wear wet jean shorts?"

She looked downright pissed as she yanked herself free from my grasp. She swam away, then stopped after reaching shallower water. Once she had her footing, she turned back to look at me. Her expression was bold, almost daring. Then, to my astonishment, she produced a pair of sopping wet jean shorts from below the surface and tossed them onto the dock. I cocked up a brow.

"Skinny dipping after all, huh?"

"Don't get any bright ideas, slick. I'm still wearing my underwear."

*Cadence. In only a wet tank top and panties.*

I nearly groaned in frustration as a visual of wet panties clinging to her body came to mind. My cock jerked to life; however, a half-naked Cadence didn't mean she'd be up for sex on the beach. Somehow, I knew if I even attempted to make a move, she'd put a knee straight to my balls.

I dove under the water and swam in her direction. When I resurfaced, she was only a couple of feet away.

"You surprised me when you lost the shorts," I said as I moved to close the gap between us.

"I think I surprised myself, too," she admitted with a nervous laugh. "My momma would wring my neck if she knew I was in the lake in my underwear–with a boy no less!"

I reached up and touched her wet hair, allowing the blond strands to slide through my fingers. The soft wet locks fell limp on her shoulder and I tilted her head up to look me in the eyes.

"What she doesn't know won't hurt her," I whispered.

Our bodies were close, nearly touching.

*What am I doing? I shouldn't touch her. Not here. Not like this. Not at all.*

I didn't know what was happening between me and Cadence, but it was bound to end badly. She and I could never be a thing. I understood my reality. As it was, my father already had me by the balls. If he found out I was messing around with the daughter of the camp owners, he'd be sure to crush them in a vice.

"Fitz?" she asked, my name barely a breath from her lips.

"Cadence," I answered back.

"I need to focus on school. I can't get wrapped up in a guy. Plus, well…I'm not that kind of girl."

"I know you're not, sweetheart." My voice was gravelly as I eyed her heart-shaped mouth. Just like I had in the cafeteria, I reached up to trace the outline of her lips. Since she'd been shy of me, I didn't want to scare her off by moving too fast. "I think that's why I'm so drawn to you. You're different from the rest."

I stared into her emerald greens with purpose, begging her with my eyes to believe me. I wasn't giving her a line. In fact, I had never been more honest in my life. She wasn't some random sorority girl who was oh-so-eager to let me get my dick wet for a night. Cadence was different.

And different was exactly what I wanted.

I had been living in a state of perpetual fury. My narcissistic and overbearing father thought he had all the control. And while he might once I got back to D.C., he didn't control me now. Not here. Not with her.

That's why I didn't stop myself from leaning in. I wanted to taste her, to see if she was as sweet as she was in my dreams. She placed her hand on my bare chest but didn't push me away. She gave me a look instead, one that tugged at the flesh of my heart. It was a small smile accompanied by the shake of her head as if she were saying, "Silly boy. It's never going to happen."

I wrapped my palm around the nape of her neck, coaxing her head closer.

"Fitz, what are you doing?"

"I'm getting ready to kiss you." She licked her bottom lip and her forehead furrowed, not sure how to respond to my statement. "Can I kiss you, Cadence?"

Without warning, she closed her eyes and pressed her lips softly against mine. It was so unexpected, I froze. I thought I'd be the one to close the remaining gap, but as her mouth began to hesitantly move over mine, I relaxed and wrapped my arms around her.

She was soft and so very sweet, just like I had imagined. Her kiss was almost chaste at first. Unpracticed. Yet it still managed to make my heart race. My tongue traced her lower lip coaxingly, searching for an opening. She gave in, parting her lips to invite me in with an eager sweetness that shot straight to my groin. When our tongues finally met, it was as if my blood turned to molten lava. It was so good… so very good.

And I was on fire.

I pressed my mouth harder against her, demanding more as I took the lead. She met me every step of the way. Water lapped around us, a gentle rocking that somehow made the kiss more erotic. My hands rubbed over her back, wishing I could remove the barrier of her tank top and feel her soft skin. Knowing I'd be pushing my luck if I tried, I cupped her head in my hands and plunged in to devour her mouth instead.

Our tongues began to dance and lap with urgency as if we were starving and couldn't get our fill of each other. When a beautiful moan seeped from her lips, I squeezed my eyes tight. We needed to put the brakes on before I did something I'd be sure to regret.

"Cadence," I gasped as I tore my mouth from hers. "Maybe we should just…you're…"

I couldn't finish the statement, barely able to catch my breath. I didn't know how to say she was driving me absolutely mad and I wasn't sure if I could control my need to touch her for much longer. I didn't want to scare her away, not after it seemed like I'd waited a century to get her here.

"I'm sorry if I was bad," she said quietly.

I stopped panting and looked at her in shock. The moon was high in the sky, illuminating her swollen lips and cheeks flushed pink. But what was most prominent was the expression on her face. She looked embarrassed.

"Bad? What do you mean?"

"Well, I don't have much experience with kissing outside of a game of spin the bottle when I was fifteen," she admitted shyly. Hesitation dimmed her eyes. "I'm sure you're used to kissing girls who've had more practice. If you don't want to kiss me anymore, I would completely understand."

Eighteen years old and never been kissed–and I mean really kissed. Teenage party games didn't count.

*Fuck…she's so innocent. Was every guy she met a fool?*

That heart-shaped mouth of hers begged to be kissed… and often. She dropped her head, almost as if she were too nervous to look me in the eye.

"Cadence, look at me. What you are in innocent and sweet, and so pretty that I can't even see straight. You are beauty looking back at me and I've never wanted to kiss anyone more than I want to kiss you. I really hope you'll let me do it again."

Her eyes brightened.

"Really?"

"Yes, really."

I leaned down and kissed her again. Summoning every ounce of willpower I could obtain, I pulled her small body tight to mine. I delved in deeper, trying to convey a message that said I wanted her. Only her. No kiss had ever felt so good. Tasted so sweet. I could kiss her for days and never tire of it.

It was wrong of me to want her, especially since I knew it could never last. If I continued to see her, we could only have the summer. The problem was, she didn't know that. Yet at that moment, with Cadence in my arms, everything felt right. The future, no matter how bleak, didn't seem to matter.

# Chapter Eight

## CADENCE

I walked down the instrument supply aisle in The Flourish and scanned the shelves. Running my finger down the list attached to my clipboard, I matched it with product holes on the shelves. Satisfied the supply re-order checklist was complete, I headed over to the cash register where my friend Joy was working behind the counter.

Joy was a year older than I was and had been working at Camp Riley for the past three summers. We had gotten to know each other while working side-by-side in the camp store. While the students were in lessons or rehearsals during the day, we often had long hours with not much to do other than chat our days away behind the counter. As a result, she and I had become fast friends almost right from the get-go.

"Next year, remind me to tell my momma to add another section to the student application. We need a list of the specific instruments they plan to bring and the replacement parts," I told Joy. "I can't seem to keep size four clarinet reeds in stock for more than a few days. Last year, it was the three and a half size."

Joy laughed, flipping one of her braided cornrows over her shoulder and leaned against the doorjamb to the stockroom.

"It's all that practicing they do around the campfires at night. I know because their ruckus keeps me up too late!"

I pursed my lips in a frown.

"I haven't heard them. Lights out is supposed to be at ten. Do I need to get on the camp leaders about it?"

"Nah," she waved off. "Girl, you know me. I like to be asleep by nine. Besides, you couldn't pay me to be outdoors at night around here. All those mosquitos! No thank you!"

I laughed at her aversion to the outdoors. Originally from Baltimore, Joy was a city girl through and through. When she began working summers here, her plan was to only stick around for two seasons. She wanted the experience to help her chances at getting into George Washington University's School of Music. Why she was back here for a third year in a row was a mystery to me.

"Oh, speaking of mosquitos, that reminds me. Bug spray is a little low on the shelves. Are there any cases left in the stockroom?"

Joy leaned back and poked her head into the room. After a quick glance around, she looked back at me and shook her head.

"Looks like only a half case is left. You should probably order more."

I opened my mouth to ask her how many cases she thought we should order, but closed it when I heard the bells above the main entrance to The Flourish chime.

Fitz came strolling in, his steps lined with power and purpose. Sweat from a hard day's work in the Virginia sun caused his t-shirt to cling to his torso outlining the six-pack beneath. His face was tanner than it was when he first arrived at camp and somehow seemed to make the chiseled lines of his face and hard jaw all that much more defined.

His eyes met mine, staring with a dissecting gray gaze that said he had a secret. I swallowed, and my heart nearly sank to my knees when he stepped up to the counter.

"Afternoon, ladies," he said, his mouth turned up on one side, offering me a glimpse of the crooked grin that caused little butterfly flutters in my belly. "Good to see you again, Cadence."

Joy looked at me in surprise. Quickly, I explained.

"Joy, this is Fitz. He's one of the guys working maintenance with Daddy this summer."

I tossed her a knowing look. I had told Joy about Fitz and Devon the day after they arrived. I warned her they were troublemakers who we needed to keep a watchful eye on. What I didn't tell her was I kissed one of them last night. A heat began to crawl up my neck from the memory. A part of me still couldn't believe it had happened. I wasn't the sort of girl to kiss boys who I barely knew. It was wrong, yet with Fitz, it seemed oh-so-right. The whole thing felt like a dream.

"Nice to meet you, Joy," Fitz acknowledged with a quick nod.

"Likewise," Joy responded before turning to me. "I was just about to run over to the bathhouse and check the supplies over there. I'll make a list of anything that needs to be ordered. Will you watch the register while I'm gone?"

"Sure thing, Joy. Thanks for saving me the trip."

Once Joy left, I walked behind the counter, put down the clipboard and tucked the pencil I had been using behind my ear. Fitz just stood there, studying my every move, not saying a word. It was completely unnerving. My stomach dipped, wishing he didn't look so damn good. He was all temptation and sin, making me want to dip my fingers right in and experience exactly what it would taste like.

"So," he eventually said. He rocked back on his heels, almost appearing nervous. For some reason, I found it charming.

"So… what?" I asked when he didn't say more.

"I'm not sure what time you get off here, but I just finished for the day," he began.

The bells for the door chimed again, interrupting whatever else he was about to say. Rachel Kane, one of the camp leaders, sauntered in. She wasn't wearing the standard issued Camp Riley t-shirt. Instead, she wore a skin-tight red University of Alabama t-shirt that had been cut off at the bottom, revealing way too much of her flat tanned stomach. The words 'Roll Tide' arced across the barely-there cotton covering her chest. Her jean shorts didn't leave much to the imagination either, putting even Daisy Duke herself to shame.

I frowned and glanced at the clock on the wall. It was nearing five which meant lessons and rehearsals ended an hour ago. That might explain her inappropriate attire.

"Hey, Fitz," she drawled out in a thick southern accent.

She made her way over to where Fitz stood, her hips swaying. She tossed him a coy smile and flipped her glossy brown hair over her shoulder in an overly flirtatious manner. I narrowed my gaze, not liking the way she was coming up on him, even if I had no business being jealous.

"Um, hey?" he replied questioningly. He glanced in my direction. I just shrugged and began to busy myself needlessly by straightening items on the checkout counter.

"A bunch of us are going into town later to check the local bars. Want to come along?" Rachel asked him.

Fitz shook his head in confusion.

"Ah, I'm sorry. I'm terrible with names. I know I've seen you around, but I don't remember your name."

I had to stifle a smile at that. He didn't even know who she was. Good.

"Oh, how silly of me. Devon mentions you so often, I feel like I know you somehow," she gushed and placed a hand on his shoulder. I rolled my eyes. "I'm Rachel. I'm a music instructor and the leader over at Clarinet Chalet."

"Well, it's nice to officially meet you, Rachel."

She moved slightly to the left, positioning herself, so she was square with him. Leaving one hand to linger on his shoulder, she placed the other on his arm. I nearly grimaced.

*For crying out loud, could she be any more obvious?*

"So, what do you say? Want to come out with us tonight? Devon will be there too," she pushed.

Fitz took a step back, putting distance between himself and the hussy who was standing way too close. He glanced in my direction, but I quickly averted my eyes.

"Actually, I kind of already have plans tonight, Rachel."

"Oh, really?" she whined. She stuck out her lower lip in a pout. It was so pathetic and made me want to vomit. I couldn't stand it when girls acted that way.

"Yeah," Fitz confirmed. "I'm meeting someone over at Creator Hall for dinner, then we'll probably chill for a bit afterward."

I raised my eyebrows, my interest suddenly piqued.

"That's too bad, Fitz. Who are you meeting if you don't mind me asking?"

Fitz tsked at her.

"Sorry, Rachel, can't tell you that. But you can tell Devon that maybe I'll catch him next time."

I struggled to keep the smirk off my face. Secretly, I was thrilled Fitz rejected her advance.

"Oh, well. Your loss," Rachel told him with a shrug. Walking over to the row of refrigerator cases, she opened one of the doors and pulled out a sixteen-ounce bottle of Mountain Dew. Taking her sweet old time, she proceeded to peruse the magazine rack. After settling on one, she came back over to us and placed the items on the counter. I looked down at the magazine she selected. Apparently, Brad was over Gwyneth and had moved on to Jennifer.

"Is that all today?" I asked.

She simply nodded, and I cashed her out on the vintage antique register. When I began to place the items in a small paper bag, she stopped me.

"I don't need a bag," she said. Removing the bottle, I handed it to her. She opened the top and took a long swig. Scooping up her magazine, she glanced back and forth between me and Fitz, eyes lingering on Fitz for a moment longer. "Y'all have a nice day now."

"Thanks. You too," I said cheerily. This time, I didn't hide my grin as she turned to sashay out the way she had come in.

"Sorry about that," Fitz said after the door closed behind her.

"About what?"

"Rachel. I swear, I've never talked to her before in my life."

"That much was obvious!" I laughed.

Silence fell again. The air seemed to buzz with a charge of

unexplainable energy. I felt pinned to the spot, enraptured by those gray eyes that were watching me so intently. I licked my lips, preparing to say something–anything to cut through the awkwardness. Fitz beat me to it.

"Eh, well, anyway…" he trailed off and did that rocking thing on his heels again. "About what I said to Rachel. You know, about having plans to grab dinner with someone later?"

"Yes."

"What do you say? Want to hang out? I thought we could grab a bite, then head back up to the lake."

*Oh my God. This boy, this older, gorgeous boy, was officially asking me out.*

My body screamed to say yes, but I knew I couldn't. My parents would never approve of me seeing a member of the staff even if he wasn't technically on the payroll. There were rules. My parents were trusting me to take on more this year. I had a responsibility, one that didn't include being accused of favoritism by other members of the staff.

"Fitz, as much as I'd like to, I can't. It wouldn't look good if we were seen hanging out together. I mean, technically I'm your boss."

He raised an eyebrow in surprise.

"Yeah, I suppose now that you mention it. I hadn't thought of it that way."

His face fell, and I scrambled to think of something fast–anything that would allow us to see each other again. Then I remembered my secret place.

"I can meet you at the lake though," I added quickly.

He grinned and leaned against the counter, cool and confident in that James Dean sort of way. Anxious flutters tickled in my belly.

"Yeah? What time?"

"How does eight sound? It will give me time to eat and get an hour of schoolwork in."

"Sounds like a plan. I'll bring some snacks." He turned away and headed up the snack aisle. When he returned, he raised both hands. One held a bag of Bugles, the other a bag of Doritos. "Have a preference?"

"Both work for me. I can bring the drinks," I offered.

Just as I had with Rachel, I rang up the snacks and placed them in a paper bag. When I looked back at Fitz, he was watching me intently. I handed him the bag and he took it with a slight nod.

"Thanks. I guess I'll see you in a bit."

"Yeah," was all I managed. All this nervous excitement seemed to have hindered my vocabulary.

When he turned to walk away, I impulsively came out from behind the counter and walked with him to the door. Once we reached it, he turned to me. His mouth tilted up on one side before turning into a full-blown smile. The corners of his eyes crinkled, and those deep grays seemed to sparkle with mischief.

"I can't wait to see you later, Cadence."

I smiled back and bit my lip nervously.

"Me too."

"Don't do that," he quietly chided.

"Don't do what?"

He reached up and traced my bottom lip that was still stuck between my teeth.

"Make me want to kiss you again, right here where anyone walking by can see."

My skin tingled from his touch before he all too quickly pulled his thumb away. Something heavy gripped at my heart. I didn't understand my reaction to him, but I couldn't stop the rush of need that engulfed my senses. His gray eyes burned into mine and I sucked in a breath when I noticed him leaning in. Instead of kissing me like I thought he would, he simply pecked my cheek lightly and headed out the door.

Stunned, I reached up to touch where his lips had brushed. My heart began to pound. Visions of childhood cartoons came to mind–the ones where the cartoon's heart was visibly beating out of their chest. I could almost see the hearts in the air around my head.

My head shouted warnings. I was acting ridiculously love-sick. This wasn't good. After only one kiss, I was clearly in over my head. I had very little experience with boys. And Fitz… well, I was fairly certain he'd been with more than his fair share of girls. Plus, he was four years older than me. Even if he weren't a member of the staff, that fact alone would make my parents absolutely freak.

However, my heart didn't want to listen to my head. There was a reason why I was drawn to Fitz like I'd never been to anyone else, and I was determined to find out what it was.

# Chapter Nine

**FITZ**

I paced along the edge of the lake, splashing water as I went. I had left my shoes on the dock, along with the bag of snacks I bought earlier at The Flourish. A quick glance at my watch said that it was ten minutes past eight. I scanned the tree line, hoping to see Cadence.

Nothing.

It was bizarre. Never in my life had I been so anxious to spend time with a girl. When I had gone into The Flourish earlier that day, my intention was just to grab a soda and be on my way. If I happened to catch a glimpse of her while I was there, so be it. What I didn't expect was to be so fucking turned on by the way she stood there with her little clipboard, looking all efficient and business-like. With her golden hair swept back into a practical braid and a pencil tucked behind her ear, it was all kinds of sexy. I couldn't resist. Talking to her, asking her to meet me tonight–I knew it was a mistake. After last night's unexpected kiss, I should have stopped everything before any kind of emotional attachment occurred, but I just couldn't do it. There was something about the way she pulled me in with those sparkling emerald eyes.

Trying to tamp down the worry that she wouldn't even show up, I picked up a flat rock and flung it across the water. One. Two. Three skips. I frowned and picked up another. That time, I managed seven skips. Just as I was about to squat down and search for a third, I heard a bark in the distance. Looking up, I saw Cadence and her furry friend emerging from the woods.

Relief flooded through me at the sight of her. She was carrying the

Boombox again, along with the sodas she promised to bring and what appeared to be folded-up towels. She struggled as she approached, barely able to juggle everything she brought while holding Dahlia's leash. I rushed to her side.

"Here, let me help you," I offered, taking the soda and bulky stereo from her arms.

"Sorry I'm late. I thought I could carry it all, but with Dahlia pulling on the leash, she made it hard." She bent to unhook the leash from the dog's collar and scratched her behind the ears. Bringing her nose to Dahlia's face, she let her lick her on the cheek. When she spoke again, her voice took on a sweeter tone as she lightly scolded her pet. "Maybe if you'd stop chasing rabbits, I would ditch the leash. But you need to learn how to behave first. Don't you, girl?"

I smiled wistfully as I watched the affectionate exchange, suddenly overcome with a wave of nostalgia over the dog I had lost so many years ago. Perhaps my father was right–maybe I was too soft. Cadence seemed to bring out all kinds of mushy emotions that I didn't even know I was capable of feeling.

"What are the towels for? Preparing yourself in case I decide to toss you in again?" I teased as we casually strolled over to the dock. I winked at her when she shoved a playful elbow into my side.

"That's actually why I was a little late. I decided to grab us a few towels at the last minute. It's still pretty hot out, so I wore my bathing suit under my clothes. I figured we might want to cool off in the lake. That is, well, um…" she stuttered. "That's assuming you want to."

I glanced at her, unsure why she suddenly sounded so hesitant. A visible flush crept up her neck until it turned her cheeks pink. Her tongue poked out to skim her bottom lip and I couldn't help but to slightly smirk. If I wasn't mistaken, that adorable blush was because she was remembering our kiss from last night.

Bending to set down the bottles of soda and radio on the dock, I flipped the switch to turn on the music. Just as it had on the first night I found her here, U2 flowed from the speakers. I returned to a standing position and faced her.

"Swimming is definitely an option." I took a step closer and placed my hands beneath each of her elbows to draw her a little nearer. "I was also hoping that a repeat of last night's kiss might be on the agenda too."

I worried for a moment that I may have come off too forward, but there was no mistaking the undeniable hope that sparkled in her emerald eyes. Her already flushed cheeks darkened to a deeper shade of crimson.

*Fuck, she's beautiful.*

"Sure, maybe. I thought we could watch the sunset first."

Her tone was guarded like she was unsure about me. Turning her head, she whistled for Dahlia. The dog was sniffing around the edge of the woods, undoubtedly in search of a stick. When she began to plod back toward us, Cadence moved away from me and began to spread the towels out on the dock. I watched her meticulously arrange the terry cloth so that each towel was perfectly square with the other. When she sat down on one of them, I took her cue and moved to join her. However, instead of sitting beside her, I sat behind her. Straddling her hips, I pulled her back to my chest.

"Is this okay?" I asked, hoping to put her more at ease.

She just nodded in response, but still seemed a little tense as she attempted to settle in against me. I breathed deep, inhaling her scent. She smelled sweet with a hint of spice, like cherry vanilla. Her head rested just below my chin, and instead of looking out over the water at the sunset, I found myself studying the braid she had woven into her hair. Varying shades of light and dark yellow intertwined with one another, creating a vibrant crisscross pattern of spun gold.

I softly ran my hands up and down the soft skin of her bare arms, only pausing once to trace my finger over the lines of her dainty shoulder tattoo. We sat in silence, neither one of us saying a word, as we watched the sun slowly settle behind the trees. After a while, Cadence tilted her head up to look at me.

"Just so you know," she began. "I don't normally do things like this."

"Like what?"

"You know, boys. I can honestly say that this is my first real date. I'm new to the whole dating thing."

*Dating? Shit. We couldn't date. This was just... What exactly was this?*

Surely it was nothing more than the beginnings of a summer fling even if she was stirring up all kinds of foreign feelings inside me. Hell, I couldn't get the girl out of my head, but I couldn't have anything more than a casual thing with her. I wasn't allowed to. Leading her to believe otherwise would be wrong. Still, the thought of ending things before they even began caused an ache in my chest, so I chose my words carefully.

"There's no pressure here, Cadence. No expectations. I just want to spend time with you. I like you, you like me. That's all this is."

*But was it?*

I didn't want to entertain the thought, so I didn't say anymore. Besides, she was so damn innocent. Because of that, I'd have to tread very carefully or risk unintentionally destroying her untouched heart.

She turned in my arms to fully face me.

"Is that how it is with other girls too? Like Rachel for example?"

She narrowed her eyes suspiciously. Her obvious jealousy made me chuckle.

"I already told you. Today was the first time I ever spoke to her. You wouldn't happen to be jealous now, would you?"

She pursed her lips, appearing annoyed that I called her out on it.

"Maybe a little," she admitted. "But that's the weird thing about this. I've always been so focused on school and helping my parents with the camp. It's not that I didn't have an interest in boys, it was only that there wasn't time for them. I certainly never had an opportunity to be jealous. Do you know what I mean?"

"Sure." I shrugged as casually as I could, afraid that the conversation might steer toward shaky ground. And, just as I feared, her next words confirmed it.

"I want to make time for you, Fitz. Considering that just over a week ago I thought you were nothing but trouble, I have to admit that you've surprised me. There's something good about you. And now, all I know is that I can't seem to stop looking at you. Can't stop thinking about you. I like you a lot," she admitted, the words scraping from her throat like a confession.

*Fuck.*

She stared up at me, her gorgeous green eyes round, innocent, and exposed as she studied me with unabashed honesty. I wanted to tell her that I liked her a lot too, but the words got caught in my throat.

"Cadence, I..." I trailed off, my voice hoarse, as a sudden realization struck me.

It was already too late. Not just for her, but for me as well. She was different. Perfect. And everything I didn't know I wanted. This girl affected me like no other. I wanted her desperately, and not just as a summer fling. My heart began to pound like it wanted to beat right out of my chest.

*Shit. I barely even know this chick.*

My conscience nagged at me, telling me to stop before things went any further. But I couldn't. I had a taste of her, and I already knew that I'd never get my fill.

She leaned in closer, taking me by surprise. Our heads were barely six inches apart. She continued to stare at me with those wide green eyes that had the ability to bring me to my knees. Uncertainty pooled within their depths. Waiting. Watching. Expecting. I was familiar with that look. I had seen it last night.

Leaning in, I closed the remaining distance between us. Wrapping my arms around her slender waist, I crushed my mouth down onto hers. She let out a tiny gasp, surprised by such a demanding kiss. Last night had been sweet and tender, slow movements against her untrained lips. Tonight, I kissed her like I'd never kissed anyone. My desperate tongue slid against hers with a hunger I hadn't known I possessed. She just tasted so goddamned good. Kissing her was like nothing I'd ever felt before. Sure, I had kissed a lot of other girls, but Cadence made me lose track of the world around me. Time seemed suspended when I was with her, making all my problems and the hell that awaited me completely disappear.

She responded by pulling back just a little to shift her position. Wrapping her legs around my waist, she straddled my hips and ran delicate fingers tentatively up my chest to my shoulders. I traced my tongue over my bottom lip, tasting her and craving more. When our mouths met once again, she came at me eagerly with a pleasing sweetness. My blood turned to gasoline, and the slide of her tongue over mine was the spark.

I cupped her head with one hand while the other roamed down her back until it reached the tiny gap between the hem of her shirt and the waistband of her shorts. Pulling her even tighter against me, I teased the small area of warm skin beneath my fingers. They slid along the hem of her shirt, needing to feel more of her skin.

Desire for her surged through me like lava. I delved deeper. Harder. More demanding. She met me every step of the way. My palm flattened against the warmth of her lower back. I wanted to move up, to feel the delicate curve of her spine, her ribs, her breasts.

I didn't think it was possible, but my dick felt ready to explode just from kissing her. And that would be fucking embarrassing. That urgent need caused me to still. Things were getting hot and heavy in a hurry. Sure, I was used to that, but it couldn't be that way with Cadence. She wasn't like other girls. She was unique in every way imaginable.

I stifled a groan and slowly broke away. Her pink lips were swollen, making that heart-shaped upper lip even more delectable.

"Sorry," I panted. "I didn't mean to be so possessive. I just said that I had no expectations, and then I practically mauled you."

I laughed lightly, hoping she wouldn't feel rejection like she had last night. God knew, I really didn't want to stop. I brought her hand to my mouth and place a feather-light kiss to the backside of it for reassurance, forcing myself to be gentle.

She smiled that shy smile again. She looked surprised, but I also saw a hint of respect.

"I didn't mind," she whispered.

This time, I didn't bother to stifle the groan. This girl would undoubtedly be my undoing.

Dahlia, who had been silent during my lip lock with Cadence, let out a soft whine. She was sitting next to us with a stick in her mouth, her tail wagging expectantly. Using that as a distraction, I took Cadence's chin in my hand and tilted her head up to look at me.

"How about that swim, sweetheart?" I asked, lightly pecking a kiss to her nose. "I think your poor pup is running out of patience."

She nodded, and I stood, pulling her to her feet along with me. As I stripped out of my t-shirt, I tried not to stare while she shed her shorts and tank top, but she made it damn near impossible. It wasn't that she was making a big production out of it. In fact, it was quite the opposite. The way she removed her clothing was hurried, her movements almost jerky. When she quickly snatched up a towel and wrapped it around her petite frame, I was reminded once again of how different she was from the rest. Most girls I'd encountered were like Rachel, brazenly flaunting their bodies every chance they got. The fact that Cadence didn't do that made me want her all the more.

We walked back up the dock and along the water's edge. Dahlia trotted along beside us. Every few minutes, I'd toss the stick for her. The pebbled sand was warm underfoot, a sharp contrast to the cool water that would occasionally graze our ankles. Cadence smiled up at me and laced her fingers through mine. The action was innocent and pure, rocking me to my very core.

So many thoughts ran through my head. I needed to tell her about me, about my past, and about what lay in store for me in September. However, each time I opened my mouth to tell her, I swallowed the words. Instead, I tried to think of a way to defy my father's demands and get out of my predicament. Other than running away to Canada, I had nothing. Besides, there would be no Cadence in Canada.

We walked around the lake until well after the sun had set. We never ended up going for that swim, but that was okay with me. We didn't talk much either. Neither one of us seemed to have a need to fill space with idle chatter. Instead, we just enjoyed the quiet of the night.

As the moon grew higher in the sky, lightning bugs danced in the air. The occasional hoot from an owl in the woods made me realize how late it was getting, but I couldn't bring myself to end the night. Our time together already had an expiration date. If I could stay here all night with her, I would. I wanted to soak up every minute I could get.

# Chapter Ten

**CADENCE**

I pushed a hand truck laden with supply boxes toward the stage set. As I approached, I could hear the faint sounds of hammering. When I got closer, the hammering stopped, and the orchestra started up. I smiled when I saw the cast rehearsing the "Make Em' Laugh" scene from *Singin' in the Rain*. It had always been one of my favorite parts.

"Cadence, bring those boxes of brushes over here," my mother called. She was waving at me to come backstage. When I approached her, she shook her head. "Thanks, honey. The heat has been brutal this year. We're four weeks into the season, and already we're behind. Paint is drying on the brushes before it even touches the wood!"

She motioned to the wooden props that were scattered all over backstage. Some were standing upright while others were lying flat. The student set designers moved around them, each one wielding a paintbrush and seemed frustrated over the fast-drying paint. I looked up and shielded my eyes from the hot Virginia sun that was shining down on us.

"What if daddy fashions a curtain of sorts to block the afternoon sun? That might help."

Her eyes lit up.

"Brilliant idea! Jamison!" she called to my father.

"Yes, dear," he responded automatically. I looked over toward the sound of his voice. He was on his knees and appeared to be fixing a few of the floorboards stage left. A hammer was in one hand, clearly signifying that he was the one causing the hammering noise I heard a few moments before.

"Is there any way to hang a curtain to shade the backstage area?" my mother asked him.

My father stood and eyed up the rafters above the outdoor stage. He scratched his chin contemplatively for a moment before nodding his head.

"Shouldn't be a problem. I can use the old stage curtains. I was just going to toss them since we have the new ones, but I'm glad I hung on to them. I'll get Devon and Fitz over here to help. We can probably have it up within a few hours."

My belly tightened at the mention of Fitz. The past few weeks with him had been perfect. Every night I had spent with him was like every girl's dream idea of a perfect date. Sometimes we'd walk hand in hand around the lake for hours, breaking only for the intermittent kiss. Other times, we'd swim or play Frisbee on the beach. On the few occasions when I had to work late at the camp store, I'd brought my homework to the lake. Fitz didn't seem to mind but simply played fetch with Dahlia while I worked. Just being around me seemed to be enough for him.

"Momma, I'm going to head back to The Flourish if you don't need anything else."

"Actually, would you stick around for a few minutes? I could use your eyes. You're good at seeing things that are out of place. While I'm directing, I'd like you to look at actor stage placement from the audience perspective. There should be windows, so nothing important is blocked."

This wasn't an unusual request from her as I had been her test audience for years. Joy had already taken her lunch break, and the store was usually quiet during this time of day. I was sure she'd be okay by herself for a while.

"Sure," I agreed with a shrug.

"Thanks. Just take a seat second-row, center stage, and I'll get started."

As my mother issued instructions to the students, I sat back and watched her. She was a genius at what she did, and I couldn't help but to notice how captivated the students were by her words. They hung on to everything she said, eager to learn from one of the best. I wished I knew the person she was once upon a time. I had only seen pictures, theater posters, and old newspaper clippings that depicted her fame. My mother had been a beautiful young woman. Her hair had been blond, just like mine, and she always appeared vibrant and bright-eyed. While sixty-two years on this earth may have grayed her hair and added lines to her face, she still looked just as vibrant and beautiful to me.

Once everyone was in their place on stage, my mother signaled to the orchestra conductor. He raised his baton and the musicians poised at the ready. The male student who played the role of Cosmo Brown began his lines, telling the actor playing Don Lockwood about the importance of not giving up.

"Come rain, come shine, come snow, come sleet! The show must go on!" he bellowed. Moving quickly over to the piano on stage right, he sat down and pretended to play. The reality was that there was a pianist in the pit playing the tune. When he began to sing and dance to "Make Em' Laugh," I laughed. And hard. His quick feet and abundant silliness were so similar to real the life actor, Donald O'Connor. The kid had major talent.

I glanced over at my mother's face. She was beaming from ear to ear, and I knew that this year's cast was destined to be great.

When the scene ended, she asked for my feedback.

"Everything looked great to me, Momma. The sound from the orchestra was good too. A few little blips, but it's early. They still have time to practice. Once the set design is complete, I think it will come together wonderfully."

"Excellent! I have one more scene I need you to watch. Again, look closely at their placement on stage. We've been struggling with the look and feel of this one. It's not the acting per se, but..." She trailed off and looked up at the sky for a moment. "Well, I don't want to influence you. Just watch and tell me what you think."

Settling back once again, I waited as my mother called the girl who was cast to play the role of Kathy Sheldon. She and the male playing Don Lockwood joined hands. I smiled wistfully when they began to sing a romantic ballad. Trying not to get too caught up in the performance, I looked carefully at their stage placement. Everything seemed okay to me as far as I could tell. My eyes roamed up and over the set, carefully assessing the lighting until my gaze settled on a more than familiar face. Fitz was standing off stage left. He wasn't watching the actors, but rather he was watching me.

Our gazes locked, and for a moment, it was as if we were the only two present. I could hear the music, but I barely saw the young students dancing in my peripheral. Blinking, I snapped myself to attention and trained my eyes back on the performers. As they tap danced across the stage, I couldn't help but steal furtive looks back at Fitz. He was still watching me, just waiting for a moment to catch my eye again. When he did, he gave me a little wink. I smiled, somewhat flattered by his attention.

I glanced over at my mother. Much to my dismay, she wasn't paying one bit of attention to the students. Instead, she was looking straight at Fitz. When her eyes flitted in my direction, her gaze narrowed. I nearly swore aloud, knowing that she had caught our exchange. She was so damn observant.

Determined not to give her more reason for suspicion, I spent the next three minutes looking at nothing else but the performance happening on stage. When it ended, I quickly stood and walked straight over to my mother. Acting as if nothing was amiss, I told her my observations.

"Considering that you've only have four weeks to work on this, the performance was exceptional. However, the sunlight on the stage seemed to wash them out. Maybe a darker wardrobe for them would help or have the tech crew shift the stage lighting," I said hurriedly. "Also, I think the orchestra should raise their tempo a bit, so the choreography is seamless and less awkward."

She watched me curiously for a moment before nodding her head.

"Yes, I agree. I was thinking similar things," she paused and looked behind me. I didn't dare turn, knowing that she was looking in the direction of where Fitz had been standing. "Thanks, dear. I'll let you get back to your work at The Flourish."

"Okay, Momma. I'll see you at dinner."

Leaning toward her, I placed a quick kiss on her cheek, before heading back in the direction of the camp store. When I was halfway there, I remembered that I'd forgotten the hand truck backstage.

"Damn!" I said aloud to myself. We had a supply delivery showing up in the morning. Unloading without the hand truck would be a bear. Turning around, I began to walk back. Up ahead, I spotted Fitz on the path. He was headed in my direction, carrying a large toolbox.

"Hey, sweetheart," he said as he approached. "Are you going back to the stage?"

"I forgot the hand truck that belongs over in the camp store. I need to go back for it."

"I can grab it later for you," he offered.

"Are you sure?"

"Yeah. No sweat. I was just headed over to the barn to swap out the toolbox. Your dad said we needed a different one for the stage pulleys. Apparently, we need to hang a curtain of some kind. Once we're through, I'll drop the hand truck off at The Flourish."

"Okay, thanks."

Since we both had to go in the same direction, we began to walk down the long winding gravel path that passed the camp store and ended at the barn.

"I forgot to mention it to you last night, but I have a favor to ask," Fitz said.

"Sure, just as long as it doesn't include winking at me in front of my mother."

I tossed him a sideways glance and he had the decency to look shamefaced.

"Yeah, sorry about that. I didn't think she'd notice, but the look she gave told me it was pretty obvious that she did."

"Well, I suppose she'd find out eventually," I said, feeling an odd mix of trepidation and excitement. A part of me wanted to tell my mother about Fitz and me. I confided in her about most things, and I wanted to share my happiness. However, I worried that she'd frown upon me getting involved with someone at camp. "Anyway, what's the favor?"

"Is there a phone over at The Flourish?"

"Of course. We might not have internet, but we aren't that archaic. There are phones all over this place."

"Not in the barn."

"Except for there," I laughed, still feeling guilty for making him sleep in the loft. If I had another option, I would have moved him and Devon. But the truth was, we really were completely booked this year.

"After work I was going to pop into the store. I need to call home. There are a few things I need and want to see if I can get my dad's housekeeper to ship them to me."

I quirked up an eyebrow with interest. Despite the many nights Fitz and I had spent together, never once had he mentioned having a housekeeper. For that matter, he barely ever spoke about his family either. I wondered why that was and, for the first time, I began to think about how vastly different our lives must be outside of Camp Riley.

"What do you need?"

"It's a secret," he said with a devilish grin.

"If that's how it's going to be, then maybe I won't let you use the phone."

He poked my ribs. It tickled, causing me to squeal and jerk away. Fitz laughed, a bellowing sound that came from deep within.

"Seriously," he said, adopting a more earnest tone. "I want it to be a surprise."

Curiosity got the best of me, so I agreed.

"Alright, I'll bite. But only because I like you," I teased. "What time do you finish today?"

"I'm hoping before five, assuming your dad doesn't hand out any last-minute jobs for me and Devon."

"I'll stick around the store until you get there. Are we meeting at the lake again tonight?"

"Do you even need to ask?"

I laughed. Our secret meetings at the lake had become part of my routine. Work, food, homework, and then sneaking off to meet Fitz. So far, this summer had been my favorite of all spent at Camp Riley. We were only one month in, but already I didn't want it to end.

"I'll be there by eight," I told him.

We walked a little further, up over the hill, until the camp store came into view. I glanced around us to make sure nobody else was nearby. Seeing that we were alone, I turned to face Fitz. Raising up to my tiptoes, I pressed a quick kiss to his lips.

"Somebody is going to see you do that one of these days," he joked after I pulled away. His hand lingered on my arm, and his eyes were intense. I was now familiar with the heat that would creep into his gaze and knew he was fighting the urge to pull me into his arms for a much longer kiss. Instead, he said, "I'll see you in a few hours."

As promised, Fitz came to the store at five to make his phone call. I let him have his privacy by straightening the shelves on the sales floor while he spoke on the phone in the stockroom. After he finished, he didn't say anything, but simply flashed me a mischievous grin before slipping out the front door of the store.

Joy watched the entire event with a suspicious look on her face. As soon as the door closed behind Fitz, she rounded on me.

"What's going on with you two?"

I looked at her in feigned surprise.

"Nothing," I lied. She gave me a skeptical look.

"Bullshit. That boy stops in here almost every day. Whenever he does, you get all flushed and start acting weird. Spill it."

I glanced around. Thankfully, Joy and I were the only ones in the store at that moment.

"Okay, so maybe I've been meeting up with him sometimes after work."

"Maybe? Sometimes?"

"Okay, so it's been a lot of times. So, what?"

"Are you two like, going out or something?"

"It's not like that. We're just friends," I fibbed again, just hoping she wouldn't see through the lie. Joy was my friend, but still. It wasn't just that I didn't want to start gossip mills among the staff. A part of me wanted to keep Fitz my little secret although I couldn't explain why.

"If you're just friends, then he obviously wants more than that. I've seen the way he watches you. Honey, that boy wants you something fierce!" she exclaimed, clearly unconvinced.

I just shrugged but didn't say anything. Instead, I went into the stockroom to grab the keys for the camp store. Coming back out, I handed them to Joy.

"It's your turn to lock up tonight. I'm going to head over to Creator Hall, grab dinner, and then head home. I want to put a bigger dent in my course load tonight. I'm a little behind on assignments."

She eyed me suspiciously as she took the keys. When I turned to walk away, she grabbed my arm.

"Cadence. Be careful."

She didn't have to say what or *who* she was referring to with her warning. Nodding, I pulled my arm free of her grasp and walked out.

Anxious to meet up with Fitz, I grabbed a sandwich of apple butter and ham for dinner and hurried home to work on my assignments. My parents weren't there. More than likely, they were still over at the stage set working and wouldn't be back for hours. For that, I was grateful. It meant I wouldn't have to see my mother's inquisitive gaze.

After working on a sociology essay for more than an hour, I was satisfied with what I had accomplished. I glanced out the window. There was another breathtaking sunset tonight, and I was grateful to be able to catch the end of it with Fitz. Still, Joy's words had hung over me the entire time I was writing my paper.

*"Are you two like, going out or something?"*

I didn't know the answer to that question and it bothered me.

*What was this thing between us?*

Shaking my head, I gathered the papers and textbooks that were spread out all over the kitchen table. I stuffed them into my backpack and brought it to my room. Dahlia, who was now familiar with my routine, stood waiting for me at the kitchen door. Grabbing her leash, the two of us set out to the lake. And to Fitz.

# Chapter Eleven

**CADENCE**

I lay upon an oversized beach blanket next to Fitz. A half-eaten bag of Bugle's was tossed haphazardly on the dock above our heads. Duran Duran's *Ordinary World* flowed from the speakers of the Boombox, filling the silence of the warm night. Dahlia lay snoring softly at our feet while Fitz and I stared up at the kaleidoscope of colors sprawling across the evening sky.

"You know, I've been thinking," I announced.

"Uh-oh. Don't hurt yourself," Fitz responded with a chuckle.

I turned my head to look pointedly at him.

"I'm serious."

"So am I," he said with a wink. He rolled over onto his right side and lazily draped an arm across my stomach. I smiled at the way he did it, appreciating the level of comfort we'd established in just a short month. We'd become familiar like he was someone I'd known all my life. However, the truth was that I really didn't know him that well at all.

"I was thinking we've spent nearly every night of the last four weeks together, but I don't know much about you. For example, what's your favorite color?"

"I'm not sure if my favorite color has anything to do with getting to know me. I don't know your favorite color, and I'm okay with that."

"Well, I'm not," I stated firmly, trying not to sound pouty. I turned on my side to face him and propped my head up with my elbow. "I want to know more about you. I think that's only normal, especially since I don't even know how to describe us. I mean, we haven't told anyone about us. Once we do, what do we say? Are we, you know, together? Do we tell them that we're boyfriend and girlfriend? If we are, how can I say that if I don't even know your favorite color?"

He pursed his lips and darted his eyes away from mine. I had a nagging suspicion that my questions were making him uncomfortable.

*Maybe he doesn't want me to be his girlfriend.*

That thought made me nervous. I knew that I was four years younger than him. I worried that our age difference might bother him. I was sure that he was used to more sophisticated women, but I also knew that I didn't want to be just a friend that he sometimes kissed. Well, maybe it was more than just sometimes. It had been almost every night, not that I was keeping track or anything.

Either way, I knew that I really wanted to be Fitz's girlfriend. It was crazy in a way. At the beginning of the summer, I told myself that I didn't have time for boys. Yet here I was spending every available free minute with Fitz.

"I think Devon has a suspicion. I haven't confirmed it, but he's not stupid," Fitz pointed out.

"Same here. I think Joy might know too. Still, Joy and Devon don't count. They're our best friends."

"To be fair, you're the one who didn't want to tell anyone about us. You wanted to keep the lake spot a secret, and you were worried about what the staff might think, remember?"

"True," I mused. I flipped back over onto my back and stared up at the sky. I still wasn't sure what he thought about our relationship. He was avoiding my questions–again. That's what happened whenever anything personal about him or the status of us was brought up.

He sat up and reached down to take my chin between his thumb and forefinger.

"Sweetheart, what's going on in that pretty little head of yours?"

"It's nothing," I said with a small smile, refusing to be that clingy girl who put demands on their boyfriend–assuming that's what he actually was.

"I have an idea," Fitz suddenly announced. His eyes smoldered when they looked down at me, the edges brimming with something brilliant and beautiful, yet held a hint of mischief. "How about I ask you ten questions tonight? You can ask me ten tomorrow night. Then we'll switch off again the next night. Sort of like twenty questions, just more drawn out. This way, when we do tell people about us, all the basics should be covered."

"Hmmm…" was my initial response. I pondered his proposal for a few moments. While Fitz waited for my answer, he reached up and popped a Bugle into his mouth. Grabbing another, he brought one to my lips. After I chewed and swallowed, he fed me one more.

"So, what's it going to be?" he finally asked.

"It's a deal. But you don't get to back out when it's your turn. Promise?"

"I promise." He tossed me a lopsided grin that made my heart flutter just a little too fast.

"Alright then. Ask away."

Fitz lay back down next to me and reached up to play with the ends of my hair.

"Well, since favorite colors seem to be the thing to know, what's yours?"

"All of them," I responded automatically.

He laughed.

"That's not fair. All of them can't be your favorite."

"Look at the sunset. I can't possibly choose just one color! They're all so beautiful."

Fitz looked out over the lake, taking in the vibrant pinks, purples, and oranges.

"Okay. I'll give you that. What about your favorite movie?"

I pursed my lips and contemplated.

"That's a tough one. I'm a sucker for oldies, so I'm going to have to go with *Roman Holiday*."

"Gregory Peck and Audrey Hepburn. Good choice," he appreciated. I looked at him, surprised that he knew of the movie. While I answered his questions, perhaps I'd indirectly get a bit of insight into who he was as well. "Favorite food?"

"Strawberries, especially with a dollop of whipped cream."

"Favorite time of the year?"

I smiled.

"It used to be Fall, but I've recently changed my mind. Now my favorite is summertime."

"Favorite sport?"

"Hockey."

"Hockey? You're killing me here," he laughed again and shook his head. "Okay, next. U2 or Pearl Jam?"

"That's a wasted question. You already know that half of my mixed tapes are filled with U2 songs. What do you think?"

"Is that a question? I thought I was the one who was supposed to be asking tonight," he said with a wink. "We're going to have to subtract that from your allotted ten tomorrow night."

I sat up straight and gave him an incredulous look.

"Hey, now that's not fair! You knew that the answer would be U2."

"You're right. I did. I just wanted to see if I could trip you up," he teased.

I scowled but eventually laid back down into the crook of his arm.

"Next question please," I requested with a sigh.

"Alright, since we're on the topic of U2. What's the best U2 song ever?"

"*One*. Hands down."

"That's a damn powerful tune. It's one of my favorites too," he confessed.

"What's not to like about it? There's love, separation, and reunification. It's complicated and painful but can mean so many things depending on the listener."

"Hmm. Interesting. I have a part B to that question then. What–"

"Whoa, wait a minute. Part B? Is that even allowed?"

"My game. My rules, sweetheart."

I raised my eyebrows.

"If that's how it's going to be, I'll be sure to remember that when it's my turn."

"Alright, you win. No part B. So where were we then?" he asked and began ticking the questions off on his fingers. "Question number eight. You said that *One* can have different meanings. I'm curious. What does it mean to you?"

I shrugged.

"Honestly, I think it's about the divisions in humanity, and about how we should remember that we're really all the same despite our differences."

He eyed me curiously as if trying to pick apart my thoughts about the song.

"I never thought of it that way. I just assumed it was about a bad breakup." He paused and scratched his head. "You think deeper than most people, if you know what I mean."

"Um, I guess so. I've kind of always been that way–searching for the deeper meaning that is."

"I admire you for that. You seem to have everything all figured out. Which, I suppose, could bring me to my next question. Where do you see yourself in ten years?"

I pursed my lips as I thought about his question.

"I have an idea, but it depends on a lot of things," I told him. "I never really thought about marriage or kids. I'd have my master's degree of course. I haven't decided if I want to go beyond grad school though. I'd definitely be working for a non-profit organization that helps those who are less fortunate. Families would be my preference. If I can make a positive change in someone's life, even if it's a small one, that change could have a rippling effect. That's why I'm in such a hurry to graduate. I have this itch to get out there, you know?"

He stared at me for a long while, his eyes searching my face, but I couldn't read his thoughts. When he finally spoke, his words were low and throaty.

"Every time I think I've got you pegged, you say something mind-blowing. I've said it before, but I'll say it again. You're different from everyone else. I've never met anyone like you," he admitted. "You're smart. Beautiful. Driven, yet completely selfless."

His tone was reverent, and it was kind of embarrassing.

"Oh, um…" I trailed off, not knowing what to say as heat flooded my cheeks. The way he was looking at me made me feel self-conscious, like he could see parts of my soul that I didn't even know existed.

"Last question, Cadence."

He reached up to run a fingertip along my jawline and stared intently into my eyes. I shivered, but it wasn't from his touch or his piercing gaze. There was something about the way he said those three little words that sent goosebumps racing down my spine and made my breathing become shallow.

"Okay, shoot," I responded, trying to sound casual even though my words came out in barely a whisper.

"Can I touch you?"

My breath caught in my throat.

*Touch me?*

*Like how? Like he was doing now? With his hand on my face?*

"You are touching me, Fitz."

His hand lowered to the hem of my tank top, skimming across the thin line of skin that was exposed just above the waistband of my shorts. He moved slowly, cautiously, as if trying to convey a message to me without using words. I may have been inexperienced in the boy department, but I knew what he wanted. I just wasn't sure how *much* he wanted.

My chest rose and fell rapidly. A weird sensation began to build in my belly, a slow burn that moved south and caused a throbbing sensation between my legs. But he didn't veer away from the spot on my stomach. He just continued to trace his finger back and forth, as if drawing an invisible repeating line between my hip bones, teasing the sensitive skin. His gray eyes bore into mine, filled with a searing heat that was palpable.

"I want to touch you in a way that I haven't before, but I won't do it without your permission, sweetheart."

That word. Sweetheart. The way he said it practically turned me inside out. It always did, even in the early days when I pretended to be annoyed at him for calling me that. I felt like my heart was about to jump out of my chest from nervous anticipation. My hands trembled as I reached up to trace the lines and curves of his face. My fingers moved across his lips. His cheeks. His strong jaw. I wanted to feel him, to have him closer, and to have him touch me in places I never wanted to be touched before. I hadn't realized how bad I wanted it until that very moment.

Patiently, he waited for me to respond.

"Yes, Fitz. You can touch me."

He released a low groan before slowly inching his hand up under my tank, but he never took his eyes from mine. His moves were hesitant, yet deliberate, as he skimmed along my ribcage. He paused when he connected with the elastic line of my thin cotton bra. Leaning in, he licked his lips and pressed a gentle kiss to my mouth. It was a cautious kiss as if he had doubts about my decision to let him touch me.

Almost involuntarily, my back arched, and I kissed him harder. I kissed him like I'd always daydreamed about but had been too afraid to. It was sweet, deep, and hungry. There was no holding back. This was my silent message to him, telling him that touching me was okay. That I wanted this to happen.

The noise he made in the back of his throat sounded like something between a gasp and a moan. But it was full of appreciation. Our kisses had never felt so good, so all-consuming. We were all lips and tongue as his hand slipped around to my back, skimming along the clasp of my bra.

Shifting his weight, he moved his body over mine. The feel of his body pressing me against the dock made all sorts of things stir inside. Keeping his one arm positioned behind my back, he pulled me closer to him. His free hand roamed up my side, pushing up my tank top as he went. With a quick pinch and a tug, my bra was unclasped. I tried not to think about why he was so good at that as he pushed up the white cotton material to reveal my breasts. He cupped one in his palm as his lips moved from my mouth to my neck, softly suckling as he went.

Pulling back slightly, he looked down at my now exposed breasts.

"Jesus fucking Christ, Cadence," he whispered, his eyes huge. The string of expletives told me that he liked what he saw. For some reason, that made me feel good. I liked him liking that part of me. I was always a little self-conscious about my small breasts that barely filled a B-cup.

He lowered his head, capturing a pink nipple between his lips. The sensation was shocking almost, but oh-so-good. His hot mouth worked over one breast while his hand molded the other. Even the most delicate touches were making me shake, causing every muscle in my body to grow tighter and tighter.

"Fitz. More," I breathed. I wasn't sure what I needed more of exactly, I only knew I had a want I couldn't define. I found myself reaching for the hem of his t-shirt. I pulled it up, craving the feel of his bare solid body against my feverish skin. My fingers trailed over the muscles of his abdomen and over his hard pectorals. Gripping his back,

I pulled his body tighter to mine and scissored my legs around his waist. I felt a tightening low in my belly. Pressing my pelvis up against him, I groaned.

Fitz stilled and lifted his head to look at me.

"Cadence," he panted. "I'm sure that I'm going to kick my own ass for this later, but we need to stop."

Reality came crashing down. We were a mess of twisted up limbs, breathless and sweaty, on the brink of catastrophe caused by over-eagerness. Of course, we needed to stop. Things had gotten way too hot in a hurry.

*God, what was I thinking?*

"You're right. I'm sorry. I don't know what got into me. I've never–"

"Shhhh," he said and silenced me by placing a finger over my lips. And then he kissed me. Once, then twice. "I know that you've never. That's why we should stop. I don't want you to have any regrets."

He pulled me up to a sitting position and reached around to refasten my bra. Once it was secure, he pulled my tank down to cover me. His actions were so tender, and I could feel myself slipping…falling. I had no experience with romance or love, but the pitter-patter of my heart told me that I was falling head over heels for him.

"Fitz," I whispered and reached up to touch his face. "You're the keeper of my heart. I could never have any regrets when it comes to you."

"Never say never," he warned. His eyes, pools of gray that were filled with desire just moments ago, were now sad. "Come on, sweetheart. It's getting late. Let's get you home."

I stared at him, confused by his sudden change in mood, and wondered if I had said something wrong. I wanted to ask, but I nodded my agreement instead and leaned in to press a chaste kiss to his lips. Tomorrow was my day for questions. Until then, it could wait.

# Chapter Twelve

**FITZ**

The sun beat down through the muggy air, the moisture feeling like liquid fire on my back as I dragged the remaining tools inside the barn. After putting them all away, I used the hem of my shirt to wipe the sweat from my brow. The day was like a sauna turned all the way up, set to full blast and would never compromise any sort of relief. I could use a shower, but Mr. Jimmy had given me extra work today, and I didn't have time. Cadence was probably already at the lake, and I was running late.

I climbed the ladder to the loft, planning to swap out my t-shirt for a clean one and put on a fresh layer of deodorant. When I reached the top, I saw Devon had recently been up there. The clothes that I saw him wearing earlier in the day were now thrown in a haphazard pile on the floor, his toiletry bag lay strewn wide open and spilling onto his mattress. The water droplets covering the shampoo bottle signaled a recent shower. It was clear he was already out for the night which meant that Mr. Jimmy hadn't given Devon nearly the amount of work that he gave me. That was unlike him. The man was always all about fair and equal work.

I frowned and wondered if Cadence's mother had told her husband about the wink she saw me give Cadence on the stage set yesterday. She probably did tell him which might explain why he doled out so many bullshit jobs to me today.

I shook my head, hoping to hell that he didn't suspect something was up between Cadence and me. If he did, today just might have been the first sign of what was to come. He had me doing everything from cleaning out the toilets to hauling firewood to all the cottages–despite the fact that each cottage still had a stack eight logs high. I ripped off the rotting two-by-fours surrounding the crumbling foundation of a cottage and replaced shingles on a sweltering black roof. I was kept so busy, I barely had time to wolf down a sandwich at lunch. And forget dinner. By the time I got to Creator Hall, dinner hour was long over.

After a quick change of my shirt, I grabbed the bag of snacks that was inevitably going to be the only sustenance I'd get tonight. I dreaded the idea of turning last night's left-over bag of Bugles into a gourmet meal, but any food was better than no food. Swinging my legs over the top rung of the ladder, I climbed down and headed toward the outskirts of the camp.

Finding the narrow tree-lined path that would take me to the lake, I stepped into the thick brush. Trees rustled overhead, swaying in the warm evening breeze. As I rounded the final bend before the lake clearing, I caught a whiff of something–vanilla and sugar. I smiled, instantly recognizing Cadence's scent.

"Boo!" Cadence exclaimed and jumped out from behind a nearby tree.

"Nice try," I laughed.

"Oh, come on! Didn't I scare you? Even a little bit?"

I dropped the bag I was holding and snagged her by the hand. Pulling her into my arms, I spun her around and buried my face in her neck.

"Not even a little bit. I smelled your perfume or whatever it is you wear. It gave you away," I murmured against her ear. "It's like a vanilla dessert."

I took her hand and kissed it, then reached up to trace my finger along her lower lip.

"Not so fast there, mister. You wouldn't want me to think the only reason you come to the lake is to steal kisses from me, do you?"

I grinned.

"Is there another reason?" I teased. Her heart-shaped lips were always a weakness of mine. Despite her protest, I leaned in to kiss her. She didn't resist for more than a second, so I squeezed her body tighter to me. After a few moments, she reluctantly seemed to pull away.

"Come on," she said, tugging at my hand. "It's my turn to ask questions tonight."

I groaned.

"Do we have to?"

"Hey, now. This was your idea, remember?"

"Don't remind me," I mumbled. "But, hey, before we get started, I need to get some of this sweat off my skin. Your dad had me working overtime today, and I didn't have time to shower."

She slipped her hand into mine and looked questioningly at me.

"Is that what took you so long to get here?"

"Yeah, he was kind of a slave driver today."

As we stepped out of the woods into the clearing, I stripped out of my t-shirt and shoes. Dropping them to the ground, I ran up the dock and dove in. The shock of the cool water over my heated skin may have been the best thing I'd ever felt. Resurfacing, I saw Cadence standing on the dock above me.

"Where's Dahlia tonight?" I asked her, suddenly noticing the absence of the playful pup that had really begun to grow on me. I was hoping to use my fetch-loving friend as a way to avoid the interrogation I was sure Cadence was about to give.

"She was out cold when I left. I think the heat wore her out today, so I decided to leave her be."

*Damn.*

Reluctantly, I swam to the shoreline and joined her on the dock. She handed me one of the towels she always brought with her.

"Thanks," I said as I shook the excess water from my hair. Water droplets rained down around me… and on her.

"Hey!" Cadence shrieked. "Who needs Dahlia here when I've got you to shake all that wetness all over me?"

Smiling wickedly, I grabbed her around the waist. Pulling her to me in a tight bear hug, my wet chest and shorts soaked her dry clothes. She struggled, but I held her firm. Her vanilla scent wafted between us, causing my mouth to water. Keeping one arm securely around her waist, I used my free hand to grip the back of her head, so I could lean in for a long, deep kiss.

Instantly, she stopped squirming and all but melted into me, her hands curling around my neck as she hungrily entwined her tongue around mine. I pressed deeper into her mouth. Shock vibrated down my spine, followed by a searing arousal only she was able to entice. A little moan escaped her mouth before she angled her head back.

"As much as I'd love to stand here kissing you all night, I think you're stalling." I only grinned and leaned down to nuzzle her neck. Her hands went to my shoulders, pushing me off. "Question time, buddy. You promised."

"Okay, okay," I laughed. It wasn't that I didn't want to play the little game I had proposed, but I was worried how personal Cadence's questions were going to be. I hadn't thought of that when I suggested it, only thinking about appeasing her concerns at the time.

I sat down across from her on the blanket she had spread out on the dock before I arrived. Music was already playing from her stereo. I hummed along to a Dave Matthews Band sax solo while Cadence tapped her chin softly. She appeared to be contemplating what she wanted to ask me first.

While she thought, I couldn't help noticing the dahlia flowers that were in full bloom along the edge of the forest.

"The flowers would make a pretty picture today," I observed. "You should have brought your sketchbook."

"Maybe, but the lighting won't last for much longer," she said, pointing to the sun was low in the sky. "If I'm going to draw them, I need to get here in the morning or afternoon."

"We're off together next week Saturday. We should plan on coming earlier. Spend the day," I suggested.

"All day?"

"It could be fun. I know I could use a day away from listening to the band rehearsing *Singin' in the Rain*. I swear I hear the song in my sleep now," I laughed. "Speaking of which, that reminds me. This afternoon, while I was working near the stage set, I wondered why you aren't part of the crew. I mean, you have amazing talent. You could help with set design."

"I'm a temperamental artist. I can't draw on command, I need to be in the mood. Sure, my mother would have loved for me to follow in her footsteps in some way or another. But outside of my sketches, there's not a creative bone in my body–at least not one I could make a decent living with. I can't sing or dance. My fingers could never get the hang of the frets on a violin or the keys of a clarinet. I tried though," she added with a small laugh. "It just wasn't my thing."

"So, what is your thing?"

"When I'm not drawing, I'd have to say it's school. Studying. Reading. I've always had a love for books. It was like I couldn't get enough of them. I've read everything from *Silent Spring* to *Wuthering Heights*. Math isn't my forte, but literature and history I love." When she caught my incredulous stare, she turned somewhat defensive. "It's not a bad thing to enjoy learning."

I smiled.

"No. It's not a bad thing at all. It's just that…well, most of the girls I knew at school planned to party their first year of college away. None of them wanted to get an early start on their thesis."

She shrugged indifferently.

"I guess I just found learning about the beginnings of the environmental movement or dissecting the relationship between Heathcliff and Catherine to be more interesting than going to parties."

I raised my eyebrows.

"I think I'm pretty well read, but you lost me there. Heathcliff and who?"

"They're characters in a book," she waved off before pursing her lips in a frown. "You seem to be asking all the questions here. Are you trying to stall again?"

"Busted," I joked and put my hands up to signal she had the floor. "I'll stop. Fire away."

She took a deep breath and studied me for a moment before speaking.

"You mentioned girls at school. If all they want to do is party, then you've clearly met the wrong ones. Have a lot of those kinds of girls been your girlfriend?"

"Sure." I shrugged. "I mean, I wouldn't call any of them steady. I took advantage of the fact I was the star basketball player on my high school team. It wasn't too hard to get girls horizontal. In college, I didn't have to be the star of anything. I was a rich party boy. Those girls either saw me as a good time or a kid who came from money."

She grimaced and seemed taken aback.

"I wasn't referring to sexual exploits. I meant just normal dating."

"Oh, sorry," I apologized awkwardly, realizing how crude I must have sounded. "I didn't mean to come across like an ass–I'm not bragging or anything. In fact, I'm not particularly proud of it now. For some reason, you've seemed to change the way I look at things."

"Oh?"

"Yeah…" I trailed off, unable to find the words to explain why she seemed to affect me so much. As the music transitioned from jazz to the more acoustic sound of Radiohead's *High and Dry*, I thought about the positive and forward-thinking outlook Cadence had on things. Perhaps it was because she didn't have any dark pockets in her life like I did or any sort of pre-determined fate to keep her from following her dreams.

"Tell me about your family. What are they like?"

*Shit. That didn't take her long.*

"You don't want to know about them, Cadence. The situation is fucked up," I told her, my tone almost a pained warning.

"No really, I do. I have such a great relationship with my parents. I know your mom died, but you always seem so bitter whenever your dad is mentioned. I'm trying to understand why."

I let out a long breath, not sure if I wanted to get into the tale. I didn't know what it was about this girl. She kept trying to get me to open up, and I didn't like it, but I was the one to set the rules of the game. I couldn't very well renege.

"I never met my father until I was eight. My mom kept his existence hidden from me," I began. "Despite his money, she wanted nothing to do with him because of the way he had hurt her. But when she got sick, she felt I had to know. My mom was an only child and her parents had long since passed. Having no especially close friends to turn to, she was worried about me becoming a ward of the state if something happened to her. Plus, she recognized the fact my father was a man of considerable means. I think she wanted me to have a piece of that pie and the advantages that came with it."

"How did he hurt her? I mean, it must have been really bad if she kept you hidden from him for all those years."

"My father had a double life. He was married when he started dating my mother. She was a clerk at a law firm owned by one of my father's attorneys. That's how they met. He lived in Maryland, but whenever he went into D.C. for business, they'd meet up. It was convenient–for him at least. My mom was in the city and his wife was nestled comfortably in his mansion in Highland, Maryland. Once my mother found out the truth, she ended it. But then she found out that she was pregnant."

"Oh, gosh! I can't even imagine." Cadence shook her head in disbelief. "What did she do?"

"She never told him. My father had been clear he never wanted kids, so she decided to raise me on her own. And she did, until she got sick with breast cancer. Stage four. She tried to be optimistic about her chances, but it didn't look good. So, she went to my father with the truth about me. At the time, he was in between wives. I'll never understand why, but their affair started back up. My mom once told me it was because she never stopped loving him despite the way he had betrayed her. It was all fairytale bullshit as far as I'm concerned."

"Sounds a little romantic to me," she said wistfully.

"No. There was nothing romantic about it at all," I snapped a little too harshly. When I spoke again, I tried to adopt a softer tone. "When she finally introduced me to him, he seemed accepting. Even kind. But then my mom's cancer took a turn for the worse. The doctors upped her chemo. She was sick all the time. Frail. I watched her slowly waste away. During all of it, my father was nowhere to be found. That's not love or romance."

I squeezed my eyes shut tight for a moment, trying to block out images of my mother in a hospital bed. I'd never forget her tired eyes, filled with so much sadness as she held my small hand and tried to assure me that everything would be alright. All those dead places inside me began to flicker. The regret, the remorse, and every old feeling I tried to keep locked down threatened to unleash all at once.

"I'm sorry, Fitz."

Grief resonated in her voice, and I fought to ignore it.

"It is what it is. After she died, he never even came to the funeral. Not being there for her was his loss. My mother was an amazing woman." I shrugged, taking on a tone of aloofness as if talking about all of this didn't bother me. "So, that's four questions. What else do you have for me?"

She blinked, and I could tell she was surprised by the coolness in my voice. I just wished she'd ask me something easy like what was my favorite color or some other nonsense. Talking about my mother's death stirred up an ache that I spent years trying to bury. This shit was too deep.

"How did you come to live with your father?"

I closed my eyes again, knowing I should never have expected mundane questions from someone like Cadence. She wasn't built that way. I sighed and continued on.

"I stayed with a friend of my mom's until the reading of the will. It stated Michael Quinn, my biological father, was to assume sole custody of me. Not wanting to risk the public embarrassment of rejecting his own son, my father took me in. However, he was no longer the nice man I met on a few occasions. He was a cruel asshole. Still is. A few months after I moved in with him, he married wife number two. The rest, as they say, is history–even if it is bad fucking history."

She nodded, sympathy and understanding prevalent in every line of her expression, but I could also see pity in her eyes. That was the last thing I wanted. I tore my gaze from hers and stared out over the water. The sun had completely set, leaving faint hints of purple to blend with the dark night sky.

Cadence moved to sit beside me and placed her hand on my chest. With a slight push, she signaled for me to lie back. Lying down next to me, she dropped her head to settle into the crook of my arm and began to trace small circles over my abdomen. Her scent was all around me–vanilla and sugar and calm. I could feel the steady beat of her heart against my side as I buried my face in her hair.

She peered up at me, and I found myself staggered by the intensity in her eyes. It felt like an eternity before she spoke.

"That was only five questions, but I think it's enough for tonight," she murmured softly.

I nearly scoffed. If she thought what I told her was bad, wait until she heard the rest of it. We were six weeks into the summer. That meant I only had six weeks left with her. I knew I had to tell her the truth about my future soon, but I couldn't tonight. Just telling her the little bit I did exhausted me, and I needed all the strength I could muster when I finally did drop the mother of all bombshells.

Never in my life had I hated my father more than I did now, yet I could see no other option. As I lay there with Cadence, quietly in the darkness, a new kind of ache began to build in my chest. I felt ashamed. Stricken. It came from knowing, no matter what I did or said, I was going to lose her forever.

# Chapter Thirteen

## CADENCE

I always loved Saturdays, going back to when I first discovered the lake at eleven years old. Since then, I would spend every Saturday of the Summer here with Dahlia, playing fetch or going for lazy swims when the heat became too unbearable. As I grew older, it became a quiet place for me to draw or read. This particular Saturday was very much the same, yet it felt different. The Virginia summer air was thick and warm yet comforting in a way I didn't know it could be. Looking down the beach, I knew everything felt different because Fitz was with me.

The two of us had just finished an exhausting game of Frisbee, followed by a quick swim to cool off. Now I was relaxing in my bikini on the dock, sketchbook in hand, while Fitz tossed a stick into the lake for Dahlia. The sight of the two of them brought a smile to my lips.

Positioning myself to face the thick forest of trees, I began to sketch the horizon. Using broad strokes, the tip of my blue pencil shaded darker areas of the sky, skipping over portions where the puffy cumulus clouds flitted by. I moved down, switching colors to begin forming the trees and the purple and yellow dahlias that lined the forest edge.

Fitz came into my line of sight, and I felt my concentration wane. Water splashed around him as he engaged in a fierce game of tug of war with my dog. A quiet laugh bubbled up inside me.

Impulsively, I decided to incorporate the two of them into my drawing. I started with Fitz first, creating the shape of an inverted egg for his head and a few simple lines to arrange the angle of his body I wanted to capture. Adding volume to the lines, I created a silhouette of him with his arm in the air like he was getting ready to throw a stick. Using the side of my pencil, I began to shade in his hairline, before switching back to the tip to start drawing the angles of his face. After a while, I didn't even have to look at him–from his chiseled cheekbones and strong jawline to the subtle curve of his lips and sharp nose, I found I already had every angle of his face memorized.

Moving on from his face, I began to detail his body. I studied his frame as he ran down the beach with Dahlia. His abs rippled in a well-defined six pack, and his shoulder muscles bunched. The taut muscles of his calves flexed, disappearing under his swim shorts as he bounced back and forth, teasing Dahlia with the stick. I feverishly drew, trying to capture every hard line that would bring the drawing to life. He truly was an incredible work of masculine art, and I could only hope I could do him justice.

As I glanced up and down between Fitz and the drawing, his gaze caught mine, and I smiled. He returned it, seeming carefree and simply enjoying the moment. Even from here, I could tell his eyes were full of happiness and love.

*Love?*

Instantly, my grip tightened on the pencil and it felt as if all the air were being sucked from my lungs. Each and every time I looked at him, my heart stuttered, and I warmed. He was the guy who steadily managed to steal more and more of me with every tease, every laugh, and every smirk. Watching him there now, playing with Dahlia, completely at ease, I saw past the gorgeous exterior that I tried to capture on paper. It caused a sudden realization to hit me.

*I love Fitz.*

I don't know when or how or why it happened so fast, but I was absolutely certain. Shock reverberated through my system, jarring open a whirlwind of emotions. The boy who had come to my camp, full of overconfidence and swagger, was that last person I ever expected to fall for. But there was something good yet broken behind all of that arrogant façade. I had seen it in his piercing gray eyes. I had felt it every time he touched me. I heard it in his words. There was no doubt. Fitzgerald Quinn had completely and unexpectedly stolen my heart. For the first time in my life, I was irrevocably in love.

When he began to walk back toward the dock, I quickly closed the sketchbook. I don't know why, but I didn't want him to see it. For some reason, the drawing made me feel inexplicably vulnerable. Until I could sort out what I was going to do with these feelings, I wanted to keep it to myself.

Fitz came to sit down beside me while Dahlia plopped down near the far edge of the dock, clearly worn out.

"Hey, beautiful," he said, draping an arm around my shoulders. "What have you been furiously scribbling in that pad of yours?"

"The sky and the trees," I replied. It wasn't a lie per se. I had started out there after all.

"Can I see?"

I shook my head.

"Nope. Not right now. I'd rather you kiss me," I told him, hoping that would be a good enough distraction.

And that it was.

He didn't make me wait for more than half a second. His mouth immediately came down to meet mine in a slow, leisurely kiss that made my toes curl. My heart swelled, feeling as though it might burst. The fact that I now knew I loved him made the kiss seem all the more powerful.

When he pulled away, he looked at me curiously. I could swear he knew what I was thinking. I looked away awkwardly and pointed toward the cooler I packed that morning.

"Do you want anything to eat? There's cut fruit, sandwiches, brownies, and sodas in there."

"Brownies? Did you bake them?"

"Oh God no!" I laughed. "It's way too hot to turn on the oven. I snagged those from the kitchen in Creator Hall. I did make the sandwiches though. There's turkey and ham. I labeled the foil wrapping with a T or an H, so we know which one is which."

Fitz leaned over to pop open the lid of the small handheld cooler and peeked inside, a short lock of dark hair falling over his brow. He reached up to brush it away. For some silly reason, the sight made my heart pound.

After deciding on a sandwich labeled with an H, he looked to me.

"Do you want one?"

"Um, I'll think just nibble on some fruit for now."

I didn't think my stomach could handle more than that–it was too tied up in little love knots. It was kind of pathetic, actually. I needed to get a grip.

We ate quietly for a while. Fitz devoured his sandwich in no time at all while I barely swallowed more than a few bites of cut up watermelon. Eventually, he glanced in my direction, his eyes curious once again.

"You okay, sweetheart?"

"Yeah, why?"

"You just seem a little quiet, that's all. Like you're thinking about something."

I wanted to scream, *"Because I am thinking! About you, about us, and about how much I love you!"*

However, those words seemed to get lodged in my throat.

"I'm fine," I told him instead, hoping my voice didn't sound as shaky as I felt.

Balling up the foil from the sandwich, he tossed it back inside the cooler. Then he turned to me with a concerned expression. Taking my chin between his thumb and forefinger, he tilted my head up until our eyes locked.

"Where did you go just now, sweetheart?"

*Oh God. I was never any good at keeping secrets. Why start now?*

Throwing caution to the wind, I just blurted it out.

"I love you."

The concerned look on his face morphed into an expression of shock. I felt my cheeks flush.

*Not very smooth or romantic at all. Way to go.*

I held my breath and stared up at Fitz.

"Cadence," he said. His tone almost sounded like a warning. I placed a finger to his lips.

"Shhh. You don't have to say it back. When or if you do, I want you to mean it."

He seemed to relax, and I tried to hide my disappointment. Still, I spoke the truth. When Fitz or any other guy said those words to me, I wanted to believe them with my whole heart. If Fitz repeated them back to me now, I might always question the sincerity.

However, the stare he kept fixed on me had me rooted to the spot with its intensity. I couldn't look away. He appeared conflicted as if there was an internal war raging inside him. I debated whether I should reassure him again, tell him there was no pressure, and it was okay. He didn't need to repeat back those three little, yet very significant words.

I felt the blush in my cheeks deepen, embarrassed by the way I had blurted out my feelings. But then, the corners of his mouth tilted up in the slightest of smiles. He reached around to cup the back of my neck, pulling my head toward his. When our mouths touched, our lips crashed together in the most unexpected mind-bending kiss.

Within moments, we were horizontal on the blanket, a tangle of roaming hands and limbs. Fitz rolled, so I was under him, kissing me deeper and harder as he settled himself between my thighs. I loved this. I loved the way he teased my bottom lip and the way his arms felt wrapped tightly around my body. I loved the feel of his bare chest and loved it, even more, when he trailed dizzying kisses down my neck. And him. I loved him the most.

I groaned, inching closer to his body, stroking my fingers across the taut flesh of his chest. He buried his face into my neck, nipping and sucking the sensitive area around my collarbone, before pulling away to look at me.

He cupped my face, pushing away a loose strand of hair that had pulled free from my braid during our hurried frenzy, and stared at me for a long moment. The torment in his eyes was now gone, replaced with irrefutable desire. Those beautiful grays flashed. He looked ready to eat me alive.

A fresh jolt of desire pounded through me. I was so undone; a shudder racked my body. He tightened his hold and plunged into my mouth again, his tongue forcing my lips apart, angling my head for the best and most instant access. The love that had been building over these past few weeks bubbled up inside me, and I felt like I'd been waiting for this moment my entire life. As our tongues danced, I was consumed with a whirl of passion and recklessness.

I wanted him, all of him. I knew I shouldn't want these things–what he was doing to me, how he was making me feel. We were moving too fast, yet at the same time, it felt like it wasn't fast enough.

"Fitz," I choked out, tearing my mouth from his. As I struggled to catch my breath, our gazes locked. My blood heated to an impossibly hot temperature. I felt dazed and completely lost in him.

"Sweetheart, I've been trying hard to do the right thing with you, but it's so fucking hard."

The agony in his eyes was abundantly clear.

"So, stop trying," I offered.

He dropped his head, releasing a sound I'd never heard from him before. When he raised his head to look at me again, I began to drown in a sea of gray. He shook his head.

"You don't know what you're saying. And if you don't stop looking at me like that, I don't know what I'm going to do."

"How am I looking at you?" I whispered.

His lips tugged at the corners.

"The same way you were looking at me when I asked to touch you for the first time."

"Then what are you waiting for?"

# Chapter Fourteen

**FITZ**

She took my hands in hers and pressed my palms to her breasts. They were soft and perfect underneath the thin material of her bathing suit. I traced my thumbs over her nipples, feeling them harden from my touch. The urge to suck on them until she was mindless overcame me. I wanted to see her skin flush with desire. There were so many things I could do to her, moves I'd perfected that would make her scream.

And damn me to hell, but I wanted to teach her every fucking one of them.

Slowly, I reached under her head and removed the little rubber band that secured her braid. Working my fingers through her hair, I spread out the woven strands, so that they splayed around her head, golden and beautiful. As much as I loved the braids she wore, there was something about her hair being down that made her look wild and free.

Instantly, my hands were everywhere, pulling at the strings of her bathing suit, kissing every inch of warm skin the moment it was revealed. Her breasts now free, I pulled back to look at them. They were perfect and pale with taut pink nipples begging for my attention.

I ran my tongue along the line of her throat. She tasted as sweet as she smelled. I kissed my way around her breasts, nibbling and sucking. She whimpered beneath me as I flicked a nipple with my tongue. Her chest rose and fell as I glanced up to her face. Her cheeks were flushed, and her lips were swollen from my kisses. She was, undoubtedly, the most amazing sight I'd ever laid eyes on.

"God, sweetheart, every inch of you is perfect."

Lifting one of her legs, I wrapped it around my hip and pressed against her. Cadence gasped and arched her back in response. Her hands gripped my hair, pulling at the strands, in the best imaginable way. Her pants were beautiful and uninhibited, not a trace of hesitation in sight.

My hand slid down over her abdomen until it reached the line of her bikini bottom. I moved my hand lower, cupping her. I could feel how hot and wet she was even through the thin line of clothing. My cock strained to break free from my shorts. I wanted to shed the barriers, to feel her naked body against mine but knew that it was out of the question. It would be too tempting. Although she hadn't said it, I knew she was a virgin. I had no business taking that from her. It was bad enough I surrendered to the carnal need I had for her, especially knowing I'd have to leave her at summer's end.

Still, what was happening between us, that was different. It was more than just lust–it was something pure and good. And goddamn it, even though I hadn't said it like I knew she wanted me to, I knew I loved her too.

I splayed my hand over her tight belly, trailing my finger along the edge of the spandex material of her bikini bottom while I sucked on the taut peaks of her nipples. I hooked a thumb just inside the elastic waist, moving to skim the line of her mound with my finger. Pausing, I lifted my head from her breast.

"Is this okay, sweetheart?"

"Yes," she panted, pushing her hips up against my hand. No word had ever sounded sweeter. I grinned and brought my lips back down to resume suckling on her nipples.

I continued to move my hand down and under until my fingers met with her slick folds.

"Shit, you're so goddamn wet," I cursed. Her thighs clenched, almost as if she were embarrassed by that fact. I nudged them apart again and moved up her neck to whisper in her ear. "That's a good thing. It tells me you like what I'm doing."

"I do like it, Fitz," she mewled.

Every time she said my name, or whispered her delight, it made me feel like I could move mountains. Being with her, watching her reactions was allowing me to see a whole new side of her. She was opening herself up to me, showing me who she was, and nothing in the world was more goddamned beautiful. Everything about this girl brought me to my knees.

It had been a long time since I hooked up with a girl who I knew for more than a few hours. And when I did, getting to the finish line had always been my number one priority. But knowing Cadence, knowing who she was inside, somehow changed things. It was hard to believe the difference it made. I actually *wanted* to make Cadence feel so many amazing things–things that would turn her inside out–even if it meant sacrificing my own pleasure. She was the only girl I ever wanted to hold on to for more than a fleeting few moments, and the idea that I was the only one who had touched her like this made everything even better. I didn't think it was possible, but that thought made me harder than I already was.

She whimpered again, and her head lolled to the side. I slowed my strokes, lingering over the one spot sure to send her over the edge. Her body tensed, and I caught her damp heat. She clung tight, nails biting into my shoulders. She was right there.

"That's it, baby. Hold on to me."

It was only a matter of seconds before she came apart in my hands.

"Fitz!" she cried out and squeezed her eyes shut tight. She flung her arms around my neck and made a sweet noise of surprise. When they fluttered open again to look at me, she looked dazed, struggling to keep her eyes open.

"You good, sweetheart?"

"Mmmm," she purred. "God, what was that?"

"What was what?"

"I felt like I was going to explode."

I chuckled, nearly forgetting how innocent she truly was.

"I take it you've never had an orgasm before?"

She smiled sheepishly.

"Um, I guess not."

I grinned and wiggled my eyebrows at her teasingly.

"Not even by yourself?"

Her face flushed ten different shades of pink, a reaction I fully expected.

"No! Of course not!" she shrieked.

I laughed and pulled her tighter into my arms.

"You're so cute when you get all embarrassed like that." I paused to rain reassuring kisses over her cheeks. Cupping her face, I looked earnestly into her eyes. "I was only teasing you. But you did you like it, didn't you?"

She nodded shyly.

"I want to feel that again," she admitted.

I flashed a devious smile as I roamed a hand down her firm, tight belly once more.

"The night's young, sweetheart. Let's see what I can do about that."

# Chapter Fifteen

## FITZ

I came to Camp Riley with the expectation my time here would be awful. As it turned out, the days were flying by, and I found myself wishing more and more for time to slow down. I didn't want to go back to my old life for so many reasons, and it wasn't just because of what my father had in store for me. There was a certain level of peace and tranquility here so unlike anything else I'd ever experienced. Each morning, I'd start the day with the arduous tasks Mr. Jimmy wanted completed. I was often dripping with sweat well before eight in the morning, but I didn't mind.

While I worked, I could hear the music rehearsals and would occasionally sneak a peek at the main stage. As hard as I was working, the students here were also putting in their time. The art students used their creative vision to build a stage set from scratch. Other students practiced their music, dancing, and performing all day. It was spectacular to watch, and I realized I hadn't given the kids here enough credit. They really were protégés of their craft.

The work day had now ended. My sweat-drenched t-shirt clung to me as I headed to the bathhouse to grab a shower. Just like every other day since arriving, my legs and back ached. However, I wasn't going to complain. I knew once I called it quits for the day, I would have the lake waiting for me. And Cadence.

Feeling refreshed from the shower, I slipped a t-shirt over my head and looked at my reflection in the bathhouse mirror. I rubbed a hand over my jawline. I could use a shave, but that would mean cutting into my time with Cadence. After running a quick hand through my hair to smooth out the unruly ends, I grabbed the bag that contained my toiletries and headed for the door.

When I stepped out into the sticky early evening air, I nearly ran straight into Devon. He was carrying a small drawstring bag, and I assumed he was about to hit the showers too.

"There you are. Where the fuck have you been?" he demanded.

"I didn't realize I needed your permission to shower," I shot back with a smirk.

"You know what I mean, man. I meant, where have you been all week? For that matter, where the hell have you been all summer? I've barely seen you."

"What can I say? I can't help it that Mr. Jimmy split up the work so now we're on opposite sides of the camp." I tried to sidestep Devon, but he put a hand on my shoulder.

"I know where you've been during the day, numbnuts. Where have you been going at night? And don't try to tell me again you haven't been seeing Cadence."

I shrugged his hand off and headed in the direction of the barn. Devon didn't take the hint and fell into step beside me. More than likely, he thought I'd gone over the deep end. He'd been nagging me for half the summer to hang out with him but hanging out with Devon also meant spending time with a group of girls who I wanted nothing to do with. However, I knew I'd have to give him something if I wanted to get him off my case.

"I've been hiking," I lied.

"Hiking?" he repeated in disbelief.

"Yeah, you know. Enjoying the great outdoors and spending time trying to clear my head."

"Clear your head of what?"

"In case you forgot, we both got into a shitload of trouble," I said dryly. "I'm trying to figure out where I go from here. Like, what's the next step? Just working out basic life crap."

That part was true–sort of. I *was* trying to figure what to do about my relationship with Cadence. I knew what I wanted. I wanted her. But what I wanted didn't necessarily mean it was possible. I had to find a way out of the deal I was locked into with my father–if one would even call it that. Other than my idea to take off to Canada, I was coming up short.

As we approached the barn, Devon shook his head.

"You've been acting weird since we got to this place, Fitz. The two of us used to always hang out. And I'm not just talking about prowling for chicks. We haven't thrown back a beer together since before coming to the camp. Come out tonight. There's this girl I want you to meet.

Her name is Rachel–pretty, big tits, just how you like them. Plus, she's been eyeing you up for a while."

"I've met her. I'm not interested," was all I said.

"Jesus, man. What happened to you? This Cadence girl is really messing with your head. I figured you would have worked her out of your system by now. What happened to staying off the radar? You're asking for trouble with that one."

I had thought similar things going in, yet I couldn't resist that forbidden fruit. I figured once I'd got past the challenge she originally presented, I'd move on. Never did I expect things to go this far with her.

"I'm fine."

"That's a load of bullshit. Does she know?"

Ice cold dread flowed through my veins, freezing everything inside. I knew what confessing everything to her would do. It would mean the end and I didn't know how to begin to tell her the truth.

"Know what?" I asked, pretending like I didn't know.

"Don't be obtuse. You know what I'm talking about. Does she know that you have to–"

"No. She doesn't know," I snapped, abruptly cutting him off. It was like he had fucking ESP or something. "Look, I know what you're going to say. I've already thought about all of it. I just haven't found the right way to tell her. She isn't like other girls, Devon. Cadence is different."

Just as I spoke the words, Mr. Jimmy stepped through the large barn doors. I quietly hissed at Devon to be quiet.

"Ah, Fitz. Just the man I was looking for. Come with me, son." He wasn't smiling. Mr. Jimmy was normally always smiling.

*Shit. Did he hear what I said to Devon?*

I glance at Devon nervously. He just shrugged.

"Catch you later, Fitz. Have a good night, Mr. Jimmy," Devon called over his shoulder and headed off back in the direction we'd come.

Apprehensively, I followed Cadence's father into the barn. He headed toward his large workbench. I eyed up the tools that littered the surface–nut, bolts, different types of drills… and a hack saw. My balls instantly tightened, the fear of being cut off very real.

"I just came from The Flourish," Mr. Jimmy began. "Seems we're sold out of Bugles. You wouldn't know anything about that, would you?"

*Fuck! He knows about us.*

Of all the things sold at the camp store, he mentioned that one. I always brought Pepsi's and a bag of either Bugles or Doritos to snack on when Cadence and I were at the lake. He has to know. There was no other explanation for why he would ask me that. I was fairly certain Mr. Jimmy wouldn't like the idea of someone like me–a much older, rich kid who'd gotten himself into serious trouble–messing around with his pristine daughter. Hell, messing around was an understatement. I'd spent the better part of my evenings for the past two weeks touching Cadence in every way possible.

"Ah, no sir," I responded, hoping he couldn't see through the lie.

He pursed his lips. I eyed the hand that still precariously rested on the workbench next to the hack saw. My heart began to pound.

"Humph. That's odd." He scratched his head in what was clearly mock confusion. "Anyway, a package came for you today."

"A package?" Much to my relief, he moved his hand away from the saw and picked up a rectangular box wrapped in brown paper, my home address listed on the return label. I nearly sighed in relief. I had been so distracted by all the noise in my head and the heavy weight in my chest, I nearly forgot. "Oh, yeah. It's from my dad's housekeeper. I asked her to send me a few things from home."

"I see." He narrowed his eyes suspiciously for a long moment before he finally spoke again. "Well, I've got to be off. The missus is holding dinner for me. Tomorrow, we need to work on the cottage on the far east side of camp. We couldn't rent it out this year because the foundation is starting to crumble. The roof is also in need of repair. You'll need to meet me there at six tomorrow morning."

There was no need to point out the time. That's what time we started every morning. I suspected his reminder was meant to be a silent warning.

*Got it. Don't keep your daughter out too late.*

"Yes, I remember."

When he finally left the barn, I exhaled the breath I hadn't realized I'd been holding. I wasn't sure if Mr. Jimmy knew the truth about why I was sent to the camp. I also didn't know if my father was checking in to get reports on me. Either way, it was now even more important for me to tell Cadence. There were only four weeks left at camp. Now that her father appeared to be sniffing around, I knew I was going to have to tell her the whole truth. I had to man up before she heard it from someone else.

My fear was once I did, our evenings at the lake would come to an abrupt halt.

---

Cadence was already at our spot on the dock when I arrived at the lake. The blanket was spread out, and I could hear Candlebox coming through the radio speakers. Dahlia was prancing around on the beach, her long, shaggy hair wet and plastered to her body. She bounded in my direction when she saw me approaching.

"Hey, girl," I said and crouched down to let her lick my cheek. "Been swimming without me I see."

I looked up when I heard Cadence laugh.

"There's no keeping that one out of the water," she called out.

I glanced back down at Dahlia.

"Is that so?" I said to the sopping wet dog. I smiled and lowered my voice to a whisper. "I'll tell you what. I promise you a full hour of fetch tomorrow night if you can give me a bit of quiet time with Cadence tonight. Deal?"

Her tailed wagged happily in response, but it didn't do much to brighten my spirits. I wasn't even sure if I could keep that promise. The knot in my stomach grew as I approached the dock. There wasn't much of a sunset tonight, a fact that seemed to only darken my mood further. The sky had been overcast most of the day and I absently wondered if we'd finally get a bit of rain overnight.

Cadence stood, facing me with her long blond hair mussed from the slight breeze in the air. She smiled brightly, and my breath caught. She was so goddamn beautiful. She was like a deity I secretly worshipped. Any thoughts I had were stolen right out of my head as I watched her with pure male appreciation.

"Hey, sweetheart. I missed you today." I set the package I was carrying on the dock and pulled her into my arms. She pressed a soft kiss to my mouth.

"I missed you too."

"Remember the surprise I told you about? It's here," I murmured against her lips.

"Oh?"

"Yeah. Rhonda, my dad's housekeeper, managed to sneak some of my mixed tapes out of my room and shipped them to me. I didn't want to tell you before because I wasn't sure if she'd be able to get them past my father." I paused, cocked my head to the side, and threw her a lopsided grin. "I figured we've exhausted nineties alternative music."

Cadence narrowed her eyes at me but smiled.

"Is that a complaint?"

"Not at all," I laughed and bent to pick up the box. After tearing off the brown paper, I opened the lid and pulled out one of the tapes. "This one has some classics on it."

"I'm scared now," she joked.

I tsked her and squatted down to the Boombox to eject the existing tape. Replacing it with one of mine, I pressed play. The track *Love Comes Quickly* sounded in the night. I looked up at Cadence. Her eyebrows shot up.

"Eighties synth-pop?" she asked.

"Don't knock it until you've heard it. This is one sweet ass song. The

Pet Shop Boys are hella good!" I stood and pulled her back into my arms, guiding our bodies to move in time with the music and leaned down to kiss her forehead. "Tell me about your day."

"Nothing too exciting. Daddy had me reordering supplies for The Flourish all day. This year's campers are wiping us out of snack foods almost daily!"

"Ah, yeah," I mumbled. "He might have mentioned something about that."

She pulled back to look at me.

"What's wrong?"

"Nothing's wrong. Just wondering what we can do tonight. I'm not sure about a swim. It looks like rain is moving in."

"Funny you should say that. I was thinking about the question-and-answer game we played a few weeks ago. You still owe me five answers, so I made something to change it up."

She stepped back and pulled a folded paper square from her pocket.

"What's that?" I asked.

"It's an origami fortune teller. Normally, you'd ask a question, and it tells you the answer, but I did it in reverse. Instead of a fortune, you'll get a question." Placing her index fingers and thumbs underneath the four corner folds of the paper, she held it out in front of me. "Pick a number."

I looked down at the folded paper. Four different numbers were ornately drawn on each of the corners. It was clear she had spent some serious time making it.

"I haven't seen one of those since Jenny Becker got it taken away by the teacher in sixth grade. Are you serious right now?"

"Dead serious. Now, pick a number."

I grinned at her, amused by the solemn set to her jaw over the adolescent game.

"Okay. Five," I said, playing along. I was genuinely curious to see where she was going with this. She moved her fingers to open and close the origami five times until it stopped on four colored circles.

"Pick a color."

"My favorite. Green, like your eyes."

"G-R-E-E-N," she spelled out. "Pick another color."

"Green again, sweetheart. Always green."

Her face fell.

"I was hoping you'd pick a different one and come to that last." With a resigned look, she unfolded the paper flap with the green dot. She glanced back up at me, her apprehension evident as she read it. "Do you love me, Fitz?"

My stomach dropped as the momentary amusement I felt took a sledgehammer to the gut. Of course, I loved her. Her touch had the ability to calm the animal raging inside me, the monster trying the break free from the binding chains. She made me a different person–a better person. But I couldn't tell her any of that while she was still in the dark about my future.

"Cadence…" I trailed off, the words getting stuck in my throat. I didn't want to drag her into my sordid world, especially since I knew better than to do it all along.

"Please, Fitz. Just give it to me straight. I need to know where we stand after the summer is over. Your father is in Highland, Maryland. My parents are in Bethesda. We'd be just over thirty minutes apart, so seeing each other shouldn't be too much of an issue. I just need to know if you *want* to keep seeing me."

I looked into her eyes. Worry and longing filled them. It nearly shredded me. But my time was now officially up. Instinctively, I pulled her hard against me as if my embrace would somehow protect her from the crushing blow I was about to deliver.

"I want to keep seeing you more than you know. The past eight weeks with you have been amazing, but I never expected it to happen. These nights at the lake, no matter what we're doing, have been the best in my life. I never expected to fall–" I stopped short of finishing the sentence and took a deep breath. "Why don't we sit down? There are things I need to tell you–things I should have told you before I ever let anything happen between us."

"Um, okay," she said cautiously before slowly lowering herself to sit. We sat cross-legged across from one another, and I took her hand in mine.

"On the day we met, you made a comment about the University of Southern California. Why did you think that's where I was from?"

Confusion crossed her face momentarily before her eyes grew wide. She began to giggle.

"Oh, that! That was just me being a smart ass. I knew you weren't from there. What I said was USC. I didn't say anything about California. You did."

"So, what does USC mean then?"

I cocked a puzzled brow at her, waiting for her to elaborate.

"What can I say? I did my research. I knew you and Devon were a couple of rich kids who got in some sort of trouble. That acronym stood for University of Spoiled Children. I'm sorry," she said earnestly. "I assumed a lot about you back then, but I'm glad you proved me wrong."

"So, if you knew Devon and I were sent here because we got into trouble, why haven't you ever asked me what happened?"

She shrugged.

"I never asked because it doesn't matter. There's no use dwelling on past mistakes. I know who you are now, and that's all I care about."

*Of course, she would think that way. Always a positive outlook.*

"In this case, it does matter. You see, you kind of pegged me right the first time around. Devon and I do come from wealthy families. I wouldn't say we're spoiled, but when you combine rich with boredom, it spells trouble. And well, we got into more than our fair of it one night. It happened at a party we threw, a big one where things spiraled out of control."

"Having a party that got out of hand isn't all that abnormal, Fitz."

"Bad shit happened that day, Cadence—on my watch. I was president of my fraternity. Devon was my VP. And yeah, we were cocky. Arrogant. We were all the above, plus I had an axe to grind against my father. If I could find a way to piss him off, I did it. Throwing a massive party, the biggest one Georgetown had ever seen, was a sure way to get the old man's blood pressure to rise. The university had been trying to crack down on Greek hazing, so rush week was non-existent. The season as a whole was pretty boring. We were itching to do something big, so that's exactly what we did."

"So, you got in trouble for throwing a party, and your father sent you here as penance? That's not that big of a deal."

"I wish that's all it was, sweetheart, but no. There was this girl. She was a freshman. I don't know when she arrived at the party. As the president of the fraternity, I was supposed to be sober and checking people at the door. Instead, I was falling down drunk, passed out on a lounge chair in the backyard by the pool of the frat house. That was typical. To this day, I couldn't even tell you how I got there. I only remember waking up to people screaming."

I squeezed my eyes shut, trying to block out the sounds in my memory. The effort was in vain. All I could see were the flashing lights of police cars behind my eyelids. I could still smell the mixed scent of weed, stale beer, and chlorine in my nostrils. And the panic. I could still feel the panic.

"What happened?" Cadence asked. I opened my eyes, her question pulling me back to the present.

"Do you remember the day I first found you here at the lake? I jumped in, looking for you, afraid something had happened. Have you ever asked yourself why I panicked so easily?"

"Honestly, no. I did think it was slightly odd, but you seemed to shrug it off, so I didn't make a big deal out of it."

"I remembered something—something I never wanted to see happen again. That girl I mentioned? Well, she fell into the pool and must have smacked her head. There was blood swirling in the water. So much blood.

I didn't think. My drunken mind just reacted. I jumped in, hoping to save her, but I was so damn drunk. I was lucky I didn't drown myself. The cops arrived at the same time I dove in. Devon, not knowing what was going on in the yard, turned off the main breaker in the house. It killed the lights, silenced the loud music. That's what we always did to warn the partygoers. The signal told them the police were there, and they had to get out. When he did that, he also turned off the lights for the inground pool. It blinded me. I couldn't see where the girl was. I swam and swam, trying to feel for her body. When the lights finally came back on, there she was. Floating on the surface. We were too late. I was too late."

Cadence stared at me with wide eyes. She shook her head in disbelief.

"That's terrible! Such a tragic accident for someone so young!"

"Yeah, she was young. And maybe it was just an accident, but the blame fell on me. The toxicology report showed her to be well over the legal limit for alcohol. They also found cocaine in her bloodstream, all things I knew to be going on at the party but ignored. Devon and I were stripped of our roles as officers but being that we were only days away from graduation, the school didn't get involved in much else. They left it to criminal court to work out."

"Criminal?"

I slowly nodded my head.

"Yes. So, I will say it again. I want to continue seeing you. I just don't think it's fair for me to lead you on. This summer, while it's been the best summer of my life, is all we can have together. Nothing more."

"I don't understand, Fitz. Once camp is over, and we go home, why can't we continue to see each other? Are you going to jail or something?"

Her tone was incredulous, and I shook my head.

"I'm not going to jail." I paused, a part of me still unable to believe the events that were unfolding behind the scenes even as I spoke. "When we went to court, it wasn't looking good. Since Devon was only the fraternity vice president and wasn't in charge of working the door the night of the party, he was looking at probation and a summer of community service. I, on the other hand, was looking at being convicted of involuntary manslaughter for gross negligence with at least a twelve-month prison sentence. I was scared out of my fucking mind."

"But you're here. You didn't get that, right?"

"No," I laughed bitterly. "Little did I know the judge was brokering a backdoor deal with my father."

"What kind of a deal?"

"A deal that makes me wonder if a jail sentence would be better than the alternative." I paused and took a deep breath, steeling myself before I had to tell her the worst of it. "You see, the judge has a daughter. I've met her a few times at political fundraisers my father dragged me to. She's a party girl who crossed the line from wild child to self-destruction practically overnight. Her father, the judge, wants to put her on the straight and narrow. Most parents would want their kid in rehab or something, right? Not this guy. He told my father if he could find her a suitable husband, that would be enough to settle her down and set her straight."

Cadence stilled.

"What are you saying?"

"I'm saying that I had to choose–marry the judge's daughter or be sent to jail."

"Wait? You're married?" she said incredulously and pulled her hand from mine. I let her, knowing I had no right to hold on any longer.

"No, I'm not married. But the date is set for this September."

A gasp raked from her lungs as horror seemed to seep from her consciousness. She jumped to her feet and folded her arms across her chest. Her gorgeous eyes were wide and steely, and her face had gone ghostly pale. She was staring at me like she didn't even know me as a civil war marched across her face.

"So, you're engaged or betrothed–whatever! You need to explain better, Fitz! I mean, marriage is a lifelong commitment! Why would you even agree to something like that?" she demanded.

She was angry and had every right to be. I never should have let things go this far. In her eyes, I was probably nothing more than a liar. The only defense I had was the truth.

"When I was given my options, I didn't know you. I didn't have a significant other at all. I foolishly thought if it didn't work out, I could always get a divorce down the line. I figured, what the hell did I have to lose? It was better than prison and a mark on my record that would follow me forever. But then I came here and saw you. I knew I only had three months of freedom. I didn't know I'd end up wanting to spend every single day of those three months with you. Now everything is fucked up."

Her eyes widened further, and when she spoke, her voice had turned to stone.

"I'm sorry to be such an inconvenience."

Anguish ripped through my soul at her words. I stood, so that I was level with her, gripping her shoulders but resisted the urge to pull her to me.

"Damn it! You're not a fucking inconvenience. You're the only good thing in my life! I'm sorry for not telling you the truth sooner. I was selfish. I'll admit, a quick summer fling was most definitely on my agenda when I first got here, but all of that changed. Before I knew it, I… we were in too deep. I decided to say to hell with my father and his plans. I wanted to feel something for once. To have it mean something. The girls I've encountered before meeting you, none of them had the ability to slither into my psyche the way you have. You were all I could think about! It messed with my head. I kept promising myself I'd tell you tomorrow. Then tomorrow came, and I couldn't find the words. Things continued to progress and grow. It all happened so fast. Then I realized…" I trailed off, afraid to lead her on further. "This isn't just a fling between us, Cadence. It's so much more than that. My only defense is I didn't know I'd end up feeling this way about you."

She shrugged out of my grasp and began to rub her arms. It was like she was warding off a chill even though the night air was just as hot and humid as it had been on the day I arrived at the camp. I knew better than to reach for her again. To kiss her. To touch her. Her eyes bore into mine with a mixed expression of confusion, hurt, and sadness.

"You knew all of this before you kissed me. Before you…before I let you touch me. Before we…I told you I loved you! Damn you! Why didn't you say anything sooner?" The crack in her voice stole the air from my lungs. I had no words to justify my actions. She was right, and I was an asshole.

"I'm so sorry, Cadence."

She turned her back me and stayed silent for a long while. I didn't say anything, knowing she needed a moment to process all I'd said. Lightning flashed in the distance and I could hear the rumble of far away thunder. Rain was definitely moving in, and I tried to gauge how much time we had before it came pouring down.

When Cadence eventually turned toward me once again, her face was pained.

"What's her name?"

"Whose name?"

"The judge's daughter, the girl you're supposed to marry?"

"Bethany."

She closed her eyes for a moment, and I knew what she was thinking. Giving a name to my future bride made it all that more real.

"Fitz, I don't know how to feel about all of this. It's crazy. I mean, we're nearing the twenty-first century. Arranged marriages–whether it be from a twisted form of blackmail or not–aren't supposed to happen. I need to think. But before I do, I need to know exactly how you feel about me and if you plan to follow through with this archaic arrangement."

"I have to. My father isn't giving me a choice. You don't understand him. He controls everything. Dictates everything. I haven't had a choice in anything since my mother died. And now… Fuck, I hate him! This goddamned wedding is literally being planned as we speak," I told her, practically choking on the words.

She stared back at me calmly, appearing almost immune to my outburst.

"You only answered a part of my question. I need brutal honesty from you, Fitz. How do you feel about me?"

I looked down at the ground. I knew I should lie to protect her, but I needed her to know the truth even if the outcome wasn't what I wanted or needed it to be. When I brought my eyes back up to meet hers, I saw tears welling up in her emerald greens. Knowing I was the cause for those tears shattered me.

"The minute I saw you, I knew there was something about you. I didn't know what it was at first. I only knew I couldn't get enough of you. You gave me a sense of hope I hadn't felt in a long time. I found myself falling hard and fast. If you hate me for everything I've said tonight, I deserve it. I knew going in, I'd end up breaking your heart–I just didn't know I'd break mine too. Because the truth is, I've fallen in love with you, Cadence, and now, I don't know what to fucking do about it."

"Fitz…"

I saw the storm roll through her emerald eyes as the tears began to spill over. Grief clutched me in its fiery hold. Incinerating. Blistering. I reached for her, but I wasn't fast enough. In a flash, she turned. Then she ran.

"Cadence, wait!" I yelled.

But she was gone. Into the woods and out of sight.

# Chapter Sixteen

**CADENCE**

I moved about the kitchen on autopilot. It was Sunday, and that meant a family dinner at home with my parents rather than in the cafeteria of Creator Hall. Sunday also signified it had been nine days since I'd last spoken to Fitz. Nine very long days where I felt this deep, unaccustomed pain in my chest. However, I knew I was right to stay away from him. When I was near him, I couldn't think. And think is what I had to do after the shock he dropped on me.

My mother had made a pot of Brunswick stew that was normally oh-so-delicious, but today I barely tasted it. I made a good show of having an appetite though, not wanting to give my mother cause for concern. She'd been giving me sideways glances, and I knew she suspected something was up. So, I made myself force down an entire bowl. Combined with the freshly baked bread my father went into town for earlier that morning, I felt surprisingly full for the first time in over a week.

Sated with his own full belly, my father retired to the living room to watch the local news while my mother and I took care of the dishes. However, he didn't go without complaining. He thought since my mother did the cooking, he should do the cleanup. My mother, as usual, just shooed him away. Secretly, I liked when she did that. It meant one-on-one time with just me and her. I didn't view the dishes as a chore when I was doing them with her. To me, it was special bonding time.

Tonight, as I dried the dishes that she washed, I listened to her hum some random tune that was in her head.

"What are you humming, Momma?" I asked. Instead of answering, she began to sing.

"You were meant for me. And I was meant for you," she sang.

"Ah, now I know," I said, instantly recognizing the song from *Singin' In the Rain*. "Was that scene being rehearsed again today?"

"It was, and I couldn't be happier about the performance! We're just about ready to move into final dress rehearsals. And let me tell you, I may as well have cast Gene Kelly and Debbie Reynolds themselves! You should stop by the set and watch them. The pair we have this year is truly remarkable. You'd think that they were actually in love!"

"Well, you never know."

My mother instantly sobered.

"Why? Have you heard something?"

I laughed.

"No, I was only joking!"

"Oh, good," she said, pressing a wet soapy hand to her heart. "The last thing I need on my hands is a teenage love affair to ruin things before the final production. I've seen it too many times. They break up, then they can barely look at each other on stage. It makes for a dreadful performance."

I thought about her words, allowing them to mull over in my head for a bit while I put away the last of the dishes.

"Momma, can I ask you something?"

"What is it, honey?"

"How did you know you loved Daddy? I mean, was it instant? Or did it take a long time for you to figure out he was the one?"

She smiled softly, recalling a fond memory.

"With your father, it didn't take too long for me to know. A few days maybe," she added almost as an afterthought.

"A few days! That's it?" I exclaimed. My mother laughed.

"Well, I suppose it was a bit longer than that. I knew he had been watching me for a few weeks before he finally got up the nerve to approach me. Then… I don't know. Perhaps it was the hurried pace of living in New York or the fast life that came with being on Broadway, but our love seemed to grow equally fast. I just always knew he was the one. We were only together for two months when he proposed, then married a month later."

"I knew your engagement was quick, I just didn't realize you only knew each other for that short of a time period. You guys didn't waste any time!" I said with a chuckle as I shook my head.

"Cadence," my mother said in a more serious tone. "Why are you asking me?"

I looked at her, only to find her watching me with a worried expression.

"No reason," I lied.

"Honey, your father and I are rare. Love has a funny way about it. Somehow, you just know. But there's a difference between love and lust. Most couples who marry as quickly as we did don't have a happily ever after. You're young. You have your whole life ahead of you. No need to rush things."

I blushed. My mother was always so observant. Although I hadn't actually told her, I knew she was aware of something between me and Fitz but had chosen to respect my privacy. She usually waited for me to open up to her about things first. While I normally confided in her about almost everything, I hadn't about Fitz, and I wasn't sure why. It was strange. Fitz was still a forbidden secret that I wanted to keep all to myself.

"I know, Momma," was all I said. Dahlia scratched at the front door. I looked over at her, grateful for the excuse to escape my mother's troubled gaze. "I'm going to take Dahlia out for a bit."

My mother came over to me and placed her hands on my shoulders. Her worry lines deepened.

"Don't be out too late," she said and pressed a quick kiss to my cheek.

I nodded once as a wave of guilt washed over me. I stepped away before I ended up spilling everything to her.

Grabbing Dahlia's leash, I opened the wooden screen door and stepped out onto the porch. Dahlia jumped around at my feet, anxious to finally go for a walk. I had buried myself in sociology homework over the past nine evenings. When I felt like I couldn't write another sentence about the social patterns in society, I picked up my worn and faded copy of *Pride and Prejudice*. That didn't go well–I just wasn't in the mood to read about the prideful conflict between Mr. Darcy and Elizabeth. On the other hand, when I switched to *Sense and Sensibility*, it got me thinking more about my relationship with Fitz. Although my circumstances were much different than Marianne's, I allowed myself to get distracted by the wrong things.

As a result of my book musings, I was sure Dahlia was feeling more than just a little neglected. I squatted down and scratched her behind the ears.

"Sorry, girl. But you know why we had to stay inside. I had some thinking to do," I whispered to her. I stood and hooked the leash onto her collar. The two of us started out down the path with only one destination in mind. The lake.

Despite my efforts to avoid Fitz, I had seen him here and there around camp. Those moments were tense to say the least. At times, Fitz looked angry, but it was impossible to know what he was thinking. Every time I saw him, I seemed to falter and shake. When I saw him today in

Creator Hall during lunch hour, I lost all focus and walked right into the side of one of the cafeteria tables, causing my plate of sloppy joe to dump all over an unsuspecting student.

And of course, the embarrassing moment just had to have happened all under Fitz's watchful eye. At the end of lunch hour, Fitz had come up to me. The only thing he said was, "Meet me at the lake tonight. Eight o'clock."

Those were the only words spoken between us since the night he told me he was to marry someone else. It was now seven o'clock. I debated all afternoon about whether I should go to him. In the end, the love I felt for him won out over the anger and hurt.

Although I made the decision to see him, I still wanted an hour alone to think things through one final time. I had thought long and hard about everything he told me, but I wanted to be sure about the decision I was about to make. The solitude of the lake seemed to be the only place I could think clearly without interruption or distraction.

Dahlia and I weaved through the wooded path that led to the lake. Once we were almost there, I unfastened her leash and let her run on ahead. When I reached the end of the path, the trees parted. The sun was low in the sky, but it hadn't quite lowered far enough to showcase the array of colors that always came with nightfall.

My gaze moved to the dock. Fitz was already there.

I wanted to feel disappointed about him beating me here. I wanted to be upset over losing an hour of alone time. But seeing him there petting a cheerful Dahlia, my heart melted a little. Any sane person would still be angry at him. After all, he hadn't been truthful and led me on. However, over the course of the past nine days, I had asked myself a series of questions.

*If I were in his shoes, what would I have done?*

*If I were in trouble like Fitz was, what would I choose to do? The phony marriage or jail time?*

*If I had met someone along the way, someone I ended up falling in love with, would I have been truthful? Or would I have tried to make the most of the time I had left?*

My parents didn't control me. They guided me for sure, but they let me make my own choices.

*What if they didn't?*

I couldn't be Fitz's judge and jury. It wouldn't be fair, especially since I may have made the same choices he had.

I slowly walked toward him and stepped up onto the dock. A beach blanket had already been spread out. The Boombox was there as well. I was so upset the last time we were here, I ran without thinking and had mistakenly left it and the blanket behind. Fitz must have taken it all back to the barn with him; however, there were a few additions tonight.

Candles surrounded the blanket, but they weren't lit. Along with the candles, freshly picked dahlia flowers were scattered around the dock.

"Hey," he said, nervously running a hand through his hair.

"Hi," I replied, unable to bring my gaze to meet his for some reason.

"I'm glad you came."

I didn't respond but moved closer to him and sat down on the blanket, calling to Dahlia.

"Come here, girl."

Dahlia's tail wagged as she plodded over to me. She lay down next to me and nudged my hand with her nose, signaling she wanted me to pet her.

"I, ah…" Fitz began as he sat down next to me. "I wanted to have this all ready before you got here, but you showed up early."

I looked at him.

"What is all of this, Fitz?"

"It's my apology. I wanted to do something nice for you."

"Flowers and candles?"

"Yeah. I mean, girls like that shit. Don't they?"

I couldn't help but laugh.

"I suppose some do. I wouldn't know. I've never been wined and dined. Is that what you're doing with me?"

"Not really. I was just trying to find some way to make it up to you. I fucked up bad, Cadence. I should have told you the truth sooner."

"I thought so at first too, but then I asked myself how I would have handled it if I were in your position. Your father has forced you into an impossible situation."

"I hate the mother fucker," he hissed.

"Fitz, stop. When you hate someone, you let them take up space in your thoughts. Every day, they claim your focus, and that allows them to control you. What happened to you, the accident, then the fallout, can't be changed. He may dictate your future, but he can't take away what we have right now." I paused, realizing my words were coming out more aggressively than I intended. His hard body sat rigid, and his perfectly chiseled jaw was set in a firm line. Despite his obvious tension, he was still beautiful. "I really wanted to be mad at you, but I don't know if I would have done anything differently."

He shook his head vehemently.

"Yes, you would have. You're too honest. I should have been upfront with you right from the beginning."

"Everything happens for a reason, Fitz. If you had told me earlier, we wouldn't be here right now. I never would have taken the time to get to know you. We wouldn't have shared all these evenings here by the lake. I wouldn't have…"

I trailed off, unable to finish the sentence. Fitz reached up to tuck a loose strand of hair back behind my ear.

"What is it? You wouldn't have what?"

I searched his eyes, losing myself in those expressive pools of gray.

"I wouldn't have fallen in love with you," I admitted. "Because yes, Fitz, even though I tried, I realized I could never stop loving you. But at summers end, I'm going to lose you. We have less than two weeks left. I don't want to spend what little time we have left being angry or passing blame. I want to make the most of it. Together. With you."

Tears brimmed my eyes, and I blinked them away.

"Oh, sweetheart. I want you more than I've ever wanted anything in my entire life. I'm sorry this is happening," he murmured and leaned in to kiss each cheek. Then my eyes. Then my forehead. "I'm so very, very sorry."

His mouth moved to my lips. I eagerly welcomed his kiss and allowed the tears to fall freely down my cheeks. All the love and lust that had ever percolated and boiled between us, spilled over onto the surface as he wrapped me tightly in his hard arms. His kiss was different from all the others we shared. It felt needy and full of desperation. The clock was ticking for us, and now that we both knew it, there was a sense of urgency that hadn't been there before.

Fitz's fingers laced through my hair as he devoured my mouth. Our tongues tangled, trying to memorize every action and every taste. He kissed me like he would never kiss me again. It made my head spin and my breathing uneven. At some point we moved from a sitting position to horizontal on the blanket. I had no idea where Dahlia wondered off to, but I didn't particularly care. I was lost as Fitz's tongue glided across mine.

The sun had lowered further in the sky, creating a rainbow mirror on the lake for the trees that surrounded it. Darkness was coming faster now as the days became shorter. To me, the fast approaching twilight was like a clock, symbolic to the little time we had left.

Magic seemed to hum in the air as Fitz's hands roamed over my body and over my breasts before coming up to cup my face. I found myself wishing that the barrier of clothing between us would disappear. It was as if I had been waiting for this moment my whole life, as if this was the piece of the puzzle I never knew was missing. There was a longing inside me that was a living, breathing thing. Fitz had reached in, pulling at that part of me until it was brought to the surface with nothing more than the soft brush of his fingertips over my face.

"Fitz," I breathed as my body involuntarily arched against him. "You once told me you didn't want me to have any regrets."

"I did," he said as his mouth moved down the line of my neck. We were both panting, his tongue flicking over the pulse pounding rapidly at my throat. I felt his hand at my waist, tugging at the hem of the shirt tucked into my shorts.

"I know I'm going to lose you, and it's going to crush me." I paused and took a deep breath. Stepping out onto a limb, I felt myself teetering until it threatened to splinter. "I never want to regret my first time. I want it to be with someone I love."

His hand froze as he lifted his head from my neck to look at me.

"What are you saying, Cadence?"

"I'm saying I love you. You are the keeper of my heart and I want my first time to be special. I want it to be with you."

Fitz sat up. His face was flushed, and I was fairly certain that mine was as well.

"I don't…" he faltered at a loss for words.

"No regrets," I reiterated.

"I understand, but Cadence." He stopped short again and then swore. "Fuck. You don't know how bad I want to. But I don't have a condom. Like, at all. Not even back at the barn. And I doubt they'd be sold at The Flourish."

My face fell. I hadn't even thought of protection, and I knew they weren't sold at the camp store. After all, I was the one who ordered the supplies sold there. But then another thought occurred to me.

"I think we're okay. I mean, I took health class and I can do the math. My period just ended two days ago," I told him. I quickly dropped my head, hoping to hide the flush that crept up my neck. I wasn't used to talking so openly about my time of the month.

Fitz closed his eyes and took a deep breath. He seemed to be fighting some sort of internal battle. In a way, I was too. What I was proposing was essentially Russian Roulette with my womb.

"Cadence, I've always used a condom, so I know I'm clean. But even if your calendar says you're safe in other ways, you're a virgin. I don't know if I can do it."

"What do you mean?"

"I've never been with a…a," he faltered. "With a virgin. What if I hurt you?"

I smiled softly, appreciating his worry and reached up to touch his striking face. My hands trembled. For the first time since meeting him, I felt like I could see all the way past the gorgeous exterior and into his huge, bleeding heart.

Rather than offer reassurances I wasn't completely confident with myself, I stood up and walked over to the Boombox. I opened the cassette player to find one of Fitz's mixed tapes inside. I pushed the cassette door closed again and pressed play. The sound of Mazzy Star filled the quiet night.

And I couldn't think of a more perfect song.

I glanced around to see where Dahlia had wondered off to. She was laying at the other end of the dock, sleeping peacefully. She'd been around for enough of my make-out sessions with Fitz to know the drill.

*Good girl. Just stay there.*

Next to the radio was a box of matches. I struck one of them against the side of the box and lit a candle. Fitz watched me curiously as I moved to light each one. There were eight in all, and I had to stop twice to light a new match. Once all the candles were lit, I blew out the match and turned to face him. My heart began to pound.

*I want this. I want to be with him in every way. No regrets.*

I repeated those thoughts over and over again as I slowly began to remove my clothes.

# Chapter Seventeen

## FITZ

Cadence stood before me, clad in nothing but a pale pink bra and matching panties. Reaching around to pull the ends of her golden hair forward, she tugged at the tie that secured the braid she had woven into it. Shaking her hair free, the tendrils fell in crimped waves over her shoulders. I loved it when she wore her hair down. It reminded me of the first day I laid eyes on her.

I looked her up and down, drinking in the sight of her. She looked nervous, almost as if she were afraid to shed the last two pieces of her clothing. The image of her standing there, uneasy yet possessing this subtle hint of bold confidence was like the dirtiest fantasy I'd ever had of her come to life. My dick throbbed, screaming at me to do something about it, but my conscious made me pause.

*Fuck, this girl is going to destroy me.*

A flush crawled up her skin, from the pale flesh just above her breasts all the way to her sun-kissed cheeks. She nervously fingered a heart-shaped pendant that she wore around her neck and cast her eyes down demurely.

"I want you, Fitzgerald," she whispered.

Hearing my full name on her lips caused my cock to strain against my shorts. I wanted her more than I wanted my next breath, but I had to be certain she was really up for this.

"Cadence," I said hoarsely. "Are you sure?"

She nodded shyly, and I reached out my hand to pull her back down to me. She straddled my hips and lowered her mouth to mine. She tasted sweet and tangy and better than anything else I'd ever tasted in my life. I brought my hands around her waist to cup her behind. It felt soft and firm beneath her panties and I nearly groaned.

*God, I shouldn't be doing this.*

I tried to talk myself off the ledge, but it was useless. Her mouth continued to move, her sweet tongue dancing with my own as she pulled at my t-shirt. I raised my arms to assist her, our mouths only parting for the briefest of seconds before crashing together once again. Her hands roamed over the lines of my chest and abs with an innocent curiosity that was an aphrodisiac like no other. Unclasping her bra, I tossed it to the side and cupped her breasts. Her hips were rocking, grinding against my waist, and I could feel her damp heat against my skin.

Rolling to the side, I shifted her body, so she was on her back, careful not to crush her petite frame with my weight. She seemed to melt into me. Her small hands wrapped around my neck as she pulled me closer with her legs, gasping when my hard erection pressed against her. Although I still had my shorts on, Cadence going off like a firecracker when touched in the right place was not a reaction I expected from her. Everything she did, every touch, every reaction was going straight to my dick.

I was losing control, and I had to get it back.

"Sweetheart," I panted. "We should think about this more."

I said the words, but I didn't believe them. The only truth I knew at that moment was how much I wanted to be buried balls deep in her. I hoped and prayed she would listen, perhaps be the voice of reason to bring us both to our senses.

"I've been thinking for nine long days. I don't need to think anymore, Fitz."

She lowered her hand to my hip and slid her delicate fingers under the waistband of my gym shorts. She reached lower and lower, sliding my shorts down farther with every inch she traveled. Her simple touch sent me flying, knowing full well I wanted things with her I shouldn't. Every thought I had about being the good and decent guy went out the window.

Almost.

"Shit," I hissed and grabbed her hand. "Cadence, wait. We can't just…I need to make sure you're ready first. Because, baby, the minute you pull that out of my pants, it's all over."

I sat up and looked down at her perfect pale skin and tiny waist. Sliding my hand up her side, I cupped one of her perky breasts, just big enough to fill my palm, and leaned down to capture a nipple between my teeth. She all but purred beneath me.

"How do you do that, Fitz? How do you make me feel so good?" she whispered.

I didn't answer but moved down her torso instead. Looping my fingers under the sides of her panties, I slowly pulled them from her body. Now that she was completely naked, I looked at her once again. She shivered in response.

*Fuck me.*

"You're beautiful."

I'd said the same thing to other girls before, but I knew for certain this was the first time I truly meant it. She had a body that would make any man stupid, and I wasn't exempt. As she stared up at me, her eyes all dreamy with lust, my brain all but short-circuited. She was looking at me like I was everything she ever wanted. Her warm body soothed any hesitation I had left. I closed my eyes to savor her, wishing this feeling could last forever.

Moving to lay alongside her, I slid my hand down over her flat stomach until my hand covered her mound. Her breath hitched as her hips arched upward. Ever so slowly, I slid a finger down to circle her opening. She was tight and tiny. And wet. God was she wet. I pushed in further. One finger, then two, stretching her to hopefully make my inevitable invasion a little less painful in the end.

She gasped, and her eyes went wide. I paused, fearing I may have hurt her somehow.

"Are you okay?"

"Yes, it's okay, Fitz," she assured. "Please don't stop."

Her hand reached up to pull my head down to meet her mouth. She kissed me desperately as I pressed in deeper to massage and stroke her walls, rubbing her clit softly with my thumb as I did so. My movements were tender at first, until her back arched and she tensed. Her breathing came faster. Shallower. She was close. I increased the pace, flexing my fingers with more urgency until I could feel the little tremors of her building orgasm. I wanted to give her this. I wanted her to feel good. She was trusting me with her body. And although I knew I couldn't keep her in the end, I wanted to make sure she would compare every guy who came after to what I made her feel today.

Her eyes grew wide, then snapped closed. I was rewarded with her gasp of pleasure as she shattered under my palm. I buried my nose in her neck, allowing her a moment to catch her breath before removing my shorts and shifting over her once more. Bracing most of my weight on one arm, I covered her body with mine. She hooked a leg up over my hip and pressed her heat up against my hard length.

I was there. I was right *there*, positioned just outside her slick entrance. I couldn't believe I was going to do this. Bareback. I'd never done that before, but there was no going back now. Not unless I wanted to walk funny until I was forty. She felt too good, and I couldn't stop this even if I tried.

She was looking down at where our bodies were so close to joining. I paused and tilted her head up to look me in the eyes. I searched them, looking for fear or apprehension, but all I saw was need–and love.

"No regrets, right?"

"No regrets," she promised.

And at that moment, I knew Cadence was the closest thing to heaven I was ever going to get.

# Chapter Eighteen

## CADENCE

The way Fitz looked at me, his gaze so hot, I may as well have been staring into the sun. He pressed small kisses to my lips. Once. Twice. Then a third time. My throat tightened with emotion. It was a strange combination of desire and fear of not knowing what was to come. I had read the first time was painful, but I didn't know how painful it would be.

"I love you, Cadence," Fitz whispered. His face was sober, telling me he understood the meaning of what he was about to do. In that moment, lost in his tender gaze, all my worry seemed to vanish.

Slowly, he pressed forward. I closed my eyes and clung to him, trying desperately to relax. It hurt, and although that was to be expected, my muscles tensed involuntarily and resisted the intrusion. Fitz was patient, pressing light kisses to my forehead and stroking my hair and shoulders as he tried to relax my body. I appreciated his willingness to be gentle even though every inch I took was a painstakingly slow process. He wrapped a strong hand around my thigh to keep it up and around his waist, then he was all the way inside.

"Sweetheart, look at me."

I opened my eyes to meet his gaze, finding a mixture of desire and worry. The combination nearly stopped my heart. The way he looked at me made me feel as if I were the only person in the world.

"I'm okay," I assured.

His warm breath heated the side of my face as his lips moved over my cheeks until eventually landing on my mouth. He continued to kiss me, repeatedly breaking the kiss to check on me. Unable to speak, I would simply nod my assurance.

His hips continued to pump forward slowly, allowing me time to adjust to his girth. I stroked his back, needing to memorize the feel of his warm body so close to mine. After a while, the pain seemed to subside. It was either that or I was just getting used to it. My body seemed to be buzzing with endorphins, and it was hard to tell.

Talented fingers stroked along my body, from my hip bone to the curve of my breast. He molded a small globe in his palm before reaching down between us to stroke my most sensitive area. He stayed there, teasing and flicking, but never once stopped moving inside me. Low in my belly, something constricted. Blood rushed through my veins. Every muscle in me drew tighter and tighter, the sensation coursing through me like the best rush of an analgesic drug. My body seemed to seize. I gasped. My vision blurred.

"Fitz!" I cried out as the most delicious sensation washed over me, thrilling and complete. It ran through my veins until I thought I might burst.

"Shh, sweetheart," he said softly and stroked my head. "I hoped to make you come, but I wasn't sure if it would be possible on your first time. While it thrills me to hear you scream my name, the night is very quiet, and sound carries."

"Oh no! You don't think–"

He cut me off by covering my mouth with his.

"No, I don't think anyone heard," he murmured against my lips. "We're far enough away, but we should still try to keep it down."

He began to move slowly inside me again. All symptoms of pain were gone, subsiding into a tender yet sweet kind of ache. I thread my fingers through his hair, enjoying the feel of his mouth moving down my neck and shoulder.

I would never forget this moment. The feel of being held in his arms. The feel of him inside me. There have been many moments in my life I'd come to cherish, and this will forever be one of them. Just seeing him here, moving above me, so gentle and tender with his touches, eradicated every doubt I may have had about who he was inside.

Pulling back, his heated gray eyes locked on mine. His movements became jagged, faster, his body tensing as he groaned. His grip on me tightened, holding me hard against him until he slumped down on top of me.

"Are you okay?" he eventually asked in a quiet voice.

"Yeah, actually. I'm good."

He reached up to stroke a hand over my hair to cup my face.

"You're the most beautiful thing in the world. I love you, Cadence."

Something broke open in my chest. The sincerity of his words nearly knocked the breath out of me. Every thought in my head disappeared. The only thing I knew was I needed him and love always found a way. We'd figure this out and find a way to stay together somehow. And if for some reason we couldn't, if this ended up being the last night we ever had, I vowed to never regret what we shared.

Fitz shifted, carefully withdrawing from my body until he was lying next to me. We lay there quietly for a while. Soul Asylum sang about a runaway train, drowning out the sounds of our heated pants as we both came down from the most incredible kind of high. He trailed a finger lazily up and down my belly, and the most strange and marvelous feeling came over me. I'd actually just had sex for the first time. I was no longer a virgin.

And like I promised Fitz, I had no regrets. Tonight was special. *He* was special.

---

When I got home that night, I was thankful my parents were distracted by the TV in the living room. As quietly as possible, I led Dahlia to my bedroom, slipped in, and soundlessly shut the door behind me. Dahlia walked over to her pile of blankets in the corner and plopped down with a loud thud.

"Cadence, is that you?" I heard my mother call.

*Shit.*

"Thanks a lot," I whispered to Dahlia before answering my mother. "Yeah, Momma. It's me. Just getting ready for bed."

I waited a beat. When she didn't knock on my door, I breathed a sigh of relief. I never lied to my parents, and I certainly didn't want to start now. Walking over to the large mirror hanging above my dresser, I examined my reflection.

The girl in the mirror didn't look any different. My hair was a little mussed and my cheeks were pink, but it wasn't anything permanent. The tenderness between my legs told a different story, but even that would go away with time. On the outside, everything seemed perfectly normal, but I knew I had emotionally changed forever. Fitzgerald Quinn was my Heathcliff, my Mr. Darcy, and my Colonel Brandon.

And he had officially put his eternal stamp on my heart.

---

The next morning, I woke up early and took a shower. I also got dressed, ate breakfast, and tried to finish up the last of my summer class assignments. All of these extraordinary accomplishments occurred as a non-virgin. Strangely, nothing much seemed to have changed. Except for the fact I now had a chirpiness about me I struggled to suppress.

My mother eyed me strangely over her morning cup of coffee.

"You're awfully bright-eyed and bushy-tailed this morning," she observed.

I smiled but said nothing as I finished the last of my Cheerios. After clearing my bowl to the sink, I filled my water bottle with ice water from the refrigerator and grabbed a couple of granola bars from the pantry. Having all I needed to get through to the afternoon, I headed out to start the workday.

As a woman. As a non-virgin.

# Chapter Nineteen

**CADENCE**

A storm had moved in earlier that afternoon, bringing with it winds and a much-needed soaking rain. The lights had been flickering most of the day, signaling that a possible power outage was coming. As a result of the inclement weather, my usual routine with Fitz by the lake would have to be cancelled. I couldn't help but feel a little desolate over a lost evening with him.

The Flourish was supposed to close at seven. Joy had left at five, leaving me to close up shop. As I'd predicted, the power went out right after she left. I phoned the cottage to tell my parents I'd stay at the store until after the power came back on. That way, if any students came in needing candles or other emergency supplies, I'd be here.

Grateful I'd brought a book with me that day, I settled in behind the counter to finish rereading the Jane Austen novel that was quickly becoming my favorite book. I'd been so wrapped up in textbooks and non-fiction works as of late, I'd nearly forgotten how much I loved classic literature. Just as I got to the part where Marianne realized she misjudged the unscrupulous John Willoughby, Fitz sauntered in. He was soaked.

I quickly put my book down and rushed to the stockroom to grab him a towel.

"Here. You're drenched," I told him as I began to pat the towel over his face, arms, and shirt. I had to force myself not to stare at the way his rain-soaked t-shirt clung to his torso. He was like my very own, very wet Adonis. It was a challenge–ever since the night I lost my virginity, I had become acutely aware of every inch of his body. It was more than just innocent attraction now. It was a blazing, burning sexual need I didn't completely understand.

"It's really coming down out there," he said, running a hand through his sopping wet hair.

I looked through the glass of the storefront windows and frowned.

"I suppose I shouldn't complain because we really need the rain, but this kind of stinks. I'd gotten used to spending my evenings at the lake with you."

"Nah," he scoffed. "A little rain doesn't have to ruin anything. We have everything we need."

"What do you mean?"

He didn't answer, and only flashed me a mischievous smile. I watched as he walked up and down the aisles, collecting various items. When he returned to the counter, he piled it all up.

"We have Bugles, soda, a blanket, candles, matches, Swedish Fish, Fun Dip, and Slim Jim's. All the essentials for a picnic."

"A picnic? But it's pouring rain outside!"

"Who said anything about going outside? Trust me, sweetheart," he said with a wink as he reached around to his back pocket for his wallet. "How much for all of this?"

Eyeing him curiously, I began to ring each item through the old-fashioned cash register.

"Thirty-seven dollars and twenty-two cents."

He whistled.

"Expensive date," he teased and tossed a few twenties on the counter.

"What in the world are you talking about?"

"I told you. Trust me."

Coming around behind the counter, he went into the stockroom, carrying all the things he just purchased. There were no windows in the stockroom, the only light from a single bulb in the ceiling, currently without power. Curious, I watched as he set about lighting candles and placing them strategically about the small room. Then he tore open the plastic packaging from the blanket and began to spread it out on the floor. Once he had the candy, dried meat, and other snacks arranged to his apparent liking, he sat down and pat the floor next to him.

"See? A picnic."

I laughed, but inside I was melting over how perceptive and intuitive he was. It was like he knew I would be disappointed having to cancel our evening at the lake, but he'd planned ahead. For me.

Still, I had responsibilities, none of which included consorting on the stockroom floor with Fitz. I nervously glanced at the front doors.

"Fitz, what if somebody comes in?"

"It's a few minutes after seven. The store is supposed to be closed. Just lock the doors."

"I have to keep them open. I told my parents I'd hang out here late just in case anyone came in for emergency supplies."

"I doubt they will," he waved off. "It's like a ghost town out there. I think most everyone has hunkered down for the night. Besides, if they do, the little bells on the front door will chime to alert us."

He was right, but that didn't do much to suppress my nerves. Almost reluctantly, I went and sat down next to him. After planting a chaste kiss to my lips, he ripped open a package of Fun Dip and held the flat little candy stick in front of my face.

"What would you like me to do with that?"

The corners of his mouth turned up and his eyes held a playful glow. The pools of gray glinted in the candlelight.

"Lick," he ordered.

Raising an eyebrow in amusement, I took the stick and gave a quick lick to each side. After handing it back to him, he dipped it into the packet of strawberry flavored sugar. Pulling it out, he brought it to my lips. I smirked and tried not to giggle as he slipped it into my mouth.

Once the sugar was sucked clean, he looked at me again. Gone was the playful expression, replaced by a heated gaze that took me whole. Overpowering ripples of lust vibrated in the air as his hand slowly caressed my thigh–back and forth, up and down. I absently wondered if he knew each stroke caused a little chill to skate my spine. It was overwhelmingly too much, yet somehow not nearly enough. I shivered with a slow release of breath when he leaned in.

"What homework were you working on when I came in?" The words were uttered so close to my ear, I couldn't stop the tremble that coursed through me.

"It wasn't homework. I was reading *Sense and Sensibility*," I told him, feeling slightly breathless.

"Is that the book about Heathcliff and whatshername?"

His teeth nipped along the ridge of my ear, his tongue making slow little flicks as he went.

"Um…her name is," I hesitated, trying to find the words to answer his question. His mouth was just so distracting, causing my mind to momentarily go completely blank. "Her name is Catherine. But, no. Catherine and Heathcliff are from *Wuthering Heights*. This one is about Marianne and Colonel Brandon."

"Tell me about it."

He threaded his fingers through mine and guided me down onto my back. Raising my arms over my head, he pinned them there as he trailed light kisses down my neck. He brushed his lips across mine. Fire blazed everywhere as his tongue tangled with mine. It was dizzying in the candlelit room, making the very air around us seem to thrum.

"I get the distinct impression you don't want to talk about books," I breathed.

He pulled back, and all I saw were eyes full of wicked glee, laced with bold confidence. It was beautiful and thrilling. A shiver raced through me.

"I can listen while I work. Let's see how good your concentration is."

His lips curved into an adorably crooked smile as he slowly pushed my shirt up. Moving down toward my belly, he kissed his way up and over my ribcage. His hands seemed to be everywhere all at once—smooth grace with lethal power.

"Um, okay," I hesitantly agreed, already beginning to writhe beneath him. "So, I guess I could start with the characters. Marianne is spontaneous and, in my opinion, somewhat flighty. She falls in love with John Willoughby."

He nipped at my breast though the thin material of my bra. I arched and brought my hands to his hair, tugging at the ends to press his mouth harder against me. Pushing down the cup, he freed one nipple. My breath hitched when his tongue began to swirl.

"I thought she was with Colonel Brandon," he murmured against my skin.

Goosebumps raised all over my body.

"Oh, not at first. But Brandon is around, biding his time, acting the gentleman until Marianne can see Willoughby for who he really is."

Another flick.

"And who is he exactly?"

I struggled with finding the answers. My heart was working overtime, doing its best to beat a hole through my chest as his hands roamed mercilessly over me. I couldn't seem to catch my breath.

"Willoughby's younger than Brandon and very good looking. He's a smooth-talking, deceitful guy who ends up choosing a woman with money over Marianne. That's how she ends up with Brandon."

More little flicks. An ache began to build low in my belly. I didn't want to talk about fictional characters anymore. I just wanted him to keep touching me. Kissing me. Licking me.

"Sounds like Brandon got the shaft. He must feel like he was second best."

"No, not really," I panted. "Marianne sees the error in her ways and comes to respect and love Brandon in a way she never could have Willoughby. Brandon is her true hero."

"Who am I like? Brandon or Willoughby?"

His hand glided up my thighs and moved around to the inside of my leg, roaming upward to release the button of my jean shorts.

"Um…a little of both I think," I said, barely able to choke out the words. "Your rugged good looks swept me off my feet, just like Willoughby did with Marianne. But over time, I found you to be more like Brandon. You have depth like he did, and that's what made me fall in love with you."

An ache began to pulse at the juncture of my thighs, the blazing need to be touched completely and utterly, consuming. I couldn't think. My mind and body were surrounded by him. Only him.

His free hand moved to the back of my neck, winding in my hair as he kissed a line down the column of my neck. I angled my head, demanding more, as he teased and tasted. His lips crashed onto mine in a kiss that was hard and dominating. I never wanted to let go. It was staggering. He made me feel so many complicated things, long-term things, that would send my carefully organized life into a tailspin. It occurred to me then I'd never felt more special and wanted. I trusted him, wanting him in a way I knew I shouldn't.

*God, how am I ever going to let go of him?*

A lump formed thick at the base of my throat, knowing I'd never survive losing this dangerous and perfect boy who had completely rocked my world.

"Do you have any idea what you do to me? How you make me feel?" he whispered low, the huskiness in his voice causing my body to quake. "The first time I saw you, you stole the air right out of my lungs. I couldn't stop looking at you. Thinking about you."

My head lolled to the side in a breathy moan. Part of it was from pleasure, but another part was from overwhelming emotion. My heart was in my throat and tears suddenly began to sting behind my eyes.

"Fitz, I don't know if I can handle losing you," I said in a slightly panicked voice. "Not now. Not ever. I know you have to marry someone else, but what if we didn't have to stop seeing each other?"

Fitz pulled away to look at me, confusion evident in his eyes. Before I could explain, the bells on the front door chimed.

"Shit!" he swore.

We rolled and scrambled to untangle our limbs. Quickly, I stood to pull down my shirt and refastened the button of my shorts.

"Stay here," I whispered. Smoothing out my hair, I left the stockroom to see who had come in.

Thankfully, it was only a couple of students looking to grab extra candles for their cottage. Too wrapped up in a fit of giggles over braving the rain storm, they didn't seem to notice anything was amiss. If it had been my parents who came in, it could have been disastrous.

After I cashed them out, they were quickly on their way. I followed them to the door, locking it behind them. That had been a close call, and I didn't want to tempt fate. When I turned to head back to the stockroom, I found Fitz leaning against the doorjamb with a concerned furrow to his brow.

"What were you saying about still seeing each other?"

"When the summer is over, what if we just saw each other on the side," I suggested. "This girl you have to marry, it's not like you love her or anything. It's just an arrangement, and it's not real. What we have is real. Let's not throw that away."

An emotion I couldn't quite place swirled in his eyes. He watched me carefully through the dimness, through the questions and madness that seemed to always surround us. After a moment, he shook his head and came over to where I was standing, cupping the side of my face.

"Cadence, no. You don't know what you're saying. My mother was my father's mistress. You don't want that life."

"But–"

"No buts. You will never be second best," he insisted. "You matter too much. The person you're going to be matters too much. I will not be the reason for you not living your life to the fullest."

He sealed his lips over mine. Lifting me from my feet, he wrapped my legs around his waist and carried me back into the stockroom. Never once did his mouth leave mine as he laid me down onto the floor once more.

Darkness had completely fallen. What little light had come in through the stockroom door from the stormy skies outside was now gone, leaving only the candles to light our way. Now locked in his embrace, I pushed away all thoughts about the future. I would bring it up again tomorrow. As we moved in a frenzy to remove our clothing, I vowed to make the most of every single moment we had left. For tonight, the only thing I would focus on was being one with him.

# Chapter Twenty

**FITZ**

Cadence was all I could think about as I piled dinner onto a tray in Creator Hall. I barely saw the food selections. The room buzzed with conversation, students and staff talking animatedly about the success or failures of the day's rehearsals. Their final performance was in one week. From what Cadence had said, parents would pour into the camp on the last day, eager to see what their kids had worked on all summer long.

The day before all that happened would mark my last full day with Cadence. We would share our last sunset, giving finality to the last night I could hold her in my arms. The weight of bricks I felt like I had been carrying all summer grew tenfold, weighing me down with every step, every hour, and every minute as I processed how close we were to that date. I knew what was supposed to happen, but I didn't want to accept it. I couldn't walk away from her. It was that simple, yet so horrifically complicated. I was in heaven and in hell–flying and burning all at the same time.

For the past week, I dragged myself through daily tasks, staggering each day to keep it together as the calendar drew closer to September. The effort to make each moment count felt like the fight of my life. I could almost hear the seconds ticking by as the sun set behind the trees, washing away the pink that painted across the sky, effectively erasing another day. We both knew it and seemed even more rushed to get to the lake after we'd finished our camp duties. Our time was running out. Every kiss, every touch, and every time I sunk myself deep inside her was precious if not a very risky gamble. Yet it was also shadowed with unspoken words about our inevitable separation.

Then there were the times when Cadence dared to bring it up. She didn't stop after that stormy night we spent in the stockroom. She was still hanging on to a small shred of hope that things could be different, and we wouldn't have to stop seeing each other after we left Camp Riley. Just last night, we talked long after the sun went down and into the late hours of the night. She tried to weigh the options, concocting every scheme under the stars that would allow us to sneak off to see each other even after I got married.

The idea was ludicrous. Sure, I wanted to stay with her, but it couldn't be in that way. She was better than that and deserved so much more. Stringing her along with a clandestine affair would be no different from what my father had done to my mother. I tried to explain that over and over again, but her naivety made her blind. For the first time since we met, the four-year age gap suddenly seemed to matter. Her innocent hope was going to make my leaving that much worse.

I brought my tray of food over to an empty table in the corner with the sole intention of wolfing it down and hurrying off to the lake. Just as I was about to dive in, Devon dropped into the seat across from me, a few fries from the tray he had been carrying spilling onto the table. Picking up his burger, he ripped into it like he hadn't eaten in a week.

"There's this place in town called Barney's," he said through a mouthful of food. "It's a local bar that seems pretty chill. A bunch of us are headed there after dinner. You coming out this time?"

I shook my head, denying his request to accompany him for about the twentieth time that summer.

"Nah, I think I'll hang back."

After swallowing his food, he leaned in and lowered his voice.

"Sneaking off with Cadence again tonight?" he asked. When I didn't respond, he continued. "Dude, I've been watching you two all summer. You try to hide it, but it's obvious. I haven't pushed too much, figuring you'd fill me in when you were ready. I've never been one to tell you what to do, but you know you can't let things be too serious with her."

I looked away and stared absently at the salt shaker that sat in the middle of the table.

"It's too late for that," I admitted. Devon let out a low whistle.

"Shit, man. We're leaving this place in a week. Does she know you won't be able to see her anymore?"

"Yeah, I told her."

"Well, then I think you should man up and walk away now. A long and messy goodbye will just make things worse."

I closed my eyes and allowed a flood of guilt to wash over me. I felt hopeless. Devon's exacting words about goodbyes seemed to ram down my throat, choking me. No matter which way I looked at things, what I had done was wrong. How I felt for Cadence was wrong. Even knowing it was wrong the entire time we were together didn't make it easy for me to stop.

"It's not that easy, Devon. I love her. Like, really love her."

Devon's eyes widened before his face turned grim.

"If that's truly the case, you know letting her go is the right thing to do. I can see this is hurting you, but better you hurt than her."

"Since when did you become such a goddamn expert?" I snapped.

Devon leaned back in his chair and held up his hands.

"Hey, I'm not trying to plan some sort of intervention here. All I was saying is–"

"I get what you're saying. I'm handling it," I interrupted and stood up. Having completely lost my appetite, I picked up the tray and dumped the contents in the nearby trash can.

There was an unfamiliar sting forming in the backs of my eyes.

*Fucking tears.*

I blinked them away, not wanting Devon to see. I hadn't cried over anyone or anything since I was ten years old–my father made sure of that. He didn't see the need to deal with anything as paltry as emotion, but just the thought of losing Cadence Riley threated to break the hardness that had been drilled into me. I couldn't stomach the idea of a life without her. But worse, I didn't know how I'd live without her.

When I turned back toward Devon, I caught sight of Cadence sitting at a table with Joy at the other end of the cafeteria. She smiled when she saw me looking at her. I smiled back, but it was only halfhearted. Guilt stabbed at me, a vicious knife to the chest that just kept twisting and turning. It was the same guilt that plagued me all summer, but I had resigned myself to the idea it was something I'd have to get used to. At the very least, it told me I had a conscience, even if that conscience was irrelevant since I didn't listen to it. Instead, I allowed myself to fall hard, fast, and furiously for Cadence.

I felt Devon's curious gaze on me. Tearing my eyes away from Cadence, I looked at him. He sat there, all calm and cool, having probably fucked his way through half the girls on staff this summer. I wanted to resent him for it, to hate him for enjoying that kind of freedom, but I couldn't. Three months ago, I would have been right there along with him. What was happening now wasn't his fault. Still, I couldn't deny this sudden urge I had to punch something.

Devon looked down, taking note of my hands that were balled into fists.

"Shit. This is bad. You're really torn up over this girl," he said.

Uncurling my fists, I splayed my palms on the edge of the table and dropped my head. Almost involuntarily, my fingers gripped the edge and squeezed until my knuckles turned white.

"I don't know what to do. This just fucking blows," I swore.

"I hear you, man. I wish I knew some way for you to get out of this deal. I mean, shit. It was just an accident. A bad, tragic accident. I even mentioned it to my dad to see if he could help. He only shook his head and said it wasn't any of my business. Honestly, I just think he was happy I got off so easy. You, on the other hand, completely got the shaft."

"Don't I know it."

Devon sighed and shook his head. Having finished eating, he tossed his napkin on his tray and stood.

"Look, if you need anything, you know I'm here for you."

I looked at my best friend, my partner in crime for the past four years. We'd crammed for tests late into the night, chased girls, and smoked way too much weed together. He'd mopped up my puke after a wild night of partying just as many times as I'd cleaned up his. We'd been there for each other during the good, the bad, and the really ugly. But this–being in love with a woman–was all new. I knew I'd be on my own for this one.

I glanced back over to where Cadence was sitting. She looked happy, chatting with Joy animatedly over something or another. Her green eyes sparkled, always so full of life. It killed me to know, in one week, I'd break her heart. I hated the feeling of helplessness. To say this summer had been the best and worst of my life would be a gross understatement. The thrill I felt over making Cadence mine only amplified the grief of having to give her up. It was as if my entire life was being ripped apart all at once and I was unable to stop it.

But perhaps Devon was right. Maybe I just needed to grow a set and do what was right– end things with Cadence now… even if it crushed me. I thought about the characters in Cadence's books. She said she had fallen in love with me because of my depth and compared me to Colonel Brandon.

*I need to be more like Willoughby.*

I hadn't read the books, but clearly, the guy was a complete dick. He foolishly gave up the girl, clearing the path for a better man. I needed to do that for Cadence, to step aside and make room for someone else who was worthy of her love.

Shoving down the anguish that threatened to rip me to pieces, I turned without another word to Devon and set off for the barn. Cadence would be at the lake within the hour. I wouldn't be. Instead, I would stay in the loft.

Alone.

She'd be worried of course, wondering why I didn't show up to meet her. It would take every ounce of willpower I possessed to stay away. Tomorrow, I'd have to come up with some excuse, but I knew deep down creating distance between us was for the best. She was desperately clinging to a futile hope, and I couldn't be selfish anymore. I wouldn't allow her to settle for second best while I was forced to share a roof and a bed with another woman. It wasn't right. I had to stop taking without regard for the consequences. I needed to do this for her.

# Chapter Twenty-One

**CADENCE**

I slammed the door to the stockroom unnecessarily hard, causing Joy to peek her head around the corner of the aisle she was restocking in The Flourish.

"Easy, girl. Whatever's bugging you, don't take it out on that poor old door. The wooden frame is older than my great-grannie," she jokingly scolded.

"Sorry," I apologized sheepishly.

I wasn't one to lose my temper, but after days of letting it simmer, I felt ready to boil over. Fitz had been avoiding me for much of the week. He hadn't come to the lake in the evenings at all. Like a fool, I would go, sit alone for hours at a time, only to have him not show up. During the day, his presence was scarce, and I rarely saw him at all. When I did, he was often tied up doing a job with my father, not giving me the chance to speak to him about what was going on. I thought about going to the barn to see if I could catch him there, but pride kept me from doing it. I wasn't about to chase him. He knew I'd be waiting for him at the lake, but he never came. All said and done, I was left to roil in my anger for far too many days.

Joy left the half-empty boxes in the aisle and came over to the counter where I was standing. She folded her arms across her chest and pointedly looked at me.

"You okay?" she asked, her tone taking on a serious note of concern.

"I'm fine," I lied. "Just tired. I didn't sleep well last night."

"I can cover the store if you want to cut out early. I don't expect the normal midday rush of students since they're all tied up with final rehearsals today. I mean, no offense, but whatever has you all riled up made you too distracted to get much of anything done around here, anyway."

I frowned and glanced at the wall clock. It was just past noon. I was supposed to work until four, but Joy was right. I had been completely useless all morning. Perhaps if I used the time to track down Fitz, we'd be able to hash out whatever his issue was, then I could come back to work.

"You don't mind?"

"I'll be fine," she assured with a shooing motion of her hands.

Not needing further words of encouragement, I thanked her as I shed my apron and headed out the door.

The days had finally cooled to a more comfortable heat level, and after spending the morning in an air-conditioned building, the warm air felt good on my skin. It made the trek around the camp in search of Fitz all the more bearable.

His avoidance had upset me, but I knew there had to be an explanation. Initially, my brain had been too muddled by my feelings for him to truly grasp the implications of what was coming. I naively wrapped myself in the present, completely tuning out the inevitable. I knew what was between us. It was good and pure. I knew he loved me. I didn't believe he was deliberately trying to hurt me. Deep down, I suspected Fitz was only trying to put distance between us so that his leaving didn't hurt so bad.

However, the conflict I felt was wearing me down. I found myself questioning his feelings for me, wondering if I had been duped. Another part of me said that wasn't the case at all, and I shouldn't be angry with him. After all, I had seen inside the shell. I knew him. He was someone who had lost, and remained terrified, hurt, and haunted by his past and unpredictable future. I understood his predicament in a way I wasn't sure I wanted to. I wanted to tell him that everything would be okay, but I didn't know if it ever really would be again. His absence had left a massive, painful hole in my chest. It made me realize, when he was finally gone forever, it would be so much worse.

Sorrow clenched down on my chest, the feeling of hopelessness overwhelming. When we met, a relationship or a summer fling was the furthest thing from my mind. Never in my wildest dreams did I think I would fall in love, nor did I think he'd be the one to claim my virginity.

But I did. And he did. And now he was leaving in less than two days. Tomorrow was the last day at camp. Tonight would be our last night. I couldn't even bear the thought of never seeing him again. He was the keeper of my heart, and I was prepared to make any sacrifice needed if it meant I didn't lose him.

A lone tear tumbled down my cheek and I hastily brushed it away. No good would come from my tears now, especially once I found Fitz. As I trudged along the winding paths of Camp Riley, I vowed to make the most of every last minute I had with him.

After forty-five minutes of searching, I finally found Fitz just outside the bathhouse. His shirt was off and tossed over one shoulder, sweat gleaming from his body as he hauled a large cart of supplies toward the main entrance. His back was to me, so he didn't see me approaching, but I saw the moment he sensed my presence. Energy seemed to race across the ground, and his spine jerked in awareness.

When he turned to face me, I saw the longing in his eyes flash, before he seemed to visibly deflate. It was an expression that surely mirrored my own. He looked beaten, and just as exhausted and hopeless as I felt. All the anger I clung to over the past few days instantly vanished.

He watched me as I closed the distance between us, not saying a word, his expression unreadable. An uneasy feeling settled into my gut as I stepped up to him.

"I've missed you these past few days," I told him quietly with a forced smile.

Pain flickered in his eyes, but he quickly masked it by grabbing his shirt and putting it back on. After he pulled his head through the hole, I stepped up to him. Not caring if anyone saw us, I wrapped my arms around his waist. I knew I shouldn't, but I needed to feel his warmth. It was the only thing that would ease my fears and make me feel safe. Any consequence I'd have to endure would be worth it if I could just feel him holding me.

But he didn't return the embrace like I wanted him to. Instead, he stiffened.

"Cadence, no," he stated gruffly. As he removed my arms from around his hips, his movements seemed tense, almost as if he had to pry himself free. He stepped away, leaving a cold and vacant space in front of me.

He seemed more than just a little off. It was as if there was a wall standing between us, separating us into two completely different worlds.

"Fitz, what's wrong? Why haven't you been to the lake?"

He took a deep breath and paused. His broad shoulders heaved, and he seemed to have to force himself to look at me. Sadness crested his features, before turning into something hard. I didn't like it. It was almost like he was psyching himself up to tell me something. I looked into his eyes, only to see a million problems flitting across them. My insides began to churn. Panic rushed my chest, a crushing force of dread against my heart that had begun to race. Before he even opened his mouth to speak, I knew I was going to hate whatever it was I was about to hear.

# Chapter Twenty-Two

**FITZ**

I hesitated, then took another step back from her. I may as well have been weighed down by quicksand, my movements were that heavy and slow. I should have known better. I should have realized what was between us was too strong, and she'd never be able to stay away. Hell, I had barely managed it myself. Even now, as she stood there with those wide, emerald eyes brimming with hurt, I wanted nothing more than to pull her into my arms. I wanted to return the embrace she tried to give and tell her everything would be alright.

But then I'd just have to chalk it up as another mistake. It would be more false hope.

"Cadence, I thought it would be better if we put some distance between us."

She nodded her head, understanding prevalent in her eyes.

"I knew that's what you were doing, but it's okay. That's why I came to find you. I completely get it, but we can figure this out. Screw your father. We'll find a way to stay together."

She reached for me again, brushing her fingers along the side of my arm. I swore I could see the air spark from the connection. Quickly, I pulled away.

"Fuck, Cadence. What don't you get? We can't. Sneaking around and having an affair? Come on now. You don't want to cheapen yourself that way."

She lifted her chin in stubborn defiance.

"It would be a temporary solution. But if it means I get to be with you, I'll do whatever it takes."

That's not what I wanted her to say–but that was Cadence. She was always so worried about me and what my father was forcing me into. She had been understanding yet optimistic maybe something would change. That optimism would keep her blind to the reality.

Changing her mind and extinguishing her hopes would need a deliberate act of cruelty. Simply avoiding her wouldn't be enough. I had to make sure she'd never want to speak to me again. I was good at that after all. I'd had years of practice, never wanting to be bothered with the latch-on kind of girl. The words had always come easy. But then again, I never loved any of those other girls. Hurting Cadence would kill me.

I looked into her eyes, memorizing every fleck of brown and yellow in the bright emerald green. I never wanted to forget the tiniest detail. In her, I found everything I'd ever wanted. A hole slashed through the center of me and I tore my eyes from hers. I stared at the ground, knowing what I was about to do would break her. After what seemed like a long, agonizing moment, I forced myself to look back up and steeled myself for what needed to be done.

"Cadence, let's stop pretending," I began, trying to come off as detached as possible. "There's no need for some long, drawn-out goodbye tomorrow. Let's just call it like it is. We had a summer fling, and it was fun while it lasted."

Her expression was guarded.

"What are you talking about?"

"Look, I like you. I like you a lot. But there's no use hanging onto a hope that things will be different. It is what it is. Besides, I'm used to a certain kind of girl–girls with money and status. You know, the blue blood types. And quite frankly, you're just not it."

A million emotions seemed to flash across her face. Disbelief. Confusion. Hurt.

"I don't believe you. You've spent the last three months convincing me of how much you enjoyed being with me, and how much you liked that I was different from the rest. You haven't suddenly had a change of heart."

I shrugged and leaned against the side wall of the bathhouse.

"Sorry, sweetheart. Me and you, it's just not working for me anymore."

She sucked in a sharp breath at my cool tone. Then she shook her head as if she didn't believe a word coming out of my mouth and glanced down at her watch.

"You get off in a few hours. Let's meet at the lake, just like we normally do. Tonight's our last night, Fitz. Things will be chaotic tomorrow once all the parents start arriving for the final performance, then you're supposed to leave right afterward. Let's make the most of the time we have tonight. I'll even pack dinner so we can get to the lake a little earlier than usual. We can talk more about all of this then."

She reached for me again, but I shrugged her hand off.

"Why bother?" I scoffed.

Just then, I saw Rachel approaching us on the path leading to the bathhouse. I prayed like hell she'd turn off in another direction, but she continued to walk straight toward us. Absently, I wondered why she wasn't on set rehearsing with everyone else but didn't bother to ask as she tossed me a wink and a flirty wave.

"Hey, Fitz," she drawled.

Cadence's face pinched up with jealousy, but she didn't say anything as Rachel continued on through the main door of the bathhouse. That jealousy caused an idea to form in my head, one that I wasn't sure I could follow through with. However, I knew I needed to nurture the seed of doubt I had already planted in her head, and this might be the only way to help it grow.

*Willoughby. Remember Willoughby.*

I clenched my fists, knowing my next words would be the most heinous of all.

"It's over between us, Cadence. No more lake. No more late-night swims. Leave me alone. I just want to enjoy my last night here."

Cadence, whose eyes had followed Rachel into the bathhouse, now turned back to me. She looked annoyed, but not angry or hurt. She still wasn't falling for any of my bullshit.

"No. Just stop this nonsense. It isn't you talking. You're just trying to end it now to make tomorrow easier. You don't need to run from me, Fitz."

I shrugged.

"Who said I'm running? Maybe I just want to spend the night with someone else for a change."

Her head jerked back.

"Like who?" she demanded, her voice laden with skepticism.

I looked at her, preparing myself to deliver the final blow.

"Rachel. From what I hear, she's always up for company."

I watched as her creamy skin turned ghostly white. She blinked several times as if not trusting what she was hearing. I stared at her hard, careful not to reveal any sort of emotion. If she had even an inkling about how much this was tearing me apart, my plan wouldn't work.

She brought her hand to her lips and shook her head, still not wanting to believe me. However, I saw it the minute my words began to sink in, when all the hurt and betrayal took root. Tears began to gloss her eyes. I couldn't bear to see them but forced myself to hold my cool gaze steady. Slowly, they started to fall, one by one, grazing the heart-shaped lips I knew I'd never get to kiss again.

"But we..." she trailed off in a whisper. "We..."

"We what? Fucked? So, what?"

She lurched back as if I'd stabbed her, yet I don't know who felt more pain–her or me. Agony spread through my body, radiating over me like heat waves held to the hot summer air. Doing this to her was utterly destroying me, but I had to keep my resolve.

Her hurt expression began to morph into something else. Anger and outrage flashed brightly. She looked ready to tear into me.

"You're a bastard!" she hissed.

Before I could react, Cadence's palm landed square across my cheek. It stung, but not nearly as bad as the sting in my heart. Looking at her pained expression, it was as if she felt I was tearing her heart from her chest with my bare hands. I wanted to comfort her, to tell her everything I was saying was just an act designed to protect her. But I couldn't. She needed to hate me so she could move on.

And I just did a damn good job of making sure she would.

Turning swiftly, she ran. Away from me. Away from my cruel words. I watched as she ran, breaking into a million pieces inside, the connection pulling with each of her steps until my soul ripped from the strain of it.

I hated myself.

My knees felt weak, and I thought they might buckle. Giving in, I bent at the waist and braced my hands on my thighs. Cadence had been the only warmth I'd felt since before my mother died. She was the light that had been missing all of these years. Now that I had deliberately and hurtfully pushed her away, I knew nothing but darkness would be in my future.

And I deserved it.

# Chapter Twenty-Three

**CADENCE**

I always wondered how many broken hearts one person could withstand–broken hearts from unexpected tragedy or broken hearts delivered by the ones who were supposed to love a person the most. I had just experienced my first, and I knew I never wanted to feel this way again.

Fitz had crushed me. I'd allowed myself to love him so freely and so openly. I fell for the good I saw inside him. I should have seen it the moment he sidled up next to me that first day at Camp Riley, all arrogance and chaos. My instincts had been right, but not necessarily about him, per se. I was only right thinking he'd be nothing but a broken heart.

Now all I felt was a hollow emptiness.

I was still grappling to understand everything. I didn't know how, in just a few short months, I could come to feel like this. Every time I closed my eyes, Fitz was there. In the silence, I heard his voice. In the darkness, I saw his face. There was no escaping it. Images flickered from the affectionate and protective person I fell in love with to the hurtful and spiteful creature he turned in to. I remembered all the arrogance and swagger he presented on day one. That side of him seemed to vanish after that first initial day yet reappeared with a vengeance as we stood next to the bathhouse. Only this time, there was calculated cruelty in his eyes. A part of me wondered if that was the true version of him all along, that I had simply been seeing things with my eyes wide shut.

Unable to stomach the idea of running into him today, I left the cottage I shared with my parents just as the sun began to peek over the horizon and had been at the lake ever since. I was certain my parents were probably wrought with concern over finding me gone that morning. For the first time ever, I would miss the final performance. But at least I thought to leave them a note, even if it was a lie. I told them I still had homework to finish, and I needed someplace quiet to complete it. I said I would be at the lake, but I'd be back in time to see the guests off.

It was so unlike me, but I didn't particularly care. In fact, I didn't really care about much of anything at that moment. I only cared about being alone and away from the crowds of people who were set to arrive that morning. Now, as the sun rose higher in the sky, I was reminded of the day I first realized I loved Fitz.

I picked up my sketchpad and flipped through the pages until I found the drawing I had started of Fitz. It wasn't complete, but that was okay. My plan today was to finish it, forever capturing the moment in time when I discovered I was in love.

As I hunched over the pad and moved the pencil over the page, a tranquil feeling settled around me. The calmness allowed me time to reflect on my own actions over the summer. Yes, Fitz had made mistakes. He lied by omitting the truth, but I also made mistakes of my own. He had obligations and a reality that was outside of his control. He was scheduled to marry another woman. I didn't know this when I gave him my heart, but I did know it when I gave him my body. I ignored all the signs, choosing to stay ignorant to the inevitable end.

A small part of me had clung to the idea he'd somehow choose me over his fate. Or even that he'd agree to see me on the side, separate from his convoluted marriage. I knew it was a foolish notion, but still, if it meant I got to keep him, so be it. I was never the sort of person to settle for second best, yet what I had proposed to Fitz was equivalent to that.

I realized now that was my mistake. He was faced with a future I couldn't even begin to fathom. I promised him no regrets, yet I hadn't followed through with that promise. His words to me yesterday, while hurtful and unkind, were empty. I knew he didn't mean them, and I was the one to push him to that point. That's why I slapped him. That's why I ran away. I wasn't truly angry at him but more at myself for hanging onto that misguided measure of hope.

The sun lowered further in the sky. The final performance was most likely over, but I had no intention of heading back into camp to see the students off. I may have told my parents I would, but I knew I wasn't really needed there now. Staff members would be saying their final farewells. Students would be making plans for dinner in town with their family members. My parents would be heading back to the cottage to recap the summer and start discussing plans for next year. We would stay at the camp for another week, so packing for us wouldn't start for another few days.

Then there was Fitz. I knew from the camp schedule a car was due to arrive for Devon and him at eight. They were probably packing at this very moment. They'd make the walk up Watercolor Way to the main entrance of the camp. Then they'd be off–Devon to wherever his life would take him, and Fitz to meet his bride at the altar.

No, there was no need for me to hurry back to the camp. I didn't need to see Fitz. I didn't need one final reminder of what would be forever lost. At that moment, as I stared down at the pencil lines and shading that shaped the man I loved, I had no regrets, and I wanted to keep it that way.

# Chapter Twenty-Four

**FITZ**

"You're going to wear out the floor if you keep pacing in that same spot," Devon said.

I paused, not realizing I'd even been doing it. I was fucking exhausted, barely sleeping a wink last night. The minutes leading up to the early dawn had seemed like endless hours. I was filled with self-doubt, wondering what I should have done differently. Despite my exhausted state, I was also restless. I knew why, but I had to face facts. I was leaving Camp Riley in a matter of hours. When I did, I would leave behind the girl who meant more to me than any sunset or every single breath I took.

Devon and I were supposed to be packing, but evidently, he thought he was finished. He was lounging on his mattress, flipping through the pages of a magazine. I tossed the remaining few belongings that I'd brought with me into my navy duffel bag. Looking around the loft, I made sure nothing else was left.

"I think that's your t-shirt," I said to him and pointed over to the orange ball of material tossed haphazardly in the corner.

He glanced at it, then lazily got up from his perch to retrieve it.

"Thanks," he mumbled, picking up the shirt and stuffing it into his own bag. Then he added, "Don't forget your box of tapes."

I glanced at the box of tapes that sat open on my bed. Their worn labels seemed to glare at me, every handwritten song title a reminder of all the nights I had listened to them with Cadence by the lake. I'd never be able to listen to them again without thinking of her.

"I'm leaving them. I can replace the music with CDs when I get home if I want to."

"Dude, are you joking? You love those damn things," he admonished. "I watched you for years, running to the stereo and timing it just right, not pressing record until the very last second when the DJ stopped talking. They're like a work of art."

"Yeah, well. Things change."

He shot me an appraising look. I felt the muscles in my jaw bulge and tense.

"I noticed you skipped the performance this afternoon," he pointed out.

"Big deal," I stated flatly. "You know I couldn't risk running into Cadence."

Earlier that morning, as the camp filled with eager parents and the students buzzed with excitement, Devon and I worked to line up long rows of folding chairs in front of the stage. I was a nervous wreck the entire time, terrified I'd see Cadence on set. I knew if I saw her, my resolve would crumble. Devon noticed my odd behavior and asked what was wrong. That was when I filled him in on everything that had happened between me and Cadence the day before.

He'd told me I did the right thing, yet now, he stood there shaking his head, his lips pressed into a tight disapproving line.

"Our ride back home won't be here for another two hours," he pointed out.

"And?"

"Just saying," he said with a shrug. "I'm going to head out and say goodbye to everyone. Most of the staff will be heading out soon."

"Alright. I'll catch up with you at the main entrance."

Devon didn't say more. He simply nodded and threw his body over the top rung of the ladder. Before descending, he paused and looked pointedly at me.

"You know…" he trailed off, hesitating. "Maybe I was wrong about breaking it off with Cadence. I mean, it is inevitable, but I didn't expect you to be such a dick about it. There's still time to fix it with her."

I gave him a death glare.

"Break it off, don't break it off! You can't make up your damn mind. I did what I had to do. What's done is done now."

Devon shook his head.

"It's your call, man."

He disappeared down the ladder, leaving me alone to contemplate his words. I looked to the bale of hay where my duffle bag and a box of tapes sat. An ache clawed at my chest as I stared. Cadence should have those. Perhaps if she listened to them, she'd be reminded of me and what we shared here in this place.

Memories of all the nights we shared flashed before my eyes. I squeezed them shut, hoping to block out the visions, only to realize they'd forever be seared into my brain.

"Fuck it," I swore under my breath.

I couldn't leave things like this with her. Grabbing the box of tapes, I rushed out to find her.

---

I started the walk toward the cottage Cadence shared with her parents. The walk eventually turned into a jog, then to a full-blown sprint until I ran into a crowd of people. I pushed my way through the horde, each one of them smiling or laughing. Some were singing songs from the musical they'd just watched. Others talked loudly, offering words of congratulations. I barely saw or heard any of it. My only focus was getting to Cadence.

After what seemed like forever, I managed to get past the crowds and raced up the path toward the cottage on the hill. My feet pounded up the wooden steps of the front porch, stopping only when I reached the door. I banged my fist against the wooden frame.

"Cadence!" I called. More banging. "Cadence!"

I anxiously paced back and forth on the porch. Much to my disappointment, Jamison Riley and Dahlia came to the door. Not Cadence. Her father looked shocked to see me standing there. I stepped back, fairly certain I looked like a lunatic.

"Fitz. What can I do for you?"

"I need to see Cadence. Um… sir," I stumbled, barely remembering my manners. Mr. Jimmy knew me even if it was only through a work relationship. Still, he was the father of the girl I loved. Making a good impression suddenly seemed to matter.

"She's not here, Fitz. She left early this morning."

*Left?*

My stomach dropped. I couldn't be too late. I had to apologize. To fix this.

"What do you mean she left? Where did she go?"

Dahlia began to whine. Mr. Jimmy opened the door to let her out, then stepped out onto the porch to stand in front of me. He crossed his arms over his barreled chest and stared at me, conflict evident in his gaze.

"Fitz, look. I like you kid. I like you a lot actually, but I think it's better if you just head on home and leave her be."

"I mean no disrespect, sir, but I need to see her. You don't understand."

"Actually, I understand better than you think. I know you've been sneaking off to the lake with her all summer long. Her mother and I aren't stupid, but we respect her privacy. She is eighteen after all. But I also know that you have certain obligations that don't really add up to me."

"Obligations?"

"Your father called nearly every week since camp started. He was checking in to see how things were going with you. Rest assured, I always gave him a good report. However, he said something last week that left me scratching my head. What's this business about you getting married in September?"

*Fuck!*

I wanted to scream. I could only imagine how the situation looked.

"It's complicated," I stated, not knowing where to even begin.

"I'll bet," he stated caustically. His tongue clicked, and I half wondered if he was literally going to pick me up by the shirt front and toss me off the porch. He didn't, and just continued on with a judgmental stare. "Imagine my surprise, to hear that the boy who's been spending all kinds of time with my daughter is supposed to be getting married. My wife wanted to murder you. At least, that was until I reminded her that Cadence is a smart girl. I thought there had to be some sort of explanation. So, tell me. Are you really getting married?"

Slowly, I nodded.

"I am, but it's not by choice. All I can say is I made a mistake, and now, I'm paying for it. I can't really say anything more."

Mr. Jimmy pressed his lips into a tight line, but he didn't say anything right away. Instead, he stood and stared, appearing to size up the situation. He looked back and forth between my eyes like he was searching for something. I could only hope he saw the truth in my words and my desperation to see his daughter.

"Does Cadence know the details?"

"She does, sir."

He grumbled something I couldn't make out. He looked out, staring absently into the woods that lined the side of the house and shook his head.

"Well, it appears you've got yourself into quite the jam, now doesn't it?" he eventually said. "I don't know what's going on, but I will say I've never seen my daughter take an interest in any boy the way she has with you."

"I didn't plan for this to happen. It just did," I said earnestly. "When I tried to break things off, I didn't do it the right way. Because of that, I need to set things right with her. I need to apologize."

He watched me contemplatively again for a moment before offering a single nod.

"If that's the case, I think you know where to find her."

*The lake.*

"Thank you, sir!"

Without another word, I turned and sprinted down the steps. I ran back though the crowd of people. It had thinned some, but they still slowed my progress. I passed Creator Hall, then the barn, finally reaching the little parting in the trees that would take me to the lake. Just as it had been all summer, the clock was ticking, and the sun was setting. Except now, I only had one hour left. There would be no tomorrow with Cadence. This was it. The minute I climbed into the car that was supposed to take me home, it was all over.

The box of tapes rattled in my arms as I ran. I finally stopped running once I neared the end of the path. Walking the last few steps to the clearing, I tried to catch my breath. When the trees parted and the lake came into view, my steps faltered. Cadence was sitting alone on the dock, her back facing me, and she had the Boombox with her. Even from this distance, I could hear the music flowing from the speakers. She had on one of my mixed tapes, the one I had left in the cassette deck the last time we were here. *Forever Young* by Alphaville glided across the air.

I felt like there was a magnet pulling me toward her. Slowly, I put one foot in front of the other. Her golden hair shone like a halo around her head. She looked like an angel at sunset. My breath caught in my throat. The pain of what I was going to lose stole all the air from my lungs.

I was halfway to the dock when she turned to face me. I couldn't tell if she was sad or happy to see me. She shook her head and held out a hand to stop me from coming any further, but I didn't stop walking until I reached the edge of the dock. Only then did I pause. She stared at me, and I at her. Emotion welled up inside me, erupting from a place I didn't know existed.

"I'm sorry, Cadence," I called out. "I'm sorry for–"

I stopped, realizing I could be here all day apologizing for the multitude of ways I hurt her.

She closed her eyes and nodded before turning to gaze out over the water for a moment. When she looked back, I could see the tears glistening in her eyes. But then, much to my surprise, she smiled. It wasn't a beaming, cheerful smile but one that came from a place of bitter sweetness.

"No regrets, Fitz."

Then, she turned her back to me once more.

I wanted to go to her, to beg for her forgiveness. But for some reason, I knew the few words we exchanged were enough.

I still clutched the box of mixed tapes in my hands. Bending over, I placed it on the worn wooden planks of the dock. This summer, I had found paradise. I'd always be forever young in this magical place. But now, paradise was gone. I knew the memories we shared would forever play in my head, over and over again. Cadence, so beautifully untouched, had trusted me. She had given me not only her body, but her heart. Saying those three words, expressing she had no misgivings, told me what I needed to know. She knew I loved her and that was all that mattered.

Stepping away, I began to walk back toward the woods. I looked back only once. When I did, I saw Cadence standing at the beginning of the dock with the box of tapes opened at her feet. In her hand, she held a piece of paper. I knew what it was. It was an unfolded origami fortune teller, one I had made at some point during the night when sleep refused to come. Inside each of the four flaps, I had written four sentences.

*Sunsets will always belong to you.*

*When it's dark, I'll remember you to find the light.*

*You will forever hold my heart.*

*Leaving you will always be my biggest regret.*

Cadence stared at me with her hand held over her heart. I did the same, each of us sending our own silent messages. My throat tightened. An ache so all-consuming slammed into my chest, nearly causing me to choke.

As I turned to walk away, I took her in one final time. Her loose-fitting tank top billowed in the breeze, causing the pale blue material to cling to one side of her body. I memorized her every curve and the way the sun shone behind her golden hair. I breathed deep, hoping to catch a hint of her vanilla scent. I didn't, but that was okay. I wished I could look into the expressive pools of her emerald green eyes once more. I couldn't, but that was okay too. I'd never forget.

Just like I'd never forget her.

# Chapter Twenty-Five

*Six Weeks Later*
*Bethesda, Maryland*

**CADENCE**

I burst through the doors of my bedroom in our old Victorian house in Bethesda and threw myself onto the bed. I didn't cry. There were no more tears left to shed. Instead, I just stared at the ceiling as a feeling of finality began to seep into my veins. Thunder rumbled in the distance and I knew a storm was moving in. The TV was on in the downstairs living room. I could hear the voice of Pat Sajak, and the click-click sound of a wheel spinning carry up the stairs. I pulled my pillow up on either side of my head to cover my ears.

It had been forty-one days and thirteen hours since I left Camp Riley. Not that I was counting or anything. In all that time, I hadn't heard a word from Fitz. I shouldn't have expected him to call or reach out to me in some way or another. I tried not to think about what he was doing or who he was doing it with. With every day of silence, the reality became more fatalistic.

Still, a part of me refused to let go of that last shred of hope. I promised myself that I wouldn't miss him. I began my classes at American University and tried to keep myself as busy as I could. However, the daily battle I had with myself to look up his phone number to call him, to beg him to come back to me was soul-crushing.

When he left me that final day at the lake, it had been a bittersweet goodbye. Still, the box of tapes he left for me rekindled a tiny flame of hope. The Chinese origami he made was still under my pillow. However, I knew now, whatever Fitz had felt for me wasn't enough to make him stand up to his father and choose me over the shitty deal he'd been given. That fact became a reality the moment I entered the living room to join my parents for a bit of TV.

Wheel of Fortune was about to come on, but there was still five minutes left of the local news. That's where I saw him again. Fitz. My Fitz–although he wasn't mine anymore. I didn't expect it to hurt so much but seeing him being photographed next to a beautiful woman in a white dress was a blow to the chest like no other.

He had actually gone through with it.

In that instant, I knew there never would be a call from him. I could never call him. See him. Touch him. He was gone forever.

The newscasters rattled on about the happily ever after for the son of a rising politician and daughter of a prestigious judge, but I didn't stick around to hear everything they were saying. I couldn't stomach it. As I struggled to breathe, the ache in my chest was so severe, I thought my lungs would collapse. Both my mother and father had looked at me with a worried expression, but I just gave an excuse about having to do homework and left the room.

I couldn't face them, especially now. They didn't know my period was late. Very late. They didn't know I had taken a pregnancy test that very morning. They didn't know how I sat on the edge of the toilet and cried at the appearance of that second blue line. There was no doubt.

I was pregnant.

The well of tears I thought was dried up began to fill again. I let them fall, streaming freely down my face as I stared up at the white ceiling in my bedroom. As much as it pained me to let Fitz go, I had to get over him. He was now officially a married man. But living here, knowing Fitz was only thirty minutes away, yet still so far out of reach, would be next to impossible. I had to work at moving on for the sake of our baby–my baby. Because, yes–I knew I was going to have to do this alone.

It would be torture seeing my parents' disappointed expressions day in and day out, and I refused to allow myself or my unborn child be a burden to them. They raised me better than that. They taught me to be independent and to stand on my own two feet. I had to show them I could do exactly that, and just hope that I wouldn't disappoint them with yet another thing. Sure, I had school to worry about, but I could sort that out later once I settled someplace. In the meantime, I had some money saved. It wasn't a lot, but it was something to get me started.

Impulsively, I jumped from the bed and went to my closet. Pulling out my suitcase, I began to toss items inside. I had no idea where I was going, but I'd figure it out. Maybe Abingdon, Virginia. It was a quiet town and I always liked it there. But then again, that meant I'd be close to Camp Riley.

And the lake.

Memories of Fitz began to overwhelm me once again. No. I couldn't go back there.

Pouring rain began to pelt against the windows and flashes of lightning peppered the blackened night sky. I struggled to muffle the sound of my sobs as I emptied the contents of my dresser. I jumped when I heard a creak in the wooden floorboards of the old house. I paused.

Glancing up from my suitcase, I spotted my mother standing in the wood doorframe of my bedroom, her eyes kind and sympathetic.

"I know why you're trying to leave, Cadence."

Maybe she did. My mother always knew everything. But what she didn't know was why I felt I had to leave.

"Momma, no. You don't understand," I sobbed. I hastily wiped my tears away, only to find more had followed. She came to me and wrapped her arms around my shoulders. As she stroked my hair, I nearly crumpled to my knees, the action soothing me during my darkest moment.

"I do understand, honey. You've never been a good liar, so you don't know how to cover your tracks very well. I saw the pregnancy test in the bathroom wastebasket."

"I'm so sorry. I didn't mean…I didn't," I stuttered.

"Cadence, look at me," she said more sternly. I picked up my head and stared into what was sure to be a future version of me. Her green eyes, while kind, were glossy with unshed tears. "All the doctors said it wasn't possible for me to get pregnant, yet here you are. You were my miracle. Your baby is a miracle. You don't have to run. We will get through this together and as a family."

"Oh, Momma," I wept, dropping my head to her shoulder once again. "But, Fitz. He's…he's married now."

"I know, honey. I know. We'll figure it out. Come now. Wipe those tears. There's a good thunderstorm moving in outside. From the sounds of it, St. Peter is having a good game of bowling with the angels. How about we go sit on the back porch and enjoy the show?"

My mother turned me and led me down the stairs. When we passed the living room, I saw my father stand up from his recliner in the corner. I couldn't look at him. I didn't want to see the worry or disappointment sure to be written all over his face. My mother shook her head at him, a silent message to let us be. For that, I was grateful even if it was only a temporary reprieve.

She led me to the back porch where we both sat down on the

wooden swing that hung from the rafters. We didn't speak, only stared out at the storm. We rocked in silence as my mother softly rubbed the top of my head. My tears still hadn't stopped, but the soothing motion of the swing combined with the feel of her hand running over my head seemed to have quieted the chaos in my brain enough so I could think.

I wanted to tell myself I'd be okay, but I didn't think I'd ever really be okay again. What I'd been through over the past four months, all the things Fitz made me feel had irrevocably changed me. I would have worked through the darkness with him whether it be fallout with his father or jail time. I believed that when I chose to give him my body, my heart, and my soul. I realized now that he never would have given me the chance to stand by him. To be there for him.

But that was okay. I made a conscious choice. I couldn't deny that I was scared of what was to come–terrified, actually. But I would never regret what happened between me and Fitz. He made me feel loved and cherished, even if it was for only a short time. I knew in my heart of hearts Fitz was my soul mate.

As the lightning flashed, my hand instinctively reached down to touch my belly. I supposed, in a way, life was like a book. It wasn't all that different from the classic tales I loved to read. I didn't get to write the ending that I wanted for my characters and could only accept what was already written on the page. For me and Fitz, the words weren't written in our favor, but just knowing I would always have a piece of him with me somehow made everything alright.

*To be continued…*

## MUSIC PLAYLIST

**Thank you to the musical talents who influenced and inspired *Untouched*. Their creativity helped me bring this story to life.**

"Bullet the Blue Sky" by U2 *(Joshua Tree)*

"Ordinary World" by Duran Duran *(The Wedding Album)*

"One" by U2 *(Achtung Baby)*

"The Best of What's Around" by Dave Matthews Band *(Under the Table and Dreaming)*

"High & Dry" by Radiohead *(The Bends)*

"Far Behind" by Candlebox *(Candlebox)*

"Love Comes Quickly" by Pet Shop Boys *(Please)*

"Fade Into You" by Mazzy Star *(So Tonight That I might See)*

"Runaway Train" by Soul Asylum *(Grave Dancers Union)*

"Forever Young" by Alphaville *(Forever Young)*

LISTEN ON SPOTIFY

Defined

DAKOTA WILLINK, LLC

*This book is an original publication of Dakota Willink, LLC*



Library of Congress Cataloging-in-Publication Data
Defined | Copyright © 2019 by Dakota Willink | Pending



Cover design by Dragonfly Ink Publishing
Copyright © 2022

# Defined

## Fade Into You Book 2

**One love. One destiny. But it only takes one person to bring the house of cards tumbling down…**

Seventeen years ago, Fitz Quinn stole my heart.
He took my innocence, then left me broken.
When a twist of fate brought us together again, I quickly learned even time couldn't dim our chemistry.
Fitz was sexier than ever—successful and provocative.
He became the man I always knew he would be, and the heat between us quickly became unbearable.

Despite the promise I made to myself, the walls to my heart started to crumble.
Before I could stop it, I fell for him all over again.
But things are so much more complicated now.
Lives are at stake.
I have to decide if sacrificing everything that defined me is worth being with the only man I have ever loved.

*To all the women who've been told they can't…*
*Actually, you can.*

"Life is about choices. Some we regret, some we're proud of. Some will haunt us forever."

— Graham Brown

# Chapter One

*Washington, D.C.*
*PRESENT DAY*

## CADENCE

I sat back in my office chair and shook my head. I just finished reading another news article that made my stomach turn. Climate change, healthcare, school shootings, immigration, government scandals—there was no escaping it. Some days I wished I could just shut out all the noise, politics, and injustices in the world. But then there were the days when I saw good defeat evil, reminding me of why I do what I do. Whenever I saw the good guys chalk up a point, it made everything worth it.

I looked up at the giant cork board hanging on the wall above my computer, filled with pictures of smiling children and families and thank you notes. There were letters of appreciation written to me and my colleagues at Dahlia's Dreamers, expressing gratitude for our work in keeping their family whole.

*Yes. It's worth it. THEY are worth it.*

I smiled to myself just as a knock sounded on my office door. Turning my gaze away from the pictures, I called, "Come on in."

Joy Martin, my best friend since our days at Camp Riley and current scheduler-in-chief, poked her head in. She was smiling broadly, her white teeth a vivid contrast to her smooth, cocoa colored skin. I returned her smile, always appreciative of the contagious grin that never failed to brighten even the darkest of rooms. The name Joy was fitting—she emitted it everywhere she went. That quality made her a true asset at Dahlia's Dreamers. The people who walked through our doors needed all the smiles they could get.

"Sorry, Cadence. I feel like I've been stuck on a billion conference calls today. I meant to check in before now. How's the day shaping up?" Joy asked as she plopped down in the chair across from me.

"Not too bad. I made a little progress on the Álvarez case after the family left but not as much as I would have liked. But then again, I became distracted by a news notification that popped up on my phone."

"Girl, how many times have I told you? Ignore it before it makes you go crazy."

"It already has," I laughed. "Anyway, I still need to go over my notes for my meeting with Simon Reed. He's due here at three o'clock. He'll get cranky if I'm not prepared."

"Actually, that's what I came in to tell you. He just called to say he's stuck in court and can't make it today. He asked if he could come in to meet you tomorrow morning at nine."

"Of course he wants to meet on a Saturday," I grunted and rolled my eyes. "I mean, I get he's doing the work pro-bono, but he's a royal pain in the ass sometimes. If he wasn't such a great attorney, I'd drop him from our list."

"Now, now, have patience," Joy said in a sing-song voice. "You know he's only a pain because you refuse to go out with him."

"Whatevs," I waved off, deliberately using one of my daughter's favorite terms because I knew it would get under Joy's skin. She hated the way the younger generation shortened words. "You know how I feel about the argyle sweater vests he's constantly *not* rocking. They're hideous. Plus, I'm just not interested in him that way."

"Yeah, yeah, I've heard it all before," she muttered.

"Don't start the 'I need to date' crap. You sound just like Kallie. And speaking of which, Reed's cancelation means I can get home early and help her get ready for tonight. I wasn't sure if I would be able to before now."

Joy cocked one perfectly shaped brow in confusion.

"What's tonight?"

"Junior prom, remember? Can you even believe it? God, I feel old. It seems like I was just there yesterday, and now here I am sending my baby girl off to her own prom. Do you want to come by and join in on all the girly prep? I'm sure Kallie would love for her Auntie Joy to be there," I added.

"I wish I could! I hate to miss it, but it's my third wedding anniversary next month. Marissa will be out of town for work, so we decided to celebrate early and made plans for a little getaway this weekend instead. We're driving up to Philadelphia tonight."

"Wow! Has it been almost three years already?"

"June twenty-sixth, baby. A day for the history books!"

"It sure was," I laughed. "How could I forget the way you hightailed it out of here the minute the Supreme Court ruling came in? You and Marissa couldn't wait to tie the knot. The two of you were like teenage kids on prom night!"

As soon as the words left my mouth, visions of my sixteen-year-old daughter doing things I didn't want to think about sprang into my mind. I paled. Joy, on the other hand, slapped her palm against her knee and burst out laughing.

"Here's hoping Kallie's prom night isn't like my wedding night!"

"Not funny. Not funny at all," I scowled, but I had clearly walked into that one.

"Oh, and another thing," Joy added once she calmed from her fit of giggles. "Your publisher called while you were meeting with the Álvarez family."

I frowned.

"Please tell me it's good news. The delay is killing us. We need that book released soon if we want to keep the lights on around here."

"Everything is back on schedule and set to release in two weeks. The final files were sent to you for review. They should already be in your Dropbox folder."

"Awesome! That's a huge relief! Let's have a look at them, shall we?"

Joy came over to my side of the desk while I opened the link to my Dropbox. Sure enough, I found a little blue file labeled *And I Smile*—FINAL. I clicked on it as a thrill of excitement seeped into my veins. When the first image filled the screen, I couldn't stop the surge of adrenaline I always felt seeing my drawings come to life in digital format. The colors seemed to look sharper and more vibrant.

But, along with the thrill, there was also a nervous feeling. Even though I had hit multiple bestseller lists in the past, there was no guarantee I'd do it again with this particular children's book. Dahlia's Dreamers, the non-profit organization I established ten years ago, relied on the success of my stories and illustrations. The financial implications that came with a possible failure always weighed heavily on my shoulders. Since everyone here made the same salary, I also had to rely on a portion of the proceeds to substitute my personal income. Nobody was getting rich working for a non-profit.

"Wow, these look amazing!" Joy gushed. "And if I haven't already told you, I love the storyline for this one. It really hits home for me. I think you nailed it."

"Hmmm…maybe," was my only response. I stared contemplatively at the text that had been merged to flow with the illustrations.

"What's wrong?"

"I don't know. I mean, I happy with it, but I wonder if I took it too far or tackled too much at once."

"No, I don't think you did, not in the least bit." Joy shook her head vehemently. "*And I Smile* touches on every aspect, showing how prejudice is a learned behavior, yet you didn't do it in an in-your-face sort of way if you know what I mean. Don't second guess yourself. There should be more children's books like this in my opinion."

"I suppose I'm just nervous, that's all. Considering our federal funding just received a drastic cut, we can't afford poor sales with this book." I didn't add that I couldn't afford it either. Kallie's school tuition bill was due at the end of the month.

Joy moved back around the desk to reclaim her seat, then leaned forward with a knowing look.

"Cadence, have a little more faith in yourself. Everything always works out. Plus, don't forget about the upcoming gala. The tickets sold out so fast, I'm sure it will be a success. You've got an amazing thing going here. Just think of all the families Dahlia's Dreamers has put back together or all the young students who were given the opportunity to be something great. Those people would never have had a chance if it weren't for you. You're loved by so many, and the new book will do great because of that fact."

I pursed my lips tightly together but didn't respond. Perhaps I was worrying too much. But then again, lives were at stake. People were counting on me and my team.

I glanced at the time on the top corner of my computer screen. It was going on three o'clock.

"Since Simon isn't coming, I'm going to finish up the few things I have left to do, then head out to be with Kallie. Do you mind holding the fort for the remainder of the day?"

"What are you waiting for?" Joy waved her hands in a shooting motion. "Go now! Prom is a special day for her!"

I laughed, thinking of Kallie's squeal after she had finally found the 'perfect' dress.

"Yeah, it is. She's so excited for it too," I added and began stacking the printouts of information about the Álvarez case. "I'll leave in a just a bit. I just want to get this disaster all over my desk cleaned up before I go."

"Well, don't take too long." Joy stood to leave. "Have fun beautifying tonight—not that Kallie really needs it. That girl has the face of an angel!" She smiled, but then her face drooped a little, regret evident in her eyes. "You'll text me pictures of her, right?"

Joy had never even so much as missed a birthday party for Kallie. I knew she was feeling a little bad about missing out on tonight. I offered a smile of reassurance, silently telling her I understood her predicament.

"Joy, it's your anniversary. Enjoy it! You know I'll text you. Hell, you can probably count on me to blow up your phone with a play-by-play later on. It will be just like you were there. Now, get out of here so I can wrap things up," I told her with a wink.

Once she was gone, I added the piles of papers I had collected for Simon Reed to a manila folder and placed it in the age-worn file cabinet drawer with our pending cases. Still left to sort were three other cases. Two of them were still in process, and the outlook was grim. However, the third one had closed yesterday, and it had a happy ending. I thought about the little boy who, after spending months apart, had been reunited with his parents. Their file went into the drawer labeled only with a smiley face. That was ultimately our job—to create smiles.

When I turned back to my desk, I noticed a legal document poking out from under a spiral notebook. It was an offer letter that came to me over a week ago. In an instant, all of my excitement about Kallie and her prom disappeared and I felt my stomach plummet.

I pulled it out and stared at it, the text nearly burning a hole through my heart. That's what happened every time I looked at the offer. It was for the last parcel of land my parents owned in Abingdon, Virginia. The property—all one hundred forty acres—had been left to me upon their passing over ten years ago. It had been their life and their dream until they died.

I sighed as a wave of sadness came over me.

"I still miss you so much, Momma," I whispered to the empty room.

I was barely twenty-four when my mother passed, my father following her less than a year later. Their deaths nearly crushed me, especially once I realized I lacked the knowledge and resources to keep their camp running. I was a single mother struggling to stay afloat. I had to prioritize. Unable to afford the tax burden, I eventually began to sell off pieces of the land bit by bit. I used some of the money to pay off my student loans and to start Dahlia's Dreamers. Later on, I sold more land to buy a modest house for Kallie and me, but the school district hadn't been the greatest. More land was parceled off so I could afford to send her to private schools.

Now there was only thirty-seven acres left. Kallie's school tuition and the fate of Dahlia's Dreamers hung in the balance. Despite the uncertainty of my financial future, I was hesitant to sell because of one major stipulation. The interested buyer refused to divide the property, which included the summer cottage I had lived in with my parents and the nearby lake.

My lake.

That was the real reason I couldn't bring myself to sign on the dotted line. It wouldn't just mean losing my childhood summer home. It would also mean giving up the lake. As good as the offer was, the thought of giving up my secret spot and the place where I'd matured from girl to woman nearly broke me. To me, it would be like selling a piece of my heart.

I'd always loved the lake. It held a certain layer of beauty and mystery that drew me in. I found the sultry summer air and sunsets to be magical. The way I had romanticized the place, it was no wonder why it was far too easy to fall in love there.

Suppressed memories tried to resurface. I struggled to push them away, but the effort was in vain. As much as I wanted to deny it, deep down, I knew that's what was stopping me from agreeing to the sale. A final sale would give me the closure I wasn't sure I was ready for. It would mean finally giving up *him*. It would mean all the memories we made together would end up being just that—memories.

# Chapter Two

## FITZ

I was sitting outside of a popular Irish pub in D.C., staring absently at the Washington Monument in the distance. It was a clear day in early May. It was warm, but the high heat of summer had not yet descended on the nation's capital.

Senator Robert Cochran was sitting across from me, opening his second pack of Marlboro Reds. As he flicked his lighter to the tip of yet another cigarette, I was convinced he only wanted to meet here because the pub allowed smoking on the outdoor patio.

It really wasn't the ideal place for us to meet. I would have preferred someplace less public, such as a private conference room or a suite at the Jefferson Hotel. Cochran said my office was out of the question and I understood why he didn't want to be seen entering my building. None of them wanted to be caught there. It would signal to anyone who was watching trouble was brewing. If he was spotted, the dogs would start sniffing around. Questions would arise, prompting a headline that would read something like, "Senator Cochran Enters Office of Washington Fixer." Then I'd have an even bigger mess on my hands.

I looked around, taking stock of my surroundings. It was in between the lunch and dinner hour, so the normally crowded restaurant was near empty. Other than Cochran and me, the only other patrons were two women seated four tables away from us. They looked young, probably fresh out of college. They were professionally dressed in pantsuits and heels, smiling and talking animatedly. I could barely hear their chatter, but I heard enough to know they were discussing politics. I shook my head.

*Nothing to be excited about, ladies.*

The young ones were always so eager. Little did they know, ten years in D.C. would harden them. They'd lose that fight—all that hopeful ambition that made them believe they could change the world.

I glanced at Cochran. He'd noticed them as well, but he wasn't eyeing them warily as he should be. No, instead of being worried about the implications of us being seen together or the possibility of our conversation being overheard, this asshole was busy checking them out. The look on his face was all too familiar—he was trying to sum up which one he wanted to bag first.

*Disgusting.*

He was old enough to be their grandfather.

"Eyes over here," I hissed quietly. "That wondering eye is what you got into trouble in the first place."

Cochran looked at me, his expression stoic.

"Boy, don't lecture me. I can handle myself," he drawled out.

"If that were true, we wouldn't be sitting here right now. While I don't particularly care who you're popping Viagra for, your wife does."

That wiped the smirk off his fat, arrogant face.

Robert Cochran wasn't anything to look at, but that didn't matter to a high-priced hooker. His money had them all vying for their turn in the sack. Patricia, Cochran's wife, was not a stupid woman. After thirty years of putting up with his philandering ways, she finally had enough and hired a private investigator. Cochran was sloppy, so it didn't take any sort of stellar investigative skills to find out what he'd been up to. In a matter of days, the PI collected hundreds of incriminating photographs—ones Patricia had no problem leaking to the press if her husband didn't pay up. For a cool five million, she'd give him a quiet divorce and the Republican Party would avoid an embarrassing scandal. The problem was, Cochran didn't want to give her a single cent.

"That's why I want to hire you and your firm to fix the problem," Cochran explained. "Your father said you're the best. He brags about his son, Fitzgerald Quinn, as being the Washington Fixer. I can't let my soon to be ex-wife fuck this up for me. She's a bitch, and she knows what's at stake. It's an election year, and we can't afford to lose a single seat."

I eyed him coolly, not caring for the way he spoke about his wife, the mother of his two college-aged sons. From what I knew of Patricia, she seemed like a nice woman. She was involved in the community, actively promoting a literacy program with the wives of other U.S. Senators. In the public eye, she appeared to be the model wife of an elected official.

While I may not know what it was like to be married to her, I did know appearances were everything. Because of that, I also knew there was no way I could put a positive spin on Cochran's indiscretions.

"My father is correct, I am the best. But he failed to tell you I won't take on clients who cheat on their wives with whores. I'm sorry, Senator, but you've come to the wrong guy."

I stood up to leave, but Cochran grabbed my arm.

"Don't give me that bullshit," he said in a loud whisper. "I know you've helped your father get out of a few jams in the past. Get off that high horse of yours!"

I nearly winced at his words but had been in the business long enough to know how to keep my poker face in place. I knew the jams he was referring to, but who my father was fucking wasn't any concern for Cochran. I pulled my arm away and brushed my sleeve like I was swatting away a fly. Reaching for my wallet, I tossed a twenty on the table to pay for the gin and tonic I had ordered but never drank.

"Have a good day, Senator Cochran," I said. Not giving him a second glance, I casually strolled away from the table. I was sure the old man was fuming, but I didn't look back and hailed a taxi.

"Where to, sir?" the cab driver asked.

"East End," I told him.

The driver took me along the Potomac, past the elaborate memorials, and entered the heart of the city. He slowed to a stop near The White House in order to allow a group of tourists to cross the pedestrian walk so they could gawk at the pristine white exterior. I had seen these sights a countless number of times, so for me, they had lost some of their luster.

Still, I always felt D.C. had a quiet strength, a force which was a constant reminder of being the home of the country's most powerful executive seat. With its vast monuments, lush green lawns, politicians, and hopeful wanna-be candidates crowding the cafes and streets, Washington sat proudly as the most dignified city in the nation. I knew the city by heart. While I could appreciate and understand its pulse, I also hated it. Yes, there was beauty, but there was also an underlying ruthlessness that couldn't be matched anywhere else. One had to understand that in order to survive here. Anyone who didn't would eventually become bait for the sharks.

As we got closer to the East End, I instructed the driver to pull over in front of my building on the corner of New Jersey Avenue NW. I paid the fare and climbed out. Crossing the pavement in a few short strides, I pushed through the double glass doors and went straight to the offices of Quinn & Wilkshire on the seventh floor.

When the elevator doors opened, our newly remodeled interior came into view. A fountain sat in the center of the waiting room, emitting the calming sound of running water at all hours of the day. Everything was pristine, including the black granite top reception desk and sleek leather furniture. The muted grays, creams, and burgundy accents gave the PR agency an air of confidence and power, matching that of the many clients who walked through our doors. From politicians to movie stars to prominent sports figures—we worked hard to promote our clients, making them appear successful, honest, relevant, and as exciting as possible.

Unfortunately, people rarely came to us when things were going well. Our clients usually came knocking *after* shit hit the fan. It ranged anywhere from a rising actress getting caught on camera snorting lines of coke to an athlete who may have celebrated too much and got a DWI. Despite what people say about there being no such thing as bad press, the reality proved time and again it wasn't true. Bad press was never good. Our job was to get them out of the negative spotlight with a positive public relations campaign. We did it, and we did it well.

As I approached my office, my secretary was there to greet me.

"Afternoon, Angie," I said with a small nod.

"Hello, Mr. Quinn. Um," she began nervously. "The other Mr. Quinn, your father, he's here to see you. He's in your office."

*Of course, he is. Fucking Cochran probably called him.*

But I didn't voice the words aloud. She might know I wouldn't be pleased to hear my father had come here unannounced, but she didn't need to know what went down today.

*Appearances. It's all about appearances.*

Instead of saying more, I gave her another nod and continued on through my office door. When I entered, I saw my father standing near the large, black-stained, maple bookshelf on the far-left wall. He appeared to be perusing the titles which I found to be extremely odd. I'd never seen him read a book in his life, despite his position with the United States government.

My father, Michael Fitzgerald Quinn, Senator of the Old Line State, strived for perfection. It often came out during public speaking events where he never failed to engage a crowd with the meticulousness of his words. That precision extended to his appearance as well. His cropped gray hair never went more than two weeks without a cut and his face was always smoothly shaved. Even his suit was always impeccable. Maryland, a state that normally voted democratic, seemed to buy this polished façade hook, line, and sinker. To anyone who truly knew him, it was nothing but a costume to hide the predator beneath the surface.

"Dad," I said, striding past him and taking a seat behind my desk. I refused to give him more courtesy than he deserved.

"Robert Cochran called," he said, not wasting any time getting to the point of his visit.

"I assumed that was the reason you got off your perch on Capitol Hill to come see me."

"Why aren't you handling this, Fitzgerald?"

"Because I don't want to," I stated matter-of-factly.

"Where's Devon? He's not as soft as you are. Put him on it."

It never failed. The man rarely spoke more than two sentences to me without throwing a cheap shot. I tossed him a look of impatience while I mentally counted to ten.

"Devon is in the Caribbean on a much-needed vacation, not that I need to explain the whereabouts of my partner to you. He's been working his ass off. I won't call him back here for this bullshit, nor will I put another member of my staff on it. Fixing a mess for a slimeball politician who can't keep his dick in his pants will never be on the firm's agenda."

"Your job is to fix negative publicity. If this goes public, the whole Party will suffer!"

I sighed, annoyed he was wasting my time and fired up my computer.

"You may have painted a picture of me as Washington's Fixer, but believe it or not, my company adheres to a code of ethics," I shot back as I watched the little apple icon light up. I wasn't about to get into it with him—been there, done that. He knew why I would never take on a client like Cochran even if he'd never understand or support it because his hands were just as dirty.

"Ah, forget it. It's time for Cochran to give up his seat anyway," he conceded. "He's been getting heat from both sides of the aisle on unrelated issues a lot lately. Sure, we don't want a scandal, but at least it gives us an excuse to push him out."

I looked up, shocked he was giving in so easily. My father never went down without a fight.

"So that's it then?" I asked incredulously.

"Why argue about it? I know how you think. You're weak, despite all my efforts to toughen you up. The only reason you refuse to take his case is because of what happened between your mother and me."

My blood began to boil at the mention of my mother. The fucking bastard never missed out on a chance to bring her up. I still hated him for what he did to her, yet he loved to remind me about it at every goddamned opportunity.

"Oh, do you mean how you left her high and dry after she got sick?"

He laughed, the sound unforgiving and cruel as he sat down in the chair opposite me.

"You need to let it go. She's been gone for almost thirty years. You think I'm no better than Cochran, but there are some things you'll never understand, son."

My fingers tightened around the computer mouse under my palm.

"Get out," I hissed, fighting the instinct to shout. I was normally calm, rational—except when it came to my father. He always knew how to push the right buttons. I loosened my grip on the mouse and pretended to click through emails, needing a distraction before I pummeled the old man.

Unfortunately, he continued on.

"You think I don't know how you feel? I know you better than you care to admit, and I know how loyal you were and still are to your mother's memory." He paused and rubbed his chin contemplatively. "But then again, we could use that to our advantage. Lost your mother when you were only a child… voters may prove to be sympathetic. We'd have to conduct a poll of course. That combined with—"

"What are you talking about?" I interrupted. His ramblings were wearing on me. I just wanted him to get to the point, then get the hell out of my office. "The voters don't care about me. They only care about the politicians who end up as my clients."

"They will care a lot about you in November."

*November?*

I eyed him warily. My father always had a self-serving agenda, and I was beginning to think he didn't come here solely for the Cochran issue.

"Why did you really come to see me today?" I questioned cautiously.

"It won't be long before Cochran announces his resignation. His attempt to hire you was simply a last-ditch effort. He knows he's out. Once he officially resigns, there will be an open seat in Virginia. You'll be the one to fill it."

I shook my head, my suspicions confirmed.

*Not this again.*

He'd brought up the subject of me running for office a few times before, but I hadn't taken him seriously. However, there was something different about his expression this time around that made my insides turn cold.

"I've already told you before, I have no interest in politics."

"It doesn't matter what your interests are. You don't have a choice anymore."

I ignored his comment and waved him off.

"Doesn't Bateman already have an itch to run?" I asked, recalling an interview I caught on one of the local news channels a few months back. "Let him do it."

"Bateman is an idiot. He's too easily swayed to the other side and he's not the for sure win. I've already talked to other members of the Party. You're the sure thing, not Bateman. You have the past and family connections to support it. People vote for those who make them feel comfortable. You're it, Fitzgerald."

"I'm happy doing what I'm doing. Devon and I have a successful and lucrative business I won't neglect. Even if I wanted to, it would be impossible. The primaries are in two months. I can't put together a campaign in that short amount of time," I insisted.

"We've already got the numbers from the exploratory committee I put together," he continued on as if he hadn't heard a word I said. "The National Republican Senatorial Committee has agreed to back you. They don't want Bateman, but they also don't want to appear biased. If he decides to throw his hat into the race, they won't stop him, but he won't get their full endorsement either. Once Cochran resigns, it will be as if the race went uncontested."

"Even without my consent, you went ahead and got the ball rolling." Feeling incredulous, I sat back in my chair and shook my head. "You're really unbelievable sometimes. You think you have this all figured out, don't you?"

"Your biggest worry will be in November. Polls are showing some woman from Richmond will win the Democratic primary. She's the only one getting in the way of you taking Cochran's seat."

I leaned forward, splayed my hands across my desk, and looked him squarely in the eye.

"I'm not running," I said for the second time in under five minutes. "And if I had any desire to do so, it certainly wouldn't be for your team."

My father stood and slammed his fist on the edge of the desk.

"Damn it! Don't try to toy with me! It's time to fucking grow up, Fitzgerald!" he shouted. "Your little business is only successful because I saw to it. I let you have your fun, but game time is over! Let Devon run the show for a while. You will do this for your country and for the Party —the Party you're registered with!"

"Or else?" I asked with a cocked brow. He could rage all he wanted. I refused to show an ounce of intimidation.

He folded his arms across his chest and tilted his chin up. His anger slowly dissolved into something icy—sinister almost—as he stared down his nose at me.

"Then I'll leak your little mishap with that girl during your years at Georgetown."

I narrowed my eyes at him.

"That was years ago, and it was a tragic accident. You know it as well as I do. I'm not a kid anymore. You can't threaten me and continue to hold that over my head."

"Can't I?" He smiled a wide, toothy grin. "I think the press will eat up a story about a poor girl who drowned because of you whether it was an accident or not. Can you imagine? Washington's Fixer couldn't fix his own mess. Daddy had to bail him out. Your life will be ruined. Your business will sink. And your son will suffer from the fallout."

I paled as a feeling of dread began to seep into my bones. I didn't give a shit about what he did to me, but my son was another matter entirely. He was my life. My responsibility. My whole reason for living.

"You wouldn't do that to Austin. You can't."

"I can, and I will. And speaking of your *son*," he spat out, emphasizing the word as if it left a bitter taste in his mouth. "It's about time you find yourself a new wife. Bethany's been gone for almost eleven years now. The voters will want to see you show strong family values. More stability."

My stomach plummeted. It was as if I were watching a rerun of my life, the past constantly on repeat. I wouldn't let him do this to me again. I rolled my eyes in a weak attempt to show I wasn't rattled by his threats.

"You've got to be kidding me. Old age must be screwing with your mind. With everything I have going on, I barely have time to date, let alone think about getting married."

"Barely? When was the last time you took a woman out?"

My gaze narrowed.

"That's none of your business."

"Well, I'm making it my business now. Don't try to play me for a chump. I know why you haven't dated. You're still pining over that girl from—how long has it been now? Sixteen years? The girl from—"

"Stop. Now. You have no idea what you're talking about," I growled. "I don't date because of Austin. He doesn't need to be confused by women coming in and out of my life. You taught me all too well what that's like. I won't follow your example."

He snorted and let out another cruel laugh.

"I have a meeting scheduled with the leaders of the RNC tomorrow night. I'll have my secretary send you the details. Make sure to be there. We need to discuss campaign strategy. The clock is ticking," he warned as if I hadn't said a word. He moved toward the door to leave. The asshole actually looked unperturbed. Confident even.

Then…he left. In his eyes, the matter was settled. I sat at my desk, feeling relatively stunned as I contemplated what in the hell had happened.

I rubbed my hands over my face, the five o'clock shadow rubbing harsh against my palms. I got up from behind my desk, moved over to the wet bar, and poured myself a stiff drink. Throwing back a swig, the Johnnie Walker Black Label burned going down and warmed my insides. Now alone with my thoughts, I walked over to the window that made up the back wall and absently stared out at the traffic.

I had no intention of running for office, but my father's threats loomed. I had to think of Austin. While I managed to shield my son from my father's cruelty, I knew he wasn't stupid. At fifteen years old, I could see so much of myself in him—some good, some bad. There was a rebellious side to him that made me worry. While I felt I had a good relationship with him, we'd been at each other's throats as of late.

*Goddamn teenagers.*

Either way, I may be able to weather the embarrassment from a near twenty-year-old scandal, but I wasn't sure if Austin, an impressionable teenager, could handle it. I also didn't think a rigorous political campaign and the public scrutiny that came with it was a better alternative.

"Fuck this," I whispered and threw back the remaining contents of my drink. I stared at the empty glass, fighting the urge to pour another. Alcohol wasn't the answer, a fact I understood all too well.

*What am I doing?*

At that moment, I needed a way to push through all the madness but drowning myself in booze wasn't the answer. A brisk jog around the National Mall was the only thing that would truly clear my head. Normally, I ran in the morning when the temperature was cooler, but a good sweat would be the perfect therapy after listening to my father's ultimatums.

Loosening my tie, I headed into the private bathroom attached to my office to change into running gear. As I stripped out of the button-down Calvin Klein dress shirt, I caught sight of my upper arm tattoo in the mirror. I stared at it as my father's words from earlier filled my mind.

*"You're still pining over that girl…"*

When he said it, I almost laughed. He didn't know about the many nights I wasted after Bethany died, drowning in a bottle of scotch and fucking any nameless body who was willing. I wasn't mourning the death of my wife like I should have been. Instead, I used the women and booze like they had the power to erase what I had truly lost. It didn't take long for me to realize I would never rid myself of the emptiness I'd felt ever since the day I left behind my first and only love.

Memories I struggled to suppress for years came to the forefront—memories of Cadence. The image of her face clouded my vision. As much as I tried, there was no forgetting a face like hers.

Our beginning may have been common and possibly forgotten if it had been anyone but her. With her long golden hair and the spark in her striking emerald eyes, no one could say Cadence was pretty. She was too stunning to use such a mundane word. Cadence wasn't just pretty. She was beautiful. And unlike most women I had come across in my thirty-nine years on this earth, her beauty wasn't only skin deep. She was unapologetic and had an enthusiasm for life that could match no other. She was delicate, yet so driven and determined.

Even at twenty-two, I knew she'd be the woman I'd spend the rest of my life looking for, but never be able to hang onto. She was exquisite—and she was still my biggest regret. We were so young, and our time together had been too short. It was one summer. That's all I was able to have with her. But it was the summer that had changed my life.

# Chapter Three

**CADENCE**

“Oh, Kallie! Just look at you!” I choked, blinking back the tears welling in my eyes. “You look so pretty!”

My beautiful daughter smiled as she descended the stairs of our modest Cape Cod style house. Her hair was swept up into a French twist, leaving just a few strands of blond hair to curl around her face. Her makeup, although she had spent an hour perfecting it, was subtle and accented her already stunning features.

After stepping off the bottom step, Kallie slowly spun in a circle. Her pale blue gown twirled around her, making the tiny sequence details sparkle in the light shining in through the bay window of the living room. If she had wings, one would swear she was an angel sent from heaven.

“Don’t move,” I said and quickly moved to the end table. I wanted to capture her just as she was, needing to freeze this moment in time. I opened up the drawer and rifled through the contents. TV remote controls, old batteries, and power cords—none of which I was looking for. “Damn it. I could have sworn it was in here.”

“What are you looking for?” Kallie asked.

“My good camera. I think it might be upstairs in my nightstand.”

“Mom,” Kallie whined. “Like, you already took a hundred pics with your phone. My friends will be here any minute.”

“Yes, but the phone quality isn’t as good. Let me just go upstairs and grab my camera. We have time. The limo isn’t supposed to be here for another ten minutes.”

"Ugh," she grunted.

"Oh, shush. It will only take me a second to grab it," I told her and raced up the stairs to my bedroom.

Sure enough, as soon as I opened the drawer, I found the expensive Nikon laying on top of a bunch of other paraphernalia. It had been a rare splurge for me, an impulse purchase I made when Kallie had begun high school. It came from a sudden realization I was running out of time. It was strange. When she was little, I used to wish for her to grow older. I wanted her to talk, walk, and feed herself. The days always seemed so long, yet her childhood had gone by remarkably fast. Now, I would give anything to have that time back. Soon she'd be a legal adult, ready to embark on the next phase of her life. Photographs would never replace the memories we shared together, but at least I would have the pictures to look back on.

I picked up the camera and was about to close the drawer, but what had been under the camera caught my eye. I paused and reached for it. It was a Mother's Day card Kallie had made for me when she was in elementary school. If memory served me right, she was eight years old when she made it.

Slowly lowering myself to sit on the edge of the bed, I stared at the faded pink construction paper. I suddenly felt very old even though I was barely thirty-five. It seemed like it was only yesterday when she came home from school with this card. She had been so excited. It had been a Friday, but she couldn't hold out until Sunday to give it to me. However, she quickly found herself disappointed come Mother's Day when she realized she didn't have a surprise to give me. Determined to make it up to me, she almost started a toaster fire attempting to make me breakfast in bed.

I smiled at the memory. It was so like Kallie. Even as a child, she always put other people first and I was proud to call her my daughter. It was hard to believe she was headed off to her first prom. Although she assured me her date was only a friend, I still worried. She was growing up way too fast.

"Mom! The limo just pulled up!" Kallie called, breaking me away from my thoughts.

"I'm coming, I'm coming," I answered and stood to make my way back down the stairs. "Hold your horses. Don't go rushing out the door. Your date should come in and introduce himself."

When I reached the bottom of the steps, I caught Kallie rolling her eyes.

"You know I love you, mom, but geez-Louise. You call yourself a feminist, but you have some really old-fashioned ideas sometimes."

"There's nothing wrong with being courted properly. It's a sign of respect," I countered.

"You did *not* just say 'courted,' did you?" Her eyes went wide with disbelief.

"Okay, okay! You got me there," I laughed. "Maybe I am a little old fashioned at times. What can I say? I'm your mom and you're going to prom. It's my job to worry about whether a boy is treating you with respect."

"I've told you like a thousand times. He's only a friend from my French class. He's doing me a favor because I didn't have a date. Besides, he's a year younger than me. I can't date a sophomore! It would be like breaking the rules or something. Girls aren't supposed to go out with younger guys!"

Tongue in cheek, I smirked.

"Is that so?"

"Yes, my friend Gabby said—"

The doorbell rang, interrupting whatever she was going to say. I barely had a moment to react. Kallie was at the door in a flash.

"Hi," I heard her say after she opened it.

"Hey, Kallie. Wow, you look great!" said a male voice. I couldn't see his face because Kallie was blocking him from view. I moved over to the door, needing to take stock of the boy who was here to take my baby girl out. When Kallie heard me come up beside her, she made the introductions.

"Mom, this is Austin. Austin, my mom."

"It's a pleasure to meet you, ah…Ms. Riley," he said with a shy smile.

I began to return his grin but faltered. There was something familiar about him. It was strange. He reminded me of…

I blinked twice, trying to shake off an unsettling sense of déjà vu. I slowly extended my hand to shake his.

"Austin, it's nice to meet you too."

My words were hesitant, cautious. I knew his face from somewhere. Those eyes. Piercing gray with flecks of dark. That crooked grin. The hair was a shade lighter, but…

*No. It can't be. I'm just feeling nostalgic from stumbling upon the Mother's Day card.*

"My mom wanted to take more pictures," Kallie said to him. "Let's go ask everyone to get out of the limo so we can get a group shot."

I blinked again.

*Yes, pictures. I need to take pictures.*

I shook my head to clear it and followed Kallie and Austin outside. After the group of twelve teenagers from St. Aloysius Prep assembled into a line, I snapped a few pictures of them all dressed up in their tuxedos and gowns. They stood formally for some while others were posed so I could capture silly shots of them jumping or making goofy faces at one another. With every picture, I tried discreetly to get a better look at Austin through the viewfinder. It was so strange, I felt like I had been catapulted through some sort of twisted time warp. A sensation of dread began to settle over me.

Kallie and her friends started to get antsy, eager to begin their big night. I had stalled them long enough. I lowered the camera and shooed them off toward the limo.

"Have a good time!" I called out to the group as they began to climb back into the waiting car. Kallie flashed me a beaming smile which only intensified the knot forming in my stomach. On impulse, I motioned for her to come over to me.

"What's up?" she asked hurriedly.

"Have fun. No drinking. Behave and be safe." I pecked her cheek with a light kiss.

"Come on, mom. You know me. I always behave."

"It's not you I'm worried about," I said, glancing over at Austin. Kallie caught the direction of my gaze and rolled her eyes.

"Relax. You don't need to worry about Austin," she tried to assure.

"You'll be home by eleven?"

"On the nose!"

She gave me a brief hug before turning back to join her friends, but I caught her by the arm. I had to know if I was just imagining things.

"Kallie, what's Austin's last name?"

Her brow furrowed in confusion at my question.

"Quinn. Why?"

My stomach plummeted to my feet and my heart began to race.

*No. No, no, no!*

The odds had to be a million to one.

It was inconceivable.

The chances were just too great.

A picture from a newspaper clipping I had saved years ago flashed in my mind. I knew Fitz had settled somewhere in the D.C. area, but I stopped following his whereabouts after Kallie was born. I had to. It was the only way I could survive emotionally.

But now this.

It could just be a coincidence, but deep down I knew it wasn't. It was possible—even probable. The similarities in physical appearance between Austin and Fitz were too close to dismiss as being a fluke. And they shared the same last name.

*This can't actually be happening to me. Not now. Not after all this time.*

As far as Kallie knew, I didn't know who her father was. I lied to protect her, and I didn't know how to tell her the truth at that moment. We were close, but she may not forgive me for this. It was her prom night, and the seventeen-year-old secret was about to ruin it and destroy every other belief she held dear.

"Mom, are you okay?" Kallie asked, her concern evident.

I looked at my daughter. So young and innocent. Just like I was once upon a time.

*God help me. What do I do?*

I gripped her forearms tightly, fighting the overwhelming urge to vomit.

"Kallie, promise me that Austin is just a friend."

Her eyes widened as if I had just grown antlers.

"Yeah! Chillax, Mom. You're way too wound up about this. It's only prom. What are you going to do in a couple of weeks when I go away to Montreal for the French class trip? I'll be fine tonight and be back before you know it."

A flash of what she said earlier about Austin came to mind. In a split second, my already frayed nerves seemed to completely tear apart.

"Kallie, you said Austin was in your French class. Is he going on the trip too?"

"Mom, stop. Maybe when I get home tonight, we can stay up late and watch an old musical or something. With popcorn? Just like we used to when I was a little kid? After all, I am sixteen going on seventeen…" she trailed off in a sing-song voice, repeating the lyrics to a song from *The Sound of Music*. She leaned in to hug me once more, but neither her words nor her embrace made me feel any better.

I looked at the limo. All of her friends had already piled inside, just waiting on Kallie.

"Sure, honey. Sounds like fun," I responded absently, feeling like I was in the Twilight Zone.

I didn't stop her when she finally stepped away. Perhaps I should have, but I didn't know how to explain it. There was no good way to tell my daughter, out of all the people in the whole wide world, she was going to the prom with her half-brother.

# Chapter Four

**CADENCE**

Once the limo pulled away, I went back into the house. Feeling as though I were in a trance, I somehow managed to put one foot in front of the other and lumbered to the kitchen. I thought about calling Joy since she knew the truth about everything, but I didn't want to be a burden while she was celebrating her anniversary. Instead, I went to the fridge in search of a drink—preferably a strong one.

Unfortunately, all I found was a half empty bottle of champagne that was left over from New Year's Eve nearly six months earlier and a few bottles of beer normally reserved for guests. I sighed and made a mental note to start stocking more alcohol in the house. Deciding a beer would be better than flat champagne, I popped the cap off and made my way upstairs to my bedroom.

On the way, I stopped in Kallie's bedroom to turn off the light she had left on. As usual, it looked like a hurricane had blown through and left clothes strewn about in its wake. I navigated through the maze until I reached the lamp. As I went to turn it off, I caught sight of the worn old teddy bear sitting at the foot of her bed. She'd hung on to it ever since she was a little girl, never once feeling teenage embarrassment over keeping her childhood companion in her bed. Love and adoration for my daughter pumped through me. She was so strong, never willing to compromise herself to please others, and it made me so proud. That pride brought a smile to my face as I reached to turn off the lamp switch before heading back out to my own bedroom.

Once there, I pulled open the door to my closet and reached for the shoebox tucked away on the top shelf. I needed to be absolutely sure before I had a full-blown panic attack over what might just be a coincidence or a faulty memory. Inside the box were letters I had written to Fitz while I was pregnant with Kallie but never mailed. I don't know why I kept them over the years. Perhaps I knew I'd be faced with something like this one day. The letters were the only proof and justification I had for keeping such a secret. Kallie wasn't the only one in the dark.

Fitz didn't know about her either.

Settling onto the bed, I placed the beer on the nightstand and blew the dust off the top of the box. Slowly, I lifted the lid. A bundle of envelopes secured in a rubber band lay on top. I pulled out the stack and set it to the side. Underneath were newspaper clippings and the playbill from *Singin' in the Rain*. I opened it up and flipped to the back to find the group photo of all the staff members from Camp Riley. Having memorized Fitz's location in the photo years ago, I easily located him and ran my finger over his image. I stared at the yellowing photo for a long while. It was a face I hadn't seen in so long, yet never managed to erase from my memory. Then tonight, that same face showed up on my doorstep to take Kallie to prom.

I placed the picture back inside the box and sifted through the other contents, spotting a folded square of paper.

*Chinese Fortune Teller.*

I didn't need to open the origami Fitz had given me on that final day to know what each fortune said. I had memorized the words he had written long ago.

*Sunsets will always belong to you.*

*When it's dark, I'll remember you to find the light.*

*You will forever hold my heart.*

*Leaving you will always be my biggest regret.*

Swallowing the lump beginning to form in my throat, I reached for the stack of envelopes. The rubber band, brittle from age, snapped apart when I tried to remove it, causing the letters to fall over my lap. It was no matter. Although they'd been stacked in the order they were written, I remember dating each and every one of them. I opened the envelope resting on top of the now messy pile. Pulling the lined paper from within, I began to read. It was the last letter I had written to Fitz.

*To the keeper of my heart,*

*I shouldn't start out this letter by addressing you that way, especially since this is more like a Dear John than anything else. Or maybe it's not a Dear John since we aren't even together. Either way, I can't help but still call you the keeper of my heart because that's who you'll always be to me—no matter what life has dictated for us.*

*Our daughter came into the world one week ago today. I named her Kalliope because the sound of her cry on the day she was born was like music to my ears. The name comes from Greek mythology and means "beautiful voice". Perhaps I'm more in tune with my mother's musical talents than I had originally thought.*

*Kallie, as I've come to nickname her, is the prettiest baby I've ever seen. I wish you could meet her, but just as sure as I'll never send you this letter, I know you'll never get to. I saw a picture of you, your father, and your wife in the paper today. It was taken at a political function in support for your father. From the sounds of it, you'll soon be the son of a United States Senator. You looked so proud in the photo, and I felt my heart bursting with admiration for your strength to endure a life you had little choice over. But the photo also made me sad. You see, I also couldn't help but notice your wife's small baby bump.*

*I wish things could have been different for us, but I accept the choice I've made. I will never regret the time I had with you. It was special and will forever be cherished. However, I've come to realize I can't keep holding on to the hope perhaps you'll rebel against your father and come back to me. I need to let you go. Being with me would only cause a scandal for your family. That sort of attention wouldn't be fair to you. You don't need your past mistakes thrown into the limelight—even if it what happened at Georgetown was a tragic accident. It wouldn't be fair to your unborn child, nor would it be fair to me or Kallie.*

*And most importantly, I realized you were right about me. I don't deserve to be "the other woman," and I certainly don't want Kallie to grow up with a cloud of illegitimacy over her head. That's why I will never tell you of her existence. That's why this will be my last letter. I have to think about Kallie now. My daughter. My new reason for living. She is my priority, just as your priority should be your new family. I need to provide a life for her even if it means creating a life without you in it.*

Tears blurred my vision and I could barely read my own signature at the bottom. The letter slipped from my fingers and fell onto my lap. What I just read, while true, were ramblings of a broken-hearted teenager who had been forced to grow up too soon. I had been too open and trusting. First love was naïve. I didn't hold back on the love I gave but willingly gave him every ounce inside of me. And he took it all—leaving no space for another man to move in. My head swam with memories as I hastily wiped the tears away.

I searched through the shoebox once again, needing to locate the newspaper article that had forced my decision all those years ago. Now, the article could potentially be confirmation Austin was exactly who I suspected. It wasn't hard to find among the neatly folded clippings. The bold headline shone like a beacon in the night.

**SENATOR QUINN PUSHES FOR LANDMARK TAX REFORM BILL WITHIN FIRST 90-DAYS**

I skimmed through the article, not particularly interested in recapping details about a bill that ultimately threw our country into a recession. I was more interested in the details about the photo alongside the article.

My eyes scanned the picture. The freeze frame was of Fitz, his father, and Fitz's young pregnant wife. Reporters were all around them with microphones trained on Senator Fitzgerald as they descended the steps of the Capitol Building. My heart constricted as an age-old jealousy welled up in me from seeing her again. She was definitely pretty, but that's not why I resented her. I didn't like the dark-haired woman because she got to have the life I had only dreamed about.

*What was her name again?*

As sharp as my memory was about that time in my life, I somehow managed to block out that little detail.

Forcing my gaze away from the photo, I ran my finger along the text of the article, stopping when I found the passage I was looking for.

> *"I can tell you we have a continued interest in building on the success of the bill. We are dedicated to improving the tax code for hardworking families and America's small businesses," Quinn said in a statement. When pushed for further details, none were forthcoming. Instead, Senatorial Candidate Quinn deflected to his soon-to-arrive grandson, using the opportunity to boast about how much the Republican party is invested in their candidate. "While I'd love to talk more about this, I have a prior engagement to get to. My son's wife is expecting a baby boy in a few months. The wives of Senate Republicans are excited about little Austin and have planned a baby shower."*

*Austin.*

That was all the confirmation I needed. There was no denying it. The boy who had shown up on my doorstep was, in fact, Fitz's son. I closed my eyes, took a deep breath, and pinched the bridge of my nose. Exhaling, I slowly looked up to the ceiling.

*Did I make a mistake all those years ago? Should I have told him? Should I have fought harder for Fitz?*

I didn't know what the answers were, but I was suddenly faced with having to justify my actions. I thought I had done the right thing at the time. I had my parents to help me through everything while Fitz had no one. My parents supported my choice. I thought I had taken the unselfish path, but now I wasn't so sure. What I once viewed as a noble decision looked like it was about to blow up in my face.

I glanced down at the now lukewarm bottle of beer I hadn't touched and followed the lines of condensation pooled around the base. A small stream of water was slowly making its way to the edge of the nightstand. There was no rhyme or reason to the pattern. It just moved closer to the edge. Water always found a way. I wished my life could be as simple, to have that gravitational force to push me toward a destination.

I was so confused. Seventeen years ago, I relied on my parents for advice. Now I sat alone, searching for guidance that would never come.

# Chapter Five

## CADENCE

I sat at my desk on Monday morning with Joy sitting across from me, her face aghast as I finished telling her about the weekend. The knot of dread that had formed in my stomach on Friday night was still there, but it was worsening with each passing hour.

Kallie had come home from the prom on time, just as she promised, and we had stayed up until after two in the morning watching our favorite musicals. I picked out *Newsies* to watch first, the story loosely based on the New York City Newsboys' Strike of 1899. The way I looked at it, nobody could resist a young Christian Bale. She picked the second musical of the night—*Mamma Mia!* Of all the things she could have picked... That was just my luck. I squirmed uncomfortably through the entire second movie, the plotline hitting way too close to home. Now I couldn't get the damn theme song from the movie soundtrack out of my head.

There were plenty of opportunities between then and now to tell her about Austin and the truth about her father, but I chickened out every time the words began to form on my tongue. I just couldn't tell her. As a result, I got to listen to a lecture from Joy.

"Cadence, this is bad. Senator Quinn is his father—the man who stands firmly against everything Dahlia's Dreamers stands for. When he finds out about Kallie and discovers what you do for a living, I'd like to say maybe he'd soften his stance, but the man just seems ruthless." Joy paused and shuddered. "Political implications aside, you need to go to Fitz. It's long past time."

"And say what? 'Hey, remember me? That stupid girl you banged one summer seventeen years ago? Well, you're my baby daddy.' Come on, Joy. He probably doesn't even remember me. I don't need to go to Fitz, but I do need to tell Kallie."

"So, why haven't you yet? She has to know before something crazy happens. Sweet Jesus! Can you imagine what would happen if she ended up dating Austin?"

I pressed my lips together in a tight line.

"Trust me, it's all I've thought about for days. I just don't know how to tell her. I went for a run yesterday morning. I needed some 'me time' to clear my head. It didn't work, so I went for another run in the afternoon. I'm sure the guys tending to the lawn around the Washington Monument thought I was nuts. I must have passed them twenty times."

"What were you doing all the way over there?" Joy asked with a furrowed brow.

"There's construction in my neighborhood and they have all the sidewalks blocked off. Running the Mall has been easier. Anyway, I was all set to tell Kallie when I returned home, but then I froze up."

Joy shook her head.

"I still think you should tell Fitz. It's not only Kallie. Austin should know too. What if he has feelings for her?"

I dropped my head and banged it on the desk.

"Did you have to remind me of that too?" I groaned.

"Hey, I know you're in a tough spot. I'm just trying to help you see it from all angles so that—"

"Hello? Is anyone there?" a female voice called from outside my office door. Joy stopped speaking and we both turned to see who it was. When nobody came in, I stood and walked out into the corridor.

A woman with a little girl was peering into the worn wooden office doors down the hall. The tiny child held a raggedy looking doll tightly to her chest. She looked around, seeming confused as the woman who held her hand dragged her from door to door.

"Can I help you?" I asked.

"Oh!" she startled. "I'm sorry. Nobody was at the desk, so I decided to see if I could find someone in one of the offices. I should have made an appointment first, but I-I couldn't wait. I need to speak with someone right away."

She had a subtle accent I couldn't quite place, but it sounded Spanish in origin. It was hard to tell with the way her voice cracked. Her expression was panicked, desperate almost. It was a look I knew all too well.

"Please, come in and have a seat," I told her. Once she stepped inside, I motioned for her to sit at the small round table in the corner.

"I'm sorry there wasn't anyone to greet you. My secretary is currently out on maternity leave. The rest of the staff has just been handling things while she's out. What can we do for you?"

The woman looked back and forth between Joy and me.

"My…my name is-is Emilia Garcia," she stuttered.

*Afraid. They always come in here afraid.*

"It's a pleasure to meet you." I took a seat across from her at the table. Over the years, I'd found it less intimidating for new clients if I sat here, rather than behind my desk. It seemed to make them feel more like we were on equal turf. I stretched out my hand for her to shake, hoping to put her more at ease. It was cool and clammy, a sure sign the woman was a nervous wreck. "I'm Cadence Riley, and this is my colleague, Joy Martin."

She nodded to Joy, then began to fiddle with the hem of her bright pink shirt.

"I, um…I'm from Richmond, Virginia."

"You're quite a way from home," I noted. If the look of anxiety on her face wasn't already enough, knowing she traveled over two hours, with a small child, without a scheduled appointment told a story about how desperate she was.

"Yes, I am," she admitted. Then she looked at me with terrified dark brown eyes, reminding me of a deer caught in headlights. "Again, I'm so sorry for showing up unannounced. I–I just don't know where to begin."

"Ms. Garcia, every person who walks through our doors comes here for one thing. Why don't you just start from the beginning?"

She looked down nervously at the little girl.

"Oh, um. My daughter. I don't like to…" she trailed off.

I looked at the little girl sitting on her mother's lap. She couldn't have been more than five years old, and I understood her hesitation. I stood up from my chair and knelt down in front of the child.

"What's your name?" I softly asked.

"Mayra," she responded shyly.

"Why, hello Mayra. It's so nice to meet you. My name is Cadence. How old are you?" She held up five fingers.

"No, no. You're not five yet," her mother chided, bending Mayra's thumb down so she only held up four. "You don't turn five for another few weeks."

I smiled, recalling how Kallie always liked to pad her age by a few months.

"Almost five? Wow! You're practically a big girl! You're not too big to color though, are you?" I asked. Her brown eyes widened with excitement as she shook her head. "Well then, if it's okay with your mom, would you like to go with Ms. Joy to find a coloring book and crayons?"

She looked up at her mother expectantly.

"Go ahead. Remember your manners," Emilia told her with a nod.

Mayra beamed and jumped off Emilia's lap. Joy walked over to her and took hold of her little hand. Once they were safely out of earshot, I returned to my seat and reached out across the table to take Emilia's hand in mine.

"Ms. Garcia," I began.

"Please, call me Emilia."

"Emilia, I can tell you're nervous. Don't be. Whatever it is, we're here to help you."

She afforded me a small smile.

"I've heard others talk of your kindness. That's why I knew I had to come here. You have to help m–me." Her voice cracked again on the last word, and it broke my heart. My only hope was that I *could* help her. Sometimes, it was too late.

"Why don't you start from the beginning, and we'll go from there?"

She swallowed and took a deep breath.

"It's about my fiancé. My daughter's father. They-they took him!"

Then she began a tale I had heard a countless number of times. With each time, the names and places were different, but the story was always the same.

Emilia's fiancé, Andrés Mendez, moved from Ecuador to the United States with his family when he was three years old. He, his younger sister, and his parents were all undocumented immigrants—a fact Andrés never knew until he was seventeen years old and preparing to attend college. He needed a social security number to apply for student loans. That was when his parents first told him the truth about where he came from.

"Andrés is so smart," Emilia said with pride in her voice. "As it turned out, he didn't need to get loans. He was awarded an undergraduate academic scholarship to attend Harvard."

"That's amazing!"

"Yes," she agreed, but then her tone turned sad once again. "He applied for a student visa and was all set to head off to Massachusetts. But that summer, I became pregnant with Mayra. I urged him to still go, but Andrés refused to leave me. He ended up going to Virginia Tech to study engineering instead. My parents were furious, but his parents didn't understand what he was giving up. They never even heard of Harvard until Andrés was accepted into the school."

I reached over to my desk and grabbed a notepad to begin taking notes. I scribbled down a few basics.

*Smart. Accepted to Harvard on scholarship. Mayra.*

"Emilia, are you undocumented as well?"

"No, I was born here. My mother was born in El Salvador, and my father was born in the States. She eventually became a naturalized citizen years after they were married."

"Did Andrés end up finishing college?"

"Thankfully, he did. It wasn't easy though. While he attended school, I lived at home. My parents watched Mayra while I worked to pay his school bills. Andrés usually took the Metro bus to his campus, but sometimes I would drive him when I wasn't working. At the time, because of his immigration status, he couldn't get a license."

*No license. Has family support.*

Having worked my way through school as a single mother, I wasn't sure if I could have done it without my parents' help. I recognized the importance of family support better than most.

"I can imagine how difficult it must have been. So, what happened next?"

"Right before Andrés graduated, we made plans to move in together. We wanted to get married first but couldn't afford a nice wedding with only my income. Andrés needed to find a job. The Dream Act had just been passed a few years before. Since he qualified, I encouraged him to fill out the DACA paperwork. I thought it was a good idea. It would mean he could get his driver's license, apply for work, and we wouldn't have to fear possible deportation anymore—and I would get to have my dream wedding. Maybe that part was selfish of me. I don't know. It took some convincing, but he finally did it. Now, I can't help but feel like it was the wrong thing to do."

"Why is that?"

"With all due respect, you know what's happening in the world. Too many in this county don't care about people like Andrés although I'll never understand why. He's a hardworking man—a good man," she spat out bitterly.

"I'm sorry about what's happening in our country, Emilia. I hope you know not everyone thinks that way. Did he get a job after he graduated?"

"Oh, of course! He's a mechanical engineer at Advanced Solutions —or at least, he was. I'm not sure what will happen now." She sniffled, and I could tell she was fighting tears. "Anyway, Andrés hated that I worked to pay his school bills, but he also knew finishing college and getting a good paying job was the best way for us to provide a good life for Mayra. He applied and the DACA application was approved. Shortly after, he landed his job at AS and got his driver's license. We found an apartment in Richmond, and he insisted I quit my job to stay at home to care for our daughter. Things were finally looking up. Until…"

*Engineer. Holds a job. Recognizes family stability. Contributing member of society.*

I scribbled the notes while I waited for Emilia to go on. She shook her head, seeming lost in thought and looked down at her lap. She began to fidget with the hem of her shirt again as a single tear trickled down her cheek.

"Until what, Emilia?"

"Andrés, Mayra, and I took a day trip to Andrés parents' house in Fairfax. It was Sunday and his mother was making pupusas, Mayra's favorite meal. We were running late due to traffic on I-95 which caused us to be in a rush to get there. Andrés was the driver. He rolled through a stop sign on his parent's street. Unfortunately, a police car was coming in the opposite direction. The officer saw it happen and pulled us over."

I knew where her story was going before she even finished. She was from Virginia, the second state in the nation to implement an agreement with the Federal government to participate in Immigration and Customs Enforcement Secure Communities program. The program was designed to create coordination between local law enforcement and the Department of Homeland Security. If an arrest was made, fingerprints were automatically run through the databases of the FBI and Homeland Security.

In the end, it would show Andrés was a DACA recipient.

"Emilia, where is Andrés now?"

She choked back a sob.

"The officer interrogated us about being so far from home, and Andrés was brought down to the police station for more questioning. He was released within a few hours but was given a traffic ticket and a court date. I went with him to court. Andrés was found guilty of the traffic violation for failure to come to a complete stop. He was given a fine to pay, which we paid before leaving. When we exited the courthouse, a man in uniform called out to Andrés by his first and last name. We didn't expect the man to be an ICE agent. There were three of them in total, just waiting for us. Andrés was detained right then and there." She stared back at me with a look of bewilderment, almost as if she couldn't believe her own story. "It took me two weeks to find out where they had taken him. Currently, he's being held by the D.C. Department of Corrections. Deportations proceedings have already begun—and all because he failed to stop at a stop sign."

# Chapter Six

## FITZ

My alarm went off at five on Tuesday. After ensuring Austin was set for school, I headed out for my morning run, leaving myself plenty of time to be to the office by eight. As my feet pounded the pavement, sweat beaded on my neck and dripped down the length of my spine. I paused at the Lincoln Memorial to stretch my calf muscles before beginning the second lap of the four-mile run. Old Abe looked lost in thought, basking in the light of the early morning sun as he stared across the Reflecting Pool at the Washington Monument. I imagined his expression matched my own. My mind was in turmoil, conflicted over my father's threats. I didn't know if he had the balls to follow through and there was a lot at stake.

I was supposed to meet with members of the RNC this past Saturday night. I bailed, and now my father was on a warpath. It didn't matter. He might think I'm weak, but he was sadly mistaken. I was no longer the pushover I once was. I had allowed him to inflict enough damage on my life and I wasn't about to let history repeat itself.

I saw a flash of movement in the corner of my eye and glanced up from the lunge position I was in. From around the corner, a blond wearing tight running gear emerged, jogging in the opposite direction from where I had come. It wasn't uncommon to see another jogger. Many people ran the Mall this time of the morning. I returned to finishing my stretch, then stood to shake out my arms. Ready to begin the next lap, I started out in a measured pace, slowly closing the distance between me and the female jogger.

As I passed her, my steps seemed to falter. I blinked, struggling with the image of the woman who had just run by me.

I stopped running and looked back. She hadn't slowed her steps, but she was looking over her shoulder—at me. When she saw I had stopped, she quickly turned away and seemed to increase her pace.

"No, it's not her," I said aloud to myself.

I shook my head. The stress I was under was causing me to see things. But still, as I watched her petite form get further and further away from me, I couldn't shake the nagging feeling it *was* her—the girl who had haunted my dreams ever since I was twenty-two years old. Impulsively, I turned and began to run after her. I had to know. If it wasn't her, I'd just make up some excuse about mistaken identity and be on my way.

She was fast, I'd give her that much. I was in a full out run and I'd barely closed the gap between us. Much to my dismay, she veered off the path and ducked around the wall at the Korean Memorial, disappearing from sight.

*Fuck!*

When I approached the wall, I looked around. Early rising tourists roamed the area, snapping pictures of the statues created to commemorate the forgotten war. I scanned the area again. She was nowhere to be found. It was like she vanished off the face of the earth.

*I'm chasing a goddamned ghost.*

Convinced I had completely lost my mind, I decided to abandon the rest of my workout routine. I'd left my Audi parked off $14^{th}$ Street. The shortest way back to it was to cut along the path that would take me through Ash Woods.

And that's where I found her.

She was approaching the steps of the D.C. War Memorial. Careful to stay out of sight, I crept around to the opposite side of the round monument. I watched as she sat down on the steps and pulled out what appeared to be a cell phone. From this angle, I couldn't see her face, only the back of her head. Her hair—the color a golden blond that brought me back nearly two decades—was pulled back into a braid. Another thing that brought me back. Staring at the woven shades of pale yellow and gold, I knew it had to be her. Only *she* had hair like that.

I could hear her speaking to someone on the other end of the call. She had the phone on speaker mode, so the conversation was loud and clear.

"For the love of God," said the voice on the other end of the line. "Girl, do you have any idea what time it is?"

"Oh, shush," the blond said. Her voice was crisp yet feminine. And so fucking familiar. "I know it's early but listen up. This is major. I saw him."

"Saw who?"

"Fitz!" she hissed my name, making me all but certain this woman was, in fact, the woman from my dreams.

"Okay, now I'm awake. What do you mean you saw Fitz? Are you sure?"

"Yes–er, well. No. His hair was a bit longer but… yes, I'm sure it was him."

"Where did you see him, Cadence?"

*Bingo. It is her.*

A wave of satisfaction came over me before another thought hit me in the chest like a sledgehammer.

*Cadence. It's really her, flesh and blood and just a few steps away from me.*

Memories of hot summer nights flashed before my eyes. I saw her again, by the lake with her green eyes sparkling and hair shimmering beneath the light of a fading sunset. I could almost feel her in my arms—even now. The warmth of her embrace, the way she whispered my name when I kissed her…

Cadence began to speak again, ripping me away from a time long past.

"I'm on my morning run," I heard her explain to the person on the phone. "He was out running too. I ran right by him, but I'm not sure if he knew it was me."

"Did you talk to him?"

"Are you crazy?" Cadence shrieked, then seemed to catch herself. She glanced around nervously for a moment and I had to duck down to stay hidden. When she spoke again, her voice was noticeably lower, and I had to strain to hear her. "Seriously, Joy. What are the odds of seeing him jogging the Mall after all this time? And especially now!"

*Joy. The African American girl who worked at the store with Cadence.*

I smiled to myself, pleased for some strange reason over the fact they'd remained friends after all this time.

"This is spooky—as in you-need-to-go-see-a-psychic kind of spooky," Joy said. "I don't know, hun. The stars seem to be aligning in a really weird way. It doesn't matter how long it's been. You need to tell him."

"Oh, God. I don't know if I can do this!"

"Well, something is telling you it's time. There have just been too many coincidences."

"You're right. I can do this. No sweat," Cadence replied, but her tone was bordering on sarcastic.

"Good. I'm glad it's settled. Now I'm going back to bed. I don't need to be at work for another two hours."

"Wait, Joy–" She stopped short, looked down at the phone, and swore. "Damn it!"

She stood up and rapidly began to pace back and forth, appearing lost in her thoughts. I followed the lines of her petite body. She looked good, really good actually. Her curves were more pronounced, her breasts and hips shapelier than I remembered yet still slender and fit. The body I was looking at belonged to a woman, not the young girl I had fallen in love with. Still, despite the years that had passed, I itched to reach out and touch her.

I shouldn't have eavesdropped on her conversation, but the minute I heard my name, I couldn't help myself. I was curious about what they were talking about and what it was she was supposed to tell me.

And I was very curious about her.

She was the girl who had rocked my world seventeen years ago so much so, I'd rarely thought about another woman since—and that included the years I spent married. As I debated over coming out of my hiding spot to reveal myself, I realized the irony of the current situation. I was spying on her, just like I had on that first day I saw her by the lake. Now here I stood today. Perhaps history does, in its own way, repeat itself. It was up to me to change its course.

"Cadence," I called out as I moved from behind the monument.

She jumped a mile and spun around, her hand going to her chest.

"You scared the shit out of me!"

"I'm sorry. I didn't mean to," I apologized as I approached her. My memory didn't do her justice. She was even more beautiful than I remembered, nearly causing me to gasp in disbelief. I didn't think it was possible for her to be more stunning than she once was. I cleared my throat. "I must say, it's fancy meeting you here."

Recovering from the shock of my sudden appearance, she seemed to remember herself.

"Yeah, ah… fancy that. I um…" she faltered. "I actually need to be off. I was just about to start my jog back."

"Wait," I said and reached out to grab her arm. When my palm made contact with her skin, she froze. So did I as the very air seemed to sizzle. I almost couldn't speak or unscramble my brain enough to move. It was the first time I'd touched her in more than seventeen years. My throat became ridiculously dry, and I had to clear it before I could speak again. "It's been a long time. How are you?"

She shrugged her arm free and rubbed the area where my hand had been. The action didn't seem to say she was offended by my touch, but rather the contact had made her feel the same way I did. Her green eyes sparkled like emeralds in the early morning sun.

*Had they always been so vibrant?*

"I've been good," she replied. "You?"

I went to speak again, but the words didn't want to come out. It was as if I was still absorbing the disbelief of seeing her again. I had to remind myself she was real, and not a crazy dream that had played on repeat for the past seventeen years.

"Not too bad," was all I managed to say.

"Well, that's good. But um, like I said. I need to get going."

She seemed nervous, but I couldn't let her walk away—not again. At least not until I found out what her phone conversation was about. When she tossed me a small wave and turned to jog away, I ran ahead to fall in step beside her. She tilted her head to eye me curiously but didn't say anything.

"Do you live around here?"

"I'm in the D.C. area, yes." Her response was cautious. I could appreciate that. After all, it had been a long time. For all she knew, I grew up to be a psychopath. Still, I needed to continue the small talk.

"I live in Alexandria, but my office is over in the East End. The Mall is convenient, and I jog this path almost every day. Strange I haven't bumped into you until now. Do you run here often?"

"No, I've only just started coming here because the sidewalks in my neighborhood are closed for construction." A strand of hair pulled loose from her braid as we ran. I wanted to reach out to tuck it behind her ear, but I refrained.

"I guess I should be thanking the DDOT then."

"For what?"

"For tearing up the sidewalks. It changed your routine and allowed us to bump into each other." She glanced sideways at me. Once again, she didn't respond, so I continued. "I couldn't help overhearing you on the phone."

Cadence stopped abruptly. When I turned back to look at her, I watched as her face paled. She looked like she had just seen a ghost. I stopped running and walked the few steps back toward her.

"You did?" she squeaked.

"Yeah, sorry. I should know better. After all, you did once lecture me on how spying isn't polite," I grinned, hoping to put her at ease by bringing up an old memory. "I am curious though. What did you have to tell me?"

"Nothing," she said, just a little too quickly.

*Interesting.*

Now I was really curious.

"Look, it's been a while, Cadence. As much as I'm enjoying this unexpected jog with you, I'd much rather talk when we aren't panting from exertion. Why don't we call it quits and go grab a cup of coffee? We can catch up."

She dropped her gaze and shook her head. When she looked up at me again, her eyes were pained. I reached out and took one of her hands, knowing instantly it was a mistake. She had always been a constant tug at my chest and the action brought me dangerously close to her. I looked down at her heart shaped lips. The urge to kiss her was undeniable.

*Christ, man. Get ahold of yourself.*

I don't know how it happened so quickly, but I shouldn't have been surprised. Even when we were younger, things had progressed fast. Now, with her small hand resting between my palms, I knew with absolute certainty, I wouldn't want to let her go. I couldn't force myself to step back.

For the first time in seventeen years, she was looking at me. I thought I'd gotten over her, but just holding her hand made me realize I hadn't—not at all. Somehow, over the course of one summer, Cadence had virtually ruined me for any other woman. I wished I could deny it, but if I tried, I'd only be lying to myself. Sure, I'd come across other beautiful women in my lifetime but none who flipped my switch more than Cadence did. The magnetic pull I always felt toward her was still there, just as charged as it was on the day we met. This could be my chance to explain myself—to apologize for not having the guts to stand up to my father all those years ago. She needed to hear me out and know not a single day went by when I didn't think of her.

"I don't think coffee is a good idea, Fitz," she whispered.

"Why not?"

"Because I…" she trailed off.

Then another thought occurred to me and I looked down quickly at the hand still in mine—no ring. I tried to hide my relief. I had been so wrapped up in seeing her again, it never occurred to me she might have given herself to someone else. Just the idea of her being with another man caused my gut to churn even if I had no right.

"It's only coffee, Cadence."

She pulled her hand free and took a step back. Her posture stiffened, and her gaze turned steely.

"Instead of asking *me* out for coffee, perhaps you should consider taking your *wife*," she stated with acid in her tone. The way she emphasized the last word made me falter. I blinked, momentarily at a loss before the light went on.

*She doesn't know.*

"Cadence, I'm not married. My wife died eleven years ago."

Her eyes widened, and she began to laugh but not in a way that sounded even remotely happy.

"Of course she died! Isn't life ironic?" She dropped her gaze to the ground. When she looked back up, her gaze was wary. "Look, Fitz, I'm sorry about your wife—truly, I am. But I don't know what you're thinking. Doing anything together is a bad idea. Running, coffee. It's all bad. There's no catching up for us. It's been seventeen years. That ship has sailed."

"Has it?" I asked.

I stared intently at her as she raised her arms in exasperation.

"We bumped into each. Big deal. Let's just say 'it was nice to see you' and move on our merry ways."

Drawn like a moth to a flame, or perhaps I was just a glutton for punishment, I reached for her hand again. She didn't pull away.

"Have coffee with me," I insisted again. "Please."

Conflict raged in her eyes. What I wouldn't give to crawl inside her brain and pick apart her thoughts. All I knew was I felt like I'd been dreaming of green eyes, soft lips, and blond hair for way too long.

"There's a coffee shop within walking distance over on Maryland Avenue," she finally said. "I only have time for a quick cup. I have to work at nine, and I need time to go home and shower beforehand."

I released her hand and motioned in the direction she was referring to.

"Lead the way, sweetheart."

Her head snapped up to look at me. I winked and tossed her a cocky grin that silently said that's right—I remember.

By the time we finished this impromptu coffee date, she would know I hadn't forgotten about anything—and I hadn't forgotten about her.

# Chapter Seven

**CADENCE**

*What am I doing? What am I doing? What am I doing?*

I repeated the question over and over again in my head as I entered Café Aroma with Fitz. Yes, Fitz. If he hadn't been the person to hold open the coffee shop door for me, I wouldn't have believed it myself. I should have been running in the opposite direction, far away from the man who had destroyed my heart—from the only one I'd ever completely given myself to. However, I never expected seeing him again would bring a whole new problem to light. With just one touch, I learned this man still had the power to make me quiver and shake and question everything I thought I knew about myself. And I hated it.

I only agreed to have coffee because I knew Joy was right. My heart didn't belong to Fitz anymore. It belonged to Kallie. I had to tell him about her—maybe. He was now a grown man. I was sure he'd changed over the years, just as I had, and I wanted to find out exactly who this man was before I told him about our daughter.

I nervously stepped up to the counter and ordered my usual.

"I'll take a triple grande one-pump vanilla non-fat latte."

"That may have been the most complicated drink order I've ever heard," Fitz said with a laugh before placing his own order with the barista. "Breakfast Blend, black."

"Mock it all you want. It's way tastier than black coffee. Gross," I countered and stuck out my tongue in disgust. Then much to my annoyance, Fitz tried to pay. I waved him off. "I've got it."

While we waited for our beverages, I watched him out of the corner of my eye. I tried not to stare, but it was a challenge. He was as gorgeous as ever and still made me a little weak in the knees. His stance was confident yet easy with one hand inside the pocket of his running shorts. Fitz had always been fit, tall and lean with a mischievous smile. Today, he had grown into that body. Wide shoulders bulged beneath the blue t-shirt that seemed molded to his skin, accentuating the hard-muscled pectorals no t-shirt could conceal.

Yes, the years had been kind to Fitzgerald Quinn. He looked perfect standing there—even his dark hair was perfect, which was a remarkable feat considering we'd just been jogging. I knew my hair was probably a wreck. I could feel the loose strands from my braid brushing the sides of my neck.

After we collected our drink orders, we headed over to a small table in the corner. Once we were seated, a silence fell. He stared at me, almost if I were a mirage that would disappear at any moment. It was unnerving. I didn't know what to say, much less even know how we came to be here in the first place.

"So, are you going to tell me about your phone conversation?" he finally asked.

"Nope," I replied automatically with a decisive shake of my head.

"You're sure?"

"Positive. Sorry, Fitz. A girl has a right to her secrets."

*And, boy, was mine a whopper.*

Until I could get a better gauge on his character, my lips were sealed. I had to think of Kallie—and not his oh-so-snug blue t-shirt. Considering that, I should have been delivering The Spanish Inquisition, but it felt weird. Everything about him was so familiar—like I knew him. But, the reality was, I didn't know him at all. I didn't know what to say. I fiddled with the sleeve of my cup anxiously before taking a cautious sip.

"How's your triple vanilla whatever?"

"Latte. And it's good."

"I would have taken you for a strawberries and cream Frappuccino kind of girl. But then again, maybe your tastes have changed over the years."

"What do you mean?"

"Do you still like strawberries?"

"Um, yeah," I said, pulling my brow together in confusion.

"With a dollop of whipped cream if memory serves me right," he added.

All the air expelled from my lungs, my heart began to thud, and my stomach clenched from a mix of emotions.

*Ten questions. Ten answers.*

He remembered.

And I remembered.

His lips curved into a smile, and his eyes crinkled at the corners. I remembered that crinkle, the natural smile lines, just like I remembered the feel of the stubble on his jaw. Today, it was perfectly shaven, the smooth lines of his face just as chiseled and beautiful as they had once been. It was like every pore, every inch of me, remembered even the tiniest details.

We stared at one another for a long moment, and I found myself unable to speak. His eyes bore into mine, and I could swear he knew exactly what I was thinking. I tore my eyes from his, incapable of withstanding his penetrating gaze any longer.

"Fitz, the past is in the past. We should leave it there."

"What if I don't want to?"

"You have to." I paused, not wanting to elaborate further. I didn't want him to know his remembrance of such a small detail from the past affected me. Switching gears, I opted to ask about him, rather than discuss memories. I was supposed to be getting to know him after all. "So, you said you wanted to catch up. Tell me what you've been up to for the past seventeen years."

Fitz sat back in his chair contemplatively.

"A lot has happened, Cadence. Seventeen years is a long time."

I glanced down at my watch.

"You have thirty minutes."

"Well then I better get talking," he said and flashed me a lopsided grin I tried hard to ignore. "I suppose I should start with Austin, my son. He's fifteen. Good kid. People say he looks a lot like me."

*Yes, I know.*

But I couldn't say that without letting on about *how* I knew.

He didn't mention his wife or anything about how she died. I wondered if he had ended up loving her and if it was too painful for him to talk about. Instead, Fitz talked mostly about his partnership with Devon. He told me about the PR company they started a year after he left Camp Riley. He spoke about their successes but not in an arrogant sort of way. He simply sounded proud of what he and Devon accomplished together.

"The original plan was to represent corporations, but my father knows powerful people, and so does Devon's father. It didn't take long before the business model changed, and we found ourselves representing more individuals than corporations. Word spread, and business boomed. Plus, people are always in need of fixing. Who would have thought a couple of punks like us would be working to fix other people's messes?" he laughed.

"You were never a punk," I replied with a small smile.

"Right. I think my father would say otherwise."

There was no mistaking the shadow that crossed his face.

"How are things on that front? With your father I mean. Is he any better?"

"Nah. The old bastard is set in his ways. He still gives me shit. I just don't take it like I used to." He paused and lifted his coffee to his lips, studying my face carefully as he did so. His gaze was intense, and I felt a blush creep up my neck. Something somber and pensive filled his expression. Lowering the cup, he looked purposefully into my eyes. "I'm sorry, Cadence. For everything."

His apology slithered over my skin, a rich velvety sound tickling my senses.

"Sorry for what?" I asked, feeling a tremble rock through the question.

I knew what he was apologizing for, but I didn't expect to see the emotions swirling in his eyes—loss, regret, grief. He ran his hands through his hair nervously. At least I wasn't the only one feeling apprehensive.

"I realized years later, everything he did was nothing more than a scare tactic. He would never have allowed me to go to jail over that accident. It would have brought embarrassment to his good name. I should have seen through it all. I was a coward. Because of that, I walked away from you. I never wanted to hurt you. I loved you. Leaving you that day was the hardest thing I've ever had to do."

Apparently, small talk was over. He wasted no time getting to the heavy stuff. Little did he know, I felt like I'd waited to hear those words for nearly two decades. Trying not to appear shocked by his confession, I waved a flippant hand in the air.

"Hey, it was a long time ago. I'm over it," I lied. As of today, it was apparent I wasn't over it at all. However, my armor was stronger now than it was when I was eighteen. At least, I hoped it was.

I'd have to be dead to be unaffected by the gorgeous man staring at me. I wasn't delusional. If Fitz wanted to make something of our unlikely meeting, he would. After all, he once pursued me with a single-minded intensity that had made my young heart flutter. But unlike my teenage self, I knew better than to give in this time. Once a shell was broken, it can never truly be repaired. The cracks would always be present, no matter how strong the glue was.

"I noticed you don't wear a ring. Have you ever married?" he asked.

Gutting disbelief thundered through my chest like a dark and ugly storm. He had some nerve asking me that. It was none of his business.

"No, I haven't," I responded curtly. "Apparently, unlike you, it wasn't in the cards for me."

I knew it was a cheap shot, but I didn't particularly care. If he was offended, he didn't let on. Instead, he eyed me, almost as if he were assessing whether to believe my façade before he continued on.

"Right. Well, anyway…back to my father. He has this grand scheme going now. He wants me to run for political office—and a senator no less!" he laughed, like he found the idea ludicrous. "I have no intention of running for anything. I hate politics. I always have. It's all about a hunger for power and the party vote. I'm sure he thinks he can strongarm me into supporting his bills."

I raised one eyebrow.

"Could he?"

"Hell, no! I mean, assuming I ran and was elected, he'd be in for a rude awakening. I'm tired of seeing things get rushed through in the name of greed if you know what I mean."

"Trust me, I know exactly what you mean," I said warily. "I'm familiar with your father, or I should say his policies."

"Oh?"

"Unfortunately, yes. I own a non-profit organization that helps DACA recipients. Your father's voting habits tend to get in my way."

"So you did it, huh? It shouldn't surprise me—you always had your life goals all mapped out. You said you wanted to work non-profit, and now here you are. You actually started your own. Good for you. Although I imagined you'd be working with kids for some reason."

"I do work with kids sometimes. More often than not, DACA recipients have children of their own. When bad things happen, it's my job to make sure their families aren't ripped apart," I explained.

"I'm sure it's more complicated than that. They wouldn't be separated if they were abiding by our countries laws."

He said it so flippantly, my back instantly went up. Fitz was right about one thing—it was more complicated. However, his oversimplification for why someone would face deportation infuriated me. I'd heard similar sentiments all too often. I tossed him an icy glare.

"Are you sure you wouldn't vote for your father's proposals if you had the chance? Because that sounds a lot like something I've heard him say on the news." He flinched as if I had slapped him, but I didn't pause in my quiet rant. "Despite the popular rhetoric these days, the people I represent are not hardened criminals, drug dealers, or rapists. They're human beings. The things I hear and see every day would make you shudder. But then again, maybe not if you think it's just about abiding by the law."

Fitz held his hands up in surrender.

"Look, I didn't mean to imply anything. I'm sure it's exactly as you say. I'll be honest, I don't know much about DACA."

"That's the problem, most people don't," I spat out.

"Hey, I take back what I said, okay? I'll even be sure to read up on it more. I'm a firm believer in knowing the facts before I speak. Clearly, I was out of line there."

Beating back my annoyance, I took a deep breath and pinched the bridge of my nose.

"Look, I didn't mean to snap. Maybe what you said was completely innocent, but this is a really hot topic for me. It's a fight I have every single day."

"No need to explain. I get it. Really, I do."

I glanced at my watch again. We had been talking for close to an hour. Now, I barely had enough time to get home, shower, and get to work on time. Plus, I would need more than just a few minutes to process everything. Seeing him, talking to him, the electric current in the air—it was strange yet familiar. It was like seventeen years hadn't passed at all. I had walked into the coffee shop a nervous wreck, but we settled into easy conversation within minutes. And it truly was easy—outside of my little political outburst.

I was beyond confused. Seeing him again and knowing he was so close had me all torn up inside. My plan to get to know him seemed to have backfired. Not only was I was torn up over what to do about Kallie, but now my brain was muddled with images of a young Fitz and the man who sat across from me. So much time had passed. The crushing heartache I felt back then should have eased with time, but seeing him again made me realize I never truly moved on. He was the father of my daughter even if he didn't know it, and he would always be the keeper of my heart because of it.

"It's been great to catch up, but I really gotta run," I told him.

He reached across the table and took my hand, his fingers warm and strong, his grip feeling just right. When he pressed his palm closer to mine, I felt something flat and smooth come in contact with my skin. I looked down.

"All of my contact information is on this card. I want to see you again, Cadence."

"Fitz, I…"

"Call me," he insisted as he stood up. His tone was firm and completely unapologetic.

Leaning down, he pressed a light kiss to my forehead. I sucked in a breath. Everything around us seemed to fade away. All the other patrons in the coffee shop were nothing more than a backdrop to him. The only thing I was aware of was the tall, dark haired, broad-shouldered man whose lips were touching my head.

The peck was brief, and he pulled away almost as quickly as he'd leaned in, but his steely gray eyes lingered on my face. His gaze was penetrating, drinking me in as if he were trying to commit me to memory. I stared back, finding myself lost in the endless universe held in his gaze. I shivered.

Then…he walked away.

I stayed there for another five minutes, looking absently at the card he gave me, having just had my orderly world completely flipped upside down.

# Chapter Eight

**FITZ**

I arrived at my office late. To say I was rattled by the events of the morning was an understatement. Never did I think I would see Cadence again. Sure, I had thought about contacting her over the years, but then life seemed to happen. I became busy with Austin and building my company. Before I knew it, more than a decade had passed.

However, she had never been far from my mind. It had been seventeen fucking years, but memories of her never stopped plaguing me. She was my silent storm, the face that had tormented my dreams for so many years. I'd never forget her sweetheart lips when she looked up at me with nothing but a shy smile or the vulnerability shown in her emerald green eyes when she'd confessed she had never been properly kissed. Knowing I had been the first person to kiss the soft curve of her neck, to feel her tight nipples against my tongue, to hear the startled cry of her first orgasm never ceased to make me hard. Now that I had seen her again, the memory of what once was came harder and faster than ever before.

It only took a brief run in with her to make me realize our time apart didn't matter—at least for me it didn't. So much about her was still the same, yet she was also different. She still had a quiet strength about her with a level of vulnerability that contrasted with the confidence in her words. Her unsurpassed beauty only seemed to intensify over time, and her passion and sharp intelligence could still cut any man down with a mere look.

During the hour we spent together that morning, I saw all of that and found myself lost in her all over again. Now, as I stepped out of the elevator to my floor, I contemplated what I should do about that fact. One thing was for certain—I wouldn't be waiting around for her to call me. I knew I would need to go to her.

"Morning, Angie," I greeted my secretary.

"Good morning, Mr. Quinn. I have a few phone messages for you," she said, diving right into business. Angie was never one to waste time with idle chit-chat. "Your father called three times this morning."

Annoyed, I pressed my lips into a tight line.

"He also called my cell. I'm sorry he bothered you too. When you see him on the caller ID, just send it to voicemail until further notice. I'll handle him."

"Yes, sir," she said with a curt nod. "Jackson Dobbs also called. He said he's running a bit late and to expect him just after eleven."

"Looks like I'm not the only one behind schedule today. It's not an issue. We've already gone over the PR strategy for him. Today we're just finalizing the paperwork. However, I do need you to hold my calls between now and then. I have something I need to do, and it may take most of the morning."

"Will do."

I entered my office and walked over to the floor to ceiling windows on the back wall. Reaching into the inside breast pocket of my suit coat, I pulled out my cell to return my father's calls. There was no use putting him off any longer. I knew why he was calling as well as I knew my own name. He was pissed off because I didn't show up for the meeting with the RNC. It was no skin off my back, but I didn't want him harassing my employees because of it.

"Fitzgerald," he barked after the first ring. "Where have you been?"

"On a run, just like every other morning," I idly stated.

"I'm not talking about just this morning. You didn't return my calls from Sunday or yesterday. I'm a busy man. I don't have time to wait around for you."

I gritted my teeth and pinched the bridge of my nose.

"What do you want?"

"I'm calling about the damn meeting you couldn't be bothered to show up for," he bellowed through the line. "Do you have any idea how embarrassed I was to be sitting there with the heads of the RNC, having to make excuses about your absence?"

"Something came up," I lied. The truth was, I hadn't done anything of importance Saturday night unless you counted catching up with the Stark's and the Lannister's latest bloodbath on HBO as important.

"I'll not have you ruin this for me. There's an order to things, Fitzgerald. You have to show up and win this damn election. I need to get my people lined up if I have any hopes of gaining Senate Majority Leader."

A sudden awareness hit me, finally able to see his end game.

*So, that's what this is about.*

"Is that your angle? I knew there had to be one. You want me on the Senate so I can vote for you to be majority leader?"

"That's right. And you'll do what you're told. If you don't, you and I both know the Quinn & Wilkshire business will suffer. Half of your clients are politicians from the D.C. area. Plus, remember what I said. You need to think of Austin."

I sighed in annoyance. I'd had enough of him trying to use my son, his own grandson and flesh and blood, to coerce me into his convoluted agenda. But then I thought about Cadence and about how she'd followed her dreams to make a difference. It made me question myself and my own role in the world. I hadn't done much of anything to make an impact. Perhaps, just maybe, this Senate seat could be an opportunity to change that.

"You can't strongarm me with threats," I told my father. "If I do this, it won't be because you threatened me. You and I both know you won't follow through because that would mean outing Judge Perkins and his role in things. I didn't show because I needed time to think about it. Reschedule the meeting. I won't miss it, but I'm not making any promises."

"We'll see about that. I'll call you when I have a new date and location. You'd better not stiff this time."

The phone line went dead.

*Asshole.*

I returned the phone to my pocket and stared out the window. My office faced southeast and I was just able to see the top of the Capitol Building from my view. The painted cast-iron dome gleamed in the morning sun, the Statue of Freedom standing proudly with her sword and shield. I frowned, thinking of all the corruption and backdoor deals that went on behind the pristine walls. We may be free, but freedom always came with a price. I meant what I said to my father. I would consider, but I wouldn't commit just yet. A part of me worried if I did this, I'd be selling my soul to the devil.

I shook my head, refusing to allow my father's antics to get to me. I had more important matters to delve into. Moving to my desk, I sat down behind it and pulled out the key to open the file drawer to my left. My hands slid over the hanging folders inside. Each file contained client information, all arranged by last name in alphabetical order—all except one. I reached toward the back of the drawer and pulled out the file that had no label. It was the file for Cadence. I hadn't looked at it since the day I buried my wife.

There had been no love lost between Bethany Perkins and me. It was an arranged marriage, a fact she had reminded me of often. Although we initially tried to play the roles of husband and wife, consummating our marriage and making the best of a fucked up situation, it was only a matter of weeks before things fell apart. She was miserable. I was miserable. I think Bethany knew I loved someone else, and it was something I felt a little guilty about to this day. Perhaps I should have tried harder with her. If I had, maybe it would have changed the outcome of things. But I didn't try at all and Bethany had quickly turned back to her old ways.

After being married for only a few months, partying and drinking became a regular part of her life again. It was no small miracle I managed to keep her sober while she was pregnant with Austin. That had been the only time we ever really got along. After his birth, she went right back to the bottle. One day, she'd blame his colic for her behavior; another day, she'd blame me, saying I didn't love her. Although I never admitted it to her, she was right. I never loved her.

Before long, her drinking became more excessive. I had suspected drugs were in the mix but I never confronted her about it. A drunk Bethany was nasty and volatile. I didn't want to deal with it, but I did have Austin to worry about. My business had really started to take off, so I decided to hire a nanny for him. It may have been the best or worse decision of my life. A nanny gave Austin stability while I worked long hours, but it also gave my wife more freedom. She took it and ran with it until she drank herself to death.

My only saving grace after the whole shit storm was Austin had very little memory of that time in his life. He had been only four when she died. While he says he can remember flashes of her, his strongest memories were with me. I made sure of that.

After Bethany's funeral, I had come back to my office. Devon and I had just moved our offices from the tiny space in the West End to the building we were in now. I remembered the day like it was yesterday and could almost still smell the paint that had yet to dry on the walls completely. I recalled sitting down at this very desk, just as I was now, staring at a picture I thought I would tuck away forever. It was a picture of Cadence from the playbill handed out to everyone on the last day at Camp Riley.

The photos of staff members and students had been taken early in the summer, right after the cast was chosen. I ran my finger along the edge of Cadence's picture. She appeared happy. At this point, she was still completely unaware I was set to marry someone else. My picture told a different story. While I had smiled for the camera, there was dread beneath the façade.

Throughout my life, I learned more from my failures than I did from my successes. Failures were the moments that stuck with a person. If they didn't, one could never learn. Leaving Cadence was my ultimate failure. When I told her I was a coward for walking away, I never spoke truer words. After Bethany died, staring at the picture of Cadence made me realize all I had lost because I didn't stand up for myself. Since that day, I stopped rolling over to my father's demands. I vowed never again to be his whipping boy, and I've held true to that promise. I did it for Austin's sake as much as my own. Doing anything less would make me an unfit father and role model. Nobody would own me again.

I placed the program back into the folder and flipped through the remaining contents. It was mostly press releases about the happenings at Camp Riley. I looked for them every Spring, hoping one of them contained a picture of Cadence. None of them did and I wondered why I had kept them for all these years. The last one was about the closure of the camp after Jamison and Claudine Riley passed away. There wasn't a lot of details about the closing in the article, other than the fact the decision was made by Cadence. It mentioned she would be putting the land up for sale. Reading through all of this again caused a pain in my chest. Not for me but for her. Selling that land had to crush her.

I replaced the folder in its hiding spot at the back of the drawer and fired up my computer. Owning a PR company came with perks. It meant I had access to personal information most people had to pay to obtain. Finding the personal cell number for Cadence took less than a minute.

I scribbled the number down on a notepad and began a new search. I typed in her name and the words 'non-profit' and 'Washington D.C.' in the search bar. I wanted to find out more about her organization and what she did. I had clearly pissed her off in the coffee shop with my comment about DACA recipients breaking the law. I had some making up to do. If I had any hopes of doing just that, I would need to get an education first. I scrolled through the search results and stopped on the fourth one down the line.

*Dahlia's Dreamers. That has to be it.*

I clicked through to the website and was surprised at what I found. The site was full of resource links, past and current projects, and stories about their successes. However, the biggest shock was seeing she was a children's book author and illustrator. Portions of the proceeds from her books went to her non-profit. I sat back in my chair, feeling awestruck and a little proud of what she'd accomplished.

Buy links were included on the site, so of course I clicked on them and purchased every single one of the thirty-two books she had published.

# Chapter Nine

**CADENCE**

Five o'clock in the morning came way too early. Normally, I'd set my alarm for six, leaving plenty of time to wash my face, get dressed, and head out for a run. I'd then come home, shower, and be to work by nine. However, with the construction on my street, taking my car to the nearest park added drive time I now needed to account for. As I turned the corner onto $14^{th}$ Street, the sluggishness of the morning began to fade, and I started to feel anxious. I had barely slept a wink. I had tossed and turned, thinking about the Garcia-Mendez case, finances, book sales, and Kallie. In the end, my worry about telling Kallie the truth about Fitz always came back to the forefront. The problem was, I didn't even have the slightest clue about where to begin.

In a rare stroke of luck, I was able to find off street parking. After I parallel parked the car, I rested my head against the seat. If I didn't have enough concerns to keep me awake long into the late hours of the night, there was also the impromptu coffee break with Fitz. I tried not to think about it, just as I tried not to think about the voicemail he'd left me late yesterday afternoon.

Reaching toward the middle console of my car, I picked up my cell and played back his message for what must have been the twentieth time.

"Cadence, it's Fitz. It was really nice catching up with you this morning. I'd like to do it again sometime over dinner. Call me."

I didn't know how he got my number, but that was irrelevant. I couldn't muster up the courage to call him back. However, what I *did* decide to do was jog the National Mall again. I told myself I would have come here regardless of Fitz, but the reality was, I could have gone to a hundred other locations to run, yet here I was again.

After a good stretch on the curb, I plugged one earbud into my ear and tucked the other one into my shirt front before setting out. OneRepublic played in my ear as I passed the giant carousel and groups of people doing yoga on the lush green lawns. The sun pierced through the horizon, sparkling through the Cherry Blossom trees as I ran down what was quickly becoming my favorite running path. I smiled politely and nodded to the other joggers who passed me.

I wasn't scanning any of their faces in search of Fitz. That would've been silly. It wasn't like he'd consumed my thoughts since the day his son showed up on my doorstep. Those steely gray eyes and strong arms didn't haunt me in the late hours of the night, just as I hadn't slipped my hand under my bedsheets imagining it was his touch. Nope. I was just out here running for my own physical work out.

That was all a lie, of course, a fact that became apparent the moment I found myself disappointed when I didn't see his face among the people I passed. I began to assume he'd only called to be polite. Perhaps I only imagined the sizzling connection between us in the coffee shop and was getting caught up with feelings of nostalgia. Fitz was my first love after all. It was only natural for me to be nostalgic, but it had been years. People change—I'd changed. The boy I'd fallen in love with was not the man I'd had coffee with yesterday. It would be unfair of me to assume he was the same person.

"Morning, sweetheart," said a familiar male voice to my left.

My steps faltered and I stopped, bringing my hand to my chest.

"Geez, you need to stop doing that! You nearly scared me out of my skin!"

"Sorry. In my defense, I did call out to you several times," Fitz pointed out. "You must not have heard me because of the earbuds."

"Only one," I said, plucking the lone bud from my ear. "I never run with both in. It's not safe."

"Not safe?"

"Yeah," I said, fighting the urge to roll my eyes. It was so typical of a man not to understand the safeties women must adhere to day in and day out. "Being a woman, I need to think of these things. Creepers are everywhere, and I need to be able to hear if anyone approaches."

He raised one perfectly shaped eyebrow in amusement.

"Creepers, huh? You didn't hear me."

"True, but I was distracted."

"Distracted?"

My face flushed, not wanting to admit I had been thinking about him.

"Yeah, I just got a case at work that's bugging me," I said, giving him only the partial truth.

"Come on, then. Let's run and you can tell me about it."

I eyed him curiously for a moment. Going for another jog with him would only exacerbate my current predicament—that much was certain. But a run may also satisfy the unexplainable burning need I had to be near him again. Perhaps if I did this, I'd be able to get him out of my system long enough to rein in my focus.

"Um, sure. Why not?" I agreed.

I started out, and Fitz casually fell into step beside me.

"So, Dahlia's Dreamers. The name's fitting."

I tossed him a sideways glance, trying to read his expression. He'd apparently done his research on me, and I worried about how far he'd dived in. However, if he knew anything about Kallie, he didn't let on. For that, I felt a small measure of relief.

"I thought so too. I was listening to all the political debate about the DREAM Act around the same time Dahlia had been put to rest. The name just sort of came to me. I started the company ten years ago. I have a small staff of five, including Joy. Do you remember Joy Martin from camp?"

"She worked in the store. Yeah, I remember her, but I thought she went to school for music."

"She did, but she couldn't find a job. When I offered her a spot, she jumped at it. She's good for Dahlia's Dreamers. It's become personal to her. It's hard to see her doing anything else now."

Fitz cut along the path that would lead us through Ash Woods, following the same trek we'd made yesterday. We moved as if we'd been running together for years, always seeming to know when the other was going to cut right or left along the path.

"Tell me about your case," he prompted.

"It's actually long and complicated, as they usually are, but this one is bugging me more because there's a little girl involved. The poor thing is barely five years old, and she has no idea where her daddy is."

I gave him a brief overview of Emilia's visit. He stayed quiet, seeming to absorb every word I said. When I finished, he sighed.

"I'll apologize again for assuming things yesterday, Cadence. After our talk, I read up on DACA. From what I gathered, I thought only a felony could revoke their status. I didn't realize a simple traffic ticket could send someone packing."

"It might not have three years ago, but new Executive Orders have changed all that. When I started Dahlia's Dreamers, our focus was to help individuals navigate through the DACA process so they could obtain legal status. Now all we do is help those very same people protect the legal status that was already granted to them. Sometimes we succeed. Sometimes we don't. Those are always the worst days," I admitted sadly.

"I mean, Christ. They have families and lives here. It just doesn't seem fair," he murmured. He shook his head and slowed his steps. When we came to a complete stop, he turned to face me. "Old Abe marks the halfway point. I usually stop here to stretch before I continue on."

Following his lead, I placed a foot on the first step leading up to the Lincoln Memorial and pressed down into a lunge. Fitz watched me, his gaze traveling from my foot, up my thigh until stopping on my face. His study of me was so intense, I became self-conscious, feeling like I was doing the stretch incorrectly.

"What? Am I doing something wrong?"

"No, sweetheart. You're doing everything right."

My breath caught, and I looked at him. His eyes were shining mischievously.

*He's flirting with me.*

If I couldn't resist those flirtations when I was eighteen, there was no way in hell I'd be able to keep away from the sinful, confident, and hot as hell man before me. Instantly, my face heated. Quickly, I returned to a standing position.

"Right, well…shall we continue on?"

"In a minute," he waved off dismissively and continued to stretch. "I admire that you went into public service. I'm curious though. Why did you choose immigrants?"

"Honestly, my interest sparked when I read a story about five young undocumented activists who were trying to transform society's attitudes about immigration. I was inspired and found myself reevaluating what it means to be an American. Then I knew someone who was personally affected," I paused, not wanting to get into a story that wasn't mine to tell. "Things just kind of snowballed after that. What about you, Fitz? What inspires you?"

"You," he replied immediately. "Watching you. Listening to you speak."

I fought the flush that wanted to creep up my neck again and forced myself to push for his answer. After all, I was supposed to be figuring out who he was, yet all the conversation was about me. A flash of a memory resurfaced, reminding me of a similar situation seventeen years ago. I supposed some things never changed.

"I'm serious. Why go into public relations?" I pushed.

"It was one of my degrees, for starters. Plus, I had a knack for it. I knew what looked good in the eyes of the public and what didn't. I grew up with that. My father was always so concerned about appearances and what could negatively influence the voters. Other than my few years at Georgetown when I didn't care about much of anything, I can barely remember a time when I didn't have to be wary of public scrutiny."

Despite all the things I knew about his upbringing, I was surprised I never realized how difficult it must have been for him. He had always lived his life under a microscope because of his father's political status. He may still live that way for all I knew. That thought made me pause. I wasn't sure if I wanted to expose Kallie to that sort of life.

"It's a shame you had to live like that. I never realized. We were so wrapped up in our own private little cocoon at Camp Riley, it was easy to forget how isolated we were from the rest of the world."

Fitz stood to face me, settling those intense gray eyes on my face.

"I miss those days. I've missed you," he admitted huskily. "I still think about you a lot. All the time actually."

My body went rigid, unable to believe his words. I wasn't going to fall for it—not for a second. If he thought he could woo his way into my panty's again, he was sadly mistaken. I took a small step back.

"That's a line," I accused, feeling uneasy.

"No, it's not."

"Why on earth would you think of me still? After all this time?"

"It's simple. You were and still are my biggest regret."

I shook my head, needing to deny the words that nearly made my heart stop.

"It was a long time ago. I was a naïve girl with foolish dreams. I get why you did what you did. It was for the best," I rambled nervously. "We both avoided a painful goodbye that way. A lot has changed since then. There's no reason to hang onto any sort of guilt."

Part of my statement was true. I truly did think it was for the best, but we didn't avoid a painful goodbye—at least, I didn't. His cruel words, even though I knew they were false, had crushed me. There was no sense in rehashing the past.

I stared down at the ground and drew invisible circles with the toe of my shoe on the concrete sidewalk. I could feel his stare on me as if somehow it was its own entity. Panic welled up inside me, knowing he was slowly taking down my walls brick by brick, but I couldn't let him in. Not again.

"You'd always been so open and honest about your feelings. Whatever promises or decisions we made all those years ago doesn't change the fact that I'm here now–that you're here." He stepped toward me, his movements lined with power and purpose. He'd always moved that way, his profound presence hitting me like a bolt of lightning. "Look at me, Cadence."

My body stayed tense, but his tone nearly seduced me into compliance. Refusing to look at him would only make me look unreasonably stubborn or scared. The last thing I wanted to do was give Fitz a reason to believe our breakup mattered. He couldn't know I measured all potential lovers against him, always finding fault with each.

And I certainly didn't want him to know, as a result, there had only been him.

Drawing in a breath, I brought my eyes up to meet his.

"What do you want from me, Fitz?"

He took another step closer, wrapped his hand around the back of my neck, and tilted my head up to study my face. His eyes moved to my lips, then back up to meet my gaze.

"I want to kiss you."

Seventeen years ago, he had asked permission. Today, he didn't. Before I could react, he covered my mouth in a greedy kiss. He didn't ease inside or wait for me to accept him. No. Unlike the days from our youth, he prowled in.

I stiffened at first as my mind shouted instructions of protest. I was confused about whether I wanted this or not. Heat clouded my judgment, and my brain seemed to disconnect from my body. It took me less than a second to realize how much I longed for him—and that scared the hell out of me. I anchored my hands on his shoulders knowing full well I should end this madness, yet I didn't push him away. Without meaning to, I kissed him back and curled my hands around his neck. He plunged in again and I willingly opened, urging him closer and tangling my tongue with his. We had moved way too fast seventeen years ago, and it appeared as though the magnetic force that had once made us impatient lovers was another thing that hadn't changed with time.

My acceptance of his kiss encouraged him to press deeper into my mouth. Tasting. Possessing. I met every stroke of his tongue as he wrapped his arm around my waist, crushing my torso against his own. The kiss rocked me to my very core. There were so many reasons the kiss was wrong, yet none of them seemed to matter. This was what I needed. It felt so good. It had been too long. For the first time in nearly two decades, I felt complete. Something I thought was long dead seemed to come alive again and I began to wonder if I'd ever been truly feeling for years. Fitz was all that seemed to matter. Somehow, over the miles and years, he'd never lost his hold on me. Now, he was unexpectedly back in my life, and I knew this was what I'd been missing. He was the essence that haunted me. Him. Just him.

"Cadence, sweetheart," he murmured against my lips. His palm caressed the nape of my neck, gliding over the slope of my collarbone. I was drowning in sensation. I could hardly breathe as a wave of dizziness made my head swim. The masculine scent of spice and earth sent my body reeling. I knew this needed to stop, but his very touch made me feel powerfully female and desired in a way I hadn't experienced since the last time I was in his arms. My fingers found their way to his hair, tugging at the dark strands until a moan escaped me.

Almost intrusively, thoughts of my daughter popped into my head.

*Shit. Kallie. What am I doing?*

I tore my mouth from his, feeling guilty for forgetting about her. But worse, I was mortified over the twinge of resentment I felt toward her. Never once had I regretted Kallie or felt like I'd been cheated in some way. She was my life. Fitz, the boy who broke my heart seventeen years ago, was not. Yet just like my teenage self, I couldn't seem to hold back from him. Fitz was my downfall and probably always would be. He extracted too many memories that had long been buried.

I tried to focus on bringing my heart rate down to a normal rhythm. If one kiss triggered these sorts of feelings, I needed to find a way to stay far, far away. I wasn't ready for this. I staggered a step back.

"Fitz, I'm sorry. I shouldn't have let that happen."

He stared at me with glazed eyes and swollen lips. I was fairly certain his expression matched my own. He reached for me.

"We've finally found each other again. Why are you pushing me away?"

"It's not what you think. I have…" I trailed off, struggling to find the right words. "I have obligations. I can't shirk my responsibilities for a quick roll in the sack."

Fitz laughed.

"Putting the cart before the horse now, aren't you? It was just a kiss, Cadence. It's broad daylight. I don't think the D.C. police would take kindly to us fornicating on one their monuments."

I blushed. For some strange reason, the thought of defiling the sacred memorials was a complete turn on. I shook my head to clear the nasty thoughts.

"It's not that. You're screwing with my head. You don't get to come back into my life now, all these years later, mucking things up."

He laughed a low rumbling sound that coiled my insides up even further.

"Mucking things up? How am I doing that?"

"In just a few minutes, you managed to twist and confuse things in a way it should never have been," I said, my brows pinched in pain. I stared absently at the ground, not wanting to admit anything else.

"Have dinner with me."

My head snapped up to look at him. The intensity in his eyes grew and I felt like I'd been thrown back in time. For a moment, it was like I was eighteen all over again. The way he looked standing there—the assured grin he wore, his t-shirt and running shorts, the way his gray eyes expressed so many things he wouldn't say. The invitation to go out to dinner may as well have been an invitation to the lake. I had been so innocent and too idealistic back then. A lot had changed since the days at Camp Riley, not only in my life but who I was as a person. Loving someone the way I once loved him had changed me deep inside.

"I don't think that's a good idea, Fitz. We can't go back. We aren't kids anymore. Things aren't the same as they were before."

"One night. That's all I'm asking for, sweetheart."

Thankfully, a buzzing in the front pocket of my yoga pants gave me a much-needed interruption to the conversation. I pulled out my cell. Simon Reed's name showed on the caller ID.

*Saved by the bell.*

"Hey, Simon," I said. I looked at Fitz. His eyes narrowed suspiciously, and if I wasn't mistaken, I thought I saw a spark of jealousy flash.

"Sorry for the early call. I just figured you'd want an update. I started work on the Garcia-Mendez case," Simon said.

"What did you find out?" I asked anxiously.

"Judge Perkins has been assigned to the case."

My stomach dropped.

"Shit! He has a hardline stance on immigration. Every time we go up against him, we lose."

"I know. I'm currently looking into his past rulings. I might be able to petition the court for a motion to remove, but I'd have to prove allegations of bias. That's going to be tough. I'd be better off filing for a change in venue since the court is far from Emilia's home address. However, that means I'd have to travel to Richmond."

I knew what that meant. Simon Reed was doing this pro-bono. To ask him to travel almost two hours would be too much.

"See what you can do about having the judge removed first."

"I'll look into it," Simon promised. "Will you be at the gala next week?"

"Helping Lives Bloom? Yeah, I'll be there. I'm supposed to give a speech to kick things off. Wish me luck," I joked.

"I'll be there too. Are you bringing a date?"

I nearly groaned, hoping he wasn't going to ask me to attend the gala with him. Simon was a decent guy even if his clothing style was eclectic at best. It was hard to keep him at bay, yet still manage to maintain a professional connection to satisfy the needs at Dahlia's Dreamers. We needed to retain all the pro-bono lawyers we could.

But then again, perhaps this was the opportunity I needed to put a little distance back between me and Fitz. I glanced over at him. He stood there with his arms crossed, studying me intently, waiting patiently for me to end my call. As much as I didn't want to push him away as he accused me of doing, I knew I had to if I wanted to hang on to any measure of control. For Kallie's sake, I couldn't afford to get lost in old teenage dreams.

"Actually, Simon. I don't have a date for the gala. Do you want to go with me?"

I kept my eyes trained on Fitz. I saw a flash of something on his face, but I couldn't quite place it. Anger? Jealousy? Curiosity?

"That sounds great, Cadence. The gala starts at six. Should I pick you up at five-thirty?" Simon asked.

"Actually, make it five. I need to get there a little early."

After I ended the call, I replaced the phone in my pocket and looked at Fitz. His expression was still unreadable.

"I'm, ah…I'm going to head back to my car," I said nervously.

"Who's Simon?"

I tipped my chin up stubbornly.

"He's a lawyer friend."

"Are you going out with him?"

"I guess you could say that. We're going to a charity fundraiser together," I replied, trying to sound a hell of a lot more confident than I actually felt.

His eyes narrowed slightly, assessing me.

"Alright. I see how it is," he said with a slight nod. "Do you want to meet back here tomorrow morning for another run?"

"Another run? For real?"

"Why not? I like the company."

I couldn't meet him again. I already had a big enough mess on my hands. Kissing him only multiplied my problems by ten, yet all I could think about was doing it again. I could still feel the tingle on my lips from his demanding kiss and the warmth from his arms as they circled my waist. I longed to be back in his embrace, lost in the essence of him.

However, I didn't admit to any of those things. Instead, I hid the smile that wanted to curve on my lips and nodded.

"Okay, Fitz. Tomorrow then. I'll meet you at the Korean War Memorial."

# Chapter Ten

**FITZ**

*Baby steps.*

That's what I told myself as I sat down behind my desk to start the workday. My cell phone buzzed in my pocket and I fumbled for it.

"Shit," I muttered when the damn thing nearly slipped from my hand. It was a text from my father stating the new meeting time with the RNC. It was set for Saturday afternoon. I was going to have to deal with preparing for it sooner rather than later, but I needed to get my head on straight first. It didn't help my mind was all kinds of distracted, a pathetic fucker singularly focused like a dog after a bone—exactly what I'd become since running into Cadence. Pathetic.

For days, my stomach had been tied up in knots from the anxiety lining my insides. She had power and energy I hadn't realized I was missing. I didn't realize how much I missed her mouth. Her taste. I had kissed her like a man deprived, igniting a fire that went straight to my dick—another thing that missed her.

Still, I'd made progress with her that morning, but it was clear she was going to make me work to gain her trust again, and I'd make damn sure to bust my ass until I got it. The years didn't matter. She belonged with me, but she was right not to trust me. Despite what she said about having no regrets, I knew I'd crushed her. I was cruel even if things seemed to end on a bittersweet note. Now, it was up to me to prove I was a different man and no longer the spineless boy she knew at Camp Riley. A fake marriage, fatherhood, and time will do that to a person.

I pressed the intercom button on my desk phone and buzzed Angie.

"Yes, Mr. Quinn."

"I need you to secure a ticket to an event for me. It's called Helping People Bloom, or something to that effect. I can't recall the exact name."

As I spoke the words, I half wondered what the hell I was doing. Cadence had thrown me so far out of balance, I didn't seem to know my head from my ass anymore. Every action felt compulsive.

"Just one ticket, sir?" Angie asked.

"Yes, just one. And if you can, keep my name off the guest list until the last minute."

I heard the click of her nails on the keyboard before she responded.

"I've got it pulled up on the computer. It looks like the Helping Lives Bloom Gala is being held at the Roosevelt Plaza Hotel. It's being hosted by five different non-profit organizations to help children of immigrant families. It says it's sold out online but getting a ticket shouldn't be a problem. I've spoken with the event's manager, Eric Ledger, several times in the past. I'm sure he'll do me the favor."

"Perfect. Thanks. Let me know if you run into any issues."

"Will do."

I hit the button to break the connection, then dialed Devon's cell. I hadn't touched base with my friend and partner in over a week. I wanted to let him enjoy his vacation in peace, but he needed to be brought up to speed on a few things.

"Devon, sorry to bug you on vacation, man," I said, pausing when I heard the telltale sound of steel drums and a male vocalist belting out Bob Marley lyrics. "Is this a good time to talk?"

"Yeah, just lying here by the pool. Nikki went down to be pampered at the spa, so I'm free to talk."

"How are things going with her?"

"Alright, I guess. I mean, we're having fun, but she's kind of high maintenance. Two weeks with her is way too long. Just this morning, she literally flipped out on our room attendant for forgetting the mints on her pillow yesterday. I'll say one thing, it was fucking embarrassing. I'll probably ditch her once I get back to the States."

"You always find something wrong with them," I laughed and shook my head.

"Hey, at least she got a vacation out of me."

"True."

"I'm sure you didn't call to talk about my trip. What's up?" he asked.

"When do you get back?"

"Sunday night. Why?"

"Just wondering so I can plan. My father's scheming and I want to run a few things by you."

"I can only imagine what the old kook is up to. What does he want you to do now? Cut off your left nut?" he laughed.

I frowned. Devon always thought it was funny when it was someone else's balls on the chopping block.

"No. He wants me to run for the Virginia Senate."

"Senator, huh? What do you think? Do you want to follow in the old man's footsteps?"

"I don't know. I'm thinking about it. I was supposed to have a meeting with the RNC last Saturday, but I didn't go. I don't know why, but I didn't take my father seriously when he first told me about it. It's since been rescheduled, but I need to make sure you're okay with my decision if I decide to run. You might need to pick up some of my clients."

Devon was quiet for a moment before he asked, "I don't get it. What's your father's angle?"

"Senate Majority Leader."

"Ah, now I see," he said, drawing out the recognition. Devon knew my father's ambitious tendencies almost as well as I did. "Hey, do what you need to do. You know I've always got your back. But I've got to say, a senator? For fuck's sake, Fitz. You hate politics."

"I know. I guess the only thing I can say is I've recently started thinking about my life. We still live in a world where there is still racism and inequality. Our country still denies minorities equal opportunity and children go uneducated. I've done nothing to help any of those things. I can't explain it, but I have this sudden urge to do something more."

"Wow. That's out of left field. You feeling alright?"

I released a long, drawn out sigh.

"I ran into Cadence, Devon."

He went silent for a heartbeat before responding.

"Cadence? As in *the* Cadence?"

"The one and only."

He let out a low whistle.

"It's been a long time since I heard that name. How did it go?"

I filled him in on all that transpired after our initial run in, including the subsequent coffee shop conversation and the research I'd done on her afterward. I finished up with the jog around the National Mall that morning but I left out the part about the kiss. I didn't know what had come over me but knew kissing her was a ballsy move. I didn't want to hear the shit he was bound to give me for it.

"So now she's planning on going to this gala thing with some lawyer. It pissed me off even though it shouldn't have. It was almost like she deliberately did it to spite me. Anyway, I've got Angie working on getting me a ticket for it."

"Hang on. Let me get this straight," Devon said with an incredulous laugh. "You see her, but you spied on her before actually talking to her. Then you go back to the office, look her up, and buy a bunch of her kids' books. Today, you go out looking for her again, then end up buying a ticket to her event but keep your name off the guest list so she doesn't know you're going to show up. I better come home soon, man. You're turning all stalker on me."

I knew he was only joking, but when he phrased it like that, I supposed it did look kind of bad. The only thing I could say was willpower was a bitch. And apparently, I still had none when it came to Cadence.

"I'm not going to let her go this time, Devon. I can't."

"What does she think about that? Does she know you want to rekindle the old flame?"

After today, I was pretty sure she knew where I stood, yet I didn't know how she felt about me. I'd always felt that Cadence was somehow out of my league, so beautiful and fierce in that soft and wistful way. She had an inherent goodness to her that was far better than me. She was grace. Beauty. My feelings for her had always been real, yet now they seemed to multiply tenfold. Every time I saw her, energy seemed to crash through the air with a torrent of emotion, resonating and pulsing through every vein in my body. I wasn't sure if it was just an echo of the past or if this was something new. Perhaps it was one and the same.

"She knows, but I think it's going to take time for me to bring her around."

"If I know you, you'll figure it out. You always were single minded when it came to her."

The light on the console of my office phone flashed, signaling an incoming call. Looking at the caller ID, I saw it was Austin's school.

"Devon, I'll have to call you back. Austin's school is calling."

"Oh, that reminds me. I've got tickets to the baseball game next week. I haven't seen the little punk in a while, so I thought I'd take him."

"Sure. I'll see if he's free."

"Cool. Catch ya later."

I hung up and clicked over to the incoming call.

"Fitzgerald Quinn speaking."

"Hello, Mr. Quinn. This is Principal Weaver calling from St. Aloysius Prep. I need you to come to the school today for a conference with me and the vice principal. Austin was in a fist fight."

*A fight?*

That sounded so unlike Austin.

"Is he okay?" I asked with concern.

"He's fine and sitting in the office with me. However, the other boy is in the nurse's office and will most likely be brought to the hospital after his parents arrive."

*Dammit!*

I shook my head, almost unable to believe it. Austin had been acting a little off lately, but I just attributed it to normal teenage mood swings. Never did I think his moodiness would lead to physical violence. I wanted to wring his neck for getting into a fight and he'd definitely have hell to pay. However, if he was having a hard time at school and I somehow missed it, this was also on me.

"I see, Ms. Weaver. I'll be there in twenty minutes."

---

Austin plopped down in a chair at the kitchen table of our home in Alexandria. His fists gripped handfuls of his shaggy dark brown hair in frustration. He'd be sixteen in a few months and was still all legs, yet he was starting to grow into his body. His arms were beginning to fill out, the wiry muscles finally showing some definition. When he looked up at me, gray eyes that matched mine flashed indignantly.

"This is total bullshit," he swore. I didn't reprimand him for using foul language like I probably should have. Instead, I leaned against the side of the table and crossed my arms. I tried to understand his frustration and knew he needed to vent.

"It doesn't matter if it's bullshit, Austin. Fighting isn't the way to solve things. You know better than that."

"What was I supposed to do? Just sit by and let the guy maul her?"

I hated to admit it, but I kind of agreed with the poor kid. When I got the phone call stating Austin had been in a fight, I assumed the worst. Then I got the full story. Apparently, he just started seeing a girl at school. He was kissing her goodbye before class. I remembered those days and didn't find it to be anything out of the ordinary for teenagers in high school. However, her ex-boyfriend saw them and didn't like it. When he started shoving her around, Austin stepped in and pummeled the guy.

"Look, I get why you hit the jerk," I began. "But breaking his nose? Come on, Austin. I saw the guys face. That wasn't just from one punch."

"Troy Adams is a dick. He deserved it," he spat out.

"Yeah, maybe he did. But still." I uncrossed my arms and began to pace, trying to decide on the best way to deal with this. I could be a hard ass, or I could go easy on him. I looked back at my son who was still scowling and staring at the ground. "I know I should probably punish you or something, but I think Principal Weaver already gave you more than your fair share."

"Yeah, she did! This blows! I mean, I get the in-school suspension part, but pulling me from the French trip? All my friends are going!"

"I know. I tried to argue with the principal about not pulling you, but you heard what she said. No extracurricular activities are allowed when you have in-school suspension. That includes the trip. If she made an exception for you, she'd have to do it for everyone." Austin just scowled some more, and I sighed. "Look, I know I've been working long hours lately. Uncle Devon is getting back from his trip next week and that should free up some time for me. I know hanging out with Dad probably won't be as much fun, but let's plan something."

He glanced up at me. I could tell that he stubbornly wanted to stay irate but saw when his expression slowly began to morph into one of resignation.

"Yeah, that could be cool I guess," he mumbled. "Maybe I can kick your butt at Madden again."

"Kick my butt! I think I'm the one who kicked yours the last time," I razzed, giving him a light jab to the shoulder.

"In your dreams," he scoffed. He stood and shook his head, shoulders still slumped in defeat. "I'm heading up to my room. I've got homework to do. What's the plan for dinner?"

It was barely two o'clock, yet the kid was already thinking about dinner.

*Figures.*

"I could probably run to the store and grab some steaks. Feel like grilling?"

"Sounds good to me. Get some of that garlic butter stuff when you're at the store too," he added. "That was good on the steak last time."

"Sure thing, kid," I said to his back as he slowly walked away from me.

After he was out of sight, I sat in the chair he had vacated and dropped my head in my hands. Sometimes, when things were going smoothly, I'd think I had the parenting gig all figured out. Then there were days like today, moments where I questioned everything I did with him, wondering if I knew anything at all. It was making me second guess whether I should continue to pursue Cadence. I knew what I wanted to happen with her—with us. I wanted to be together again. However, I worried if bringing a woman into my life was right for Austin at this stage in his life.

For the first time in a long while, I allowed myself to miss my mother. Somehow, I knew if she were here, she'd know what to do. At least I'd like to think she would. I'd been only ten years old when we shared our final memories. It was possible she wasn't the woman I'd envisioned her to be at all. Either way, I was alone now. I would just have to figure things out on my own.

# Chapter Eleven

**CADENCE**

Nine days flew by remarkably fast, one day blurring into the next. My daily jog around the Mall with Fitz continued. With each day, it felt as if one more brick in my wall broke free. It terrified me to know I was leaving myself vulnerable to heartbreak. There wasn't any more kissing, which I was thankful for and disappointed about at the same time. It was so confusing. Every time we talked, he'd eventually bring the conversation back to where we began over seventeen years ago. It was like he was trying, ever so subtly, to remind me of all the good we once shared. Little did he know, I had never forgotten. Nor did I forget all the pain that came with that good.

Still, his words always seemed laced with sexual undertones. The sound of his voice stayed with me long into the night. I couldn't get him out of my head. I wanted him in ways that made my body ache. Perhaps it was something to do with the change of hormones women experience in their thirties, but I still couldn't believe I had broken down and bought my very first vibrator. I told myself I had bought it just in case. It still sat in the package, burning an embarrassing hole in my nightstand drawer—I had yet to summon the courage to actually use the damn thing. Still, I knew a rubber toy, combined with the memories of what once was and the present day, would be a poor substitute for the real thing. I'd never fantasized being with someone the way that I was with Fitz. I was so distracted by my thoughts of him and constantly had to remind myself of the predicament I was in.

Before I knew it, Friday was here. Kallie was set to leave for her

French class trip to Montreal in the morning and I was helping her pack. With all this confusing emotion surrounding Fitz, I didn't know which way was up. I no longer knew if I was trying to rediscover him for Kallie's sake or because of my own selfish need to take back what had once been mine.

As I listened to her debate between a green wool sweater and a blue one, my heart tightened from the swell of love that engulfed me. What I felt for her was so powerful. She was the center of my heart. My world. She was a gift given to me when I thought I couldn't go on, reminding me of the bigger purpose in my life. It wasn't about protecting my battered heart that had once been broken to pieces. It was about her. Everything I did was for her.

"I think the green one," I told her. "It will bring out your eyes."

"Yeah, but blue looks good on me. I think I'll pack both."

I laughed.

"Just remember to save enough room in your suitcase for souvenirs."

"I will. Austin made me promise to bring him something back."

My stomach sank. She hadn't mentioned his name since the prom, and I still wondered if he was going on the class trip. Perhaps this was my opportunity to tell her the truth. But then again, I wasn't sure if telling her and then sending her off to another country was the right move.

"Austin? Is he not going?" I pressed, taking advantage of the opening she left me.

"No, he can't anymore."

"Why not?" I asked, trying to sound as casual as possible.

"He got in trouble in school. He was kissing Jessica Bradford and Troy Adams saw them. Troy is Jessica's ex," she explained. "Troy and Austin got into this big old fight because Troy was pushing Jessica around. All the other kids circled around them and were chanting 'fight, fight.' It was childish in my opinion. They shouldn't have been egging Austin and Troy on, even if Austin was in the right. Anyway, they both got yanked down to the principal's office and now Austin can't go with us to Montreal."

She rattled off the high school gossip so quickly, I struggled to keep up. As her words began to compute, a feeling of relief washed over me.

*Good. Kissing another girl. Not my daughter. I still have time.*

"Oh, that's too bad," I said, but internally I was doing fist pumps.

"Yeah, it stinks. The whole group from prom was going to be there. Austin will be the only one missing," she said. She looked sad, but it only appeared to be a general disappointment and not the longing expression a girl would have if she were going to be missing her boyfriend. Although I didn't like to see her unhappy, her expression gave me another thing to be relieved about. I was finally beginning to believe Austin and Kallie really were only friends.

"I know what will cheer you up," I offered. "Aunt Joy and Marissa are going to stop by later to see you before your trip. I asked them to pick up a birthday cake on their way over. Since you'll be in Montreal when you turn seventeen, they wanted to do a little something for you before you go."

"That's so sweet of them! I haven't seen them in forever! How are they?" she asked excitedly.

I didn't point out she'd just seen them three weeks ago. In the eyes of a sixteen going on seventeen-year-old girl, I was fairly certain three weeks was equivalent to an eternity.

"They're good. They went away to Philadelphia a couple of weekends ago for an early anniversary celebration. When they were there, Marissa finally convinced Joy to adopt. They haven't started the process yet, but we may have a new baby to spoil before the end of the year."

"Ooh! A baby!"

"Yes, but mums the word. I don't know if I was supposed to share that with you. These things are complicated and not all adoptions go through as planned. They may want to keep it quiet until something is for sure."

"My lips are sealed," she promised, sliding her finger across her mouth as if there was an imaginary zipper.

I felt my phone vibrate in the back pocket of my jeans. Pulling it out, I saw a familiar number flash across the screen. It hadn't been programmed into my phone, but I'd listened to the voicemail that went along with it enough times to know who exactly was calling—it was Fitz.

*Shit! Should I answer it?*

Panic seized my chest and I glanced at Kallie. She was still rifling through drawers in search of the perfect articles of clothing to bring.

"Kallie, I've got to take this call. I'll be right back."

"No problem," she waved off over her shoulder.

Moving as fast as I could down the stairs, I practically hurdled over the banister in a rush to get out the back door. As soon as I stepped out into the early evening air, the vibrating in my hand stopped.

I stared at the motionless phone, watching the screen fall dark. I didn't know if I should call him back. Before I could decide what to do, the phone lit up and began to vibrate again.

"Hello?" I answered tentatively.

"Hey, sweetheart."

"Hi…um, why are you calling me?"

"Shouldn't I be?"

"I don't know. We normally just chat during the morning jog. We aren't phone people."

He laughed.

"Maybe not yet, but that could change. I wanted to talk to you about something."

I glanced nervously behind me to make sure Kallie wasn't lurking anywhere, then moved further into the backyard.

"What is it?" I asked.

"I didn't tell you about this during any of our morning runs because I needed to think things out. Everything is fine now, but my son got in trouble at school last week. He was in a fight, trying to defend the honor of some girl. Teenagers," he scoffed.

I already knew this of course, but I couldn't let him know that.

"That's too bad," was my only reply.

"What I needed time to think about was you. I want to see more of you. The time we spend together in the morning is great, but I want more. I know you do too. I can feel it. However, we need to talk this out. It's not just me in the game. I have to consider Austin. Teenagers are so impressionable. I'd like him to meet you one day, but I need to do it right if you know what I mean."

*Oh, I know what you mean alright. Especially since I've already met your son.*

I didn't voice the words, but I was beginning to feel the walls closing in around me. My heart began to pound rapidly in my chest. I wasn't used to lying and knew I couldn't keep this up for much longer. He was going to have to know the truth sooner rather than later.

"I get it, Fitz. But let's not stress about it. I'm good with how things are for now. Keep it casual," I stated, working my hardest to sound as offhanded as humanly possible.

"I'm not okay with that, Cadence," he said in a low voice before he unexpectedly swore. "Dammit. I didn't want to do this over the phone."

"Do what?"

"I never expected to see you again. But now—after bumping into you, seeing you, spending time with you—I feel like I've been waiting my whole life for this moment. I'm ready to take the next step and see where it leads."

My breath caught in my throat.

"Fitz, don't…" I warned.

"Hear me out. I never got over you. I tried, but there wasn't a woman on the planet who could hold a flame to you. Even when I was married, I thought of you. She knew it too. She didn't know your name, but she always knew my heart belonged to someone else."

A wave of shock reverberated through me. The girl inside me wanted to leap through the phone and into his arms. But the woman in me didn't know if I should believe it. He said he loved me the day he took my virginity. Less than two weeks later, he left me broken, alone, and pregnant.

"We weren't together long enough for you to hang on to me all these years," I whispered. Tears stung the backs of my eyes. I couldn't let them fall.

"Yes, we were, and you know it."

I did, but I didn't want to admit it. There had been men over the years, casual dates that fizzled out to nothing. I'd always been afraid to go the final step, not allowing anyone to touch me. I told myself a sexual relationship with a man would spell trouble for me and Kallie. It would complicate the life I'd so carefully built. However, I always knew the true reason deep down. Opening up physically and mentally to another man would mean moving on from Fitz. It meant letting another man claim a place only Fitz had been.

"Fitz, I can't do this with you right now. I have to think about…" I trailed off.

"Think about what?"

*Kallie!* I wanted to scream, to finally come clean with everything. However, this wasn't a conversation that could be had over the phone. I gave myself a mental kick. This deserved a face to face. I needed to look into his eyes and physically see his reactions.

"I have to think about my responsibilities, but I agree. We need to talk about things."

"So, what do you say? How about having that dinner with me?"

"Yeah, I guess that could work," I conceded.

"When is good for you?"

The doorbell rang, interrupting my response. I heard a chorus of shrieks and looked back toward the house. Through the windows, I could see Kallie racing to greet Joy and Marissa in a huge group hug.

"Fitz, let's talk about this more on our next run together. Tomorrow morning," I told him in a rush. "Friends of mine just arrived so I have to go."

I didn't wait for him to respond and managed to end the call just in time before hearing Kallie call out to me.

"Mom! They're here!"

"I'll be right in!"

As I turned to head back toward the house, I paused to allow myself a moment to compose myself and looked around the yard. The lush green lawn was bathed in moonlight. The wooden fence I had installed when Kallie was a little girl cast long shadows over the grass, occasionally interrupted by the flicker of a firefly. Kallie and I had planted the small garden flourishing in the far-left corner. Along the fence line, we dug the dirt to make room for a long row of dahlias which were now just starting to bud. My eyes traveled the fence to where the flowers ended, marking the grave where I had buried Dahlia's ashes. The yard had been an oasis for Kallie and me as she grew up, often spending our evenings reading books or making up our own fairytales while swinging on the hammock hung between the two large oaks.

I sighed and continued on to the house. I tried to protect Kallie over the years, to shelter her from the monsters in the closet, both fictitious and real. It crippled me to know there was no way I could protect her from the firestorm of emotions she would feel learning who her father was. There was nothing I could do. My life with my daughter, as perfect and as precious as I tried to make it, was about to be blown apart.

# Chapter Twelve

**CADENCE**

I lugged Kallie's two-ton suitcase through the noisy and congested crowd toward the check in counter at Reagan National Airport. Well, it wasn't two tons, but it was heavy enough for me to worry about whether she'd be within the airline weight restriction guidelines. It also didn't help I was bone tired. Between thoughts of Fitz and worrying about Kallie's trip, I'd barely slept much at all the night before. I looked at my daughter who was weighed down with a carryon bookbag on one shoulder and a large duffel on the other.

"I swear, you did not have this much stuff packed last night, Kallie. What in the world did you add?"

"Sorry," she moaned. "I looked up the weather. The temps up there are all over the place this time of year. I didn't want to be too cold or too hot. I called Gabby this morning, and she said—"

"Never mind. Forget I asked," I sighed. I didn't have the patience to listen to a 'what Gabby said' rambling. Sweat was beginning to form on my brow and my patience was beginning to thin. Ever since Kallie was little, large crowds tended to make me jittery. I think it came from the fear I'd lose her. Either way, that anxious feeling never seemed to go away even as she grew older.

Thankfully, bag check went smoothly without any issues. As I walked Kallie to security, a new sort of anxiousness came over me. The longest Kallie and I had ever been separated was when she stayed overnight at a friend's house. Now I was letting her go for a full week. When I thought about it, just sending her to kindergarten practically sent me into cardiac arrest. I had to be out of my mind to allow her this trip.

"Here we are!" Kallie sang with cheerful excitement once we reached the back of the long line for security. This was the end of the road for me, and I couldn't stay with her any longer. My heart began to pound uneasily in my chest.

"Do you have your passport?"

"Yep. It's in my bag."

"And your cell phone and extra chargers?"

"All set."

"What about your toothbrush?"

She frowned.

"Come on, Mom. You double checked that yourself this morning. We can't stand here going through everything. My friends and teachers are probably already at the gate."

"You know your gate number, right?"

"Yes," she said in exasperation. "Can I go now?"

I smiled sadly, knowing I'd have to get used to this. She was almost grown up. Before long, we'd be sharing many more goodbyes.

"Come here, baby girl."

I swept Kallie into my arms, my devotion to her bubbling through me like the gentle flow of a stream. My heart no longer felt like it was going to fail because I had my reason for living in my arms. She was all that mattered. I pressed a tender kiss to her forehead, and she squeezed me tight. I felt her heart beat against mine, the thrumming in perfect sync to each other. I clung to her, knowing I was hanging on a little too tightly, as overwhelming emotion caused tears to sting my eyes. It wasn't every day a mother sent their only child off on a plane to Canada.

I pulled away and swallowed back the lump in my throat.

"Have fun and be good," I told her, knowing I didn't even need to mention the latter.

"Love you, Mom."

"I love you too, honey. Call me when you land."

"I will."

I stood there watching her for a while, making sure she got through security okay. She looked so grown up as she handed her passport to the TSA agent for approval, and once again I began to feel old. Time went by way too fast.

As I walked back to my car, my mind drifted to Fitz. For the first time, I began to feel guilty about all the time he'd missed with her. When the time came for me to tell him about her, I would need to do something to try to make up for it.

---

Thirty minutes later, I entered the building that housed Dahlia's Dreamers. For me, Saturday and I had a love-hate thing going on. While I didn't like working on what was supposed to be my day off, I loved it because I usually had the place to myself. That meant uninterrupted research, organizing, and strategy time. However, I knew someone else was in the office as soon as the elevator doors opened on my floor. I smelled coffee and heard the telltale gurgling of a fresh pot being brewed.

Joy sat at the reception desk looking at something on the computer.

"It's Saturday. What are you doing here?" I asked, making a beeline for the coffeemaker. Thankfully, I remembered to wash my favorite mug yesterday. The black ceramic cup with 'The Future is Female' in boldface type sat next to the brewing machine, just waiting to be put to good use.

"Marissa's working, as usual. I swear, the investment firm she works for is going to put her in an early grave. I'd wish she'd just quit and go back to teaching pre-school. I keep telling her money isn't everything."

"No, but it does make things easier."

"You sound just like her. Something's going to have to give if we get approved for this adoption. She knows it, but she's afraid to rip the bandage off. Anyway, I thought I'd pop in here and work on a few things since she wasn't home. We got a birthday invitation in the mail," she told me. I glanced over my shoulder to see her waving a pink card in the air.

"Oh? For who?" I asked as I stirred sugar into the coffee.

"It's for Emilia's daughter, Mayra. The two of them are staying in Fairfax with Andrés' parents while they wait to hear news about what's going on. It's closer to the holding center and more convenient. Mayra is turning five and they're throwing a little birthday party for her."

"That was nice of them to think of us."

"Yeah, I thought so too. I'll talk to Marissa to see if we're free. I'd like to go." She paused when I turned toward her, her face assessing me. "Geez, Cadence. You look exhausted."

"I haven't been sleeping well. I think I need a new pillow. Until then, a fifth cup of coffee will have to do," I joked, holding up the mug.

"A new pillow, huh? How did it go with Kallie this morning?"

"I didn't start balling like a baby if that's what you're asking."

"Well, it's a good thing you saved your tears. I'm sure they'll be falling fast the minute you step into your office."

My brow pulled together in confusion.

"Why is that?" I asked, glancing down the hall toward my office door.

"You'll see."

Curious, I stepped away and headed down the corridor. When I rounded the corner, I was shocked to find bouquets of dahlias everywhere. Vases of them literally covered almost every available surface, creating a sea of yellow, purple, blue, and pink. It wasn't unusual for us to get flower deliveries, dahlias in particular since it was the name of the organization. However, we never received so many at once.

"Who in the hell…" I began to ask, trailing off when I saw a note card sticking out from the bouquet in the middle of my desk. I crossed the short distance and plucked the card out from the petals.

*You once told me all colors were your favorite, so I couldn't choose just one. Instead, I chose the ones that reminded me of a sunset. I missed you this morning. I hope that wasn't your way of telling me you weren't up for going to dinner. Call me.*
*Yours, Fitz*

Without thinking, I had told Fitz last night over the phone we'd discuss dinner plans at our next morning run. However, I forgot about having to take Kallie to the airport when I said it. When I didn't show up this morning, it was only natural for him to think it was because of something he did or said. Now, as I stared at the hundreds of gorgeous dahlias that flooded my office, a million emotions swept over me—guilt for unintentionally standing him up, delight at his thoughtful gesture, and a kind of schoolgirl giddiness at his request for me to call him. As I processed it all, sadness also crept in. Tears blurred my vision as I tried rereading his words a second time. It was like he was trying to untie this string inside me. I was terrified if he pulled hard enough, I'd completely unravel. This man, the keeper of my heart, made me feel so much, and I didn't know what to do about it.

"Secret admirer?" Joy asked. Startled, I stuffed the card back into the envelope.

"I guess so," I replied, my voice hitching. I blinked, hoping to hide the tears.

She raised one very skeptical eyebrow and leaned against the door frame.

"You're a terrible liar."

I plopped down in the chair behind my desk. Shifting the bouquets to peer at Joy between the vases, I let out a shaky breath.

"Apparently, I'm a very good liar. I've been doing it for seventeen years!" I looked around at all the beautiful arrangements, fighting back the tears that wanted to spring into my eyes again.

"Honey…" Joy said softly. With just that one word, the floodgates burst open and every worry I experienced over the past two weeks came rushing forth.

"I don't know what to do, Joy!" I sobbed and began to ramble. "I don't know how to tell Fitz. I don't know how to tell Kallie. I'm still torn over selling the last part of my parent's land. I'm worried about our heavy caseload and the families who are at risk of separation. I'm stressed about our finances—or lack thereof, I should say. Then tonight, I have to go to this gala with Simon Reed, all because I stupidly asked him to go to keep Fitz at bay. Everything is a mess! I don't know anything anymore. All I know is I've been jogging with Fitz every day for nearly two weeks. I told myself it was because I was trying to get to know him again before I brought Kallie into things, but now everything is so confusing. I'm feeling things I don't want to feel for him—can't feel for him!"

Joy came over and squatted down next to my chair. Grabbing the box of tissue that must have been hiding somewhere within the gale of flowers, she handed it to me.

"You asked Simon Reed to the gala?"

"Of all the things I said, you picked up on that most?" I asked incredulously, hiccupping through a sob.

"Forget about Simon. Although I really hope for your sake he doesn't own an argyle tuxedo."

I laughed through the tears.

"Knowing my luck, he probably does!"

"Just breathe. Everything will be fine," she tried to reassure. She held up a hand and began ticking things off on her fingers. "Let's back it up one step at a time. Kallie is in Montreal for the next week, so you don't have to worry about telling her right away. The Austin thing seems to be sorted out, so no worries there. Our caseload will get easier in a few weeks when Victoria gets back from maternity leave. As for the families, that worry will always be there as long as there are immigrants in this country. You can't make yourself sick over it. Only focus on what's within your power. The money situation is fine. I literally just read an email from the publisher. *And I Smile* drops on Tuesday, and presale numbers show it's on track to hit the *New York Times* list. No need to sell your parents' land right now."

I peeked at her over the tissue I held to my nose.

"It is?"

"Yes. So relax. The only thing you truly need to worry about right now is Fitz. Telling him about Kallie is important, but I think you need to sort out whatever these feelings are you're having for him first. Tell me, what's going on in that big heart of yours?"

"It's hard to explain, Joy. It's almost like we picked up where we left off, yet it's so very different. He makes me mixed up inside. He remembers things, little things that should have been insignificant, yet he remembers them all the same." I paused and handed her the note card for her to read. "He called me last night. It was right before you showed up at the house."

"Is that why you were out in the backyard?"

"Yes."

"I knew something was off when you came in. What did he say?"

"He wants to talk about things, about meeting his son in particular. I nearly laughed, having already met the kid! What kind of person does that make me? Then he tells me he never got over me, and thought about me even when he was married. I should have found it appalling, but I was thrilled!" I practically shrieked. "So you see? I'm a terrible monster!"

As a fresh wave of sobs wracked my body, Joy started to laugh.

"You're not a monster. You're human is all."

"He asked me out to dinner."

"You said yes, right?"

"No…ah, yes. Kind of, I guess. I don't remember now. See? I told you he was messing with my brain!"

"Oh, honey. You are one hot mess," she said with a chuckle. "Get yourself together. Go to dinner with the man. Allow yourself a minute to feel, explore this thing going on with you two, and see what happens."

"But don't you think that will make things worse? It's one thing for me to have feelings for him again, but I can't very well let him have the same for me while I'm holding onto such a big secret."

"I think it's too late for that. I mean, look at all these flowers, girl! The guy is obviously already head over heels for you. If Fitz is worth his salt, he'll understand once you explain why you did what you did. It probably won't be easy at first, but I'm confident if he meets Kallie, whatever hard feelings he might have will disappear."

"What about his father?" I asked, suddenly remembering a huge potential obstacle. "I'm worried about that too. Not only do I lack elite social status, I'm speaking tonight at a gala fundraiser where I'll be mingling with politicians who vote against his anti-immigration proposals."

Joy nodded, her expression somber.

"That could complicate things. However, that's politics. This is personal."

"Politics are personal, Joy. You know that. Your favorite President said it," I pointed out.

"I'm trying to say what's between you and Fitz has nothing to do with your beef with Washington. Cut the crap and stop looking for excuses. I think you're ready for more than you're willing to admit. I also think you're a lot stronger than you give yourself credit for. Go to dinner and enjoy yourself. I mean, look around you! These flowers had to cost a fortune. I highly doubt a man like Fitz will take you to the Capital Burger. Let yourself be wined and dined. You never know where it's going to lead."

I glanced around the room at the abundance of dahlias, overwhelmed by the sheer number of them.

"That's exactly what I'm afraid of," I whispered.

I knew where it would lead. I'd most likely get distracted from telling him the truth, too busy getting lost in the endless depths of his beautiful gray eyes. After the way he kissed me last week, with all that power and dominance, I learned exactly how weak I was when it came to him. However, my heart didn't have room for more breaking. I had barely recovered the first time. Joy was wrong about my strength. I didn't have it in me to withstand a second broken heart. My body wanted him something fierce—the physical attraction so strong, I ached—but I wasn't emotionally ready to end up in his bed, assuming that's where things led to. Not to mention, I couldn't allow that to happen while he was still in the dark about Kallie. The problem was, I knew if faced with the choice, I wouldn't be able to stop it.

# Chapter Thirteen

**FITZ**

I struggled to shake off the foul mood I was in as I walked into my father's house in Highland, Maryland. Cadence hadn't shown up for what was quickly becoming our routine morning run. I worried my call to her last night had scared her off and could only hope the flowers I sent would make up for anything I might have said wrong. However, as much as I wanted to track her down, I couldn't at the moment. I needed to focus on this meeting with the committee members from the RNC.

My father—in an attempt to make up for my absence at the last meeting—rescheduled it to be in his own home. It was rare for my father to host anything, he was usually too selfish to be bothered. However, when he did host something, no expense was spared. As I walked across the oriental rug in the foyer, I spotted my father's housekeeper coming down the stairs. Her hair was swept up into her usual tight bun, looking slightly grayer than I'd remembered. She was holding a feather duster in her hand, and she beamed when she saw me.

"Afternoon, Rhonda."

"Boy, where've you been? I haven't seen you in ages!"

Hurrying over, she wrapped her slender arms around me, her familiar scent filling my nose. It was a combination of lemon Pine-sol and cherry pie, reminiscent of my time growing up in this house. Rhonda had been the one to tuck me into bed and pack my school lunches. She'd bandaged my knees when I'd fallen off a skateboard and cried when I went away to college. She'd been my anchor and the only good thing about living here. I felt guilty not coming to see her more often. The truth was, in an attempt to avoid my father, I hadn't stepped foot in this house in nearly two years.

"I'm sorry I haven't been around, Rhonda. Work has kept me busy."

Her kind brown eyes were soft when she pulled away. She just smiled at me again, allowing me to have my lie.

"Well, it's good to see you again finally. All the men are already in the dining room. I trust you remember the way?"

"I do, thanks."

I didn't promise to visit more often. She knew I wouldn't and understood the reasons. However, I made a mental note to invite her over for dinner in the near future.

As I made my way to the dining room, I smelled the aroma of garlic and thyme wafting from the kitchen. I suspected a top D.C. chef had been hired for the occasion. Still, when I walked into the dining room, I barely noticed the silver plates and sparkling crystal goblets spread across the long mahogany dining table. I was too busy looking at the people who sat around it.

Thomas Hagel, Rick Thurmond, Fred Gramm, James Helms, and my father sat around the table. Despite the early hour of the afternoon, they'd already been into the scotch. However, I noticed their glasses were practically down to the rocks. I glanced at my watch. It was going on one o'clock, the exact time I was told to arrive. Clearly, they had started well before I got there. That fact rattled me a bit, but I shook off the apprehension.

"Gentlemen," I said with a slight nod, refusing to show an ounce of intimidation.

I did the formalities and went around the table to shake each man's hand.

"Fitzgerald, it's been a while. We're looking forward to this campaign. Your father has said great things about you," Hagel said.

*Funny, he's never said them to me.*

The words were on the tip of my tongue, but I just smiled and moved on to the next person. I recognized many of the men from various functions in support of my father. I was young at the time, and more often than not, I got a pat on the head as they showed obligatory tolerance for a child they knew was only there to help sway the voters. Now, I was a grown man, and they were all pushing seventy, some even older. No females were present, but that was typical. My father tended only to surround himself with the good ole boys club.

I sat down, and my father's staff began to bring out the food. The committee leaders began to talk about potential campaign strategies, and what *they* thought should be the most important things for my agenda.

I quietly listened, hardly enjoying the lobster frittata the chef had prepared for lunch. It wasn't that the food didn't taste good, but more because I was too engrossed in their convoluted ideas about how the country should be run. It was a joke. They were so far behind the times, it was actually sad. My youth might actually give me the upper hand in this charade. The Party needed a drastic change. And if it meant it had to start with me, so be it. When they brought up immigration reform, I finally spoke up.

"I understand your concerns about border security. What I don't understand are the reasons you're all so eager to kick out the people already here—especially if they are contributing members of society. Every person in this country is more interlaced than ever before, yet we're still divided. Have you forgotten this country was founded on immigrants?" I asked pointedly, looking directly at my father. It was a bold move, but I didn't break my stare, almost daring him to challenge me in front of the other men. "The people you're going after came here as infants and children who didn't have a choice. I think uprooting them from everything they know is inhumane. I won't support that, nor will I agree to use it as a campaign talking point to get votes."

The room fell silent and my father's face turned red. Every person in the room supported my father's attempt at dismantling DACA. Thanks to Cadence, I knew all of this from the research I'd done. However, based on what I'd heard today, my father had only just gotten started.

It was Thurmond who broke the silence first by clearing his throat.

"Well, perhaps that's not the right campaign platform for you. We shouldn't have assumed that just because your father…" He trailed off with an awkward laugh, his bushy eyebrows giving him the appearance of constant annoyance. "There are plenty of other options to choose from. There's tax code reform, voting system standards..."

I tuned him out, zeroing in on my father's expression. The vein in his neck pulsed, and his gaze was piercing and cold, but I didn't back down. Through the remainder of the meal, the two of us seemed to have this silent power exchange—me telling him I wouldn't be his puppet while his eyes shot daggers coated with bloody threats.

After dessert was served, the conversation turned to the official campaign kickoff party and advertising strategies. I paid close attention to this part since not one person here seemed to realize I hadn't even said yes to running.

"We have the kickoff party already planned," Helms explained. "It'll be held two weeks from today on the rooftop of the Marine Gate Hotel. We'll start with your formal announcement. After that, cocktails and hors d'oeuvres. During this time, you'll need to connect with lobbyists, high ranking union officials, and private campaign donors. We'll be there to help of course, but all eyes will be on you. We've hired a couple of speechwriters who worked for the second Bush administration. Once we draft talking points for you, we're confident the cash will flow in. We don't have a lot of time to work with here, so we're going to need the funds for the aggressive television and radio campaign we have planned."

I held my hands up, signaling him to stop. This was all getting to be way too much.

"Alright, we need to slow down here. If I'm going to do this—and that's a really big if—I'm going to do it my way." Many eyes widened in surprise, but I continued. "TV ads and mailers will only go so far. I work in PR, remember? Image is everything. A flyer doesn't show personal investment. I'd want to give voters that in-person connection. I'd want people canvassing neighborhoods and not just for 'knock' count. I've been around my father's campaigns long enough to know the drill. Campaign operatives who rush through neighborhoods, hurrying to rack up an impressive number of knocks get nowhere. You won't reach voters that way. Real conversations will."

Gramm, who had been silent almost the entire meal, piped up.

"Sounds like a great concept, but your inexperience is showing. Do you know what that takes? First of all, there isn't time for a boots-on-the-ground style campaign. Secondly, there's a lot of strategy involved. We've got to come up with scripts to ensure the conversation isn't awkward. We'd need to facilitate training, hire supervisors. It's too monumental a task to put together in a short amount of time."

I shrugged.

"If you want me, you'll make it happen."

His laugh was almost condescending as he shook his head and continued.

"I don't think you understand how things work around here. If you do things our way, you'll find your opportunities can be quite lucrative."

"I'm not following you," I said cautiously.

They all looked at one another like they had a secret I wasn't privy to. Finally, my father spoke up.

"Tell him, Gramm," he said. Then he glanced at me with a smug expression, signaling he was getting ready to throw his ace on the table.

I looked back at Gramm who leaned back in his seat, running one hand over his round, overstuffed belly while the other fiddled with the end of his gray mustache. His eyes narrowed on me like he was assessing whether I was trustworthy. I wasn't intimidated, but I had to admit there was something sinister about him that made my skin crawl.

"The RNC has been hacked," he began. "It's not public knowledge yet. We're still investigating it and are looking to hire a PR firm to deal with the news once it breaks."

"What kind of hack?"

"Emails of top-ranking members. Cybersecurity was alerted to the breach four months ago as was the FBI."

"Four months ago? And nobody else knows about this yet?"

"We're trying to keep the hack quiet for as long as possible. We don't want public scrutiny to compromise the investigation and possibly sway the election," Gramm explained. "However, reporters have begun to sniff around. It will only be a matter of time before they draw some far-fetched conclusion that a foreign body is trying to influence the election."

I raised an eyebrow.

"Is that the case?"

Gramm just smiled, but there was something disturbing about it.

"The RNC is prepared to pay five hundred thousand dollars to the PR agency that takes on the mess," he told me, rather than answer my question. "If all goes well, another two hundred fifty thousand will be given as a bonus. So you see, Fitzgerald, cooperating with us can prove to be very beneficial to you."

I looked back at my father, disgusted by how little the man actually knew me. When he couldn't persuade me by threatening Austin and my reputation, he thought offering to buy me would secure the commitment he needed.

"Three quarters of a mil, you say? Well, I've got news for you. I won't be bought," I told them, ensuring I made eye contact with every man at the table. Standing, I tossed my napkin on the seat of my chair. "I get to choose my platform and campaign promises. I'll also want to be kept apprised of all advertising strategies. There won't be any smear campaigns on my watch. If you're good with all of that, I'll be at the kickoff party to make my formal announcement to run. If you're not good with it, you have until then to find a replacement. Gentlemen, I'd like to say it's been a pleasure, but I think illuminating is a better word to describe this meeting."

With that, I turned and walked out of the room, not stopping until I reached the Audi and was seated in the driver's seat. I gripped the wheel in an attempt to stop the angry tremors coursing through me. If I weren't in the room to hear what they had to say, I almost wouldn't have believed it myself. Every single suspicion I'd ever had about D.C. politicians had come to fruition in under two hours' time. Slamming my head back against the seat, I swore quietly to myself.

"Fuck! What the hell have I gotten myself into?"

I could only imagine their reaction once they found out I was in attendance at the Helping Lives Bloom fundraiser tonight. I supposed I could make up some bullshit excuse about trying to scope out the competition, but the explanation would be weak at best. They'd never buy it. At the end of the day, I knew I wasn't cut out to play their games. The whole thing was nothing but a goddammed circus orchestrated to get the votes they needed to push their agendas. They mercilessly exploited the working class while sleeping all fucking cozy in their beds purchased with inherited money. It was sickening.

If I truly wanted to make some sort of difference in the country, I'd never do it as long as I was saddled with this lot. Independent might be the only way to go, but there wasn't time to launch into a campaign like that now. I didn't have the power, nor did I have the political backing. Hell, I still wasn't even convinced this was how I wanted to go about things. If I wanted to make an impact, there were plenty of other ways I could do it. For now, I would just have to wait and see where the chips fell.

# Chapter Fourteen

## CADENCE

As I stepped off the stage at the Helping Lives Bloom fundraiser, the crowd was still applauding. I ducked my head to hide my blush, moved by their reaction to my speech. Public speaking was never part of my comfort zone. All I did was speak from the heart, recapping stories of the families who Dahlia's Dreamers had helped. I didn't deserve their applause as much as the families who survived devastating heartbreak did.

"You killed it, girl!" Joy said as I approached her and Simon Reed. She wrapped her arms around my shoulders in a congratulatory hug.

"I agree. If donors don't open up their wallets after that, I'll be surprised," Simon said.

As I was about to offer my thanks, Simon leaned in for his own hug. I stiffened, feeling unnecessarily uncomfortable with the quick embrace. I had hugged Simon many times in the past, more often after we scored a big win in court. But today, it felt different. Perhaps it was the flowers he'd given me when he picked me up before the gala. Roses. I hated roses. It had been an awkward moment, and I hoped to hell he didn't view our being here together as an actual date.

"Thanks, Simon," I said, taking a compromising step back when it seemed like he wanted to hang on a little too long. I glanced over at the computerized flower filling the large projector screen on the wall. The stem was lit green to the bottom leaf. The goal was to raise enough money throughout the night so the flower's head would bloom. "Ann Marie from Families United is supposed to speak next. Hopefully, she'll get us to the next leaf. The sooner that flower blossoms into color, the sooner I can relax."

"The really hard part is over. At least now you can grab a drink and mingle," Joy said, holding up her apple martini. "You've got catching up to do!"

"Good idea. I'll go grab us something," Simon offered as he pushed up the wire rimmed eyeglasses that always seemed to be slipping down his nose. "What would you like?"

I contemplated what I wanted to drink and glanced down at my dress. I supposed I wouldn't look very classy holding a beer bottle while wearing a black evening gown. Spaghetti straps and rhinestones just didn't seem to jive all that well with Budweiser.

"I'll have what Joy's having," I told him.

"One apple martini coming right up!"

As Simon walked away, I turned to Joy.

"You need to save me," I pleaded. "I think Simon thinks we're here as more than friends."

"Paisley bowtie isn't doing it for you, huh?" Joy laughed. "He'd have to be dead not to want something more. Have you looked in a mirror today? You look amazing!"

"Right," I said and rolled my eyes. "With the expense of Kallie's French trip and the tuition bill due, I couldn't spring for a new dress. This was the only suitable thing I had. My closet mostly consists of power suits and yoga pants."

"Either way, I don't think Simon cares if your dress is old or new. But I think you're right about him, he's been standing a little too close to you. If you want saving, I have an idea." She turned and pointed to the left corner of the room. "Marissa is over there talking to John Hasting from McGann and Hasting's Law Firm. Simon's been trying to get in there for years. If I have her make introductions, I guarantee he'll be out of your hair for the rest of the night."

"You're a life saver!"

I glanced around the ballroom and thought about the guest list, looking for potential donors who I had to try to connect with throughout the night. While I looked, I couldn't help taking in the elegance of both the crowd and the room. Chandeliers sparkled in the dim lighting of the room. Round tables were spaced across the floor, with ivory tablecloths and centerpieces of glittering flowers and scrolling vines. This event, hosted by Dahlia's Dreamers and four other non-profits, was the first of its kind. We split the cost of hiring an event planner as none of us had the experience to put on a gala. The hope was to raise money for our organizations as all of us had taken a big hit when our Federal funding was slashed.

A lot of time went into the planning—and a lot of money too. I worried we wouldn't get people to buy the expensive tickets, but the event planner assured me our ticket prices were in line with other similar fundraisers. From the size of the crowd alone, it was obvious the planner knew what they were doing.

As I scanned the large space, the hired band began to warm up, preparing to entertain guests between the planned speeches. I noticed a few members of Congress in attendance who were on our side. That made me happy to see. We needed their support now more than ever. I made a mental note to thank them at some point during the night.

My eyes continued to roam until I was suddenly overcome with the feeling of being watched. I could feel it blazing from somewhere on the other side of the room. It was like a pulsing energy that was all too familiar. I should have known better than to look, but there was nothing I could have done to stop myself. For some reason, I knew who I'd discover standing there. I turned to face the blistering heat, and my mouth dropped open in a sharp gasp. All that energy crashed like the flares of the sun, searing as the flames licked my skin.

*What was he doing here?*

My legs seemed to wobble on my four-inch heels. My hand shot out to clutch Joy's arm, bracing myself so I didn't fall. Joy grabbed my hand and searched my face.

"Honey, what's wrong?"

The words seemed to lodge in my throat and I felt starved for oxygen as my gaze locked on the man who stood across the room. I cleared my throat and turned my back to him.

"He's here," I whispered.

"Who?" she asked, scanning the crowd of people.

"Fitz."

"Are you freaking kidding me?" she hissed. Her stylish braided updo bobbed when she turned back to me. "Where is he?"

I pointed in a general direction over my right shoulder. She looked behind me for a few moments before recognition flashed across her face. I wanted the floor to reach up and swallow me whole. It wasn't because I didn't want to see him—it was because I *couldn't* see him. Not here. I had a job to do. Networking with donors needed to be my focus, and I knew his presence would be a distraction I might not be able to keep at bay.

"God, Joy. I can't have this right now. Not tonight."

"What do you need me to do? Do you want me to tell him to leave?"

"No. Just let it be. I'll... I'll figure something out."

"Good. Because girl, if I were batting for the same team as you, I'd be hightailing it right over there. That's one fine specimen of a man. He makes Chris Evans look like a troll."

I turned around to look at Fitz again, but Simon stepped in front of me, blocking my view. He held up a martini glass filled with pretty green liquid and a flower topped stir stick.

"Oh, um…" I faltered, having already forgotten he'd gone to get a drink for me. "Thanks."

"Simon," Joy said, linking her arm through his. "My wife is over there talking to someone who I'm sure you'd like to meet." She pointed toward Marissa and Simon followed the line of her finger. When he spotted John Hasting, his face lit up. Joy winked at me.

"Oh, you definitely need to talk to him," I gushed, hoping I didn't sound too obvious.

"Aren't you going to come with us?" Simon asked.

"Oh, no. You go on with Joy. I have some people I need to catch up with."

He seemed conflicted, but only for the briefest of moments before he and Joy walked off. Breathing a sigh of relief, I looked back to the place I'd seen Fitz. Deciding to confront the situation head on, I moved in his direction. I didn't think he had spotted me yet. If he did, he was making a good show of pretending otherwise. He didn't appear to be here with anyone and looked like he was trying to find someone. The young girl in me wanted to believe he was looking for me, but the grown woman in me knew better than to get my hopes up.

I was used to seeing Fitz dressed casually in a t-shirt and shorts. Today, he had traded the look for a fitted, expensive black tuxedo over a crisp white shirt and platinum tie. He looked so different wearing it, appearing even more broad shouldered than usual. His casual hair was styled in a sophisticated way around his gorgeous face, accentuating his strong jaw and prominent cheekbones. A shiver ran down my spine at the sight of him.

When he turned his head, I knew the moment he saw me. His eyes locked on mine. I felt pinned beneath them and had to remember to put one foot in front of the other. His lips curved into a smile so gorgeous and plush and made for kissing. I suddenly found it hard to swallow. A flash of the old love I once felt for him ricocheted in the depths of my heart. It was a love I convinced myself I had given up on, knowing that waiting for him to come back to me would cause me to lose myself completely. Yet here he stood, appearing taller, broader, older. It made my heart flutter. He watched me as if he knew what I was thinking, his expression full of something dangerous, possessive, and alive.

All of those things combined with a young girl's emotions only made him that much more appealing. I wondered if that appeal was messing with my brain, or if what was quickly building between us was so much bigger.

# Chapter Fifteen

**FITZ**

Since the moment I met her, she always had the power to drop me straight to my knees. Time hadn't altered that. She was so stunning, I went stupid, a reaction I seemed to have whenever she was around.

Tonight, her golden hair was styled in loose curls, allowing it to cascade down her back in silky waves. Even from where I stood, I would swear I could feel the warmth emitting from her very essence. She moved with devastating graciousness combined with a body wrapped in a silky black dress meant for sin. Those tempting curves had been my sin once upon a time. Taking her, then leaving her had been the biggest mistake of my life. Nevertheless, here I was again, feeling that same intense lust overtake me. It was so forceful, it made me dizzy.

I sucked down a breath and took a few steps toward her, closing the remaining distance between us.

"Small world," I remarked with an impish smile. I took her hand and brought it up to softly brush my lips over her delicate fingers.

"Small world indeed. It's funny, I didn't see your name on the guest list," she noted, eyeing me suspiciously. My hand migrated to her wrist, giving it a subtle squeeze before releasing her.

"That's because I wanted to surprise you. Did it work?"

"Oh, it worked alright. Thank you for the flowers by the way."

"You're very welcome."

"They're beautiful, but next time, I think just one bouquet will get your point across," she noted, her perfect lips slightly tilting up in a demure smile. Turning her head, she surveyed the room. "I didn't think this was your kind of crowd."

"Maybe it is, maybe it isn't. God knows, I'm going to be in a world of trouble for being here tonight," I admitted with a light laugh.

She cocked her head to the side, emerald eyes sparkling with curiosity.

"Why is that?"

"I had a meeting with the RNC today about taking a shot at the Senate seat. I'm not sure if I'm going to do it yet. Their agenda leaves a lot to be desired and I told them as much. I'm sure my being here tonight will only add to the uphill battle I could potentially have," I added warily.

"So, then why come?"

"I wanted to see you," I answered matter-of-factly before glancing up at the stage. The band had finished their warm up and struck up their first song. I took the glass Cadence was holding and placed it on an empty tray that passed by. With an exaggerated bow and a teasing wink, I said, "Please allow me the honor of the first dance, my lady."

She giggled—like actually fucking giggled. The sound reminded me of our days at Camp Riley when she'd been so carefree and innocent—when she'd been mine.

"I'm sorry, Fitz. I can't. While the band is playing, I need to be on the floor talking to donors. They'll play for thirty minutes, then we'll break for our next speaker. Do you see that big flower over there?" she asked, pointing to a wall-sized flat screen television. "I need to make it bloom. I can't do that if I spend all night dancing with you."

"Just one dance," I insisted, wrapping my arm around her waist and leading her to the dance floor anyway.

"Fitz…" she warned. I chuckled and pulled her against me just as the band's female vocalist began to sing. Splaying my palm firmly against her lower back, I guided her into a slow dance.

"You look beautiful tonight, sweetheart."

She blushed but tried to conceal it with a roll of her eyes.

"Stop that," she scolded.

"So, where's your date?" I asked, not bothering to hide the hint of jealousy that crept into my voice.

"Simon? Oh, he's off with Joy talking to some fancy law firm," she waved off.

That was good to know. Her date was a fool as far as I was concerned. If I had brought her here, I wouldn't have let her out of my sight. But that was okay. His loss turned into my good fortune.

"So, tell me, what's Simon to you? Colonel Brandon or John Willoughby?"

She jerked her head back in surprise.

"Oh, well…neither I guess," she faltered, blinking in confusion. "He's just a friend. He does a lot of pro-bono work for us. Why?"

"I was only wondering. I have to know my competition, that's all. You used to say I was like a little of both, Brandon and Willoughby that is. Is that how you still see me?"

"Fitz, those are just characters in a story. It's not real life. Besides, what I said back then was nonsense and nothing more than ramblings from a teenager girl."

Her body moved with mine to the music as I led her around the dance floor. Our feet shuffled in time effortlessly as if she were made to be dancing in my arms.

"I don't agree. You see, I've thought about the characters and I think I've gotten to know them pretty well. I think if we crossed storylines, say *Wuthering Heights* with *Sense and Sensibility*, the two of us are more like Heathcliff and Elizabeth Bennet."

"What? You can't cross stories like that! It's preposterous. And don't you dare mess with Colonel Brandon. He's good and steady, and—" She stopped short when I started to laugh.

"I love when you get all literary. It's good to know that hasn't changed."

She started to say something, but then a look of incredulity suddenly crossed her face.

"Wait a minute. Are you telling me you actually read those books?"

I chuckled again and pulled her tighter against me, not caring about who was watching—including the asshole named Simon. I leaned in close to whisper in her ear.

"I've read every single one."

I felt the shiver run down her body and grinned in satisfaction, knowing I was getting to her and breaking down those walls she tried so hard to hold up.

"Why did you read them?" she asked, a hint of disbelief still in her tone.

"Honestly? I read them because they reminded me of you during the lowest time in my life. Not to bring up ancient history but being married to Bethany wasn't a walk in the park." I saw her flinch but continued, needing her to know exactly how much I thought of her over the years. "She was a raging alcoholic, always out partying. She was a terrible mother, choosing to get completely annihilated with booze or pills instead of taking care of her own son. When she was out trying to find the next good time, I was home with Austin. His colic was bad. Rocking him was the only thing that seemed to calm him, so that's what I did for hours on end every evening. I took to reading to pass the time. Those stories you always talked about weren't necessarily my preference in genre, but they brought me solace when I needed it most. They always brought me back to you."

I watched her as we moved ever so slowly across the dance floor, the beat of the music somehow matching the beat of my heart. Her expression went from astonishment, to hopeful, to sadness all in a split second, but then I saw regret.

"Why did your wife die, Fitz?"

"Car accident. She was wasted, drunk and high on whatever poison she decided to put into her body that night. She hit a telephone pole head on. Died instantly."

Shock registered on her face.

"Oh my gosh, I'm so sorry."

"Don't be. As bad as it sounds, her death was the best thing that could have happened to me and Austin," I shrugged off, speaking words that couldn't have been truer.

"Did you ever love her?" she asked hesitantly.

I paused at that, afraid of her judgment if she knew the truth. I wondered if she'd think I was a monster if I said I never loved my wife, the woman who gave birth to my son. I'd never felt anything for Bethany other than disgust.

"Would you think I was a bad person if I said no?"

"I think you were put into an impossible situation. I don't think you'd be a bad person for not loving her."

"Well, I didn't. Not even a little bit," I admitted. I hesitated, not sure how she would take my next statement. "It was always you, Cadence. Just you."

As if on a cue, the band changed songs and a male vocalist took the mic. I instantly recognized the steady drumbeat and synthesizer as it rippled across the room. A high, sustained guitar was soon followed by the lyrics to *With or Without You* by U2.

I looked down at Cadence, studying her face. Her eyes were wide and glassy. She blinked rapidly, almost as if she were fighting back tears.

"That was one dance, Fitz. Thank you, but I have to go now," she all but whispered and pulled away.

"Wait," I said, reaching out to her. She didn't pull away again but let me guide her slowly back into my arms.

"Just one more," she whispered the warning like she didn't really mean it. She knew what I was feeling—she felt it too.

The moment, the song, it was all too real. It brought me back to another time and another place. It was reminiscent of all we once shared together—the sunsets, the slow and tender touches, the mixed tapes we listened to for hours on end. Even the smell of her was the same— that vanilla scent I'd never forget. A lump formed in my throat, and I swallowed it back, wanting to beat myself for wasting so much time. Too many years had passed.

"Do you know how many times I thought about finding you? I went to your parents' house once. It was right after Bethany died. Your father answered the door. I begged him to tell me where you were, but he said I'd had my shot. He told me you were happy and had moved on with your life."

She sucked in a sharp breath.

"I never knew."

"I left the house thinking it was for the best. I was trying to deal with the mess Bethany left behind, my business, and Austin. I wasn't in the right frame of mind. Years passed and I tried to forget you. It didn't work. I never should have left you in the first place. I've spent my whole life regretting that decision, but you have to know I'm not the same man I was then. I was twenty-two years old with more baggage than I knew how to carry."

"Shhh…please don't. I can't. Don't ruin this moment by talking about the past."

We fell silent and moved to the music, her body moving with ease against mine. The song began to come to a close all too soon, and I didn't want to let her go. When she began to pull away for a second time, I didn't hold her back. She had a job to do and it was wrong of me to get in her way.

"U2 revived the *Joshua Tree* tour," I said offhandedly, trying to break the intensity in the air. "They're playing FedEx Field. I should see about getting tickets for us."

"Yeah, maybe," she said so quietly, I barely heard her over the final guitar riff from the song. She took another step back. "That was two dances, Fitz. I really need to go work on lighting up that flower."

She stared at me for a beat, her expression unreadable. Then without another word, she turned and walked away.

I must have stood there like a fool for another three minutes at least, stunned by the connection I still had to this woman. I shouldn't have been surprised. It had always been there, but now it was burning brighter than the sun. I shook my head, forced myself to leave the dance floor, and made my way over to the bar. I needed a fucking drink.

After ordering a Jamison's neat, I scanned the crowd until I spotted Cadence. I watched her work the crowd for a while, completely in awe of her ability to move efficiently around the expansive ballroom, never lingering too long with one guest before moving on to the next. She was beautiful—the whole package—and not just in appearance. It was her whole persona and the way she presented herself. There was so much goodness in her, and I wondered if she even knew it. I always saw greatness in her, and tonight was proof.

The music stopped, and another speaker took the stage, but I barely heard a word of the speech. I was too focused on watching Cadence. I never wanted her more than I did right then, to feel her pressed against me in another dance. I recalled the feeling of her tight little body, the way she moved with me in time to the music, and I began to envision more. Being with her again. Inside her. Hearing her scream my name. I could almost picture her just as she was that summer, eyes wide with startled desire. I wanted to see that look on her face now, but this time as a grown woman.

I looked up at the flower on the flat screen. The stem was completely lit, the lights just barely grazing the petals. The sooner the flower bloomed, the sooner I could have Cadence all to myself.

On impulse, I headed over to the area where workers were accepting donations.

"How much more do you need to make that thing light up?" I asked the young girl behind the table. She looked down at her computer screen, then back up at me.

"Only thirty-eight thousand more to go!" she announced cheerfully. "Would you like to make a donation? You can do it right here or we have a website set up where you can donate anonymously right through your smartphone."

"Does the website take credit cards?"

# Chapter Sixteen

**CADENCE**

The entire ballroom erupted into cheers, causing me to pause the conversation I was having with Tyler Mansfield, the hopeful candidate for Maryland's second district. I turned around to see what the commotion was all about and saw the donation flower had bloomed. Bright pink, blue, and yellow petals lit up the flat screen to illuminate the entire room.

"Congratulations, Ms. Riley!" Tyler said. I looked back at him, my mouth turning up in an ear-splitting grin.

"Thank you!"

"I guess you don't need my donation after all."

"It's funny you should say that. You see, I was just speaking with Erin Brooks from the California Teachers Association. Word is, national support will go to all candidates who step up to protect students who are impacted by the recent DACA changes. You do realize that Learn to Dream is one of the non-profits to benefit from tonight, right?" I hinted.

He offered me a wry smile.

"Alright. You've made your point," he chuckled. "I'm going over to the donation table right now."

I laughed as he walked away but startled when I heard a loud shriek from behind me.

"Ah! You did it!" Joy exclaimed. I turned toward the sound of her voice. She and Marissa were coming up to me with glasses of champagne. I looked behind them. To my relief, Simon was still talking to the associates from McGann and Hasting's.

"No, *we* did it," I laughed. "Can you believe it? It's barely eight o'clock!"

"I was just over at the donation table," Marissa chimed in. "Apparently, an anonymous donor came through and brought the team to the final goal."

"You've got to be kidding me! Wow! And here I was worried about the expense of tonight!" I shook my head in disbelief and accepted the offered glass, holding it out in a toast. "Cheers to a successful event and many more after!"

The three of us clinked glasses. After taking a sip, I scanned the room for the heads of my partner organizations in this endeavor. They were gathered with their staff in celebration as well. I smiled to myself, thinking of all the people and families we'd now be able to help.

*Today is a good day.*

The band took the stage for another set, this time starting out with an upbeat tune to match the excitement of the crowd.

"Now that your work is complete, I believe you have more time for dancing," said a low voice from behind me. I slowly turned to meet the intense gray eyes I'd felt on me all night.

I glanced at Joy. Both she and Marissa were watching me with knowing looks.

"What are you waiting for, girl? You earned it. Go dance!" Marissa told me as she pulled Joy by the hand toward the dancefloor.

I looked back at Fitz and smiled, feeling overcome with excitement from the jubilation that emitted throughout the room.

"You heard the lady. Apparently, I earned it!"

Not needing further encouragement, he grabbed me by the arm and twirled me out onto the floor with the other dancers.

Another hour passed in what only seemed like five minutes. We danced and talked, our conversation jumping from one topic to the next. Some dances were fast while others were slow, but the slow dances were different from the first two we shared. There was this buzz in the air that made it seem like everything had a sexual undertone. Fitz hadn't lost his playful side. His flirtations were deliberate as were his hands which shamelessly roamed over my back and hips. He made all the little hairs on my body stand on end, and my nipples went painfully hard every time I pressed against him. With only a single look from him, my body seemed to hum to life.

After a while, we both needed a break and decided to head over to the bar. Once our drinks came, Fitz turned to me and leaned in close to my ear.

"Room twelve-ten. Fifteen minutes," he whispered. Then he pressed a plastic card to my palm before leaving me alone and slack-jawed with a keycard to a hotel room in my hand.

As I stared down at the black plastic, my heart thudded loudly in my ears. I wasn't naïve. I knew what the invitation meant without him even saying it.

*Oh God. No. I can't do this.*

I still had too many secrets. While I managed to bury them for a little while tonight, I couldn't take that next step with Fitz. He had no idea. He probably thought we were rekindling an old flame. Little did he know it was so much more. If I went to his room, if I slept with him before he knew the truth, he'd hate me and think I was nothing but a liar. In a way, I was.

Overwhelming panic consumed me. I searched the room for Joy. I needed my friend, my sounding board to help me work through this and hold me up in the way she always had. I spotted her with Marissa, the two of them line dancing to a cover song of Shakira's.

*Shit!*

I didn't want to interrupt their fun for my self-imposed drama. I took a long swig of apple martini number two. I wasn't a big drinker, so having already consumed a martini and a couple of glasses of champagne, this one was going straight to my head. I set the glass down on the bar, knowing I needed a clear head to work through this.

Tonight had been fun with Fitz, but I was flirting with danger and couldn't shake the overwhelming feeling of dread. Things had shifted so fast with us, and I had to put it in perspective. I needed to stop this before I got to a point of no return—I feared I already had. A part of my soul told me no attempt on my part would be able to stop the avalanche of emotions sure to ensue. There was no easy way to tell him about Kallie. I was terrified I wouldn't tell him the right way, or I'd say the wrong thing and risk losing him forever. My heart broke at the thought.

After ten minutes of indecision, I knew what I had to do. I couldn't hide from the truth anymore. Stepping onto the dancefloor, I made my way over to Joy and tapped her on the shoulder. Turning toward me, she leaned in so she could hear me over the music.

"Can you cover for me?" I asked. "Tell Simon something came up and I had to leave."

"Sure, but where are you going?"

"To talk to Fitz."

"Good, I'm glad. The two of you left so much unfinished, Cadence."

"Yeah, we did," I admitted sadly and looked down to stare absently at the way the strobe lights glinted off the toes of my silver heels.

"Hey, look at me," she said, lifting my chin to meet her gaze. "I've been your friend for a long time. Trust me when I say he needs to know how you feel. This is bigger than just your secret about Kallie. After watching you dance with him tonight, you owe it to yourself to find out what's going on between you two."

"No, Joy. I'm not going to talk about my feelings," I told her sadly. "It's time for me to come clean. About everything."

---

My hands trembled as I fumbled to insert the keycard into the slot of the hotel room door. My chest ached with a heavy feeling I couldn't shake, knowing I was about to do the hardest thing I'd ever done in my life. Nerves gripped me as I pushed the door open, the shaking in my hands taking over my entire being.

When I entered, I found more than just the average hotel room. He had reserved a suite, complete with a sitting area, dining room, and separate bedroom. Music played softly in the background. Fitz stood near the couch, filling the space with everything him. He'd removed his tuxedo jacket, leaving it tossed haphazardly on the back of a settee. His tie was loosened at the neck, and one hand rested in the pocket of his pants while the other ran anxiously through his gorgeous dark hair. His presence pummeled me, so powerful and raw, and energy seemed to crawl the walls.

Hesitation was evident in his eyes as he took me in, but there was also desire.

"I'm glad you came," he said huskily.

Memories—flashes of another time—ricocheted through the depths of my being, causing a shiver to race down my spine. I could see the lake, candles and dahlias on the dock, a young Fitz looking nervous and apologetic. I forced myself to blink it all away and took a step forward. Struggling to gather myself, I tried to find the courage for what I needed to do.

"Fitz, we need to talk about some things."

"And we can. Over strawberries and cream."

My brow creased in confusion until I looked down at the coffee table in front of the sofa. An entire platter of strawberries had been set out, each one artfully arranged to surround a bowl of whipped cream. Champagne had been poured, the little bubbles slowly rising to the surface of two crystal glasses.

*Oh, no…what is he doing?*

I didn't expect this. This had disaster written all over it, and I couldn't let us get any deeper than we already were. It just wouldn't be right. I needed to remember the reason I came to this room in the first place. It was about the truth. His seduction was not supposed to be in the cards. I'd never be able to withstand him.

"I, um…" I faltered, words just seeming to ramble from my mouth. "I don't know…Fitz. I can't, I'm not…"

I felt rooted to the spot, undecided whether I should stay or flee from the room. As it turned out, I didn't have to make the decision because Fitz made it for me. He was already moving closer, possession in each measured stride. He leaned in and pressed the gentlest kiss to the curve of my neck. His spicy and masculine scent clouded my senses. I trembled when he reached up, his fingers softly brushing along the side of my cheek. I dared to look into his eyes, gray pools that swirled with something fierce.

"You wanted to talk?" he asked huskily. When it was clear I'd been rendered speechless, he laughed. "Come on, sweetheart. Let's sit down."

He led me over to the couch, and we sat. I stared at the plate of strawberries, my mind in a daze. I blinked once, then twice, in an attempt to push away the fog. I should have known this was coming the minute I decided to come to his hotel room. We could never ignore what was between us. Joy was right. Fitz and I had left too much unfinished. There were parts of me I tucked away, hid from and ignored, but they would always belong to him. Acknowledging those parts only made the guilt I felt for lying that much worse.

"Fitz," I began, attempting to find the strength to say the words on the tip of my tongue. But anything I might have said was silenced by the strawberry he brought to my lips.

"Taste," he demanded.

*Oh God…*

So much more was laced in that one little command. My already pounding heart began to race faster and faster, knowing I was already losing the battle after only being in his presence for a mere few minutes. Every single dirty fantasy I'd ever had about Fitz wanted to come to life right here in this room. I thought I might combust just from the images conjuring in my head. I needed to rein it in—to try harder.

"When you left, I didn't know—"

"It killed me to walk away from you," he interrupted. Stark vulnerability oozed from his truth. My throat tightened from his expression, filling my head with an onslaught of emotions I wasn't ready to admit to him, yet I couldn't stop the words from tumbling from my mouth.

"You took a piece of my heart when you left."

"And I left my whole heart with you," he confessed, grief written in his expression. I nearly broke from his words as his head dropped to rub his nose against the side of my face.

"Fitz, I'm terrified of you hurting me all over again. There's too much at stake this time," I began again, ready to lay it all out on the table. My mouth felt dry. I unconsciously ran my tongue over my lips to moisten them so I could speak. Fitz's eyes dropped and followed the path of my tongue, before finally making their way back up to mine. Just as I was about to speak, his lips crashed down on mine.

I didn't even attempt to protest, surrendering to a merciless kiss that set me on fire. Our tongues quickly found each other, his more aggressive than mine. This was not the kiss of a college boy I once knew nor was it like the kiss we shared near the Lincoln Memorial. This was so much more. It had the ferocity of a hot-blooded male taking complete and utter control.

"I never meant to hurt you. I'm so sorry, sweetheart. So sorry," he murmured against my lips. Tears sprang to my eyes, confusion winding through the very depths of my soul. Layer by layer, he was stripping me bare, peeling away the hurt to expose all the love.

"I would have waited for you," I whispered in between kisses.

"I couldn't let that happen, Cadence. You deserved more. So much more."

His hard contours pressed against the softness of my body and I found myself reaching up to thread my hands through the hair that skimmed along the edges of his collar. Fitz groaned when I tugged, and he pulled me tighter against him. I'm not sure when or how it happened so quickly, but we went from kissing to feverishly groping each other in a matter of minutes.

My fingers found the buttons of his shirt and I worked my way down, a desperate need to feel his bare flesh under my palms all consuming. He caressed a hand down my back, along the zipper of my dress, and settled at my waist. Shivers raced down my spine, wishing he'd just tug the zipper down.

*Why did he get to me like no one else ever could?*

I was too far gone to answer that question. I'd worry about tomorrow when tomorrow came. Every time he was near, I felt an unexplainable connection between us like an invisible line that remained unchanged over time. I wanted to be with him more than anything else.

*No. I need to tell him about Kallie. I'm not supposed to be doing this.*

I pulled away quickly, leaving us both panting.

"Wait," I breathlessly told him, the one syllable word coming out pained. I leaned back and adjusted the strap of my dress that was slipping down my shoulder. Fitz was a disheveled mess, his hair sticking up wildly. His shirt twisted up, only having been partially removed. His chiseled abdomen rippled as he shrugged impatiently out of the rest.

Once it was off, he reached for me again, but I froze when I caught sight of a tattoo. It was high on his right arm, a thorny vine that wrapped around his bicep up to his shoulder. In the center was a light blue dahlia, so similar to the one I had inked on my own shoulder. Except with his, the words *Fade Into You* were scripted underneath.

I felt like I'd been punched in the gut. It was the name of the Mazzy Star song that had been playing when I gave myself to Fitz for the very first time. I brought my eyes up to meet his, terrified of what I'd find but still desperate to see his expression. He pressed his forehead to mine. I almost couldn't breathe.

"When did you get that?" I whispered, fearful of what his answer might be.

"Six years ago. I told you, Cadence. I've never stopped thinking about you. I've never stopped loving you," he said, his voice low and throaty with emotion.

I clutched a hand over my drumming heart. All the oxygen seemed to suck completely from the room, replaced by him—only him. If he'd said that to me a few weeks ago, I would have accused him of lying. I would have assumed it was some fairytale designed to dupe me into dropping my panties. I pulled back a few inches to study his face. I saw the torment in his eyes, but there was also devotion and love. I couldn't doubt his words. He was speaking the truth.

I choked back a sob.

"Fitz, I…"

"I don't want to live in the past anymore, Cadence. I want what I have here. Right now. I want to be with you."

Elation raced through my veins like a potent drug. He was all around me, his presence thick and consuming in a way only he could be. It had been so long since I'd wanted—and I mean, really wanted. It was too much. It would be so easy to give in. I'd fantasized so many times about what it would be like to make love to Fitz again, but never in my wildest dreams did I think I'd have the opportunity. I closed my eyes as he pressed soft kisses down the line of my neck. He exuded testosterone, drugging my senses until I was high on him. I soared, my blood heating, my flesh on fire. My brain tried to tell me I should push him away, but I was no longer in control. My body had completely taken over.

When he brought his lips to mine, he hovered over them, barely touching. My lips parted and we breathed together, slowly inhaling each other's need. I'd never loved anyone the way I had loved him. At that moment, I realized I never stopped. It was still there even after all this time.

Everything was so wrong, yet oh so right. I knew I should end this madness—I should tell him about Kallie first—but I couldn't bring myself to do it. I feared his anger and was afraid to lose him again.

Perhaps if I allowed myself to have tonight, if I gave into this burning need I had for him, I'd find the courage I needed to do the right thing. But for now, I only wanted him. My body, the shell that had lain dormant for seventeen years, had finally awakened because of Fitz. My Fitz. Only he could make me feel this alive.

I gave in and felt my body melt into him, burying the fear and surrendering every ounce of resistance.

# Chapter Seventeen

**FITZ**

I sensed the moment she surrendered. Her cheeks flushed and her eyes darkened, the color turning a deep green and brimming with possibilities.

*There it is. There's my sweetheart.*

It was wrong for me to take things so fast with her again. I knew I should be taking my time despite the electric heat burning through my system. I had planned to take her out to dinner first, then maybe to see a show at the Kennedy Center. I had wanted to give her romance like I never did all those years ago. But then tonight happened. After feeling her warm body pressed against mine and her hips gyrating against me on the dance floor, I threw all thoughts of taking things slow right out the window.

Now, I could barely believe she was here in my arms. We had left so much undone and so much unsaid. It had taken me years to figure out, but I knew what I had with Cadence was nothing but pure and good. It was real. My biggest mistake was I'd allowed too much time to pass. I missed her. I missed this. The other women I'd held over the years had always felt awkward because Cadence was the only person I'd ever truly wanted there. Nobody had ever felt the way she did.

"It's been too long. Just too damn long," I whispered against her mouth before running my tongue over her heart-shaped lips, demanding she open to me. I kissed her. Tenderly. Passionately. Desperately. I wanted her to feel everything I felt, to feel the relief from finally having something we'd denied ourselves for so long, and to breach the distance time had left between us.

My arms banded tightly around her, and I hauled her to my chest, lifting her petite body to carry her to the bedroom. I never took my lips from hers, guiding her as I plundered her mouth. Once there, I carefully set her back on her feet and turned her around to press her back against my chest. I held her close, palm splayed across her abdomen as I leaned in to graze her ear. My breath was hot on her neck as she tilted her head so I could nibble down to her shoulder. I felt a shiver rock her body and she moaned.

"Fitz…" she sighed and tried to turn to face me. I stopped her, keeping her back firmly against me. I wasn't in a hurry. I wanted to savor every moment with her.

"I don't want to be rushed. I want to take my time. To make you feel good."

"I need to touch you," she persisted.

"We'll get there. First, I want to relearn your body. I want to feel every curve of you, to memorize you with my hands. With my tongue. I want to taste every inch of you."

She shuttered again as I moved my hand up her back to the zipper of her dress. Slowly, I tugged it down to expose the delicate curve of her spine. Looping a finger under each strap at her shoulder, I slid them down until the silk pooled at her feet.

I pressed my lips to her shoulder, trailing soft kisses along the hollow at the side of her throat as I reached around to cup her breasts through the black strapless bra. The material was rough against my palms and felt nothing like the basic cotton she had worn all those years ago.

This was mother fucking lace.

Sexy.

Intimate.

And all woman.

My cock strained in my pants and I thought I might come on the spot. I wanted nothing more than to toss her on the bed and fuck her senseless. Reining in the mad desire I had for her, I forced myself to do exactly as I'd promised, memorizing every delicious inch of her body. My mouth moved across her shoulders, working my way down her back and over her hips.

More lace. And a thong no less.

I groaned.

"You're unbelievable. You don't know what you do to me," I uttered as I raked my tongue over the curve of one cheek, then the other, before moving down and up each of her legs. "I've missed this so much. Your taste. Your scent. Your goodness. You've always been my light even when all I could see was the dark. I'm going to take care of you now. Show you how sorry I am. It's just me and you, sweetheart. That's all it ever was."

Working back up her body, I finally turned her to face me. Pure lust thrummed through my veins, and I felt my jaw tighten, desperate to see everything that was underneath the few scraps of black, sexy lace. I reached around to her back with slow, purposeful grace and unclasped her bra. Those perfect mounds and dark pink nipples spilled free.

I cupped her neck and ran my tongue down the base of her throat until I captured one hardened peak in my teeth, relishing in her startled cry as I rolled the other nipple between my thumb and finger. I lured her back toward the bed until the backs of her knees hit the mattress. Legs buckling beneath her, she sat down.

"Lie back," I told her. She hesitated, her eyes fraught with worry, and my stomach sank. I nearly swore, hoping like hell she wasn't having second thoughts now. "Cadence, don't look at me like that. Don't tell me to stop."

"Then don't talk. When you apologize…" she trailed off. Her expression was pained before a flash of determination sparked. "I don't want to be confused about the past. I want this, Fitz. I need it. I need you. No more talking. Just touch me, please."

"No talking? I'm sure I can think of something to keep my mouth occupied," I teased as I coaxed her back, eager to remove that final barrier of clothing so I could taste her like I never had the chance to all those years ago. If she didn't want to remember the past, that was okay. I didn't want the chains of history to hold us down any more than she did. I would give her this moment and show her all the pleasure we could share. Seventeen years ago, we had been a mess of fumbling limbs. Now I wanted to teach her all the things we could become.

Sliding down the lace, inch by beautiful inch, I tossed them aside and dropped to my knees between her legs. Grabbing her ankles, I pushed her legs apart, careful to gauge her expression as I did. Desire pooled deep in her emerald eyes, the delicate blush moving from her cheeks to her breasts, and I knew she wanted this.

Tearing my gaze from her face, I allowed myself finally to look down at her now exposed sex.

*So fucking gorgeous.*

I slid the pad of one finger gently over her clit. Her back immediately arched and an elicited gasp wrenched from her throat.

"Oh!"

I parted her folds and slowly sank one finger inside her heated well, a sharp hiss escaping me.

"God, you're exquisite. So wet. So ready. So dammed tight." I slid another finger in, stroking her inner walls while my thumb traced slow, leisurely circles over that pulsing bundle of nerves. She gasped again, and I sank down to her, unable to go another minute without tasting her. "Tell me you want me, sweetheart. Tell me you want this."

"Yes, yes! I want it," she shamelessly begged.

Wedging my shoulders between her legs, I rested my face against her inner thigh and inhaled her scent. Dipping down, I swiped my tongue over her entrance in one long lick. She tasted as sweet as she smelled. Her hands reached down and grasped the ends of my hair, searching for something to hang onto as I explored every nook and crevice of her most intimate parts. I dipped into her core before laving her oh-so-sweet spot, making her writhe beneath me. I pressed my tongue flat against her, rolling until that beautiful nub began to pulse. It was only a matter of time before she came apart.

"That's it. Let go, baby. Let me taste you on my tongue. I want you to feel it. I want you to feel all the things I was meant to make you feel."

"Oh God. Please!"

She pushed up against my mouth. I glanced up to find her head lolling from side to side, golden hair splayed out on the bed, desperate for the release that was so near. Cadence without inhibition was intoxicating. I could drown in her. Her hips bucked, but I held her still and brought her to new heights.

I felt her body stiffen and heard her sharp inhale. When she came, she screamed out my name, and it was the most glorious fucking thing I'd ever heard. The way she responded so readily to me was one of the things I remembered most about her. I loved her carefree trust and the way she allowed me to take her to places she'd never been. Before long, she'd realize I'd only taken her for a stroll around the block. I had a trip around the world planned for her tonight.

I toed off my shoes and shed my pants, leaving only my boxer briefs in place. I eased her body up the bed and blanketed her with my weight, sinking us deeper into the mattress. My throbbing cock pressed against her abdomen as I worked my hand up her thigh, peppering light kisses along her collarbone.

"Do you feel how hard you make me?" I whispered.

"Fitz, I…I," she panted through glazed eyes. I lifted my head to look at her. A mix of embarrassment and longing stretched across her features. "It's been so long. There's only been…"

She trailed off, hesitating as she traced a finger over my arm tattoo. I trembled from the contact, remembering the yearning I'd felt for her on the day I'd gotten it.

"There's only been what, sweetheart?" I prompted.

"You, Fitz. I don't know how to do this with you now," she told me, her voice just a husky whisper. "I've only ever been with you, but I'm sure there were all kinds of women for you between then and now. It's crazy. I didn't seem to care about my sexual inexperience when I was eighteen, but I care now for some strange reason. Go easy on me, okay?"

I froze at her words, seeing the raw vulnerability in her eyes.

*There's only been me?*

*Fuck.*

There was something caveman-ish about the way that fact thrilled me. She was mine. Just mine. I was the teacher of everything. But it was also scary to know how easily I could hurt her. I desperately didn't want that to happen. If things didn't work out with us for some insane reason, it would be so, so bad. It could be even worse than seventeen years ago.

She knew this, yet she was here, trusting me once again with her body. We had so much history and so much hurt we were up against. That didn't make our situation ideal, but there was just something about her. Something about the way she curved into me, the way she smelled like vanilla and sunshine that made none of the what-ifs matter. She was the only woman I could ever remember wanting to hold on to for more than a fleeting moment of time. I knew, without a shadow of a doubt, I still loved her. We belonged together. As bad as things could potentially be, I also knew there'd be so much good.

"Cadence, I love you. I've never stopped loving you. All other women were nothing but a temporary high. Every time I closed my eyes for the past seventeen years, I was with you. It's always been you. I'll stop now if you want me to, but sweetheart, I've never wanted anything more than I want you right now."

She reached up to cup my face.

"Then what are you waiting for?" she asked, echoing the words she had spoken to me so many years before.

Not wanting to spend another moment hesitating, I got up from the bed and opened the nightstand drawer to remove the box of condoms I had placed there earlier.

"Were you planning this all along, Mr. Quinn?" she teased, but there was a hint of suspicion in her question as well.

I chuckled.

"I know how it looks, but no. I shot over to the corner store while you were schmoozing donors. After dancing with you, I figured I should grab them just in case."

I shed my boxers and made quick work of the condom. Before climbing back onto the bed, I took a moment to appreciate her naked form spread out before me. Cadence was always beautiful, but a naked, luminous Cadence was something poets could write sonnets about.

I crawled up her body and she bent her legs, cradling me between. Positioning myself at her entrance, I pushed forward, barely sliding through the arousal between her lips. Her slender arms clung to my neck encouragingly and I pushed all the way in. I sucked in a gasp so hard it made my lungs hurt. The effect she had on me hit me like an earthquake. Lacing my fingers through her hair, I captured her mouth with mine.

"Fitz," she whimpered as my forehead rocked against hers.

"Do you remember what I told you the first time you gave yourself to me?"

When she responded, her voice was thick with emotion.

"You said I was beautiful, and you loved me."

"I meant what I said then, just as much as I mean it now. I love you, Cadence. Nobody has ever fit me the way you do. You've haunted my dreams for seventeen years. I've wanted to touch you. To feel you. To kiss you. To fuck you. I let go of you once. I won't ever do it again," I declared, the words a breath of a whisper against her lips.

She moved her hips, matching my thrusts as she gripped my shoulders. The girl I once knew was innocent—untouched. But this… this was Cadence defined. It was like she couldn't get close enough, and it was a feeling I understood all too well. I felt it too. I had to remind myself to go slow when every fiber of my being wanted to fuck her hard and claim her as mine once and for all.

Her nails raked down my back to my ass. I felt the bite of them against my skin as she made those little gasping noises that made me impossibly hard. Nothing had ever felt or sounded so damn good. She was perfect—my treasure. There was just the right amount of give-and-take as I drove into her deep and hard. The air in the room seemed to come alive—the energy and the connection the truest thing I'd ever felt. I could worship her all night long.

I tried to keep some modicum of control, but it was to no purpose. I could feel her body building, the pleasure mingling with my own as she moaned my name. Our bodies were slick with sweat, pleasure bound, and full of need. When I felt her start to come apart again, I pinned her arms above her head. I plunged into her, possessing her, the tightening of her perfect body making me feel like I could live forever.

My body raced, my dick pulsing with need, hard and desperate. Hunger ravaged through my veins and every muscle in my body tightened, rippling with an unbearable force. I slammed home and my world flashed white. So bright. A blinding light that left me quaking in her arms.

We lay there panting for what seemed like hours, but it was probably only minutes. After a time, I rolled off of her and she snuggled into the crook of my arm. Her arm draped across my torso, so warm and familiar. It was where she was meant to be.

She looked up at me, her eyes searching for something. What it was, I didn't know. I reached out and brushed my thumb across the bottom of her swollen lip. Old hopes mingled with new ones filled my mind, thoughts of what once was and what could be.

"You're beautiful," I said softly. She reached out and pinched my arm. It wasn't a hard pinch, but it surprised me nonetheless. "What was that for?"

"Just making sure you're really here. Is this real? Are you really with me?"

"I was a fool to walk away from you, but I'm here now. This is as real as it gets."

"I need you, Fitz. I've always needed you," she whispered into the quiet room. "No matter what happens, don't ever forget that."

# Chapter Eighteen

**CADENCE**

Sunlight streamed through the sheer white curtains on my bedroom window. I looked at the red neon numbers on the clock and saw it was after eight. I rarely slept in that late. But, then again, I had quite the workout last night. I gave in to a good stretch and all but purred as I recollected the memories.

I'd heard tales from female friends about how the best part of sex was oral, but I'd always had my doubts because it seemed a little too intimate for my tastes. However, last night I learned how wrong it was to assume. Fitz had taken me to new and impossible heights. I didn't think it was possible to orgasm so many times in one night. He'd taken me on the bed, then again on the sofa in the sitting area where he licked strawberries and cream from my body as if I were a feast he wanted to savor.

My experience with him had shaken the foundation of my very soul. Nothing could have prepared me for it. It was more than just sex. The way we moved together and the way he demanded I yield everything to him had caused sensations to take over so much more than just my body. He'd taken over my heart as well. The young man who stole my heart when I was a teenager had done it once more. I had, without a doubt, fallen in love with Fitzgerald Quinn all over again. Only this time, it was stronger.

The hours had passed much too quickly. I could have stayed wrapped in his arms all night long, but around midnight, I reminded

Fitz why we should leave. His son would probably do more than just raise an eyebrow if he found out his father had been out all night.

I crawled from my bed and headed to take a shower. As I allowed the hot stream to flow over my head and shoulders, I recalled the conversation from the night before. Fitz had insisted on taking me home while I insisted on handling it myself.

*"Let me take you home," he said.*

*"I'll just grab an Uber."*

*"No, Cadence. It's late. You're a beautiful woman. You shouldn't be all alone at midnight. What did you tell me about creepers? My car is already here. I'm taking you home."*

*"Still trying to save me, Mr. Quinn?"*

My teasing jest ended up delaying us for another hour as Fitz felt the need to take me again right there on the floor. As a result, I didn't get home until well after one in the morning. Allowing him to bring me home had been a mistake. I'd been too drunk on him to actually think it through. While I currently didn't have the risk of him running into Kallie, his knowing my address made me vulnerable. It meant I truly only had a little less than a week to tell him the truth. I couldn't risk him coming here unannounced and possibly finding out about her before I was ready.

After I finished the shower, I put on a t-shirt and yoga pants before pulling my hair back into a French braid. I didn't bother with makeup, having no plans to leave the house. Today was for catching up on house chores—especially laundry, which was piled a mile high in the first-floor laundry room off the kitchen.

I flipped on the stereo and began to separate the mountain into piles of colors and whites. After tossing the first load into the washer, I went to the closet in the front hall and pulled out the vacuum. Just as I was about the start it, a knock at the door sounded behind me. Turning, I peered out the sidelight. My stomach sank when I saw Fitz smiling at me through the narrow window.

*Shit! What is he doing here?*

It was exactly what I'd been afraid of happening. For a moment, I debated not opening the door, but he already knew I was inside. I glanced around the room. Framed pictures of Kallie were literally everywhere. Panic jarred my bones. There was no way he could come in.

Slowly, I stepped up to the door and unlocked the deadbolt. Opening the door just a few inches, I smiled and tried to hide my apprehension over his being there.

"Fitz, what a surprise!"

"I brought breakfast," he said with a crooked grin, holding up a bag with the logo of a popular bagel joint stamped across the front.

"Um, actually. I was just cleaning. The house is kind of a mess. Can I get a raincheck?"

"Don't be ridiculous. I don't care if the house is messy," he insisted and moved to push open the door. I braced my foot firmly at the bottom so he couldn't push it open without a lot of force. I scrambled to think of an alternative plan—one that didn't include Fitz stepping foot inside my house—all while ignoring the little voice in my head screaming at me to tell him the truth.

"No, really. How about we take it over to Arlington Ridge Park instead? It's a nice day out," I suggested, hoping like hell I sounded convincing.

He cocked a puzzled brow but nodded.

"Alright, I guess that could work too."

"Perfect. Let me just go change, and I'll be right out." Quickly, I shut the door in his face. Locking the deadbolt again, I pressed my forehead against the back of the door. I said a silent prayer to anyone who would listen, begging for some kind of guidance. It was clear I had no idea what I was doing.

Less than ten minutes later, I sat in the passenger seat of Fitz's sleek black Audi as we headed toward Arlington Ridge Park. Tension filled the space due to my refusal to let him in the house and it made for awkward conversation. When we didn't turn off George Washington Memorial Parkway when we should have, I turned to him in confusion.

"Where are we going?"

"To my house in Alexandria."

My eyes widened in fear, the earlier panic I'd felt coming back in full force.

*Shit! Austin.*

I couldn't let him see me.

"I'm not ready to meet Austin yet, Fitz," I rushed out, unable to cover up the high-pitched sound of anxiety.

"He's not home. He's out shooting hoops with a few friends and will be gone for most of the day." He reached across the middle console to give my hand a light squeeze of reassurance. "I won't push you until you're ready. It'll be okay."

I leaned my head against the car window and exhaled a sigh of relief. Still, I couldn't help but worry about the possibility of him returning home early. It would be disastrous. Fitz pulled his hand away, but his touch lingered on my skin long after and his words remained in my head.

*It'll be okay.*

"Just give me a heads-up next time, okay?"

We stopped at a red light, and Fitz turned to me. I could feel the heat of his gaze, and I slowly looked his way. Gray, stormy eyes met mine.

"What are you so afraid of, sweetheart?"

"Who said I'm afraid?"

"After last night, I thought…" he trailed off, and the light turned green. Turning his attention back to the road, he hit the accelerator. Reaching toward the dash, he fiddled with the dial of the radio. "I think we could use a little music. Current or throwback?"

*Oh God. No throwback.*

I couldn't handle being catapulted back in time any more than I already had.

"Current is good."

He settled on a station, and I listened to Imagine Dragons sing apologies about everything they'd done as we drove the rest of the way in silence.

*Jesus Christ…I should have picked throwback.*

When we pulled into his long driveway, I nearly gasped at the size of his house. When I compared his home to the modest house I shared with Kallie, we might as well have lived in a cardboard box. White pillars flanked the front door of the stone and stucco, two-story home. Meticulous landscape lined the walkway and steps leading to the main entrance, following the front of the house and disappearing around a stone wall that ran the length of the property. I barely had a minute to take it all in before he pulled the Audi into a large three-car garage.

Fitz killed the engine, then walked around to my side of the car to open the door for me. I took a moment to compose myself, not wanting to appear like I was gawking. It was only a house after all—albeit, a very big house—but still just a house. He'd told me he ran a successful business. I guess I just hadn't realized exactly how successful it truly was.

When we entered the house, I wasn't surprised to see the stunning interior. The kitchen was a modern design with brushed stainless-steel appliances, black granite countertops, and tall white cabinets. Light fixtures hung from the ceiling at various heights. They appeared to be there more for ambiance than light, softly illuminating the six bar stools wrapped around the kitchen's center island. Through the door to the kitchen, I could see a large family room leading to a sun porch and the backyard. I couldn't see beyond the porch but could somehow envision Fitz playing with a young Austin on the lush, green lawn surrounding the house.

"You have a beautiful home, Fitz."

"Thanks. I'll give you the tour after we eat," he replied as he placed the bag of bagels on the counter. Moving to the refrigerator, he peered inside. "Looks like Austin polished off the apple juice. Is orange juice okay?"

"That's fine," I murmured, feeling relatively uncomfortable in this posh space.

Fitz came back over to where I stood, pulled out a barstool, and motioned for me to sit. After retrieving a couple of plates, he sliced the bagels apart and spread cream cheese over the halves of each one. I took a tentative bite and stared out into space, unsure of what to say.

He watched me curiously and seemed to sense my uneasiness because after we finished eating, he took my hand and led me through the living room toward the sunporch. As we walked, I couldn't help noticing the many photos dotting the surfaces of end tables and walls. Most were pictures of Austin throughout the years, growing from a boy to a young man. It wasn't all that different from what was in my house. A family lived here—Fitz and Austin, father and son. My heart ached, feeling I'd been robbed of something precious, wishing pictures of Kallie were among his collection.

Once we stepped out into the warm morning air, Fitz turned to pull me into his arms. The raw strength of him enveloped me. A calm stillness held fast to the air as the sun rose closer to its peak in the sky. He pressed his forehead against mine and softly ran his hand up and down the curve of my spine.

"What's wrong, Cadence? You've been acting strange since I showed up at your house this morning. And please, don't tell me it's because you didn't want me to see a mess."

There was an acute worry in his voice, a kind of brokenness that seeped into my reply.

"Why did you bring me here?"

"Because I wanted you to see another part of me and to tell you more about Austin before you meet him. I also wanted to talk about us—where things stand and our future together."

*Our future together.*

My knees nearly buckled, struggling to find balance as my throat thickened. This man was making me wish for things I had no business wanting. A heavy ache began to build in my chest.

"What about our future?"

"I've decided I want to make a go for the Senate seat, but I want to make sure you and Austin are okay with it before I tell my father. I haven't spoken to Austin about it yet. I figured I'd talk to you first."

I shook my head, unable to comprehend how things progressed so fast. He was speaking to me as if we were in this together—like I had a say in his life choices.

"You don't need my permission, Fitz."

He shifted back a step and stared out at the horizon. Raising a hand, he ran it through his dark hair and inhaled a deep breath. When he looked at me again, uncertainty clouded his features.

"Actually, I do. I want to be with you. If you're a part of me, people will want to know about you."

"What do you mean? What people?" I asked cautiously.

"The RNC will dig into your background to make sure there isn't any kind of embarrassing scandal that could potentially hurt my campaign. It's for my protection and I won't be able to stop them from doing it. I can try to shield you from the press, but your photo will inevitably be taken by journalists whenever you're around me. This is why I need your permission. I want you by my side, but you're more important to me than a Senate seat. If you're not on board, I won't do this."

His words caused fear to rake over me in a rough caress. I stared at him in shock, unable to believe he was thinking so long-term about our future. But more, realizing what would be uncovered when they began to dig into my past terrified me. I had allowed Fitz to crawl back into my heart, and clearly, he'd allowed me to do the same. That was the problem when someone affected you. It caused you to entertain all kinds of foolish ideas about what could be. Now we were at a crossroad.

Telling Fitz about Kallie was now irrelevant. I would still have to come clean of course, but everything he said put a new spin on things. This campaign—the scrutiny that came with what he wanted to do—would throw us into a spotlight I didn't want. Kallie would be the subject of only God knew what. Plus, I had to consider Dahlia's Dreamers. My organization was built on years of sweat and blood. It was my heart and soul. Joy wasn't far from the mark when she spoke about Fitz's father. He had already made it his mission to make life miserable for organizations such as mine. The minute he found out I was the cause of scandal for his son, I knew he'd destroy everything I worked so hard to build. I might be able to handle whatever was thrown at me, but I would never allow Kallie or the good people at Dahlia's Dreamers get caught up in this.

My shoulders fell as I processed the implications, never feeling more defeated than I did at that moment. I should have thought this through better. Just as he had seventeen years ago, Fitz's father would once again stand in our way. My head shook back and forth in denial, unwilling to accept the idea of having my world picked apart by the very man who went against everything I believed in. I slowly backed away from Fitz, bringing one hand to my heart, the other to cover my mouth. Angry tears began to well in my eyes as I processed the terrible twist of fate life had thrown at us.

"Cadence, what's wrong?" Fitz reached for me, but I pulled away.

"I'm sorry, but I can't be a part of this."

"I understand why you might have reservations. We can talk about it. But, sweetheart, there's no reason for you to get so upset."

"There's nothing to talk about. I can already see how things will play out." I turned to go back into the house, but he grabbed my arm to stop me, forcing me to face him. "Please, Fitz. Don't make this any harder. I need to go home and think about things. I can't do that here—with you."

"There's something you aren't telling me. I can feel it. What's really going on?"

I could only stare at him, overcome with confused emotion as I grappled to put what I was feeling into words. I wanted to scream and yell about all the injustices in the world. I wanted to hate Fitz for leaving me and marrying another. I wanted to hate myself for not running away like I should have all those years ago. Perhaps if I had, Kallie wouldn't have met Austin, and none of this would be happening. I wanted to meet Fitz's father, so I could rip into him for the way he'd destroyed his son's life, my life, and for his daily attempts to crush the opportunities for so many hardworking immigrant families. Too many tears were shed because of him. He was the epitome of everything I tried to shield Kallie from. My daughter represented everything good in the world. I'd die before giving Fitz's father the chance to manipulate her like he had so many others. I didn't want him anywhere near her.

"It's your father, Fitz. He wants to destroy everything I stand for!"

His eyes widened in surprise, disbelief clouding every inch of his beautiful face.

"That's why you're upset? Because of him?"

"He's gotten in the way of us before. Mark my words—he'll do it again. I don't know how, but he will. Once he finds out who I am, it'll be gloves off. He'll dig into my past and manipulate the situation until you want nothing to do with me. I allowed the man to dictate my future seventeen years ago. I can't sit by and watch him do it again. I need to protect myself and everything else I hold dear."

His fists balled in frustration.

"Dammit, Cadence! I'm not my father, and I won't lose you because of him. Not again—not when I've waited this long to find you. I won't let him stand in the way of us."

"Please, just bring me home," I pleaded again.

"You don't need to run from me. I won't let him manipulate anything. Things are different from what they once were."

He was right. Things were different—so much different. We were no longer kids who could pass our nights away making love as the sun dropped low behind the trees. We were adults with real-life responsibilities that couldn't be ignored.

For every action, there was an equal and opposite reaction. And while I was acutely aware of Newton's Third Law, there was one force that had remained unchanged over time—the connection between Fitz and me. I half wondered if I was focusing on all the wrong things. Perhaps, if our connection had defied the laws for this long, I could dare to hope.

"Why do you want to run for Senate, Fitz?"

He released his hold on me and let his arms fall to his sides. Pinching the bridge of his nose, he moved to sit down on a white wicker loveseat and motioned for me to join him. After I sat, he put his arm around my shoulders and pulled me close.

"I feel like I've been coasting. Sure, I have a good life. I got through all the bullshit from the past. I have a successful business, a beautiful home, and an amazing son. But I always felt like something was missing—like I'd yet to find my true purpose. When I ran into you, something shifted in me. I can't explain it, but I found myself needing to do something more. After that, everything strangely began to align. When my father proposed the Senate seat, my initial response was a firm no. But then, because of you, I've spent my evenings reading about the DREAM Act, border security, and everything else in between. In the process, I learned how far the Party has fallen off the moral compass. I feel like I can change all that, but I can't do it alone."

I couldn't help smiling at his words.

"Moral compass, huh? You sound like a liberal."

He shrugged.

"Perhaps it's not liberal at all, but common sense. I know all the ugliness that can come with politics and can handle swimming with the sharks, but I'm not well-versed on the interworkings of the government. Proposals are one thing, but actually enacting good policy is completely different. I worry I'm making the move too soon and I'll be in over my head. I'm not naïve. I know I have a lot to learn." He paused and twisted in his seat so he could look down at me. "I want you to help me, Cadence. You've been in the thick of this for years and I could use your guidance and wisdom."

"Fitz, you're shooting for a Republican seat," I said, shaking my head. "I appreciate your enthusiasm about making a change, but I hope you're not taking this on to try to impress me. You have no idea what you're up against."

"I know better than you think. I may need you to help me to navigate the ins and outs, but I can handle the rest."

I shook my head again.

"If you're really hell-bent on doing this, you should get to know the people you're planning to fight for."

"That's part of my campaign strategy. Knocking on doors—"

"No, it's more than that," I interrupted. "I mean *really* get to know them. Do you remember me telling you about Andrés Mendez? The man who's facing deportation for a traffic ticket?"

"Yeah, why?"

I hesitated, not sure if I should extend an invitation that could put Emilia's future in-laws at risk. They were still considered undocumented after all and it was rare for people in their situation to extend invitations to outsiders. They trusted me to keep their secret safe, but they didn't know Fitz. However, if Fitz truly wanted to help, he'd have to embrace the passion that would inevitably fuel his fight. To me, the best way he could attain that was to make a personal connection to the people he was fighting for.

"Emilia, his fiancée, invited me to their daughter's birthday party on Thursday night. Her name is Mayra and she's turning five. You should come with me and learn the human side of things."

He cocked his head to the side curiously before slowly nodding in agreement.

"That's a good idea. I'd like that."

"After the party, I'll be curious to hear your thoughts. If you come out of it with a fire in your belly that's even remotely close to mine, I'll help you."

I bit my lower lip, feeling nervous about the promise I'd made. While it was a promise I intended to keep, I wasn't sure he'd still want my help after all was said and done. I crossed my fingers superstitiously, hoping I didn't make an already precarious situation so much worse.

# Chapter Nineteen

**FITZ**

I pulled in the driveway to a little Cape Cod-style house in Fairfax with Cadence at six o'clock on Thursday evening. Through the large front window, I could see people milling about and hear their jovial chatter carrying through to the outside.

"You ready for this?" Cadence asked, giving my hand a slight squeeze as we walked up to the front door.

I grinned and looked down at the box wrapped in pink unicorn paper tucked under my arm. That morning, Cadence and I had met for our routine run. When she mentioned the present she bought for Mayra, I realized I probably shouldn't show up to the party empty handed and went out during my lunch hour to get a present for the birthday girl. Clueless on what to buy, I scanned the shelves of purple and pink frill for what seemed like an hour before Google ultimately saved the day.

"Yeah. Thanks for the invite, sweetheart. I'm excited to meet them."

"Don't thank me yet," she laughed. "Kid birthday parties can get a little rowdy."

Cadence knocked on the door and a short woman with dark brown eyes opened it a moment later.

"Ah, Miss Riley! I am so glad you came!" the woman exclaimed, her subtle Spanish accent coming through in the way she added importance to her vowels.

"Please, Emilia. I've told you before to call me Cadence," she laughed and embraced the woman in a brief hug before we were ushered inside. "Emilia, this is Fitz. I hope you don't mind I brought him along."

"Not at all!"

"It's nice to meet you," I said and extended my hand. After we exchanged pleasantries, Emilia stepped in between Cadence and me and looped her arms through ours.

"Please, come with me to the kitchen so I can introduce you to the family."

Swarms of kids ran past my legs as we walked through the living room toward the kitchen. Balloons drifted around aimlessly on the floor and happy birthday banners draped the walls. A stack of unopened presents piled high in the corner of the room. I didn't think I'd ever seen so much pink in my life.

When we got to the kitchen, loud conversation and laughter assaulted me. In a mix of Spanish and English, everyone seemed in competition to be heard, each person practically shouting over the next. I half wondered how any of them knew what the other was saying.

Emilia clapped her hands loudly.

"*Atención*! Everyone, this is Cadence Riley, the wonderful woman who is helping to bring Andrés back to us. This is her friend, Fitz."

I nodded to the crowd of men and women who simultaneously called out "thank you for coming" and "*bienvenido*" before returning to their previous shouty conversations. I couldn't help but smile. I never had big, loud family gatherings growing up and had only witnessed them on TV. However, being in the thick of it was something else entirely.

"Oh, good! I'm glad you made it," I heard Cadence say. I turned to see who she was speaking to and recognized Joy and the woman I'd seen briefly at the fundraiser gala. "Fitz, you already know Joy. This is her wife, Marissa."

As more hand-shakes where exchanged, a strange look passed between Joy and Cadence. Joy looked almost wary while Cadence's eyes widened with an unspoken message.

"Uh-oh. I saw that. Is there anything I need to know?" I joked.

"Nothing at all!" Joy's dubious expression evaporated, and she laughed. "Unless you don't know about Mrs. Mendez's specialty."

"Ah, yes! It's delicious!" Emilia said with an excited nod. She pointed to a platter of what looked like green leafy packages wrapped in twine on the center of the kitchen table.

My brow furrowed, trying to figure out what it was, and Cadence began to laugh.

"Your expression is priceless, Fitz. Those are tamales."

"They only get made on special occasions because they take so much time to prepare," Emilia explained. "Would you like to try one?"

I shrugged.

"Sure. Why not?"

She scooped up one of the green bundles, removed the twine and outside leafy part, and set what was inside a plate for me.

"The plantain leaves are only meant to preserve the flavor. What's inside is the good part. Think of an enchilada but less saucy," Cadence suggested.

I took a hesitant forkful only to find myself pleasantly surprised by an odd combination of chicken, cheese, tomatoes, and some other kind of meat. Slowly, I nodded my appreciation.

"This is really good!"

"I'm glad you like it," Emilia beamed. "Please, make yourselves at home. Now that everyone is here, I'm going to round up the children. Mayra is very excited to open her presents."

As if she had ears in the walls, the most adorable little girl with wide brown eyes came whizzing into the kitchen. She was sporting pigtails with bows and a pink animal print dress. This had to be Mayra.

"Present time?" she asked excitedly.

"Yes, *princesa*. Now go get your cousins and sit nicely in the living room."

After we finished our tamales—which was probably one of the most delicious things I'd ever tasted—Cadence and I followed the other guests into the living room. Joy and Marissa were already there chatting it up with an older woman on the sofa. Kids circled, seeming to materialize out of nowhere, vying to get the best seat next to the birthday girl.

Mayra opened each present one by one, stopping in between to politely thank the person who'd given it to her. After all of her gifts were opened, everyone piled back into the kitchen to sing happy birthday. And again, there was more pink. The platter of tamales had been replaced by a huge cake decorated with pink icing and rainbow hearts.

"*Feliz cumpleaños*, Mayra," the group began to sing. I didn't know the Spanish words, so I just hummed the birthday tune along with them.

Cadence stood on her tiptoes to whisper in my ear.

"I love how they've hung on to their culture and traditions, yet still embrace the American way. That's what makes this country so great. This is what I wanted you to see."

"What are you two whispering about?" Joy asked. I turned, not realizing she had been standing behind me in the doorway.

"I was just telling Fitz how I liked that they haven't completely abandoned their heritage to fit a mold." An indecipherable look passed between them before Cadence said, "I'm sorry, Joy. That wasn't directed at you."

"I didn't think it was. You're right though. It's nice to see them staying true to who they are."

"What did I miss?" I asked, feeling completely confused.

Cadence glanced at Joy but fell silent.

"It's okay," Joy said with a nod. "He can know."

Cadence turned to me, placed her hand on my arm, and leaned in closer so as not to be overheard.

"Joy's family is originally from Colombia. In the late seventies, before Joy was born, they fled to find sanctuary in the United States to escape the Colombian conflict. All of them, including her older brother, were undocumented. Joy's parents are still undocumented, which is why I was hesitant to speak. Undocumented people don't generally like to have their status broadcasted."

My brow furrowed, still relatively perplexed.

"Okay… so what does that have to do with traditions?"

Both Joy and Cadence glanced around with worried looks as they scanned the room.

"Why don't the four of us go back to the living room while everyone else enjoys their cake? It's quieter in there," Joy suggested. Unsure what the big secret was, I followed the three women into the living room. Once we were seated comfortably on the overstuffed sofa, Joy turned back to me. "My family name is actually Martínez, not Martin. It's a name my parents stopped using once they came to the U.S. They wanted nothing to do with where they came from—including the language. To this day, I've never heard them speak a word of Spanish. Cadence knows it has always bothered me to think about the customs my family chose to wipe out. That's why she apologized even though I knew she didn't mean anything by her comment."

"I gotcha now. Why did your parents do it? Was it to fit in?" I asked.

"Partly. Being a black family in America in the seventies already had its challenges. Add a language barrier to the mix and it would have been even worse. However, with my parents, it was more about forgetting all the bad things they left behind. They wanted to start anew, but everything came to the forefront after my brother's arrest."

I raised my eyebrows in surprise.

"His arrest?"

"Yes. That's the reason I wanted to come in here where it was private. I didn't want to scare Emilia or the family any more than they already are," Joy explained and looked sadly toward the kitchen door. "My brother was arrested when he was twenty-five years old. He was still undocumented. My parents didn't want him to apply for Deferred Action. They were afraid the application would be denied, and he'd be sent back Colombia. So, he never filed. As a result, he didn't have the same opportunities I did. It's amazing what having a social security number can do for a person. People don't realize how those little nine digits define their rights, freedoms, and opportunities."

"So I'm beginning to see," I murmured, thinking about all the conspiracy theories I'd read about undocumented immigrants. They weren't eligible for the same benefits afforded to legal citizens. That was a fact, yet, so many believed otherwise.

"Anyway, he wasn't a bad kid, but he had his struggles. One night, he got caught up in a bar fight over something stupid. He and four others were arrested and charged with assault. Within in a matter of weeks, my brother was sent back to Colombia." Her voice cracked, and she paused to take a deep breath. A single tear slid down her cheek and Marissa squeezed her hand encouragingly. A look of understanding and sympathy passed between them before Joy continued. "We tried to speak to him over the phone, all while trying to find a way to get him back. He managed to find a place to live and we sent him money until he could find a job. Then one day, we couldn't reach him. One month later, we found out he'd been killed. He was shot dead while sitting outside a local store, an innocent bystander caught in the crossfire between the store owner and one of the drug cartels. That's when my parents finally decided to open up about the place they'd escaped. The things they saw and lived through were terrible. It was no wonder they wanted to bury it all."

I had no words as I tried to wrap my head around the horrific story. Other than the momentary tear, Joy told the tale with little emotion. She spoke matter-of-factly as if she were numb to recounting a story she knew all too well. I'd read similar stories in recent months, but somehow it was different hearing it from someone I knew.

"That's why Joy really came to work at Dahlia's Dreamers," Cadence added. "It wasn't because she couldn't find a job. She had a great job teaching high school music in Baltimore. She gave it up in order to help others from meeting the same fate as her brother."

I wanted to ask more questions, but the crowd from the kitchen began to gravitate back into the living room, effectively ending the conversation. I looked around the room at Andrés Mendez's family members, feeling as if I were seeing them in a whole new light. They'd welcomed me graciously with open arms and treated me like one of their own.

However, as the night wore on, I was able to see past their display of happiness as they celebrated little Mayra's birthday. When I looked closer, I could see sadness and worry about Andrés in their eyes. I saw the sorrow when Mayra asked if her daddy would be there soon. I saw the concerned glances they gave Emilia when they thought she wasn't looking. I wondered how she was holding up through all of this. They were a family who felt the same love, devotion, and worries as anyone. That simple fact was overlooked by so many, the human side easily cast aside and overruled by fear of the unknown.

I draped an arm over Cadence's shoulders and fiddled with the end of her braid. For the first time, I truly began to understand what drove her to help these people. I didn't think it was possible, but my love for her—for this remarkable, unselfish woman—seemed to grow even stronger. I didn't know what I did to deserve this second chance with her. She'd been the one who got away, but there was no chance I would let her go again. I pulled her tight to my side and vowed right then and there to do something to try to help this family and the poor little girl who didn't know where her father was.

I sat quietly, listening to the warm chatter between family and friends and attempted to think of ways I could help. I knew my asshole father would be of no use, but he wasn't the only one with political connections. Leaning in closer to Cadence, I whispered in her ear.

"What's the name of the judge?"

She angled her head up to look at me.

"What judge?"

"The one handling the Garcia-Mendez case."

Her face screwed up in disgust as if just the thought of the judge turned her stomach.

"Judge Perkins."

My head snapped back in surprise.

"Perkins? As in Jonathan Perkins?"

"Yeah, I think so. Why? Do you know him?"

I knew him alright. That shady bastards backdoor deal stole years of my life. He and my father schemed to throw every possible criminal charge at me, deliberately scaring me to accept the nuclear option. Because yeah—my fake marriage had been nothing but fucking nuclear. My hatred for Jonathan Perkins surged. His crooked ways bound me to his daughter and to a life I never wanted. The only good thing to come out of it was Austin, the grandson who Perkins had little to do with over the years. Considering all the man had put me through, I'd say he owed me more than just a few favors. Perhaps it was time I played his own game and called one of them in.

I looked down at Cadence and met her curious emerald eyes. If I told her my thoughts, she'd get her hopes up. I didn't want to do that until I knew whether Perkins would even hear me out. I hadn't spoken to the man in years.

"Yeah, I know him. Let me see what I can do," was all I said.

My phone buzzed in my pocket signaling an incoming text. I pulled it out and glanced at the screen, frowning.

"What is it?" Cadence asked.

"It's Austin. Devon took him to a Nationals game tonight. Traffic is a bitch going over the bridge, so they decided to stay in the city at Devon's condo. Austin's going to crash there for the night and Devon will just drive him to school in the morning."

"Oh. Is that a bad thing?"

"No, I'd just planned on spending some time with Austin after I left here. I wanted to talk to him about the campaign and get his thoughts on it. It's no biggie. I can just talk to him tomorrow night." My gaze dropped to her pink, heart-shaped lips. I took in the subtle sheen of gloss coating them as I thought about the possibilities of being kid free for the night. "Come home with me."

Her eyes widened in surprise.

"What?"

I leaned in close to her ear and breathed her in. She smelled like vanilla and desire—it was intoxicating. The seriousness of the past thirty minutes seemed to melt away.

"You heard me. Austin's gone for the night, and I have the house to myself. It's fate, who are we to argue with it? Stay the night with me."

"Fitz," she hissed in a low whisper. "I can't stay the night with you!"

"Yes, you can, sweetheart. Come home with me," I repeated before lowering my voice to a breath below a whisper. "I want you naked. I want to taste you. I want you screaming."

Her eyes darted about the room nervously as she looked for anyone who may have overheard our private conversation. I knew my words were highly inappropriate for a kid's birthday party, but I didn't give a shit. Nobody could hear me, but they would eventually see the tent threatening to pitch in my pants if I didn't get out of here soon. Just thinking about a naked Cadence did all sorts of things to me.

Her demeanor shifted, and her eyes glimmered with a barrage of conflicted emotions—desire, longing, apprehension. She squirmed slightly but didn't say yes or no to my request. Instead, she stood up and walked over to Emilia.

"Emilia, it's been a pleasure. Fitz and I are going to take off."

*Hell, yeah.*

I smiled to myself and followed her lead. After we exchanged farewells with everyone, we headed for the door. Cadence turned to me as soon as we stepped outside.

"I'm not going to stay the whole night, but I will come for a few hours."

"I can do a lot in a few hours, sweetheart."

"I'm sure you can, Mr. Quinn, I'm sure you can."

# Chapter Twenty

**CADENCE**

During the car ride to Fitz's house, the air crackled with inexplicable sexual tension, and we barely managed small talk. Once we got into the house, we stumbled up the stairs to his bedroom like a couple of teenagers in a hurried frenzy.

When we reached the upstairs hallway, his arm snaked around my back and he lifted me effortlessly. It was as if I weighed nothing more than a feather in his arms as he carried me to his room. Setting me down on the center of his bed, he cradled my face in his hands and pulled back. We both stared into each other's eyes.

"I love you so much it hurts," he whispered.

I wanted to repeat his words more than anything. I'd loved this man my whole life, but I couldn't voice the words while I was still looking for excuses to hide the truth. I stared into his deep gray eyes and my chest ached. I wanted him. I loved him. I *needed* him. My throat thickened with overwhelming emotion.

"Fitz, I…" I paused when I felt a lonely tear slide down my cheek. Fitz leaned down and kissed it away.

"God, Cadence. Don't cry, sweetheart."

"They're happy tears," I explained. "I'm just so happy here with you. This moment. I… kiss me, Fitz."

He grabbed my head and yanked my mouth to meet his. My heart felt like it would explode. Everything in my body tensed. I breathed him in and felt his heat. He made me feel so much all at once. I felt frightened, happy, desperate, and hopeful. My tongue danced with his and I poured every single thing I'd ever felt for him into the kiss. This was where I belonged. I'd found my place again—and it was in his arms. It was home and there was no place I'd rather be.

We kissed frantically—nothing had ever felt so good. His tongue collided with mine and my back arched. I moaned into his mouth. I had no sense of time as we began to claw at each other's clothing. In a matter of seconds, I was down to my bra and panties feeling breathless as I tried to recover from his merciless kisses.

"Holy shit," he panted.

"Yeah, I'll say," I replied as I tried to slow my racing heart. My body was buzzing as I stared at the pulse beating at the base of his throat. I kissed it, needing to taste his skin with my tongue. When I pulled back, his gray eyes were burning with desire as they raked over my face.

"I want to taste you."

"As much as I'd love that, not yet. Roll onto your back," I told him.

He did as I asked without question. I climbed over him and straddled his hips. His hands came around to cup my ass as I leaned down. I pressed my lips to his chest, slowly moving my hand down his torso to push down his box briefs and wrap my fingers around his length. Working my way down, I trailed kisses over his abs. The last time we were together, Fitz had gone down on me. It was an experience I'd never forget. Tonight, I wanted to return the favor.

When I reached his thick member, I hesitated and licked my lips. I'd never done this before and hoped like hell I wouldn't screw it up. I only knew everything in the past seventeen years had brought me to this moment. He was the person who had walked me home because he was worried about my safety, the one who planned a picnic on the floor of a stockroom so I wouldn't be disappointed, and the man who had shown gentle tenderness when I gave myself to him for the first time. He'd always lived in my heart. His touch reminded me of the girl I once was and made me believe in the woman I was today.

"You don't have to, sweetheart."

"Shhh… don't make me lose my nerve."

I tentatively swiped the head of his cock with my tongue.

"Jesus fucking Christ," he hissed as he gripped my head. His fingers tangled in my hair and I felt a heady rush of power. Growing bolder, I sucked the head into my mouth.

I'd never felt such an intense need to pleasure someone, but with him, everything was different. Skills I never knew I had came to the forefront as I took in more of him. I ran my tongue around the smooth crown. He groaned and it gave me the courage to lower my head further. He was thick and soft on my tongue as I sucked, his ridges sliding back and forth over my lips.

He thrust himself deeper and forced a steady rhythm. I opened my throat to accept him, sucking and twisting my tongue around his thick shaft, using my hand to pump faster. I felt desperate and unable to get my fill of him. I swallowed and opened my throat even more to take in every inch I could. I pushed my head forward, taking him deep with my swallow and held steady.

He inhaled sharply.

"Cadence, stop," he panted. "I'll never last if you keep that up. I don't want to come in your mouth. I want to be inside you when I do."

I flipped back onto my elbows and watched as he stood up to slide his boxer briefs the rest of the way down his muscular thighs. He was way too attractive for his own good. When his cock sprang free, I took in his length and girth as he sheathed his hard shaft with a condom. There was nothing I liked more than looking at him. We might have been well into our thirties, but Fitz's chest was just as broad and ripped as it had been when he was twenty-two.

Suddenly, I became self-conscious of my own body. I'd been so wrapped up in the moment the last time we were together, I never paused to consider my breasts weren't as perky as they'd once been. I'd tried to stay in relatively good shape by religiously jogging every morning. My legs and ass were decent, but my belly was definitely a lot softer than it used to be. Fortunately, I'd escaped horrible stretch marks during my pregnancy with Kallie and only had a few faint lines which had mostly faded over the years. Still, my body wasn't nearly as tight, and I couldn't help but wonder if Fitz found the looser version of me to be just as beautiful as he once did.

Without thinking, I closed my eyes and pulled the bed comforter over to cover myself.

"Cadence, what's wrong?"

"Nothing," I responded quickly.

Climbing back onto the bed, he blanketed me with his body.

"Sweetheart, look at me." My eyes fluttered open. "You're beautiful. I don't ever want you to hide your body from me. It's flawless."

"How did you know what I was thinking?"

"I can read it on your face. I can see it in the way you tensed up and tried to hide. There's no reason to hide from me. All I see is how perfect you are."

My heart swelled as I brought my legs up to surround his waist. I felt his erection grow impossibly bigger as it pressed against my core. Shamelessly, I rocked my hips up, relishing the friction from his iron hard length against the lacey material of my panties. My sex clenched, and I buried my insecurities, imagining his length thrusting inside me.

Reaching beneath me, he wound his hands behind my back and unclasped my bra. My breasts spilled free and he cupped them instantly, rolling the peaks between his thumb and forefinger until I thought I might buck right off the bed. I struggled to find coherent thoughts. Moans and pants took their place. The air smelled of sex mixed with his cologne, making an all-encompassing vapor designed to intoxicate. Heat flooded my core, needing to feel him inside my body more than I needed to breathe.

I allowed my fingers to explore the ripples of his abdomen—touching him, needing to feel the heat of his skin. Our lips danced, and our hearts beat wildly against each other's. He led, then I led, each of us giving and taking. My insides tightened, and I whimpered.

He prowled down my torso, his mouth moving over my belly and kissing the inside of my knee. Fire shot right through me when he pushed aside the crotch of my panties. He slipped a long, thick finger deep inside and every part of me came alive.

"God, sweetheart. You're so fucking wet."

His finger worked through my folds, lightly grazing over my clit. Electricity flowed through me causing every nerve ending in my body to stand at attention. He teased me for a minute or so before pushing another finger inside of me. Every part of my body sizzled. Fire burned through my bloodstream. I panted toward the ceiling and closed my eyes. My hands fisted in the sheets as a feeling of ecstasy began to build. Time seemed to stand still. My muscles tightened, and heartbeat quickened. It beat so hard I could feel it in my ears. I was already close. So close.

All at once, he removed his fingers from my body. I gasped from the sudden stop of pleasure and snapped my eyes open. He was looking at me with intense arousal as he brought his fingers to his mouth. I watched as he licked my juices from his fingers and something inside me quickened.

"Please, Fitz! Don't… I need to feel you!"

He didn't listen to my unashamed begging but instead, brought his fingers to my lips. Without question, I opened my mouth and tasted the tanginess of my own essence. Leaning in, he pressed his mouth to mine in a blind assault of lips and tongue, moving in perfect harmony.

His hands slid down to my waist, and he looped his thumbs through the sides of my panties. He slithered down my body and ripped them down my legs with a ferocity that made my head spin. I gasped from the heat that blazed across my skin.

"Say it again," he growled. "Tell me what you need."

"You, Fitz! I need to feel you inside me."

A groan rumbled from somewhere deep in his chest as I guided him to my willing, wet sex, bringing him to the place only he had been. He plunged inside.

"Fuck," he growled. "Your body. The way you feel. It's like you were made for me."

He pushed harder and faster, riding me in a way he never had before. I thought I might combust from the pleasure of it.

"God, you feel so good!" I gasped.

Something in him seemed to snap, releasing whatever measure of control he had been trying to hang onto. A scream escaped me as he plunged forward. Each thrust was deeper than the last, filling me completely and bringing me to new heights of ecstasy. I was lost, floating weightlessly and I didn't care if I ever came down.

His fingers laced through my hair and he tugged, causing my scalp to tingle in the most delicious way. He was everywhere—inside me, touching me, kissing me. I couldn't feel anything except him. He was a part of me, and I was a part of him. It was an overload of sensations, consuming me with inexplicable, mind-altering need.

Rolling our bodies, Fitz pulled out and flipped me onto my stomach to take me from behind. Strong hands gripped my hips as he pulled me to meet him thrust after thrust. He molded my ass with his palms and pleasure wound fast. When his thumb raked across the most sensitive part of my behind, I sucked in a sharp breath. I jumped, unable to process he would touch me in such an intimate spot. More shocking was my disappointment when he moved his hand away. Alarm gripped me as I realized how deep I'd fallen. I was ready to submit every last part of me to him.

I didn't know what it was with him. Whatever it was made me forget about everything—the past, my responsibilities, the lingering unspoken truths. It was as if we were destined to be together, bound in the most fundamental ways—like nothing could have stopped our reunion from happening.

Holding fast to my hip with one hand, he reached around with the other to circle my clit with his finger. Tremors rolled through my limbs as he pounded into me. My arms wrapped around a pillow, trying to find something to hang onto as he drove me higher and higher. Shockingly, he pulled out and flipped me onto my back once more.

"I want to see your face when you come, baby," he said huskily, his lips curving up in a way that read pure sex.

In an instant, he was back inside me, plunging with a ferociousness that took my breath away. Pulling all the way out, he pushed in again all the way to the hilt. He wasn't gentle in any sense of the word. I raked my hands down his chest, then back up to grip his shoulders. Drenched with sweat, he fucked me and fucked me, over and over again. Dizzying shimmers of color began to dot my vision and I cried out.

"Fitz! Oh, oh!"

"Look at me. Keep your eyes on me."

Noises I'd never made before ripped from my soul. I moaned and drowned in the waves of ecstasy. My legs started to quake, and the earth stilled. Energy spiked, my core clenching in a blissful state of euphoria as the orgasm rocketed through my body.

"Let go, Fitz. Let me feel you come," I rasped.

Dropping his head to mine, his hips brutally continued to snap in and out. The intensity billowed, making us one. I'd never felt more connected to him as I did the moment his body began to tremble. He jerked and shook as he swelled and pulsed inside me, crying out my name over and over again. I felt him shudder before he finished, his body going still.

I didn't want to move and break our connection. I think he felt the same because he groaned in disappointment when his softening cock slipped from my body. Rolling onto his back, he shed the condom and tossed it into the wastebasket next to the bed. He slid his arm under my head, pulling me tight to his side, and I curved into him. We laid there for what seemed like the longest time with my hand resting on his pounding heart.

As I listened to his breathing slow to a steady rhythm, I forced myself to separate the euphoria of the present moment and think about the reality I was faced with. I'd allowed myself to get lost in him once again, but things had gone on for far too long. I should never have come here tonight. At the rate our rekindled relationship was moving, no time had seemed like a good time to tell him about Kallie and she was due home on Sunday. I only had a few days left and I couldn't put off the truth any longer. However, now wasn't the right time. I needed a concrete plan before I brought the avalanche of passionate emotions surging between us to a screeching halt.

An idea about how to tell Fitz began to form in my mind as he traced slow circles with his index finger over my tattoo.

"Fitz," I said into the quiet room.

"Yeah, sweetheart."

"There are a lot of things we need to talk about. I know you said you wanted to hang out with Devon tomorrow night, but I was wondering if you'd want to stop by on Saturday morning? Maybe do breakfast?" I suggested.

"That sounds like a great idea," he murmured against my head. "I have a lot of questions after meeting the Mendez family tonight. We can go through them, then maybe go over my speech. I was emailed the drafts for the kickoff party this morning."

"Yeah, maybe," I replied weakly.

*Assuming he still wanted me to attend the party after he learned the truth.*

I had to believe he would. The connection we shared wasn't something years could sever. When two people loved each other the way we once had, there was no chance of ever being the same again. It was too strong. My heart had finally found its way back to him, but I had to tuck it away again—even if it was only for a little while. It didn't matter what was present in every look, touch, and kiss. It was time he learned everything.

---

When I got home later that night, I went straight to my bedroom and pulled out the box of letters I had written to Fitz all those years ago. Carrying the box down to my tiny home office on the first floor, I set it on the old maple desk and bent to open the safe situated underneath. I rummaged through the contents, pulling out any document related to Kallie—her birth certificate, hand and feet prints taken at the hospital where she was born, old report cards. One by one, I placed each paper on the scanner and printed out a copy. After collecting various pictures of Kallie taken over the years, I put everything I'd gathered inside the box.

Replacing the lid, I brought it back to my room and set it on the dresser before changing for bed. After turning off the lights and climbing into the comfort of my cotton bedsheets, I stared up at the shadowed blades of the ceiling fan swirling round and round. I thought about all that had happened tonight, the past few weeks, and all the way back to a young love that had blossomed under a setting sun.

Whenever I was with Fitz, I saw flashes of the young man I once knew coming out in the older version of him. There were so many memories between us, and I could recall all of them. It reminded me of a time when life was easy. I was so carefree, spending my days with Fitz as if nothing could touch us. Now, things weren't so simple. There were no guarantees my plan to tell him about Kallie would work, but I couldn't spend the rest of my life wondering. I could only hope he'd come to understand.

# Chapter Twenty-One

**FITZ**

I left the office an hour early on Friday afternoon. End of the week rush hour traffic in D.C always brought out a special brand of crazy. When combined with the thunderstorm that rolled in thirty minutes earlier, the commute was a nightmare.

On the way home, I stopped by the grocery store to grab a four-pack of Guinness for me and a two-liter of soda for Austin, then hit the local pizza joint to pick up dinner. I was looking forward to getting home and spending some long, overdue quality time with my son.

"Austin, I'm home," I called when I came in. "I've got pizza and those parmesan breadsticks you love."

"Sweet! I'm starving!" he yelled back.

I shook my head. The kid always thought he was starving. I headed down the hallway off the garage and rounded the corner into the kitchen. Austin was standing at the kitchen table riffling through the contents of a large box.

"Get some plates from the cabinet, will you?" I asked and set down the pizza so I could grab two clean glasses from the dishwasher. Cracking open a can of Guinness, I poured the dark liquid until a nice, creamy head formed, then filled Austin's glass with Pepsi. "I'm just going upstairs to change out of my suit. I'll be right back."

After shedding my sports coat, tie, and dress pants, I threw on a pair of jeans and headed back down to the kitchen. Austin was still standing over the box at the kitchen table and hadn't gotten the plates.

"Dad, why did you order all of this?"

"All of what?"

"These kid's books. I know the lady who wrote them. She's my friend's mom."

Somewhat annoyed he hadn't followed my direction about the plates, I went to the cabinet to grab them myself.

"No, it can't be your friend's mom. I know the person who wrote them. She's a friend from a long time ago. She doesn't have any kids," I replied absently. With the pizza box and plates balanced in one hand and my glass of beer in the other, I motioned my head toward the soda. "Come on. Grab your glass and the two-liter. Let's head down to the basement."

"You're wrong, Dad. I'm telling you it's the same lady," he insisted. Sighing, I walked over to where he stood. Opening one of the books, he pointed to the author photo in the back. "The girl who I went to the prom with, that's her mom. I've met her."

He pulled out his wallet, removed a picture from a plastic sleeve, and held it out to me. Setting my load down on the table, I took the photo from him.

"What's this from?" I asked impatiently. My stomach began to rumble. Apparently, I was just as hungry as Austin was.

"It's a group shot of all of us at prom," he told me. He pointed at a pretty blond in the middle of the group standing next to him. "That was my prom date, Kallie."

The smiling girl in the photo was practically a spitting image of Cadence. If she wasn't Cadence's daughter, I'd be a monkey's uncle. I frowned. If this was, in fact, her daughter, I didn't understand why she hadn't mentioned her before.

Suddenly, a thought hit me—one so blinding it was as if I'd been sucker punched. As a sophomore in high school, Austin wasn't old enough to go to the Junior prom on his own, and his date had to have *been a Junior.*

*One year older than Austin.*

*She looks* just like Cadence.

All the air deflated from my lungs and my hand began to shake. I allowed the picture to fall free from my grasp and jammed my hands into my pockets, not wanting Austin to see how rattled I was.

"Austin, how old is Kallie?" I tried to ask as casually as possible.

"She's a year older than me. Why?"

I looked dow*n at the phot*o again.

Could it be?

I shook my head. No, Cadence would have told me. There was no fucking way she would have *hid my daught*er from me.

My daughter.

For some reason, just thinking those two words made the possibility all too real.

"No reason," I lied and plastered on a fake smile. "Ready for me to kick your butt at Madden?"

Austin grinned.

"Yeah right! You won't be kicking anything, old man! It's on!"

We made our way to the lounge area in the secluded basement which was basically set up as a man-cave with couches, a large flat screen television and a pool table. I was a good place to unwind or for Austin and me to take turns kicking each other's asses in a video game. Normally I enjoyed the time we spent here together, but I couldn't find the usual appreciation today. I was too busy trying not to be sick from the realization seeping in.

Cadence lied, and she'd been lying for seventeen fucking years.

Austin turned on the TV and the PlayStation. The Madden intro music began to play as we both grabbed a slice of pizza and settled into the gaming chairs in front of the TV. The food tasted like ash in my mouth. The shock I'd felt in the kitchen had begun to subside, slowly being replaced by the worst feeling of betrayal.

I stared at the TV, absently selecting my team and players, but when it came time for the opening kick-off, I barely registered what was on the screen. Conversations rushed in as I considered all the things Cadence had sai*d to me over the past few weeks.*

*"I can't shirk my responsibilities."*

*"I'm terrified of you hurting me all over again. There's too much at stake this time."*

*"I need you, Fitz. I've always needed you. No matter wh*at happens, don't ever forget that."

I recalled the phone conversation I overheard her having with Joy on that first day *I ran into Cadence jogging the Mall.*

*"The stars seem to be aligning in a really weird way. It doesn't matter how* long it's been. You need to tell him."

I remembered the strange, panicked behavior in the car when she told me she wasn't ready to meet Austin. I didn't understand it then, but I now realized it was because she'd already met him. If he saw her, her secret would be out. Then there was the way she seemed to want to push me away and the refusals to let me into her house. All the signs she was hiding something had been there, but I didn't see them. Now, it was blatantly clear, and it all made perfect sense. I felt like an idiot. Her words and push back weren't meant to put me off. They were meant to conceal the truth.

Looking at my son, another thought struck. I racked my brain, trying to remember the name of the girl Austin had been kissing at school when he got into the fight.

"Austin, the girl you got into a fight over—the one you just started seeing—what's her name?"

"Jessica. Why?" he asked through a mouthful of food.

I exhaled in relief, but that still didn't mean his teenage hormones weren't active on prom night. I'd already had sex with a few girls by the time I was h*is age,* and it occurred to me I'd never had the talk with him.

"You didn't do anything with Kallie *on prom night, did you?"*

*"What do you mean?"*

*Christ,* was he really going to make me spell it out?

The referee in the game whistled and the ball snapped. I tried to defend against Austin's three-man route combination, but my brain was too damn distracted. I cleared my throat, hoping I didn't sound as awkward as I felt.

"You know, fool around. Did you make out or anything like that?"

His face pinched up as if he found the mere idea completely disgusting.

"Hell, no! Trust me, Dad. We're only friends. That would be like kissing my sister or something," he assured as he maneuvered his players down the field. "Touchdown! Yeah, baby!"

I glanced back at the screen, the chee*ring from th*e virtual crowd a dull buzz in my ears.

His sister.

His words made me want to vomit and I had to swallow the bile forming in the base of my throat.

"Nice play," I weakly congratulated.

"Dad, what's up with you tonight? It's never that easy. I basically just wiped the field with you. You let me hold your safeties, leaving a huge opening."

I closed my eyes and pinched the bridge of my nose. I didn't know how to respond to him. Anger at what Cadence had done leached into the marrow of my bones. Blinding, white-hot rage flashed. My brain scrambled to organize every feeling and thought I ever had about her, trying to make sense of it all.

"Sorry, kid. Just distracted tonight. Can we pick this back up in a few hours? There's something I need to do."

"Ah, yeah, sure," he slowly agreed, his expression perplexed. "I'll text my friend, Jace. Maybe he'll want to play a game online or something."

I gave his shoulder a light squeeze before standing to walk back up the stairs to the kitchen.

I looked around the kitchen. The children's books Austin had pulled from the box were strewn all over the kitchen table, the mess symbolic to the shambles my life had become in the blink of an eye. Once again, my life had been sucked into a violent twister, barreling down an uncharted path. Where it would spit me out was anyone's guess.

# Chapter Twenty-Two

**CADENCE**

After I got home from work, I called Kallie to wish her a happy birthday, then went through the pile of bills that needed to be paid. Once I was through, I set out to clean the house top to bottom. I wanted everything to be perfect for Fitz when he came by the next day. It was strange, but I felt if I showed him a neat and tidy environment, it might somehow show I was a good mother and ease the blow about Kallie. I thought I did a good job with raising her and wanted him to feel confident about that.

The air was thick with humidity, the crisp spring air beginning to change over to summer heat, and rain showers had moved in a few hours earlier. The weather, combined with my mad dash to make everything in the house sparkling clean, made my skin sticky with sweat. I needed to shower before I could relax and unwind. Tomorrow would most likely be the most emotionally draining day of my life and I needed to be well rested if I had any hopes of getting through it.

After a quick shower, I felt more refreshed as I combed through my tresses. Slipping into a pair of cotton shorts and a tank top, I went down to the kitchen, happy I had remembered to grab wine at the grocery store on my way home. I uncorked the bottle, poured myself half of a glass of red, and went to the living room to see what old movies might be showing on the TV.

Deciding on *Casablanca*, I settled back into the plush couch pillows. Lightning flashed outside, and thunder boomed. Rain pelted loudly against the windows and I had to turn up the volume on the television to hear it better. Just as Humphrey Bogart discovered his old flame was in town, a loud bang caused me to jump. The booming continued, and it took me a minute to realize it wasn't thunder, but someone repeatedly knocking on the front door.

"Who in the hell…" I muttered.

I walked to the door and peered out the side window. My heart stopped when I saw Fitz standing on my doorstep in jeans and a crisp, white button-down shirt with the sleeves rolled up to the elbows. His eyes flashed angrily as he ran a hand through his already messy hair.

"Open up!" he barked.

Startled by his uncharacteristic behavior, I cautiously cracked the door a few inches.

"Fitz, I thought you weren't coming by until tomorrow."

"We need to talk, Cadence. Now!" he stated gruffly without any sort of greeting. Not waiting for me to invite him inside, he pushed past me. I barely had a minute to react. He looked around the house, almost as if he were searching for something.

*Or someone.*

My stomach plummeted to the floor and my palms began to sweat. I was going to tell him about Kallie in the morning anyway, so I didn't attempt to hide the pictures of her. Perhaps I'd end up telling him tonight instead. Still, I'd never seen him this angry and couldn't help but think he might already know. Not wanting to contemplate what this unexpected visit could mean, I nervously moved to the end table and picked up the bottle of wine.

"Drink?" I asked.

His head snapped around to look at me.

"No. I prefer not to drink when I'm fucking pissed off," he spat out.

My stomach twisted and turned into a million knots. I drew in a shaky breath.

"Fitz, what's wrong?"

"Where is she? Is she here?" he demanded in a gruff voice.

"Who?" I feigned, hoping like hell this wasn't what I feared.

He moved toward me with purpose, closing the distance between us in just a few short strides. Once we were toe-to-toe, he grabbed me by the shoulders and startled me. He didn't hurt me, just held me still.

"You know who I mean, damn it! Kallie!"

I felt all the blood drain from my face. My worse fear had come to fruition. He was so angry and I could tell he didn't even want to look at me. His eyes flitted back and forth between pictures on the walls seeing them for the first time, his expression guarded and hurt. Sadness washed over me in waves. I didn't know how he found out, but I should have been the one to tell him. He deserved to hear it from me first. Regret nearly stole my breath.

"Fitz…"

"Why?" he demanded. The single word was forced, laced with pain and disbelief. I could see the war waging inside him.

"I'm so sorry. I know I should have told you sooner."

"You're damn right you should have! You lied to me. I've spent all these years believing you were perfect, good, and honest. I loved you…I love you so fucking much but you didn't even have the decency to tell me the truth! What else are you keeping from me?"

He squeezed my shoulders hard and I winced. A look of mortification crossed his face as soon as he realized what he was doing. Almost immediately, he dropped his hands to his sides. Taking a step back, he slammed frustrated hands through his hair and began to pace.

"I'm not hiding anything else. I swear it. I was planning to tell you," I whispered.

"When?" he bellowed. "Exactly when were you going to tell me we had a child together?"

"I was…I was going to tell you tomorrow when you came over."

"Why? It didn't fit into your schedule seventeen years ago?"

I flinched and tried to think of a way to explain it all.

"It was a long time ago, Fitz. I was barely eighteen years old—scared, broken, and alone. How did you find out?"

His eyes continued to dart around the room, and he didn't look at me when he answered.

"Austin. I ordered your kids' books. When they arrived in the mail, he found them. He saw your picture and it didn't take long for me to put the pieces together. When I finally did… fuck, Cadence! I felt as if my entire life had been snatched away from me. All that time…" He trailed off, his voice breaking, unable to find the words to express more. "Where is she now?"

"On the French class trip."

A look of recognition came over his features and he nodded.

"The French trip…Austin was supposed to go on it." He paused his pacing and looked pointedly at me. His eyes flashed angrily. "But you already knew that, didn't you?"

I looked away guiltily. Slowly, he walked over to the end table to pick up a framed picture of Kallie. It had been taken her sophomore year in high school. He stared at it for a long while, neither one of us speaking. An impenetrable expression hardened his beautiful face. Finally, unable to take the silence any longer, I sucked in a steeling breath and spoke up.

"She has your smile."

His head snapped up and regretful eyes raked over me. It was as if he were processing a million thoughts. In them, I saw all of his pain and heartache.

"I know what it's like to be a parent, Cadence. I've practically raised Austin on my own. I watched him play and grow. I taught him the rules of basketball and helped him with algebra. We've argued and fought, laughed and cried. We've shared birthdays and Christmases together. We established traditions—lots of fucking traditions! But, with Kallie—my daughter—I'll never have any of those things. You stole that from me."

I knew full well how important all of those things were. I covered my mouth and tried to choke back a sob, but there was no stopping the tears that began to fall freely down my cheeks. I never meant to steal those opportunities from him. I just did what I thought was right.

"Fitz, you don't understand. Like I said, I was eighteen and scared. The day I found out I was pregnant with Kallie was the day you got married. What was I supposed to do?"

"Tell me the truth, dammit! That's what you should have done! If I had known, I would have…" he trailed off.

"You would have what? Come back? You left, and we both know you wouldn't have come back to me. I had to accept that."

"I don't know what I would have done, and you can't assume!" he snapped. "You didn't tell me. You didn't think I deserved to know—to have that chance. How could you look at me again after all these years and not tell me right away? I can't believe you'd betray me like this!"

Memories of all those days I'd waited for him rushed to the surface. It forced all the anger, heartbreak, and frustration that had been buried deep for seventeen years to come to a head.

"Betray you? How dare you sit there on your high horse and make accusations? I went back and forth about whether I should tell you during my entire pregnancy. There were days when I was sure I'd contact you and days when I hated you for leaving. I understood your hands were tied, but it didn't make the reality hurt any less. I cried almost every night, knowing I wasn't enough for you—that I wasn't enough to make you stay. If I told you I was knocked up, and you came back, it wouldn't have been for me. It would have been because of a baby. That would have made me no different from your father."

"How so?"

"It would have been another part of your life where you had little choice. Was I wrong for not telling you? Maybe, but I was so scared! I wasn't perfect. I was practically a child myself, being forced to make impossible decisions. No answer was the right answer, so I made the choice for both of us to protect Kallie. I had the sense to realize a baby wouldn't have made a damn bit of difference. You would have stayed married and nothing about the situation would be any different. If I'd found out I was pregnant before you got married, maybe things would have played out differently. But like I already said, I didn't know until it was too late. I was so mad, upset, and lost. I loved you, and you broke me. You have no idea what it was like for me. You don't know how bad I hurt!"

"Don't I?"

His eyes bore into me, flashing with accusation. I was swiftly filled with unexplainable resentment. Spine stiffening hard and straight, I glared right back at him and snapped.

"No, you don't! You can be angry at me for not telling you a few weeks ago, but you don't get to be pissed off at me for not telling you years ago. You made the choice to leave. You put everything else ahead of me. I used to be the girl who believed in fairytales and happily-ever-after. When you walked away, all of those grand ideas about Prince Charming were destroyed. There were options, and you didn't take any of them! While you were reciting wedding vows, I was left home to cry and worry about my future. Do you know how hard it was to give birth to Kallie—to our daughter—knowing I'd be reminded of the only man I'd ever loved every day for the rest of my life? I could have given her up, but I didn't. Instead, I worked to bury the bitterness and regrets. I promised you no regrets, and I was determined to keep that promise. I persevered through all the challenges and raised a remarkable young woman. I built my own damn castle and raised Kallie to believe she can breathe fire—and I did it all by myself!"

Something regretful flashed in his stormy gray eyes.

"You didn't give me much of a choice, now did you?"

"Just as you didn't give me one," I bit out.

Running his hands through his hair again, he violently tugged at the ends and swore.

"Fuck, Cadence! I can't do this with you!" he thundered and shook his head. "I need to get out of here. I shouldn't have come here unannounced like this. God, if she'd been here… I should have considered the possibility before banging down your door."

"Yeah, you definitely could have handled this differently," I sardonically stated.

"Wait—you think *I* handled this wrong? You're unfucking believable."

I took a deep breath and hastily wiped the tears from my face. This bickering was pointless.

"Look, I'm sorry. We both screwed up. I'm just trying to explain why I did what I did all those years ago. Fighting about it now isn't going to change anything," I tried to reason.

His eyes locked on mine.

"No, arguing won't help. But I can't ignore the fact you lied to me for more than seventeen years. I need to think."

He quickly moved passed me toward the front door, but I couldn't let him leave—not like this. I needed to make him understand. Rushing to him, I grabbed his arm to stop him.

"Fitz, wait a minute! Wait right here." Not waiting for a response, I dashed up the stairs to retrieve the box I had put together the night before. When I came back down, he was already walking down the porch steps, into the rain. "Here. Take this. It might help you understand."

He turned around, pain crashing over his features and lancing at my heart.

"Understand what?"

"Understand I've loved you since I was eighteen years old. When you left, a huge, aching hole was punched through my heart. A part of me died. You were the first man to really kiss me. To touch me. To make love to me. For me, there's never been anyone but you. I still love you. It was always you, Fitz. I just hope the contents of this box will make you see that. If not, then walk away. That's what you do best at after all."

It was a cheap shot, but I couldn't hold it back. Taking a hesitant step forward, I shoved the box in his direction. Ever so slowly, he took it from my hands.

"It's you who doesn't understand, Cadence. I've carried guilt over leaving you for half my life. I've struggled to forgive myself. I loved you more than anything. For me, loving you is like breathing. But this betrayal… I don't know if I can survive this."

My stomach dropped, and I nearly sank to my knees. The finality in his words was more than I could bear, knowing once he left this time, it may be forever.

He stared at me for a moment longer before turning away once more. He walked slowly down the driveway, seeming oblivious to the pouring rain, and climbed into his black Audi. Then he was gone.

# Chapter Twenty-Three

**FITZ**

I had spent most of the week in a full-blown rage, not knowing if I was coming or going. I was agitated, pissed off, and confused. I ignored calls from everyone, barely making it through the workday only to have to come home and pretend everything was normal in front of Austin. Devon had been giving me strange looks all week, but I didn't give a flying fuck. I'd basically operated on two frequencies all week—pissed off and really pissed off. Even now, I was supposed to be going over my speech for the kick-off party. It was already Thursday, and I had less than two days to make it satisfactory, but I couldn't focus on the words. As hard as I tried, there was no caging the blinding fury racing through my veins. I couldn't stop wondering what my life would have been like if Cadence had told me about our daughter. Yes—our daughter. It was just too much to wrap my head around.

When I finally felt calm enough to analyze the situation, I sat down at the desk in my study and opened the lid of the box Cadence had given me. I hadn't wanted to look inside it before now. For some reason, hanging onto the anger had just been easier.

On top of the pile, I found everything to do with Cadence and me from seventeen years ago. There was the origami I'd given her on the last day at Camp Riley, the mixed tape which included the song *Fade Into You*, and the playbill for *Singin' In The Rain*. I pushed it to the side irritably, not wanting to be distracted by what was once between us.

Underneath the old memorabilia, I located everything I could ever want to know about Kallie. There was a copy of her birth certificate, listing her full name as Kalliope Benton Riley. I liked the way Cadence had incorporated her mother's maiden name. It had a nice flow to it—almost whimsical.

Kalliope was born on the twenty-first of May, seventeen years ago. I looked at the calendar on my desk. Her seventeenth birthday had been the day I discovered her existence.

*Another birthday I missed.*

The father was marked as "unknown." Seeing the word caused a pain in my chest, but I pushed on, only stopping when I got to the school pictures. Over and over again, I flipped through the photos of Kallie taken over the years. The transition as she grew from year to year was inconceivable, and I couldn't help but be angry over all that lost time.

*More regrets.*

Austin taught me what it was like to be a parent—to have that unconditional bond—knowing I would sacrifice anything for his well-being. Raising him hadn't been easy. Between building my company and dealing with his drunk mother, he and I had definitely gotten off to a rocky start. However, things got better over time, growing easier as we settled into our groove. He was a good kid who I was proud to call my son—but 'son' was the keyword. I could relate to Austin man to man. I didn't have the faintest idea about what to do with a girl.

*Would I have been a good father to her?*

I flipped through the pictures again. My heart swelled every time I looked at her adorable little face, then filled with pride to see how she'd grown into a beautiful young woman.

I set the pictures down and moved on to the next thing in the box—a stack of envelopes that had aged yellow over time with my name written in flowing script across the front of them. Removing the paper inside the first one, I began to read.

*To the keeper of my heart,*

*It's only been a few days, but already I miss you so much. My heart is broken. I know why you had to leave, but I don't know if I'll ever accept it. I'll always love you, and you'll always be the person I gave myself to so openly and freely. Despite your words, I'll never stop seeing the good in you. Now that you're gone, all I feel is a hollow emptiness. I don't know how I came to feel like this in just a few short months. Every time I close my eyes, I see you. In the silence, I hear your voice. In the darkness, I see your face. I don't know if I'll ever escape it. I wish you'd come back to me. I wish you had picked me over your father's demands. I'll try to accept things for what they are, but until then, I'll keep writing to you with the hope one day we'll be together again.*

*All my love,*
*Cadence*

I poured through letter after letter. She had written to me almost every single day since the moment I left Camp Riley. I read about the day she found out she was pregnant and about the support her parents gave her. Sometimes, her letters were sad. Sometimes they were angry and bitter. But then there were the happy letters—like the day she felt Kallie kick in her belly for the first time. A pain of grief hit me, wishing I'd been there to place my hand over her stomach and experience the moment with her.

Although the letters were written to me, they were more like a dear diary of sorts. In between the letters were newspaper clippings mainly about my father but had my name thrown into the text for some reason or another. As I continued to read, I began to understand her struggles and fears. I could feel the way she battled with herself to seek me out but worried about the fallout I'd suffer. That's what it always came back to—me. She'd denied her wants and desires in order to protect me. Until the end. In the end, she did it to protect Kallie.

When I began to read the letter dated one week after Kallie was born—when Cadence finally decided to say goodbye—I felt my throat tighten.

*I wish things could have been different for us, but I accept the choice I've made. I will never regret the time I had with you…*

I'd left her isolated and scared. I could only imagine what seeing a picture of me and my pregnant wife did to her. Based on the transition of her letters, it was obvious Cadence had gone into survival mode and it was all because I'd left her alone. What she had gone through was not all that dissimilar to what my own mother lived through. The irony of it all wasn't lost on me. My mother made a choice to keep me hidden to protect me. Cadence had done the same for Kallie a generation later. I couldn't fault Cadence for that. She did what she had to do. Yes, I could be angry, but my anger had been misguided. I was the one who was truly to blame. I was the one who had left.

I still loved her so much—that fact would never change. I just didn't know how to handle what I was feeling. I couldn't articulate the pain and loss, and I certainly couldn't make any decisions about my future in this state of mind. I had no idea where to go from here, but one thing was certain. I couldn't waste any more time. I had to meet Kallie. Her mother and I had a lot to work out, but while that happened, I didn't want another day to go by where I didn't know my daughter.

*My daughter. What would it be like to meet her? To know her?*

A knock on the door jarred me from my thoughts. I scrambled to shove everything back inside the box, shoved it under my desk, and hastily wiped away the moisture in my eyes.

"Come in," I called, assuming it was Austin. I was surprised to see Devon poke his head in.

"Hey, man. How's it going?" I closed my eyes and dropped my head into my hands. "That bad, huh?"

"Devon, you don't even know the half of it."

"I could tell something was up this week. At first I thought you were just all keyed up about the kick-off party coming up on Saturday, but when you went ballistic on Angie today I knew it was more than that. I figured I should come by your place to run interference."

"Yeah, I owe her an apology," I guiltily admitted.

"No, dude. You need to give your secretary a goddamn raise. I didn't think the poor thing would make it until five o'clock when you finally decided to drag your miserable ass out the door. What's going on?"

I sighed and reached back under my desk to pull out the box. Opening the lid, I handed Devon Kallie's birth certificate. He gave it a quick glance, then looked at me in confusion.

"That's a birth certificate for Kalliope Benton Riley—Cadence's daughter," I explained.

"Her daughter?" He paused and looked at it more closely. He raised a hand and began to do mental math on his fingers. "Wait a minute. She would have gotten pregnant the year we…the summer…"

"The summer we were at Camp Riley," I finished for him.

"Are you telling me you have another kid? A daughter?"

"Yeah, but keep your voice down. I don't know how in the actual fuck I'm going to tell Austin. I've barely processed it myself."

"Shit, man. Lady luck just doesn't want to blow your way, does she?" I didn't answer. Instead I slid the last letter Cadence had written to me across the desk for him to read. When he was through, he shook his head. "This is nuts. I'm pretty sure Steve Holy sang a country song about this."

"Great," I scoffed. "As if I didn't already despise country music enough. I guess I'll need to buy myself a pickup truck and a dog."

"Hey, now. Remember what they say—play the song backward, and the guy gets everything back," Devon chuckled. "So now what are you going to do?"

"I don't know. I've been asking myself that all week."

"Well, what do you say I go to the fridge and grab us a couple of beers? We can figure this out. God knows, we've been in more than our fair share of jams. This should be a piece of cake, right?"

I laughed, but the situation was far from amusing.

"Sure. I think I've got a Guinness or two left and a bunch of those IPAs you like."

After Devon left the room in search of beer, I took a deep breath. I felt as if my entire life had been a current—every time I tried to swim against it, it just swept me away. I refused to be dragged down any longer. The problem was, I was currently drowning, and I didn't know how to fight this kind of undertow.

# Chapter Twenty-Four

## CADENCE

I dragged myself through the work week, fighting to keep it together. It had been the fight of my life, trying to hide the quiver in my voice and the tears constantly threatening to break free. Despite the fact I didn't think the situation could get any worse, it had. I hadn't heard from Fitz all week long. I knew I'd messed up and figured it would be best to give him time to think things through, but it had been seven long days. I didn't know how much more time he needed.

I fretted over whether I should tell Kallie, but I was terrified Fitz might be gone for good. I didn't know how to give her the truth if it meant I'd have to turn around and say he wanted nothing to do with her. I never wanted her to think she was unwanted or unloved by anyone.

Then there was this ache. It was an ache I knew I'd feel but never imagined it would be this bad. I missed Fitz so much, the pain just as present as it was one week ago when he'd left my house in anger. It clawed at me as I pulled the car into my driveway.

Throwing the car in park, I glanced in the rearview mirror. The makeup I'd slapped on that morning was still somewhat intact, but no amount of concealer could hide the dark circles under my eyes. I'd barely slept a wink all week, but at least it was Friday. If I really wanted to, I could stay in bed all day tomorrow.

Climbing from the car, I slowly walked toward the front door. I glanced at the flower planters flanking the porch steps. The dahlia blooms were wilted and in need of water. I usually watered them as soon as I got home from work, but all motivation to do much of anything had completely disappeared. A pint of Ben and Jerry's and comfy pajamas just seemed so much more appealing. As a result, the poor flowers hadn't had water for days.

I focused on putting on a happy face and stepped through the front door. I called out to Kallie.

"Kallie, I'm home!"

I shook my head as I took in the evidence everything was back to normal since she'd arrived home from her trip. She'd been back for only a handful of days, but I may as well kiss my clean house goodbye.

Her bookbag laid open on the couch, spilling papers out over the cushions. Her shoes, as usual, were left where they landed, and the maroon cardigan embroidered with the St. Aloysius logo was strewn haphazardly over the back of the recliner. Her suitcase still sat near the foot of the stairs by the front door, unzipped and clearly rifled through. I kicked her shoes to the side so I didn't trip over them and walked toward the kitchen. Kallie was a good kid but getting her to pick up anything around the house was like pulling teeth.

I found her sitting at the kitchen table pouring over college brochures.

"Anything pique your interest?" I asked. When she didn't respond, I walked over to her, plopped my purse on the table, and plucked an earbud from her ear. She looked up in surprise.

"Sorry, Mom, I didn't hear you come in."

"Perhaps, you would have heard me if the music wasn't so loud. You're going to damage your ears," I gently chided.

*God, I sound like my mother.*

"Check this out," she said, holding a brochure for some school in Colorado.

"Later. Right now, I want you to clean up this mess. I love you, girl, but you're a slob. I asked you to put that suitcase away the night you came home." I pointed toward the front door. She flashed me a guilty look but got up to do as I asked without argument. Before she left the kitchen, she paused and turned to me.

"Mom, are you okay?"

I didn't know how to answer that. I should tell her I was fine, but the truth was, I didn't think I'd ever be okay again.

"I'm good, sweetie. Why?"

"You've been looking like a sad-faced emoji all week."

*Had I been that obvious?*

Kallie inherited my mother's intuitive traits and easily spotted when something was amiss. It was no surprise she'd picked up on my melancholy mood, but I didn't think I'd been that transparent. Still, she didn't need to be burdened with my problems—at least not yet. Since it was now my turn to look guilty, I turned away from her and busied myself with getting a glass of water.

"A sad-faced emoji, huh?" I tried to laugh off.

"Yeah. I'm kind of worried."

"I'm fine—really. I just have a lot on my plate right now."

I leaned back against the counter and took a long drink water. I wasn't all that thirsty, but rather wanted to use the glass to hide my expression. My mother always said people could read me like a book.

"Do you know what I think? I think you've been alone for too long. You need to find a hot guy and go out on a date," she announced.

I nearly choked on the liquid pouring down my throat.

"A date?" I squeaked.

"Yeah, you remember how to do that, right? I mean, I'm probably going away to school in a year. I don't want you to be here alone after I'm gone. Aunt Joy and I were talking about it. She agrees with…" she trailed off and narrowed her gaze. "Oh my gosh! You have been on a date, haven't you? You're blushing, Mom! Do you have a boyfriend?"

There was no mistaking the excitement in her voice over the possibility. I needed to shut this down immediately. Knowing Kallie, it would be less than five seconds before the next question came pouring out. I set the glass down on the counter and brought my hands to hips.

"I'm not blushing. It's just warm in here," I tried to deny. However, from the suspicious look on her face, it was obvious she wasn't buying it. "I think Aunt Joy needs to mind her own business, and I think you have a suitcase to unpack."

I donned a stern expression and pointed toward the living room again. She continued to look skeptically at me for a moment longer, then smiled this small, knowing grin before turning to head out of the room.

I tilted my head toward the ceiling and closed my eyes. Taking a few deep breaths, I forced myself to try to relax. I needed to get out of the funk I'd been in. Life went on and I'd have to figure out a way to deal with it sooner rather than later.

While Kallie was cleaning up her belongings, I opened the freezer to pull out chicken breasts for dinner. I was deciding what to do with said chicken when my cell phone began to ring in the purse I'd set down on the kitchen table. Digging it out, I looked at the caller I.D. It was my real estate agent. She was probably calling about the buyer for the land in Abingdon. I had yet to give her an answer about whether I was going to sell it.

"Hello?"

"Cadence, it's Savannah Sterling."

"Hey, Savannah. What's up?"

"I'm calling about an offer made on the property in Virginia."

"I assumed that was why you were calling. I've actually thought about it. I think I'm going to hold off for now."

"No, there was another offer—one that might make you change your mind. It came in just this morning from a completely different buyer. It's a corporation called TDP and they're willing to pay three times the market value. I really think you should consider."

*Three times?*

I thought about all the things the money could buy. I could give the long overdue raises to the people at Dahlia's Dreamers, pay off my mortgage, and the last few installments of Kallie's school tuition. I might even be able to take her on a little vacation before she started college. Still, despite the generous offer, I wasn't sure if I could emotionally part with my childhood summer home. With everything currently happening with Fitz, I wasn't in the best frame of mind to make permanent decisions and I didn't want to do anything rash I might regret later.

"Email me the offer and I'll look it over Monday morning when I'm back in the office. No promises though, Savannah."

"I know, I know. I get it. Some things have sentimental value that no money can replace."

I didn't think truer words had ever been spoken. After thanking Savannah for the call, I pressed the end button on my phone and went back to preparing the chicken. Peeling off the cellophane wrapper, I popped it in the microwave to defrost. My cell phone rang again.

"Oh, for crying out loud! Can't a woman cook dinner in peace?" I shouted to no one who was listening. This time, it was Simon Reed. Inwardly, I cringed. I hadn't spoken to him since the gala, and I was nervous he might be upset about the way I'd abruptly left him that night. I debated whether I should answer the call, but ultimately decided I should in case it was work related.

"Cadence, I've got great news!" he said excitedly after I picked up.

"What is it?"

"It's the Andrés Mendez case. The judge dropped the charges against him. ICE is processing his paperwork now. His status is safe. Emilia can pick him up at the holding center within the hour."

Happy relief washed over me, excited to hear the first good news I'd had all week.

"Oh my God! Are you kidding me? That's great! What happened? Why did he change his mind?"

"I don't know the all details. The judicial assistant called my office fifteen minutes ago. I know the guy pretty well, which is probably the only reason I was able to get a few tidbits. You know how judges are normally super tight-lipped about their decision-making process. Anyway, all he said was Judge Perkins got a phone call from some guy named Quinn. A few minutes later, the judge came out of his chambers and announced he was dismissing the case."

I heard everything he said, but I could only focus on one word.

*Quinn.*

*Did Fitz do this?*

"You said Quinn, right? Do you have a first name?"

"No, it wasn't mentioned. Why?" he asked. I stared absently into space as I tried to wrap my head around what this might mean for Fitz and me. "Cadence, are you still there?"

"Yeah, Simon. I'm here. Thanks for the update and all your work on the case. I'm going to call Emilia now—she'll be absolutely thrilled!"

After I ended the call, I took a moment to process the information. I recalled the faraway look Fitz had when I'd told him the name of the judge. Then I remembered how upset he was when he left my house last week. I didn't know if he called the judge before or after our argument.

I made the call to Emilia, then to Joy. Both were just as ecstatic as I was over getting to add the Mendez file to the drawer with the smiley face sticker. However, I couldn't help but feel my excitement glow with a little something extra. The possibility Fitz had called the judge *after* we had our fight might mean there was a sliver of hope for us.

As I went about preparing dinner for the third time, I tossed the chicken in a marinade and sliced and diced the vegetables for our side dish. Except now, I felt a bit lighter on my feet.

---

I crawled into bed around eleven. Just as it had all week, sleep eluded me. I tossed and turned for forty-five minutes before turning on my bedroom television. As I flipped through the channels in search of old sitcom re-runs, my cell phone chimed on my nightstand. I ignored it, assuming it was an email coming through. When it chimed again a few minutes later, I glanced over at it curiously and picked it up.

My heart began to race when I saw it wasn't an email at all. It was an incoming text from Fitz. Quickly, I typed in my password to unlock the screen and pulled up my messages.

11:56 P.M.
FITZ: WE NEED TO TALK.

11:59 P.M.
FITZ: I KNOW YOU'RE AWAKE. I CAN SEE THE LIGHT FROM THE TV COMING THROUGH YOUR BEDROOM WINDOW.

*What? He can see…*

Scrambling from the bed, I ran to the window and drew up the blinds. Across the street, Fitz was leaning against his parked car. When he saw me, he looked back down at his phone. Glancing down at mine, I saw the three little dots signaling he was typing.

12:01 A.M.
FITZ: GLAD I GUESSED RIGHT ABOUT THAT BEING YOUR ROOM. I DON'T THINK OUR DAUGHTER WOULD TAKE KINDLY TO A STRANGE MAN STARING UP AT HER BEDROOM WINDOW.

*Our daughter. He said our daughter.*

My heart ached, and hope bloomed deep within me. I didn't know what his words could mean, but I had to find out. Standing here staring out the window and texting wasn't going to get me the answers I needed. Acting on impulse, I dashed from the room, into the hallway.

I came to a screeching halt in front of Kallie's bedroom door, needing to make sure she was asleep. As quietly as I could, I slowly inched the door open to peek inside. The lights were off, and she seemed to be fast asleep. Relieved, I silently closed the door once more and continued my mad dash down the stairs.

When I got outside, I slowed to a more reasonable pace and walked across the street to where he stood. When I reached him, the day-old stubble covering his jaw and his expressive gray eyes took my breath away. I had to fight every bone in my body to stop myself from touching him. Whenever he was around, I was unable to resist being close to him. But with everything happening between us, I hesitated. For some reason, he seemed so far out of reach. We stared at each other in silence. I knew I had to say something one way or the other, but fear of getting the words wrong rendered me speechless.

"Hey," he said, shifting his weight, one foot to the other. He appeared as nervous as I felt. The air was wrought with tension. His being here could mean so many things, but I was afraid to hope.

"Simon Reed called me today. Andrés Mendez is free to go," I told him, attempting to break the ice with small talk. When he only nodded, I added, "Thank you, Fitz. I don't know what you did but thank you."

"The judge was Bethany's father. He owed me a favor or two." My eyes widened in shock at the coincidence. He laughed bitterly. "Yeah. It's funny how things work out sometimes."

"Yeah, I'll say." I studied his face, desperately trying to read the conflicting emotions. I couldn't tell if he was mad, unhappy, or relieved to be standing outside my house. "Fitz, look. Kallie…she doesn't know about you yet or else I'd invite you inside. Do you want to go sit in the backyard and talk instead?"

“No. It’s late. I just wanted to see you for a minute.” He paused and reached up to tuck a stay lock of hair behind my ear. The action seemed automatic before he seemed to catch himself. Shoving his hands into the pockets of his jeans, he rocked back on his heels.

“Why are you here, Fitz?” I whispered.

# Chapter Twenty-Five

**FITZ**

I stared at her, completely forgetting my reason for coming by. She looked hot as hell in her little tank and cotton shorts. Her golden hair was woven into the braid she always liked to wear, and I could tell she was braless, reminding me so much of that first night I'd spent at Camp Riley.

But then I remembered nearly two decades had passed. The sky was now dark and there wasn't a sunset at her back. There was no lake. There was no dock. This was the present and things were so much different.

"I'm here because I couldn't stay away," I began, my words coming out hoarse. Her mouth opened to form a delectable little O, but I cleared my throat and continued. She deserved the humble pie I was about to dish up. "I went through the box you gave me."

"And?" she asked nervously. Looking down, she began to fiddle with the hem of her shirt.

Moving closer, I stepped toe-to-toe with her and placed my hands on her slender waist. Stormy, emerald green eyes moved up to meet mine.

"I feel like every turn I've made in my life has sent me the wrong way down a one-way highway. I try to dodge the oncoming traffic, yet I know a crash is inevitable. It's time for me to get off that stretch of the road and travel the right one."

"What's the right road, Fitz?"

"You are. I'm so sorry, Cadence. I understand now. When I came here last week and flipped out, I didn't have a fucking clue. I never stopped to think about what you went through all those years ago. As much as I'd like to, I can't turn back time. You have the right to say you don't want anything to do with me—I deserve as much after leaving you alone all those years ago. All I know is I've never looked at another woman the way I do you. When I closed my eyes, it was you I saw. Even when I was angry with you for keeping Kallie from me, I still saw you. If I have to walk away knowing we don't have a chance in hell, I'll wait for you because there has never been anyone else *but* you."

Her lips parted, and my stomach squeezed. I leaned down and kissed the top of her forehead.

"Fitz, I…"

"There are a lot of things I have to come to terms with and I know we have a lot to work through. It won't be easy, but I want to give it a shot. Tomorrow night is the campaign kick-off party. The invitation is still open if you'd like to go. It should wrap up by nine, and I thought we could go for a drink afterward and talk. But you should know, Austin will be at the party. As far as he knows, you're an old friend. He doesn't know Kallie is his half-sister."

She stepped back, wrapped her arms around herself, and shook her head.

"I don't know if me being there is a very good idea. We always seem to rush into things and think later. We can't do that anymore. Austin aside, I assume your father will be there. What will he say? Or what about the scandal in the press when they find out about Kallie? Aren't you worried? I mean, I don't know if I want Kallie to be dragged through the mud because of what you're doing politically. It's my job to protect her."

I felt the corners of my mouth turn up, appreciating the mother lion presence in her tone.

"I've thought about that too, but I think I can avoid a PR mess. It's what I do for a living, remember?" I reminded her with a wry smile. "I went over things with Devon last night and brought him up to speed on what's going on. I'll handle my father. Don't worry about him. As for the press, we can spin this a few different ways so there's minimal to no damage."

She curiously cocked her head to the side.

"How so?"

I paused for a moment, unsure of how she'd take to the ideas Devon and I came up with.

"We could just say you're my girlfriend, and Kallie is your daughter. Her birth certificate says as much. Nobody has to know she's mine." I tried to keep my expression blank, needing to hide the pain I felt over option one.

She shook her head again.

"No, I don't like that. I can't handle any more lies, Fitz. It wouldn't be fair to us or to Kallie and Austin."

Not realizing I'd been holding my breath, I exhaled in relief. God knows, I didn't want to deny my daughter any more than I already had.

"Good. I'm glad you said that, but I thought I owed it to you to give you the choice. Since we both agree burying it is out, it leaves two other ways to play it. We can say we were together years ago, you got pregnant, we had a falling out, but ended up reconnecting years later. That's as close to the truth as we can get without getting into the shady details about my father and Judge Perkins."

She squeezed her eyes closed as if she were trying to visualize how everything would play out. When she opened them again, her expression was pained.

"Why do you still feel the need to protect them?"

"It's not about them, sweetheart. It never has been. It's about Austin. I don't want him ever to know he was the result of blackmail. I never want him to feel like he was unwanted."

She nodded her head slowly.

"I can understand that. I had similar sentiments this past week. I didn't tell Kallie about you because I wasn't sure if you were coming back. No child should feel unwanted or unloved." She sighed and rubbed her arms as if warding off a chill, despite the fact the night was warm and humid. "What's the third option?"

"I back out of running for Senate."

"Back out? But why?"

"After talking with Devon, it seemed like the most obvious choice. It will give us time to sort through this openly and honestly without putting the kids through a possible media circus."

"Fitz, I don't want our children to suffer embarrassment, but I also don't want to stand in the way of your aspirations. You have the chance to do something good. You shouldn't give that up."

"So, what if we go with option two then? I campaign as planned while we work through the rest. What's the worst that could happen?"

"People could get hurt—me, Kallie, Austin. You don't know what the future holds."

I took a hesitant step closer and brought her to my chest. Thankfully, she didn't pull away as I feared she might, but placed her hands on my shoulders and stared at me with those wide, emerald eyes.

"You're right, sweetheart. I don't know what the future will bring. But I do think it's worth taking a chance to find out. When I ran into you after so many years apart, it was like my world settled. Everything finally began to make sense, but then I found out about Kallie and it completely flipped upside down. Now—just seeing you tonight—I feel it beginning to calm again. People say everything happens for a reason. Maybe things didn't happen seventeen years ago because they weren't meant to be. Maybe we wouldn't have been able to make it work back then. I may not know what will happen down the road, but I know I see you in every part of the journey. You were always supposed to be in my life."

Her eyes brimmed with tears and she shook her head. I couldn't tell if she was happy or sad.

"Fitz, I…I don't know if..."

She stared off, appearing lost in thought. I waited a beat before pressing her to finish.

"Tell me what you're thinking. I need to know where your head's at, Cadence. Can we make a go at this one more time?"

"I don't know. I want to say yes, but I'm confused about what the right choice is. I want to be with you with all my heart, but maybe we should think about this more. Plus, I need to find a way to tell Kallie, and you Austin."

"Tomorrow then—after the party. We can figure out the best way to do it, but I don't want to do it alone. I think we should tell them together."

She rested her head against my chest.

"I'm scared, Fitz," she whispered.

"About what? Talking to the kids?"

"No. I'm afraid of you. You left once before. I accepted it, but now… when you stormed out last week, it was as if you ripped my heart out all over again. But this time, it was so much worse. I've fallen completely in love with you all over again and you can hurt me worse than you know. If you leave again, it will destroy me."

She'd always been so open and honest about her feelings. Tonight was no different and her words tore at my chest. I'd fucked up way too many times with this girl. It didn't matter what I did—I always seemed to mess it up.

"I won't hurt you, Cadence."

"You can't promise that."

I leaned back and tilted her chin up to look at me.

"No, I can't. But I can promise you I won't walk away easily. I love you, Cadence. I'll earn that place in your heart again and remind you that, despite all the time apart, sometimes the reward is worth the wait."

# Chapter Twenty-Six

**CADENCE**

I checked my reflection in the full-length mirror behind my bathroom door one final time. Slowly, I spun in a circle.

"I don't know. Are you sure I look okay?" I asked Joy. She was currently propped up on the counter on FaceTime. I turned back toward her, allowing her full view of the cream-colored pantsuit I'd chosen.

"Honey, you look great. If you don't believe me, ask Kallie."

"I would if I could. She's at a friend's house until eight. I left her a note telling her I'll be at Marine Gate for the evening and would be back late." I paused to fiddle with the chunky gold necklace at my neck. I frowned and looked at Joy through the phone screen. "Too much?"

"A little bit. Maybe wear your silver necklace with the tiny pearls. It's dainty and feminine, not too ostentatious."

"Great idea."

After swapping out the necklace, I began fussing with my hair, even though I'd already spent close to an hour styling it.

"Stop messing with it. It looks good," Joy scolded. "Your hair is perfect, your makeup is perfect, and you're dressed to kill. Your nerves are what's going to ruin it all."

"Am I that obvious?"

"Just a little," Joy laughed. "Try to relax. I know you're worried about Fitz's father, but you have to remember—you know who he is, but *he* doesn't know who *you* are. Just take a deep breath. Your biggest concern should be about the afterparty."

"I'd hardly call drinks with Fitz to discuss how we should tell our kids a 'Once Upon a Time at Camp Riley' story an afterparty," I stated dryly.

"You know what I mean. Either way, you're going to be late if you don't get a move on."

"You're right. Thank you, Joy. I'll text you later."

After ending the video chat, I took off down the stairs, slipped into my nude pumps, and headed out the door.

Traffic was surprisingly light, and I made decent time. It was a good thing too because finding parking was a bitch. After twenty minutes of circling the block, I ended up having to park in one of the expensive ramps. I checked my reflection in the review mirror one final time and took a few calming breaths.

*Time to get this show on the road.*

I walked up to the Marine Gate Hotel and entered through the glass turnstile doors. Almost instantly, I spotted a sign that read 'RNC Event, Rooftop Patio, Elevator C' and followed the direction to where it pointed.

I walked past the hotel check-in desk and down the corridor leading to a bank of elevators. There were two security guards positioned outside the elevator I needed to take. One was checking off the names of the guests who were waiting to go up. The other loomed ominously over the line of guests as he discernibly looked each person over. When I got to the front of the line, I gave my name.

"Cadence Riley."

Security guard number one scanned his finger down the list.

"I'm sorry, ma'am, but I can't allow you to go up."

"What do you mean?" I asked in surprise and pinched my brows in confusion.

"It means you can't go up," he reiterated.

"That can't be right. Mr. Quinn is expecting me."

He pursed his lips in annoyance—as if he'd rather be doing anything other than dealing with me. He made a shooing motion with his hand.

"Please step aside so I can check in the other guests."

Ignoring his request, I crossed my arms stubbornly and dug in my heels.

"Check the list again," I demanded.

He sighed, huffing out a long and exaggerated breath as he absently glanced down the list again.

"There. I checked again, and you can't go up. Don't make this harder than it needs to be. I'm just doing my job—and it includes keeping out unruly protesters. So again, please step aside so I can check in the other guests."

I blinked and angled my head to the side feeling somewhat taken aback.

"I'm not a protester. I'm…" I trailed off, not sure how to describe what I was to Fitz. "It's like I said. Mr. Quinn is expecting me."

Another impatient sigh.

"If you must know, Mr. Quinn specifically has you down as someone who's not allowed to enter."

I shook my head.

"No, that can't be right," I repeated. The second security guard leaned over to look at the list, then whispered something to the guard who wouldn't let me pass.

"My apologies ma'am. I misspoke. Mr. Fitzgerald Quinn had your name on the approved list. However, we work for Senator Michael Quinn. He's the Mr. Quinn who said you're not allowed to enter. I'm sorry, but we can't let you up."

There were murmurs from the people in line behind me, and I felt my face flush in embarrassment. Apparently, Senator Quinn knew who I was after all.

"He did, huh? Well, we'll see about that." Stalking away, I took my cell phone from my purse and dialed Fitz. There was no answer. "Dammit!"

I walked back toward the hotel lobby and tried him again. When it went straight to voicemail, I sat down on a cushioned bench, pressed against the wall, and took a moment to think. I didn't want Fitz to assume the worst if I didn't show up. There had to be another way to get up to the roof.

"Excuse me, Miss," said a voice to my left. I looked up just as a luggage cart ran over my foot.

"Ouch!"

"Oh, I'm so sorry!" said the bellman who ran me over.

I pinched my eyes closed, leaned down to remove my pump, and rubbed my smarting toes.

"It's fine," I waved off.

*Just add this to the list of things that had to go wrong this week.*

The bellman apologized again and continued on his way without another word. I watched him push the cart down the corridor and swipe a key card to open a set of large double doors. When the doors opened, I spotted a service elevator just inside.

*Service elevator. That's it!*

Moving as quickly as I could, I slipped my shoe back on and managed to wedge my hand between the doors to stop them from closing. The bellman never looked back but continued down a corridor leading to who knew where, completely unaware of the doors that failed to shut behind him. Once he was out of sight, I slipped inside and hurried to the service elevator.

I hit the button for the highest floor. When the elevator stopped, I stepped out and glanced up and down a long hallway. From the look of things, I'd been dumped off on the twelfth floor and not the roof. There was a window to my left and a long hall to my right. There had to be a staircase somewhere that would lead up to where the party was being held.

I walked down the hallway, peering in door after door, hoping to find a stairwell. The floor was obviously not meant for the public. Instead of hotel guestrooms, I found office space and supply rooms. The place was a maze of corridors branching off in various directions. Finally, I noticed a little sign on the wall with a picture of stairs, a stick figure person, and an arrow pointing up. Hoping this would lead me to my destination, I began to climb the steps.

# Chapter Twenty-Seven

**FITZ**

White satin sashes, peppered with silver and red glitter, hung from the glass guardrails of the rooftop patio. Spherical oil lanterns were strung between the metal poles dividing the glass panes, their flames flickering in the subtle breeze. I stood next to Devon by the podium that had been set out for me, the two of us taking in the crowd beginning to gather.

"Are you sure about this?" he asked.

"Nope, but I'm here now," I laughed. "Keep an eye on Austin for me tonight, will you? He told me he was cool with my decision to do this, but I want to be sure."

"No problem. Where is he now?"

I glanced over toward the bar where Austin stood eating a plateful of hors d'oeuvres and sipping on a Pepsi.

"He's over there by the bar. Cadence should be here any minute. He knows she's Kallie's mother, but he still doesn't know my connection to her. He might get curious and ask questions once he sees us together. Until I can work out how and when I can tell him the truth, I have to be careful."

"Have you decided how you're going to tell him?"

I reached up to grip the back of my neck and sighed.

"I don't know yet. Cadence and I are supposed to go out later on tonight to talk about it. It's not going to be easy. I mean, Christ. How in the hell do I tell him he took his sister to the fucking prom?"

"That's no joke, man," Devon acknowledged and shook his head.

"Don't worry about it tonight. You've got enough to focus on. Just do what you need to do. I'll take care of the kid. After we get through this dog and pony show, maybe I'll take him to see the new *Avengers* movie or something."

I placed my hand on Devon's shoulder, gave it a brief squeeze, and patted him on the back. I didn't think I'd ever appreciated his friendship as much as I did at that moment.

"Thanks, Devon."

After Devon walked off to be with Austin, I pulled my speech from my breast pocket and skimmed through it once more. Every few minutes, I'd pause to sweep the room for Cadence. I'd expected her to be here twenty minutes ago and began to worry she'd had second thoughts.

"I know who you're looking for. She isn't coming."

I turned to see my father had come up beside me.

"Who do you think I'm looking for?"

"That stupid girl who fucked everything up years ago," he said quietly through his teeth as he nodded politely to anyone who passed by.

"I don't have time for your mind games. I need to think about my speech. I'm supposed to talk in ten minutes." I turned to walk away, but he grabbed hold of my arm and plastered on a smile. To anyone who was watching, it may have looked like he was offering me words of encouragement. However, I was familiar with the malice showing in his eyes. His grip tightened.

"Listen to me, boy. Forget that woman. Do you think her coming back now is a coincidence? Your political career will never survive the scandal she'll bring. It will destroy you."

I released an impatient sigh.

"I don't know what you *think* you know, but what's between Cadence and me is none of your business."

"Oh, believe me. It's absolutely my business. I know all about her and what her endgame is. She's had a hell of a time financially for years—putting that daughter of hers through private schools, starting that ridiculous organization. Because of your obsession, I've had to keep tabs on her. Now she's back and looking for trouble. You've got money and power, and she wants a piece of it."

I froze.

"What did you just say about her daughter?"

"Don't play stupid. Do you honestly believe I wouldn't know about the love child you spawned?"

Ice slithered down my spine as I grappled with what he was saying. I didn't believe his accusation—Cadence wasn't suddenly back in my life for financial gain. I knew better than to believe that to be true.

However, his mention about keeping tabs on her raised the hairs on the back of my neck.

"Are you trying to tell me you've known about her daughter—my daughter—for years and you never told me?"

"You fool! Keep your voice down! People might hear," he hissed. Taking my elbow, he led me toward the edge of the rooftop. I went along willingly, needing to find out what else he'd kept from me over the years.

"Answer my question," I demanded through gritted teeth. "Have you always known?"

"Of course. I've known about her since the day she was born. They call you The Fixer, but it's always been me doing the fixing. That Riley girl has always been a threat. You need to cut her out of your life now before she does real, permanent damage."

I didn't want to believe even *he* could lie about something this monumental. His lie was jarring and couldn't have come at a worse time, yet I shouldn't have been surprised by what he'd done. Just when I began to feel like I could put the pieces of my broken world back together, he made room for more devastation by punching right through to the center of my chest and ripping out my bleeding heart. That's what he always did. I didn't think it was possible for me to hate him more than I did at that moment.

"You son of a bitch!" I hissed. "I thought I knew the depths you would stoop to for power, but this is a new low—even for you. How could you keep that from me?"

"It wasn't a matter of keeping something from you. You need to look at the bigger picture. It only takes one person to bring the house of cards tumbling down. This was about protecting you!"

I glared at him, suddenly seeing everything with perfect clarity.

"If you call fucking with my life protection, you really are delusional. I'm out."

"What do you mean you're out?"

"It means I'm not running. I've got seventeen years of catching up to do—no thanks to you—and I don't have time for your games, this campaign, or the Senate. I'm out."

"If you think you're going to pull out of this campaign, guess again. It's time you take your rightful place. The Senate seat is only the beginning." He gripped my arm, and his eyes flashed with something that bordered on maniacal as he raved. "You have the makings of a president, Fitzgerald, and it's high time you realize that!"

I stared in shock, unsure if I should take him seriously.

*The fucking presidency?*

I nearly laughed, shook my head, and ripped my arm free from his vice-like grip.

"I wanted to do something good—to make a positive change—but there's been something off about this whole damn thing right from the get-go. I'm not doing this with you. Maybe I'll consider again in the future, but I won't be doing it for you. I'll be doing it for me, my children, and my wife." When his eyes widened in surprise, I smiled. "That's right, Pops. I'm going to marry Cadence. It's what I should have done all those years ago."

Turning away from him, I scanned the room for Devon. I needed my wingman now more than ever.

"Devon!" I called when I spotted him. He paused the conversation he was having with Austin and looked in my direction. I motioned my head for him to come over. When he approached, I stared directly at my father when I spoke.

"Do me a favor. Get Austin, take him home or out to see the movie you mentioned earlier. This show is over."

I didn't know what Devon's reaction was because I was too focused on my father's expression. It morphed from shock to anger in a split second.

"Don't you dare do this, boy."

"Watch me."

I walked over to the podium and stepped up onto the riser. For the very first time, I was finally going to take back full control of my life.

# Chapter Twenty-Eight

**CADENCE**

I spotted Fitz as he took the podium and watched him scan the crowd. There was a gray-haired man standing near him, trying to get his attention. On closer inspection, I recognized the face I'd seen countless times on television.

It was Fitz's father.

My stomach sank, and I tried not to let apprehension get to me. I watched another man approach Senator Quinn and usher him off to the side. It only took me a moment to realize Devon Wilkshire was the second man. Even from here, I could tell the years had been kind to him. He still had that rugged handsomeness he'd had when I'd known him at Camp Riley. The two men put their heads together in quiet conversation and walked away while Fitz adjusted the microphone on the podium and scanned the crowd again.

When his eyes landed on me, a small smile turned up the corners of his mouth. The confidence and ease in which he stood made his presence known throughout the entire rooftop patio. His eyes didn't stray from me, his gaze intoxicating. We stared at each other for a moment, a gentle kind of understanding passing between us. I smiled back encouragingly, silently telling him I had his back. I believed in him with all my heart.

The wind kicked up, blowing my hair across my face. Brushing it aside, I focused on Fitz once more. He was no longer looking at me but up and to my left. I turned toward whatever had caught his attention, only to see a string of oil lanterns break free from the high poles surrounding the patio.

It was like I was watching a video on slow motion. Liquid poured from the lanterns, soaking the white and red sashes lining the glass surrounding the roof before they crashed to the ground. Instantly, the material ignited. In no time at all, the flames seemed to leap from the sashes to the furniture, setting fire to the nearby tablecloths and chair seat cushions.

"Oh my God!" I brought my hands to my mouth in disbelief.

People began to scream. I froze to the spot and stared in horror as the fast-moving fire got closer and closer to the propane patio heaters. Everyone rushed toward the exit on the other side of the room, their once pleasant chatter now cries of pure desperation. I moved forward, intent on following them when someone grabbed hold of my arm.

"Oh, no you don't," said a gruff voice from behind me. I turned around to see Fitz's father behind me, his face glowering with hatred.

"Senator Quinn," I said in surprise. I felt another small gust of wind. Heat licked the back of my neck, and I looked behind me. The flames had already spread across the middle of the rooftop, creating a barrier between me and the exit. Fitz was on the other side trying to push through the surging crowd to get to me. He couldn't break free, so I yelled, "Go with them, Fitz! I know another way out!"

"That boy is pathetic risking his neck to get to you. Goddamn fool!" the Senator spat out. I barely heard his words as I wracked my brain, trying to remember which way I had turned through the maze one floor down.

"Please, sir, we need to get out of here! Follow me."

"Not so fast." Gripping my arm tighter, he steered me back down the narrow hallway and down the stairwell that led to the lower floor. "You and I need to go someplace private and have a little chat first. You're not going to fuck this up for me."

He turned left at the base of the stairs, pulling me along with him. I shook my head, knowing we needed to either continue down the stairs or go the other way to reach the service elevator.

"Senator, I can assure you, I have no idea what you're talking about. There's a fire! We need to leave! This is the wrong way!" I pulled, trying to break his hold, but he only tightened his grip. "Ouch! You're hurting me!"

"Shut up!" he snapped. He continued dragging me down the hall, my feet sliding along the floor as he pulled. I could hear little explosions coming from the roof overhead. I prayed it wasn't the propane tanks. I'd never heard a gas explosion before, but I imagined it would be louder.

When we reached the end of the hallway, he shoved me down a

dimly lit corridor and into a dark room. I swore as my ankle rolled all the way to the side, causing me to stumble forward.

"Shit!" I yelped, throwing my hands out to stop myself from falling. I wasn't fast enough. My face collided with something hard that made a loud clanging sound. Pain splintered up my leg and my head rang. I clutched my head to stop the ringing and felt something warm and sticky under my fingers—blood.

I fought nausea and forced myself to turn around. I blinked, waiting for my eyes to adjust to the dim light. Brooms, mop buckets, and other cleaning supplies filled the space. I appeared to be in a large janitor closet of sorts.

"If you care about your daughter at all, you'll keep that bastard child away from my son. Do you understand me?"

Confused by what was happening, I could only stare at the broad frame of Senator Michael Quinn filling the doorway. I barely had time for his words to register before a loud boom shook the entire building. My ears rang, and I screamed.

*Propane tanks.*

The first boom was followed by a second, then a third. A loud crack echoed through the corridor, bringing with it thick, black smoke. The smell began to get stronger, filling my nostrils until I began to cough. I wasn't an expert, but if I had to guess, the fire on the roof was now on this floor and spreading fast.

Panicked, I lunged and tried to push him out of my way, not caring about anything other than escape. Our bodies collided, and we stumbled against one of the metal shelves causing everything resting on it to go clanging to the floor. I tripped over a bottle of something rolling on the floor. I spiraled down, bringing both of us crashing to the ground.

The smoke was getting thicker and I could barely breathe. He gripped my shoulders and I began to kick and claw, panic and desperation overtaking all common sense.

"Let me go! We have to get out of here!"

"Fucking wild bitch! You've always been wild. Nothing but trash. Your mother was a stage whore and you're no different!"

A loud roaring sound muffled his words and I saw a flash of light. His hold on me slackened and we both turned our attention toward the light. To my horror, I saw flames licking around the edge of the doorframe. I looked back at Senator Quinn and saw his eyes widen as realization of the danger suddenly sank in. Pushing himself off me, he made a beeline for the door. I scrambled to stand up, intent on following him out. My twisted ankle screamed in pain as I got to my feet.

Fitz's father seemed to assess the fire beginning to climb the walls of the hallway before turning back to look at me. Something evil flashed across his face as he stepped out into the fiery corridor and closed the door behind him. Instantly, I was thrown into pitch blackness.

"No!" I screamed. Moving as fast as my ankle would allow, I reached out to grab hold of a shelf. Using one hand to steady me, the other fumbled through the dark in the direction of the door. When my hand reached the smooth surface, I found it hot to the touch as I skimmed along searching for the doorknob. When I found it, I prepared to rip the door open, but instantly pulled my hand away—the metal handle was fiery hot. The flesh on my hand burned, and I squeezed my eyes closed. I was trapped.

*Think! Think!*

Falling to my knees, I felt around the floor, pushing through the mess of cleaning supplies until I felt the familiar satin material of my purse. Fumbling with the clasp, I pulled out my cell phone. The screen lit up. Fingers shaking, I dialed 9-1-1.

"Please hold for the next available operator," said a computerized voice on the other end of the line.

"Please hold! It's fucking 9-1-1!" I screamed to no one. Hanging up, I dialed again.

"All circuits are busy. Please try your call again."

*God, no. This can't be happening.*

Using the flashlight app on my phone, I angled the light toward the door. Fire glowed through the tiny crack at the bottom, and smoke billowed up toward the ceiling. Adrenaline and fear thundered through my veins. Moving the light around the small room, I looked for anything that might help me. I spotted a pile of folded white rags and a gallon-sized jug of distilled water. Staying low to the ground, I crawled over to the items. A fire alarm began to sound, and I nearly laughed, wondering why in the hell it hadn't gone off twenty minutes ago.

My throat and lungs burned as I poured water over the rag. It was getting hot—so hot I wanted to scream. Covering my mouth with the soaked material, I crawled back to lay against the wall furthest from the door. Sirens wailed in the distance, but I knew they'd never find me in time. The smoke was beginning to thicken, swallowing me whole. Black. Suffocating. I took deliberate, shallow breaths, knowing I had to reserve my oxygen as I tried to call 9-1-1 for a third time.

When I still didn't get through on the fifth attempt, I decided to try reaching the only other person I could think of—the one man who had always tried to save me. I began to cough violently, my lungs burning and fingers trembling as I dialed his number. I could only hope and pray he wouldn't let me down now.

# Chapter Twenty-Nine

**FITZ**

I had only made it down two flights of stairs when my phone began to ring. I would have ignored it but knew it was Cadence calling by the ringtone I'd set specifically for her. I struggled to get my phone out of my pocket as I was shoved this way and that by panicked people fighting their way down the stairs.

"Sweetheart, where are you?"

I could barely hear her through the loud rush of the crowd.

"Fitz…twelfth floor…maintenance closet." Her voice was raspy and low, barely able to choke out the words.

"Wait, what?" There was no answer. "Cadence!"

I pulled my phone from my ear to look at the screen.

"Come on, man! Keep it moving!" said some guy from behind me as he pushed me forward. The sudden jolt knocked the phone from my hand, sending it flying until it was swallowed up within the sea of people.

"Shit!"

Panicked, I looked around for Austin. He was well ahead of me with Devon in the hastening crowd.

"Austin, stay close to Uncle Devon! I'll be right behind you!"

Turning back, I ignored the curses from the people trying to get down the stairs as I pushed my way up toward the door that would open up to the twelfth floor. When I finally reached it, I yanked it open as much as I could, slamming into anyone who wouldn't move out of my way and slipped through. Plunged into a wall of suffocating smoke, I brought my arm up to cover my mouth.

I didn't know how she'd gotten to the twelfth floor. The last time I saw her was right after the lanterns fell. My father had been standing next to her, but I'd lost sight of them in all the commotion.

"Cadence! Cadence!" I yelled, then waited a beat hoping to hear her respond. The only thing I heard was the thrumming of my heart and the shrill sound of the building's fire alarm.

*Fuck!*

The smoke was so damn thick, I could barely see a thing. Feeling my way along the walls, I paused at every door hoping to find her location. None of the rooms were set up as hotel guest rooms, giving the appearance I was on a floor reserved solely for hotel operations. I passed laundry rooms and storage rooms, but nothing that resembled a maintenance closet. Flames glowed brightly up ahead. If she was anywhere near there, I'd never be able to get to her.

I continued to open door after door but no Cadence. My lungs burned, and I began to cough. Stepping into a room filled with rows upon rows of kitchen supplies, I closed the door behind me. The air wasn't as smoke-filled, allowing me a minute to catch my breath.

Running toward the shelves, I began to rummage through storage bins with the hope of finding something to cover my mouth. I just needed to buy time—just a few more minutes of air—so I could find her. I frantically dumped the contents, watching as they scattered all over the floor. The search was futile.

I slammed my fist against one of the metal shelves in frustration. The entire floor was a maze full of shit. There wasn't anything here, and I was wasting time. Inhaling a huge gulp of air, I covered my mouth with my arm once more and prepared to go back out into the smoky hell. As I moved to open the door, something red in the corner of the room caught my eye. I turned and spotted a neat row of at least ten fire extinguishers. Relief flooded through me as I rushed to grab one of them before going back out.

I pushed through the door, only to smash into something. The impact knocked me back into the room, flat on my ass. The fire extinguisher clanged to the floor.

"What the…" I looked up. I didn't run into something—it was someone. My father stood above me, coughing and sputtering as he tried to make sense of who was on the ground at his feet.

"Fitzgerald?"

"What the hell are you still doing in here? Where's Cadence?

"Forget that damn girl. She's gone," he choked out as I got back to my feet.

"What do you mean she's gone? I saw you with her."

"It means she's gone. I took care of her just like I took care of the last one."

"The last one? What are you talking about?" I asked impatiently as my worry over finding Cadence grew. I didn't want to hear one of his rants. I just wanted to get to her and get the hell out of this inferno.

"I'm talking about Bethany, your drunken little problem. She was a liability—a problem to be dealt with," he paused to succumb to another coughing fit. After he recovered, he glared at me, his gaze maniacal.

"I don't know why the fuck you're talking about Bethany, now of all times. I need to find Cadence! Now, where is she?"

My father ignored me and carried on like I hadn't even said a word.

"I mean, I'll admit I didn't plan on the car accident," he rambled. "That was just a fortunate accident. But getting the pills in her hands was the easy part. That idiotic girl was all too eager to buy pretty pills from a stranger she'd just met."

His mumbled words were incoherent, insane babblings I barely understood. We both began to cough again as I tried to decipher what he was saying.

"You're responsible for what happened to Bethany?" I asked incredulously. There was a loud crack and a hiss to my left, but I didn't bother to look to see what caused it. I was too busy staring at my father who stood there, grinning like a Cheshire.

"Problem solved," he boasted, then brushed his hands together for added effect—like the mother fucking asshole was actually proud of what he'd just admitted to doing. I gaped at him in disbelief as I thought back to that time in my life.

*Bethany. Pills. Car accident. Cause of death. The toxicology report.*

If what he said was true about Bethany, nothing would stop him from harming Cadence. My fists curled until all I saw was red—thoughts of vengeance and retribution entwined tightly around my heart. I couldn't let him hurt her. Not now—not ever. She and Kallie were innocent pawns in his fucked up game. It was time for this all to end.

"You've gone completely mad! Where is she? What did you do?" I tried to scream the words, but they came our hoarse and raw, my lungs burning from more smoke inhalation. My father coughed again and didn't answer me. Instead, he bent down to pick up the fire extinguisher I'd dropped and took off running. The problem was, he was headed straight toward the corridor where I'd seen the fire. "No! That's the wrong way!"

I cursed under my breath, trying not to acknowledge the fact the asshole cared more about saving his own skin than anything else and hurried back into the kitchen supply room to get another extinguisher.

When I came back out, there was a deafening boom. Instantly, I was knocked flat again from the impact of some kind of explosion. My body slammed to the ground, knocking what little air I had from my lungs. My ears rang as I struggled to make sense of what was happening.

I heard someone scream, but everything was muffled through an echoing ring. Everything was so hot—so hot I thought my skin would melt from my bones. I rolled to the side and tried to focus.

When my vision cleared, I saw him.

The blast had thrown my father down the hall and back toward the kitchen supply room. He was on his back, still and unmoving as an avalanche of burning plaster and metal collapsed just a few feet ahead of him. I blinked, time seeming to move in slow motion before it rushed back in to match real time.

"Dad!"

I got up as fast as my stunned body would allow and limped over to him. From the looks of it, he'd taken the flash head on. Every part of his exposed skin was charred black and bloody. The pungent odor was unbelievable, and I had to fight the bile welling in my throat as I leaned over him. His eyes moved to meet mine, but his body remained motionless. I watched in horror as a small trickle of blood fell from the side of his mouth. Slowly, he raised a shaky hand and pointed. I looked in that direction, but all I saw was fire and smoke.

"What is it? Is that where Cadence is?" He didn't answer. His arm fell to the floor and his eyes went vacant. "No! No, no, no! Wake up, damn you!"

I shook his burned body, needing him to tell me where she was. He didn't respond or move and a part of me knew he was already gone. Still, I pressed my fingers to the side of his neck, fighting to ignore the way they sunk inside his charred flesh as I attempted to find a pulse. There was nothing.

My body went still as everything I'd ever felt for him came crashing down around me. I saw flashes of myself as a boy meeting him for the first time. I remembered how kind he'd seemed and how my mother softened whenever he entered the room. Then I remembered how he wasn't there when she died. I remember the early years when I lived with him—the cruelty, the punishments, the way I longed for a parent but got nothing from him. I remembered the fight we'd had on the day I got married. I'd told him I wouldn't go through with it and said I was going back to Cadence. He just issued more threats—more ultimatums. I hated this man with every fiber of my being, but nonetheless… he was my father.

"Ah! Fuck!" I screamed and slammed my fist to the floor. I looked down at his lifeless body once more as the conflict raged inside me. I had to sort out my feelings later. He was dead. There was nothing I could do for him now and I was running out of time. My only hope was to find Cadence.

Leaving my father's body to the will of the fire, I took off in the direction he'd pointed, praying like hell he had been trying to tell me where she was. My lungs screamed as I ran through the smoke, my throat burning despite my arm covering my mouth.

*I have to get lower to the ground.*

I dropped to my knees and army crawled as fast as I could. The only thing I could see was orange and yellow glowing bright. Everywhere I looked there was fire—in front of me, behind me—bubbling the wallpaper and eating away at the plaster and wood. Panic seized my chest.

"Cadence!" I called out, ignoring the pain the hoarse cry brought to my chest as I moved closer and closer to the flames.

I neared the end of the hall and could see the faint outline of one final door. Flames slithered along the walls across from it, seeming to jump back and forth to teasingly lick its surface. I crawled along the floor and heat moved across my skin—so hot, I wanted to scream. Instinct told me should get out. It wasn't the fire that terrified me, it was the smoke. I wouldn't survive if I breathed it in for much longer. Every second that passed meant I was running out of time.

But desperation made people do desperate things. I had to know if she was there. If I turned around now, then found out that's where she'd been all along, I'd never forgive myself. My only thought was to get to her. She had to be there. I could feel it in my bones like some sort of sixth sense.

*Just one more door.*

When I got to be a few feet away, I realized the fire damn near surrounded the frame. Pulling the pin from the fire extinguisher, I aimed the hose and squeezed the handle, clearing the flames with frozen snow just enough to close the remaining gap. I reached up for the door handle but jerked back from the burn.

"Fuck!"

I shook my hand, not even thinking about the blisters that were probably forming as I pointed the hose at the area around the doorknob. Disoriented, I tried to focus as I ripped off my suit jacket. Using the material as a shield for my skin, I turned the knob and pushed the door open.

I scanned the dim room lit only by the flames that threatened to burn me alive. Through the smoke, I spotted a head of golden hair, lying motionless against the far wall.

"Cadence! Baby! Sweetheart!" I cried out, shimmying my body across the floor to get to her. Fear gripped me like a vice as I scooped her lifeless body into my arms. A white cloth tumbled from her hand and her head fell back limp. "No, God no. Please!"

Just as I had with my father, I pressed two fingers against her throat. She had a pulse—weak, but it was there.

I looked back at the door. Flames bloomed and were beginning to engulf the entire opening, radiating heat and asphyxiating smoke. I blinked rapidly, trying to bring moisture to my burning eyes as I glanced around the tiny room that felt like the inside of a furnace. A half empty gallon of water and a pile of rags lay next to where Cadence was. Realizing that may be the reason why she was still alive, I dosed another one for myself. I refused to allow this place to become our hell.

Acting on pure instinct, I grabbed the fire extinguisher one final time. Squeezing the trigger, I screamed through the dripping wet rag and sent white foam to smother every single threatening flame.

My lungs heaved, and I knew I probably only bought us a few minutes. Turning back to Cadence, I stood and cradled her in my arms. Moving as fast as my smoke-inhibited body would allow, I stepped out into the blistering hot hallway and ran toward the direction of the stairwell.

The smoke was thick, and I had to use the walls to find my way. When we finally reached the entrance to the stairs, I pushed through the door and ran down the first flight.

*She has to be okay. She has to be okay. I can't lose her now.*

I repeated the chant over and over again as I rounded the corner of a landing. Every gulp of air I took was a challenge. Unexpectedly, water rained down from overhead when we reached the tenth floor. I swore under my breath.

"Fucking sprinklers."

I didn't have time to think about why they hadn't been working on the twelfth floor. My only concern was getting Cadence out of there. It seemed to take forever, but I finally reached ground level and pushed through the emergency exit door to the outside.

Clean, smoke-free air assaulted me. Sirens and flashing lights were everywhere—firetrucks, police cars, ambulances. I barely processed the scene as I collapsed to my knees and gasped for air. I couldn't breathe. Everything hurt so bad as I fought to stay coherent and awake.

*I need to keep moving. Cadence needs medical attention.*

I knew this, yet I couldn't find the strength to stand back up. Instead, I laid her lifeless body down on the grass. She was still—so still. Her golden hair covered her face—soaking wet and streaked with black. I pushed it aside.

I heard someone yell, "There they are!"

More voices shouted.

I didn't look up to see who it was.

I felt arms come up behind me and pull me to my feet. I couldn't take my eyes off Cadence.

People surrounded her. Someone was doing CPR.

*Oh God. Please no!*

My already failing heart seemed to stall, and my vision began to blur. I opened and closed my eyes several times in an attempt to keep focus.

An oxygen mask was placed over her face.

*That was a good sign, wasn't it?*

Someone put one over my face. I batted it away, only for it to be replaced once more.

My vision blurred again, then all went black.

# Chapter Thirty

**CADENCE**

I choked and coughed while voices shouted around me. My throat and chest hurt so bad, I felt like they were on fire as I gasped for air. My head throbbed. There was pain in my ankle and leg. And my face—there was something on my face. I reached up to grab it, but my arms felt like lead weights as I attempted to pull it away.

"Oh, no. You need that," said a female voice.

Slowly, I opened my eyes and turned my head toward the sound of the voice. A paramedic was standing to my left and repositioning whatever was on my face. I blinked and tried to get my bearings.

*It's an oxygen mask.*

I shifted my gaze to the person hovering above me. A very disheveled looking Fitz stood looking down at me. His face was filthy, and his hair was sticking up wildly in all directions. I looked behind him to see flashing lights, more paramedics, and firefighters rushing about. Fitz breathed a sigh of relief.

"You scared the hell out of me, sweetheart," he said, his voice was hoarse and raspy.

"Fitz, I…what happened?" My words were muffled through the mask as I tried to sit up. Pain ripped through my skull in a blinding ache.

"Shhh. Lay down. You don't need to talk now," he told me.

"She got lucky. I don't hear any rattling in her lungs, and there's minimal swelling in her airways," the paramedic said. "I'm going to go see about helping some of the other victims. Please make sure she leaves the oxygen mask on for a little while longer and give me a shout if you need anything. I won't be gone long. Are you sure you don't want a painkiller for that hand? It's a nasty burn."

"I'm okay. Thank you for your help," Fitz said with a nod.

After she walked away, I took in Fitz's appearance again. His white shirt was covered in black soot, appearing burned in some places, and his left hand had been bandaged.

"Are you okay?" I asked.

He lifted my hand with his unbandaged one and brought my fingers to his lips.

"I'm fine. Just a little burn to the hand is all."

That's when it all came flooding back.

*There was a fire. I was trapped. Senator Quinn.*

I shifted the oxygen mask down so I could speak without restriction. He tried to stop me again, but I pulled my head away and forced myself to sit up. Ignoring the throbbing in my temples, I gripped Fitz's arm.

"Listen to me, Fitz! Your father," I choked out the words, feeling as if I had nails in my throat. "He closed the door on me. I was trapped."

Sadness filled his expression as he reached up to stroke my head.

"I know, sweetheart. But he's gone now. He can never hurt you again."

"What do you mean he's gone?"

"He was killed in the fire. There was a blast…" he trailed off as conflicted emotion clouded his features.

Burning tears formed and blurred my vision as I contemplated everything that had happened tonight. I remembered my mother once telling me God only gives what one person can handle. If that was the case, I'd reached my capacity. I looked at Fitz, my emotions a jumbled mess. All I knew was I needed to be close to him. I needed to feel some flicker of hope to know everything was going to be okay. The welling tears spilled over and streamed down my face.

"Hold me, Fitz. Please, just hold me."

Resting one hip on the side of the gurney, he sat down next to me. He pulled me close and I closed my eyes, giving in to the sobs that wracked my body. Resting in the safety and security of his arms, I tried to find balance and allowed the calmness of his embrace to wash over me. He stroked my back and murmured quiet assurances, his hypnotic and soothing voice chasing away my fears. He was like a snowstorm, blanketing me in white, covering me. I was buried, trapped, yet still warm at the same time. My fingers gripped his shirt, hanging on with everything I had. I never wanted to let go. He was everything I needed at that moment—protector, savior, lover, friend.

Finally feeling like I had an ounce of strength, I opened my eyes again. When I did, I spotted Devon and Austin standing a few feet away. Austin was looking at the ground and toeing his shoe around in the grass. Quickly, I looked at Fitz. He very subtly shook his head.

"No, he doesn't know," he murmured quietly. "But I'm sure he suspects something is up. I'm going to need to tell him soon, but I'll let you call the shots on this one. I've wasted half my life without you. I'm not going to do anything to fuck it up again."

"Mom! Mom, is that you?" I turned my attention to my right and saw Kallie and Joy racing across the lawn. Fitz released his hold on me and stood but kept his bandaged hand on the small of my back.

"Cadence, you scared the life out of us, girl!" Joy exclaimed once she reached my side. "I heard about the fire on the news. When I couldn't reach you, I called Kallie and found out she couldn't get a hold of you either. Neither one of us wanted to sit there and wait, so I picked her up, and we came straight here. But then the police wouldn't let us through the barricade and…"

She trailed off, and her eyes widened as she took in my appearance for the first time.

"I'm okay," I croaked out. Looking to Kallie, I noticed her concerned expression and grasped her hand in mine. "Don't worry. It's just a headache and a little sore throat. Nothing I can't handle. Mom's made of steel."

Her hand tentatively reached up to touch my shoulder.

"I don't want to hurt you or anything, but can I…can I give you a hug?" Kallie asked.

"Of course. Come here, baby girl." Reaching out, I pulled her in as tight as I could. Over her shoulder, I turned my head to watch Fitz's expression carefully. Despite the chaos of the situation, the fact he was seeing his daughter for the first time wasn't lost on me.

After she pulled away, Austin took a step closer.

"Hey, Kallie," he said.

"Austin, what are you doing here?"

"That's, ah…" He pointed awkwardly toward Fitz. "That's my dad. I was here with him for this event thing he had going on tonight."

Kallie looked at Fitz. He just stared, appearing stunned into silence before eventually reaching out to shake her hand with his one good one.

"It's nice to meet you, Kallie. You look… you look just like your mom."

My daughter observed him curiously as she shook his hand, her eyes following the line of his arm that was still resting behind my back. She narrowed her eyes suspiciously.

"Is this him, Mom? The boyfriend you tried to deny having?"

I nearly laughed but instantly found it was a mistake. My lungs screamed. Devon cleared his throat obnoxiously loud and Fitz tossed him a dirty look. The corners of my mouth turned up slightly when I realized how some things never changed.

*Batman and Robin.*

I looked back at Kallie. Her big, green eyes were full of young, innocent excitement. I had worked tirelessly over the years to protect that innocence. The world was full of ugly truths and I'd always felt she shouldn't be burdened with any of it. Glancing back at Fitz, I realized there was nothing ugly about our truth. She didn't need my protection from this. The love Fitz and I shared should be celebrated. It had lasted the sands of time and everything else in between.

"Well, honey. It's funny you should mention that," I began, struggling to find the right words. I was sitting on a gurney outside of an ambulance in the middle of pure mayhem. This was not the time nor the place for this discussion. "There's a lot I need to talk to you about but not here."

"That's right. Not here," Fitz agreed and wrapped a protective arm around my shoulder. He looked down at me, eyes brimming with a mixture of happiness and worry. "It can wait. You need to go to the hospital and get checked out first."

"I'm fine, Fitz. I'll admit, I'm exhausted, but what I want more than anything is a shower. I just need a few minutes to feel like a human being again. What time is it?"

"It's just after eight," Kallie answered.

"Joy, if you could take Kallie and me home, that would be great. I'll come back to get my car from the parking garage tomorrow."

"You really should go to the hospital, Cadence," Fitz warned.

"You heard the paramedic. She said I was lucky and appeared to be okay. If I think I'm not for any reason, I'll go." I raised my eyebrows and looked pointedly at him, hoping to convey a message that said I didn't want to put this off any longer. "I need to get cleaned up and get the stink of fire off me. Do you and Austin want to come by the house for pizza in about an hour? I know it might be a little late, but I'm sure nobody has eaten dinner yet."

"I'm up for pizza," Austin said.

Fitz shook his head.

"Why am I not shocked by that?" he chuckled. Looking to me, he whispered, "Are you sure about this, sweetheart?"

"I've never been more sure of anything."

Then, taking me by surprise, he leaned in to place a chaste kiss to my lips.

"Whoa! I knew it!" Kallie exclaimed. "He is your boyfriend!"

When I answered her, I never took my eyes from Fitz. He stared back, making me feel like I was the only person in the world. All I could see, hear, and feel was him.

"No, baby girl. He's not my boyfriend. He's the keeper of my heart."

# Chapter Thirty-One

*Abingdon, Virginia*
*3 MONTHS LATER*

**CADENCE**

Anxious butterflies danced in my stomach as Fitz drove us down the long stretch of road leading to Camp Riley. The GPS on the dash said we were three minutes away. I hadn't been to the property since my parents died. I just couldn't bear to come here. The place held too many memories I'd wanted to keep buried. While things with Fitz and me were better than ever, it was still hard to visit my childhood summer home and not see my mother and father hustling about in the thick of a musical production.

When the sign for the camp came into view, my stomach dropped. The wood plank that once boasted bright gold lettering was now worn with age and neglect. I should have expected as much but still. I supposed I should be grateful the sign was there at all. So much else had completely changed.

The gravel road that had only been used for pedestrian traffic or service vehicles was now paved with blacktop. Trees had been cleared to widen the road, leaving room for two-way motor vehicle traffic. To the left of the road, a housing development had been built. Modern homes and lush green lawns took up the space that had once been miles of forest interspersed with quaint little cottages. To the right of the road, the tall moss-covered oaks and pines stood tall and untouched. That portion of the land still belonged to me—even if it was only for a little while longer.

After a long debate with myself, I'd decided to sell it to the corporation that offered me three times the land's worth. Fitz, knowing how hard my decision was, offered to come here with me to finalize the sale. I couldn't in good conscience let sentimental value get in the way of doing what was best for Dahlia's Dreamers. The company was holding up just fine on its own through private donations and my book sales. In fact, *And I Smile* broke my personal record when it hit the *New York Times* bestseller list for the ninth week in a row. However, the office space and furnishings for my non-profit could use some serious tender loving care, but it hadn't been in the budget. It was a reality I had to accept when a client sat down in one of our waiting room chairs only to have it collapse beneath them.

"I don't know who the head of the TDP corporation is, but I wish he wasn't so insistent on meeting me instead of my real estate agent to inspect the property. It's five o'clock in the evening on a Saturday. By the time we get back home, it will be after midnight. We should have gotten a hotel room," I complained. I knew I sounded whiny, but I was too miserable about what I was about to do to even care.

Fitz glanced at me curiously as he maneuvered the Audi down the smooth black pavement toward my parent's old cottage.

"You okay?"

I sighed.

"Yeah. It's so depressing coming here now. It will be strange without my parents. I know selling is the right choice, but that doesn't make it an easier to accept."

"Don't be depressed, sweetheart." Reaching over, he squeezed my leg reassuringly before pointing to a green street sign on the corner. "Look! They used the path names for the street names. It's still Watercolor Way. See? It's like I've said before—everything happens for a reason. Things are going well. The kids are happy, we're both in a good spot professionally, and we're together. Everything will work out just fine."

I looked out the window at the passing scenery without really seeing it. I knew Fitz was right. The ugliness of the past finally seemed to be behind us. We buried Fitz's father with a lot less fanfare than the Senate would have liked. A delegation of Members of Congress wanted the ceremonies to be held within the halls of Congress itself, but Fitz politely declined their offer without revealing his reasons. In private, he told me he didn't think his father—a man fueled by paranoia, grand delusions, and greed—deserved to lay in state in the Rotunda, a place shared with Presidents, Vice Presidents and Generals. I couldn't agree more and supported his decision to hold a smaller affair. We avoided the media and didn't comment when the President ordered the flag to be flown at half-mast over the Capitol Building through the day after the funeral. When the Senate passed a more elaborate resolution on the Floor noting the accomplishments and distinctions of the late Senator Michael Quinn, Fitz turned off the news coverage. Watching *Game of Thrones* just seemed so much more appealing.

Kallie and Austin had taken well to the news about me, Fitz, and our history. Kallie was more accepting than I expected her to be, taking every chance she could to get to know Fitz better. Fitz had been over the top, spoiling her rotten in an attempt to make up for lost time—not that Kallie minded in the least bit. Austin and I were getting along well, but he was a little more cautious. However, it was for reasons Fitz and I hadn't predicted. Austin requested we keep things on the 'downlow' until after he graduated high school. I couldn't blame him. Kids could be so cruel, and he'd most likely get ripped to shreds by his peers for taking his half-sister to the prom.

Out of respect for Austin's wishes, Fitz and I both agreed to keep our relationship quiet. There would be no political campaigns in the near future if at all. Fitz was beginning to learn he could make more of an impact in the private sector rather than the public. As a result, Quinn & Wilkshire decided to spearhead a pro-bono PR campaign focusing on local non-profit organizations to raise awareness. It was set to launch next week.

When the car came to a stop in front of my parent's brown clapboard cottage, I didn't wait for Fitz to come around to open the door for me like he always did. Instead, I quickly climbed out and approached the porch steps. The buyer was supposed to be here in fifteen minutes, and I wanted to get this over with as soon as possible.

The wood beneath my feet creaked as I climbed the stairs. Reaching into my purse, I fished around for the keys to the front door. When I couldn't locate them, I looked back toward the car. Fitz was approaching behind me holding up a silver ring with keys dangling from the end.

"Looking for these?"

"Yeah, thanks. I could have sworn they were in my purse. Where were they?"

"On the floor of the front seat of the car."

Assuming they'd just fallen out of my purse, I took the keys from Fitz's outstretched hand, unlocked the front door, and entered the kitchen. The old table still sat in the middle. Other than the smattering of cobwebs and the dust lingering on the surface of everything, the kitchen looked just as it had the last time I was here—except my parents were missing.

A wave of nostalgia came over me. I expected it to happen, but I didn't expect tears to come along with it. Fitz's strong arms came from behind me to wrap me in his warm embrace.

"I'm sorry," I sniffled. "I don't know why I'm crying. I guess it's because I still miss them so much. I'm being silly when I should be wiping down the table. We can't very well sign a contract on a table full of dust."

Fitz turned me to face him and tilted my chin up with his index finger.

"Sweetheart, I don't mind a little dust."

"You might not, but the buyer will."

Stepping back, he reached into his back pocket to produce a thick envelope and handed it to me.

"Trust me, the buyer doesn't care about dust or anything else. Things are fine just the way they are. See for yourself." His eyes gleamed with the most peculiar look, almost playful. I glanced at the envelope curiously.

"What are you talking about?" I asked as I took it from him.

"Open it."

I sighed, thinking I should be cleaning instead of indulging Fitz in whatever game he was playing. I slid my finger along the seal and pulled out the stack of folded papers. I skimmed through the text and immediately realized it was the purchase contract between me and TDP for the sale of the land. Automatically, my hand dropped into my purse to feel for my copy of the contract. When my hand made contact with the envelope, I knew what Fitz had handed me wasn't mine.

"Why do you have a copy of this?"

"Isn't the buyer supposed to get a copy?"

"Well, yes. But…" My stomach twisted and my eyes widened. "Are you TDP?"

"No, sweetheart. *We* are TDP."

"I don't understand."

He grinned.

"It's kind of a funny story actually. Do you remember me telling you about the night Devon came over and I told him about Kallie? The two of us had been trying to find ways to spin the story with the public if needed."

"Yeah, I remember. Why?"

"Well, we had a few too many beers and one subject jumped to the next. That's always a dangerous combo. Anyway, we got off topic and started talking about our taxes and charitable contributions. Things kind of just spiraled after that. Why don't we take a walk, and I'll tell you about it?"

Genuinely confused, I shook my head.

"I can't go for a walk. They buyer will be here soon and—"

"Cadence, nobody else is coming here today. Now, come with me."

When he took my hand, I eyed him questioningly. He didn't explain further, and simply led me out of the house.

"Where are we going?"

"To the lake."

"The lake! That path has to be so overgrown by now. I'm not wearing shoes suitable for hiking."

He glanced down at my navy ballet flats and shrugged.

"So, I'll carry you if I have to. Now, if you'll stop arguing, I'll explain everything when we get there. Trust me."

# Chapter Thirty-Two

**FITZ**

As we walked down the hill toward the lake, birds chirped in the still of the trees overhead. Rays of light streaked through the branches, bending over the path like a living canopy. With Cadence's hand in mine, it felt like we'd walked this way to the secret spot a thousand times. Although I hadn't been here in years, it was still familiar. The path was overgrown like Cadence predicted, but it wasn't nearly as bad as it could have been, and we were able to navigate it with relative ease. I was actually thankful for the overgrowth. With the new housing development not that far away, I worried about the possibility of someone intruding on us. However, it was clear nobody had traveled this path regularly in a long while.

"Fitz, are you going to tell me what the hell you were talking about back there?"

I chuckled.

"I will when we get to the lake."

She pulled her hand from mine and stopped dead in her tracks.

"I'm not walking any further until you tell me what's going on. Who or what is TDP?"

I shook my head and pulled her to me.

"You have no patience," I chided and pecked a light kiss on her forehead. Moving my lips to her hair, I inhaled deeply. Her vanilla scent mixed with the surrounding pines brought me back—way back. "Mmmm… you smell good."

"Fitz, don't you dare try to distract me," she warned.

I laughed again and pulled away.

"Fine. You win. TDP is a brand-new, non-profit corporation. If you flipped through to the back of the papers I handed you, you would have seen your name listed as the president. It's just waiting for your signature of acceptance."

Her brows pinched together in confusion.

"Another non-profit? I'm sorry, maybe I'm a little slow on the uptake here. You'll need to explain better."

"Quinn & Wilkshire was behind on quarterly donations. To catch up, Devon and I decided to donate a big chunk of money to TDP. A large portion of that money was then used to place a sizable offer on this land. I have ties to this place too, Cadence. I couldn't let you sell it. There are enough structural buildings and land left to make this into something again. My thought was to keep it a summer camp, but on a much smaller scale than Camp Riley. It wouldn't be a performing arts camp, but a literacy youth camp for low income families. When we made the donation, we also made sure enough money would be left over to get a new camp up and running."

"But who would run it? I certainly don't have the time. Plus, Abingdon is over five hours away from D.C. As great as this all sounds, I can't be in two places at once."

"I've thought about that too. I went over things with Joy—"

"Joy? She knows about this?"

"Yeah. Your best friend is pretty amazing," I appreciated with a smile. "After talking to Joy, we came up with a plan. With her and Marissa looking to adopt soon, Marissa plans to quit her job and go back to teaching preschool. Since she'll be off during the summer, she's willing to come here to work the youth camp. She actually excited about it. If Joy and Marissa happen to adopt along the way, Marissa will be able to bring their new son or daughter with her to the camp and supplement their income in the process."

"But that would mean summers away from Joy. I can't imagine they'd want to be separated right when they are trying to establish a family, and I can't afford to have Joy take entire summers off from Dahlia's Dreamers."

"That's already been worked out too. We'd keep your parents old place for ourselves and use it as a summer getaway. Joy wants to snag one of the remaining cottages and turn it into a summer home as well, then convert one of the other ones into a satellite office for Dahlia's Dreamers. It's all been worked out, sweetheart. All everyone is waiting for is your stamp of approval."

She shook her head in disbelief as she took it all in. If there was one thing I'd learned over the past few months, it was Cadence was an organized planner. Her ducks were always lined up in a row, and I was pretty sure I just sent them flying all over the place.

"I can't believe you did this. I'm having a hard time wrapping my head around it all…" She trailed off, and her eyes suddenly went wide. She gripped my arm and shrieked, "Oh my God! This means I don't have to sell the land!"

"Well, technically you do, but you'll be selling it to yourself in a way. You just have to–"

My words were cut off as she threw her arms around my neck and rained kissed all over my face.

"I love you, I love you, I love you so, so much!"

"Had I known I'd get this reaction from you, I wouldn't have waited to get the details ironed out. I would have told you two months ago," I laughed.

When she pulled away, her emerald eyes sparkled with delight.

"Thank you, Fitz."

"Anything for you, sweetheart."

I only hoped she was just as excited for the next surprise I had planned. Taking her hand in mine once more, we continued walking to our lake spot.

"What does TDP stand for?" she asked as we approached the end of the path.

"I thought you'd never ask," I smiled and pulled out my phone. Opening the picture app, I scrolled to find the image I was looking for and held it out for her to see. "It stands for The Dahlia Project. This is just a mockup of the sign I had designed, but eventually, it will replace the worn Camp Riley sign out on the road."

Her sweet, sexy mouth tipped up at the corners.

"The Dahlia Project?"

"Yeah, I couldn't help myself. I had a real fondness for that dog. This place isn't quite the same without her. It seemed appropriate."

When the trees parted to open up to the vast lake, the sun was low in the sky, but it hadn't quite fallen behind the treetops yet. I looked out toward the dock and smiled. Joy had set up everything perfectly for me. A beach blanket was spread out and unlit candles surrounded it. Along with the candles, freshly picked dahlia flowers were scattered around the dock. Seeing it all as it had been on the day Cadence first gave herself to me quickened my heart. The only thing missing was the Boombox. Neither Joy nor I managed to get our hands on one, but it was okay. That's what smartphones were for.

I heard Cadence's sharp intake of air when she spotted what was on the dock.

"Fitz, how in the world did you manage to do this?"

"Well," I drawled out. "I had a little help. Joy might have been here already today."

"Might have?"

"Yeah. Just like I might have given her a list of instructions…and she may have made up your old room so we have a place to sleep tonight too."

She laughed as we stepped up on the dock.

"Well, aren't you a little schemer? No wonder you weren't worried about getting back so late or booking a hotel room. Either way, I think it's perfect! It's just like it was when we were younger! Now all we have to do is wait for the sun to get a little lower so we can see all the vibrant colors."

She let out a little squeal of excitement, held out her arms, and twirled around. I thought my heart would burst, seeing her so happy. Grabbing her around the waist, I pulled her into my arms, cupped her face, and our lips connected. Gliding my tongue across that pouty lower lip, she sighed into the kiss. I pulled her closer and pressed deeper, dominating the kiss until she felt like putty in my arms. My pulse raced from the passionate way she kissed me back. This woman never failed to steal the breath right from my lungs.

"I think we might be able to find something to do to pass the time until the sun sets," I murmured against her smooth skin as I nibbled along the line of her jaw.

She pulled back and gave me an impish grin.

"I'll admit, it was sad seeing my parents place so empty, but the lake will always belong to you, Fitz. You didn't have to open an entire corporation just to get me here. If you wanted to do it on the dock again, all you had to do was ask," she joked.

"Do it, huh? Is that what you want to do?" I teased back. I loved when we shared flirty moments like this. It gave me a glimpse into the future and what could be between us.

"Maybe."

I lightly traced the line of her collarbone with my fingertip.

"Hmmm…let's see what I can do about that."

I skimmed a hand up her waist, sliding under the loose-fitting material until I could capture her breast. Shifting the cup of her bra down, I rolled the already hard nipple. She let out a little whimper and closed her eyes. Lowering us down to the blanket, I pressed her back to the dock.

I held her face between my palms and pressed my mouth to hers once more. Her lips moved to meld with mine. I kissed her desperately, our tongues sliding deep to clash and taste. She was wearing a pencil skirt—the tight little thing had driven me insane with lust all goddamn day. I could have easily shifted it up and gone right for the gusto. However, I wanted to take all the time in the world to savor her.

As I kissed her, I slowly removed the clothes from her body, only breaking our connection when I had to slip her shirt over her head. Once she was naked, she reached for the buckle on my pants.

"No, sweetheart. Just lay back and let me do the work."

She did as told without question and just watched as I stood to light the candles. Once they were lit, I dug into my pocket for my phone and pulled up the music library. After connecting to the little Bluetooth speaker I'd asked Joy to bring, I selected the playlist I'd made just for this occasion and set both devices down on the dock. The music that sounded in the quiet, early evening air wasn't anything we'd listened to in the past. We may have circled back to where we began, but tonight was about moving forward and making new memories.

Once I was stripped out of my khakis and polo shirt, I laid back down, covering her body with mine. I needed to feel her bare skin against me—the other half of two souls on fire. I could sense Cadence's desire and her longing for more. She purred beneath me as I trailed kisses down each of her thighs, calves, ankles, and toes. This woman was perfection, and she was all mine.

I moved back up her body, my lips trailing over her hips and across her smooth stomach. I closed my eyes and inhaled the scent of her skin, needing her more and more with every breath I took. She squeezed my biceps and urged me closer.

"Fitz, please…" she mewled. I looked into her expressive emerald eyes. She looked so unguarded and exquisitely tender when she whispered, "Take me. I need you."

Her words almost broke me, and my heart began to hammer in my chest.

I took her hands in mine and kissed each of her fingertips before pulling her arms above her head and locking them in place. The weight of my cock pressed against her warm and velvety heat. My blood surged from the desperate need to possess her. Thankfully, Cadence had gone on the pill two months ago. Since then, there had been no more barriers between us. When we connected now, we were truly one.

Her gaze glowed sultry and provocative as I slowly slid into her waiting body. Instantly, I was lost in all-consuming heat. I began to move slowly and deliberately, absorbing every sensation and savoring her every reaction. We made love tenderly, each of us exploring each other as if it were the first time—and in a way, it was. Being together again as grown adults in the place where we first began felt different somehow.

I continued to push into her with long, languid strokes, fighting with every shred of my being to hold on—to wait for her. She felt so damn good. I was so close but knew she wasn't there yet. Knowing what she needed, I increased my pace and her hips rose to meet mine. I could only hope beyond hope she would get there soon.

When her eyelids began to flutter, I knew she was nearly there. Her head dropped to the side and her eyes rolled back, her expression reflecting one of imminent pleasure.

"That's it. Come for me, sweetheart."

I drew back once more, then pushed forward again and again. Her fingernails clawed down my back and I felt her brace beneath me. Our gazes locked and we both launched to the brink of ultimate pleasure.

At her shattered cry, my orgasm burst forth in an explosive stream of both agony and ecstasy. I choked out a strangled moan, pouring myself inside her. It was a moment of derailing intensity, a perfect blending of heart and mind.

I collapsed down on top of her, careful to balance my weight so I didn't crush her. My cock jerked as she vibrated around me, still giving up the last remnants of our release. Once our breathing returned to a steadier rhythm, I reluctantly withdrew from the heated clutches of her body and pulled the excess blanket over to cover us. We laid there for a while, listening to the music as the sun dropped low behind the trees.

"Do you love me?" I asked her.

She tilted her head up to look at me. Skimming a finger along the lines of my tattoo, she smiled softly.

"You know I do."

"Hmmm… I'm not so sure. Let's see if you can prove it." Pulling myself up to a sitting position, I reached for my pants and dug in the front right pocket until my fingers connected with a folded-up square of paper. Tugging it out, I handed her the origami fortune teller. "You up for a game of questions?"

Her eyes sparkled with humor, and she sat up.

"I don't know what you're up to, but I'll play." Plucking it from my hand, she laughed as she placed her fingers under the flaps. "Okay, pick a number, Mr. Quinn."

"Four," I said right away, knowing it didn't matter which number I picked. Everything would lead to the same question.

She counted the origami four times and held it out to me once more.

"Pick a color."

"Green, sweetheart. Always green."

"G-R-E-E-N."

Once the origami landed on its intended destination, she shifted the paper to unfold the flap. As she read the question, her hands began to shake.

"I would have gotten down on one knee, but we're already sitting down so…" I trailed off, trying desperately to read her expression. Her eyes were still fixated on the origami and she had yet to look at me. Reaching for my pants once more, I dug into the left pocket and removed the tiny black box. She looked up and our gazes locked. This wasn't a silly game of questions from years past. This was the real deal.

"Fitz, I…" she whispered, bringing a trembling hand to her lips.

"Nearly two decades have passed, but when I look back, I can remember every single moment of the first summer we spent together. It was a time I'll always cherish because it brought me strength through the years when I needed it most. I didn't plan on falling in love with you back then, just as I don't think you planned on falling for me. But once we met, it was clear we couldn't control our feelings. We both fell in love despite the obstacles. For me, a love like that has happened only once. When I got it back—when I got *you* back—I vowed to never let that love go again. What we have is rare and beautiful, sweetheart. I can't replace the time we lost, but I want the chance to be your Colonel Brandon and everything else in between." Taking a nervous breath, I asked the most important question of my life. "Will you marry me, Cadence?"

# Chapter Thirty-Three

## CADENCE

He sat a foot away from me, his eyes searching mine. Every time I looked at him, something deep twisted in my heart. A shiver raced down my spine and energy crashed through the air like a thunderbolt. My love for him was bigger than anything else I'd ever felt. It was intense and potent—just like he was. As I stared into his expressive pools of gray, I saw something in our future that would go on forever.

I wanted to leap into his arms and scream yes, but we both had to remember we weren't alone in the decision to make a lifelong commitment.

"We should talk to the kids about this, Fitz."

He grinned sheepishly.

"I already did. I asked Kallie's permission first. Once she gave it, she, Austin, and I went ring shopping."

"You went shopping for a ring with them?"

My heart wanted to explode with love. The fact he'd asked Kallie made my heart swell. Tears of joy filled my eyes.

"Yep. Austin wanted me to get this gaudy solitaire while Kallie was eyeing up too much bling. In the end, I chose this."

He flipped open the lid of the small box in his hand. I gasped. Nestled in a bed of black satin sat a princess cut diamond set in an intricately twisted vine of gold and pavé diamonds.

"Oh, Fitz! It's beautiful."

"It reminds me of the braids you always wear."

"My braids? I didn't think you really noticed the way I wore my hair," I laughed.

"I always notice you, sweetheart. Even when you think I'm not looking." He paused and inhaled a shaky breath. Taking the ring from the box, he held it out. "I've loved you for more than half my life. You are my forever. I want us to be a family—me, you, Austin, and Kallie. So what's it going to be, sweetheart?"

Tears began to fall freely without any chance of stopping. I don't know how it happened, but we were really here. I glanced out over the lake, taking in the picturesque scenery. The trees were dense, and the rolling hills were just as breathtaking as ever. The sun had finally dropped to the perfect level, leaving pink and orange hues to paint the sky. It made everything around us feel warm. I allowed the heat to encompass me and looked back at Fitz. This wasn't a dream, but my perfect reality. Second chances don't happen often, and I would forever be grateful for ours.

"I love you, Fitzgerald Quinn. I've loved you since I was eighteen years old. From the very first kiss we shared, I've been yours."

"Is that a yes?"

I pressed a hand to his heart.

"With you, it will always be yes."

Taking my hand from his chest, he slipped the ring onto my finger. It was a perfect fit. Years of wrong suddenly shifted to right, and it was because of this man. I had no reservations. Without him, a piece of my heart had been missing. Now that my keeper had put the piece back, there was no doubt—he defined me.

## MUSIC PLAYLIST

**Thank you to the musical talents who influenced and inspired *Defined*. Their creativity helped me bring this story to life.**

"Mamma Mia" by Maryl Streep *(Mamma Mia! The Movie Soundtrack)*

"Feel Again" by OneRepublic *(Native)*

"Could You Be Loved" by Bob Marley *(Uprising)*

"Out of the Dark" by De Lune feat. Jason Zerbin *(Out of the Dark)*

"With or Without You" by U2 *(The Joshua Tree)*

"Waka Waka" by Shakira *(This Time for Africa)*

"Dangerous Night" by Thirty Seconds to Mars *(America)*

"Hi-Lo (Hollow)" by Bishop Briggs *(Church of Scars)*

"Shots" by Imagine Dragons *(Smoke + Mirrors)*

"Love Don't Run" by Steve Holy *(Love Don't Run)*

"The One" by Kodaline *(Coming Up for Air)*

"A Thousand Years" by Christina Perri *(A Thousand Years)*

LISTEN ON SPOTIFY

Endurance

Dakota Willink, LLC

*This book is an original publication of Dakota Willink, LLC*



Library of Congress Cataloging-in-Publication Data
Endurance | Copyright © 2021 by Dakota Willink | Pending


Formatting by: Dragonfly Ink Publishing

# Endurance

## Fade Into You Book 3

*Sloan*

As the son of a Formula One racer, the need for speed was in my blood. But in the blink of an eye, my life in the fast lane came to a screeching halt.

That's when I met her—Kalliope Benton Riley.

She wasn't my usual type at all. She was a total hippie, packaged to perfection with flowy dresses and rainbow-colored hair wraps. She had outlandish ideas about the stars, the moon, and predetermined destiny. Ridiculous.

Yet, I couldn't turn away from her mesmerizing green eyes. She was more than a pit stop. She was my addiction—my checkered flag.

*Kallie*

A psychic gypsy once told me I was cursed when it came to relationships and romance. She was right.

But her warning only prompted the universe to say, "Hold my beer."

Enter Sloan Atwood. He was arrogant and cocky. Avoiding him should have been easy, but all his sexy rough edges were impossible to ignore. Before long, my heart knew I couldn't box this lap. There would be no winners in this race. Total shut down was the only way to prevent permanent damage.

"Like shining stars, every one of us has the potential to light up the darkness with our own particular brilliance."

— Unknown

# Prologue

*Kallie*

Bright neon lights lit up the starless night and excited chatter echoed across the extensive field covered with carnival tents, rides, and games. The smell of popcorn and fried dough filled the air as eager kids dragged their parents from one location to the next. The Arlington County Fair had always been one of the most extraordinary weeks of the year for me, where I'd made countless memories with my mother. But this year, things were different. It was no longer just the two of us parading in and out of funhouses and craft tents, sampling fried Oreos and gorging on kettle corn. Our family of two was now a family of four—and soon to be five.

I glanced at my semi-blended family as we waited in line for funnel cakes loaded with powdered sugar and cinnamon. My father was staring adoringly down at my mother as if she were the only person in the world. He was smiling with his hand resting on the slight curve of her belly. As tiny as she was, my mother couldn't disguise the baby bump swelling at her middle for much longer. She thought I didn't notice, but I did. I wondered how much longer they would wait to tell Austin and me.

My gaze traveled to my half-brother. Austin, completely oblivious to the new sibling on the way, was being a typical eighteen-year-old male. His eyes were glued to the ass of a brunette who'd just passed by us. I could almost see the wheels spinning in his head, wondering if he'd be able to sneak away from the family to chat it up with her. I shook my head and snorted a laugh.

"You're a little too obvious, Austin."

He glanced at me and grinned sheepishly.

"I have no idea what you're talking about," he denied.

"Kallie, leave him alone," my mother chimed in. "It's only normal—especially when they're that pretty." She chuckled and winked at Austin. It didn't surprise me that she'd noticed his wandering eye. She rarely missed a trick with me while I was growing up. Austin, even though she was still getting to know him, was no different.

After we got our funnel cakes, the four of us aimlessly roamed across the fairgrounds, taking in the sounds and sights of the night. Eventually, we ended up in front of a giant purple tent with gold lettering boasting gypsy psychic readings. Smoke machines had been strategically placed around the temporary structure to give it a creepy yet mysterious aura, seeming deliberately over-the-top by hitting all the classic stereotypes. It was Madame Lavinia's tent—my least favorite place at the county fair.

"This is new," my father observed.

"Nah, it was here last year," Austin said. "Don't you remember Kallie freaking out about Gabby's broken arm?"

I gasped upon recalling with happened to my friend.

"Freaking out? That gypsy predicted Gabby would have a tragic accident. The next day, she broke her arm. I was right to freak out!"

"Oh, yeah. I kind of remember that happening," my mother mused. "Fell off a diving board, right?"

"Yes," I confirmed. "I warned Gabby not to go into that tent, but she didn't listen, and look what happened."

"Don't forget about Charlie-Charlie," Austin reminded me.

"There was that too! The Charlie-Charlie game said Gabby would injure herself in 2013, and the gypsy predicted the same!"

I gulped, thinking about the game my Aunt Joy taught me. Gabby and I used to play the paranormal game all the time, spending many of our nights calling on a Mexican demon named Charlie to answer all of our questions. It was a simple game consisting of two pencils crisscrossed perpendicularly to form four sections on a piece of paper labeled with words like yes and no, or years and months. We'd then press the ends of the pencils until they started moving without our control—something Austin regularly mocked us for believing. He insisted that someone was always controlling the game by pushing a pencil one way or another to get the desired answer to the questions asked.

"Charlie also predicted that the guy who kisses Kallie during a sunset would be her soulmate," Austin added with a smirk. I huffed out an impatient breath and slapped his arm.

"I'm serious about this."

My pragmatic mother shook her head and rolled her eyes. She could think I was acting silly all she wanted. It wasn't just about the Charlie-Charlie game. My mother hadn't been there to see the ominous eyes of Madam Lavinia when she whispered the warning to Gabby.

"Kallie, I'm sure it was just a coincidence. Games and psychic gypsies can't tell your future any more than the origami fortunetellers I used to make when I was younger could."

"I don't know about that," my father said. "The origami you made for me once upon a time was pretty accurate."

"Oh, don't give Kallie any more reasons to believe in this nonsense, Fitz. Besides, I was the one who made the origami and asked all the questions. Therefore, I controlled the outcome." She paused then, giving in to a yawn, before looking at my father. "I'm getting tired. Ready to call it a night?"

"I'm ready if you are," he replied.

"But we still need to ride on the Zipper," Austin complained.

My gaze traveled to the opposite end of the carnival, where the Zipper's oval frame rotated like a Ferris wheel with free-spinning cars suspended from the sides of the boom. It was one of my favorite rides.

"Why don't you two head home?" I suggested to my parents. "Austin and I can catch an Uber."

"What's an Uber?" my mother asked.

Now it was my turn to roll my eyes. "You see, Mom. There's this little app you can put on your phone that makes cars just magically appear to take you wherever you want to go."

"Okay, smarty pants. I might not be up on all the—"

"Cadence, don't get yourself all wound up," my father interjected. "We can leave if you want to. If these two want to stay and have their brains rattled around in that Zipper contraption, so be it. Besides, we haven't had the house to ourselves in quite some time." He flashed her a crooked smile and waggled his eyebrows.

"Ewww, gross!" Austin and I yelled in unison.

My mother laughed and slipped her arm around my father's waist.

"Kallie, don't stay too late. You have to start packing in the morning."

I groaned, not needing the reminder. As excited as I was to start my freshman year at the University of San Diego in a few weeks, I was dreading all the work that went into packing for a cross-country move.

After my parents walked away, I turned to Austin.

"Alright, let's go get zipped!

"Not yet," he said and took hold of my arm. "Let's go see the gypsy first."

My eyes widened as he began to pull me toward the tent.

"I'm not going in there," I said with a vehement shake of my head.

"Chicken," he taunted.

"So what if I am?"

"Come on, Kallie. We're both leaving for college in a few weeks. Who knows when we'll be able to go to the county fair together again?"

"Um…next year, when we're home for summer break," I pointed out sardonically.

"Maybe—assuming neither of us gets a job and decides to stay on campus. Come on. Stop being a baby and do something memorable this year."

"Do you honestly think a chat with a crazy fortuneteller is going to make today more memorable somehow?"

"I do," he said with a curt, all-knowing nod before pulling harder on my sleeve.

"Austin, I said no!"

"You're acting like a scaredy-cat. It'll be fine, you'll see."

Before I could protest further, Austin shoved me through the opening of the purple tent. I blinked as my eyes adjusted to the dim lighting.

When my gaze landed on Madame Lavinia, I froze. She stood next to a round table covered in an intricately embroidered tablecloth. Incense and candles burned in every corner of the tent, causing a smokey haze to billow around her. Her clothing was exactly as I remembered it from the year before. Her puffed-sleeve blouse with a low neckline flowed over the waistline of a long, colorfully pleated skirt of bright chiffon. Gold hoop earrings, bangle bracelets, and jewels weaved through her long black hair to complete her appearance, but it was her eyes—one ice blue and one brown—that stood out the most to me. They stared unblinkingly, and when her unwavering gaze darkened, I felt a shiver race down my spine.

It was like she could see straight into my soul.

Austin nudged me forward again, and I staggered as if I had two left feet. I was about to protest, but the gypsy spoke.

"Tarot cards or the crystal ball, my dear?" she asked in a deep, raspy voice that made her sound much older than she appeared.

"Oh, um…ne-neither," I stuttered. "We were just headed over to the Zipper. Sorry to have—"

"Tarot cards or the crystal ball?" she repeated.

"She wants the crystal ball. Right, sis?"

Austin bumped me again. I looked in his direction and noticed his mocking smirk. I scowled, wanting to do nothing more than smack him. My brother didn't believe in superstitions and had slept through the lesson in history class when Mrs. Beecher talked about Nostradamus. Predictions and prophecies were real and could be dangerous. I didn't know if this fortuneteller was the real deal or not, but after what happened with Gabby last year, I wasn't going to take any chances.

"No, really. I should go," I said with a weak smile as I turned toward the exit.

"You have heartache in your future," Madame Lavinia announced. Slowly, I turned back to face her. A pit formed in my gut, and I was afraid of what she might say next.

*Damn you, Austin!*

"Wha-what do you mean?" I hesitantly replied.

The gypsy took a few steps toward me until she was close enough to reach out and take my hand. Her slender fingers turned my palm, so it was face up. Her grip was so cold; it caused goosebumps to rise on the surface of my skin.

"I see travel in your future. And the sun—the sun setting in the west."

I stifled a tiny gasp.

*How does she know I will be traveling?*

It had to be a coincidence.

"Last I checked, the sun always set in the west," I told her, trying my best to sound skeptical, even though my heart was starting to race.

"You're a Gemini?" she asked.

I frowned. She had a one-in-twelve chance of getting my zodiac sign right, but still…

"That's right. Lucky guess."

She smiled knowingly at my aloof reply, then looked down at my hand where she had begun tracing a red-painted fingernail along the creases in my palm. After a few moments, she clasped my hand between hers and led me over to the chair in front of a table supporting an eerie, glowing crystal ball. Smoke swirled inside the glass orb as it pulsed with multicolored light. I tried to remind myself that it was probably only trick magic.

But what if it wasn't?

"Sit," she ordered. My breath quickened, and my pulse pounded in my ears. I was suddenly too terrified to do anything other than comply as she rounded the table and took a seat across from me. "Now tell me, what fortune do you wish to hear from Madame Lavinia?"

I glanced back at Austin. He stood near the entrance to the tent, looking gleeful. I scowled at him before turning back to the gypsy.

"Well, just a basic fortunetelling, I guess. Just don't tell me anything bad."

"I can't guarantee that. Your destiny is your own." Her eyes narrowed, and I sat transfixed, unable to look away from her shrewd stare. She stayed silent for what seemed like hours, but it was probably only a few seconds before moving both hands to hover over the crystal ball.

"I see something—something that is very important to your future. Destructive and doomed love surrounds you. Remember the weaknesses of a Gemini, my dear, or you'll be destined for a life of heartbreak. Your eagerness to express your emotions will be your downfall," she warned.

My eyes widened, not sure what she was getting at.

"My downfall?"

Madame Lavinia slowly nodded her head but never took her eyes off the glowing sphere.

"You will fall in love under the bright sun in the west, giving someone the power to destroy you. And make no mistake—destroy you he will."

"What do you mean by…by destroy me?" I whispered.

The wind outside the tent picked up, rustling the thin walls and causing the candle flames to flicker. The gypsy inhaled sharply and snapped her head up to look at me. Her two different eyes turned black as night as she reached across the table to grip my hand tightly.

"The man who tastes your lips under a California sunset will be the one to break you."

# Chapter One

Six Years Later

*Kallie*

"Good night to the old lady whispering hush. Good night, stars. Good night, air. Good night, noises everywhere." I slowly closed the *Goodnight Moon* cardboard book and looked down at my five-year-old little sister, Emma. Her eyes were closed, and her breathing even. I smiled at her sleeping, angelic little face. She had inherited my father's dark hair but had my mother's green eyes and creamy complexion. Although I was more than twenty years her senior, there was no denying the bond I shared with her. She had brought so much joy to our family and was the symbol of a long-awaited happily ever after for my parents.

As quietly as I could, I placed the book on her nightstand and tiptoed out of her room to go back downstairs to the living room where my brother and best friend were waiting for me. Austin was lounging lazily on the couch, and Gabby sat with one leg draped over the arm of the chair across from him.

"She's out cold," I told them after I entered the room.

"Where did your parents go tonight, anyway?" Gabby asked.

"It's their anniversary, so I offered to keep Emma overnight for them."

"Gotcha. So, are you finally going to tell us why it was so important for us to come over tonight?"

"Yeah, what's the big news?" Austin pressed. Popping a few potato chips into his mouth, he frowned with his mouth full. "I rescheduled my Madden football tournament with the guys for this. Whatever it is, it better be good."

I waved him off.

"Football, shmootball. I promise you—this is important. And stop being a slob with those chips. You're getting crumbs all over the couch." I pushed Austin's long, muscular legs off the couch and brushed bits of potato chips from the cushions. Taking a seat next to him, I snagged a chip from his bowl, then looked meaningfully at each of them. "It's about Dean."

"What about him?" Gabby prompted.

"He proposed."

"Oh, my god! You're kidding me! I can't believe it!" Gabby gushed. "Tell me all about it. Did he get down on one knee?"

"Well, no. He just…" I glanced to my left, noting Austin's silence. He'd gone perfectly still, watching me curiously, as he waited for me to continue. Feeling uncharacteristically nervous, I leaned toward the coffee table and topped off my half-empty glass of wine from earlier. "Well, you know how Dean is. He's always so practical. He just explained how this was the natural next step. He probably didn't feel the need for all of that fancy wedding proposal fluff."

"Well, what do you expect from a doctor? As you said—he's practical," she agreed.

"Dean's not an actual doctor. He's a dentist. It doesn't get more boring than cleaning people's teeth for a living," Austin said with a smirk. His opinion mattered so much to me, and he was clearly not impressed. Taking a long swig of his beer, he gave me a pointed stare. "I hope you didn't expect skywriting or some shit like that."

"Oh, who really cares about that stuff?" Gabby chided. "Dean's a great catch—nobody can get it all. I'd rather have a nice practical guy over hearts and roses any day. So, did you set a date?"

"No. Not yet."

"What are you waiting for?" she admonished.

"Well, I haven't exactly said yes."

Gabby froze, with her wineglass halfway to her lips, then glanced down at my hand.

"Is that why you aren't wearing the ring? Wait." She stopped short, closed her eyes, and took a deep breath as if she were trying to find patience. "Please tell me you at least *have* a ring."

"Um…" I hesitated. "Not exactly. Dean thought it would be better for us to pick it out together and make sure it was the right size."

Austin audibly snorted. "Typical Dean. Such a dud."

"Dean's a sweetheart, Austin. You're just mad that he beat you at golf," I pointed out, rubbing salt in a wound that my brother refused to let heal.

"It's not that at all, Kallie. You two are just an extremely odd match. Dad says you're like the exclamation mark at the end of a sentence. I mean, look at you. You're all about flowy skirts, rainbow hair, free love, and world peace. Then there's Dean, my-middle-name-is-boring, rocking sweater vests and scraping plaque all day."

Taken aback, I unconsciously reached up to touch the clip-in rainbow extensions braided through my natural blonde hair.

"Gee, Austin. Say what you really feel, why don't you?" I snapped, then looked to Gabby for support. To my surprise, my best friend was frowning and nodding her head in agreement.

"He's got a point, Kals."

"Ugh, you guys. I'm serious! I want to make sure this is the right decision. I mean, I never want to get divorced, so I asked him to give me forty-eight hours to think about it."

"Think about what? Don't you love him?" Gabby asked.

"We've been dating for over two years. Of course I love him."

"So, why not give him an answer? We've been friends for as long as I can remember, Kallie. I know you always act first and think later. Why are you waiting this time?"

"I'm not waiting. I'm reflecting."

"Did your tarot cards tell you to do that?" Austin quipped.

"Shut up, Austin," I snapped in frustration. He wasn't helping. "I knew I shouldn't have invited you over. But if you must know, I haven't looked at my deck in over a month."

"I'm just teasing you. Come on, Kallie. I'm your brother. It's my job to razz you. You know I've always got your back. I just want to—"

My cell phone rang, cutting off whatever else Austin was about to say. I glanced down at the coffee table where the phone sat. My father's name showed up on the caller ID.

"Hold that thought. It's Dad. He's probably calling to check on Emma." Grabbing my phone, I headed into the kitchen and answered. "Hey, Dad! If you're calling about Emma, don't worry. She's tucked in for the night and fast asleep."

My father chuckled.

"No. I trust you have things handled with her. She loves sleepovers at your place. I'm actually calling about a business matter."

"Please don't tell me you're working during your anniversary dinner. Mom will kill you."

"I'm not," he assured. "We haven't even gone out yet. We had to push back our reservation time because your mother got an urgent call and had to go into the office."

My heart sank. My mother ran Dahlia's Dreamers, a non-profit organization that aided immigrants with a legal path to citizenship. Urgent calls usually meant someone was in jeopardy of being deported.

"Is everything okay?"

"Yeah, everything is fine for now. She just got back. But you know how it is around here—never a dull moment. We were about to head out when Devon called me about a new client in need of immediate assistance."

"Who's the client?" I asked.

"His name is Sloan Atwood."

"I've never heard of him."

"To make a long story short, he's a race car driver in Los Angeles whose career ended rather abruptly. I don't know all the details. All I know is that he's been on a bender. His agent, Milo Birx, called me to fix it. I was hoping you could help."

I thought about the long hours my father put in at his PR firm, Quinn & Wilkshire. While he always made plenty of time for our family, I'd seen first-hand how trying the job could be almost as soon as I started working for him. After receiving my MBA in public relations, I wanted to work for the best. My father's nationally known firm was precisely that—and people rarely came to him when things were going well. It wasn't until after something went wrong did clients want the firm to run damage control. Despite the perception, bad press was never good, and our job was to get people out of the negative spotlight with a positive public relations campaign. Quinn & Wilkshire did exactly that, and we did it well, no matter what time of the day it was.

"What do you need me to do?"

"Honey…" he hesitated. "I'll be honest. Since your sister was born, I've been trying to limit the hours I spend with clients to have more family time. But you know how it is—it's tough. Devon just got back from a thirty-day stint with an NBA player. Now he has a baby on the way. If he adds Sloan Atwood to his client list, his new wife just might kill him."

"And rightly so. He works like crazy," I said with a laugh.

"Well, considering that, Devon and I have been in discussions for the past month about lightening our workload in general. Do you remember how you mentioned one day becoming a partner at the firm?"

"Of course, but I figured that would be decades away."

"Yeah, well… This commission is huge—too big for the firm to pass up. If you can handle Atwood, we might be willing to speed up that timeline by a few years, so you don't have to wait decades. But, before you agree to anything, there are some things for you to consider."

"Such as?"

"Milo emailed me a file on Atwood. After looking it over, Milo and I both decided we can't manage this from the DC office. This is a major commitment. If you take Atwood on as a client, you'll have to go to California."

"That's not a big deal. After all, I lived there for four years, and I travel all the time for clients."

"Six months, Kallie. You'll need to be in LA for a full six months. There would be a bonus payout of twenty thousand dollars for you after the completion of the contract. Milo is serious about this and wants a solid commitment from someone who can be there daily. He won't get that with a long-distance rep, which is why I don't think Devon or I should take him on."

I blinked, pausing to soak in his words. Quinn & Wilkshire never had a client who required that kind of time commitment, as far as I could recall.

"Why so long?"

"Milo worked out some deal with a charity out there called Safe Track. It involves working with foster kids over the span of a few months, and Milo is terrified Atwood will screw it up. I'll email you the file after we hang up so you can see why. You'll need to be Atwood's shadow. When he eats, you eat. When he sleeps, you sleep. When he shits—"

"I get the picture, Dad," I said and rolled my eyes. "Six months is a long time, though. I'll need to talk to Dean."

"Of course."

"When do you need to know by?"

He hesitated again.

"Tomorrow morning at the latest. If you say yes, I'll have our travel coordinator get you on plane by late afternoon or early evening."

I puffed out a breath. Twenty-four hours to decide on a cross-country move wasn't very long, even if it was temporary. However, I knew my father. Fitzgerald Quinn would never ask this of one of his associates if it wasn't necessary. There was also the big fat carrot he'd dangled. The bonus was a definite perk, but fast-track to partner was something Quinn & Wilkshire never offered—especially to anyone who was a friend or family member. Nepotism was frowned upon and taken very seriously. Considering his firm belief in starting at the bottom and working your way up, I knew this must be bigger than he was letting on.

Financially, this was huge for me. While my parents had paid for my undergrad, I was on the hook for graduate school. The twenty thousand dollar bonus would more than cover my remaining loans.

Plus, if they made me a partner at the firm, the raise I'd receive would ease the financial burden I was currently facing with my hefty mortgage. The townhouse in I'd purchased in Georgetown didn't come cheap, and my bank account could prove it.

"Let me take the night to decide. I'll let you know in the morning," I eventually said.

After ending the call, I went back into the living room. Gabby was channel surfing, and Austin was, once again, sprawled across the entire couch. Rather than push his legs aside again, I took a seat on the floor and threw back the rest of my wine in one long swig.

Gabby eyed me curiously. "Everything okay?" she asked.

"I'm not sure yet. My dad wants me to go to California for six months."

"Kallie's going to Cali," Austin said with a laugh. "Nice."

"You're such a turd," I said and tossed a throw pillow at him. "Add this to the list of decisions I need to make. Adulting sucks. I miss our college days when my biggest decision was which class to register for."

"I'm assuming this is a work thing," Gabby absently remarked, and she continued to flip through the channels on the television.

"Yeah, some race car—oh, wait!" I sat up straight and pointed to the TV. "Back up to the last channel. I love that movie!"

Gabby clicked the remote until *Singin' In The Rain* was on the screen.

"Aww, come on! It's bad enough you fed me tofu for dinner. Don't make me sit through a chick flick," Austin complained.

"This is a classic, Austin. Besides, our parents fell in love at summer camp while putting on this production. You have to love it because of that."

"Yeah, I know the story. Dad loves to tell it every year on your birthday," he grumbled.

"Hush!" I waved him off. "This is my favorite part."

The three of us fell silent just in time to hear Don Lockwood say, "You sure look lovely in the moonlight, Kathy." He'd just finished setting the stage—quite literally—to create a romantic atmosphere so he could profess his love to her in a song.

As he sang the romantic ballad and stared adoringly into the eyes of his beloved, a feeling of melancholy settled over me. Dean never looked at me the way Don Lockwood was looking at Kathy Seldon. I knew it was just a movie, and actors were supposed to be convincing, but still... The song lyrics came from somebody's real-life experience—an experience I wanted to have. If truth be told, I didn't have that kind of chemistry with Dean.

I thought back to Gabby's question.

*"Do you love him?"*

Undoubtedly, the answer was yes. However, what Dean and I

shared wasn't anything like what I witnessed on the television screen. While I knew not everything could be like it was in the movies, I still knew what true, undying love looked like. I'd had a front-row seat to it for years with my parents. After a seventeen-year separation, their love never faded. My baby sister in the next room was proof of it. But with Dean, I'd always felt like something was missing between us. There were no gentle touches or furtive glances. The new relationship flutters of excitement had long since disappeared. There was no anticipation because Dean was always predictable. He was practical, and he was safe. I may have loved him, but I wasn't convinced I wanted to settle for safe.

That's why I told him I needed to think about his proposal. I didn't know what was more important to me—the relationship security Dean would surely provide or the idea of being swept up in song and dance with the person I loved. I wanted both, but I wasn't sure if that was asking for too much.

As I continued to listen to Don Lockwood sing about how his beloved was meant for him, I asked myself if the same was true for me.

*Were Dean and I meant for each other?*

I didn't know the answer. Tears began to well in my eyes from the realization, and I quickly blinked them away. Perhaps the opportunity to go to California was fated. At the very least, it would give me time to work out these conflicting emotions and let destiny guide the way.

"Kals, you okay?" Austin asked, eyeing me curiously.

"Yeah, I'm good." I offered him a forced smile and turned my attention back to the television, wishing real life were like it was in the movies.

# Chapter Two

*Kallie*

After two hours of listening to me weigh the pros and cons of marriage and a temporary move to California, Austin and Gabby bid their farewells.

"I love you, sis. I'll keep my ringer turned up. If you need to call and hash out your thoughts in the middle of the night, I'm here for you," my brother said, pulling me into a fierce hug.

"Thanks, Austin." I squeezed my brother tight. Despite our constant teasing, I knew Austin would do anything for me. He understood the magnitude of the decisions I was facing and would support whichever choices I made.

"That's ditto for me," Gabby added.

I let go of Austin and embraced my friend. "Thanks, you guys. I love you both so much."

As they headed for their cars, I stood in the doorway of my townhouse, watching until their taillights disappeared. After closing and locking the door, I headed upstairs toward my bedroom. Along the way, I passed by the guest room to check on Emma. I smiled when I saw her tiny arms wrapped around the purple plush teddy bear that I'd given her on her fourth birthday. Her breathing was deep and even, assuring me she was still asleep.

Giving in to a yawn, I gingerly closed the door and went to my room. Austin's mention of my tarot deck had been on my mind ever since he'd said it, and I was looking forward to the quiet solitude and reflection they always seemed to bring.

Sitting on my bed, I opened my nightstand drawer and pulled out the cards. Settling in, I tapped the deck twice, then gave them a thorough shuffle before cutting the pile three times. I was fairly new to tarot reading by most standards. I'd dabbled in college but had recently become more serious with general readings for myself. They helped to give me perspective on the past, understanding of the present, and insight into future possibilities.

Focusing my intent and energy, I fanned the cards into an arc across my bedspread. After selecting the first eight that called to me, I placed them in formation face down. Flipping over the first one, the Judgement card lay before me. It was upright, symbolizing reflection and awakening, and would be the theme for today's reading. Reflection was fitting for my current situation, as I'd been doing a lot of that lately.

Leaving the card in place, I turned over the next card to reveal the reversed Moon, symbolizing confusion. I frowned. Tarot cards were always open to interpretation, but it was almost scary how much they were in tune with my energy.

Flipping over a third card, it revealed an upright Temperance card. I closed my eyes and called on my intuition, trying to see how the symbol of patience applied to my current situation. After turning over the first two cards, I'd felt anxious and found myself taking a few deep breaths. Perhaps that's exactly why the card presented itself. I needed to maintain a sense of calm and balance to better channel my energy.

Turning the fourth card, I let out a small gasp when I saw the upright Tower card—a symbol of disaster in my future. My heart began to race again, and I quickly flipped over a fifth card. It was the upright Devil, which meant addiction and materialism.

With only three cards left, I slowly reached to flip over the one that would give me insight into external influences. It was the reversed Lovers card. My stomach dropped, knowing this was more than just an omen. It was something I'd already been feeling—a sense of imbalance in my relationship with Dean. This card told me that a move to California could have a very negative impact on my relationship.

After talking with Austin and Gabby, and before taking out my tarot deck, I'd been almost certain of my path. I thought I would go to California, then return in six months to marry Dean. If our relationship was meant to be, we would get through the separation.

Now I wasn't so sure.

In all honesty, I'd been shocked by his proposal. Perhaps it was because I had a history of failed relationships. Everyone who came before Dean was either a cheater, a self-indulgent bad boy, or a suffocating control freak. I'd often thought back to the gypsy's warnings so many years ago when she told me I was cursed in romance and destined for a life of disappointment and heartache. When I met Dean, I had thought the curse was broken because he was the complete opposite of the other guys I'd dated.

"Did I settle too easily?" I wondered aloud to the empty room.

Reaching for the second to last card, I flipped it to see an upright High Priestess. Her appearance could signify that it was time for me to listen to my intuition rather than prioritizing my intellect and conscious mind. Considering that, I remembered what Dean had said about marriage being the next practical step. A part of me began to wonder if I was actually *in* love with Dean. I feared that I might only love him more as a friend but was simply falling in line with society's natural order of things.

I shifted my gaze to the final card. Considering that all of my cards so far had been Major Arcana, signifying impactful and life-changing events, I was almost afraid to turn it over. When I did, I found myself staring at the upright Fool. I sighed at the foregone conclusion and tapped my finger on the jester's face.

"You just had to show up today of all days, didn't you?"

In love, the Fool tarot card signaled that I needed to experience new things to find the romance I desired. It meant taking risks to find love in the most unlikely places. The card could also mean new beginnings in my career, and I should welcome the chance to be bold when starting a new journey.

As I stared at the imagery on the cards to determine the story they were trying to tell, my cell phone began to ring. Rattled by the sudden noise, I didn't even look at the name on the caller ID before answering.

"Hello," I said absently.

"Kallie, it's me," Dean replied, effectively snapping me to full attention.

"Dean! Hi…um, I didn't expect to hear from you tonight." I paused and glanced at the clock. It was nearing midnight. "You never stay up this late."

"I'm in bed, but I can't sleep. I started thinking about the plans to tell my mother we're engaged. I thought—"

"Tell your mother? But I haven't even said yes yet," I interrupted, trying to keep my voice light.

"Doll, you and I both know that's just a formality," he said with a chuckle. "After we get the ring, I thought we should take her out to a nice dinner and give her the good news."

*A nice dinner?*

I nearly scoffed. When Dean proposed, we'd been sitting at his kitchen table. He decided to pop the question over Thai take-out. Now here he was, saying he wanted to treat his mother to a nice dinner so we could tell her about our *non*-engagement when all I got was subpar vegetable pad thai in a cardboard container. I inhaled a deep, calming breath and forced myself not to sound petty with my reply.

"Look, Dean. We need to talk. My dad called earlier about a job in California. We picked up a client who lives in L.A. It's a lot of money and I think I'm going to take it, but I'd have to leave tomorrow."

"Well, that's great, doll! More money is always good and I know how much you like to travel, so—"

"It's for six months, Dean. I'd have to move there temporarily."

"Six months? But I have the American Dental Association dinner next week. I need you to be there."

"I'm sure you'll be fine without me."

"It's not about whether I'll be fine or not. It's about how it will look if I show up without a date. Everyone will be there with spouses or significant others. You can't expect me to go alone."

I pinched the bridge of my nose.

"Honestly, Dean. I don't know why you would want me to be there anyway. You know I hate those things because I can never be myself. The charade is exhausting."

"Kallie, we've been through this. It's not a charade. You just don't understand acceptable decorum."

I pursed my lips in annoyance. For Dean, acceptable decorum at formal events meant no colorful hair extensions, always remembering to place my napkin on my chair when I left the table, and only speaking when spoken to. Heaven forbid I say something that could embarrass him in front of his peers.

Feeling frustrated, I glanced down at the tarot cards spread out over my bed. I absently pushed them together until they were in a neat pile and placed them back inside my nightstand drawer. Regardless of what the cards were trying to tell me, I knew in my heart what needed to happen. I had to figure out if Dean and I were meant to be together—and this conversation was definitely not helping. Marriage should be forever. It wasn't fair for me to waste his time or his life if I was having doubts. I believed everything happened for a reason, and I did not doubt that California was fated.

"I'm not going to debate acceptable decorum with you. Our views on that will always be different. As for my move to California, I think it's a sign that we should put the wedding plans on hold. We can discuss it when I get back."

"That's not going to work for me, Kallie. I need you at that dinner," he stated matter-of-factly as if that settled the matter. An angry heat flooded my cheeks, and no matter how hard I tried to tamp it down, my temper began to simmer.

"Why do I feel like you're dismissing me—as if I'm no more than a woman on your arm for your stupid event?"

"Oh, stop it. You know you mean more to me than that."

"Do I? I mean, never once did you say you'd miss me if I were to be gone for six months. No. Instead, your first instinct was a black-tie dinner."

"You're not being fair. Of course I would miss you."

I sighed, knowing I was acting slightly irrational, even if my feelings were justified.

"Alright. Let's not fight. I don't want to leave with things on a bad note."

"So you're going? No discussion?"

I paused, unsure of how to respond. When my father called about the job opportunity, my first thought was to talk it over with Dean. However, at some point over the course of the night, I'd already made up my mind. I was going with or without Dean's approval. What did that say about me and my relationship with him? In a roundabout way, I was acting just as dismissive toward Dean as he was to me.

"Yes, I'm going. My father wouldn't have asked if it weren't important. We'll just have to work through the separation. What's six months? It will go by faster than you think."

He stayed silent for a long moment that seemed to stretch on forever. Just as I was about to ask him what he was thinking, he finally spoke.

"Fine," he said curtly, clearly unconvinced. "What time is your flight tomorrow?"

"I don't know yet. After I hang up with you, I'll shoot my father a text to let him know I'm in. He has a travel agent that will handle all of the arrangements for me. Once I know, I'll forward you the itinerary."

"My appointment schedule is full tomorrow, so I probably won't be able to see you off."

My heart sank—but not for the reason it should have. I was disappointed because, deep down, I knew Dean wouldn't have been there even if he didn't have a packed schedule. He was never a big believer in nonsensical, tear-filled goodbyes. I'd gone on numerous short business trips in the past, and rarely did he see me off. If I saw him at all, it was simply to give me a ride to the airport, and I never expected more than a quick peck on the lips before he drove off.

"Okay. I'll text you when I land then," I replied, desperately trying to keep the sadness out of my voice. "Goodnight, Dean."

"Night."

The line went dead. There were no I love you's or air kisses through the phone. Just silence.

I tossed my phone to the side. Shaking off feelings of melancholy, I stood from the bed, walked over to my closet, and tried to focus on something positive. Buried behind a plethora of shoes and handbags were a couple of suitcases. I pulled each one out and laid them on the bed.

Unintentionally, I found myself humming the tune of "Leaving on a Jet Plane" by Peter, Paul, and Mary as I began to pack my clothes. Was I still frustrated after my phone call with Dean? Yes. I was sad too. But I also couldn't help feeling a little excited about whatever possibilities lay ahead.

# Chapter Three

*Sloan*

There was a particular atmosphere that came with a good beach bar. It was more than just the music blaring from a jukebox loaded only with beach-vibe songs. With a fruity drink in hand and toes in the sand, people were able to leave their worries behind, lay back, and enjoy a carefree life—even if just for a few days. The Soggy Sand Dollar in Long Beach offered precisely that. It was the reason their crowd ranged from tourists showing off their new vacation clothes to local sea-drenched surfers with tanned cheeks. Everyone was happy. There was no misery—just an escape from everyday life.

And I loved it here.

Location was key, and a bustling boardwalk on a white sandy shoreline made for prime real estate. The front of my favorite hole-in-the-wall bar was wide open to the beach and always packed, day or night. Not only were the drinks cheap and readily flowing, but the cabanas out back were a convenient place to crash for the night after having a few too many. All I had to do was slip the bartender a fifty, and a cabana under the stars was all mine. It had become a regular thing for me, and today would probably be no different. I had arrived at three in the afternoon and managed to get a steady buzz going by five. With any luck, I'd be well past drunk in an hour. After all, it wasn't like I had any place to be.

The more beers I knocked back, the less I found myself caring that

I had been served the cheap kind. I looked down at the silver can in my hand. Beach rules dictated that The Soggy Sand Dollar maintain a no-glass policy, making aluminum and plastic part of the official serving ware. Coors Light was watery and barely even beer, but it was getting the job done—especially when I poured it into a red Solo cup with a shot of Jack Daniels and chugged it as a boilermaker. Fortunately for me, that was on the menu today.

"Johnny!" I called out to the bartender. "I'm almost empty."

The aging, lifelong bartender glanced my way and grinned. His eyes crinkled in the corners, and I wasn't sure if it was because of too many late nights slinging whiskey or too much time in the sun. Perhaps it was a little of both.

"Almost is the keyword, my friend. Don't worry. I've got you covered," Johnny assured.

I returned his smile, then shifted on the barstool to gaze out at the beach. Waves crashed into the surf, and there was a slight breeze in the salty air, whispering just enough to make the blazing California sun more tolerable. I decided right then and there that my night would be spent in the cabana. Tonight, I planned on being lulled to sleep under the stars by the sounds of the ocean.

My cellphone vibrated in my pocket. Pulling it out, I glanced at the screen. The sun was so bright, and I couldn't read it. Turning back toward the bar, I leaned forward and balanced my elbows on the polished oak top. I blinked a few times, struggling to focus. The words were fuzzy, the letters seeming to blur together momentarily. I thought about the painkiller I took after I'd first arrived at The Soggy Sand Dollar. I probably shouldn't have popped prescription oxy on an empty stomach. I would need to order up a couple of the chef's famous fish tacos sooner rather than later. Combined with the booze, I was feeling the effects of the pill more than usual.

Forcing myself to focus on the cell phone screen, I groaned when I saw it was a text message from my agent, Milo Birx. He had an annoying habit of checking in on me daily. Not bothering to read his message, I switched over to my voicemail inbox. Scrolling down the list, I selected a voicemail I'd received a month earlier and brought the phone to my ear.

"Mr. Atwood. This is Dr. Haskell. After going over your test results with your physical therapist, I'm sorry to say this, but I can't clear you to race again. The risks are just too great. Please call the office at your earliest convenience. I'd like to schedule an appointment to go over the test results in more detail, as well as discuss alternate options for pain management."

Just as it had on the day when I first heard the message, my stomach sank. I'd had to replay it three times before I grasped the words. I squeezed my eyes shut, trying to will away the memories from over one year ago, but the effort was in vain. Flashbacks from the crash assaulted me, reminding me once again that my life was now permanently altered.

I could still hear the crunch of metal on concrete when I swerved to avoid a slowing car, spun out, and hit the wall—driver's side first—at high speed. The screeching tires and the scraping sound of the car along the wall until it finally slid to a complete stop would not be something I'd soon forget. I'd been conscious when my crew arrived to cut me from the wreckage but passed out before making it to the ambulance. I barely remembered the weeks and months that followed.

I raked my hands through my hair, painfully yanking at the roots in an attempt to drown out the sounds in my memory. I shouldn't have listened to the doctor's message again. I wasn't sure what compelled me to do it. I certainly didn't need a reminder of all that was lost—I'd spent every day of the past month trying to escape it.

I looked down at the drink in front of me, realizing I wasn't just buzzed—I was drunk—just like I wanted to be. A few more boilermakers and I could be out back, fast asleep in a cabana.

"Johnny!" I called out again.

"I hear ya. I'm coming."

As I waited for my refill, I let my gaze wander over the faces throughout the bar. I'd been all over the world, and if there was one thing I'd noticed, it was that everyone looked the same as they did everywhere else. Short, tall, thin, overweight. Blonde, brunette, old, young. They may have had different skin tones or worn different clothes, but they were still all very much the same.

Until now.

Out on the beach, a woman emerged from the water, sparkling in the sunlight where the surf kissed her skin. Rainbows flowed from her head and cascaded over her shoulders as she moved across the sand, stopping only to tie a turquoise-colored wrap around her shapely waist. She moved without purpose, defying gravity, and I wondered if her feet were even touching the ground. I couldn't be sure. It was as if I were staring at a mystical mermaid sent from the depths of the ocean straight to me. I didn't know where she'd been or where she was going—I only knew I wanted to go to wherever she was headed.

"Who is that?" I whispered to myself, her gravity pulling me until I was locked in. Everything around me seemed to disappear, and all sounds fell away until I could only focus on her. Gone was the boardwalk, the loud chatter of people, and the music from the jukebox—it was only me, the white sand, and my rainbow mermaid. She alluded grace and confidence, the sensual sway of her hips so fluid it was as if she were still moving in the water and not on land.

She looked up and seemed to catch my eye. Before I could think to wave or motion her over, she disappeared—gone, poof—as if she were no more than a mirage. The world came rushing back into focus. I blinked, then scanned the beach, wondering if I'd only imagined her.

Johnny appeared to set a new Solo cup and a can of Coors Light in front of me, then began pouring a shot of Jack Daniels. Turning my attention away from the surf, I looked at him.

"Did you see that woman?" I asked.

"Working here, I see a lot of women," Johnny said with a laugh.

"No, I mean the woman with the rainbow hair out on the beach. Bikini, all curves, walked like she was floating on air. She was like a… I don't know… a mermaid or something."

"A floating mermaid? I've seen many things in my years, but I ain't never seen a floating mermaid. You're seeing things, my man. Are you sure you can handle another shot of whiskey with this beer?"

Pursing my lips into a frown, I nodded.

"Yeah, give me the shot. I wouldn't be able to drink this piss you're serving any other way."

Johnny chuckled.

"Owner was trying to cut expenses, and the regulars aren't too happy. I'll be sure to pass on your complaints," he said as he poured the beer into the cup, then dropped in the shot of whiskey. "You take it easy now. I'll save a cabana for you, but you need to use your own two legs to get there. I don't care how famous you are, Atwood. I ain't goin' to carry your ass out there."

The sound of a hand slapping down hard on the top of the bar caused Johnny to startle. Both of us turned in the direction of the noise.

"I knew it was you!" said a man three stools down. He thumbed in the direction of a beefy man sitting beside him. "I just said to my friend, 'Hey, that's Sloan Atwood!' He didn't believe me, but sure as shit, I was right!"

I gave the two men a short, two-finger wave, then turned back to my drink.

"So what? I don't fucking care if it's Sloan Atwood," the beefy guy said.

"Dude, he was a god behind the wheel! Do you know how many championships he won?"

I tried to tune them out, not wanting to listen to their critique of my racing abilities as if I weren't sitting right there. Picking up my beer, I chugged it back, taking three long swigs until the cup was empty. Since my anonymity was now lost, it was time for me to pay my tab and leave.

Reaching into my pocket, I fished out my wallet and removed a one-hundred-dollar bill. Motioning with my chin, I signaled to Johnny, my sole focus being anything other than the discussion the two men were having about me.

"I'll ah… I'll take that cabana now," I said.

"Really? It's early, man."

"Yeah, well…" I trailed off when I realized I wasn't able to focus on the bartender's face. Everything was foggy, and the room seemed to tilt. "I just gotta get out of here, Johnny."

Moving to stand up, I swayed and grabbed the edge of the bar to steady myself. I knew I was feeling pretty good, but my struggle to stay upright made me realize I was drunker than I'd initially thought.

"See what I'm saying? Just look at him," the man down the bar prattled on. "Atwood ain't no Tony Stewart. He's a washed-up has-been."

Slowly, I turned my head to look at man number two and gave myself a moment to focus. My initial impression was that he was beefy, but that implied muscular and powerful. This guy was anything but. He was overweight and out of shape, trying to hide his gut by puffing out his chest like a goddamned neanderthal.

"Who the fuck are you calling a has-been?" I challenged.

"Atwood," Johnny warned.

I ignored him and took a few unsteady steps toward the fat asshole. He stood up from his stool and glared at me.

"I'm talking about you, Atwood. You have a problem with that? It's a shame, really. You're not even thirty years old yet."

"Shut the fuck up," I snarled.

"Aww, poor baby. What's the matter?" he said in a cooing, mocking tone. "Don't like hearing you're all washed up?"

No matter how valid his words were, I reacted without thinking. Stepping toward him, I lunged at him and swung what I thought was a well-aimed punch.

It wasn't.

Completely missing my mark, my foot caught the edge of the step leading to the boardwalk. I stumbled forward and tried to regain my footing, but the effort was in vain. I twisted, grappling for something to hang on to, only to find fistfuls of air. Falling backward, everything in my line of sight passed in a blur as I went down. I heard the startled cries of the people around me.

Then, everything went dark.

---

Six hours later, I leaned my head back against the couch in my less-than-tidy living room in Beverly Grove. Milo had just dropped me off, but not before giving me a lecture about pulling my shit together.

Much like the months following the crash, today was a complete haze. Details about how I got into a bar fight were a blur in my memory. I knew what happened, yet I didn't. It was as if the essential scenes in my mind were veiled behind a thin gray curtain, where only distorted shapes and shadows could be seen. The combination of oxy and too much booze can do that. Synergism was what Milo had called it. One minute I was sitting at the bar, then the next minute, my drunk ass was in a jail cell.

According to Milo, my attempt at punching a man who'd been goading me had failed. When I pulled back to take a swing at him, I'd fallen over, smacked my head, and taken out a little girl in the process. She'd been walking on the boardwalk with her mom, and neither of them even saw it coming. I'd been too drunk and high to pay much attention to anything, let alone notice innocent bystanders. All I cared about was bloodying a man's face. As a result, a young girl ended up in the hospital with a broken arm and a bunch of cuts and scrapes that needed stitching—and I ended up behind bars.

Thankfully, Johnny knew to call Milo right away. My agent showed up at the holding center soon after, and I was lucky to have only spent a few hours in the slammer. Still, the damage was done. Milo had made it clear that the parents of the little girl would most likely sue me. There was no going back from tonight, just like there was no going back to before the crash.

*Consequences. There are always consequences.*

No matter which way I looked at it, my life was screwed.

I stood up and went to the living room credenza, where I kept my liquor stash. I was still more than just a little buzzed from earlier but not drunk enough to fall asleep—and I was fucking exhausted. I hadn't had a good night's sleep in what felt like forever. Every time I tried to rest, my mind would start to race. I was consumed with too much regret. If I had any hopes of sleeping tonight, I learned months ago that a nightcap or two was the only sure way. It would mean no dreams, no sounds of crunching metal, no ache in my hip. Jack Daniels was the only thing that seemed to quiet the noise and dull the pain. If I happened to combine it with a bit of oxycodone now and then, so be it. I knew I was on a collision course with no off-ramp. Yet, I couldn't find the energy to care in the least bit.

Bottle of Jack in hand, I went back to the couch and set it down on the coffee table. I eyed up the bottle of deep amber liquor, standing proud next to the prescription oxycodone. There were only two pills left in the little orange bottle, and I knew Dr. Haskell wouldn't prescribe more—especially after Milo told him what happened tonight.

I shifted my gaze to the clear plastic envelope sitting beside the bottle of amber-colored whiskey. It contained the personal effects returned to me by the police after Milo sprung me from my cell. The sight of it disgusted me, knowing that I—Sloan Atwood, race car driver extraordinaire—had been reduced to drug and alcohol-induced violence. That wasn't me—or at least, it wasn't who I *was*. I shook my head, knowing the old Sloan Atwood died on the track over a year ago. I'd never be the same again.

I poured a shot, then threw it back. I barely felt the burn as it went down, yet I still poured another and knocked that one back as well. Slamming the shot glass on the table, tiny droplets of brown liquid splattered over the surface. Finally feeling tired enough to go to sleep, I dragged myself out of the armchair and stumbled my way up the stairs. With any luck, I'd be pulled into a dreamless sleep within minutes.

Stripping out of my shirt and pants, I crawled into bed naked. I didn't bother to set the alarm. After all, it wasn't like I had anything to do in the morning.

I fought off the sensation of the room spinning, closed my eyes, and welcomed the weight of sleep. My alcohol-clouded mind thought about the past year, the physical rehab, and time spent going to countless doctor appointments. Every minute had been filled with a hollow emptiness. I had nothing anymore.

Without racing, I was no one.

# Chapter Four

*Sloan*

Waking up after drinking too much was always a challenge. The pounding in my head was killing me. I peered at the clock to see it wasn't even eight o'clock in the morning yet. I didn't want to be awake. I'd been dreaming, and for once, it wasn't a nightmare. Mr. Sandman was kind last night, bringing me visions of a beautiful rainbow mermaid. I rolled over onto my stomach and groaned, determined to go back to sleep, and wondered why I'd woken up so damn early.

The answer to my unspoken question came in the form of a loud, intrusive knock on the front door. Then the doorbell rang, the sound piercing through my sensitive eardrums and causing my head to pound even harder. I opened my eyes again and squinted against the bright sunshine coming in through the balcony's glass doors off my bedroom. I silently cursed myself for forgetting to close the curtains before going to bed.

Another knock sounded on the door—this one louder than the last.

*What. The. Fuck.*

Dragging myself out of bed, I pulled on a pair of gray sweatpants and headed downstairs to see who the unwelcome guest was. I assumed it was a salesman or someone pushing religious literature. I was in no mood to listen to a vacuum sales pitch or hear why I needed salvation.

I yanked open the front door, my body tense from being pulled unwillingly from the comfort of my bed. I was ready to give an earful to whomever was standing on the other side but stopped short when I saw it was a beautiful blonde. Her bright green eyes were wide with surprise —probably from the way I practically ripped the door from the hinges when I opened it.

I was about to lash out but stopped short when I noticed her hair was pulled to the side in a loose braid. Multi-colored strands had been braided through it—rainbow strands. As if my dreams had come to fruition, I gaped at her in disbelief. She was my rainbow mermaid.

"It's you. What are you doing here?" I asked, unable to stop looking at the colorful braid cascading over her shoulder and breasts—and what a fine set of breasts they were. I couldn't help but notice the way they accentuated the tempting curves of her waist. What can I say? I was a man, and I loved tits, and when they were right in front of me, I was definitely going to look.

Clearing her throat, she angled her delicate face to the side.

"I'm sorry?" she asked, seeming confused.

"You're the woman from the beach. I saw you and thought…" I didn't finish the sentence, quickly realizing how ridiculous it would sound if I said I'd thought she was a mermaid.

"I'm not sure what you're referring to. I don't believe we know each other. Are you Mr. Atwood?"

"That's me. Who wants to know?"

"My name is Kalliope Benton Riley. I'm a public relations agent from Quinn & Wilkshire. Milo Birx sent me."

I scratched my head, feeling foggy from the rough night, and I wasn't sure if I'd heard her correctly.

"My agent sent me another agent?"

"Well, I suppose you could look at it like that, but he doesn't handle PR. I do."

I took a second look at her. She was slight of build and relatively short when compared to me. I estimated her to be no more than five feet two inches. My six-one frame towered over her, yet her small size still managed to have a commanding presence in my doorway. Her bohemian dress attire didn't suggest business professional in the least bit. The tribal-print blouse hung just low enough to see the swell of those breasts I'd been admiring. The shirt was knotted at the waist, where a long apricot-colored skirt flowed over her hips, stopping to skim the tops of her sandaled feet. Large silver hoops hung from her ears, with matching bangles on both wrists. She reached up to tuck a loose piece of hair behind her ear, revealing a certain amount of careless grace in her movements.

Her overall look had a hippie vibe to it, and as much as I wanted to punch Milo for sending a PR rep to my house so early in the morning, at least he had the sense to send someone who was sexy as sin. The fact that I'd spent the night dreaming about her made it even better, and I couldn't push away the intrigue I felt. She made a definitive impression, seeming small-town yet worldly, innocent yet cunning, and beautifully exotic in every sense of the word.

Feeling more than just a little bit curious, I cocked my head to the side and offered her a small smile.

"Okay. Despite the early hour, I'll play along, Ms… What did you say your name was?"

"Kalliope Benton Riley. But you can call me Kallie."

"Well, then you can call me Sloan. You might as well come on in." I stepped aside and allowed her to enter, noting the subtle mix of patchouli and vanilla that emanated from her as we made our way to the kitchen.

*Holy hell, she smells damn good too.*

I motioned for Kallie to sit at the kitchen table while I put on a pot of coffee. If I wanted to get through this with a clear head, I needed a boost to wake my ass up. So consumed with needing caffeine in my veins, I was barely conscious of the takeout containers littering the table and floor until I saw her disapproving stare. My house had an open floor plan, leaving the mess of clothes, empty bottles and cans, and car magazines scattered about the living room in plain sight. I tried to ignore her as my need for caffeine suddenly turned into a need for something much more substantial.

"Can I get you anything?" I offered. "Coffee? Soda?"

"I'm okay, but thanks," she replied.

"Suit yourself." I shrugged, scrapped the idea of making coffee, and grabbed a Pepsi from the refrigerator. Caffeine was caffeine, no matter what the form. Cracking it open, I casually leaned against the wall and took a long swig.

"Mr. Atwood, before we begin discussing business matters, I must insist that you put some clothes on."

Glancing down at my bare chest and tattered Formula One sweatpants hanging low on my hips, I grinned awkwardly. I hadn't looked in a mirror, but I must have been quite the sight. I absently brushed my fingers over the three-day-old stubble on my face. If the taste in my mouth was any inclination to how I must smell, I could only imagine what she was thinking. Her tone was light, but I could sense the condemnation. I reached up and smoothed out my hair as best as I could, slightly embarrassed to be seen this way. Still, I couldn't help but notice her furtive glances at my torso.

The side of my mouth quirked up. I couldn't say why, but something about this woman made me want to toy with her. I wasn't naïve. I knew how women looked at me—and Kallie didn't seem to be immune. I took a step closer and leaned down, so one hand was pressing on the table.

"I would have dressed, but I wasn't expecting company. Does my naked chest make you uncomfortable?" I teased, deliberately lowering my voice to just above a whisper. She glanced at my chest again before quickly averting her eyes. My cock stiffened when I caught sight of a delicate blush sliding into her cheeks.

*Fuck, is she ever gorgeous.*

When she swallowed hard, blinked, then crossed and uncrossed her legs nervously, I half wondered who was actually toying with who. I barely knew her, yet all I could think about was spreading her out on my kitchen table so I could taste every inch of her creamy skin.

Seeming to catch herself, she frowned. Angling her chin in defiance, she gave me a cutting stare.

"If you had checked your messages, you would have known I was coming," she replied, effectively side-stepping my question. She tossed me a warning look, and the meaning couldn't have been any clearer. She was letting me know that my interest in her was duly noted, but it wasn't going to be reciprocated.

Standing upright, I returned to my position against the wall and shrugged. "Yeah, well… I've been preoccupied with a few things."

"Mr. Atwood—"

"Sloan," I reminded her.

"Sloan, why don't we get right down to the reason I'm here?"

I almost chuckled.

"Not one to waste time with idle chit-chat, are you?"

"Not particularly. You have a mess on your hands, and I'm here to fix it."

Taking another swig of Pepsi, I eyed her suspiciously over the rim of the can, still unsure what to think about her. "Your accent. It's not Californian. Where are you from?"

"I live just outside of Washington D.C."

I raised my eyebrows in surprise.

"You're a long way from home. PR firms are a dime a dozen in these parts. Why would Milo enlist the help of someone from across the country?"

"Because Quinn & Wilkshire is the best—and you're wasting my time. Can we please get down to business now?" she asked with an air of impatience, but it was nearly impossible to take her seriously. The multicolored strands intertwined with her golden blonde tresses made her look like a princess who just stepped out of a fantasy book—or in my experience, a rainbow mermaid emerging from the ocean. It was a stark contrast to the tightness of her jaw and determined expression, but it may have been the sexiest combination I'd ever seen.

"Fine. Have it your way," I conceded with a shrug. "We'll skip the small talk, but I'm going to take a shower first. Sit tight, Rainbow Brite. Give me ten minutes, and then we'll talk."

Without giving her a chance to respond, I set my empty pop can down on the table and headed toward the bathroom.

As promised, I finished showering and shaving in less than ten minutes. I brushed my teeth and exchanged the old sweatpants for a pair of jeans but deliberately skipped putting on a shirt. Instead, I slung a plain white t-shirt over my shoulder and made my way back into the kitchen. Perhaps it was a dick move, but I had rather enjoyed watching her squirm uncomfortably after the way I had caught her looking at me earlier.

However, when I entered the kitchen, she wasn't the one squirming uncomfortably—I was. In the short time I'd been gone, she'd cleaned up the mess of Styrofoam containers and beer cans that had been lying around. The trash was now piled into the garbage can, and the aluminum cans were neatly lined up in the recycle bin outside the utility room near the kitchen.

*Well, shit.*

I really wished she hadn't taken it upon herself to clean up. Now I'd have to play nice—within reason, of course. Scrapping the plan to saunter in like I was James fucking Dean, I pulled the t-shirt off my shoulder, slipped it over my head, then grinned sheepishly at her.

"You didn't have to do that," I told her, motioning to the now tidy space.

"I know. I was just bored waiting for you to come back, so I made myself useful. Don't get used to it. I'm your PR rep, not your maid."

I cocked one eyebrow at her straightforward tone, then shook my head and smiled to myself. I was more than just a little captivated by the delectable woman sitting at my kitchen table. Her heart-shaped mouth, round emerald-colored eyes, and easy blush made my dick twitch. She was leaving herself wide open, and I couldn't resist another opportunity to see that delicate blush again.

"Oh, I have plenty of thoughts on what you could be for me, Miss Kallie. Maid wasn't one of them."

Just as I'd hoped, a flush began to creep up her neck again. I grinned as I took a seat in the chair across from her, knowing I was getting to her.

*Mission accomplished.*

She sighed, ran a hand over her colorful braids, and met my eyes again.

"Listen, Sloan. I'm not here to play cat and mouse. Your agent warned me about what I might find when I got here, but I didn't expect this." She paused, seeming to collect her thoughts. "To put it bluntly, after being here for barely twenty minutes, it's plain to see that you're a train wreck. Enough beer cans and whiskey bottles are lying around this place to fill an entire dumpster. Drinking yourself into a stupor every day isn't going to get you very far."

I bristled at her condescending tone.

"What I do isn't any of your business."

"Everything about you is my business now. I know what you've been through. Milo sent me a file that outlined it all. It was a tough road, and I get that. I also know any man who was able to endure what you did is better than this. However, cleaning up your act is up to you. I can't force you to do anything. I can only work with people who have the will."

I scowled, pissed about the drastic turn in the conversation. I no longer wanted to casually flirt with this mermaid apparition who'd played a starring role in my dreams last night. Instead, I wanted to put her over my shoulder and toss her judgmental ass out the front door.

"Cleaning up my act, huh? I'm not sure what you think you know from my supposed file, but a few paragraphs aren't enough to even scratch the surface of what I've been through."

"I'm sure it doesn't. So, why don't I tell you what I do know, then you can fill in the blanks?" When I didn't respond, she held out a hand and began ticking things off on her fingers. "I know you were in a terrible accident just over a year ago. Your car hit a wall during a practice session. You fell unconscious, were airlifted to a hospital in critical condition. The doctors said you had less than a twenty percent chance of surviving your injuries."

"Yet, here I am," I interrupted, extending my arms as if to prove it.

"I'm not finished," she stated curtly before continuing. "The left side of your body was immobile, and your skull was fractured. You had a collapsed lung, several broken ribs, and a shattered hip. You spent three months on a ventilator in order to breathe. Despite the odds, you pulled through after nearly a year of intense therapy—but it wasn't enough. The damage to your hip was too great, and you were told you could never race again. After receiving the news, you fell into a depression, started drinking, and popping too many painkillers. The result? Milo phoned me this morning to tell me that a little girl named Tanya Griffin is in the hospital because of your drunken rage. This morning's newspapers have painted you as a monster, and I expect a lawsuit from the girl's family to be filed any day now."

I winced as I listened to her recap the traumatic events of the past year. She'd barely taken a breath as she listed everything in chronological order up until this moment. I wasn't sure what Milo sent her, but there had to be a bunch of HIPAA law violations somewhere in there. As for possible lawsuits, I couldn't care less about those—I deserved them and would forever be plagued with guilt over accidentally hurting an innocent child.

But while Kallie's summary was correct, I was still right about one thing. The file she read didn't even scratch the surface. Never once did she acknowledge what I'd truly lost in the crash that happened one year and three months ago. There were some things I'd never get back—the feel of the engine revving, the wind as it whipped around the car, the roaring of the tires, the adrenaline rush that always came when I got behind the wheel.

Or the euphoria felt during the victory lap after a big win.

"You think you know everything, but you know nothing about me or what I had to give up," I said through gritted teeth. "Milo's intentions were good, but I think it's time for you to leave. I had a late night, and a bottle of ibuprofen is calling my name."

Her stiff posture softened, and to my surprise, she reached across the table to cover my hand with hers. Her bright green eyes appeared concentrated as she stared back at me, and a strange sort of energy passed between us.

"I told you I was going to list the things I knew, and then you had to fill in the blanks. I'm not insensitive to how you might be feeling. You were in the prime of your life, only to have it all ripped away. I won't pretend to understand what that feels like, but I can try if you'll let me. The sooner I figure out who you are, the better I can do my job." She stopped, seeming to come to some sort of realization, then cocked her head to the side contemplatively. "Sloan, I'm a big believer in fate. The destiny of every single person on the planet is written in the stars. There's a reason I was sent across the country to help you. Maybe you can consider this a new beginning."

I stared back at her, soaking in her words. She wore a curious expression, and I had to wonder if her comment about fate was actually about her—not me. But it was her earnestness about a predetermined destiny that made me pause. As ludicrous as the idea was, she made me believe it. Something flashed in her deep pools of green. I wasn't given a chance to figure out what it was before she stiffened and pulled her hand away from mine.

"Kallie, I want to help you out here, but I don't even know where to begin. There are just some things that can't be explained on a piece of paper. Racing was everything. I don't know who I am without it," I admitted with total sincerity. "I'm not sure how a fancy PR firm is going to help me get past that."

She pursed her lips as she considered me with inquisitive eyes.

"It won't, but it will help your less-than-savory reputation. Milo lined up a volunteer opportunity for you with Safe Track, a company sponsored by NASCAR that handles the fostering of young boys. He hopes to reverse the media spin that you somehow hate children. It's a good start, but I have a few other ideas up my sleeve as well. If you're willing to give this a go, let's start tomorrow at Motor Club Speedway in Fontana. A man by the name of Cooper Davis will be there tomorrow with a few of the boys from Safe Track. Meet me at ten o'clock."

"I'm familiar with the track, and I know Cooper. He's a friend of mine."

Her expression brightened, and I could almost see the wheels spinning in her head.

"Good. That should make things easier. I've put together an informal photoshoot and plan to invite the media."

"No," I stated firmly and adamantly shook my head. "No media. They spent years worshipping the ground I walked on, then turned on me in a hot minute after the accident. I haven't seen today's newspapers, but I'm sure it's even worse now. I don't trust them. They'll be looking for me to screw up."

"Well, then, Mr. Atwood, I guess you shouldn't screw anything up."

Kallie stood and swung her crocheted purse over her shoulder, signaling she was about to leave. When she turned and began walking toward the front door, I quickly followed her, overcome with a strong desire to ask her to stay. For what, I didn't know. It was odd considering that just fifteen minutes earlier I'd wanted to throw her out.

When we reached the door, she opened it, stopped just outside the threshold, then turned to face me. I stared down at her and our gazes locked. And there it was again—gravity, just like I'd felt when I saw her on the beach. She pulled me in, and I thought I might drown in the green sea of her eyes. I'd just met this woman, but there was something about her I couldn't quite place. She was familiar yet so unfamiliar at the same time. She was a stranger, yet I felt like we knew each other intimately, as if we were two infinitely magnetic souls.

I took a deep breath, attempting to get ahold of myself, but it didn't help. Her vanilla patchouli scent filled the air, and it was practically making me high—on her.

"Kallie, why did you agree to come all the way here?"

"It was a job assignment. I had no choice."

For some reason, her response pissed me off. Perhaps it was my ego, but I wanted her to be here for me and not just another job assignment. My feelings were ludicrous. From the way she spoke, she most likely never even heard of me until my agent hired her—yet that might be the most appealing thing about her. She didn't seem affected by my fame. She didn't have stars in her eyes or look at me as a meal ticket. There was no fangirling or gold-digging to worry about. I was a stranger to her in a way that I wasn't to so many other women.

I reached out and wrapped my fingers around her slender arm. Electricity seemed to sizzle under my palm, shocking me so much, I nearly pulled away. Yet, somehow, I held my grip firm as I stared down at her pink heart-shaped lips. My only thought was keeping her here—I didn't want her to disappear like she had yesterday. I wanted to make this rainbow mirage become a reality.

Without giving it further thought, I leaned in and planted my mouth on hers.

# Chapter Five

*Kallie*

I stiffened in protest as my mind grappled with this unexpected development.

*Is this happening? Is he really kissing me right now?*

I anchored my hands on his biceps, intending to push him away and end this madness—he was a stranger in almost every sense of the word. However, the heat I still felt from seeing him shirtless clouded my judgment, and my brain seemed to disconnect from my body. I was confused and didn't know what to do. I didn't want this…yet I did at the same time.

Without meaning to, I found myself kissing him back. My hands shifted from his shoulders to curl around his neck. My acceptance of his kiss encouraged him to press deeper into my mouth. Tasting. Claiming. His masculine scent of spice and earth sent my body reeling. I met every stroke of his tongue as he wrapped his arm around my waist, crushing my torso against his.

His fingers caressed the nape of my neck, gliding over the slope of my collarbone. I was drowning in sensation. I could hardly breathe as a wave of dizziness made my head swim. I knew it was wrong, but his possessive, animal touch made me feel powerfully female and profoundly desired. I felt it from the top of my head to the tips of my toes, and every molecule was consumed in molten heat. This was what

I'd not even known I'd needed, and it felt so damn good. I finally knew what had been missing between Dean and me—it was chemistry and unbridled passion.

*Oh my God. Dean.*

Almost intrusively, thoughts of my potential fiancé popped into my head. I tore my mouth from Sloan's, shocked at myself and awash with feelings of guilt. I stepped back, only to see his heavy breathing matched my own. His short dark hair was mussed, and I half wondered if I'd been the one to do it or if it had just dried that way after the shower.

*What in the world has come over me?*

The kiss had only lasted a few seconds, but it still took me a moment to calm my racing heart. I tossed him an accusatory glare.

"Why did you do that?" I demanded.

"Do what?"

"Kiss me like that!"

Leaning against the door jamb, he looked me up and down. His piercing blue eyes seemed to say he had a secret only he knew, while the side of his mouth quirked up in the sexiest lopsided grin I'd ever seen.

"Would you have preferred me to kiss you in a different way?"

"No! You had no business kissing me at all!"

"Remind me again. Why did you agree to come to all the way to California?" he asked.

I puffed out an impatient breath, not sure why he wanted me to repeat what I'd literally just said a minute earlier. "I said it was a job assignment. I had no choice."

"Well, then that's my answer too."

My brow furrowed in confusion. "What are you playing at, Sloan? That's your answer to what?"

"You wanted to know why I kissed you. The answer is, I had no choice. Your lips are just too irresistible." He shrugged, tossed me another crooked smile, then took a step back. "I'll be at Motor Club Speedway tomorrow morning at ten. I'll see you then, Kalliope Benton Riley."

Without another word, he closed the front door.

I stood there for a solid minute, completely shocked over what I'd allowed to happen with a total stranger. Too stunned to do much else, I slowly turned and walked down the driveway toward my rented BMW. As my astonishment began to dissipate, my fury began to mount. Once I was safely inside the confines of the car, I slammed my palms against the steering wheel and let out a scream of frustration.

"Argh! Of all the nerve! Who does he think he is?"

I glanced at my reflection in the rearview mirror. My cheeks were flushed pink, and I wasn't entirely sure if it was because I was mad or still turned on from Sloan's kiss. Knowing it was probably the latter only infuriated me further.

I took one last look at Sloan Atwood's contemporary-style home and wondered what I'd gotten myself into. With its oversized glass windows, sleek lines, and lack of any sort of feminine touch, the large Beverly Grove home was nothing more than an overpriced bachelor pad. Someone who lived in a place like this was probably used to getting their way with women without consequence.

I scowled at the house, then started the ignition and backed down the driveaway. As I made my way toward the interstate that would take me back to my rental house in Santa Monica, I tried to force myself to keep my temper in check and focus on the road ahead. However, my effort was in vain. The I-10 was bumper to bumper. I'd nearly forgotten how bad California traffic could be, no matter what time of the day it was. What should have been a twenty-minute drive could turn into a two-hour drive in the blink of an eye. Crawling along at five miles per hour gave me plenty of idle time to get lost in my thoughts—and the more I stewed, the angrier I got.

People didn't just run around kissing other people without permission. The presumptuous jerk didn't even know me. Never mind that I'd kissed him back—he never should have advanced on me that way in the first place. He was a client, for crying out loud—not to mention that I was engaged.

*Sort of.*

I glanced down at my hand where an engagement ring should have been.

"Damn it!" I spat out. I angrily beeped the horn for no other reason than because everyone else was doing it. It felt good to vent some of my frustration. I cursed Dean for being practical—for not giving me a ring that I could use as a shield against unwanted advances. Perhaps if he'd given me one, I might have said yes to his proposal. But I also cursed myself for welcoming a stranger's kiss.

There was no doubt that Sloan was a man who knew what he wanted and took it. I could appreciate that because I was like that too in certain situations. It wasn't about wielding power and control. It was merely about being driven to achieve.

But what happened on his doorstep was none of the above.

Sloan emitted a kind of sexual energy I had never before encountered, and he managed to ignite every desire I hadn't known existed. With every look, every breath, and every word he spoke, my insides tightened with inexplicable arousal.

And I had loved every second of it.

I'd wanted Sloan to kiss me the minute he returned fresh from a shower wearing nothing but a pair of blue jeans. My stomach clenched as I recalled his appearance. His hair had been wet, the deep brown waves shedding tiny droplets of water onto his broad shoulders and chest. He had a face any male model would die for and a body to match. When he'd finally pulled on his white t-shirt, that only made my attraction to him even worse. His t-shirt had stretched tight around his arms, the sinewy muscle bulging from the sleeves. Seriously—the man's biceps could be considered arm porn. He hadn't just looked good, but he smelled good too—like the smell of the earth after a fresh rain, with just a hint of spiciness that made my toes curl.

The reaction he'd sparked in me was so out of character, and my response was unexpected. It had been near impossible to ignore the chemistry that threatened to knock me off my feet.

As a result, I was now a cheater.

I'd never cheated on anyone in my life. I knew what that betrayal felt like, and it sucked. It didn't matter if I'd already been questioning my relationship with Dean. I'd crossed a line by welcoming a kiss from Sloan.

While I had no intentions of repeating what happened in the doorway to his house, it didn't mean I could escape my guilt. I had to tell Dean the truth—and not just about the kiss. I needed to be honest with him about everything. One kiss with Sloan confirmed everything I already knew to be missing with Dean. What I'd felt with Sloan in just the briefest of moments was something I'd never experienced with the man who wanted to marry me. I now knew that Dean and I were not meant for each other, and I owed it to him—to both of us—to be truthful.

When I finally arrived at the house Quinn & Wilkshire arranged for me to stay at, I was a ball of nerves over the phone call I knew I had to make sooner rather than later. So, when I entered the quiet house, and my cellphone began to ring, I nearly jumped out of my skin. Fumbling through my purse, I pulled it out and saw Austin's name on the caller I.D. I sighed with relief. I wasn't ready to talk to Dean yet—at least not until I could get my thoughts together.

"Hey," I answered.

"Hey, Kals. I'm just calling to check in and see if you're all settled. Dad was telling me about the house he set you up in, and it sounds nice."

I looked around the spacious two-bedroom home. The owner was a financial advisor who had recently accepted a consulting contract working in Europe for a year. Rather than sell the house, she decided to rent the fully-furnished home. She'd been explicit in the rental agreement—she would only rent to a business professional, and no kids or pets were allowed. The minute I walked through the front door, I could understand why. The house impeccably maintained house had everything from custom drapes and luxury furnishings to an inground swimming pool in the back yard surrounded by immaculately manicured landscaping. Not a single detail had been missed, and it was easy to see why the home was the owner's pride and joy.

"The square footage is about the same as my townhouse in Georgetown, but it's all one level here, so it looks bigger. I like it a lot. It's very chic and a whole lot better than the hotel I was staying at. What a creep show that was!"

Austin laughed.

"You're so dramatic. I highly doubt your two-day stay at the Hilton was that bad."

"Trust me. You weren't there. The hotel itself was fine—it was the people in it. I went down to the gift shop my first night there to get myself a bottle of wine. I smacked right into someone wearing a lime green rubber bodysuit. Everyone else was decked out in weird garb too. You know me—I'm all about individual expression, but this was extreme on so many levels. I don't know if there was a costume event of sorts going on or what. All I know is that I felt like I was walking through the Capitol in *The Hunger Games*."

Austin laughed again, this time harder and longer, and I smiled. I missed him so much already, and I'd only been gone for a few days.

"Alright. I get the picture. L.A. is weird," he granted after he finally stopped laughing.

"Not weird. It's just different in a way I didn't expect. I mean, I was in Southern Cali for college for four years, but I never ventured north much. It's a whole different world here—the sounds, the smells, the air." I paused and looked out the large glass patio door. There had been an air quality alert today, and seeing the gray smog blocking the otherwise blue sky hurt my heart. "I guess I'll get used to it."

Austin fell quiet for a moment before speaking again.

"What's up, Kals? You alright?"

"I suppose so. Why?"

"Normally, you get excited to experience new things—even if they are weird. You seem hesitant right now… I don't know. Off, I guess you could say. I just want to make sure you're doing okay out there."

I sighed. Austin had the uncanny ability to read me—even from twenty-six hundred miles away.

"I met my client today."

"And?"

"He's an arrogant jerk, but nothing I can't handle."

"Is that it?"

"No…" I hesitated. "I have to call Dean later. I'm going to break things off with him."

"Oh, really?" He tried to sound surprised but had difficulty masking the glee in his voice.

"I know you aren't a big fan of his, but you could at least try not to sound so happy about it," I said dryly.

"I'll be honest. I can't say I'm disappointed, but I do wonder what brought this on."

My hand automatically moved to brush my fingertips over my lips. My mouth began to tingle as I remembered Sloan's kiss. I didn't understand my reaction to him, and I couldn't stop the rush of need that engulfed my senses as I recalled the memory. There was a reason I was drawn to Sloan in a way I'd never been to anyone else, and I was determined to find out what it was. But I couldn't tell my brother any of that for obvious reasons. Austin would think I'd lost my mind.

"There's always been something missing in our relationship. I just think it's the right thing to do. I feel like I'm being pulled—like my destiny is shifting by cosmic force. I just can't tell which direction I'm supposed to go."

"Here we go…the moon, stars, and planets are aligning," he teased.

"Oh, hush. I know better than to talk to you about this stuff. I should hang up now and call Gabby. She gets it."

"Speaking of Gabby, I ran into her at the grocery store this morning. She mentioned that she has some vacation time she needs to use and was thinking about coming out to see you."

I perked up, excited about a possible girls' weekend—or maybe a whole week—with my friend.

"Really? When?"

"She wasn't specific, but I got the impression it would be next month sometime. Call her and ask."

"I'll give her a buzz later after I talk to Dean. I'll probably need her ear after I make the call to him."

"I wish I could head out for a visit too, but my company recently picked up a project in Japan. I just found out I'll be crossing the globe a lot over the next three months. It will be hard planning anything in between."

Austin was an engineer who worked for a worldwide company that focused on everything from aerospace to defense systems. He frequently traveled for his job, but multiple trips to Japan were a lot—even for his company.

"What's in Japan?" I asked.

"It's an amusement park subdivision. The mouse is looking to expand again. Lots of new rides mean a shit-ton of hydraulics and motion control systems."

"Sounds boring."

Austin laughed but followed up with a sigh.

"Enough about me. Getting back to Dean—my feelings about him aside—I think you're making the right decision. You just…I don't know. You deserve better. I can't explain it."

"I hear you. And thank you."

"Alright, I've got to run. I leave in a few days, and I'm not sure if I'll talk to you before then. With the time difference and because I'm not sure where the hell I'm going to be on any given day, email is best if you need to reach me."

"Will do. Be safe. I love you, brother."

"Love you, too."

After I hung up the phone with Austin, I went into the living room and sat down on the couch with my laptop. It wasn't even noon yet, and I wanted to get a few hours of work in before calling Dean. I told myself it wasn't stalling but prioritizing. A call to him would only distract me from accomplishing much of anything today, and it was better to do it later. After all, I'd come to California for one reason—to fix a client's reputation. To do that, I needed to learn more about him.

Typing Sloan's name into the search engine, Atwood Racing Enterprise was the first thing to populate. After only a few minutes of reading, I learned that Sloan had once been an intimidating force in the world of racing. He'd won multiple championship races and was the youngest driver to win three consecutively. He was more than just a big deal. When he'd said racing was everything to him, my search results showed me that was the understatement of the year. It was almost hard to believe I hadn't heard of him until I was assigned as his rep.

After thirty minutes of reading, I found myself unable to stop staring at an image of Sloan on the screen. In the picture, he was decked out in his racing gear with his helmet at his hip. It was as if he were looking right back at me with those smoldering blue eyes. Desire burned hot in my belly, flipping and twisting like anxious butterflies.

Almost immediately, I felt guilty.

*What am I doing?*

I didn't know how I could have such a strong attraction to a man I'd literally just met when, just a week ago, I thought I was in love with Dean. Closing my eyes, I took a deep breath. When I opened them, I knew I couldn't put off the inevitable anymore.

Setting my laptop to the side, I picked up my cell phone from the coffee table and called Dean. As the phone rang, I began to feel the sting of tears. While I knew I was doing the right thing, it didn't make the call any easier. This deserved a face-to-face conversation—not a phone call from thousands of miles away. I should have been honest with myself long before coming to California and broke it off with Dean months ago when I first started having doubts.

But, as the phone rang, I reminded myself once again that

everything happens for a reason. It was time to end this chapter because I knew in my heart that Dean wasn't meant to be my whole story. When he finally picked up after the fifth ring, I steeled myself for what I had to do.

"Dean, it's me. We need to talk."

# Chapter Six

*Sloan*

My head was still pounding. I should have gone back to bed after Kallie left, but there was no way I could sleep after what happened. I couldn't stop thinking about the taste of those pouty, heart-shaped lips or the power and energy that seemed to radiate from her when she submitted to my kiss. When she'd abruptly pulled away, I found myself feeling foolishly stunned. Catching me off guard was rare, yet I'd nearly been knocked on my ass by an eccentric goddess who could make my head spin with just one look.

I didn't know why I impulsively kissed her. I'd never done anything like that before in my life. In fact, I'd always considered guys who did things like that creepy. By doing what I did today, I'd officially crossed the line into the creeper zone. There had been nothing during our conversation that hinted she was interested in me at all, yet her body language told a different story, so I just acted on it without thinking.

While I knew I'd overstepped my bounds, I didn't regret it—not for a minute. My only regret was letting her walk away. We had only just met, but two people with a connection like that were not meant to stay strangers.

The crazy thing was, she wasn't my usual type at all. Tall brunettes, curvy in all of the right places, sultry with just the perfect amount of naughtiness, was the kind of woman I usually went for. Kallie, on the other hand, was the complete opposite. She had a wholesome vibe to her—and she was a total hippie. With her flowy skirt and rainbow-colored hair, she spoke of outlandish ideas about fate and predetermined destiny. It was ridiculous. Yet, for some reason, I couldn't turn away from her mesmerizing green eyes. And after just one taste of her lips, I knew she would be more than just another brunette pit stop. She would be a challenge, and that made me want to win her over all the more.

Resisting the urge to take a cold shower, I grabbed the keys to my Chevy Camaro and began driving to Motor Club Speedway in Fontana. As I navigated the highway, I couldn't help missing my Alfa Romeo Spider. It had been my favorite car over the years, but just like everything else, I'd been forced to give it up after my accident. I hated driving the Chevy. It just screamed douchebag with a mullet. If my hip injury didn't dictate the necessity for the custom paddle technology that only Chevy offered, I wouldn't have been caught dead in the car. I preferred the sweet and seductive features of the Alfa Romeo's unique design over the Chevy any day. Every time I complained about it, I forced myself to remember that I was lucky to have found something even remotely sporty. I could have been stuck with a Buick.

Just over an hour later, I arrived at Motor Club Speedway. I hadn't been to the track since before the doctor called and told me I couldn't race again. It was too painful, and I knew if I ever returned to any race track, it would have to be on my terms—and preferably not under the watchful eye of Kalliope Benton Riley. With any luck, Cooper would be there, and I could talk to him about my current predicament with the girl who completely upended my morning.

When I walked through the main doors, I spotted Benjamin Dunn, the Crew Chief for Cooper's racing team, as I made my way through the main gates.

"Hey, Ben!" I called out to him. He glanced in my direction and smiled when he saw me.

"Atwood. Well, well! It's been a while. I didn't expect to see you here today," he drawled in a thick Southern accent.

"What can I say? I'm like a bad penny. I always turn up," I joked and clapped him on the shoulder. I was surprised by how good it felt to see him. "Man, you're a sight for sore eyes. How are things around here?"

"Same old since you were here last. You?"

"Eh, the same old for me too, I guess," I replied as casually as I could. Even though we both knew how drastically different things were in my life, there was no use talking about it. "I'm actually here to see Cooper. Is he kicking around?"

"Yes, sir. He's here—and his knickers are in a knot over something. Last I saw him, he was up in the box yelling at the newest pit crew member. I'm telling you… some of these kids coming in here lately have me shakin' my damn head. Porchlight is on, but no one's home."

I grinned, knowing exactly what Benjamin was referring to. Some new hires were better suited for selling team merch than holding a wrench.

"Got it. Thanks for the warning. I'll head that way."

I tossed Benjamin a quick wave, then walked down the corridor to the steps that would take me to the box seating area of the clubhouse. When I got there, I found Cooper with his arms crossed, staring down at the track. His shoulders were tense, and his jaw was set firm. He looked nothing short of furious.

"Rookie forget one of the lug nuts?" I asked as I approached.

Cooper glanced in my direction. Shock registered in his eyes before he quickly masked it and turned back to the track.

"No, but he could have if he'd been down with the rest of the crew."

"Why? What happened?"

"He was up here in the box, sleeping off a hangover. He's just lucky I got to him before Ben did."

"Oh, shit. Not good." I shook my head. Fatigue for any pit crew member was dangerous on a normal day—compounded by an alcohol-induced hangover, it could be deadly. "Did you cut him loose?"

"Nah, he's a good kid. He's been on the job for about six months and always brought his A-game—until today, that is. After I was through with him, he knows better than to come here hungover again. If he does, he's out. The crew is only as strong as its weakest link."

"No truer words have ever been spoken," I agreed. I looked down at the track and watched the crews bustling around as they prepped for a practice race. If just one of them missed a step, it could throw an entire race—or worse. I felt Cooper's eyes on me and turned my head to face him.

"How are you holding up, Sloan? You haven't been here in quite a while. I'm sure you didn't stop by to hear about a rookie fucking up."

"I'm fine."

"Now that's a whole load of bullshit, and you know it. I called Milo this morning after I heard about what happened in Long Beach. I'm worried about you. We all are."

I pursed my lips in annoyance. I could always count on Cooper for his no-bullshit way of getting straight to the point, but that's not what I needed now. I didn't want to talk about how fucked up my life was. I wanted to speak to him about Kallie and what I should do about her.

"What happened yesterday in Long Beach won't happen again. I'm more concerned about the little girl, Tanya. I can't tell you how bad I feel," I admitted.

"I'm sure you feel awful. If it's any consolation, from what I've heard, she's going to be fine."

"It doesn't matter," I retorted. "It shouldn't have happened."

"You're right on that front. It definitely shouldn't have happened. The Sloan Atwood I know is better than that. You've got to get your shit together. You're driving too fast on a dead-end road, brother. You need to change tracks completely."

I sighed, knowing how right he was.

"Milo hired a firm to help me out. The PR rep showed up at my house this morning. They lined up some shit to clean up my image—whatever that means. That's the reason I came here today. I haven't been here in quite a while, and I wasn't sure how it would feel coming back. Plus, the chick with the PR firm…" I trailed off, trying to find the words to describe what happened with Kallie. "After she came by the house this morning, I decided that I'm not sure if she's going to work out."

"Why not?"

Before I could respond, I heard a thunderous noise coming from the track. I drew in a sharp breath and turned to see the cars moving into their starting positions. The rumble of their engines caused a quiver deep in my bones. I was instantly overwhelmed with jealousy and desperate longing. I wanted to be down there—not up in a box talking about bullshit with Cooper. I craved the feeling of the tires roaring beneath my legs, the high that came during every turn, and the euphoric rush that was produced only when I hit top speed. I shifted my weight just enough to feel the dull ache in my hip—a reminder of why I'd never be behind the wheel of a race car again.

I bitterly tore my gaze from the track and turned back to Cooper. I tried to ignore the pity in his eyes. He knew without explanation what I'd just been thinking about.

"She's not going to work out because I don't want her help," I told him as if the answer were really that simple and not about the consuming need I had for the mysterious rainbow mermaid who'd taken up residence in my psyche from the moment I first saw her.

"You never were one to ask for help," Cooper said warily and shook his head. "All I can say is to give this woman a chance. PR is her thing, after all. Maybe she can help you get around the bend."

"It isn't about not accepting the help—I'm open to it. God knows I need all the assistance I can get right now. I just don't want *her* as my rep." I paused and rubbed my thumb and index finger over my chin, thinking about all of the other ways I *did* want her. "She might not want to represent me anymore anyway. I may or may not have screwed things up with her this morning."

"How so?"

Lowering my hand, I looked squarely at my friend.

"I kissed her."

Cooper's eyes widened.

"You what? I mean, not that I'm one to throw stones, but didn't you just meet her?"

"I guess you could say that. I saw her on the beach yesterday, but we never actually met until this morning. I don't know what came over me. Hell, she isn't even my type. All I know is that she was on the beach, then I couldn't stop thinking about her. When that very same woman showed up at my house this morning, I was shocked to see her there. It felt like too much of a coincidence. We talked, and before she was about to leave, I realized I didn't want her to go. So, I went all caveman-like, grabbed her, and kissed her. I can only imagine what she thinks now."

Cooper started to laugh.

"Ballsy move. Did she kiss you back at least?"

A slow grin spread across my face as I recalled the memory of her petite hands curling around my neck.

"Oh, yeah. She definitely kissed me back—at first. Then she seemed to remember herself and pulled away. I think I caught her off guard. Supposedly, Milo gave her a file on me, and I'm pretty sure the file didn't list presuming playboy as a character description."

Cooper let out a low whistle.

"Fuck, man. Now what?"

"I told her I'd meet her here tomorrow morning. I guess I'll find out then. She's got something set up with Safe Track. I'm not sure if your wife has anything to do with it."

"Rochele mentioned she would be here tomorrow for a photoshoot with the boys. I didn't realize it had anything to do with you, though. What's the name of this PR agent?"

"Kallie."

Cooper scratched his chin contemplatively.

"Hang on. I have a better idea, one that might make things less awkward—you know, soften Kallie up, so she gets to know you a little better before tomorrow. I mean, I know how much you like your women, but you aren't a total dick."

I frowned.

"Okay. So… what's your idea?" I asked hesitantly. I wasn't sure where Cooper was going with this.

"It makes sense to get her and Rochele together since they'll be working together tomorrow. I think the four of us could all have dinner tonight—you, Kallie, me, and Ro."

"I don't think I can call her up and ask her to dinner at this point," I said with a laugh.

"You don't have to. I can ask Ro to set it up. Nothing fancy. We'll keep it casual with the goal of discussing the photoshoot. I don't know who Ro is planning to bring, but it's a good idea to brief you on each of the boy's situations. What do you say?"

I pursed my lips and considered his proposal. It wasn't a bad idea. I was familiar with Safe Track and knew they fostered boys from all backgrounds, many of which included extreme trauma with long-lasting effects. Having a better understanding of what I would be walking into would be a good thing. Plus, the idea of seeing Kallie again so soon was more than just a little bit appealing. The problem was, I wasn't sure how she would react to a night out with me after what happened this morning. Hell, I didn't even know if she still wanted to be my PR rep. A new agent might have already been assigned to me for all I knew, and she could be on a plane back to D.C.

My heart constricted at the thought of never seeing her again. It felt strange to be so affected by a woman—to want her so desperately despite barely knowing anything about her. My conscience nagged at me, telling me to rein things in before they went any further.

But I couldn't.

I'd had a taste of her, and I already knew I'd never get my fill.

"Alright. I'm in. Have Rochele set it up."

# Chapter Seven

*Sloan*

Five hours later, I pulled into a parking space in front of an eclectic sushi restaurant named The Lucky Koi. I'd never been there before and was surprised when Cooper texted me this as our dinner location. I wasn't a huge fan of sushi and hoped they had something mainstream on the menu. Still feeling slightly hungover, my body craved anything deep-fried and greasy over raw fish and seaweed.

When I stepped through the restaurant's doors, I was greeted by a formally-dressed Japanese woman standing behind a narrow podium.

"Welcome to The Lucky Koi," she said with a nod.

"Thank you. I'm meeting Cooper Davis, party of four. I'm not sure if they've arrived yet."

The woman looked down at her clipboard.

"Yes. I see two members of your party have arrived. Right this way, please."

Walking down a dimly lit hallway, I looked around. The place wasn't too fancy, but definitely more upscale than the local hamburger joint. When we reached the end of the hallway, the space opened up to reveal what looked like an Asian garden built into the Pacific coast. The walls were nothing but glass, giving a full view of the surf crashing into miles of sandy beach. Inside, slated stones, tall bamboo, and lanterns decorated the seating area.

I spotted Cooper and Rochele sitting at the far end. Cooper gave me a short nod when he saw me.

"I didn't take you for a sushi kind of guy, Cooper," I joked as I took the seat across from them. "Was there something wrong with the Crab Shack?"

"Not my choice. Blame Ro. She picked the place."

"I thought it would be better to cater to Kallie's tastes since this is supposed to be a business dinner," Rochele explained. "When I called to invite her, I asked about any dietary restrictions. She told me she was a vegetarian. I knew this place had plenty of vegetarian options, so here we are."

I shook my head.

"Of course Rainbow Brite is a vegetarian," I remarked, not bothering to suppress an eye roll.

"No rainbows tonight. Sorry to disappoint you," said a familiar voice.

Startled, I looked up to see Kallie had come up behind me. It had been less than ten hours since I'd last laid eyes on her, yet I felt as if I was seeing her for the first time. Gone were the rainbow streaks in her hair, replaced by purple strands that matched her dress. She wasn't wearing bohemian attire like she'd been this morning. Now she wore a thin-strapped, long bright orchid satin dress that whispered over her curves, giving me a glimpse at tiny details that I'd missed before. With her arms bare, I was able to see a delicate moon tattoo lacing over her right shoulder with little stars cascading halfway down her arm. There was writing as well, but I couldn't make out what the scrolling font said at a quick glance. The dark ink should have been too bold against her creamy skin, yet somehow it made her seem elegant and even more mysterious.

"Kallie, I didn't realize you…I, um…" I stuttered, uncharacteristically stumbling over my words as I quickly stood to pull out her chair. I was both surprised to see her standing there and amazed by how fucking gorgeous she looked. "I…ah, you look great—different. Please, have a seat."

Cooper attempted to laugh but had been mid-sip with his water and started choking. Once he caught his breath, he grinned from ear to ear.

"I never thought I'd see the day," he said with unmistakable humor in his voice.

"Shut up, asshole," I muttered.

Rochele pursed her lips and threw Cooper a scolding look, but she didn't comment. Instead, she stood and extended her hand to Kallie.

"I'm Rochele, but you can call me Ro. It's a pleasure to meet you, Kallie."

"Likewise. It's nice to put a face to the voice," Kallie graciously said as she returned Rochele's handshake.

Glancing back to where I stood waiting to push in her chair, Kallie smoothed her hands over her hips and sat down. She moved with devastating grace, her body wrapped in a satin dress meant for sin. Intense lust threatened to overtake me, so forceful it made me dizzy.

Shaking my head, I returned to my seat next to her, and an uncomfortable silence fell over the table—or perhaps I was the only one feeling awkward. I needed a minute to just fucking relax. I didn't know what the hell was wrong with me. It was as if Kallie had put some sort of weird voodoo spell on me. Thankfully, our waiter was efficient and came over to take our drink orders relatively quickly.

"What can I get for you, Miss?" he asked Kallie. She glanced at me, then placed a hand on my shoulder.

"Mr. Atwood and I will just stick with ice water. Thank you," she replied.

I blinked, not sure if I'd heard her correctly. I was about to speak up, but she squeezed my shoulder as if in warning. I looked at her curiously, and something about her expression compelled me to stay silent.

"And for you, Miss?" the waiter asked Rochele.

"I'll have a gin and tonic, extra lime."

"And I'll take a Sapporo," Cooper added. I eyed him questioningly, not realizing he was a fan of lighter Japanese beer. Cooper shrugged when he caught my eye. "When in Rome…"

When the waiter walked away, I rounded on Kallie.

"What was that all about? Is there a reason I couldn't order myself a damn drink?" I demanded a little too harshly. God only knew, the longer I sat at this table next to this spellbinding goddess, the more I felt like I needed one.

However, if Kallie was taken aback by my tone, she didn't seem upset by it. She simply picked up her water glass to take a sip of it. I noted how graceful the movement of her hand was, never hesitating but fluidly gliding as it would have if I hadn't just snapped at her. She raised one perfectly shaped eyebrow and eyed me knowingly.

"Do you see that guy sitting alone at the table over there?" She angled her head slightly, lifting her chin to the left. I turned to see who she was referring to.

"Yeah, I see him. What about him?"

"He's a reporter."

"How do you know that?"

"It's my job to know these things. Your every move is being scrutinized. If you want to fix your reputation, you'll take my advice and drink water tonight."

Cooper glanced in the direction Kallie had motioned. Turning back to face us, he released a low chuckle.

"Oh, she's good, Sloan. I recognize that guy. He's a reporter from the *Racing Beat.* I'd keep this girl around if I were you. She'll be able to clean up your image in no time."

Kallie smiled and nodded her head knowingly. She didn't look smug to be told she was correct but humbly confident in her ability to see things. I narrowed my eyes at her. A part of me wanted to signal the waiter back to the table and order a double scotch on the rocks just to spite her, but another part of me knew she was right. The newspapers were having a field day with headlines about me, many of them speculating why I fell into a bottle after the crash. The last thing I needed was to give them more ammunition.

Still, there was no way I was going to let Kallie win this power play. Leaning in closer so only she could hear me, I asked, "Are you trying to fight with me?"

"No, why?"

"Because if you are, you should know it's turning me on."

To my satisfaction, her eyes widened, and her face flushed ten shades of crimson. The way it crept up her neck and blossomed over her cheeks was like catnip for my soul—addictive and immensely satisfying. But even more rewarding was the unmistakable flash of desire in those endless pools of green. Sitting back in my chair, I crossed my arms and allowed myself a moment to enjoy her discomfort.

Rochele cleared her throat. She may not have heard what I said, but she was not oblivious to Kallie's recognizable blush.

"Yes. Well, speaking of your image, Sloan, let's talk about tomorrow," Rochele suggested.

"Fine. Let's talk about it," I agreed, choosing to accept the small victory over Kallie as I smugly—albeit begrudgingly—picked up my glass of ice water from the table and took a sip.

The two women dived right in. Cooper and I barely got a word in edgewise. As I listened, I found out the two boys Rochele planned to bring to the track were new to The Residence, the place where the orphaned boys lived after losing their parents. While I'd met several of the boys staying at The Residence in the past, I was never introduced to the two who would be joining the photoshoot.

"Marcus has been with us for about six weeks," Rochele said. "He's ten years old and has been bouncing around in the system for years—that is until recently when a spot for him opened up at The Residence. His biological parents both died of drug overdoses."

"Oh, that's awful!" Kallie said regretfully with a shake of her head.

"I really hope we can bring him some stability. He desperately needs it. Eli is the other boy I'm going to bring. He's nine years old and has been with us for about a month longer than Marcus. He's been through a lot. His father is unknown, and his mother was a prostitute. She was murdered by one of her johns right in front of Eli."

I frowned, unable to mask the anger I felt from hearing the boys' stories. I'd been through my fair share of shit, but I couldn't imagine seeing my mother murdered in cold blood. A wound like that ran deep and would have long-lasting scars.

The waiter returned with Cooper and Rochele's drinks, then took our food orders. Cooper and Rochele decided to share a sushi sampler platter, and Kallie ordered something equivalent to rabbit food—edamame, avocado salad, and a vegetable sushi roll. I, on the other hand, managed to find the only thing that looked remotely edible on the menu—steak teriyaki.

The conversation continued to be about the two boys Rochele planned to bring to tomorrow's photoshoot, but I was only tuned in with half an ear. I was too preoccupied with the shades of purple twisted through in Kallie's braid. The two times I'd seen her before this, her hair had been rainbow-colored, and I wondered how or why she changed the colors. There was a lock of hair that always seemed to spring free near her left ear. She was forever tucking it back, and I couldn't tell if it was a nervous habit or if it was a hairstyle that refused to stay in place.

I had so many questions about her. She was like a riddle I had to find the answer to—but it was a riddle that certainly wasn't going to be solved over just one dinner.

When the food arrived, I shook my head as if to clear it, and I forced myself to focus on the conversation at hand.

"When Eli first came to The Residence, Ro said he wouldn't let anybody touch him," Cooper was saying. "I didn't realize how bad it actually was. I'm talking about full-on screaming fits. I saw it happen once when one of the younger boys at The Residence tried to be nice and hug him. It was brutal. My heart broke for the little guy, but they've made great progress with him."

"Thanks to Cooper," Rochele added. "Eli's love for race cars helped us break through some of his barriers."

"I was planning on keeping the photoshoot candid—nothing staged," Kallie said. "I just want everyone to relax and have a good time while the camera clicks away. Considering Eli's issues, that's probably a good thing. From what you've described, I don't want a photographer to accidentally trigger him when trying to get a group pose."

Rochele nodded her head in agreement.

"Eli's therapist, Dr. Dellaneve, assured me that he would be okay for tomorrow. Just remember that there can be no physical contact with him, and all should be good," she warned. My ears perked up upon hearing this.

"And if he's not?" I asked. "Kallie is insisting on having the press there. What if something goes wrong?"

"Let me handle that," Kallie said. "There are plenty of other things you need to focus on, including getting me a list of other possible problems that could arise."

"Such as?"

"Crazy ex-girlfriends, a falling out with a friend, bad blood with a family member—stuff like that."

"Right!" Cooper scoffed. "Like Sloan has kept any woman around long enough for her to collect dirt on him."

"Well, there was Skylar," Rochele reminded with a teasing wink. "I think she lasted, oh… maybe two weeks? Then there was Erica. How long did you keep her around for, Sloan?"

"Alright you two. Enough. What can I say? I'm a busy guy. I don't have time for the latch-on types."

I glanced at Kallie, feeling slightly uneasy. I wasn't sure why I cared about her opinion so much—I just did. Sure, I'd been around the block more than a few times, but I didn't want her to think I was some kind of philandering skirt-chaser. Although, after my advance on her this morning, I'm pretty sure that's exactly what she thought.

"Two weeks or two months. It doesn't matter," Kallie waved off, then looked directly at me. "I need to know about any skeleton in your closet that could give you negative publicity. I've got six months to make it disappear. I also need to know about anything that could help you. What is your relationship with your parents like?"

I instantly stiffened and felt my jaw clench. An uncomfortable silence fell over the table.

"I'm sure that information is in the file you have on me," I responded coolly. Kallie's eyebrows pushed together in confusion.

"Actually, I don't recall reading anything about them."

"Well, Miss Know-It-All, I don't know what to tell you then. I guess Milo was slacking."

Kallie's head snapped back, and she blinked twice, her expression showing that she was clearly offended by my words and tone.

"Sloan, is there something I need to know?"

Before I could respond, the waiter approached the table with the check. Taking advantage of the distraction, I signaled for him to hand it to me.

"I've got dinner covered," I told the group and reached into my back pocket for my wallet.

"Nah, man. You don't have to. I'll split it with you," Cooper said.

"I insist. You can get it the next time."

Kallie didn't say anything but continued to look perplexed. I could practically see the wheels turning in her head. It didn't matter. A basic Google search would tell her everything she needed to know.

"I'm going to use the ladies' room before we head out," Rochele announced with a pointed look at Kallie.

"I think I will, too," Kallie immediately replied, and both she and Rochele stood from their seats.

After they walked away, I turned to Cooper.

"Why do they always go to the bathroom in pairs? It's fucking weird."

Cooper laughed.

"Not weird at all. I'm pretty sure Ro planned that after the way you snapped at Kallie. My guess? She's in there explaining your shitty behavior."

"I didn't snap."

"Yeah, you did. I felt that arctic chill from across the table. Cut the girl some slack. How is she supposed to know about what happened?"

I looked in the direction of where the two women disappeared and blew out an aggravated sigh.

"I suppose I owe her an apology," I murmured more to myself than to Cooper.

My friend laughed again.

"An apology is a start. I mean, yeah. She's your PR rep, but it's more than that. You've got it bad for this girl. I've never seen you like this."

"No need to point out the obvious. I don't get it either. I barely know her—not that I knew any of the other women I was with all that well either. But Kallie is different somehow." I paused and pursed my lips together, trying to find the words to explain the unexplainable. "I know what you're thinking, and you can say it. I'm fucked up."

"Nope. I think it's voodoo pussy."

"Jesus, Cooper. I haven't even been with her in that way. Yeah, it's like she put a spell on me, but there's no magical pussy taking hold of my dick—at least not yet."

"It doesn't matter. It was like that with Ro and me. I saw her and immediately wanted her. There was no rationalization for why I couldn't get her out of my head. It just was. I'm not saying what's going on with you and Kallie is anything like Rochele and me but trust me on this—if you want a chance to find out, you probably need to be a little nicer."

The waiter returned with my credit card, and as I put it back in my wallet, I considered Cooper's words. Before my accident, I was never a big drinker, and I never took drugs. Sex was my only vice. I'd had more than my fair share of women, but I wasn't a playboy. I merely appreciated the high that came with being buried deep inside a beautiful woman. It was an instant stress reliever.

After the accident, I'd felt more alone than ever before in my life. Cooper had been the only one dumb enough to stick around and put up with my miserable ass. When I found out I couldn't race again, I'd used alcohol and painkillers to dull the physical and mental ache no doctor could heal in an operating room. I shut out everyone and anything that reminded me of my previous life, including my ability to get laid with just a snap of my fingers. Depression took over, and I'd assumed no woman would want a broken has-been. In the process, I'd mastered the art of being an asshole.

Then Kallie showed up at my door.

A part of me wondered if the only reason I felt so drawn to her was that she was the first woman I'd allowed myself to be around for more than a passing minute since the crash. I wasn't certain, but I would have to heed Cooper's advice and start being a little nicer to Kallie if I wanted to find out.

# Chapter Eight

*Kallie*

I stood in front of the restroom mirror and reapplied a thin layer of gloss to my lips. Rochele walked up next to me, leaned her hip against the counter, and gave me a small smile.

"I'm not sure what you're thinking, but I want you to know that Sloan isn't normally a complete jerk," she said.

"No. I don't think he's a total jerk. But I do think he's arrogant and assuming."

"Still mad about the kiss he planted on you this morning?"

"You know about that?" I asked, feeling shocked and embarrassed at the same time.

"Cooper might have mentioned it," she admitted with a knowing grin. "I have to say, I've never seen Sloan act like this before. You had him tongue-tied quite a few times over dinner."

"I don't know about that. He didn't seem to have any issue biting my head off just now."

"Don't hold it against him. There's a reason he turned cold there at the end. Once you get to know the real Sloan, you'll understand why he reacts the way he sometimes does."

Dropping my gloss into my purse, I snapped it closed then turned to face her. "Help me out then. What am I missing?"

Rochele sighed and crossed her arms. "How far back into Sloan's past did you dig?"

"I didn't dig much at all yet. I haven't had the chance to. All I know is what was in the file Milo gave to me and what I pulled up in a quick internet search."

Her face hardened.

"Milo…" she trailed off and shook her head. There was no mistaking the element of disgust in her expression. "I've never been a fan of his, but it doesn't matter what I think. He did right by enlisting your help. Sloan doesn't deserve the headlines he's getting. He's been through enough."

"I read about it. The crash, the rehab—all of it is so traumatic."

"No, I'm talking about *before* the crash."

"What do you mean?"

She hesitated for a moment, seeming unsure if she should say more.

"Look, most of what happened right before Sloan's accident isn't anything that's not already publicly available on the internet. I just don't think you've come across it yet. If you dig a little deeper, it's all there. I don't think I'll betray any confidences by telling you about Sloan's parents and why he won't talk about them."

"What about them?"

"Sloan's father, Jeff Atwood, was a Formula One racer who died in a traffic accident on Ventura Freeway near Pasadena. It was a ten-car pileup about twenty years ago. From what I read about it, it was pretty awful. Six people died in total. Sloan was just a kid when it happened. He had always idolized his father, but after that day, he chose to continue his father's legacy and started racing."

"I didn't know his father raced too. I can understand why it must be hard for Sloan to talk about him."

A sad look spread over Rochele's pretty face, and she shook her head.

"No, that's not why he doesn't talk about him—or his mother for that matter. The morning before Sloan had the crash that pulled him from racing, he discovered a hard truth about his father. I was there when it all happened." She paused and seemed to be recalling the memory. "The song, "Ventura Highway," was playing from a Bluetooth speaker in the pit lane. It was just something Sloan did before every race, whether it be a practice lap or the real deal. It's a superstition he has. Cooper has superstitions too—in fact, most drivers do. Anyways, a reporter showed up and started asking him questions about his father, saying Jeff Atwood had been drunk and was responsible for the accident on the freeway all those years ago. Sloan shooed the guy away, and none of us paid much attention to what he was saying. However, Sloan must have been thinking about it. When his mother showed up right before the practice run, he asked her about it. It turned out to be true. His father had been drinking and driving—a fact his mother had kept hidden from him for years."

"Oh, no…"

"Sloan was furious to find out he'd idolized a man whose intoxication resulted in the death of five innocent people. He argued with his mother about it in front of everyone. There was a big shouting match in the pit lane, and Sloan ended up behind the wheel in a rage. Fifteen minutes later he spun out and crashed into the wall."

"Oh my gosh!" My eyes widened in shock as I tried to envision how the scene unfolded. Sloan had to have second-guessed every decision he made that day. Not to mention, his mother must have been beside herself with guilt. I knew I certainly would've been. "Does Sloan blame his mother for what happened?"

Rochele shrugged, the expression on her face letting me know I had yet to hear the worst of the story.

"I don't know. I never asked him because it was a touchy subject. His mother killed herself three days after the accident."

I gasped.

"She killed herself?"

"Yeah. That's why he snapped when you mentioned his parents. He's still furious about what she did. It's assumed that once Sloan's mother heard about his extensive injuries, she couldn't handle it. He was in really rough shape, and nobody expected him to live. With his mother gone, all he had was his friends to help him fight his way back. Being able to race again became his sole focus and the reason he fought so hard on his road to recovery."

I thought back to what Sloan had said to me. It felt like I'd heard the words a lifetime ago, not just that very morning.

*"You think you know everything, but you know nothing about me or what I had to give up… Racing was everything. I don't know who I am without it."*

Suddenly, the pieces started to fall into place.

"Then the doctor told him he could never race again…" I let my words linger in the air, not needing to complete the sentence.

Rochele nodded knowingly. "That's why I said not to be too hard on him. Just give him a chance, Kallie."

---

Before leaving the restroom, I asked Rochele to say goodbye to Sloan and Cooper for me and left the restaurant alone. It was easier to make a quick exit rather than go back to the table to face Sloan. Now that I had a bit more insight into his past, I needed a moment to reflect on my newfound knowledge.

I was always a sucker for a sad story, and this was no exception.

Considering how weak I was under Sloan's gaze, it would only make it worse at a time when I needed to focus on the job at hand. As much as I was a spontaneous kind of person, I'd never been a big risk-taker. I was methodical with any decision I considered life-altering, especially when it came to my career. I loved my job and was grateful for the opportunity to work for my father's firm. I'd worked way too hard to allow my hormones to mess it all up, and I didn't want to do anything that could jeopardize it—especially considering the money that was at stake. If I wanted to stop pinching pennies, I needed to keep my eyes on the prize.

I'd taken an Uber to the restaurant since parking near the Santa Monica Pier was so expensive. However, I was beginning to wish I'd taken my own car. Standing out there waiting for an Uber inevitably meant I'd see Sloan when he came out. Glancing back and forth between the door to the restaurant and the beach, I made a split-second decision to head toward the water and began walking across the sand until I reached the Pacific shoreline.

The large Ferris wheel on the Santa Monica Pier could be seen in the distance, and the setting sun cast an orange and red glow, making the people on the beach look like nothing more than dark shadows. Everything felt hushed as the water lapped at the sand. I'd spent a lot of time on the beaches of Southern California when I'd been in college, enjoying the tranquil setting the sand and sea offered. I'd nearly forgotten how much I loved it.

A young couple holding hands walked past me. They looked fresh out of high school, oblivious to everyone around them as they ducked their heads together and laughed at their private joke. I smiled to myself, appreciating their young and innocent love. But at the same time, seeing them also made me feel sad. It reminded me of the phone call I'd made to Dean earlier and all the failed relationships that came before him. Perhaps the gypsy was right—I was doomed when it came to love.

As if the mere thought of Madame Lavinia stirred something in the air, the hairs on the back of my neck stood on end. I felt something—like a presence—that caused goosebumps to rise on my arms despite the warm evening air. Instinctively, I slowly turned to look behind me.

Glancing in the direction of where I'd just come from, I saw Sloan standing on the edge of the restaurant's walkway. Wrapping my arms around myself, I shivered. It wasn't Madame Lavinia's presence I'd felt—it was Sloan's.

Even at this distance, I could see that he'd loosened the collar of his white dress shirt. It was now unbuttoned at the neck, and he had one thumb hooked into the right front pocket of his jeans. He stood tall and confident, oozing with power and an irresistible bad-boy vibe. The way he turned to look up and down the shoreline was almost as if he were searching for someone.

*Is he looking for me?*

I wasn't sure, but I knew the minute he spotted me. Turning away, I continued down the beach, suddenly feeling very self-conscious of the way I walked through the sand with my sling-back heeled sandals. Without skipping a step, I slipped off each shoe, looped the back straps around my index finger, and continued walking.

A moment later, I heard my name called, and my heart began to race. Resigning myself to the inevitable, I turned around to see Sloan standing directly behind me.

"It'll be dark soon. You shouldn't be down here alone," he said.

"I'm a big girl."

I expected a retort of some kind, but he didn't give one. Instead, he surprised me by reaching up to tuck a loose strand of hair behind my ear. His touch seemed to surge with electricity, causing my body to quiver from the brief contact.

"Do you like the beach, Kallie?"

"I do. But then again, I don't know anyone who doesn't. There's just something calming about the ocean."

"Very true," he said thoughtfully, then angled his head to the side curiously. "I saw you yesterday in Long Beach. At least, I'm pretty sure it was you."

I looked at him in surprise, suddenly remembering what he'd said on his doorstep that morning. He thought I was a woman he saw on the beach.

"That's right. I was there yesterday. I don't remember seeing you, though."

"It's probably good that you didn't. My head is still fuzzy about what happened, but I definitely remember seeing you. You looked like a mermaid coming out of the ocean. And the rainbows—there was no mistaking that when you showed up at my door. That's how I recognized you this morning. I really liked the rainbow weaves you'd had in your hair. Why did you change the color?"

I shrugged and thought about how much Dean despised the way I changed the color daily.

"I change the color based on how I feel that day. Some people wear clothes dictated by their mood. I swap out hair extensions. Ultimately, it's an expression of myself. Rainbow is for when I'm feeling optimistic—when I'm trusting destiny to take hold and make anything happen."

"Destiny, huh? And the purple? What does purple mean?"

I hesitated, unsure about how much I wanted to divulge. I couldn't tell him I wove purple through my French braid when I was getting ready for dinner because of how his kiss had turned me inside out—

especially when I didn't understand it myself. Instead, I gave him the partial truth, but no less honest.

"Purple is when I'm confused or feeling conflicted over something. I also wear purple when I'm nervous."

He eyed me questioningly.

"Do you feel nervous?"

"No," I lied, albeit a little too quickly. In an attempt to recover, I brought the conversation back to business. "I'm conflicted about the right way to handle your PR strategy."

He nodded his head, but there was a glint of amusement in his eyes.

"I'm not so sure about that. I get the feeling there's more behind the purple today. Am I right?"

"Maybe."

Turning away, I continued my walk down the beach. Sloan fell into step beside me.

"Is that all you're going to give me? Come on, Kallie. We're going to be working together a lot over the next few months. At dinner, you wanted me to tell you everything about myself so that you can help me, but it's kind of hard to do that if I don't know anything about you. Give me something here."

*Give him something? Why would I give up anything about myself when I know he is keeping things from me?*

I stopped walking and turned to face him, the words on the tip of my tongue. I wanted to repeat what Rochele had told me, but instinct held me back. I knew Sloan would need to tell me his version of the story in his own time, not because I demanded it.

*It's too personal.*

Besides, it wasn't like he had the opportunity to share the story about his parents. It wasn't fair of me to accuse him of hiding things considering the length of time we'd known each other. Until he decided to open up about it, I'd just have to work with what I knew.

Shaking my head, I began walking again. "I'm not here because of me, Sloan. It's about you."

He fell quiet as he walked beside me, the only sounds coming from the waves crashing into the shore or the occasional laughter of people in the distance. "So… are you going to tell me the real story behind the purple hair?"

I pursed my lips, frustrated with his persistence.

"Since you insist on knowing, fine," I said with an exasperated sigh. "Before dinner tonight, I broke things off with Dean, my longtime boyfriend. He wanted to marry me, but I knew I couldn't go through with it for reasons I don't feel like explaining. Even so, my decision didn't come easy, and I have conflicting emotions about it."

"Oh. I didn't realize you were involved with someone."

"How could you? We literally just met this morning."

"Well, either way, the decision had to be tough. I'm sorry."

"Don't be. I mean, the breakup was inevitable. When I called him, he wasn't even shocked. He told me he'd expected it. He said pinning me down would be like trying to pin down a cloud."

"So you're a real-life Fraulein Maria, are you?"

I smiled. "You're familiar with *The Sound of Music*. I wouldn't have guessed that."

"It's not by choice," he admitted with a laugh. "My gram was into musicals and used to torture me with them when I was a kid."

"My mother loves them, too. It's in her blood. My grandmother, Claudine Benton-Riley, was a stage actress on Broadway. My mother grew up with show tunes all around her." I paused, feeling pensive as I thought back to what Dean had said. "I don't know. Maybe Dean is right. Maybe I'm too flighty."

"Do you want to know what I think?" he asked, and without waiting for an answer, he continued. "I think that bit about comparing you to pinning down a cloud was his ego talking. He probably just didn't want to admit rejection."

"No. You don't know him like I do. He's always so practical, right down to the engagement ring—or lack thereof." I let out a bitter laugh as I thought back to the other things Dean had said during our phone conversation. Even though I'd just told Sloan I didn't want to explain it all, I found myself divulging more than I should. "Dean originally told me he didn't propose with a ring because he wanted me to help him pick one out. I thought it was considerate of him, even if it wasn't very romantic, but I should have known there was a more logical reason behind it. The truth came out after I ended it. Apparently, he'd assumed I wouldn't say yes right away and didn't want to lose out on the interest he'd earn on the cash in his brokerage account while waiting for my answer."

Sloan stopped short, and I turned to see him looking at me with disbelief. "He actually told you that? The guy sounds like a real dick if you ask me."

I shrugged. "No. Not a dick. There wasn't any malice when he told me. It was just a statement of fact. At least now I know the truth. It's for the best."

Sloan cocked his head to the side with an expression of concern. "I hope that um… our kiss this morning. You have to know I don't normally do things like that. It sounds like things weren't too great with the two of you, but I hope what happened with us isn't the reason you broke up with him."

"No—yes. I mean, no. It wasn't the main reason. Our breakup was bound to happen. What happened between you and me, no matter how inappropriate, was eye-opening for me. But more importantly, I'm the PR agent representing you. That can't happen again."

"Hmm," was all he said, and I narrowed my eyes suspiciously. He had the most peculiar look on his face. He appeared both smug and elated at the same time.

"Why are you smilking at me like that?" I asked.

"Smilking?"

"It's like a smile and smirk at the same time," I explained. "Don't do that."

Sloan threw his head back and laughed long and hard.

When he eventually quieted, we stood looking at one another for the longest minute of my life, neither of us sure of what to say. It was as if my admission about breaking up with Dean suddenly left endless possibilities—none of which we could possibly explore. He was my client, after all. Not to mention, my father would have my head if I got romantically involved with Sloan.

But oh, how I wanted to—badly—and I couldn't understand why.

"I suppose you're right," he said.

"About what?"

"About us. It was rather presumptuous of me to kiss you like I did. Allow me to start over by properly introducing myself." Taking my hand, he brought it to his mouth and brushed his lips softly over my knuckles. Warmth spread throughout my body. "My name is Sloan Atwood, the audacious asshole who ravaged you without permission on his doorstep."

While his words were teasing, his gaze was intense. Energy crackled in the air, and I felt mesmerized by the sea-blue irises of his eyes. Unfortunately, the spell broke all too soon when the sound of a band began to play. I blinked to reclaim my focus, pulled my hand away, and looked up toward the street. A beachfront restaurant not far from the sushi place where we'd just had dinner had suddenly come to life. Twinkle lights crisscrossed above the patio like electric spaghetti, illuminating the guests circling on the dance floor. In the middle of the group there was no mistaking the white ball gown of a bride. She was in the arms of her groom, moving together to a smooth yet powerful stream of strumming guitar strings. A moment later, the lead singer began to sing a cover of "Marry Me" by Train.

"It's their first dance," I murmured.

Sloan followed my gaze. "That song is so cliché," he said.

Turning away from the dancing couple, I looked quizzically at Sloan. "I like that song. How is it cliché?"

"Just listen to the lyrics. They are cheesy as all hell."

I pressed my lips together and looked back at the couple. "I don't think so. Those lyrics were born out of somebody's experience. You can't write words like that without having felt them. It's about love and romance and dreams coming true."

"Nah, I don't buy it. Love songs are just a hoax designed to play on people's fantasies. It's all garbage. Romance and dreams are for fools."

I shook my head at his statement, unable to look away from the couple as they danced.

"Dreams aren't garbage—they define every one of our unforgettable moments. Everyone has them, and I'm sure you've had thousands. Those were all dreams that came true."

Sloan stayed quiet, and I wondered what he was thinking. Turning to face him, I saw that he wasn't watching the couple as I had been, but instead was looking out at the ocean.

"More often than not, my dreams turn into nightmares," he said quietly. His tone was so hushed, and I wasn't sure if he was talking to himself or me. If Rochele hadn't told me more about his past, I might not have understood the full implication of his statement—but I did, and my heart broke for him. Reaching out, I placed a gentle hand on his arm.

"Fate may have put you on a different path, but you owe it to yourself to forge ahead and make new extraordinary moments. Just look at where we are right now. The beach, the people, the sunset… this could be an unforgettable and extraordinary moment if you allow it to be."

He looked down into my eyes, his gaze penetrating. "I'm sorry for snapping at you earlier in the restaurant, Kallie."

I smiled. "It's okay. I forgive you."

Casting his gaze down to my extended arm, he raised a hand to run a finger over my shoulder, tracing the lines of my tattoo.

"What does this say?" he asked.

I automatically looked down at my exposed shoulder to where the tattooed stars and words swirled to disappear behind me. I angled my body so he could see the entire thing.

"It says, 'Loving in the moment is something luminous.' It's a song lyric by Alice and the Glass Lake."

"From what I know about you, it seems fitting. I… Kallie…" He hesitated and swiped a frustrated hand through his hair. He looked truly aggravated. For what reason, I had no idea. His eyes flashed with something unfamiliar before he turned my body until we were standing toe-to-toe. Heat clouded his expression, and my heart began to race. For a moment, I thought he was going to try to kiss me again, but then he spoke. "Ah, screw the rules and whatever you think about the level of appropriateness. Dance with me."

That was the last thing I expected him to say, and I couldn't stop the laugh that bubbled from my lips.

"What?"

"You heard me. I said dance with me."

Without giving me a chance to respond, he wrapped an arm around my waist and pulled me to him. Enveloped in his scent, I couldn't think straight. Before I knew it, he coaxed me into a gentle sway.

The slow melody changed only a short moment later when the band kicked it up with a cover of "I Want You To Want Me" by Cheap Trick. However, Sloan didn't increase his movements to match the tune. Instead, he continued to rock slowly, entirely out of sync with the music.

Then, to my astonishment, he began to sing.

It was quiet at first, almost a hum, until he began to form the words. I was completely enthralled—and not because of the quality of his voice. It was because of the way he said the actual words. It was as if he was trying to send me a message I knew I shouldn't want to hear. I half wondered if I was making more out of this moment than what it really was—as if I were fantasizing about the idea of sharing uninhibited passion with this man rather than acknowledging my reality. And the fact of the matter was, I barely knew Sloan. I was solely here to do a job.

I understood passion and chemistry could be like living, breathing things. When two people were cosmically compatible, one's existence could light up in life-altering ways. I believed destiny was written in the stars, and when the stars were perfectly aligned, things could seamlessly fall into place.

But I didn't believe in insta-love.

The pull I felt had to be imagined. It was the only thing that made sense. What was happening now was unadulterated lust and nothing short of pure insanity. I tried to resist the feelings, but it was like fighting a powerful undertow. The more I fought it, the quicker I'd drown. It was easier to float to wherever the tide took me, hoping that destiny would deliver me to solid ground.

When the song ended and transitioned into another, Sloan wrapped his hand around the base of my neck and tilted my head to look up at him. Emotion squeezed at my heart until I felt it might burst.

"You may be onto something with this whole romance thing. The sunset is so much prettier with you in it. You just might make me a believer," he murmured. "I'm glad you decided not to marry that guy."

"Why is that?"

"I might not know a lot about you, but I can easily see you deserve somebody who will love you and leave you wild."

He leaned in, and I knew the kiss I so desperately wanted to feel again was coming, but his words jolted me back to reality. Untangling myself from his arms, I took two steps back and gazed out at the seemingly endless ocean and the setting sun. The gypsy's words from so long ago echoed off the crashing waves.

*"The man who tastes your lips under a California sunset will be the one to break you."*

I looked back at Sloan. His breathing was uneven, and his piercing blue eyes were dark pools of desire. His hair was slightly mussed by the gentle salt breeze that curled around us, which somehow made all of his rugged sexiness even sexier. My stomach clenched, my breath caught, and my heart seemed to still. God, how I wanted this man, but even though my body physically ached for him, I couldn't do this with him. Business relationship aside, nothing could happen here. Not in this place—not unless I wanted to risk a broken heart.

"I have to go," I said abruptly, then turned to walk away. If I hadn't been afraid of tripping over my own two feet in the soft sand, I would have run.

"Kallie, wait." He took hold of my arm and forced me to meet his gaze. He looked irritated, yet there was no mistaking the longing in his eyes.

"Sloan, please. Let me go. We can't."

"You can fight this all day long, but I say fuck this 'you're my client' bullshit. There's something unexplainable between us that you know you can't resist. Mark my words. One day, you'll be begging for it—begging for us—to happen."

"Don't be so arrogant. Believe it or not, my choice to not let this go any further has nothing to do with you."

"So what does it have to do with then?"

I glanced at the last sliver of the setting sun.

"A warning. You and I—we'll never work."

# Chapter Nine

*Sloan*

When I walked onto the track the following day, I was exhausted, which was nothing new, but the reasons behind it were entirely different. Last night, I'd been consumed with images of Kallie.

Every time I tried to close my eyes, all I could see was her gorgeous face, shadowed by the fading rays of sunset behind her on the beach. The majestic picture she'd painted had haunted me all night long. And when I remembered how good she'd felt dancing in my arms, it took every ounce of control I had not to rub one out. She was a spellbinding, gorgeous beauty who made everything around her come to life with her mere presence.

I couldn't make sense of it, how a girl I hardly knew had gotten so far into my psyche I couldn't even sleep. At three in the morning, I'd considered getting out of bed and pouring myself a drink but ultimately decided against it because I knew Kallie would disapprove. I didn't need the alcohol. It was just a bad habit I'd gotten into by telling myself it was the only way to make it through the night. Recognizing how quickly she had influenced my decision-making only served to keep me awake longer. Then there were her words about a warning. She was afraid of something. Of what, I didn't know, but I'd made a personal vow to find out.

Shaking off the concern that I'd done something to spook her, I shoved a hand through my hair and jogged my way toward the pit lane.

A group of people was gathered near an open-wheel car. I spotted Rochele, Cooper, and two young boys who I assumed were Eli and Marcus next to a photographer assembling his gear. Milo was also there, off to the side and talking to Benjamin, but I didn't see Kallie anywhere.

Glancing at my watch, I noted that it was fifteen minutes past ten. I was a little late, and I'd expected her to beat me here.

"Sorry I'm late," I told the group. "Where's Kallie?"

"Don't look so worried, man. She's here," Cooper informed me with a laugh. "She just went inside to wash up. She touched something and got grease all over her hands."

Masking my relief, I simply nodded. "Gotcha. So, are you going to introduce me to the boys?"

"Sloan, this is Marcus," Rochele said, patting her hand on the shoulder of a young boy who looked to be no more than ten years old. Then she pointed to the other boy, a sandy-haired kid who was tracing an invisible circle on the ground with his foot. "And this is Eli."

I noticed she didn't place her hand on Eli's shoulder like she did when introducing Marcus. I recalled the conversation at dinner the night before and remembered Eli was the boy who didn't like to be touched.

"It's nice to meet you," I told them.

"Both of them just took turns with Cooper on the track, but now they are ready to work."

"That's right, boys," Cooper chimed in. "Races are won and lost in the pit lane. It's not all about driving a fast car, isn't that right, Sloan?"

"That's right," I agreed, trying to ignore the cameraman who was five feet away and snapping pictures. Doing my best to act casual, I squatted down a few feet in front of Eli. "What do you say, champ? Want me to teach you how to change a tire?"

Eli looked up from the ground with wide eyes. There was a hint of a smile on his face as he slowly nodded.

"Can I help too?" Marcus asked excitedly.

Instantly, Eli stiffened.

"We'll take turns, Marcus. I'll have you stand right over here," I said, pointing to a spot far enough away from the car so I didn't have to worry about him accidentally touching Eli. "After Eli changes a tire, you guys can switch places, and it will be your turn."

"Sweet!" Marcus said and jumped up in the air. Eli remained quiet but seemed to relax.

Taking the lead, I grabbed an impact wrench, then sat down on the ground next to the car. Patting the spot next to me, I motioned for Eli to sit down.

"The guys in the pit crew have an extremely tough job," I told him.

"I used to work with a pit crew a long time ago before I started racing. It might not be quite as fun as driving a fast car, but it has its own kind of excitement. Guys in the pit have to work under pressure at lightning-fast speed, which is part of the reason they need to use these fancy tools."

"What is that?" Eli asked, pointing to the impact wrench.

"It's a kind of wrench that uses compressed air to remove and replace lug nuts as quickly as possible. But I have to warn you. It's loud. You might want to cover your ears."

Eli's eyes grew impossibly wide once again as he quickly held both hands over his ears. I mouthed the word 'ready,' and he nodded his head rapidly. I smiled, pleasantly surprised at how much I was already enjoying this, and pressed the wrench to one of the lug nuts. In five seconds, I had all but one of them removed, deliberately leaving it for Eli to practice.

"Who's making all the racket over here?" I heard Kallie say from behind me.

Feeling like I'd connected with a live wire, electricity sparked through my veins at the sound of her voice. I slowly turned to meet her gaze. She smiled brightly, and my breath caught. She was so goddamned beautiful—like a deity I secretly worshipped. Any thoughts about changing a tire were stolen right out of my head as I watched her with pure male appreciation. Bright green eyes sparkled back at me. I returned her smile, immediately noticing the rainbow hair was back. It wasn't braided today but pulled up into a high ponytail, allowing the Skittle-colored strands to flow with the golden blonde hair down past the base of her neck. All I could think of was the candy commercial, and it made me want to taste *her* rainbow.

Setting the impact wrench on the ground, I stood to greet her. Leaning against the hood of the car, I raked my gaze over her body. Clad in tight jeans and a wispy yellow tank, the sun glinted off her large gold hoop earrings, making her look like a sun-kissed gypsy.

"Why, hello there, Rainbow Brite."

"Hello, yourself."

"Feeling optimistic today?"

"Maybe," she replied coyly, and her face turned a pretty shade of pink. There was a hint of mischief in her voice, and I couldn't help but think she might be flirting with me. That was definitely a good sign. It meant she probably wasn't upset with me about last night.

"I heard you made a mess of yourself," I said, motioning toward her hands.

"Hardly. Just a bit of grease that washed off easily enough. What did I miss?"

"Nothing much. I'm just teaching the boys how to change a tire.

Isn't that right, Eli?" I turned around only to find Eli picking up the impact wrench. "Eli, no. Don't touch—"

Before I could finish my sentence, Milo lunged forward to take the wrench out of the boy's hand. In the process, he grabbed hold of Eli's arm. I froze, immediately recognizing Milo's mistake. Instantly, Eli began to scream—but it wasn't just any scream. The sound from his mouth was the most gut-wrenching thing I'd ever heard. It was grief, fear, and hurt all rolled into one.

All at once, everyone scrambled to calm the screaming boy. Cooper roughly pushed Milo away from Eli to make room for Rochele. She was at Eli's side in two seconds flat, ensuring a safe distance as she whispered soothing words to him. Kallie stood wide-eyed, clearly in shock over the rapid shift of events, while I looked around for the photographer. Thankfully, he seemed just as stunned as the rest of us and had lowered his camera. However, the photographer was here on our dime and was the least of my concerns.

"Kallie, where's the press?" I asked frantically.

"They aren't here yet. I told them eleven o'clock. I figured that would give us time to get acquainted with the boys first."

I breathed a sigh of relief. The last thing I needed was a write-up about a kid who'd lost his mind while he was on my watch.

It seemed to take forever but was realistically only a few minutes before Eli quieted. Appearing satisfied that he was okay, Rochele turned to Kallie and me.

"Cooper and I are going to take Eli up to the box and get him something to eat and drink. He needs a break. Do you mind staying here with Marcus?"

I shrugged, not sure what other choice I had. I was just thankful the screaming had finally stopped. Still, I couldn't help but feel for the kid. I'd never heard or seen such a display of anguish, and my heart broke for him.

Squatting down in front of Eli, I held up my hands. I wasn't sure why I raised them. I just didn't want to do anything to upset him further, and it seemed like the right thing to do—as if by letting him see my hands, he would find it reassuring and remain calm.

"Eli, are you cool with that?" I asked softly. "I'll let Marcus finish up your turn. Then you can come back to help when you're ready."

Eli nodded ever so slowly, the action somehow making him look hopelessly frail, before turning to walk away with Rochele and Cooper. Getting to my feet, I rubbed a hand over my face, grateful the crisis seemed to be over.

"Rochele shouldn't have brought him here," Milo barked after they were out of earshot. "He's got issues. That kid is all sorts of fucked up."

My head snapped back, shocked by the harshness in Milo's tone.

"Geez, Milo! Go easy on the little guy! If you hadn't touched him, none of this would have even happened," I pointed out.

Milo snorted.

"You think this is my fault? Maybe if you weren't too preoccupied with a piece of tail, the kid wouldn't have picked up the wrench in the first place."

"What the hell are you talking about?"

"I'm not blind, Atwood. I saw the way you looked at her," he said, motioning toward Kallie with a lift of his chin. "I hired her to help you, not to fuck you. I have half a mind to call her agency and have her replaced—unless screwing clients is part of her PR strategy."

"Hey! Who the fuck do you think you're talking to?" I stepped up to him, ready to lay him flat, but Kallie moved between us.

"Gentleman, you have an audience," she reminded.

I glanced to my left and saw Marcus staring with apt curiosity.

*Shit.*

I took a deep breath and shook my head. Stepping away from Milo, I turned toward Marcus.

"Ignore the grownups. We can be dumb sometimes," I told him, annoyed that I'd lost my head so easily. "Come on over here, Marcus. We can't afford to lose focus when there's work to be done. And last I checked, we have tires that need changing."

I glanced at Kallie, and she gave me an approving smile. Milo, on the other hand, didn't say a word but simply walked away in a sulk.

*Fuck him.*

Milo was the best agent around, having mastered the art of obtaining endorsements and sponsorships for drivers all over the country. He was the most sought-after agent in the racing circuit—but he was also known to be a complete asshole. At the height of my career, I ignored the ugly rumors because I'd needed him, but there was no need for me to do that now. I wasn't entirely sure why I kept him around anymore. I should just fire him and be done.

*But firing him would mean admitting your racing career is officially over.*

Ignoring that thought, I sat down on the ground with Marcus and got to work.

# Chapter Ten

*Sloan*

"I'm glad things ended better than they started," Kallie said as we walked along the long corridor circling Motor Club Speedway. "I was happy Eli calmed down enough to come back. The two of you working together was pure gold. The press ate it right up."

I shrugged.

"It wasn't hard. I mean, I'll admit I was nervous because so many eyes were on me. I just kept reminding myself that Eli is a good kid who was dealt a shitty hand. Focusing on that helped."

"Well, it worked. I've got to say, though, I didn't breathe for a full solid minute after you accidentally touched his hand when trying to maneuver the compressor."

I laughed, appreciating her sentiment.

"You and me both. Thankfully, he was so concentrated on the task he didn't seem to notice."

"Oh, I think he noticed. I just don't think he minded. He seemed comfortable around you." She stopped walking and placed a gentle hand on my arm. When she looked up at me, her eyes were soft and filled with pride. "Seriously, Sloan. You were really great with him. When you and Cooper were cleaning up, Rochele told me she was impressed with how you handled Eli. PR aside, you did a good thing today. You should be proud."

I looked past her toward the entrance to the track, unsure how to handle the gushing compliment. I didn't think I did anything special. At the end of the day, the sole reason I was here was for a PR stunt. Kallie was making more out of it than it was.

"Let's just hope the morning papers have something nice to say."

"Oh, don't count your chickens before they've hatched. You've got a long way to go before all is forgiven," she reminded me and took a step back. "I'm going to take off. I'll give you a buzz later on today, and we can discuss your PR schedule for next week."

"Wait. You're leaving?"

"You didn't expect me to stick around here all day, did you?"

"Well, no. I guess not. What are you doing after you leave here?"

"I've got some calls to make and research to do. I need to dig up info on local events that may be good for you to get involved in."

"No rest for the weary," I teased. "I guess I should be thanking you. I'll walk you to your car."

We stepped out into the bright sun, and Kallie pointed to the left. "That's me right over there. The red BMW."

"Nice ride, but I'll admit, it's not the car I expected you to drive. A car like that screams arrogance."

"I'm not sure how a car can say so much," she replied with a chuckle.

"A car says a lot about a person."

"I'll admit, it wouldn't have been my first choice. It was what the rental agency gave me. At home, I drive a Prius. It's better for the environment."

"Now *that* I expected. Saving the world one mile at a time, Kallie?"

She shrugged.

"Just trying to do my part. Taking care of Mother Earth is important to me. In fact, that's why I'm a vegetarian. I originally went to college for Environmental Studies. I changed majors my sophomore year after I learned how small the job field was. Unfortunately, the government moves at a snail's pace when it comes to climate change, and there's not much money to be made in the private sector."

"With all the talk about global warming, I think that will all change soon enough."

"I think it will eventually, but opportunities wouldn't have opened up before my student loan bills came due. Who knows? Maybe one day I'll go back to school for it. But for now, Public Relations it is. I can't complain, though. I love what I do."

When we reached the car, Kallie unlocked it and moved to get inside. However, when she stepped back to make room for the door to open, she bumped into me and stumbled. Instinctively, I caught her by the waist, entirely unprepared for the electric current that began to sizzle at the point of contact. It surged through my veins, robbing me of breath. There was a pulsing—an invisible thrum—and I couldn't be sure if it was the beating of my own heart or if what I felt between us was somehow its own living being. The soft scent of her hair wafted tantalizingly under my nose, and I felt her shiver. Despite the warm temperature, I could see goosebumps rising visibly on her arms.

*She feels it, too.*

"Easy now," I whispered against her ear.

"I'm sorry. I wasn't paying attention, and…" Her voice was breathy as she let the sentence go unfinished.

I knew I should step away or come up with something smart-assed to say, but I couldn't break the searing connection. Turning her to face me, I boxed her in against the car with both arms. I didn't want her to leave my side. I wanted her someplace where she couldn't run so easily from me as she had last night. Something had spooked her on the beach. What it was, I didn't know, but I wasn't going to let her run off like that again. The very thought of her leaving—of not seeing her until tomorrow, or next week, or whenever the hell she deemed appropriate—felt like a sucker punch to the gut.

"I don't want you to go home alone to make calls. Come to my place. We can make whatever calls you need to make together."

She blinked a few times as if gathering her thoughts, then shook her head.

"Sloan, that's not a good idea." Gone was the breathy voice, replaced by her professional demeanor.

"Why not?"

"Because you and I…" She paused, seeming at a loss for words, before motioning back and forth between us. "I'll be honest. I don't know how or why, but things got complicated in a hurry. All I know is that we really need to focus on what's important—and that's cleaning up your image."

"Right now, I don't care about my image. All I care about is being somewhere alone with you."

"Sloan, how can you say that? You barely know me."

"I know enough."

"Well, I don't. I have work that needs to be done. Going to your fancy lair is the last thing I should do."

"My lair? You make me sound like Tony Stark," I said with a smirk. "I may have been able to fly around the track, but that's as far as it goes. No Ironman super suit is hiding in my closet."

Looking down at the ground, she puffed out an exasperated sigh.

"Sloan, I—" she stopped short, seeming to notice something. "Well, would you look at that? Damn it. I somehow managed to get grease on my hands again. I'm going to run back inside and wash it off before I get it on my clothes or all over the interior of the car."

Without warning, she ducked under my arm and hurried back toward the entrance to the track.

*Oh, hell no.*

Following close behind her, we closed the distance and entered the building. When I saw her disappear behind the door to the women's restroom, I looked around to make sure the coast was clear, then slipped in and locked the door handle behind me.

Kallie was standing at the sink washing her hands and looked up in surprise when she saw me. "Sloan, what are you doing? You shouldn't be in here."

"Why not?"

"Because it's not…it's not," she stammered. "It's not appropriate."

I grinned as I slowly advanced toward her.

"I don't care about being appropriate, Kallie. You should know that by now. I've never been one for decorum, so you'll have to do better than that."

"Well, I also don't trust you to be in here alone with me. You're…" She trailed off, appearing flustered, as she focused on scrubbing the nonexistent grease from her hands.

"I'm what?"

"You're dangerous for me," she blurted out.

"Dangerous?" I chuckled. "Oh, baby, you have no idea how dangerous I can be—especially when I want something. You've read my file. I like to win, and there's nothing I want to win more than you. If you tell me you don't want me, I'll walk out that door, and we'll keep it professional. But I don't think you will. I think you want us to happen just as much as I do. I don't know why you're fighting it."

"You're wrong. You don't know enough about me to know what I may or may not want. And I'm telling you I don't want this."

She wouldn't meet my gaze but instead moved over to the electric hand dryer and placed her palms under it. Hot air buzzed from the machine as I stepped up behind her and rested my hands on her hips. I lowered my head to her ear, speaking just loud enough to be heard over the dyer.

"I think you're lying. I saw it all over your face when we were out by the car. Even now, you're flushed, and your breathing is erratic. Am I wrong?"

The dryer finished, and she lowered her hands to her sides. She didn't attempt to move away from me, but she also didn't answer and instead seemed to be lost in contemplation. I needed to see her face—to read her eyes and know if this fantasy I had of being with her was just one-sided. For all I knew, her erratic breathing was from frightened nerves. The last thing I wanted was for her to be afraid of me. Spinning her body so that we were standing toe-to-toe, her bright green eyes stared up, and I held her gaze steady.

"It doesn't matter if you're right or wrong, Sloan," she finally said. "Yes, I know there's this weird, inexplicable energy between us, but you don't understand. I can't be with you."

"Stop letting a stupid contract get in the way of things. It doesn't change the way I feel. I haven't been able to stop thinking about you since I first saw you in Long Beach."

"You don't understand. It has nothing to do with our contract. Well, maybe it does, but that's not the main reason."

"Does the main reason have something to do with the warning you mentioned last night?"

"It has everything to do with the warning. Please, trust me on this," she pleaded.

"The only thing I trust is my gut, and my gut is telling me there's only one way this is going to end."

"And how is that?"

I pulled her closer, pressed my lips against the delicate skin of her earlobe, and whispered with heated breath, "With me buried deep inside of you."

She gasped in surprise, and I wrapped one hand around the base of her neck.

"Sloan, I don't think we know each other well enough to be having this conversation."

"Then let's stop talking about it. I'm going to kiss you now, Kallie. Please don't deny me."

To my satisfaction, she didn't pull away. Her cheeks flushed, and her eyes darkened to a deep green and brimmed with possibilities. I leaned in so close, and I could feel her breath on my lips. Yet still, I waited. I couldn't force her. She had to be the one to close the remaining distance.

I sensed the moment she surrendered when her breathing became shallow. I could feel the pulse in her neck quicken under my palm as she angled her head, pushed up on her toes, and brought her lips to mine. They felt soft and full, and I enjoyed every single trembling breath she took as she gained the courage to apply more pressure. Electric shockwaves coursed between us, and she let out a small whimper. I responded by pushing my mouth harder against hers.

Parting her lips, she allowed our tongues to begin a slowdance. I suppressed a groan of satisfaction, not wanting to gloat about being right. It hadn't been just my imagination. She wanted this as much as I did, and her need tasted so goddamned good.

As I kissed her desperately, my only focus was to make her feel everything I felt. Adrenaline coursed through me and my heart began to pound. I pulled her tightly against my chest, and she seemed to melt into me, giving me all the encouragement I needed to lower my hand and squeeze her firm, jean-clad ass.

"I shouldn't want this," she murmured against my lips.

"But you do," I said, my voice low and raspy as I stated the obvious. She released a soft moan, and it was as if my words bolstered her courage to explore further. Her fingers curled through my hair, then moved down to my shoulders and back, touching as if she couldn't get enough.

Moving our bodies in unison, I turned until the large block privacy windows were at her back. Lifting her onto the window's ledge, I positioned myself between her legs. There was no hiding how turned on I was in this position. My cock was rock hard, and when I heard her small gasp, I knew she could feel it through our clothing. That just made me burn for her all the more.

I devoured her, our tongues twisting and tasting. I wanted more. I *needed* more. Tearing my lips from hers, I took a second to read her hooded green eyes. All I saw was desire and longing behind those thick lashes.

"Oh, Mother of Stars… Sloan, what are you doing to me?" Her words sounded like the sweetest of sighs, and I groaned.

"Not nearly enough."

"Everything about this moment feels right, but…"

"Shhh," I hushed, placing a finger over her lips. I cupped her face and stroked her cheeks, unable to get enough by simply touching her. I knew how she was feeling. This was wrong on so many levels, yet it just felt so damn right.

"I don't want to regret this, Sloan."

"You're overthinking, Kallie. Just feel. Tell me what you want." When she didn't respond, I slipped a hand under her tank until I felt the creamy skin of her waist. It was warm and soft and everything I'd imagined. I pressed my lips to her shoulder, trailing soft kisses along the hollow at the side of her throat as I moved my hand up to cup one of her breasts. I began to massage over the lacy fabric. "This—is this what you want?"

"Yes," she breathed.

Covering her mouth with mine once more, I didn't give her a chance to say anything else. With one hand clamped on her hip, I used the other to greedily pull aside the cups of her bra, and her breasts spilled free. I pushed the thin tank up to her neck and lowered my head to capture a nipple between my teeth. She gripped my head with both hands and arched, encouraging me to take my fill. When I began to circle my tongue over her supple areola, she moaned, and I nearly came on the spot. There was no doubt Kallie would be like volcanic molten lava in bed. Even though I knew I wouldn't take things that far today, I wanted to take this moment to discover a few of the places that would make her erupt.

"Tell me what you want, Kallie," I repeated, speaking the words into her cleavage as I moved my mouth between each tit, refusing to let one get more attention than the other. "I can't assume. Not now. I need to hear you say it."

"I just want you to touch me."

"Where, Kallie? Tell me where."

"Everywhere!" She gasped out the word as if it hurt her to say it.

Sliding my hand from her hip, I positioned my thumb at the apex of her thighs and began to rub. Even through her jeans, I could feel her heat. She was driving me fucking wild.

Moving from nipple to nipple, I enjoyed the way she lifted her hips against my hand to get better friction. Her hands snaked around the base of my neck as she arched her back, searching for more, and I was determined to give her exactly that.

Banding my arms tightly around her, I slid her off the window ledge and carried her petite body back by the sink, where I pressed her back against the wall. I swiftly unbuttoned her jeans and dipped my hand under the waistband of her panties. When my fingers connected with her wet slit, we both gasped.

"God, you're so fucking wet," I murmured against her lips. I circled her hard clit for a moment, then drove a finger inside her heated well. Her breath hitched and her hips pushed upward, taking what I offered with fevered urgency. I increased my tempo, building momentum until she was whimpering with need.

"Come for me, baby. I want you to come on my hand."

She kissed me frantically, and my fingers thrusted deeper to massage and stroke her walls, only pulling out to trace wet circles around her throbbing nub. I felt her body tense, and her shallow breathing began to come faster. She was close. I quickened the pace, flexing my fingers with more urgency until I could feel the slight tremors of her building orgasm. I wanted to give her this—to make her see that if she gave us a chance, we'd be explosive.

When I knew she was almost there, I tore my mouth from hers so I could see her face. I wanted to watch her as she fell apart. Her eyes grew wide, then snapped closed, and I was rewarded with her cry of pleasure as she shattered under my palm. Her ecstasy faded to enfolding aftershocks, and her eyes slowly fluttered open. Burying my nose in her neck, I allowed her a moment to catch her breath as I inhaled her scent—that vanilla mixed with patchouli that was already becoming so familiar.

Once her breathing began to regulate, she clasped my face between her palms and pulled my head down to hers for a slow, languid kiss. When she pulled away, there was no mistaking the glowing embers in her gaze.

"Sloan, I've never felt this way before. I'm not the kind of woman who *does* things like this. I don't know what came over me, but—"

A rattling sound at the door cut off her words. We both stilled.

"That's strange. It's locked," I heard Rochele say from the other side.

"I'll get a janitor to unlock it," I heard Cooper tell her. Their voices were muffled, but there was no doubt it was them.

"Shit!" Kallie hissed, scrambling away from me to adjust her shirt and button her pants. When I began to laugh, she shushed me and frantically whispered, "Be quiet! They'll hear you!"

"Relax. If you think Cooper and Rochele haven't had more than their fair share of clandestine hookups, you're sadly mistaken."

"That's not the point," she snapped. "As I said, I don't do things like this. Plus, I'm your—"

"Yeah, yeah. I know. You're my PR rep. You have a serious hang-up over that. It's all good. Trust me," I said and moved toward her. She backed away, rapidly shaking her head.

"Jesus H. Christ, Sloan. They're going to be back at any moment now, and I can only imagine what they'll think if they find us here together. Quick. Hide in one of the stalls."

"I am not—" I didn't get a chance to finish before Kallie pushed me into the tiny bathroom cubicle. She may have been only a couple of inches over five feet, but she was mighty strong for such a little thing. Or perhaps I was just too busy laughing to put up much of a fight.

"Lock the door," she whispered. "And for the love of all the spirits, stay quiet!"

Feeling amused, I complied just as I heard keys rattling in the door lock. A moment later, I listened to the water from one of the sinks running, followed by Rochele's voice.

"Kallie, I didn't realize you were in here. The door was locked, so…"

"Oh, yeah. Sorry about that. The bathroom I'd used earlier near the pit was just a single stall. When I came in here, I had assumed it was that same way. I didn't think to unlock it when I realized there were private stalls in here."

*Single stall?*

I smirked, entertained by Kallie's inability to concoct a lie that didn't sound ridiculous.

"Oh, gotcha. Got to love those single-stall bathrooms," Rochele replied, but the skepticism in her voice was clear as day. Not to mention, all Rochele would have to do is glance at the floor to spot my red-and-white men's Reeboks flashing like bullseyes under the stall door, and she'd know I was here.

"Are the boys gone?" Kallie asked, continuing the small talk. Her voice had a slightly elevated pitch, giving away how nervous she was.

"Yes. The director of Safe Track just came by to pick them up. There's a movie night planned at The Residence."

"That sounds like fun."

I heard the flushing of a toilet, then water running. It was somewhat awkward hiding out in the women's restroom waiting for them to finish their business, but it was what it was. It's what Kallie had wanted, so all I could do was stare at the gray metal walls of the stall and wait it out.

Within a few minutes, the two women exited the restroom. I waited until it was safe to assume all was clear, then opened the cubicle's door. I wanted to catch Kallie before she left the premises, but when I hurried out to catch up with her. I came face to face with Cooper. He had been leaning against the wall opposite the restroom waiting for me to come out. His knowing smile was wide as he shook his head.

"Looks like Ro owes me twenty bucks," he said with a laugh. "But seriously, man. There's a hotel just up the way. Probably cleaner than the restrooms here at the track. Just saying…"

Without another word, he turned and walked away, but his low chuckle could be heard echoing off the concrete walls of the corridor as he left the building.

# Chapter Eleven

*Kallie*

I sat at the kitchen table with my laptop, staring at the slew of emails I needed to respond to. Three were from Milo Birx, barking at me to get something or another lined up for Sloan. I didn't like the man at all. To say he was rude, arrogant, and downright nasty didn't even begin to cover the bad vibes I got from him—and it went well beyond his lack of compassion for the orphan boys who lived at The Residence. There was just something evil about him. He gave me the creeps.

My inbox also contained bills that needed payment, their flashing due dates reminding me why this job was so important. I couldn't wait until the day I would gain extra pocket money after paying off my student loan debt with the bonus following my contract.

Follow-up emails from the D.C. office needed tending to as well. The bulk of them were from former clients who needed assistance in some form or another. However, I couldn't seem to focus on any of it. Only one client was first and foremost in my mind—and that was Sloan Atwood.

It had been four weeks since our hookup in the women's restroom—four long weeks of strategically making sure I was never left alone with Sloan again. When I agreed to take him on as a client, my father had instructed me to be Sloan's shadow. For the most part, I was. I'd gone through the motions of scheduling more one-on-one events with the boys at Safe Track and orchestrating in-person media interviews. I'd made sure Sloan's calendar was full, and I had been present for every single engagement.

The only problem had been coming up with ways to avoid any sort of physical contact. He was everywhere I turned, and if I so much as brushed up against him, it was complete agony. My insides would begin twisting with desire, reminding me of what his hands had felt like on my body. He knew no boundaries. I couldn't believe how a man I knew so little about had the power to possess me the way he did.

Recognizing my weaknesses, I was careful only to see him in public settings, not allowing him the opportunity to whisk me off into some kind of hidden broom closet where he could have his way with me again. It wasn't that he didn't try. I just made sure to be one step ahead of him since I clearly couldn't keep my head around the man. I needed to regain my balance after being kissed senseless twice—and then some—within just thirty-six hours of meeting him. The easiest way for me to maintain focus was to bury myself in work. Sloan and my father's firm were counting on me to concentrate on the job. Nobody would win if I lost sight of my priorities so early in the game.

Clicking out of my inbox, I pulled up the information for Drift, a professional racing school that I was hoping to get Sloan involved with. While I'd managed to keep him busy, his schedule was on the lighter side for the upcoming weeks. I didn't want him to have too much free time on his hands, and I could only do so much with local charities to fill his calendar. Perhaps working as an instructor at the school would help fill the void racing left and help his reputation in the public eye.

Picking up my cellphone, I dialed the phone number for the operations manager listed on the website.

"Drift Racing School. This is Sheila. How can I help you?"

"Hi, Sheila. My name is Kalliope Benton Riley. I represent Sloan Atwood. I was wondering if I could speak with Joel Freidman, the operations manager."

"Just one moment, please."

After being placed on hold, I tapped a pink-painted nail on the edge of my laptop while I waited. A few minutes later, a gruff voice came on the other end of the line.

"This is Friedman."

"Hello, Mr. Friedman. My name is Kalliope Benton Riley. I represent—"

"You can save your breath, darlin'. My secretary told me. Atwood, right?" he asked in a thick Southern accent.

"That's right. I saw on your website that you're looking for instructors. Is there a time when Mr. Atwood could come in to speak with you about that? Possibly an interview?"

Joel Friedman burst out laughing as if I'd just said the funniest thing he'd ever heard. After a moment, he coughed, then calmed himself enough to speak.

"Look, I don't mean to laugh, but Atwood is the last person I want around these parts. You're wasting your time."

"But Mr. Friedman, if you'll just—"

"Atwood is a drunk, and I won't have my students put at risk. Not to mention, you've called the wrong school. Atwood isn't a drift racer. He's an open-wheel racer. I suggest you figure out the difference before you call around looking for jobs for him."

While I knew there were different types of racing, my knowledge was limited and didn't extend beyond what I'd seen in *The Fast and the Furious*. I mentally kicked myself for not doing more research. I'd just assumed racing was racing. However, I should have known better than to assume anything in the PR business. Even still, I couldn't stop the feelings of indignation—and not because I was upset over him pointing out my lack of knowledge. I was mad over what he'd said about Sloan.

"I can assure you, Mr. Friedman—Sloan is not a drunk. I've spent the past month with him, and he hasn't had one ounce of alcohol. You can't judge or assume things based on one mistake he made."

"Oh, it's more than that. I've seen those pictures of Atwood with the kids at the track in the newspaper. If you think a few photo ops with orphans are going to change what happened, you're sadly mistaken. Blood is thicker than water, darlin'. There's no changing that. His old man was deep into the bottle for years until it finally caught up to him. He was an arrogant SOB, too—thought the sun came up just to hear him crow. I imagine his son isn't much different."

I bristled, feeling thoroughly annoyed on Sloan's behalf. While he still hadn't opened up to me about his father or his feelings surrounding his own accident, I knew enough to know that Friedman's harsh judgment wasn't warranted.

"What Atwood senior did should have no bearing on Sloan's character. While I can understand how he might not be a good fit as an instructor because his racing experience isn't right for your school, it's wrong to make a son suffer for the sins of his father."

"Maybe, maybe not. But it's a chance I can't afford to take. I appreciate the call, but I'm a busy man. Good luck to you. Bye now."

"Mr. Friedman, wait—" The line went dead. "Ugh!"

Frustrated, I sat back in my chair and pinched the bridge of my nose. As Sloan's PR agent, I knew I needed to push him to tell me about his father so I could have a prepared response in situations like this. However, the more I got to know Sloan personally, the more I hesitated to confront him about it. It just seemed too personal—like an invasion of privacy—and I felt it would be better for him to tell me when he was ready.

My stomach rumbled, and I glanced at the time. It was nearing two o'clock, and I'd skipped lunch. Pushing the laptop to the side, I decided it was time to take a break and get something to eat. I walked into the kitchen, opened the refrigerator door, and scanned the contents. Deciding on a spinach salad, I pulled out all of the fixings. After I finished layering the greens with walnuts, mandarin oranges, and feta cheese, I went back to the table with the bowl, intent on making it a working lunch.

As I ate, I returned to focusing on the job at hand. Next to me on the table was a copy of a newspaper from a small local press. On the front page, Sloan's face was all smiles in a picture captured outside The Residence with Eli and Marcus. He really was handsome, with his dark hair and blues eyes—eyes that made me feel like he could see right through me. He was sporting day-old stubble on his face when the picture was taken, adding to his sexy, rugged appearance.

We had been there for a barbeque—a last-minute invitation from Rochele at Eli's request. The press hadn't been notified, but there was always someone around with a cell phone camera waiting to catch an image of a famous race car driver. In this case, it was a neighbor. I was just as shocked as Sloan was at seeing his picture in the paper the following morning. Alongside the picture was a glowing article titled, "When Kindness is Winning."

Positive PR was always good—and when it was organic, it was even better.

Sloan was a natural with the boys, and I found myself thinking about the conversation I'd had with Joel Friedman. Friedman had been too punitive with his judgment. Sloan may have screwed up when he relied on alcohol and pills to cope, but it didn't have to define him. Perhaps if he used his experience for good, people might view him differently. That thought brought an entirely new idea to mind—one that had me pushing away my salad and tackling the keyboard once more.

---

An hour later, I was feeling incredibly accomplished. A targeted internet search had opened up a ton of possibilities, and I'd been fortunate to score right out of the gate. Jeremiah Lanford, the owner and head counselor at Wings Halfway House, had been all too willing to let Sloan come in and work with the teens who struggled with alcohol and drug addiction. He readily offered to have Sloan be a guest speaker at a public event they had planned for next week.

The problem was, I wasn't sure if Sloan would be on board with it. He didn't seem like the type who would jump at giving a keynote address, but I could work with him on it. This could be an excellent opportunity for him. After spending the past month with him, I didn't believe he had an addiction problem, but he had been on a dead-end road that could have ended in catastrophe if it wasn't for the wake-up call he'd gotten in Long Beach. He could use his experience, as well as his notoriety, to possibly influence a struggling teen.

I closed my laptop, ready to call it quits for the day, but a knock at the door made me pause and look down at my attire. Even though it was after three in the afternoon, I was still wearing booty shorts and the tank top from my yoga workout that morning. My hair was an absolute wreck, piled in a messy bun on top of my head. While the exercise was part of my morning routine, I typically showered right afterward. This morning I'd been so focused on getting straight to work, I had completely lost track of the day. As a result, I was a hot mess.

"Crap," I cursed under my breath, not happy about an unexpected visitor. Moving to the front door, I peered through the security peep hole to see who it was. A man in a tan uniform shirt was on the other side, holding a bouquet.

*That's odd. Who would be sending me flowers?*

Feeling curious, I unlocked the deadbolt and opened the door.

"Delivery for Kallie?"

"That's me," I replied and took the arrangement from him. "Thank you."

After signing for the delivery, I closed the door and brought the beautiful arrangement of sunflowers mixed with vibrant roses, lilies, and snapdragons to the kitchen. Placing the bouquet on the counter, I removed the envelope from the vase.

*Hey, Rainbow Brite! I know you've avoided being alone with me. I won't apologize for anything, but I think we should start over—for real this time. I've been patient, and the planets have aligned. Dinner at my place tonight. – Sloan*

I smiled after reading what he'd written on the card. I wasn't sure what he meant by the planets aligning, but I had no intention of going to his house. It was a sweet gesture, yet a precarious one, and I couldn't help but feel a little sad about it. It would be so much easier if I could simply trust destiny to guide the way and give in to Sloan's advances.

But I couldn't.

A round with my tarot deck last night confirmed as much. The upright Strength card had presented itself, reminding me to stay disciplined—especially during times of great adversity. Putting the job ahead of my desires for Sloan had been proving to be more than just a little bit difficult. It had been nearly impossible.

As I was about to put his note back into the envelope, I noticed a cream-colored satin pouch tied around the neck of the vase. Loosening the drawstring tie from the bag, I dumped the contents into my palm. It was a beaded chakra bracelet with a notecard explaining its meaning. I didn't have to read the card to recognize that the different colored beads represented the planets.

"Is that what he meant by the planets aligning?" I said aloud to myself.

Before I could contemplate it further, my cell phone buzzed. Walking back to the kitchen table, I saw Sloan's name on an incoming text.

Today
3:32 PM, Sloan: *Hey. What are you up to?*
3:33 PM, Me: *Researching things to make you look like a choir boy.*
3:33 PM, Sloan: *Anything good?*
3:34 PM, Me: *Maybe.*
3:35 PM, Sloan: *Did you get the flowers?*
3:35 PM, Me: *I did. Thank you.*
3:38 PM, Sloan: *I picked the sunflower bouquet mixed with all the different colors because it reminded me of when you wear your rainbow hair.*

I smiled, flattered by his attention to detail. I'd suspected Sloan had a sweet side to him on the first day we met after he'd pulled me into a dance on the beach. I'd slowly learned over the past month that there was so much more to him than the assuming arrogance that was often on display. He kept things close to the vest—that much was certain. But when he let his guard down, especially around the boys at The Residence, I was able to catch a tiny glimpse of his huge heart.

Almost instinctively, I went back to the counter to retrieve the chakra bracelet. I pressed it between my palms, closed my eyes, and focused on the beads' energy. After a few moments of meditation, a sense of calmness washed over me, and my cloudy destiny seemed to clear a bit. From behind closed lids, all I could see was Sloan. My stomach began to flip. Opening my eyes, I stared down at the beads and chewed on my bottom lip, wondering if I'd been paying attention to all the wrong signs.

My hookup with Sloan at the track was so much bigger than he realized. For me, it was like I could feel him in every molecule of my body, his unbridled passion taking me to heights I'd never been before. It had been foolish of me to let things go so far—a moment of extreme weakness. I simply fell into the moment with little thought about the consequences. Afterward, all I could do was recall the gypsy's warning. I thought back to what she had said to me all those years ago.

*"I see travel in your future. And the sun—the sun setting in the west."*

At the time, I thought she was referencing my move to California for college. Now I wondered if she had been looking beyond my college years toward something more meaningful, as the words she'd said afterward were too much of a coincidence to be ignored.

*"Destructive and doomed love surrounds you. Remember the weaknesses of a Gemini, my dear, or you'll be destined for a life of heartbreak. Your eagerness to express your emotions will be your downfall."*

My breakup with Dean, followed by a hasty makeout session with Sloan in a public restroom, made her words ring true. I'd allowed my emotions to rule me in typical Gemini fashion, which was exactly what the gypsy had warned me about. As silly as it may have sounded, I couldn't shake off all she had said. Her words were like a pulsing neon sign in my head telling me to run away.

*"You will fall in love under the bright sun in the west, giving someone the power to destroy you. And make no mistake—destroy you he will. The man who tastes your lips under a California sunset will be the one to break you."*

Goosebumps pebbled on my arms as I thought back to the sunset on the beach with Sloan. While I had stopped him before he could kiss me, I couldn't ignore the magnetic pull I'd felt toward him that night and every moment after that. Whether I denied him a sunset kiss or not, I knew then that he had power over me. And after our encounter in the bathroom at the track, I was sure that, if given the opportunity, the man could destroy me.

However, regardless of the fortuneteller's warning or what my tarot cards said, I knew deep down that I could not continue to run from this. Sloan possessed a fierce determination that I would have to face one way or another. And if I were honest with myself, I knew I couldn't fight him off for much longer. My heart and body wouldn't let me. I wasn't even sure why I was fighting it anymore. After all, I was a grown woman with a strong mind and a desire to go after what I wanted. Was it so bad that I wanted Sloan? It didn't have to be anything serious. I wasn't looking for that. As long as I set the pace, a psychic warning could only come to fruition if I allowed it to.

Placing the bracelet back inside the bag, I felt extraordinarily conflicted despite the clarity about the inevitable. I sighed and picked up my phone to reply to Sloan's last text.

3:39 PM, Me: *The flowers are beautiful. And the bracelet too. That was very nice of you.*
3:40 PM, Sloan: *And what about dinner?*

I didn't have to have psychic abilities to know that question was coming next. I glanced at the vase of flowers. The radiant yellow petals of the sunflowers were reminiscent of bright sun rays on a clear day.

Mixed with the perfect combination of bold colors and gorgeous florals, they were an instant mood lifter. That was why I always associated the rainbow with optimism—something that Sloan knew because I'd told him as much. I could only guess that he aimed for an optimistic vibe when he added the note to have dinner tonight.

3:43 PM, Me: *I don't think dinner at your place is a good idea. But I do have something to discuss with you. How about we go out?*
3:45 PM, Sloan: *Doesn't work for me. I want to enjoy a meal and a nice California wine with you without having to worry about reporters stalking every beverage I taste. My place.*

I bit my lower lip as I considered his proposal. He had a point. It would be nice talking freely without worrying about prying eyes and eavesdroppers. However, the idea of going back to his oversized bachelor pad was intimidating. I wasn't sure why—it just was. I looked around at my surrounding space, then glanced outside to the inground pool. The thought of inviting Sloan into my space felt safer for some reason.

I looked down at my phone and reread the entire text thread. Instead of responding to his invite, I walked down the hallway to the master suite. Once there, I went over to the dresser and pulled my tarot deck from the box. Anxious butterflies danced in my stomach as I tapped the deck twice, then gave the cards a careful shuffle. After cutting the pile three times, I broke with tradition and committed to turning over one card only. I had no intention of going through an entire formation trying to interpret the meaning of each card. I already knew what my gut was telling me. I just needed one more sign to let me know if I should follow it.

When I flipped the top card, the upright Star presented itself. I audibly sighed with relief to see a symbol of hope and love in romance. The optimistic energy I'd been feeling so powerfully was reinforced by the Star card. It was telling me that I shouldn't ignore it but use it to rebuild my confidence so that I could move on to the next chapter—and my inner goddess was telling me if I allowed myself to turn the page, the next chapter included Sloan.

"I can control the pace," I reminded myself.

Impulsively, I typed my reply to Sloan before I could change my mind.

3:57 PM, Me: *How about you come here? I have wine.*
3:59 PM, Sloan: *That works. I'll bring the food and text you later for your address. Does 7:00 sound okay?*
4:00 PM, Me: *I'll see you then.*

Feeling remarkably satisfied that I'd come to a decision about which path to take, I turned away from the cards and moved to the closet. Along the way, I spotted the homeowner's smart home system and decided to take advantage of it.

"Alexa, play upbeat music," I called to the little Echo Dot sitting on the dresser.

"The station, Dance Party Favorites, free on Amazon Music," the computerized voice replied.

Instantly, "Don't Stop Believin'" by Journey began to play.

*Perfect.*

I smiled to myself and opened my closet to pick out something to wear. As the music played, I eyed up a light pink halter sundress. The airy, breezy ruffle design was flattering on me and appropriate for an evening sitting by the pool. Paired with a long necklace, stacked bracelets, and pink hair extensions, the outfit completely suited my current mood. Satisfied with my choice, I pulled the dress out of the closet and laid it flat on my bed. After telling Alexa to turn up the volume, I sang along with Steve Perry and headed to the bathroom to take a shower.

# Chapter Twelve

*Sloan*

With a takeout order from The Lucky Koi in hand, I climbed into the black leather driver's seat of the Camaro with a satisfied grin on my face. I felt like I was finally making headway with Kallie. Even though she hadn't given me the opportunity to touch her since our encounter in the track's restroom, I'd used the time to pay attention to every little detail about her and knew my efforts were starting to pay off. From remembering the food she preferred and the jewelry she wore to her beliefs in the stars and the moon, it was like the meticulous prep work that went into a race—and no detail was too small. Except now, I was preparing for an entirely new kind of race—the race to Kallie's heart.

Her unpredictability over the past month had been a challenge for me. She went from red hot to ice cold in the blink of an eye, trying her hardest to keep me at arm's length. Two weeks ago, she would have flat-out rejected a private dinner invitation from me. Her willingness to accept it today, even if it was at her place, signaled I might finally have her attention for something other than business.

Still, I knew I had to be careful. She was a wild card. One wrong bump and our tandem could be wrecked. She was the antithesis to every woman I'd ever been with, yet the attraction I felt for her was no less irresistible—it was downright consuming. Her uniqueness just made me want her all the more, and I'd committed to doing whatever I had to do to have her.

I pulled out of the restaurant's parking lot, shifted lanes, and followed the GPS map to the address Kallie had texted me. With the top down, I hit the accelerator and drove up Ocean Avenue toward North of Montana. Within fifteen minutes, I was turning onto Kallie's driveaway. Killing the engine, I grabbed the bags of food and walked up the walkway leading to the single-story home. Kallie opened the front door before I reached it.

Instantly, my breath caught, and I slowed my steps, wanting to take in every inch of her. Her emerald eyes were shadowed darker than usual, and her lips were coated in a thin layer of gloss. Her feet were bare, with pink painted toenails that matched the pink in her hair and color of her dress—and what a dress it was. It was casual and shouldn't have been nearly so devastating, but in that, she looked like a goddamned sex goddess. The halter V-neck accentuated her breasts, and all I could think of was how they had felt in my hands, how her nipples tightened with just one flick of my tongue. It would only take one tug at the tie at her neck to set those gorgeous globes free.

"Hey, there," she greeted with a smile. Her green eyes twinkled, reminding me of fuchsite sparkling under a setting sun.

"Hey, yourself." Stepping toward her, I reached with my free hand to twirl a pink lock of her hair around my finger. This was the first time I'd seen anything other than purple and rainbow colors. "No rainbows today. What does the pink mean?"

"Happy."

I cocked up one eyebrow. "What are you so happy about?"

She shrugged as if to say, 'why wouldn't I be,' and smiled. "I guess I'm just happy about the progress I made today, and I'm happy you're here. Come on inside. I've already uncorked the wine."

Enjoying the subtle sway of her hips as she walked, I followed her inside to an open concept kitchen, dining, and great room. She breezed past the interior rooms and led me to a connected outdoor living space with an inground pool. Next to the pool, I saw she'd set a patio table for two. A bottle of wine sat chilling in an ice bucket next to a plate of cheese, olives, and crackers. I set the takeout bags down on the table and glanced around.

"Nice setup you have here," I mused.

"Thanks. Make yourself comfortable. I just realized I forgot the utensils. I'll be right back."

As I waited for her to return, I rolled up the sleeves of my black button-down and went to work on emptying the contents of the takeout containers. The food selection included more rabbit food for Kallie and beef hibachi for me.

"I can't take credit for the menu," I said after she returned. "But I knew you liked the restaurant we ate at with Cooper and Rochele. I hope this is okay."

"Looks great to me. You'll have to let me know if the wine is any good. I'm not up on the best California vintages," she admitted as she began to pour the chilled white into two glasses.

"I'm no wine snob—I prefer a good whiskey or an IPA over anything else—but I can recognize a quality *vino*." I paused to accept the glass she held out and took a sip. The flavor was crisper than some of the other white wines I'd had, but I liked it. "It's smooth—not as sweet as I would have expected, but good."

We took our seats at the table, and it was hard not to notice the way the slit in Kallie's long flowy dress opened to reveal her shapely thigh. I wanted nothing more than to reach over and slide my hand all the way up, but I knew any attempt to do that just yet would be a mistake. Getting her to open up to me—both literally and figuratively—would take finesse.

Tearing my eyes away from her sexy legs, I focused on the food in front of us. Kallie began to pile forkfuls of green onto her plate, and I tried not to wonder how any of it could possibly sustain her as I added a hefty portion of beef to my plate.

We ate quietly for a time. She seemed content to enjoy the peaceful evening while I, on the other hand, used the absence of conversation to get a better read on her mindset. I wanted her—badly. Things were going well, but I knew one wrong move would shoot our delicate balance straight to hell.

"This avocado salad is so amazing," she said after we were halfway through our meal. "I can't believe you remembered what I ordered the last time. I wouldn't have."

I glanced down at her plate. Though she'd said her food was good, I found her to be moving it around her dish more than she ate.

"You've barely eaten anything," I pointed out.

"I had a late lunch. Plus, I'm distracted at the moment, so that isn't helping my appetite."

"Oh? What about?"

"Well, I think we should establish some ground rules for tonight," she announced.

I paused midchew and eyed her quizzically. "Rules?"

"Yes, rules. I came to a conclusion earlier today."

I grinned at her businesslike tone. When she talked all professional, I found it sexy as hell. "Should I be nervous?" I teased.

"No, but I do think it's important to get this off my chest. I invited you here on the pretense of business—which we do need to discuss—but after dancing around it for a month, we both know tonight won't be all work and no play. You were right when you said there was something strong between us. There have been signs, and while I'm not entirely sure if I'm reading them correctly, I'm tired of denying the attraction I feel for you. Plus, I know how you operate, and I can predict where this night will go. If I didn't, I wouldn't have invited you here."

I nearly dropped my fork, totally taken aback by her unexpectedly relaxed stance. I was used to aggressive women coming on to me, but Kallie had always been different. Up until two seconds ago, I'd fully expected to have to work to win her over. Now she was saying there were… signs?

"What are you trying to say, Kallie?"

"I'm saying that I'm open to the possibility of there being an us, but there are important business things to go over first before you try to get in my pants."

I sat back in my chair and crossed my arms, unable to hide my amusement. She looked thoroughly satisfied—as if her declaration somehow made the inevitable easier for her to accept.

"You're not wearing pants," I pointed out.

She flushed, and I felt my amused grin widen.

"You know what I mean. It's just an expression. Would it have been better if I said, 'under my skirt?'"

"Much better. Does that mean you're going to *let* me try to get under your skirt later?" She didn't answer but merely smiled in return before taking another forkful of salad. "Alright, since you're going to play coy, why don't you tell me about these signs you speak of?"

"Nope. I already told you—business first. You need to have patience."

"Patience is the most overrated virtue."

"Maybe it is," she replied with a shrug. "But you don't have much choice in the matter now, do you?"

I eyed her curiously for a moment before going back to my food. "Fine. Have it your way. You want to talk shop, then I've got some news for you."

"Oh?" she asked, looking up from her plate with interest.

"Do you want the good news or the bad news first?"

"Yikes. That sounds scary. I didn't realize there were both. Let's get the bad news out of the way first."

"Milo called. He—" I stopped short when I saw her cringe. "What's wrong?"

"Nothing. I just don't like Milo. I mean, I've only been around him a handful of times, so it's not like I know him all that well. It's just a feeling I have. I'm not surprised his name is attached to whatever bad news you have to tell me. I've deliberately not looped him in on some of the events we had scheduled with Safe Track because I don't trust him. Whenever he's around, he gives off negative vibes."

I pressed my lips together in a tight line, understanding her astute observation perfectly.

"You're not alone there. Not many people like him, but he's good at his job." I paused, unsure if I wanted to fully commit to the words I was about to say. "I don't really need him anymore. I can cut him loose if it makes you feel better."

"No, it's okay. We all have to work with people we don't like. What did he want when he called?"

"Tanya Griffin's parents filed a lawsuit."

Kallie froze, her fork hovering over her plate.

"That's not good, Sloan. After all the work we've put into—"

"Hang on. Let me finish. We both knew a lawsuit was coming. That's the bad part, but not a surprise. The good news is, because of all the positive press you've been getting me, my lawyer thinks we'll be able to settle reasonably out of court."

Kallie's shoulders sagged with relief. "That's good to hear. That last thing I wanted was to face a public trial while we're trying to rebuild your image. People don't need a reminder of what happened. Any news on the little girl?"

"She's fine, from what I've heard. Full recovery. That fact helps my case a lot too."

"That's also good, which brings me to tell you about the opportunity I lined up for you earlier today that could heighten your positive PR even more."

Having finished my food, I pushed the plate away, topped off our wine glasses, and sat back in my chair. "More positive press is good. Let's hear it."

"Well," she began, seeming somewhat apprehensive. "Have you ever heard of Wings Halfway House?"

"The name rings a bell. Why?"

"It's a place for teens struggling with drug and alcohol addiction. I spoke with a man named Jeremiah Lanford, the owner and head counselor over there. Considering your accident and what happened afterward, I thought speaking to the teens about your experience would be an opportunity for you to do some good. Jeremiah thought it was a great idea too."

I pressed my lips together in a frown. I understood what she was trying to do, but public speaking wasn't exactly in my wheelhouse. Talking to a reporter after a race was one thing, but reciting carefully-orchestrated words to a crowd of teenagers struggling with addiction was different altogether. I may have been on a collision course, driving the wrong way on a one-way street, but I didn't know enough about addiction to give advice. The most I could say was, "Hey, kids. Don't fuck up like I did."

"I'm not sure if that's the right gig for me, Kallie. Isn't there something else you can set up with Safe Track?"

"I already have stuff lined up with them. Wings would be different. Given your past, you understand the destruction that can come with excessive drinking and drugs." She paused and reached over to place a hand on my knee. "Not to mention, your notoriety could really make a difference for one of these kids. Jeremiah offered to let you come in and speak with them sometime within the next couple of weeks. If all goes well, he said he'd be interested in exploring mentorship opportunities too."

I hesitated, not sure what to say. Yes, I could probably tell my story easily enough, but that wasn't what worried me. Kallie didn't know about my father. If she did, she would know that something like this had the potential to open up a can of worms. I didn't want to do it, yet there was something in her expression that made me feel like I had to. She was pushing at the walls I'd constructed around myself since the accident—and I was letting her.

Standing up from my chair, I turned away from her intense gaze. Looking out past the pool, I stared at nothing in particular as I contemplated what she wanted me to do. After a moment, I shook my head, then turned back to her.

"Fuck, Kallie. I can't mentor a teenager. My own life is barely on track. Up until you showed up, I was off the rails, on a road to nowhere. I just don't think I'm a good fit for that kind of thing right now—possibly ever."

"Can you at least think about it? I told Jeremiah that I'd need to talk to you about it first, but he agreed to keep the guest speaker spot open until he hears back from me. Perhaps if you meet with him and tour the facility, you can make up your mind then."

"Alright. I'll think about it."

Her ability to twist me to her will was astonishing. This girl was going to be the death of me at this rate.

"If you find yourself struggling with a speech, I can help you and—"

"Kallie, don't get ahead of yourself. I said I'd think about it. No promises."

She beamed, and I felt myself soften. Standing up, she came over to where I was standing and placed her hands on my forearms.

"Thank you."

I looked down at her wide smile. Her green eyes twinkled in the low sun, and I couldn't stop myself from reaching up to touch her face.

"I've traveled all over this country for more races than I can count.

I've seen thousands of faces and just as many smiles. But yours, Rainbow Brite… your smile is my favorite."

Her grin widened, and she began to laugh—and I mean, really laugh. The sound was full and deep, the freedom of who she was coming to the forefront. Even when she quieted, there was still a slight twitch to her lip as if she were still mulling over the humor in her head.

"You've got some smooth lines, Sloan. I'm sure you've used that one on all the ladies."

"No. Just you," I admitted sincerely. The humor faded, and she flushed a subtle shade of pink. Tilting her head to the side, she eyed me with curiosity.

"I can't help but think about what Cooper said about you not keeping women around for very long. I don't know where things will go with us, and I'm not looking for anything serious, especially considering I'll only be here for another four and a half months. I have a life in D.C., and when our contract is over, I'm going back. But you should know in advance that I don't know how to do casual flings. When I give, I give one hundred percent of myself and won't be able to separate sex from emotions. Even if I try for casual, it may not end up that way for me, and when I think about where things may lead tonight…" She wavered, and her apprehension was evident by the worry lines on her forehead.

"Look, I know what Cooper said. He's not wrong—I don't do serious, but it's not for the reasons you might think. I'm not anti-commitment. It's just that racing life is—" I pinched my brows together, trying to think of the best way to describe what it meant to spend countless hours on the road, living in trailers, and working my ass off to win one qualifying race after another. "Racing life is hard, Kallie. There's nothing glamorous about it—especially when you're first coming up. I traveled a lot, and I saw the relationship strains other drivers had with their significant others. I just wanted to focus on racing. It was all that mattered to me."

"I was never up on who was who in the racing world," she admitted. "But with minimal research, I learned what a big deal you were. When I read something that compared you to the Tiger Woods of racing, I was shocked to realize I hadn't heard of you before."

"I don't know about that particular comparison, but I do know I was at the top of my game at the time of the crash. I still hold the record of being the youngest driver ever to win three consecutive championships, but the money and fame that came with it didn't happen without sacrifice. I would never have achieved any of it if I'd had the distraction of a serious relationship."

"And now?

"Well, I'm not racing at the moment now, am I?"

"At the moment?"

"I'll always want to be behind the wheel again, Kallie. That will never change."

"I know the doctor said you couldn't race anymore, but considering how medical technologies advance, I have to ask. This is going to sound so contradictory—especially since I just said I don't want anything serious—but I'm more than just a one-night-stand kind of girl. If given the opportunity to get back into racing, where would that leave me?"

"If you're wondering that, it seems like you are, in fact, looking for something serious."

"Not necessarily. I just want to know where I'll stand if you start racing again."

"If I answer that, you might not like it, Kallie."

"Try me."

*Fuck.*

Unable to meet her stare, I stepped away and turned to look out over the pool once more. I didn't know how we got to this point, but I knew I had to give her an honest answer. I didn't like mind games, and I hated liars. I prided myself on speaking my mind, and people always knew where I stood. Giving her brutal honesty might ruin any chance I had with her, but I gave it to her, nonetheless.

"Racing was, and still is, my first love."

"I'm okay with that," she responded.

I spun to face her again, shocked to hell by her acceptance. "You are?"

I didn't know any woman who would be okay with being told she was second fiddle to a motorsport. I expected to have to explain more.

"Sounds crazy, right?" She sighed and began to pile up our dinner dishes. "The thing is, I appreciate the honesty. I just got out of a serious relationship, and as I said, I'm not looking for another. However, I needed to make sure I wasn't going to be a one-shot deal for you. Being another notch in someone's bedpost has never worked for me. Your response may not be acceptable for some women, but it's enough for me. I know my limitations, and now I know yours. If I think I'm getting in too deep, your honesty tonight will help me keep my emotions in check. I only want something real and authentic—someone who wants to be with me for who I am and not an idea of what they want me to be. Does that make sense?"

Taking a few steps toward her, I stopped her from clearing the table and turned her to face me. Using one finger, I tilted her chin up until her eyes met mine. "I told you once before that you deserved someone who would love you and leave you wild. I meant what I said."

She didn't respond but looked away, seeming somewhat nervous. I followed the direction of her gaze to see the sun had lowered further in the sky, creating a rainbow mirror on the pool for the surrounding landscape. When I looked back, I saw worry lines creasing her forehead again. She took a step back and returned to clearing the dishes, but I stopped her by wrapping my arms around her waist.

"Sloan, the dishes. Let me just—"

"What is it? Tell me what's bothering you."

"I…it's…" she faltered. "It's the sunset."

"What about it?"

She released a small laugh and shook her head. "You'll think I'm nuts."

She pulled away once more, but this time I didn't stop her. Following her lead, I helped bring the dirty dishes into the house. We cleaned up in silence as I waited for her to explain. When the last plate was stacked into the dishwasher, I took her hand and led her back out to the patio. Taking a seat on one of the lounge chairs near the pool, I pulled her onto my lap.

"Kallie, what's with you and the sunsets?" I asked, pointing to the sun that had almost completely disappeared. "You had the same look on your face that night on the beach."

Apprehension momentarily clouded her features before being replaced by a look of resignation.

"It goes back to something a gypsy fortuneteller told me at a carnival when I was eighteen. Her name was Madame Lavinia. I didn't want to see her, but my brother, Austin, literally pushed me into her tent, and I didn't have much of a choice. Austin knew how much I believed in destiny and fate, and he used to get a kick out of it. Still, if I'd had any sense, I would have run right out of there."

"What did she say?" I asked with genuine curiosity. I had a feeling that whatever she was about to say would give me a bit more insight into the free-spirited woman who could drive me wild with just one look.

"She said destructive love would surround me, and the man who kissed me under a California sunset would be the one to break me. That's why I ran before you could kiss me on the beach. As for tonight, I was hoping it would be dark before… Well, before anything happened."

I raised my eyebrows and grinned, amused by the solemn set to her jaw as she told her outlandish tale.

"A gypsy fortuneteller. You're serious right now?"

"I knew you would think I was nuts," she mumbled, then let out an exasperated sigh and stood up to pace. "Forget I said anything."

"No, I'm glad you told me. All this time, I thought I'd done something to spook you," I said, trying my damn hardest to stifle the laugh threatening to burst forth. "I'm happy to hear it was just a… a carny influencing you."

She stopped pacing and narrowed her eyes at me.

"You can think it's funny all you want, but it's more than what she said about being kissed at sunset. It's also about what happened with us right out of the gate. I'm a Gemini and tend to let my emotions rule me. Madame Lavinia predicted that would be my downfall. I broke up with Dean, then the very next day, I got hot and heavy with you—a virtual stranger at the time—in a public restroom."

As ludicrous as it all sounded to me, I could tell her concern was wholly genuine, and I tried to adopt a more somber tone.

"Kallie, I don't believe in psychics. I decide my fate—nobody else. But you've obviously had considerable worry over this. What can I do to help you get past it?"

"You don't have to do anything. I decided earlier today that I was going to let it go and just live in the moment—as long as there's no sunset involved."

I glanced in the direction of the setting sun. It had completely disappeared behind the landscape, having left behind a rainbow watercolor painted across the sky. Reaching up, I clasped her hand.

"Kallie, I don't care about the sunset. I want you. Here and now."

Her long lashes dropped before lifting to boldly meet my stare. Her demeanor shifted, and her eyes glimmered with a barrage of conflicting emotions—desire, longing, apprehension.

But when I tugged her hand to pull her back onto my lap, she didn't resist.

# Chapter Thirteen

*Kallie*

"*I want you. Here and now.*"

His words ricocheted through my body. Small shadows chased across his face in the dim lighting, making him look dangerously sexy. Our eyes met for a brief second, and I took in the darkness dancing in his gaze.

*Holy Mother of Stars…*

It was all I could think before he covered my mouth with his. I knew this moment was coming, but I'd hoped to put him off until it was completely dark—when the sun had safely hidden away behind the earth. But now none of that seemed to matter. I wanted this man in a way I'd never wanted anything else in my life.

His kiss was light at first—just a graze that drove me completely wild. I whimpered against his lips, and he responded by gripping the back of my head and pressing his mouth more firmly to mine. Within mere seconds, the kiss went from tentative to feverish, passionately demanding to take what he needed.

Our tongues danced as the rainbow sky faded into a deep purple on the horizon. His hands moved possessively up and down my back, progressing over my ribs and to my waist, skimming the sides of my breasts on the way down. I felt myself shiver at the contact, my desire building and causing a fervent ache between my legs.

Shifting my position, I arranged my skirt so I could straddle his hips.

His breath was hot on my neck as he nipped his way across the line of my jaw, moving down my neck to my cleavage. He tugged the strings securing my halter with one hand while his other ran up my leg, then slid under my dress. He massaged my thigh, shoving my skirt further up as he went, brushing past the strap of the lace thong at my hip and around to cup my nearly bare behind. He held me firm and pulled the top of my dress down to expose my breasts.

"No bra," he murmured. My nipples pebbled from the appreciative way he stared at them. A moan escaped me as his magical lips leaned in to kiss the area around one tightened peak. He kneaded my breasts, pinching the erect nipples between his thumb and forefinger before capturing one with his teeth. At the same time, he slid his other hand from my backside to slip a finger under my panties. The throbbing between my spread thighs intensified, and I ached to be satisfied.

"Touch me, Sloan."

"I will, baby, but there's something in my way. I want no barriers this time. I've been fantasizing about seeing you bare for far too long." He grabbed hold of my hips with little effort and lifted us both from the chair until we were in a standing position. Looping one finger through the side of my thong, he said, "I want these off."

He tugged the thong all the way down to my feet and I willingly stepped out of them. He kissed his way back up my legs, starting near my ankles, then over my knees until he reached the apex of my thighs. A fire burned fierce in my belly, and I couldn't think straight. I was nearly naked with him holding my dress up around my hips, the fabric barely clinging to my body by the elastic band under my bustline. When he began to pull that down, too, I grabbed hold of his hand.

"Sloan, maybe we should go inside," I breathed. "Somebody could see. The trees only hide so much."

"No. I want you here. Naked. If someone's out there, let them watch." To prove he was serious, he quickly yanked my dress down and it pooled around my ankles, leaving me completely exposed. It was an extraordinary sensation to feel the soft coastal breeze dance lambently across every inch of my skin as I stood there, stark naked, with Sloan. It was incredibly liberating. Stepping back, he admired his handiwork for a moment before breathily whispering, "You're so fucking gorgeous."

Then he lunged for me and began the merciless attack on my mouth once again. Pulling my naked form tight against him, he coaxed me back onto the lounge chair. Pressing me back, he hovered over me and positioned his body between my legs. Using one hand, he raised my arms above my head and leaned in to nip his way around my collarbone. His free hand softly brushed along the curve of my breast, pausing only to flick at a rigid peak, then slid down over my stomach to the juncture of my thighs. When he ran a finger through my wet slit, my breath caught, eliciting a gasp of unadulterated pleasure.

Never before had I felt so uninhibited and free. I didn't care about the gypsy's words, my tarot cards, or the fact that there were still dark purple streaks across the sky from the setting sun. I didn't even care about the possibility of being seen. It was as if nothing in the world mattered except for his touch.

"Oh, God… Sloan. I feel like I've waited a lifetime for this."

Releasing my arms, he sat up and used both hands to spread my thighs further apart. Continuing a slow exploration of my most intimate parts, he lazily circled my clit with his thumb, spreading the moisture around before sliding two fingers inside. I wanted to cry out from sheer ecstasy, but I worried about the neighbors possibly hearing, so I held back. My back arched, and my stomach tightened. I was coming apart at the seams.

"You like this?"

"Yes, don't stop!" I shamelessly begged.

Lowering his head, he pressed his mouth against my folds. Instantly, an electric shock surged through my body, eliciting a moan from my lips. His tongue moved against the pulsing nub, flicking up and down and filling me with the most intense pleasure I'd ever felt.

"I want you to come, Kallie," he murmured between licks. "Then we're going to take this party to the pool. I want to feel your naked, wet body sliding against mine."

Fire coursed through me at his words, the ache turning into something vicious, and I could only moan again in response. I wanted him—desperately. I needed to know what he'd feel like inside me. I'd never before had a lover linger in all the right places in order to find my most sensitive areas. If his hands and tongue could work so much magic, I could only imagine what it would be like when we officially joined for the first time. Images of Sloan and I moving together in unison in the pool filled my mind. It was enough to send me reeling over the edge.

"I'm going to come!" I gasped. The words had barely passed my lips when wave after wave of the sweetest, most intense ecstasy rocketed through me. It started low and deep, bursting forth in a kaleidoscope of colors that took my breath away. My body shuddered and convulsed, but Sloan wouldn't let up on the merciless flicks of his tongue against my throbbing bundle of nerves. I squirmed, but he held me to the spot with his firm grip on my hips.

"Be still, baby. Just feel," he ordered.

I was so sensitive to his touch that my natural reaction was to pull away. Still, even if it was nearly impossible, I did as he told me. I loved the way he made me feel but hated it at the same time. It was as if my mind, heart, and body were not my own, but something only he commanded.

Holding as still s as possible, I focused only on the tightening sensation that was quickly building deep in my belly once again. His fingers circled my walls as his tongue applied pressure to my clit. I could feel a second orgasm on the horizon, but he kept me on edge, never quite allowing me to get there. I bucked involuntarily, craving the relief I was so close to getting. I was beyond the point of wanting. He was driving me insane, and I was desperate, completely lost in an ocean of sensations.

He must have sensed my urgency because he plunged his fingers deeper into my core and increased the intensity of his tongue. My insides constricted, and my mind went hazy. In one blinding moment, white-hot pleasure shot through my veins. I cried out, unable to suppress my screams.

Time passed. I didn't know if it was seconds, minutes, or hours. I was only aware of the tingling sensation all over my body as I slowly opened my eyes to meet his. His lips parted slightly, and his deep blue eyes were a violent inferno of desire. Moving up my body, he took the lobe of my ear between his teeth before tracing the outline with the tip of his tongue. A shiver ran through me.

"Let's go to the pool," he whispered.

Climbing off the chair, Sloan began to unbutton his shirt.

"No, let me," I told him. My legs felt weak as I stood from the lounge chair, but I kept myself steady as I closed the gap between us and reached for the buttoned seam of Sloan's shirt. Starting at the top, I unfastened each button to expose his chest at a painstakingly slow pace. As much as I wanted to rip the clothes from his body, I wanted to enjoy this moment of seduction even more.

Once his shirt was removed, I lightly trailed my fingertips over his rock-hard abdomen to the line of muscle leading to his groin. I heard his sharp intake of breath as I reached to undo the buckle of his belt, allowing me easy access to unzip the fly of his jeans and release his straining cock. After pushing his pants down his legs, I took a step back to admire the hard lines of his body. He would make any sculptor weep. I could see the faint lines of his scars on his left hip and arm, and I wondered how many came from the crash and how many were from the resulting surgeries that followed. The imperfections somehow made him look more rugged and sexy. He was magnificent in every sense of the word—from his muscular thighs to the rippled power of his rock-hard abs and broad, bronzed shoulders—the perfect specimen of the alpha male.

I took in the dangerous glint in his eyes before allowing my attention to travel down past his tapered V to settle on his long, thick erection that looked impossibly hard. Moving forward, I gave him a slow and lazy kiss. He wrapped his arms around my waist to pull me closer, but I shook my head.

"It's my turn, Sloan. I want to taste you."

Lowering to my knees, I took his virile cock into my hand. His breath hissed between his teeth as I closed my lips around the lush head, flicking my tongue leisurely before taking him further into my mouth. He was hot, silky, and soft. His taste ignited my senses, and I greedily sucked, worshiping his manhood. Sloan fisted his hands through my hair, encouraging me to take more, so I pushed forward until I felt him hit the back of my throat. Tightening my lips, I pulled back to swirl my tongue, then pressed deep to suck him in long, drawing pulls.

"Holy fuck, Kallie. I'll never last at this rate," he groaned and pushed forward into my mouth. My sex tightened in pleasure from his words as his thick veins throbbed against my tongue. His thighs tensed and I could feel his shaft swell deep in my throat. His breathing became ragged, and I knew he was close.

I pulled back, not wanting him to come just yet. I wanted to feel him inside me when he did. I looked up at him and our gazes locked. The raw hunger in his eyes mirrored my own as he hauled me to my feet. I saw him reach down and snatch a condom from the pocket of his jeans before moving to lift me effortlessly. He positioned my legs, scissoring them around his hips. As he walked us to the pool, I swiped my tongue up the side of his throat, relishing in the intoxicating smell of his cologne and the subtle saltiness of his skin.

Lowering us to the top step, he sheathed the condom over his length, then captured one of my nipples between his teeth to tease the hardened point. With me straddling his hips, he trailed kisses up my neck, fisting his hand in my hair and yanking my head back to ravage my mouth like he was starving. Water lapped around my knees, and a fire began to build low and deep in my belly. It flowed through me, hot like lava.

With my knees firmly planted on the top step of the pool, I tightened my legs against his hips. I could feel his erection pressing hard against my heat as his teeth bit into my lower lip, the sharp sensation cutting through me and intensifying the ache in my belly. I needed him inside me—now. Slick with anticipation, I reached between us to position his tip to my entrance, then lowered onto his scorching heat with painstaking restraint. He pierced me, stretching me inch by divine inch until he was rooted deep in my essence. Our unification was more fulfilling than I could have possibly imagined, and I could almost see actual sparks flying in the air.

"Magic," I breathed.

"You can say that again," he agreed as he pushed up and gripped my hips.

I tightened around him. My already rapid-heartbeat increased in tempo, fueling my veins with even more desire for him. With my hands braced on the concrete behind his head, I began to move. As if the gods had created us for each other, we easily found our rhythm. His motions were determined, matching me thrust after thrust. We rocked together and the water sloshed, adding an erotic melody to our union. I kissed him again, our breaths mingling as we rose to new heights.

I gripped his shoulders, needing something more than concrete to hang onto, and felt his rippled muscles bunch beneath my palms. Before long, I was overflowing with arousal.

"Oh, God!" I gasped. I was so close.

"Fuck, Kallie," he growled with a satisfied groan. "You're driving me wild. Give me your orgasm. I need to feel your sweet pussy tighten around me."

Reaching between us, he began to circle my clit with his thumb as he pushed up harder inside of me. My muscles clenched involuntarily as he brought me closer to that glorious peak. I was amazed at how he knew exactly what to do to please me—how to torment me with delicious pleasure, teasing me just long enough to ensure my climax would be cataclysmic.

With every inch of his length buried inside me, I dug my nails into his shoulders. I was right on the cusp and could barely think.

"I'm almost there," I panted. Tightening my legs around him, I braced myself for that delicious moment when I would be sent over the edge. I trembled, losing more of myself with every passing moment. I became desperate, the promise of release all-consuming.

"Now, Kallie. Give it to me now!"

Strong hands gripped my hips, pulling me down as he pushed up in a hard thrust. Over and over again, he plunged impossibly deeper. As he continued to power upward, that slow build in my belly burst. I was mindless, wildly grinding against him as I split apart at the seams. I tossed my head from side to side and let out a harsh cry of fantastical release. My sensitive tissues rippled until I began to spasm uncontrollably in a long, shattering, heart-pounding orgasm.

"Sloan!" I cried out and unraveled around him, overcome with a sensation of blinding heat. Colors flashed before my eyes as the rush surged through me.

My fingernails clawed at his back, pulling him closer when I felt him tense beneath me. I clung to him, waiting for the moment he would follow me into the abyss of mindless release. With one last plunge, his body convulsed before momentarily falling still. When his breath hitched, and I felt the delicious pulsating of his cock, we spiraled together and his climax burst forth.

A rush of air escaped my lungs as my hammering heart worked its way back to a normal rhythm. With his arms banded tight around me, the raw strength of him enveloped me. I slumped down and wrapped my arms around his broad back. A calm stillness held fast to the air as he pressed his forehead against mine, then softly ran his hand up and down the curve of my spine.

"Goddamn," he murmured into my ear. "I knew the moment I met you that you'd be a firecracker, but I had no idea... That was pyrotechnics on steroids."

I smiled and let his words linger in the air for a moment.

"I think you were right when you said the planets have aligned. Venus and Mars definitely played their part tonight." I felt the rumble of laughter in his chest more than I heard it and pulled back to look at him. "Why are you laughing?"

"I'm laughing because I have no idea what you're talking about."

"Mars is the planet of sex. Venus is the planet of love. When they align, they promote sexual attraction and compatibility."

His grin widened, and he placed a light kiss on the top of my nose.

"Whatever you say, Rainbow Brite."

"It's true!" I protested.

"Maybe it is. Why don't we go inside and see if your theory is correct?"

"We could, but the outcome depends on certain things."

"Such as?"

"Your birthday. When is it?"

His brows pinched together in confusion.

"May 2nd. Why?"

I eyed him knowingly as a slow smile spread across my face.

"You're a Taurus. That's a good match for me—a Gemini—especially if you want to test my theory," I told him before leaning in so I could whisper in his ear. "Because make no mistake, you'll need great endurance in the bedroom to keep up with me."

# Chapter Fourteen

*Kallie*

My eyes fluttered open at the sound of floorboards creaking. I yawned and rubbed the sleep from my eyes. Rolling over onto my back, I saw Sloan standing at the foot of the bed in the morning light, completely in the buff and entirely shameless. He had just come from the shower and was towel drying his wet hair, the action causing droplets of water to rain down from his head and glisten on his shoulders and chest. I sighed inwardly. He was truly magnificent.

"Good morning, gorgeous. Did you sleep okay?" he asked.

Perfectly content admiring his physique, I let my gaze roam over his body one more time before answering.

"Really good, actually. What time is it?"

"It's almost nine."

"Nine! I never sleep that late. If I were home in D.C., I would have already finished my morning yoga routine and be in my office by this point."

"Don't beat yourself up over it. I kept you up late—you know, that whole endurance thing," he added with a wink, then flashed me one of his cocky and swoon-worthy smiles. "Besides, skipping yoga once isn't going to hurt. You proved last night how flexible you could be."

I nearly melted as I recalled the heights he'd taken me to during the night—over and over again—once more in the pool, then twice in my bed. But now, my body was craving something else. Holding the sheet up to cover my naked chest, I sat up.

"I can't handle your tricks pre-caffeinated and on an empty stomach. I need sustenance."

"My tricks?" he asked as he slipped into the jeans he'd worn last night. They were tight in all the right places, yet slightly faded in spots, as if he'd spent countless hours working on cars while wearing them.

"Yeah. And you're doing that smilking thing again. Cut it out."

"Oh, so you like that, do you?" he countered with a suggestive smile, emphasizing his smilk even more until my toes wanted to curl.

I frowned and tossed a pillow at him.

"Food first."

Catching the pillow in the air, he laughed and tossed it back.

"You're cranky in the morning before you eat. Good to know. I'll go whip up some grub while you get dressed."

"You don't have to do that," I told him, but it was too late. He was already out the door.

I rolled out of bed and did quick work in the bathroom. Within twenty-five minutes, I was showered and dressed in frayed jean shorts and a gray off-the-shoulder T-shirt. I'd skipped putting on makeup but clipped my pink hair extensions into my ponytail before heading out to the kitchen. Once there, I saw Sloan had managed to find all the tools he needed and was working on our breakfast. Wearing those oh-so-snug jeans and nothing else, he looked glorious standing over a pan of eggs sizzling in a frying pan—like my very own sexy chef.

"Do you want help?" I offered as I watched him pull bread from the toaster.

"Not unless you can procure bacon out of thin air."

I scrunched up my nose in disapproval.

"Pigs will never be on the menu in this house as long as I live here. Sorry, not sorry."

"I'm just teasing you. I'm good with this. Have a seat. There's coffee in the pot," he said, pointing to the coffee maker on the counter. "I would have made you a cup, but I wasn't sure how you take it."

"I'm not a big coffee drinker. I prefer black tea."

He cocked his head to the side, looking perplexed.

"Oh. I'll drink it then. When you said you needed caffeine, I just assumed you meant coffee. I didn't realize…"

He didn't have to finish his sentence to remind me about how few personal details we knew about each other—right down to the basic things like coffee or tea. Yet here I was, consumed with unyielding seismic feelings after a night of unbridled passion. While we might not have been total strangers anymore, there was still so much we had yet to learn. Pushing the nagging worry aside, I filled the tea kettle with water and placed it on the stovetop to boil.

"Don't sweat it, Sloan. How could you know?"

"Next time—and there will be a next time—I'll remember," he promised as he placed two plates of piping hot eggs on the table for each of us.

*Next time.*

Anticipation coursed through me after hearing just those two words, only to be replaced with disgust as I watched him douse his eggs in ketchup.

"You put ketchup on your eggs?" I asked incredulously.

"Along with fifty-four percent of Americans."

"That's gross," I said with a laugh.

"I honestly prefer hot sauce, but you didn't have any in the fridge. Ketchup isn't bad, though. It's pretty tasty. You should try it."

I grimaced.

"No thanks. A little bit of salt and pepper is good enough for me."

Suddenly feeling ravenous, I focused my attention on my own plate and speared a piece of the scrambled egg with my fork. We ate in the quiet for a while, content to enjoy our start-of-the-day meal. When we finished, I stood to clear the dishes. As I was stacking them into the dishwasher, the doorbell rang.

"That's strange," I mused. "Who would that be?"

Sloan cocked up a curious brow, then shrugged and continued to sip the remains of his coffee. Drying my hands quickly on a dishtowel, I made my way to the front door. When I opened it, my mouth dropped open. Gabby was standing there beside a suitcase on the other side.

"Surprise!" she said with a wide grin. Without giving me a second to absorb my shock, she rushed in and wrapped me in a tight hug.

"Gabby! I'm so glad to see you! I wasn't expecting—" I stopped short when I felt her stiffen. Taking a step back, I followed her gaze and saw that she'd spotted Sloan. He was still sitting at the kitchen table, in all of his shirtless glory, looking just as stunned as I was.

"I wanted to surprise you, but it looks like I should have called," Gabby said somewhat indignantly as she pushed a lock of chestnut hair from her forehead. To say there was tension in the air was an understatement. I could only imagine what the scene looked like to her—and it was exactly as it appeared.

"No! I'm glad you're here. Austin mentioned that you were going to visit, but I wasn't expecting that to be for another few weeks. Come in. There's someone I'd like you to meet." Pulling her inside, I closed the door, took her suitcase, and wheeled it off to the side. I stood there between Sloan and Gabby like a pickle caught in the middle, then nervously motioned to Sloan. "Gabby, meet Sloan. Sloan, this is my best friend, Gabby."

Standing up, Sloan approached us and extended his hand to her.

"It's a pleasure to meet you, Gabby."

"Likewise. Kallie has told me all about you."

Sloan cocked up an eyebrow in surprise.

"Has she?"

"Yeah," she replied with a slow nod of her head. "She apparently skipped a few details."

I cleared my throat uncomfortably, knowing I owed Gabby a huge explanation. While I had talked to my friend several times over the past month, I'd never once mentioned my physical involvement with Sloan. All she knew up until three minutes ago was that he was my client.

"Gabs, I'll fill you in later. Right now, Sloan and I were just finishing up breakfast. Are you hungry? I can make you something."

"No, I'm good. I snacked on the plane. But thanks," she said, never taking her eyes off of Sloan. She seemed to be sizing him up. Her watchful gaze was suspicious, but Sloan seemed unruffled. If Gabby thought she could intimidate him, she would be sadly disappointed—Sloan was the master at intimidation.

"How about coffee then?" Sloan offered. "There's still some left in the pot."

"Coffee would be great. My flight left at five this morning, east coast time. I could use the boost."

Without another word, Sloan nodded and went back to the kitchen. After pouring Gabby a mug, he looked over his shoulder and said, "Cream? Sugar?"

"Just a little bit of cream, please," Gabby told him.

He handed her the mug of steaming java.

Thanks," Gabby said, and her scrutinizing stare seemed to soften. The fact that Sloan was shirtless, showing off his impeccable abs, was definitely helping the situation. Gabby was never one to shy away from a fine specimen of male beauty.

"No problem," he replied easily. "Well, ladies. I hate to cut this introduction short, but I should be heading out. I'm just going to grab my things, and I'll be off."

While Sloan was in the bedroom getting what I could only assume was his shirt, an awkward silence fell over the table. I offered Gabby a slight shrug and a smile, almost apologetic, as I waited for us to be alone so I could explain. She smiled at me in return, but her grin didn't quite meet her eyes.

When Sloan emerged from the bedroom, he was fully clothed with his keys in hand. Leaning over, he kissed the top of my head.

"I'll call you later," he said. I moved to stand and walk him to the door, but he stopped me. "It's all good. I can see myself out. You two have catching up to do. Gabby, it was nice to meet you. I hope to see you again soon."

I silently watched him walk to the front door. Once the door was closed, I turned back to Gabby. She had gotten up from the table to snatch a leftover piece of toast off the counter. When she looked back at me, she placed one hand on her hip and stared at me with accusation.

"You have some explaining to do," she said, pointing the piece of toast at me like it was a jousting lance. She sounded mad—and rightfully so.

"I know, I know. I should have told you. The problem was, I didn't even know how to explain it to myself, let alone somebody else. It just sort of happened."

"Happened? Last I knew, you broke it off with Dean and wanted to take time to reflect on things. I bumped up my vacation time and booked a flight here, assuming you would appreciate some girl time after just breaking up with your *fiancé*," she said, emphasizing the last word.

"He wasn't my fiancé," I reminded her.

"Whatever. Who cares about the technicalities—he proposed," she waved off, then tossed the uneaten toast back onto the plate on the counter. "Bottom line is that you and Dean were *serious*. Yet, when I get here, I see you're shacking up with the hottest guy I've seen since Bradley Cooper. Now spill it. And I want *all* the tea. How long has this been going on for?"

I chewed on my bottom lip, hesitant to tell her the truth. I was a terrible liar, and if I wasn't forthcoming from the beginning, she'd find out eventually. So when she narrowed her eyes with suspicion, I knew honesty would be best. Getting up from the table, I went into the family room and plopped down on the couch. Gabby took a seat in the armchair adjacent to me, crossed her arms, and waited not-so-patiently for me to continue.

"It began the first day I met him. I went to his house to introduce myself, lay out the PR strategy, and all that jazz. We talked for a while, then… Well, to make a long story short, when I was leaving, he kissed me. Don't ask me to explain how it happened—it just did."

"He kissed you! Wait—you were still with Dean at that point, right?"

"Yes."

"Did you kiss him back?"

I groaned.

"Yes, I kissed him back. And you don't need to remind me—I know I'm a terrible person."

"No. I don't think that. I just think you and Dean weren't meant to be. Everybody around you knew it. You just had to figure it out for yourself. Go on," she prompted with an impatient twirl of her finger.

"After I left his place, I knew I never would've let that happen if I was truly in love with Dean. Later that same day, I called Dean to break it off. You know all about that part."

"Yeah—and he was a complete dick about it, in my opinion. Not buying the ring because he was worried about losing interest in his bank account? I mean, really," she scoffed. "I still can't believe he admitted that to you."

"It doesn't matter," I brushed off, refusing to disclose how much it stung. I'd made my choice and felt confident it was the right one, but it was hard knowing the person I'd been with for over two years appreciated his money more than me.

"So, on day one, Sloan kissed you. Where did it go from there?" Gabby prompted.

I tossed her a meaningful look, unable to contain my smile.

"Well, we may or may not have had a super-steamy hookup in a public restroom…" I trailed off as her big brown eyes went wide. Her jaw dropped open, and she began mouthing words that wouldn't come out. For once, I'd made her speechless, and her disbelieving stare made me laugh.

"You did not!" she exclaimed after finding her voice.

"We did—but I immediately regretted it," I hurriedly added. "He's my client, after all, and getting romantically involved is so unprofessional. My father will kill me when or if he ever finds out. Not to mention, if things go south with Sloan, I risk forfeiting a bonus payout that I could really use. With all of that in mind, I avoided being anywhere alone with him for weeks afterward. It wasn't until last night when we finally made it… official, I guess you could say."

"Had sex?"

I rolled my eyes.

"Yes, Captain Obvious."

"So, how was it?"

I gave her a pointed stare, then made a zipper motion across my lips.

"Nope. I never kiss and tell."

"Aww, come on, Kallie! I haven't had sex in months. Just one little detail?"

I laughed.

"He was still here this morning. If it was bad, do you think I would have let him spend the night? But I will tell you this." I paused, looking for the right words. "With Sloan, there's this inexplicable connection. It's like I can physically and mentally feel my destiny shifting by cosmic force. The pull is so strong, I can't deny him—can't deny us. It's like we were meant to happen. I never felt that way with Dean."

"Oh, shit. This is serious, Kals."

"I know."

"So, now what?"

"Well, now that I gave in to it, there's nothing I can do but let the Fates take the reins and enjoy the ride."

Gabby smiled and cocked her head to the side thoughtfully. After a moment, she set her coffee mug on the table and came over to wrap me in a hug that warmed my soul.

"I've missed you so much. And I'm happy for you—really, I am. You seem content—relaxed even. I can see it in your face and your posture. And, more importantly, this is the first time I've heard you *sound* like you in a long time. You've always had this energy about you that people could feel before you even uttered a single word. It was like Dean was suppressing that and all of the little quirks I love about you. I'm so happy you're back."

I squeezed her tight and blinked back tears of joy. I was grateful for her friendship, knowing I could count on her to always see me for who I was. Her presence brought balance to my world, and it felt so good to have her there.

***

Four hours later, Gabby and I were lounging outside on the patio, drinking piña coladas, and poring over the twenty-seven tabs we had opened between both of our laptops. She was only here for a long weekend, and I'd decided to dip into my limited savings and plan a short trip north to Napa Valley to make the most of my time with her. As she hemmed and hawed over which bed and breakfast we should stay at, I sipped on the coconut rum cocktail and mapped out wineries.

"I know this is super last minute. Are you sure you can get away?" she asked.

"It's not a problem. I don't have anything booked for Sloan until Monday afternoon. It's just over a six-hour drive to Napa Valley, not accounting for any traffic we're likely to encounter. If we leave tomorrow morning, that will give us Friday evening, all day Saturday, and the first half of Sunday. It's too bad there aren't any last-minute flights into Sacramento."

"A drive is fine with me. I hate flying—and even more so after the flight out here. The turbulence was brutal. Besides, I have to get back on a plane on Monday. The fewer flights I have to take, the better." She paused, clicked a few keys on the keyboard, then put her feet up on the empty chair next to her, showing off her perfectly manicured red toenails. "Okay. The B&B is all booked. We check in tomorrow at three. Checkout is Sunday at one in the afternoon."

"Perfect!"

"Did you decide on the wineries we should hit?"

"I don't think we should drive around ourselves—especially since we'll be drinking. I was thinking about booking this wine train tour—scenic views, antique rail car, wine tastings. It sounds fun."

"Yes—book it! Ooh, I'm so excited!"

Raising my frosted glass to clink it with hers, I grinned ear to ear. "Road trip!"

# Chapter Fifteen

*Sloan*

I woke up Friday morning feeling like something was missing. I rolled to the side, reached out, and came up with a fistful of cold sheets. It put me in a foul mood. After spending only one night in Kallie's bed, it already felt strange to wake up without her in my arms. I wanted her with me—always—and as I remembered her call last night to tell me about her weekend trip with Gabby, it made my mood sink even lower. I wouldn't get to see her again until Monday.

Flipping so I was flat on my back once more, I stared at the ceiling. Practice races were happening at Motor Club Speedway later on today. A day at the track would be better than sitting around my place sulking. The sooner I showered and headed out, the sooner I'd be able to push Kallie's absence from my mind. Shoving a frustrated hand through my hair, I swung my legs over the side of the bed. When I stood, a stabbing pain shot through my hip.

"Shit!" I yelled to the empty room, grabbing the nightstand to steady myself. Chronic pain after any joint replacement was common. For me, mornings were always the worst because that's when the muscles surrounding the joint were the stiffest. I knew better than to put too much weight on my left leg right away. Instinctively, I opened my nightstand drawer to reveal the little orange bottle of painkillers. There were still two remaining pills. I hadn't taken one since before meeting Kallie.

Guilt clawed at my chest, knowing she would disapprove if I took one—especially since I didn't really need them for pain management anymore. It usually took a good thirty minutes or so for the muscles to naturally loosen, but once they did, I was generally fine as long as I made sure not to put too much weight on that side of my body throughout the day.

Slamming the drawer closed, I decided to wait out the pain. After a few minutes, the sharp stinging began to subside into a dull ache. Carefully moving toward the master bathroom, I looked forward to the long, hot shower that was sure to help loosen me up.

---

"Something feels off," Cooper said, elevating his voice to be heard over the music blaring from the grandstand of Motor Club Speedway. "The Distance" by Cake was always a staple as pit crews scrambled to prepare for the next practice race, but the music seemed extra loud today.

I'd just arrived at the track twenty minutes earlier. I hadn't expected Cooper to be there, as his team wasn't on the schedule today. However, he'd been invited to observe and give pointers to a racing team as they practiced. The driver was a friend of ours, Tyler McDermott. His recent success in the European circuit made him a favorite to win the Motorsports International Legacy League, more commonly known as the MILL.

"Feels off in what way?" I asked.

"Shit has been going wrong all day," he explained. "The crew just replaced the rear bearings for the second time today, and the car has only been around the track a few times. That shouldn't be happening. I'm trying to think of what the team might be overlooking."

"Has anyone on the team looked at the clutch plate? When I first arrived, I noticed the car sliding around a bit."

"Yeah, everything checked out."

"I'm sure it's fine, Cooper. Tyler has a good team. They'll figure it out."

"I hope so. Tyler needs everything to be perfect for the MILL. Bets are on him to win, but he needs the money more than the title."

I frowned and turned my gaze away from the track to look at Cooper. There was an urgency to his voice that made me think there was more to the story.

"The money? Tyler makes a good buck from endorsements. I heard Kapton Motor Oil paid him a mint to promote their product. Don't tell me he blew through it all."

"You didn't hear?"

"Hear what?"

"Man, you really have been out of the loop, haven't you? I'm talking about his wife, Amy."

"What about her?"

"She was diagnosed with an aggressive form of cancer about six months ago. I don't remember what kind, but the prognosis is bad. My heart breaks for both of them. They've spent almost every penny they have on her chemo. Tyler said he wanted to take her to Switzerland for some experimental treatment, but the price tag is insane. So, as I said, he could really use the prize money from a win—not to mention all the extra endorsement money that will follow."

I shook my head over the devastating news.

"Wow… I didn't know. Tyler and I used to talk all the time, but I haven't spoken to many people since my accident. I feel bad that I didn't know. I should call him."

"You had a lot going on. I'm sure he didn't want to worry you."

"Still, Tyler is a good guy. I met Amy a few times—a real sweetheart. For both of their sakes, I hope he wins this." I stared absently at the track and rubbed my chin thoughtfully. "What about doing a fundraiser? If we pulled in enough drivers, I'm sure we could raise the money he needs."

"Ro is looking into it, but I'm not sure if she made any headway. Maybe you could ask Kallie to get with her on it."

"That's not a bad idea. I—"

The rumbling sound of a car engine cut me off. Whatever was wrong with the rear bearings must have been fixed because Tyler's car pulled out onto the track once more. Cooper and I moved up to the bottom row of the spectator stand to watch the open-wheel single-seater take position.

Within minutes, the car was moving around the track at a blistering speed. I thought Tyler took the cornering speed a little too slow, not utilizing the aerodynamic downforce the car naturally generated to push the car down onto the track. I was about to comment on it but paused when I saw he hadn't gotten back up to speed on the straightaway. Then I spotted the smoke.

Instinctively, I gripped the railing in front of me until my knuckles turned white. Everything happened so fast. The only thing I could do was watch helplessly as Tyler's car—its back end on fire—spun out of control and crashed into the center barrier.

Everything around me glitched into slow motion. Cooper hopped the rail and took off running. The fire marshals scrambled. I heard screams from the observers and yelling from the pit crew, but it was all a distant echo. I couldn't move or look away from the wreckage. Completely frozen to the spot, it was as if Tyler's crash were my own, and in that moment, I was unable to prevent myself from being thrown back in time to that day.

*I slip my arms into the sleeves of my flame-resistant racing suit and zip up the front. Walking over to the waiting open-wheeled race car, I use all the energy I have to push down my anger over the information I found out about my father. My sole focus must be on the practice race I'm about to run.*

*I climb into the car and allow a crew member to adjust the Hans device until I am safely secure in the head and neck restraint. Gripping the steering wheel, I wait for Benjamin to signal me out onto the track to join the pack of ten cars. Once he does, I move into position at the back of the group. The purpose of today's practice is to teach the rookies how to take the lead from behind. Nothing else matters except the cars on the track.*

*When the flag drops, so does my foot on the accelerator. Moving the steering wheel from left to right, I weave between cars and make my way to the front. I keep my eye on who I'd pass, knowing I've yet to reach Tripp Lucas, an arrogant S.O.B. who is still a few cars ahead. Little does he know, he's about to get schooled.*

*The engine revs as the wind whips around the car. I feel the tires roaring beneath me as I nose just ahead of Tripp. I shift, and the car lurches. A rush of adrenaline surges, making me feel alive in ways only racing could. The only thing that could make it better is if this wasn't just for practice but the real deal.*

*As I creep past Tripp, he taps the gas and pushes slightly ahead of me. I do the same, the noses of our cars playing a virtual tug of war. When he gets the advantage, I don't bother to chance a glance in his direction. I know the cocky bastard is probably smirking. He doesn't know I'm just toying with him. Making him think he is winning is all part of the psychological game. I haven't even begun to push my car to its limits yet. The rookie has a lot to learn.*

*As we whip through the first lap, I catch a glimpse of my mother standing next to Cooper and Benjamin in the pit lane. The image of them is fleeting, their forms nothing but a blur as I speed past—and it's a good thing, too. The last thing I want is to see her. My teeth clench as I tamp down my anger once more and focus on the turn ahead.*

*I bank left around the bend and prepare for the straightaway. Easing my foot off the clutch, I shift into final gear and press the gas pedal to the floor. I can see Tripp's car losing speed in my peripheral, and I grin. I have him now. When I think it's safe to look, I cast my gaze in his direction. Sheer panic is written all over his face, knowing he is about to be lost in my dust. Instinctively, my grin widens.*

*However, my smile is short-lived. It takes me less than half a second to realize Tripp's panic had nothing to do with losing the race and everything to do with the smoke billowing from the engine of a slowing car up ahead.*

*"Son of a bitch! Where's the goddamn caution flag?"*

*I have a split second to decide. If I swerve left, I will hit Tripp's car. If I brake too hard, I will risk being hit by the two cars right on my tail. My only hope is to ease off the gas, slowing just enough for Tripp to pass me so I can get around the smoking car. I remove my foot from the gas, hoping Tripp will take the cue. Thankfully, he does—but he isn't fast enough.*

*The slowing car comes closer and closer. A shiver of fear races down my spine. Officially out of time, I have no choice but to bank left. I hear a crunch and immediately know the front bumper of my car connected with Tripp's rear. My car spins out, skidding along the track backward. I am all but blind as I brace for impact.*

Whether a few minutes or a few hours had passed, I couldn't be sure. All at once, everything seemed to fast forward into real time. I saw Tyler's body being carried away on a stretcher. Cooper appeared at my side, his breathing heavy.

"He's alive. I'm not sure of the extent of his injuries. They're taking him by helicopter to Bayfront Hospital. It'll take me a while to get there by car. I'm going to leave now. Do you want to—" Cooper stopped short and grabbed my arm. "Sloan. Hey, man. Are you alright? You're as white as a sheet."

Slowly, I turned my head to look at him.

"Yeah, it's just that… the crash. It reminded me…"

Cooper released my arm, stepped back, and shook his head.

"Shit. I can't imagine what seeing that must have been like for you. Don't worry. Tyler was conscious and talking. I don't think his injuries are life-threatening. It was nothing like your accident. Do you want to ride with me to the hospital?"

"It's all good. You go on. I'm going to hang back. Maybe look into what went wrong with the car."

Cooper seemed wary as he studied my face, but I ignored him and turned my focus back to the track where the fire crew was still dousing the flames.

"I don't like the idea of leaving you here alone. Are you sure?"

He sounded torn.

"I'm sure. Tyler needs you more than I do," I replied without looking at him.

At some point, Cooper must have left. I didn't remember him walking away, nor did I remember the long drive back to my house. One minute I was at the track, and the next minute I found myself at my kitchen table with an unopened bottle of Jack and my last two remaining oxycodone pills sitting in front of me.

# Chapter Sixteen

*Kallie*

Three hours into the drive to Napa Valley, Gabby and I sang along with The Ataris—completely off-key and not caring one little bit. "Boys of Summer" was one of our favorites, and it brought back so many memories from our younger years.

Having just driven through the flat and dusty terrain of Bakersfield, we'd finally gotten past the obstruction of oil pumping units and agricultural fields to a more scenic route—if one could call it such. The narrow asphalt road on which we traveled was full of twists and turns, with steep drop-offs. I nervously looked ahead, seeing nothing but tumbleweeds and potholes to avoid.

"You seem antsy," Gabby said.

I eyed her questioningly.

"Antsy?"

"Yeah. I wonder why they call it that anyway—antsy. It's kind of a dumb word when you think about it. Ants don't seem anxious. They seem pretty calm and hardworking when building their little anthills."

I laughed.

"I guess I never thought about it. But then again, why do we call someone 'nutty' when they're acting crazy? Or what about harebrained? I don't think the peanuts and rabbits of the world would take kindly to the reference," I pointed out.

"True."

Glancing at my cell phone mounted on the dash, I flicked my finger against it as if somehow the action would spark cell service. My phone had been fading from one bar to no bars ever since we got off I-5 and headed toward Bakersfield.

"Gabby, I have no clue where we are."

"Just keep driving toward the mountains, then we'll double back the way we came."

"Mountains? All I see are big brown hills. What looked like mountains from a distance turned out to be a whole lot of nothing."

"Because we haven't gotten there yet. Besides, it's an adventure! For someone who's usually so free-spirited, you're worrying too much. Just go with it."

"I don't think we should go any further. I'm going to turn around. I'm getting really nervous about being in the middle of nowhere without a cell phone signal. I mean, what if—" I was interrupted by a loud thud from underneath the car. "Oh my god! Did I just hit something?"

"I don't think so. I didn't see an animal or anything."

My heart sank, thinking I may have run over a furry critter when I distractedly looked at the GPS map.

"Gabs, I'm pretty sure I just killed Thumper."

However, the drumming sound continued, making me all but certain I hadn't hit anything. I began to wonder if there might be something wrong with the car itself. My concern grew as the incessant thump-thump noise continued over and over again in a steady rhythm.

Gabby turned down the radio to hear where the sound was coming from. Then she laughed and pointed to the side view mirror.

"No, you didn't kill Thumper, but you may have run over a nail or something sharp. Or maybe it was the pothole you hit a mile back. I'm pretty sure you have a flat tire."

"A flat! Why are you laughing? That's not funny!" I scowled, annoyed that she somehow found this humorous, and cautiously maneuvered the car to the side of the road until it came to a stop. Looking at my phone once again, I saw the words 'no service' where the little bars should have been. "Do you have cell signal?"

Gabby pulled her phone from her purse and glanced at the screen.

"Nope."

"What are we going to do now? Without cell service, neither one of us can call AAA."

"I can change a tire. No sweat. I've got this, *chica*. Pop the trunk."

I looked under the dash in search of the trunk release as Gabby climbed out. After finding it, I killed the engine and joined her at the back of the car. She stood with her hands on her hips, staring down into the trunk, seeming perplexed.

"What's wrong?" I asked.

"Tools. There's a tire and a jack here, but no lug wrench."

"So what does that mean?"

"It means I can't change the tire."

"You have got to be kidding me." She just shrugged, and I threw up my arms in exasperation. Pinching the bridge of my nose, I began to pace. I knew I shouldn't have listened to her and stayed straight on the route to our intended destination. Turning back to the car, I opened the door to the backseat, pulled our luggage out, and set the bags down on the side of the road.

"What are you doing, Kals?"

"I'm looking for tools. Maybe the rental agency put them in the backseat for some reason."

"I doubt it," she said skeptically.

Glancing back at her, I let out a breath in frustration.

"Maybe, maybe not. Are you just going to stand there watching me, or are you going to help me look?"

Gabby went to the opposite side of the car and began to search around. We lifted the floormats and flipped down the back seat but came up empty-handed.

"Damnit!" I cursed, slamming my hand on the top of the car.

"I'm sorry."

"Not for nothing, but when you spotted the mountains and wanted to take pictures, my gut told me it was a bad idea. But no—instead, I listened to you when you said, 'We have time, Kallie. Just detour through Bakersfield.' Now, here we are, somewhere on route 178, with a flat and no way to call for a tow. Even if we could fix it, I have no idea how to get us back."

"I'm really am sorry, Kallie," she repeated. "But, in my defense, the rental company is to blame for the missing tools. I would have been able to change the tire if it weren't for that."

"We should have just stuck to GPS. At least then we wouldn't have ended up in the middle of nowhere," I grumbled. "The last thing we passed was a gas station about ten miles back."

"Someone is bound to come down this road eventually. Until then, I packed wine."

I tossed her a skeptical look.

"Wine? How is that supposed to help?"

"Wine always helps," she said, her voice full of optimism as she began rummaging through her suitcase on the side of the road. "When I went out this morning to grab snacks for the trip, I picked up a couple of bottles for us to drink at the hotel."

As I watched her struggle with the corkscrew, I couldn't help but laugh and hoped she was right. Someone would have to drive by eventually. Until then, all we could do was wait it out.

Closing the trunk, I climbed onto the back of the car and took a seat. The sun was blisteringly hot, and my hair was sticky on my neck. Using the hair tie I had wrapped around my wrist, I bound the pink and blonde into a loose bun on top of my head. Feeling the heat just as I was, Gabby mimicked my actions and then handed me a bottle of white.

"I didn't think to pack cups," she told me after she took a swig straight from a bottle that she'd kept for herself.

"I don't think we need to worry about being civilized when there is literally no sign of civilization anywhere," I joked. Holding up my bottle, I clinked it to hers, then took a sip. "If it weren't so damn hot, I'd suggest we walk back to the gas station."

"I second that. I'm not walking anywhere in this heat," she agreed.

"What did you buy for snacks?"

"Lots of stuff." Reaching into the backseat, she procured two large Ziplock bags of goodies, then took a seat next to me on the back of the car.

"If Sloan were here, I'd bet he would be able to change the tire without tools," I said through a mouthful of kettle chips.

"There's no way to MacGyver your way through changing a tire. I don't care how sexy he is—he's not a miracle worker. What we need is a fairy godmother to come bibbiti-bobbiti-boo us out of this."

"Maybe. Chip?' I offered, holding out the bag.

"Sure." As she crunched away, her expression was thoughtful.

"What are you thinking about, Gabby?"

"Honestly? I'm thinking about you and Sloan. I'm still a little surprised by it. I mean, I'm not judging you in the least bit—that man is fine as hell. But I am curious about what's going through your mind. Is this just a fling to get over Dean, or is it something more? Rebounds can be fun but also destructive if you aren't careful."

I considered her question for a moment, not entirely sure of the answer.

"It can only be a rebound if I had a broken heart. The crazy thing is, I never felt like I did. Sure, I was sad for a few days after Dean and I split, but I wasn't sad because I missed him. I was sad because I felt like I wasted two years of my life with someone who didn't make me happy. As for how I feel about Sloan… It's tough to say. It's not just a fling, but it's too early to tell if there's more to it. I just know I felt something strong the minute I met him. I've been thinking about the gypsy's warning a lot too. You remember Madame Lavinia, right?"

"Yeah. How could I forget? She predicted I'd have a tragic accident, and then I broke my arm the next day. I know it was just a coincidence, but it was super spooky at the time."

"What if it wasn't a coincidence?"

"You can't be serious." She paused and looked at me incredulously. "Kals, please don't tell me you've been carrying around what she said to you about sunsets and doomed love for all of these years."

"I can't help it. There are just too many coincidences to ignore. She's one of the reasons I spent a month avoiding being anywhere alone with Sloan. I was nervous. But I have to wonder—"

"Kallie, listen to me. It's not—"

"No, hang on. Just hear me out. I recently began to think I misinterpreted the warnings. Getting lost in my emotions and worries may be the reason she predicted destructive love. Perhaps I've been the one who's been getting in my own way by overthinking everything. Maybe it has nothing to do with Sloan—or any other guy who may have kissed me at sunset—and everything to do with the way I let my emotions rule me."

Gabby's eyes grew wide, and she looked genuinely worried. When she spoke, her tone was apprehensive.

"Oh, no… You've been stressing way too much about this, Kals. I need to tell you something, but you have to promise you won't get mad."

I chuckled.

"How can I promise that if I don't know what you're going to say?"

"Good point," she responded with an ironic smirk. "What I have to tell you has to do with Austin."

I rolled my eyes.

"Oh, God. What did my brother do now?"

"I swear, Kallie. I thought you knew, or I would have told you. I didn't know you were carrying this around all of this time and—" She stopped short, and I narrowed my eyes.

"And what? What did he do, Gabby?"

She sighed and shook her head.

"When we were in high school, the two of us used to play Charlie-Charlie all the time. One of the times we were playing, Austin wanted to join in. Do you remember that?"

"Yeah, why?"

"Austin sort of… well, he moved the pencil to make you believe that the guy who kissed you during a sunset would be your soulmate."

"Sort of?" I said with a laugh. After taking another sip from my wine bottle, I smiled. "When we were playing, I suspected Austin of deliberately pushing the pencil. Why would I be mad about that? It was just a silly game. I haven't really thought about it since."

"Well…that's not all, which brings me to the psychic gypsy. Austin knew how freaked out you were about my so-called tragic accident, so he may or may not have paid off the psychic to tell you all of those things."

I froze, unable to find words as I processed what she was saying. When I finally found my voice, the words came out slow and laced with disbelief.

"May or may not have paid her off?"

"Kallie, as I said—I swear I thought you knew. I would have told you before now had I known. Austin thought it would be funny to get the gypsy to say the opposite of what the Charlie-Charlie game said. He knew it would mess with you. His logic was to make sure you didn't get too serious with a guy when you went away to college. I suppose it was his twisted way of being an overprotective brother, but I thought he would have told you the truth by now. Are you mad?"

I stayed quiet, looking down at the busted-up asphalt road for a moment before bringing the wine bottle to my lips. I took a long pull. I always knew there was a possibility that the psychic was a fraud, just as I knew there was potential to change any negative reading from happening in the future by my own free will. I just never thought I would be betrayed by Austin that way.

"No, I'm not mad. Just feeling stupid, I guess."

"If it makes you feel any better, I don't think Austin thought you were still hanging on to this either. It was only a joke—we were practically kids at the time. You know he wouldn't deliberately hurt you."

I gave her a small smile.

"I know he wouldn't."

I stared at the endless road covered in dust and tumbleweeds feeling disempowered. I felt foolish and even found myself second-guessing my tarot cards. Something that once gave me peace, comfort, and guidance during difficult times suddenly seemed childish and trivial. It was as if everything I believed was just an illusion.

---

Darkness had fallen hours ago, yet not a single car had passed. We'd consumed most of the snacks, and there wasn't a drop of wine left. Resigned to spending the night in the car, Gabby and I decided to sleep in shifts. It was my turn to keep watch. We agreed that at daybreak, before it got too hot, we'd walk back to the gas station we hadn't wanted to walk to when the sun was high in the sky. Our only saving grace was knowing we had a few bottles of water in the car to get us through the hike.

I looked out the front windshield at the star-filled sky. Being so far away from the city lights, thousands of twinkling dots could be seen as far as the eye could see. For me, stargazing was like dreaming with your eyes open. I was convinced that our destiny was written on the very stars which I looked upon, and no matter what anyone did to change it, the outcome was always fated. I'd always been someone with immense energy and an ambitious drive, and I believed anything was possible if I just followed my path. But after hearing about Austin's ruse, I now felt disenchanted, and it upset me on a profound level.

As I sat there in the dark, I began to wonder about every single aspect of my life. I had obsessed for years over the tiniest details, always trying to find the deeper meaning to reassure me of my path to happiness and success and also help to prepare me for anything terrible looming on the horizon.

*What if it's all a bunch of hocus pocus and misguided intention?*

It was too much to process in my exhausted state, and I fought back a yawn. The combination of the hot sun during the day and consuming too much wine was a terrible mix for someone who needed to stay awake half the night. I glanced at my phone to check the time. It was after one in the morning, and I wasn't due to wake Gabby until two.

My eyelids felt heavy, and I blinked rapidly in an attempt to keep them open. I thought about getting out of the car to stretch but was nervous about doing so after hearing the high, quavering cries of coyotes from somewhere nearby. Inside of the car was safer, especially since luck was clearly not on my side today.

*Perhaps if I closed my eyes for just a minute…*

# Chapter Seventeen

*Kallie*

I woke to the sun blazing through the windshield. I blinked, becoming aware of a relentless knocking on the driver's side window. Turning my head, I nearly jumped out of my skin to see a gray-bearded man with a wide-brimmed hat peering through the window. Glancing at Gabby, I noticed she was still fast asleep.

"Gabby!" I hissed as I shook her. "Wake up!"

Groggily, she opened her eyes and jumped the same way I had when she saw the man.

"Shit! What time is it?" she asked.

"I don't know," I told her as I turned the key in the ignition so I could power down the window. Glancing up at the man, I smiled and said, "Hey, there! Sorry. You startled me."

"It's alright. Everything okay?" he asked.

I pointed over my shoulder in the direction of the deflated tire.

"We caught a flat tire last night, and we couldn't get cell service to call for a tow."

"You ladies slept here all night? Holy smokes—that wasn't too fun now, was it? You never know who could come around the bend in these parts. You're lucky nothing happened to you," he added with a shake of his head. "You got a spare? I can change it for you so you can be on your way."

"I have a spare, and it's so nice of you to offer, but unfortunately, the tools are missing from the trunk."

"That's no problem. I keep a toolbox on the tractor," he told me and thumbed toward a large-wheeled yellow farming tractor parked on the opposite side of the road. "Just give me a minute to get what I need."

"That would be great! Thank you so much!" I said, not hiding my immediate relief. After he walked away, I turned to Gabby. "It looks like our fairy godmother sent help."

"Thank goodness, too. I'm stiff as hell," she complained as she opened the passenger door to stretch her legs. I followed her lead and watched as the man walked back toward my car, lugging a large red toolbox. When he reached us, he set the box down and extended his hand to me.

"I should have introduced myself. My name is George Calhoun."

"I'm Kallie, and this is Gabby. Believe me when I say it's more than just a pleasure to meet you," I joked. "If you hadn't shown up, we'd be walking ten miles to the nearest gas station to find a payphone."

"I can believe that. Cell phone service around Bakersfield is known to be the worst in the country. There's not much around these parts. Where were you ladies headed to, anyway?"

"Napa Valley from Santa Monica, but we took a minor detour and ended up a little lost," Gabby said.

"A minor detour? You're halfway to Death Valley. I'll say you were lost!"

He shook his head and chuckled, then sat on the ground next to the flat tire and began to work. Fifteen minutes later, the full-sized spare was secure. George stood up and wiped the dirt off his hands on his tan coveralls.

"You should be all set now. The air in the tire is a little low. You'll want to fill it at the next gas station. Just try to avoid any potholes in the meantime."

"I can't thank you enough," I told him. "Is there anything I can do to repay you? I have a bit of cash on me and—"

"Don't you worry your pretty little head about it. You don't need to give me anything. I'm happy to help," he assured, then smiled to reveal the deep age lines on his tanned face. After he collected his tools, we bid our farewells and watched as he puttered down the road on his tractor.

"Man, did we ever catch a break!" Gabby said.

"For sure. At the rate we were going, I thought we'd never make it to Napa Valley. You ready to go?"

"Yes, but…about Napa Valley." She hesitated, and I was pretty sure I knew what she was thinking. By the time we got to Napa and checked into our room, the wineries would most likely be closed for the day—

and forget making it there in time for the wine tour by train. While we could still go on as planned tomorrow, it seemed pointless to drive all that way for just one day.

"Do you want to scrap the trip and just head back to my place? I'm sure we can call the B&B and get a refund if we explain what happened."

"Kals, I'm so glad you said that! After yesterday and last night, I just can't get excited about it anymore. I was afraid to say so because it was my idea to detour in the first place. I just think I've had enough adventure for a while," she said with a small laugh. I couldn't agree more.

As I drove back in the direction we came, Gabby repeatedly checked our cell phones for service. We stopped at the next gas station to add air to the tire just as George suggested we do, asked for directions, then continued on our way. The clerk's explanation of how to get back to where we needed to be was meandering and hard to follow, so I just tried to follow the landmarks I remembered passing, even if they were scarce.

When we reached Bakersfield, I sighed with relief to know we were heading in the right direction. And when our cell phones started chiming with notifications, I nearly wept.

"Finally, we have service!" Gabby announced. "It's weak, but it's something. I'll pull up the directions back to your place, then screenshot them in case we lose service again."

"Good idea."

"You've got a bunch of voicemails on your phone. Want me to play them on speaker?"

"Sure."

My mother's voice was the first to sound through the speaker.

"Hey, Kallie! It's mom. I was just calling to see if you and Gabby got to Napa okay. Call me when you get this."

My mom was a forever worrier, so her message was no surprise. However, the following message was unexpected.

"Kallie, it's Cooper Davis. When you can, give me a call back."

As he rattled off his phone number, I wondered how he'd gotten my number but then realized he must have gotten it from Rochele. When my inbox advanced to the next message, I was shocked to hear Cooper's voice again.

"Kallie, it's Cooper again. Hey, I'm sorry to bother you, but I can't reach Sloan. I was wondering if you've heard from him. Give me a buzz back."

I frowned as a computerized voice told me it was the end of my messages. I glanced at Gabby in confusion.

"That's strange. I wonder why he's trying to get a hold of Sloan."

"Kals, I just looked at your call log. That guy Cooper called three more times after the last message. Sloan called once, too, but didn't leave a message. You don't think something bad happened, do you?"

My stomach did a nervous flip, and I bit my lower lip.

"I don't know. Can you dial Sloan for me? His number is in my contacts."

"Sure."

I waited as the phone rang. After the fourth ring, a loud beeping sound came through the line signaling the call had failed.

"Lost service again," Gabby said.

"Damn it. Did you manage to pull up the driving directions at least?"

"Yeah. I grabbed them on my phone while your voicemails were playing."

"Good. That's all that matters. I can try calling Sloan again when we get home."

Still, despite my words, Sloan *did* matter, and I was concerned over why he wasn't answering his phone when Cooper called him. Whatever it was, it must have been serious enough for Cooper to reach out to me. What it could be was anyone's guess, but I couldn't shake the angst-ridden feelings for the remainder of the drive back to Santa Monica.

---

"The idea of a shower never sounded so good," Gabby said as we dumped our bags in the front hall of my house. "I'm going to take one if that's okay."

"Go for it. I'm going to try to reach Sloan again. I'll shower after. Just don't use up all the hot water," I added, knowing Gabby's penchant for long, hot showers.

"I won't," she promised, but I knew better. If I she wasn't quick, there was no doubt I'd be washing under lukewarm water.

After Gabby disappeared down the hall, I pulled my cell from the back pocket of my jeans and dialed Sloan's number. It was my third time calling him since we gained steady signal strength, but there was no answer once again. I began to pace. Feeling frustrated, I pulled up my missed call log to locate Cooper's number. He answered after the second ring.

"Kallie, hey. I'm glad you called back."

"Yeah, sorry. I just got your messages this morning. I was on a road trip, got lost, and had no cell service. It's a long story. Anyway, I've tried calling Sloan, but he hasn't picked up for me either. Is everything okay?"

I heard Cooper sigh on the other end of the line.

"There was an accident at the track. A friend of ours, Tyler McDermott, was banged up pretty good and was sent by helicopter to the hospital."

"Oh, no! Is he okay?"

"He'll recover. But he's not the reason I called you. I'm worried about Sloan. He was at the track when it happened. I left him there to go to the hospital, but I didn't like how he looked. I think the crash really shook him up. When I called him later, and he didn't answer multiple times, I started to get even more worried. I have a meeting that I can't miss this afternoon, but I planned to head over to his place to check on him as soon as I finish. I should be able to get over there by three."

Glancing up at the clock hanging on the kitchen wall, I saw it was nearing noon. If I hurried in the shower, I could be to Sloan's place by one.

"No, it's okay. Thanks. I'll head over there myself in a bit."

"Are you sure? I don't mind. I just want to make sure he didn't do anything stupid."

"It's all good. When I see him, I'll make sure he gives you a call."

After thanking Cooper for reaching out, I ended the call and went to the front hall to grab my suitcase, then began rummaging quickly through it to find my shower toiletries. A few minutes later, Gabby came down the hall with a towel wrapped around her head.

"Fifteen minutes. That might be a record for me!" she joked. "There should be plenty of hot water left."

"Thanks, Gabs. Listen, I hate to leave you alone since you'll only be here for a short time, but I need to go out for a bit. I just spoke with Cooper, and I'm worried about Sloan. I'm going to check on him. Will you be okay here for a few hours?"

"I'm a big girl. Do what you need to do. While you're gone, I'll take advantage of that glorious pool you have in the yard."

"Are you sure?"

"Positive."

I smiled, grateful for her easy understanding, then hurried to the bathroom to shower.

# Chapter Eighteen

*Kallie*

Shortly after one, I pulled into Sloan's driveway. His black Chevy Camaro was parked haphazardly in the middle of the drive. It was at an angle, and I couldn't pull up all the way. That wasn't a good sign. After ensuring my back end wasn't sticking out in the street, I parked near the end of the drive, then got out and walked up to the front door.

After ringing the bell four times, it was clear he wasn't going to answer, so I walked around to the back. Thankfully, the gate to the backyard wasn't locked. As I rounded the back corner of the house, my steps faltered when I saw a patio chair tipped on end and the glass patio doors partially open. My stomach dropped, and panic began to set in.

I hurried toward the open doors. Once inside, I looked around but didn't see Sloan. The place was a mess—but in a different way than it had been when I was there the first time. Takeout containers and clothes no longer littered the floor, but almost every piece of furniture had either been shifted to awkward angles or knocked over. One of the end-table lamps had toppled onto the floor, and the glass top of the coffee table had slid to balance precariously on the frame. Automatically, I bent to reposition it so it didn't fall and break.

As I stood back up, I froze when I spotted an orange prescription bottle on the floor. The lid was off, and it appeared empty. Picking it up, I read the label.

It was oxycodone.

The pit in my stomach grew.

"Sloan?" I called out in alarm. I listened for his answer as I picked up the lamp and put it back in its proper place on the table. Stepping over an empty bottle of Jack Daniels, I made my way upstairs with the hope of finding Sloan there.

I tried not to worry about what the empty pill bottle and liquor could signify, but my anxiety only grew with every step I took. Halfway to the top, I heard a loud bang, then a thud. I gasped and began to sprint up the last remaining stairs. I hurried along the hallway toward the sounds. At the end of the hall, I came to what I could only assume was Sloan's bedroom. The bed was unmade, and the room reeked of whiskey—but that wasn't what caused fear to wrap like a vice around my heart. It was seeing Sloan lying face down on the floor that made my blood turn cold.

"Sloan!" Rushing to him, I skidded to a halt and tried to flip him over. His dead weight made it a struggle, but I eventually got him to shift onto his back. He looked up at me with glazed eyes, almost as if he couldn't focus. Judging by the smell of him, he probably couldn't. His pupils looked normal and not constricted like I'd expected them to be. That was a good sign. It meant he might not have taken the prescription drugs after all.

I pressed my lips together in a tight line, glanced around the room, and tried to think of what to do. There was a balcony off of Sloan's bedroom, and he was lying just inside the open doors. The wrought-iron curtain rod hanging over the door had been pulled from the brackets, falling until it skewered one wall. My quick guess was that he tripped coming inside and tried to grab ahold of something to stop himself from falling. The rod puncturing the wall was most likely the source of the bang I'd heard, and the loud thud was probably Sloan's heavy body hitting the floor.

He groaned and attempted to sit up. I quickly shifted to help him. That's when I noticed he had another bottle of Jack—this one half-empty—clutched tightly in his hand. Despite his fall, he managed not to spill a drop. I did a mental calculation, combining the bottle he was holding with the empty one at the base of the stairs, to figure out how much he'd likely consumed since last night.

Fighting to push himself up with his free arm, the two of us managed to get him into a sitting position. Shifting his body, he leaned back against the side of the bed, almost as if it were too much of an effort to stay upright on his own. Dark circles shadowed his eyes, and his face was pale. He looked fragile and broken.

*Have I been blind over the past month? How did I not know he could be triggered so easily?*

Speechless, I could only stare at him. I was kicking myself for failing to ask more probing questions about his accident and what happened with his mother and father. As a trained PR agent, I knew how to ask the hard questions, yet I'd avoided them and allowed my personal feelings to get in the way.

After a moment, he seemed to regain some semblance of focus and glared at me.

"What are you doing here?" he slurred viciously. I flinched from the venom in his voice. I'd never heard him talk to me like that before.

"I talked to Cooper. He told me about the crash. I was worried when you didn't answer the phone, so I came here to see if you were okay."

At my words, his face momentarily softened.

"I called you."

"I know, but you didn't leave a message. Sloan, what happened?"

"No rainbows," he mumbled instead of answering me. Reaching up, he fumbled the blue extensions I'd clipped in today. "Why blue?"

"Blue is when I'm sad. I was sad when Cooper told me what happened. I'm even sadder now to see you like this. Why, Sloan? Why did you do this to yourself?"

Instantly, his menacing look was back. He scowled and tried to stand up. I quickly moved to help him, but he batted my hand away.

"I've got it!" he snarled. Once on his feet, he swayed a bit but didn't topple over like I thought he might. With him standing at full height, I was able to take in his appearance. He was clad in nothing but a pair of boxer briefs, and there was a long cut extending from his right shoulder to his sternum. It wasn't deep, but it would still need tending to.

"Sloan, you've scraped yourself up pretty good. Let me get something to clean—"

"If you've come here to save me, you can forget it. I don't need you to fix me anymore. Get out!"

"You're drunk!" I snapped back. It was foolish to point out the obvious, but I couldn't think of anything else to say. I'd never seen him in such a state, and I didn't know how to handle it.

"Well, thank you for pointing out what I already knew. In my opinion, I'm not drunk enough. Now get out so I can finish this here—" He stopped slurring to point a wavering finger at his bottle. "This here bottle needs to be finished."

He took a few swerving steps toward the balcony doors. I moved, afraid he might fall on me, but I was also scared of him going outside near the railings.

"Wait. You shouldn't go out there. It isn't safe in your condition. Please, Sloan. Stay in the house," I begged and placed a hand on his arm. He glanced down at it with disgust, as if it were an annoying fly he wanted to swat away.

"Why do you even care? You're wasting your time. You can't stop history from repeating itself. I am who I am, baby. It's in my blood!" he shouted and jabbed a finger into his chest.

*History? His blood? Is he talking about his father's drinking?*

"What are you talking about?"

"Jesus Christ! I told you I don't want you here! Don't you have someone else who needs fixing?" Ignoring me, he continued another few steps toward the door. I knew he was only acting like an asshole to get me to leave. It stung but little did he know, I wasn't going anywhere.

"Sloan, stop this right now. You're not your father!" The words were out before I could think. Sloan's steps faltered, and he turned his head to glare at me through narrowed eyes.

"What did you say?"

"Nothing," I responded hurriedly, not wanting to say anything else to upset him. "Just forget it. Let's go downstairs. I can make some coffee and—"

I stopped short, my breath catching in my throat as my fears came to fruition. When he reached the balcony door, his foot caught on the threshold and caused him to stumble. Before I could think to react, he grabbed hold of the doorframe to stop himself from falling. In the process, he dropped the bottle of Jack Daniels. The glass bottle hit the tiled floor of the balcony and shattered into hundreds of tiny glass pieces. The brown liquid slithered like a toxic snake to disappear over the edge.

"Fuck!" he hissed.

Throwing his arms up in a rage, his forearm hit my face, and I stumbled back a step. It smarted only a little, and I knew it was an accident, but that didn't change the fact that I wanted to cry. The shock was the only thing preventing my tears from falling. I couldn't believe I was seeing him like this. The person standing before me wasn't the man who was kind and patient with orphan boys, the man who slowed danced with me on the beach, or the man who called me Rainbow Brite and whispered sweet flirtations into my ear.

No. This was a man who had his whole life ripped away from him in one tragic moment, and he was spiraling out of control as a result—and breaking my heart in the process. I didn't want to be anywhere near him, yet I knew I couldn't leave. I couldn't abandon him at a time when he needed me the most—and not as his lover, but as his agent.

Tucking my emotions away, I donned my professional hat.

"Enough. You're a complete train wreck, and I know you to be better than this. Time to sleep this off. No more talking until you've sobered up."

He glowered at me, looking as if he wanted to argue, but couldn't muster up the energy. When I took his arm, he didn't push me away this time but allowed me to lead him to the bed. Once he seemed settled comfortably, I pulled the blankets up to cover him.

"I don't know why you want to be with someone like me. I'm sorry, Kallie," he mumbled quietly. I didn't respond, too afraid my voice would crack if I did. I wasn't mad at him—although I knew I should be. I just couldn't be angry when my heart hurt after seeing this powerful and captivating man be made small by things he had no control over.

I waited until his breathing was even, signaling he was asleep, then exhaled a sigh of relief. Moving to the chair in the corner, I sat down quietly and allowed myself a moment to relax for the first time since before getting the flat tire yesterday. It was strange to think I'd been stranded on a road to nowhere mere hours ago. It felt like it had happened weeks ago.

Remembering that I was supposed to update Cooper, I took my phone from my purse and shot off a quick text to him.

Today
1:37 PM, Me: *Hey, Cooper. I just wanted to let you know I'm with Sloan. He's okay. He indulged in too much whiskey and is currently sleeping it off.*

His response came almost immediately.

1:40 PM, Cooper: *Dumbass. Thanks for letting me know. I'll call him later. If you need anything, you know where to find me.*
1:41 PM, Me: *I appreciate it.*

After dropping my phone back inside my purse, I set it on the ground near my feet. My gaze shifted up to wander over Sloan's glorious body. His face, typically so intensely alert, was peaceful and relaxed while he slept. He no longer looked like the cocky race car driver who could make me feel exposed and naked with just one look. Instead, he appeared young and innocent.

I stifled a yawn as exhaustion from a restless night of sleeping in the car began to set in. I leaned my head back, knowing a quick nap would be needed if I wanted a clear mind after Sloan woke. Closing my eyes, I tried not to think about the conversation I would need to have with him and surrendered myself to sleep.

---

A rustling sound awakened me from my slumber. The unfamiliar surroundings disoriented me at first. It took me a solid fifteen seconds to realize where I was. I glanced out the balcony doors at the setting sun. I'd slept the entire afternoon and most of the evening.

*Crap!*

I hadn't planned on being here that long. I cast my eyes to Sloan. He was still asleep but stirring. The sound of his movement must have been what prompted me to wake. Reaching down into my purse, I retrieved my cell phone to check the time. When I looked at the screen, I saw there were three missed text messages from Gabby.

Today
4:03 PM, Gabby: *Any thoughts about dinner? I thought maybe we could go down to the pier.*
4:33 PM, Gabby: *On second thought, I don't feel like going anywhere. I'm perfectly content to stay lying by the pool. How about we order pizza instead? Veggie toppings only, of course.*
7:14 PM, Gabby: *Hey, is everything okay? I'm getting worried.*

Guilt washed over me, feeling terrible about leaving her after she'd flown all the way here to see me. Typing as fast as my fingers would allow, I sent back an apology.

8:06 PM, Me: *Gabs, I'm really sorry. When I got here, Sloan was a bit of a mess, and I didn't want to leave him. I'm not sure how much longer I'm going to be.*

I saw the three little dots on the screen, signaling she was typing. A few seconds later, my phone vibrated with her response.

8:08 PM, Gabby: *I figured as much. Don't worry about it. I was starving, so I went ahead and ordered the pizza. There are leftovers here for you.*
8:09 PM, Me: *I feel awful. Thanks for understanding. I'll text you when I leave here.*
8:11 PM, Gabby: *Don't feel bad at all! I'm fine. I already assumed you'd be spending the night with that hottie. I'm completely jealous, by the way. Take your time. I won't wait up. Have fun!*

I glanced at the bed, then at the bent curtain rod and the hole in the wall.

*Fun?*

If Gabby only knew half of what had gone on here, she'd be screaming at me to get out. There was nothing fun about what happened earlier, and I didn't expect things to get any better after Sloan woke.

# Chapter Nineteen

*Sloan*

There was a stabbing pain piercing from one temple to the other. I tried to blink to rid myself of it, only to be blinded by rays from the setting sun coming through the balcony doors. Rolling away from the sunlight, I brought my hands up to my head and squeezed. My stomach pitched. It felt as if I'd been run over by a Mack Truck.

I lay there for a moment, waiting for the churning in my stomach to subside. As I did so, a feeling of awareness came over me, almost as if I were being watched. Slowly opening my eyes, I allowed them to adjust to the light. When my vision finally came into focus, I saw Kallie sitting in a chair in the corner of the room—and that's when it all came flooding back.

The whiskey.

The argument with Kallie.

*Shit! What the fuck was I thinking?*

Almost as soon as the question popped in my head, I knew the answer. Memories of my crash had blended with Tyler's, bringing back the terrible moment when my life had ended for all intents and purposes. I squeezed my eyes shut tight, trying to block out the images.

"How are you feeling?" Kallie asked.

I peered at her through squinted eyes.

"Like hell," I mumbled.

"I would imagine. How much did you drink?"

"I'm not sure."

"I saw the empty prescription bottle downstairs." Although she said it as a statement, I could tell she was fishing for an answer about whether I'd been under the influence of oxy too.

I closed my eyes again and tried to recall the order of events after I got home last night. I remembered sitting at the kitchen table, pouring shot after shot. I'd tried going to bed, but memories of the crash plagued me, and I couldn't sleep, so I came downstairs and drank some more. I recalled getting the bottle of oxy and struggling with the childproof cap. I was completely wasted by that point and had fumbled the pills, causing them to roll across the hardwood floor and disappear under the couch. I looked for them for a bit but gave up and opened another bottle of Jack instead. Everything was somewhat of a blur after that, but I was almost certain I hadn't taken them.

"Kallie, if you are wondering if I took the pills, I didn't. I thought about taking them, but I dropped them somewhere in the living room. I think they rolled under the couch."

"That might explain why the living room looked as if someone had tossed it. Do you feel like getting up? A shower and some food will work wonders."

"Maybe."

"I'll go downstairs and see about throwing together something to eat," she told me and stood up from the chair. "While I do that, you can clean up, then come downstairs to put something other than whiskey into your system."

There was no missing the level of disdain in her voice, but her expression told a different story altogether. She was looking at me with a mix of sadness and pity. I turned away from her, embarrassed by my behavior. I didn't deserve her sympathy. I only had myself to blame.

After she went downstairs, I slowly made my way to the bathroom. Turning on the faucet, I stripped down, then stepped under the showerhead. Bracing myself against the tiled wall with two hands, I let the water stream over me and tried to think of a way to rationalize what happened with Kallie. I knew I'd been awful to her during my drunken rage. If being an asshole was an art form, I'd mastered it. After the way I'd treated her, I owed her an explanation.

Once I was showered and dressed, I felt significantly better but not great. Making my way downstairs, I found a steaming cup of coffee and a bottle of water sitting on the kitchen table. Kallie walked toward me, carrying two plates with sandwiches and potato chips. After she set the plates down on the table, I inspected the food more carefully. One sandwich was piled high with salami, and the other appeared stacked with lettuce and tomatoes only.

"A lettuce and tomato sandwich?" I asked in confusion.

"I had to make do with what was in the fridge. No worries. I didn't expect to find Tofurky in your house," she said with a laugh. "Just think of it as a BLT without the B."

"That can't possibly taste good."

"Not my favorite, but it's fine for now. You also have some blocks of cheese in there. I can cut that up if either of us is still hungry after we have this. Now, sit. Eat," she ordered and pointed to the food on the table.

After we both took a seat, I watched her from the opposite side of the table as she sprinkled salt and pepper on the tomatoes, then dug into the blandest sandwich imaginable like it was the best thing she'd ever tasted. I shook my head and picked up my salami on rye.

"What are you doing here? I mean, I thought you were going to Napa Valley with your friend, Gabby."

"I caught a flat tire, so plans changed. It's quite the tale, to be honest," she added with a laugh. "But I think it was fated. After Cooper called, I—"

"Cooper?" I interrupted. "Why did he call you?"

"I mentioned it to you earlier, but you must have forgotten. Cooper is the reason I came here today. He was worried about you after the crash you witnessed yesterday."

I pressed my lips together in a tight line, annoyed to know Cooper had needlessly bothered her.

"He shouldn't have worried. I'm fine."

She arched up one eyebrow, her expression skeptical.

"Are you really?"

I wasn't, but I didn't want to get into it with her. Instead of answering, I focused on eating. Following my lead, she did the same. Neither of us said a word until the food had been cleared from our plates. Decidedly done, Kallie pushed her plate away and sat back in her chair. Her bright green eyes looked thoughtful, and I could sense her hesitancy before she finally spoke.

"Sloan, I want you to tell me about your accident—and I don't mean the technical stuff I can read about online. I want to know more details about the pain you experienced from your injuries, the rehab, your feelings during that time, and all the rest. I should have pushed you to tell me before now, but I allowed my personal feelings to get in the way. As your agent, I need to know every tiny detail—including the details about the argument you had with your mother over your father."

My head snapped up in surprise, suddenly remembering what she'd said about me not being like my father. In my drunken stupor, I couldn't focus enough to press her on it. But now I was more than ready to.

"How the hell do you know about that?" I demanded.

She blinked, and it was easy to see she was shocked by the coolness in my voice. For me, it was an automatic response. Talking about the accident and my parents stirred up an ache I'd spent a year trying to bury. When she eventually spoke, it was apparent she was choosing her words carefully.

"How I know doesn't matter. Your feelings about it are all I care about. I only know a little of the story—and certainly not enough to protect you from any negative press. People talk, but I want to hear the whole thing from you. If I understand, maybe I can help you rewrite the stars."

I nearly scoffed.

*Rewrite the stars. Right.*

I closed my eyes, knowing I should never have expected a mundane response from someone like her. She wasn't built that way. There was always a deeper meaning.

"Kallie, I really don't want to talk about it. I've spent the better part of a year trying to forget it."

"Maybe that's why you can't get past it and why you got so drunk last night. Maybe you *need* to talk about it."

"Kallie… I can't."

She moved over to sit in the chair next to me and placed her hand on my knee. She peered up at me, and I found myself mesmerized by the intensity in her eyes. Her touch could calm the monster inside of me trying to break free. She made me a different person—a better person.

"Talk to me, Sloan," she murmured.

My throat clogged with emotion, and I tore my gaze from hers. A war raged in my head, wanting to tell her everything yet wanting to keep it all buried at the same time. She didn't understand. She couldn't hear the sounds of screeching tires and crunching metal that haunted me by day and slithered into my dreams at night. She didn't know I could still taste blood in my mouth, the metallic hints as fresh as it was on the day of the crash. Then there was the agonizing pain—both physical and emotional—that followed for months afterward.

Her warm hand shifted from my knee to cover my hand, ripping me away from a dark time and back to the present. I looked down at her slender fingers, then up her arm until my sight landed on her angelic face. Kallie stared back with eyes full of concern.

"Alright. I'll tell you," I conceded.

She smiled tentatively, seeming pleased but also cautious.

"It's a nice evening. If you're through eating, why don't we take this conversation outside?"

I nodded my agreement and stood up from the chair. Leaving the remains of our dinner on the kitchen table, I allowed Kallie to take my hand and lead me outside. Once there, I took a deep breath. The fresh air felt good and helped to clear my head. It made me realize how stifling it had become when we were in the kitchen.

I looked around and noticed one of the patio chairs toppled over. I had a vague recollection of shoving it aside in a fit of anger, but I couldn't remember beyond that. Bending over, I grabbed the arm of the chair to flip it upright. I motioned for Kallie to sit down, then took a seat next to her.

"Where do you want me to begin?" I asked.

"I don't know. It's your story." Sympathy and understanding were prevalent in every line of her expression, but the pity was also back in her eyes once more. It was the last thing I wanted. Tearing my gaze from her, I stared out across the yard. The sun had set entirely, leaving faint hints of purple to blend with the dark night sky.

"I suppose I should start with the morning of the crash. That's when everything went bad. I was heading up a practice session at Motor Club Speedway. Before we got into the cars, I'd instructed one of the crew members to play America's "Ventura Highway" on one of the portable speakers we kept in the pit. Like you believe in the stars and the moon, I have my own superstitions. I never race—for practice or competitively—before letting the song play through." I paused, not wanting to admit that hearing the song now just made me want to vomit. "Anyways, this punk-ass reporter showed up and started asking me a bunch of questions about my father. I didn't want to talk to him, and I was pissed that he was interrupting my pre-race routine."

"What was he asking you?"

"It was the usual bullshit questions at first, but then he wanted to know why I never apologized for what my father did. I didn't know what he was talking about, and I tried to ignore him, but he was a persistent fucker who wouldn't let up. Back in the day, my father was a big deal in the racing world. He was a Formula One racer—a really good one. Still, he wasn't unlike every other racer. He worried about fatal crashes on the track but tended to think he was invincible on the open road. Before hitting the height of his career, he died in a ten-car pileup on Ventura Freeway. Hence the reason "Ventura Highway" was my jam—it was kind of like a salute to him. Naturally, reporters speculated about my chosen career path because of that, but this reporter started saying stuff no other reporter had."

I eyed Kallie for a moment, noticing that she didn't look surprised by anything I was saying.

"Go on," she prompted.

"Do I need to? It looks like you already know everything I'm saying."

"Not everything."

"Have it your way." I shook my head and sighed. "Anyways, the reporter accused my father of being responsible for the accident on the freeway. He said my dad was drunk at the time of the crash. I was taken aback since that was the first time I'd ever heard anything like that. My mother happened to be at the track that day, which wasn't uncommon whenever I was practicing or competing. I immediately confronted her about it. She was hesitant to tell me at first but couldn't deny the reporter's accusations in the end. They were all true."

"I can't imagine that was easy to hear."

"No, it wasn't. It was a blow like I can't describe. You have to remember that there wasn't internet back then, so any reporting on his accident was all in newspaper archives. Why would I think to dig up the information when I thought my mother had already told me all I needed to know? I was just a little kid when my dad died, but I'd idolized him all my life. It pissed me off to find out my mother had lied, and I wanted more details, but it was time to get behind the wheel. I stormed away. And then…" I trailed off and raked my hands through my hair as I tried to tell the story without hearing the sounds that lived in my memory. "Then the crash happened fifteen minutes later. If you've ever been in an accident, you know the sound of metal crunching. I can still hear it to this day. Everything just happened so fast—one minute, I felt cocky about schooling a rookie, and the next, I was spinning out. I have a vague recollection of the spectator crowd cheering like crazy after they pulled me out of the car, but that's all I remember."

"I'm so sorry, Sloan."

"For what? I knew better than to get behind the wheel when distracted. I preached to my crew, and other drivers about the importance of staying focused all the damn time, yet I didn't follow my own advice. That was one the first thoughts I'd had when my crew arrived to cut me from the wreckage—that I'd fucked up and lost focus."

"What about what happened after? With…" She hesitated. "With your mother."

"My mother," I spat out bitterly. I paused and took a deep breath, steeling myself before I had to tell her the rest. The mere mention of my mother grated on my nerves, but it also caused the most severe kind of ache—a contradiction of emotion I had never been able to sort out. Closing my eyes, I pictured her blurred face as I raced by her on the track right before the crash. It was the last time I saw her, and my words preceding that had been laden with anger. "Why do you want to know about my mother?"

"Well, I know she committed suicide," she answered softly.

"Fuck. Is there anything you don't know? What else did Cooper tell you when he called?" I demanded, feeling incredibly betrayed.

"Cooper didn't tell me anything. I've never discussed any of this with him. Rochele is the one who told me the night we all went out for dinner. She was trying to explain why you got so snippy with me when I'd asked about your parents."

Pushing up from the chair, I shoved a frustrated hand through my hair and began to pace the patio.

"That was over a month ago, Kallie. You've known this whole time?"

"As I told you, I only know a bit. I didn't press you because I thought you would talk about it in your own time. Rochele wasn't able to explain how you feel—only you can do that."

"Yeah, well—she's got some fucking nerve. Rochele knows what it feels like to be plagued by memories of a car accident. She's been through it. She had no business telling you anything about what happened."

"Sloan, please. Don't be mad at her. She was only trying to help."

I wanted to be angry, but I couldn't be. Kallie was right. Rochele didn't do anything wrong. I was glad Kallie had heard it first from someone I trusted, rather than reading tabloid articles full of half-truths. I was just upset because I didn't want to be talking about this. It made me feel unsettled and vulnerable, knowing that every protective barrier I'd built to protect myself was violently crashing down with every word I spoke.

I turned my back to her and looked out across the yard. The sky was now dark and bleak, the only light coming from the moonbeams peeking out occasionally from a passing cloud. It matched my current state of mind—as if Kallie was the only ray of light cutting through my darkness.

"My mother killed herself three days after the accident. She slit her wrists in the bathtub," I said quietly, not entirely sure if I was talking to Kallie or myself. "I'd been put in a medically-induced coma and didn't find out about what she did until a month later. When the doctors said they didn't think I would survive my injuries, it was assumed that she couldn't handle losing me on top of losing my dad. I don't know that for sure, though—as I said, it's just an assumption. She didn't leave a note or any other form of explanation. Some claim that people take their own lives due to mental illness, but all I can see is her selfishness. There's no excuse for what she did. What kind of mother abandons her son when he's fighting for his life?"

I felt a hand press softly on my arm and glanced over to see Kallie looking at me with sad eyes.

"I'm sorry, Sloan. She should have been there for you."

"You're damn right she should've been! I was alone, stuck in a hospital bed, with the left side of my body completely immobile. I had a concussion, several broken ribs, and needed a ventilator just to fucking breathe. When the doctors woke me from the coma and removed the vent, I was scared out of my mind. I was terrified I'd never walk again. I couldn't even hold a goddamned spoon with my left hand. It took eight months of rehab, five days a week, to get me back to almost normal—almost being the keyword," I added bitterly.

"Tell me what 'almost' means. Why did the doctor say you can't race anymore?" she asked tentatively, almost as if she were afraid to voice the question. I understood her hesitancy—I felt it too. I was scared to say the prognosis out loud for fear it would somehow make it truer than it already was.

I turned to face her and found nothing but patience in her wide emerald eyes as she waited for me to continue.

"About a month before you showed up, the rehab facility arranged for me to go into a car simulator. I was pushing the docs hard to clear me for racing. Dr. Haskell, my surgeon, conferred with the physical therapists, and they decided to test my reflexes to see how I'd fare before giving me clearance. I didn't pass their test."

"Why not?"

"I suffered too much loss of stamina. I couldn't press the gas or brake pedals for long periods without experiencing extreme pain in my left hip. Even now, I have to be careful with the way I stand. Mornings are the worst, though, because that's when the joint is the stiffest.".

"How do you manage to drive a regular car?"

"Custom paddles on the steering wheel. I only switch over to them when my hip is acting up. The technology is great and has helped me a lot, but it isn't up to snuff for race cars."

"I never would have known. You've never given any inclination that your hip bothered you."

"Most days, it's fine. I was relentless with my PT to make sure of it."

"It had to be a tough road, and going through all of that without family..." She trailed off, looking thoughtful. "My mother has always been so supportive of me—and my father too, even though I didn't meet him until I was seventeen."

I cocked a curious brow at her. "Seventeen?"

"Yeah. My parents are kind of a not-so-perfect second-chance romance. If you ever meet my father, I'm sure he'll tell you—right down to his *Fade Into You* tattoo that ended up being my parents wedding song."

"Mazzy Star. Good tune," I mused.

Kallie smiled wistfully for moment, almost as if she were lost in a memory.

"He loves to tell everyone about the summer he met my mother by the lake at Camp Riley. They fell in love under the stars but were tragically separated until he became—as he likes to joke—her very own Colonel Brandon seventeen years later. He gets all sentimental about it, but that's a fairytale for a different day. My point is, I've always had parental support. I can't imagine having to go through what you did all by myself."

"It wasn't easy. Before my mother killed herself, she had always supported me. She never missed a single race. I may have been mad at her for not telling me the truth about my dad, but I would have gotten over it with time. However, I don't think I can ever forgive her for leaving me alone when I needed her the most. I'd always been independent, even as a kid. But this time, I couldn't do it by myself. There were moments of both debilitation and exhilaration as I fought to take a step or hold a utensil just to feed myself. It was humbling in ways I can't explain. I'm just grateful I had good friends to help me through the worst of it. Cooper was there a lot when the rehab got really tough. He understood racing was all I had left and knew why my recovery was so important. I fought so damn hard and did everything I was told to do in order to get behind the wheel again, but now…"

I let the sentence go unfinished, unable to articulate what 'now' meant for me anymore.

"I get it, Sloan. Really, I do."

I shook my head, needing her to understand how I'd gotten to this point.

"Before my accident, I rarely drank because I thought it clouded the mind. I hated not feeling in control. It seemed like drinking was the only thing I *could* control after my accident, and it gave me an escape. When I saw Tyler crash, everything just came flooding back. All I could think of was making those memories go away. I didn't want to feel anything, so I came home, grabbed a bottle, and—"

"You don't have to explain anymore," she interrupted and wrapped her arms around my waist.

Grateful she was giving me a reprieve, I pulled her tight to my chest and buried my face in her hair. I was emotionally spent, yet I also felt like I could finally breathe. Perhaps she was right—after holding it all in for so long, maybe I did need to get this off my chest. I suddenly realized how much of a struggle things had been and how exhausting it was to go through the motions day in and day out, knowing racing was forever out of my reach. Since meeting Kallie, those endless moments felt easier to endure, as if she alone had the power to keep me grounded.

She pulled back to look at me and afforded me a small smile. At that moment, I was completely lost in her. I returned her smile and silently wondered what it was I did to deserve this eccentric rainbow goddess. Reaching up, I touched a blue lock that was intertwined with her natural blonde, recalling what she'd said about the blue.

"I hate knowing that I made you sad. I don't want to see you wearing blue ever again, Rainbow Brite. If it means I can never have another drink again, so be it—no more drinking, no more worry about pills. You deserve better."

"Sloan, when I came here today and saw you the way I did…" She trailed off, seeming to collect her thoughts. "I can't explain what it felt like. I just know I can't do anything like that with you again. If there's a repeat of what happened earlier, I'll be on the first plane back to D.C. I need you to promise me—no more getting completely wasted and no more pills."

"I promise."

Placing a finger under her chin, I tilted her head up so I could lean in and press my lips to hers. She tentatively opened for me, her tongue sliding over mine. After the turmoil of the past twenty-four hours, she tasted so damn good. All I wanted was her.

# Chapter Twenty

*Sloan*

Our slow kiss quickly evolved into frantic heat. It was as if all the strained emotion from the past hour had suddenly combusted into a flame. I pulled back, wanting Kallie to understand how desperate I was for her at this moment. I cradled her face in my hands and stared into her eyes. Her cheeks were flushed, and her gaze was like molten fire. The passion burning in those expressive pools of green was almost too much to bear. I'd never felt this way about anyone before—never felt so desperate. I didn't know how or when it happened, but I was falling hard for this woman. I needed her more than she realized. My throat thickened with overwhelming emotion.

"I want you, Kallie."

Tracing her fingertip along the neckline of my t-shirt, she gave me a coy smile.

"So, what are you waiting for?"

Within a matter of minutes, we were stumbling up the stairs to my bedroom, tearing at each other's clothes with an animal-like frenzy. She kicked off her shoes as I yanked her shirt over her head. By the time we made it to my room, she was wearing nothing but her bra and thong panties.

Snaking my arm around her back, I lifted her effortlessly and set her onto the bed. After shedding what remained of my own clothes, I climbed naked on top of her and brought my face down to her breast, biting at a taut nipple through the thin lacy material of her bra. She gasped and threw her head back. Her need was just as hot as mine. Her bodily responses to my touch were the strongest of aphrodisiacs, driving me to the point of madness.

I flicked my tongue up the side of her neck and stopped to nip at her ear. The rapid succession of her breath matched mine, both of us fueled with nothing but pure carnal need. Moving back to her mouth, we kissed frantically, tongues colliding as her back arched. She moaned into my mouth, causing my body to buzz with endorphins.

Reaching beneath her, I wound my hands behind her back and unclasped her bra. Her glorious tits spilled free, allowing me to roll each peak between my thumbs and forefingers. The air already smelled of sex, creating an all-encompassing vapor designed to intoxicate—and I was drunk on her as her hands unabashedly roamed to explore my body.

I prowled down her torso, my mouth moving over her firm stomach, all the way down to kiss the inside of her knee. When I pushed aside the crotch of her panties, I found her already wet for me. I smiled, loving the way we could go from zero to ten on the Richter scale in just a matter of moments. I slipped a finger inside her heated well and began to stroke her walls. She all but rocketed off the bed, hands fisting in the sheets as her ecstasy slowly built. I slid another finger in and began to flick my tongue over that hard bundle of nerves. Her hips pushed up against me, trembling and fraught with desire, searching in desperation for quick release.

"Oh, Mother of Stars..." she breathed, writhing and panting beneath me. "Please, Sloan. I don't want to wait. I need to feel you inside of me."

Her begging for it may have been the biggest turn-on yet. I grunted, not wanting to waste another minute. A fire burned through my bloodstream. My need to be inside her was fierce.

Pulling my fingers from the clutches of her body, I brought them to my mouth. She watched me with intense arousal as I made a slow act of licking them clean. She whimpered and reached for me. Leaning in, I kissed her, allowing her to taste the sweet tanginess of her essence on my tongue before moving to sit up. Sliding my hands down her waist, I looped my thumbs through the sides of her panties and pulled them down her legs.

Now that she was completely naked, I took a moment to appreciate every line and every curve. She had a body that would make any man lose rational judgment, and I wasn't exempt. As she stared up at me with eyes filled with unadulterated lust, my brain all but short-circuited.

"Tell me again, Kallie," I growled. "Tell me what you need."

Her eyes flashed with desire, causing my cock to throb and ache, knowing I was so close to feeling her snug heat. She didn't hesitate with her response.

"I need you inside me—now!" she gasped.

After making quick work with a condom, I positioned my body to hover over hers. Bracing one hand on the headboard for balance, I used the other to notch my throbbing tip to the outside of her waiting entrance.

"Are you ready for me, baby? This won't be gentle."

"Sloan, please," she begged again.

In one quick thrust, I plunged my shaft through her tight clasp until it was completely sheathed. She cried out and brought her legs up to wrap them around my hips. Pulling me in closer, she gave me all the leverage I needed to drive all the way home. A low groan rumbled from somewhere deep in my chest.

"Fuck, Kallie. It's like you were made for me." I drove into her again, and she let out another gasp as her body worked to accommodate my girth. "That's it. Take me. All of me."

The rippling of her heat drove me wild, but I held steady as I waited for her to get there. I hissed through clenched teeth and pushed harder. By the time I felt her building orgasm clench around me, I was ready to explode. Invigorated by the feel of her slick walls, I increased the speed of my thrusts.

"Sloan!"

"That's it. Scream my name as loud as you want. No neighbors can hear you this time."

Over and over again, I impaled her as she came, each plunge deeper than the last and filling her completely. She met me thrust after thrust, her eyes rolling back as her moans surrendered to screams. Her fingers laced through my hair and tugged in the most erotic way.

The woman in my arms was all fire, and I was entirely lost in her flame. It was an overload of sensations, consuming me with inexplicable, mind-altering need. She made me forget about everything—the past, my injuries, racing. It was as if all her talk about fate was true, and we were destined in the most fundamental ways—like nothing could have stopped us from being together.

She raked her hands down my chest, then back up to grip my shoulders. She squeezed tight, and I could feel her second orgasm begin to pulse around my cock. When she burst apart, something inside me seemed to snap, releasing whatever measure of control I'd been hanging onto. Her cry of ecstasy was all I needed to lose myself. It was my turn.

Dizzying shimmers of white began to dot my vision. I sunk deep and hard, filling her completely, until my seed erupted. Energy spiked, and I came with such a violent force that I was left shuddering and trembling in her arms.

Our hearts beat wildly against each other. I didn't want to move and break our connection but knew I needed to remove the condom before long. Rolling onto my back, I shed the rubber and tossed it into the wastebasket next to the bed. Sliding my arm beneath Kallie, I pulled her tight to my side. Her heated body curved into mine as we allowed our racing hearts to return to a normal rhythm. We lay there perfectly content, her hand resting peacefully on my chest while I traced the lines of her tattooed shoulder.

I couldn't be sure of how much time passed before the tranquility was broken by the ringing sound of my cell phone coming from downstairs. I ignored it and continued tracing small circles around Kallie's tattoo. The ringing stopped, only to begin again a few minutes later.

"You should get that," Kallie murmured. "It could be Cooper calling to check in."

I groaned in irritation.

"Fine, but don't move. I'll be back in a few."

Swinging my legs over the side of the bed, I pulled on a pair of boxer briefs and made my way downstairs. It took me a minute to locate the phone because I didn't remember where I'd left it. When it began to ring again for the third time, I ended up finding it on the floor next to the couch. Still feeling annoyed over having been ripped from Kallie's arms, I snatched up the phone. My aggravation only grew when I saw Milo's name lighting up the screen.

"What's up, Milo?" I briskly answered.

"Sloan, what are you doing on Monday?"

I scratched my head and tried to remember if Kallie had anything lined up for me.

"Ah, I'm not sure. I'll have to check. Why?"

"Whatever you have going on, cancel it. It turns out Tyler McDermott is going to be out of commission for at least a month. He's banged up pretty bad—concussion and a few fractured ribs—but he's expected to make a full recovery."

"That's fantastic news," I said with relief.

"Yeah, well… not for his sponsors. McDermott won't be cleared in time to race the Motorsports International Legacy League in San Antonio. They're pushing hard for a replacement driver, opening up a huge opportunity for you."

"For me?" I asked in confusion.

"Yeah, you. NASCAR was willing to make an exception and allow a replacement driver in a similar situation a while back. The MILL is following their example. Tyler's car did well in the European circuit, and his sponsors think it could do even better in the U.S. After evaluating the damage, it turns out Tyler suffered more harm than the car did. Mechanics are working around the clock, and the car should be fixed and ready to go within the week. The only thing the sponsors need is someone to drive it. That's where you come in."

I froze, fixating on a proverbial carrot dangling just out of my reach. Substitute drivers were a gray area. Technically, the car qualifies—not the driver. Some argued that replacement drivers made sense for racing teams going for owner's championships. Others said replacement drivers shouldn't be allowed because it isn't fair to fellow competitors who fought hard to earn titles all season long. However, all of that stopped mattering for someone like me the moment my doctors labeled me a disabled driver.

"Milo, you know I can't race."

"Why? Because of a little hip pain? Come on, man. It's one race. I can get you what you need to numb the pain. Don't worry about that."

I knew Milo's offer to help me "numb the pain" ultimately meant one thing—prescription oxy. However, oxy didn't only mask pain with a temporary high. It also slowed the user's reflexes which could have catastrophic consequences for anyone operating a vehicle, even under normal conditions. Milo obviously didn't understand that. I may have stupidly popped a few pills when I shouldn't have, but I'd been aware of how easily someone could become addicted to opioids and recognized the dangers of building a tolerance. I'd been lucky up until this point, and I wasn't sure if I wanted to risk traveling that road again.

"Milo, the entire racing community knows I haven't been cleared to race."

"They don't know shit. For all they know, you took early retirement. Just let me handle the technicalities. This prize money is too big to pass up. All I need to know is if you're in. If you are, I'll need you to report to the track at eleven on Monday morning so we can begin practices and prep. You'll need to get acquainted with a new car and Tyler's crew, as well as get fitted for new gear and schmooze the sponsors. You know the drill."

I fell quiet. Milo's mention of prize money made me pause—not for myself, but Tyler. I recalled what Cooper had said about Tyler's wife, Amy. If I did this and won, I could give the prize money to him, and Amy could get the experimental treatment she needed in Switzerland. However, it was more than just that. Charity aside, I wasn't a saint. The idea of getting behind the wheel again was more than just appealing—it was like being offered the forbidden fruit I couldn't refuse. To know I could feel the rumbling of the engine again in just a matter of days was almost too much to wrap my head around.

As I considered Milo's offer, I began to think about the possibility of pushing through the pain on my own. The occasional painkiller could help if the ache in my hip became too unbearable, just as long as I was sober when I was behind the wheel. I didn't know if that was even an option because I had yet to try—but that's what practice was for.

*What if I could prove the doctors wrong? Maybe I can race again.*

"Let me think about it," I finally said.

"I need to know by tomorrow."

"Alright, I'll call you."

I ended the call and stared at the blank screen, unsure how to process the turn of events. Setting the phone on the coffee table, I went back upstairs to where Kallie lay naked and waiting. Perhaps if I talked to her about it, she'd help me work through the decision. But on second thought, there was a very good possibility she wouldn't approve—especially if racing meant I had to kill the pain with pills.

"Who was that?" she asked when I entered the bedroom.

"Milo."

"Oh, what did he want?"

I hesitated with my answer, buying time as I shed my boxers and climbed back into bed beside her. Pulling her to my chest, I kissed the tip of her nose. I moved my lips over her cheek, across her jawline, and down to her neck. My cock hardened again, anxious to feel her slick heat once more. I shifted my weight, pulling her on top of me until she was straddling my hips.

"Why he called isn't important," I told her. "The only thing that matters right now is you riding me for the victory lap."

# Chapter Twenty-One

*Kallie*

Gabby shuffled into my family room on Monday morning with a loud yawn.

"Ouch! That looks like it hurts," she said when she spotted me standing in a triangle pose in the middle of the room. "I don't know how you do that so early in the morning."

"It's after eight-thirty. It's not early. In fact, it's late for me," I said with a laugh. "Yoga in the morning increases blood flow, stretches your mind, and sets the tone for the day. It's energizing, Gabs. You should try it."

"Mediation does a lot of that, too. Personally, I'd rather sit and meditate with a cup of coffee and let the caffeine stretch my mind—especially after staying up so late," she joked as she pulled the bag of coffee grounds from the cabinet.

"We did get to bed late, but at least we got to make up for the lost time. I still feel horrible about Saturday," I said guiltily, thinking about how I didn't get home from Sloan's house until after one in the morning. To make it up to Gabby, I'd spent all day with her on Sunday. I took her shopping in L.A., and we did the not-so-glamorous walk on Hollywood Boulevard, looking at the terrazzo and brass stars embedded in the sidewalk. We had dinner afterward at an eclectic little restaurant on the Sunset Strip, then came home and talked about everything and anything under the sun long into the night.

"Will you stop stressing about it? I've already assured you—I was perfectly content by the pool all day," she repeated for what must have been the tenth time in the past twenty-four hours.

Standing up, I wiped the sweat from my brow.

"I'm going to take a shower. Your flight leaves at three-thirty, right?"

"Yeah."

"Alright. That gives us the morning together. I thought maybe we could head over to the Santa Monica Pier and—" I stopped short when the sound of my cell phone vibrating on the end table interrupted me. I snagged it and looked at the caller ID. I didn't recognize the number.

"Hello?"

"May I speak to Kallie, please?" said a male voice on the other end of the line.

"This is she."

"Kallie, it's Jeremiah Lanford from Wings Halfway House."

"Oh, hi! I didn't recognize the number. What can I do for you?"

"Last we spoke, you said you would get back with me on when would be a good time for Sloan Atwood to come in and speak. As it turns out, I have a cancelation for this week Friday. Do you think he would be interested in filling it?"

I mentally went through Sloan's calendar for the week. A few engagements were on the schedule with Safe Track, the first one being later on today, but I was reasonably certain Friday was open. Still, I remembered Sloan's hesitation about speaking with the teens.

"I think Friday will work, but I'll need to get with Sloan first. I'll ask him and get back to you within the hour."

"Excellent! I'll look forward to your call."

After I hung up, I immediately called Sloan. When he answered, he sounded half asleep.

"Let me guess. You need me to pose for a picture in an hour," he said groggily.

"Not exactly." I laughed. "Sorry to call you so early, but I just got a call from Jeremiah Lanford, the guy who runs Wings Halfway House. He wants you to speak on Friday."

"Kallie, I—"

"Before you say no, hear me out. You don't have anything scheduled until four this afternoon. I thought that maybe after Gabby leaves for the airport, the two of us could pop over to Wings for a quick tour. You could get a feel for the place, then decide."

"Yeah…about this afternoon." He paused, and I sensed his hesitation. "Something came up. I need you to cancel everything on my schedule for the next couple of weeks, maybe longer."

My brow furrowed in confusion.

"Cancel? But why?"

He hesitated again.

"I'm going to try racing again, Kallie."

I blinked several times, trying to figure out if I'd heard him correctly.

"But you can't, Sloan. The doctors said—"

"I know what the doctors said, but there's a chance I might be able to push through it. I won't know unless I try. Tyler McDermott's accident means his sponsors need a driver to replace him. I thought about it and told Milo yesterday that I would do it. Racing in the MILL is huge, Kallie. I can't pass up the opportunity without trying."

I had no idea what the hell racing in the MILL meant and didn't waste time trying to figure it out. Instead, I zeroed in on one thing—Milo. My jaw clenched at the mention of him. I thought back to Saturday night when he'd called Sloan. I'd have bet my last dollar that this sudden opportunity was discussed on that call—and Sloan hadn't said a word to me about it.

"It would have been nice if you'd clued me in," I said somewhat curtly. As his agent, I was annoyed that he'd kept it from me, yet knew I had no right to be mad on a personal level. He was a grown man who could make his own decisions. Still, I couldn't help but think about his past injuries and worry that he could somehow hurt himself. After everything he went through, a setback could be devastating.

"Kallie, don't be upset."

"I'm not upset," I lied.

"Yes, you are. I can hear it in your voice."

I sighed and pinched the bridge of my nose. I spotted Gabby out of the corner of my eye, looking at me with concern.

"I just don't want to see you have a setback. Against all odds, you've made almost a complete recovery, but you still have issues with your hip—you told me so yourself. There's a reason the doctors didn't clear you."

"I told you why the doc didn't give me clearance—it was only because my stamina pressing the gas and brake pedals was shot. It had nothing to do with the replacement joint and everything to do with the pain I experienced. I want to see if I can work through it."

"But Sloan—"

"Look, Kallie," he interrupted impatiently. "I'm headed to the track in a couple of hours. This week is just setup and practice. The MILL isn't for another six weeks. Why don't you come down to the track with Gabby? You can see for yourself how it all works. I promise to know my limits. And when you come, make sure to wear your rainbows. I need your optimistic energy."

Before I could respond, the line went dead. I pulled the phone away from my ear and stared at it in exasperated disbelief. I hated being hung up on—especially when I wasn't through talking. Fighting off the urge to throw the phone across the room, I tossed it on the couch where decidedly much less damage would occur.

"Damn, he can be so infuriating," I grumbled.

"What? What did he do? What happened?" Gabby hurriedly asked.

I looked at my friend's alarmed expression and sighed in resignation.

"Want to hit the race track today? I can explain on the way there."

When Gabby and I arrived at the track a couple of hours later, we stood off to the side of the pit lane and watched the flurry of activity. Fans dotted the stands, excited by the possibility of seeing celebrity race car drivers, while AC/DC blasted from the speakers strategically placed around the track. Even though there wasn't a race today, there was no denying the exhilarating energy in the air. Everywhere I looked, people buzzed about. Judging from their various tasks, I could guess who the crew members were, but the two men talking to Sloan were a mystery. They were decked out in expensive suits, making them stand out among the crew members wearing tattered jeans, stained T-shirts, and baseball caps boasting various racing emblems.

"Who are those men Sloan is talking with? That one guy in the navy suit is F-I-N-E fine," Gabby said appreciatively, and I laughed.

Sloan must have heard me because he turned away from the two men and glanced in our direction. The confidence and ease with which he stood made his presence bigger than the entire track. When his eyes landed on me, he smiled and didn't bother to mask the heat in his stare. I watched his gaze skirt up and down my body, causing butterflies to flip in my stomach. I loved the way he looked at me sometimes, as if he were picturing me naked beneath him, touching and exploring every inch.

His intoxicating gaze lingered on me for a moment longer before turning back to the two men and pointing to where Gabby and I stood.

"I'm not sure who those guys are, but it looks like we're about to find out," I said. "They're headed this way now."

"Kallie," Sloan said as he approached. "Just the woman I was looking for."

"Oh?" I said in surprise, looking from Sloan to the other two men.

"Yeah. I want you to meet Wyatt Bates and Joe Corbin, representatives from Kapton Motor Oil, the head sponsor for Tyler's car that I'm going to race." I raised an eyebrow but didn't comment on Sloan's certainty about whether he *could* actually race or not. Instead, I extended my hand to the two men.

"It's a pleasure."

"Wyatt and Joe, this is Kallie and her friend Gabby. Kallie is my…" Sloan trailed off, not seeming to know how he should introduce me. In truth, I didn't know either. I supposed we could have assumed I was his girlfriend. However, we had yet to discuss making our relationship public. I thought it was best for Sloan's reputation to keep it quiet, and until I told my father about us, it was best for me too. The last thing I needed was for him to hear about me carrying on with a client from the press.

Smiling, I took the lead and broke the awkward silence.

"I'm Sloan's P.R. agent. Gabby is a friend of mine. She's in town visiting, and I thought I'd bring her down to the track to see what the fuss was all about."

"It's nice to meet you," Gabby said.

Wyatt held out his hand for her, which she readily took. He was the guy in the navy suit who she'd been eyeing up, and I could easily see why. The man oozed sex appeal, and if his arrogant stance was any indication, I thought he knew it too. He gave Gabby a flirtatious wink, and she all but swooned at his feet. I wasn't sure if I wanted to laugh or roll my eyes.

"Is it safe to assume I'll be working closely with your company over the next few weeks?" I asked, hoping to save my friend from embarrassing herself.

"Yes, ma'am. We're expecting good things from Sloan," Wyatt said.

"We were thrilled when he agreed to come out of retirement and fill in for Tyler," Joe added.

*Retirement?*

"Yes, well… I guess everything happens for a reason," was all I could say as I discretely flashed Sloan a questioning look. He didn't notice my confusion, nor did he seem surprised by what Joe had said.

"We should plan a time for you to come down to the Kapton Corporate offices and meet with our marketing team," Wyatt suggested. "We have our own PR strategy already in the works, but since you know Sloan better than we do, we'd like to pick your brain on ways we might be able to heighten that PR."

"That sounds great," I agreed and reached into my purse for a business card. "My number is on here. Give me a call, and we can set something up."

"We'll look forward to it," Wyatt said as he pocketed my card. "Sloan, we're going to head out. Ace Apparel should be here in an hour to fit you for new gear with the Kapton logo. The car should be ready to go by Wednesday. Joe and I will be back then."

"Sounds like a plan," Sloan said. The three men shared a hearty handshake, then Joe and Wyatt walked away. Sloan turned back to Gabby and me. "Come on. I want to show you something."

"Wait. I need to go over a few things with you first. Before driving here, I made some calls to change your schedule. I've canceled your Safe Track events for this week and put off Jeremiah for the time being." I paused, suddenly remembering what Joe Corbin had said about Sloan coming out of retirement. "Also, why does Kapton think you came out of retirement? What was that all about?"

"Milo told them that, and I just went along with it. I didn't get into the details with him."

"Well, don't you think you should, especially since it's not entirely true?"

"Kallie," he interrupted, clasping my face between his palms. There was a mischievous sparkle in his eye that piqued my curiosity. "Thank you for clearing my schedule, and as much as I'd like to debate with you about what Milo said, does it matter? I'm more interested in something else right now. I'm going to try racing again, and that's all I'm focused on. Are you with me?"

"Yeah, Sloan. I'm with you."

"Good." He beamed and reached for my hand, but I pulled away and shook my head.

"I think it's best if we keep our relationship on the down-low for now," I explained. "You'll be in the spotlight again soon enough, and we don't need to give the press any reason to speculate more than they already will."

Sloan shrugged.

"Whatever you say. You're the boss. But just so you know, it's going to be hard keeping my hands off of you if you continue showing up at the track in those little shorts."

I flushed, and Gabby snorted a laugh, which only caused my blush to deepen. I looked down at my black t-shirt and cut-off jean shorts. I hadn't expected to conduct business today, or I would have dressed more appropriately. I'd deliberately worn these clothes, knowing I wouldn't care if I accidentally brushed up against grease like I had the last time I was at the track.

Seeming oblivious to my embarrassment, Sloan turned to walk away. Gabby and I followed him across the track and toward a set of tall, wide double doors.

"I think it's pretty ironic that Kallie, of all people, is going to be working side by side with a motor oil company," Gabby pointed out as we walked.

"Tell me about it. I was thinking about that when I shook their hands. I know it's part of the business, but I'm going to have a hard time overlooking the fact that they're one of the biggest culprits of air pollution. I'm going to have to make a sizable donation to Greenpeace just to ease my conscience."

"Just remind me not to tell you what the gas mileage is for these babies," Sloan said with a chuckle as he slid open the large metal doors. A parking lot opened up on the other side, revealing four large red trailers, three of them built around matching semi-trucks. They stood tall, sleek, and shiny, with the Kapton Motor Oil logo emblazoned in black and silver lettering along the sides.

"Fancy," Gabby remarked.

"This is how we'll get to San Antonio, Texas for the race. International races would have a different transportation system for obvious reasons, but U.S. races typically travel by road. That right there," he said, pointing to a windowless trailer, "that's the hauler. It's how the car will be transported. The other three are totor homes for the top-ranking crew members. Most likely, additional haulers will be added for equipment, but these are to showcase."

"Showcase?" I asked.

"The sponsors can go a little overboard with these things. It's like there's this unspoken competition to see which team can pull up looking the best. The drivers never mind because it's to our benefit." Reaching up, he unlatched the door to the totor home that had Tyler McDermott's name written on the side, and I wondered if the name would soon be changed to Sloan's. "Step inside, and I'll show you what I mean."

Climbing aboard, I looked around the surprisingly luxurious layout. There was a spacious kitchen and dining area, complete with smaller-than-average stainless steel appliances. Black leather armchairs and a couch occupied what could only be described as a living room, with a large screen T.V. hanging on the wall adjacent to them.

"Wow! You weren't kidding about these being a showcase!" Gabby gushed, sliding her hand over the black and silver veined marble countertop in the kitchen area. "It's gorgeous in here."

"The sides pop out, which makes for more room. It can sleep up to eight, but the king bed in the back is reserved for the driver. That's me," he added with a wink.

I eyed him curiously, once again biting my tongue about whether or not he could even race, as I followed him toward the back. He sounded so happy and excited. I'd never seen him quite like this before—he was like a little kid on Christmas showing off his new toys. Who was I to kill his spirit?

When we reached the back room, a small master suite with a private bathroom came into view. The composite wood walls were painted a muted gray, and the bed was covered with a plush red comforter and black throw pillows. It matched the overall sleek and extremely masculine style of the upscale RV.

"I like it," I said as I stepped past Sloan to get a better look at the room.

Moving to the left to make room for Gabby to enter, Sloan took advantage of the tight space by placing his hands on my hips. With minimal effort, he pulled me back, so the curve of my spine was against his hard chest. He leaned in, and I could feel his breath hot on my neck while he not-so-subtly slid one hand under the hem of my T-shirt to connect with the bare skin at my waist. I shivered at the contact but quickly pushed his hand down and cast a side-eye at Gabby to see if she'd noticed. She was looking around the room, seemingly unaware that Sloan was trying to feel me up right in front of her.

"I can't wait to feel you naked in that bed," Sloan whispered softly into my ear. I stifled a gasp as I felt his fingers graze under my shirt once more.

"Um," Gabby said, making a loud show of clearing her throat. "I'll just step outside and leave you two to it."

"No, it's fine!" I said hurriedly and slapped Sloan's hand away. "Sloan just needs to learn how to behave."

I angled my head to give him a pointed stare. He laughed and held up his hands in mock surrender.

"Hey, don't blame me. I told you what I think about those shorts."

"We should head back anyway," I told them and stepped back out of the bedroom, away from Sloan's wandering hands. "The apparel people will be here soon, and Gabby needs to get to the airport by—"

"Sloan!" yelled a male voice. Startled, I turned and saw Milo poking his head inside the door to the totor home.

"What's up, Milo?" Sloan asked.

Milo looked right past Gabby and me as if we weren't even standing there and motioned with his head toward the track.

"Stop fucking around in here. You can have a threesome *after* the race," he snapped. My spine instantly stiffened in indignation. "Ace Apparel just arrived. You need to go get fitted."

"I'll be right there," Sloan replied.

"When you're through with that, I need to talk to you. Meet me in the sponsor's lounge." Milo paused, his gaze quickly flashing to my face, before looking back at Sloan. "And when you come, come alone."

Then he was gone, leaving the totor home door to slam closed in his wake.

"I really don't like that man," I murmured.

"I'm pretty sure the feeling is mutual," Gabby observed.

"Milo just hates it when his drivers are distracted by women," Sloan rationalized. "I'm sorry, Kallie. I know he can be a real dick, but I can't cut him loose now. I wouldn't be here today if he didn't land this opportunity for me. I'll talk to him, though. He needs to cut that shit out. There's no reason for him to be so rude to you."

"Don't worry about it. It's not worth it," I tried to assure. However, inside I was seething. I never wanted to slap someone as much as I did Milo. He was an asshole—plain and simple. There was no other word to describe him.

The three of us exited the totor home and made our way back to the track.

"Things are moving along pretty quick, Sloan. Have you talked to your doctor or physical therapist about all of this?" I inquired as we walked.

"Not yet."

"Why do I get the feeling that you're not going to?"

"I'll think about it. How long are you two planning on sticking around the track?" he asked, clearly trying to change the subject.

"Not much longer. I thought Gabby and I could take a quick walk around the inside corridor, maybe stop at the gift shop, then leave for the airport."

"So, I'll see you later then?"

I shrugged.

"Possibly. The day sort of flipped upside down on me. I haven't thought much past bringing Gabby to the airport."

Sloan stopped walking, forcing Gabby and me to look back at him.

"Gabby, if you don't mind," Sloan said as he grabbed my hand. "She'll be right back."

Without warning, Sloan all but dragged me a few yards away toward the spectator stands until we rounded the corner into a small secluded alcove behind the seating area.

"Sloan, what are you—" I protested but was immediately silenced when he pressed my back against the concrete wall.

I gasped, but he stifled any protest I may have had by covering my mouth with his. Within a matter of seconds, heat exploded through my veins. His kiss was deep and demanding. I didn't care about who might walk by and see us or about what they might think of a returned celebrity racer caught in a liplock with his PR agent—all that mattered was the passionate power of his lips on mine.

I surrendered to him, allowing his tongue to push past my parted lips. Pulling my hips sharply against him, he forced my back and neck into a slight arch and angled his head to get better access. He groaned against my mouth, the vibration causing my nipples to stiffen in response.

"God, Kallie. I'll never get enough of you," he murmured, then continued to ravish me like a starving man who couldn't get his fill.

I reached up to tangle my fingers through his dark waves, pulling him closer and encouraging him to take more. But much to my regret, he broke the kiss and pulled slightly away. I was breathless from the electrifying sensations coursing through my body, leaving me charged with nowhere to go.

"Well, that was some goodbye kiss," I joked in between pants as I tried to catch my breath.

Pressing his forehead to mine, his blue eyes bored into mine with such intensity that goosebumps formed on my arms.

"That wasn't a goodbye kiss, Kallie. That was a promise of later."

Stepping back, he flashed me one of those lopsided, sexy grins I loved so much, then turned and walked out toward the track. I was left momentarily stunned. Shaking my head to clear it, I followed his path only to find Gabby staring at Sloan as he passed by her. She had a look of total bewilderment on her face.

"What the hell was that all about?" she demanded. I shrugged sheepishly but didn't answer. I couldn't take my eyes off Sloan as he sauntered away. I didn't want him to go, yet I couldn't stay. All I knew was that, after I dropped Gabby off at the airport, I would be counting down the seconds until I experienced Sloan's promise of later. It was crazy how much I always looked forward to our time together. He'd quickly become the reason my sun and moon rose and fell. He was why the stars seemed to twinkle a little brighter and…

*Oh my God.*

A heaviness began to build in my chest, welling in my throat until I thought I might choke. And at that moment, a sense of perfect clarity burst forth.

*I'm falling in love with him.*

I knew when I agreed to pursue this thing with us, it would be risky. My emotions had a mind of their own, and I knew I could fall for him. I just never anticipated I would fall this hard and this fast. The realization crashed over me like a tidal wave, crushing me upon impact.

At first, I was flooded with happiness—until the brutal reality washed it all away as I remembered the gypsy's words. Gabby may have told me that Austin paid the fortune teller to say those things, but what if it wasn't all a ruse? What if her words were a real premonition, and I was setting myself up to be broken? If that was the case, it was too late to turn back now. I had a full heart—full of blossoming love for a man who I wasn't sure would love me back. Our relationship was supposed to be temporary. I would be going back to D.C., and if all went well, he'd be going back to his first and only love—racing.

I didn't know how much time had passed, but I was brought to attention by a hand waving in front of my face. I blinked and focused my gaze on a wide-eyed Gabby.

"Sorry, Gabs."

"Shit. You've got it really bad for him."

I studied Gabby's face and wondered if I should share my thoughts.

"I do—I *really* do. I'm not sure what to do about it either," I admitted.

"What do you mean?"

"This is going to sound so stupid, especially after you told me the truth about what Austin did, but what if the gypsy wasn't faking her predictions after all?"

"Oh my God, Kallie. Stop right this minute."

"I told you it would sound stupid," I said with a small laugh that I didn't really feel. "I guess it's been such a foundational belief in my life for so long that it's hard to shake the foreboding feelings about what the gypsy said. Even though I now know it was all a ruse, it's almost like the damage has already been done. Plus, I just can't help considering my history of falling for the wrong guy. I have no illusions when it comes to Sloan. We aren't a fairytale. In a few months, my contract will be over, and we'll go our separate ways. And when that happens, it will be just like the gypsy said, regardless of whether she knew it then or not—my heart will be broken."

"Who says you have to leave when your contract is over?"

"Gabby, I can't stay here. I have a whole life in D.C., and I could never stay away permanently. I'd miss my parents and little sister too much. Emma is growing so fast. I wouldn't miss that for the world."

Gabby tilted her head, seeming to contemplate something for a moment, before giving me a small smile.

"Do you know what I think?" she asked.

"What?"

"I think everything you've experienced in your life has brought you to this moment—the gypsy, Austin's prank, Dean, the job transfer to California, and even the dumb Charlie-Charlie game we used to play. I think the universe was preparing you for something bigger. And maybe, just maybe, Sloan is that something. You'll never know unless you take a chance."

# Chapter Twenty-Two

*Sloan*

Kallie and I entered the front door of my house after having spent the morning at the track. I'd been behind the wheel practicing almost every day of the past two weeks, and my hip was feeling the result. Kallie had been by my side for it all. I loved having her there, but I hated it at the same time. Her constant presence made it difficult to disguise the pain when it got really bad. I wasn't sure why I continued to try to hide it. Perhaps it was my ego not wanting to make me look weak. She'd been so supportive, and I didn't want her to worry or second guess my decision to do this.

Deliberately falling behind to stay out of her line of sight, I followed her into the living room with a slight limp as I attempted to shift my weight away from my left hip. I managed to make it to the couch just before she turned toward me.

"How are you feeling?" she asked.

"I'm feeling great," I lied and flashed her a bright smile. "I'm happy with the progress we made today on the track. Tyler's crew and I have really clicked. They're starting to feel like my own now. It's always a good day when we manage to shave a few seconds off the clock."

Her expression was doubtful, but I didn't let my grin falter.

"If you say so," she said with a shake of her head. She walked over to the patio doors, folded her arms, and stared out across the yard.

"Don't believe me?"

"Not really." She sighed, then turned to face me once more. "You try to hide it, but I can see you're hurting, and I don't understand why you're pushing yourself so hard. I get that you want to race again, but why push so quickly for this race in particular? There are other races you can enter, ones that would give you more time to prepare. As it stands right now, you've barely gotten through the past two weeks, and there are still four more weeks to go."

I knew she was right, and I should probably do as she suggested. The pain I felt after only one day behind the wheel had been enough to give me a reason to reconsider. However, after the conversation I had with Tyler a few days earlier, I quickly realized it was too late for me to pull out. He needed me to win this.

"The thought has definitely crossed my mind, but I can't. Not now. It's not just about me, Kallie. It's about Tyler McDermott too."

"Tyler? What about him?"

I leaned back and rubbed my forehead, remembering the anguish in my friend's voice when he talked about Amy.

"It's his wife. She has cancer. After Tyler got home from the hospital last week, I called him. Amy, his wife, is in rough shape—much worse than I realized. He's been in touch with some doctors about an experimental treatment available in Switzerland. He wants to take her there, but the price tag is insane. It's basically going to cost him two-hundred grand just to walk in the door, then seventy-two hundred dollars per treatment after that, spanning three days a week for four months. His wife qualifies for the trial, but he needs the prize money from the MILL to do it."

"I'm not following you. If you race, how does it help him?"

"If I win, it's three million dollars, minus the crew and Milo's cut. That doesn't include any contingency dollars put in by sponsors. Even if I don't win but finish in the top ten, there's still a sizable amount of bonus money to be paid out. Obviously, I'm going to race to win, but I don't plan to keep any prize money. I don't know how I could after hearing about Amy. Tyler is desperate. I'm going to give any winnings I get to the McDermotts so they can get Amy the treatment she needs."

She just stared at me for a few seconds, seeming to take a moment to absorb what I'd said, then walked over to where I was sitting.

"That's a lot of money to give up, Sloan."

"It is," I agreed.

Taking a seat next to me, she placed a soft kiss on my cheek.

"You're a good man," she said softly. "I can't believe you're going to give it all away. I don't know anyone who would do that."

"Don't kid yourself," I brushed off. "I might be doing a good thing, but I have selfish reasons for doing it too. Competing in the MILL will give me the exposure I need to reinstate myself into the racing world. There will be other purses to win."

She eyed me thoughtfully, then clasped my hand between hers and stood up.

"Maybe, maybe not. I just hope you don't kill yourself in the process. You need to be careful with that hip. That said, come on. Let's do some of the yoga techniques I taught you. You need to stretch after racing this morning."

*Fuck.*

Stretching was the last thing I wanted to do right now. I could barely move from the red-hot pain blistering across my left hip. If I stood up and attempted to twist myself into a pretzel as she did, she would immediately know how bad I was hurting today.

"I will later," I told her. "Right now, I just want to chill for a bit."

"Alright. Take your time. Just make sure to do it. If you don't mind, I'm going to use your shower. I need to get the stink of exhaust out of my hair. I have to meet with the marketing team at Kapton Motor Oil at three, and I don't want to walk in reeking like their product."

"The shower is all yours. I'll take one afterward."

She narrowed her gaze suspiciously, and I knew what she was thinking. Kallie had spent more time at my place than hers as of late. She'd taken numerous showers here—many of which I'd climbed in to join her. However, just the thought of doing that today made the stabbing pain in my hip seem all that much worse.

If she was questioning my sudden lack of libido, she didn't voice it. Instead, she quietly made her way upstairs to the master bath. It wasn't until I heard the faucet turn on that I let out a quiet groan. Shifting my weight, I stood up. Pain shot down my leg, and I winced as I slowly made my way to the kitchen for an ice pack. Alternating cold and heat seemed to work the best when it got this bad.

After securing the ice pack inside the waistband of my tactical racing pants, I went back to the couch. Twenty minutes later, I heard Kallie turn off the shower. Thankfully, my hip was feeling remarkably better—not great, but at least I could stand up without wincing. All I needed to do now was quickly get heat on it, and the shower usually worked best to loosen it up. After I did that, I would attempt the stretches Kallie had suggested.

Placing the ice pack back inside the freezer, I made the seemingly impossible hike up the stairs. When I entered the bedroom, I stopped dead in my tracks. Kallie was standing by the bed digging through her overnight bag, her hair wrapped in a towel, the ends of her hair dripping water down her shoulders onto the carpet. The afternoon sun was shining in through the balcony door, casting a glowing halo around her. She looked like a beautiful, blonde angel.

Not bothering to fight the gravitational pull I always felt from her, I walked over to the bed and sat down on the edge.

"Come here, gorgeous," I said.

When she turned to face me, I reached up and began to pull the towel from her body, but she caught my hand to stop me.

"Sloan, we don't have time. I have to—"

"Shhh. I know you have to leave soon. Trust me and just sit down," I told her and patted the bed next to me. Doing as I asked, she released my hand, allowing the towel to fall from her body. I caught it as she moved to sit naked beside me. "Turn so your back is to me."

Again, she did as I'd instructed. I loved that she was so trusting, even when in the most vulnerable state. It only made me want to be buried balls deep inside of her. If it weren't for the pain in my hip, I'd tell her to blow off the meeting with Kapton so I could do precisely that. I'd spread her wide and savor every inch of her until the sun came up the next day. However, that wasn't my current reality, so I settled for second best instead—and touching Kallie in any way was always at the top of my list of things to do.

Using the towel that had been wrapped around her, I brought it up to dry her hair, then moved down to wipe away the droplets of water from her arms. I took my time drying her, slowly brushing the soft cotton over her upper body, suddenly overcome with the need to take care of her just as she had been taking care of me for the past couple of weeks.

Leaning in, I kissed along her shoulder, over the delicate outlines of her star and moon tattoo, until I reached her neck. Her breathing became short, coming out in little gasps when I moved the towel around to dry her breasts. My cock grew hard in my pants, and I had to shift to make room for my girth. My movement caused her to turn her head and look at me. Passion had ignited in her emerald greens, a fire burning so hot, my dick instantly stiffened to a near painful level.

"Fuck, Kallie. You can't look at me like that."

"Like what?"

"You know what. You'll never make it to your meeting if you keep it up. You're too damn tempting."

Pulling her naked body against my fully clothed one, I brought my lips to hers. She moaned against my mouth, moving her body against mine to deepen the kiss. I gripped the back of her neck as her hand ran over the span of my chest, digging into the muscles. Sliding her hands under my shirt, her fingertips skimmed the tips of my nipples.

"Shit," I hissed, knowing I wasn't going to be able to put off the inevitable for much longer at this rate. And when she moved her hand to cup the bulge in my pants, I was reminded of how this beautiful, rainbow mermaid goddess could destroy me with just one touch.

Almost reluctantly, Kallie pulled back. Her cheeks were flushed, and her lips were swollen from our kiss that had been cut short.

"Promise me we'll finish this later?" she asked.

"I don't need to promise anything, baby. I can guarantee it."

"I need to get dressed. I have to be out the door in twenty minutes."

Reaching around to squeeze her backside, I gave it a light slap before giving her a quick peck on the nose.

"You better hurry then. Kapton is waiting."

Climbing from the bed, she grabbed her overnight bag and rushed into the bathroom to get ready. I lay back on the bed, suddenly realizing how much I enjoyed having her here. In fact, I didn't like the idea of her *not* being here. While we'd barely been together long enough to say we should move in together, I couldn't help but fantasize about making that a reality one day. When we weren't lighting the sheets on fire, we'd developed into an easy relationship. Sometimes we would talk long into the night. Other times we didn't need to speak at all, and I never found those moments of silence to be awkward—it was golden. She knew who she was, what she was, and she owned it. And more importantly—she knew who I was and accepted it.

When Kallie emerged from the bathroom fifteen minutes later, she'd been completely transformed. I sat up, only to feel pain spread through my hip. I winced but pushed down the ache to take a moment to appreciate her. Dressed in a long skirt and an airy peach blouse, she'd pulled her hair back into a rainbow braid. I looked forward to unraveling all of those multicolored locks later.

"Okay, I'm off," she said as she slipped into a pair of sling-backed heels. "I'm hoping we can wrap this meeting up in a couple of hours. Fingers crossed."

Coming over to where I sat, she planted a quick kiss on my lips, then hurried out the door. I stayed seated on the bed and watched her leave, needing to be sure she was out of sight before I attempted to move. The shooting pain I'd experienced a moment earlier made me terrified to stand up. I should have gotten into the shower sooner. I mentally kicked myself for getting distracted and giving the joint time to stiffen.

I waited a few minutes until I heard the opening and closing of the front door, then gingerly moved to stand. Instantly, pain like molten fire radiated from my hip.

"Fuck!" I hissed as I took a few steps toward the master bath. My body shook, and I had to grab the doorframe for support. I gripped it so hard, my knuckles turned white as I allowed a few minutes for the pain to subside. Once the tremors settled, I slowly continued until I reached the vanity. Yanking open the drawer, I pulled out the bag Milo had given me that first day at the track. The reason he wanted to see me alone in the sponsor's box—without Kallie—was because of the contents in the clear plastic Ziplock. Inside, there were fifteen pills of oxycodone.

I recalled Milo's words as he shoved the bag into my hand.

*"I can get more if you need it. All you have to do is ask."*

I shouldn't have accepted them. I should have thrown the pills in his face instead.

But I didn't.

Although I wanted to push through this on my own, there was a small part of me that knew I might need them one day—and that day had arrived. With a shaking hand, I unsealed the bag and pulled out a single pill.

I stared at it for what seemed like forever before looking up at my reflection in the mirror. Pain was clearly written across my face, my eyes seeming hollow from the days spent trying to endure it. With the race still four weeks away, I had to do what I had to do. After that, I could take a break and give my body time to heal again. There was no point in suffering this way if I had something readily available to numb the agony. As long as I wasn't under the influence of the pills when behind the wheel or downing them with a shot of Jack, what difference did it make if I took them? It wasn't like before when I searched for the pleasant emptiness only the opioid pills and booze could bring. This time, I wasn't trying to chase a high—I just wanted to douse the excruciating fire in my hip so I could race. It was the only thing that mattered.

Looking back down at the pill nestled in the center of my palm, I brought it to my mouth and placed it on my tongue.

# Chapter Twenty-Three

*Kallie*

Over the past three weeks, Sloan and I had settled into an easy routine. Since I was needed at the track for various reasons, I'd chosen to do as much as I could remotely from my laptop rather than work from home. Each morning, we would drive to and from the track together. It had been my idea, suggesting it would be better for the planet if we drove my car since it got better gas mileage, and he had readily agreed. While I always cared about the environmental impact of my choices, this time, it had merely been an excuse. Doing all the driving also meant Sloan didn't have to drive home after a hard day of practice.

While he practiced with his crew, I would head up to the sponsor's box and strategize. Never before had I been so devoted to a client. I'd been his shadow, essentially working fifteen to eighteen hours a day ever since he returned to the track. I spent my time working diligently on setting up events to increase public awareness of Sloan's accomplishments. Carefully-orchestrated press releases and public appearances with Safe Track brought positive attention from community leaders, resulting in additional photo ops with prominent members of local society. I worked hand-in-hand with Kapton Motor Oil's marketing executives to spotlight the Atwood Racing and Kapton brands through various media platforms. And thanks to Cooper's connections, I even managed to get Sloan a guest spot on Jimmy Kimmel the week after the MILL.

Through it all, I somehow managed to avoid Milo. I let him handle the endorsement opportunities flooding in from numerous motorsport products, all vying for Sloan's face to appear in their commercials. The endorsements were dollar signs, and I'd quickly learned that was all Milo cared about anyway.

The only problem I ran into while working remotely was the interruptions. From the people coming in and out of the sponsor's box for various reasons to the loud rumbling of the cars on the track, it was hard to concentrate at times. Popping in a set of earbuds tended to drown out most of the noise, but that didn't always work. The constant distractions often meant I had to write press releases and respond to emails late into the night—much to Sloan's complaint.

While I hadn't actually moved into his place, I found myself spending more nights at his house than mine. It seemed to work better with the routine we'd established. It also allowed me to keep a closer eye on Sloan's physical condition after a day of hard practice—and by the look of his current state when he entered the sponsor's box where I was working, today had been a tough one.

He smiled as he approached, and I pulled my earbuds from my ears. I studied him, seeing the way he was trying to cover up his limp. He couldn't fool me. He was hurting again but trying to hide it.

"Hey, Rainbow Brite. Listening to anything good?" He asked, and leaned over to plant a kiss on my forehead.

"Ruelle. How are you feeling?" I asked—just like I had every day since he decided to get back behind the wheel. Before he spoke, I knew what his reply would be.

"I'm feeling great," he predictably answered.

*Liar.*

I didn't voice the thought out loud because it wasn't worth the argument.

"You don't look too great."

"Thanks for the compliment," he sardonically replied. "Are you ready to go?"

"Yeah, just give me a minute to get my stuff together." Glancing back down at my computer screen, I saved the press release document I'd been working on, then closed the laptop. After gathering my things, Sloan and I headed out.

Out the corner of my eye, I monitored him as we walked across the parking lot at Motor Club Speedway toward my car. When we reached it, he opened the driver's side door of the BMW for me, then made his way around to the passenger side. As I buckled my seatbelt, I watched his movements while he climbed in. He was cautious, and I caught his wince when he thought I wasn't looking.

We were supposed to leave for San Antonio, Texas in two days. The big race wasn't for another week, but my concern for Sloan had grown steadily with each passing day. I wasn't convinced he'd be able to pull it off. He practiced hard, but the actual race would be even more challenging, and it would come with more risks. It was one thing to practice in a controlled environment with a couple of other cars on the track, and something completely different to be going up against forty or more other racers on race day. I suspected Sloan might have been thinking the same, as his mood had become increasingly sullen over the past week.

"Have you thought any more about calling your doctor?" I asked. "PT might help considerably right now."

"Kallie, don't. I told you. I'm fine," he replied irritably. He ran a hand through his dark waves, and his eyes flashed. It was impossible to miss the fiercely determined set to his jaw.

I pursed my lips and shook my head in frustration. He was as stubborn as a mule and resolved to see this through. The only thing I could do was continue to support him.

"I packed a hemp extract in my overnight bag. It's a pain relief cream. When we get back to your place, you should rub some of it on that hip. Afterward, I can help you stretch," I offered rather than push the issue further. "I'll need to stop by my place at some point too. We leave for San Antonio in two days, and I still need to pack."

He turned his head to look out the window but didn't respond. Suppressing a sigh, I turned the key in the ignition and began the drive back to Sloan's house in Beverly Grove. An awkward silence fell between us, and I flipped on the radio for some background noise. After fiddling with the controls, I settled on an alternative music station. Green Day's "21 Guns" began playing through the speakers.

I tried to focus on the lyrics, but my effort was in vain. All I could think about was how much it hurt to see the man I fell in love with suffering so much. While I hadn't told him I loved him yet, I was sure about the depths of my feelings. I just hadn't found the right time to tell him amidst the insane schedule we'd been keeping. By the time I finished work for the night, it was almost always close to midnight. We'd fall into bed, make love into the early hours of the morning, only to have the alarm go off all too soon, and we'd start the routine all over again.

However, deep down, I knew I could have found the time to tell him. My excuse was really only for myself because I was terrified of Sloan's reaction once I told him. It could significantly complicate things if my feelings weren't reciprocated. Neither of us needed that kind of strain a week before his race. It would be better for all if I kept my feelings to myself for a bit longer.

When I pulled into Sloan's driveway almost an hour later, we still hadn't spoken. After I killed the engine, Sloan began to climb out of the car. I turned to look at him. Pain was prevalent in every line of his face, distorting his perfect features with dark shadows. I hurried out and walked around to his side of the car to help him. I reached for his arm, but he pushed it away.

"I've got it," he snapped, letting his pride outweigh his need for help.

"No, you don't. Stop being a fool," I told him and wrapped an arm around his waist. "I might be small, but I'm stronger than I look. Put your weight on me."

He didn't protest this time and leaned into me. When we got to the front door, I reached into his front pocket for the keys to his house.

"Careful. If you dig deep enough, you might find something else," he teased.

"You're incorrigible," I said with a small laugh. "You can barely walk, yet you zeroed in on the least important thing at the moment. Is sex always on your brain?"

"Only when it comes to you."

We entered the house, and I led Sloan over to the couch. After he sat down, he released a small groan. I worried my bottom lip, hating to see him this way.

"Stay here. I'm going to run and grab that hemp cream I told you about."

"I can assure you—I'm not going anywhere."

Not wasting another minute, I hurried up the stairs and into his master bathroom to where I'd left my overnight bag. After locating my makeup tote, I pulled it out and sifted through the contents until I found the cream. I hoped that the combination of hemp and other organic ingredients, including menthol and arnica, would soothe the muscles supporting his joint. Since he still refused to work with his doctors and therapists, the cream combined with stretching would have to do for today.

"Here you go," I said after I returned to the living room. "Just scoop out a good dollop with your fingers and rub it directly over the painful areas. While you do that, I'm going to head back upstairs and change into clothes more suitable for stretching. Do you want me to grab you a pair of shorts or something while I'm up there?" I asked, not wanting him to do the stairs if at all possible.

"Please. There are gym shorts in the second drawer of my dresser." I turned to walk away, but he called out. "Kallie?"

"Yeah."

He hesitated, and his brow furrowed. His expression held a certain amount of sadness mixed with resolve. But there was also a longing I had never seen before.

"Thank you," he eventually said. "I'm not sure if any of this would be possible if I didn't have you with me."

I smiled, but my concern for him prevented the smile from reaching my eyes. I was worried sick. As much as I tried to understand his reasoning, I wished he would end this insanity.

"Of course," was all I could say, then hurried upstairs to change.

When I returned to the bathroom, I quickly stripped out of my jeans and slipped into a pair of yoga shorts. I left my red Atwood Racing Enterprise T-shirt on, a recent wardrobe addition I'd snagged from Sloan's latest merchandise shipment, then pulled my hair back into a ponytail.

"What is this crap, Kallie? It smells weird," I heard Sloan yell from downstairs.

I chuckled to myself as I smoothed my hair fly-aways with a brush.

"Just put it on," I called back. "I'll be down in two minutes after I put my stuff away."

I moved to toss the hairbrush back into my bag. In my haste, I banged my hand against the marble top of the vanity.

"Damn it!" I cursed when I saw I'd broken a nail. It was only partially torn, but it had broken near the nail bed. Reaching into my makeup tote, I dug around for nail clippers but came up empty-handed. Wondering if Sloan had any, I opened the bathroom vanity drawer and began rifling through the contents. I didn't see a pair at first glance, so I bent to look into the back of the drawer and pulled the contents forward.

I didn't find nail clippers, but I did find pills—and they didn't appear to be the over-the-counter kind. They weren't cold pills or aspirin, nor were they in a bottle from a pharmacy. Instead, the little white tablets were in a clear plastic Ziplock bag. Upon closer inspection, I saw letters and numbers carved into the pills. My heart began to pound in my chest.

Bending down to where my jeans lay on the bathroom floor, I pulled my cell phone from the back pocket to do a quick Google search. I forced myself to relax, hoping beyond hope the pills were not what I suspected. Maybe I was wrong—perhaps it was just flu medicine or something of the like. However, deep down, I didn't think that was the case. Copying the indented text from the pills, I typed "white tablet M 05 52" into the browser and waited for the results to populate. Once they did, I sucked in a breath and felt my eyes widen in disbelief. Although the internet pictures varied slightly, an educated guess said the bag in my hand was full of oxycodone.

The betrayal was a slap in the face—both personally and professionally. On a professional level, I worried about what would happen to the Quinn & Wilkshire name if this got out—especially after all I'd done to bolster Sloan's image. While improving his reputation was in my job description, it was what I did during off-hours that made Sloan unique to any other client—that was personal.

I'd spent the past month watching him silently suffer, unable to do anything but show my support in every way I knew how. Hours upon hours had been spent caring for his physical condition. From learning his PT exercises and teaching him yoga to researching the best natural remedies for pain, I'd done everything in my power to make sure he could get out of bed each day and do what he loved most. But it was more than how much effort I had poured into this—he had made a promise to me. No more booze. No more pills.

And I had believed him.

*Have I been nothing but a fool?*

My heart felt heavy, my emotions twisting up into a knot. I loved Sloan with my whole body and soul. To know he would disregard his promise to me and risk everything for a few pills not only made me feel betrayed but angry. Fury at what he had done surged through my veins and pulsed at my temples. My brain scrambled to organize every feeling and thought I ever had about him, trying to make sense of it all. I knew he'd been in pain, but I hadn't realized it was so bad that he had to resort to taking painkillers.

*Why didn't he just tell me?*

I hurriedly tossed the rest of my things into my overnight bag, then stalked out of the bathroom with the bag of pills in hand. Going downstairs, I found Sloan sitting on the edge of the couch with his pants pulled partially down on one side, massaging cream into his hip.

"This stuff isn't half bad," he said. "I already feel it working."

"Sloan, what are these?"

He glanced up and frowned as he focused on what I was holding. The moment he realized what it was, his furrowed brow raised, and he momentarily froze. Shaking his head, he looked back down at his hip to return to the task at hand.

"It's nothing," he brushed off.

"I don't think these are nothing. Is this oxy?"

His head snapped up, and regretful eyes raked over me. It was as if he were processing a million thoughts. However, whatever he was thinking was quickly masked with a blank expression.

"So what if it is?" he challenged.

"Are you serious right now? I had to practically scrape you off the floor after you saw Tyler's crash. You drank yourself into a stupor, admitted to wanting to take painkillers but decided—." I stopped short as a new realization came over me. "Or maybe you did take the pills after all. Is that why you promised me no more booze *and* pills?"

"Kallie, listen to me. I—"

"No. You listen to me! I've bent over backward to make sure you've received positive coverage by the press. I'm going above and beyond what is expected of me based on our contract. I get that you want to race again, but this isn't the way. I thought I was helping you, but you've been lying to me this whole time!"

He slammed frustrated hands through his hair, then stood up to adjust his pants back into their rightful place and began to pace.

"Kallie, it's not what you think. Milo gave them to me and—"

"Milo!" I covered my mouth and choked back a sob. "Of course he gave them to you. Why the hell would he give two shits as long as you win and he gets a chunk of the prize money? What's his cut in all of this?"

"Ten percent, but that's beside the—"

"Ten percent! Wait a minute—who's paying Quinn & Wilkshire for me to be here? You or him?"

"I don't see why that matters."

"It matters because it lets me know how much stake Milo has in all of this."

"Technically, I'm paying for it. Milo just signs the checks."

I wasn't sure what I thought about that. I never thought to ask before now, but now that I knew, it somehow made me feel like an overpriced prostitute. That just infuriated me further.

"I still can't believe you would do this for him. That man is a snake!" I snapped.

Sloan stopped pacing to look at me. His face hardened, and his eyes bore into me, flashing with accusation. "At least he knows how to get me behind the wheel again. And he also doesn't throw around baseless allegations—which is more than I can say for you!" he thundered.

My head snapped back in surprise as the meaning of his words sunk in.

"Are you saying you didn't take the pills?"

"Maybe I did, maybe I didn't. Why would you care either way? All that matters is that I look good in the public eye. Isn't that right?"

Spine stiffening hard and straight, I glared right back at him and snapped.

"It's not just about the press coverage, and you know it. It's about everything I've done to help you *personally*—all because I fucking care! I've spent almost every day of the past three months with you, and a good portion of one of those months was spent doing your PT exercises and practicing yoga to make sure you were doing this the healthy way. And this," I said, pointing to the bag I held up, "this is not healthy."

"What does healthy even look like, Kallie? For fucksake, healthy isn't the way I was living a few months ago. It felt like I was walking on broken glass day after day, and the only way to numb the pain of what I'd lost was to escape into a bottle. I was miserable—resigned to the fact that my life had been ruined. But now, things are different. I have a chance to do what I love again. I told you before that racing was my first love, and I'll do anything I have to do to hang on to it. If you want to be by my side for it, fine. If not, you know where the door is."

I stilled, his immobilizing words cutting me to the core, slicing open my heart, and draining all the optimism I'd felt about our future together. Staring at him with wide eyes, I saw all of his pain and heartache for his one love—and that clearly wasn't me. My eyes stung, and I shook my head in disbelief, suddenly filled with indescribable resentment. There was no stopping the tears that began to fall freely down my cheeks. I always wondered how many broken hearts one person could handle. Whether broken hearts from unforeseen disasters or broken hearts delivered by those I loved the most. I'd experienced many—but this was, without a doubt, the absolute worst.

I'd foolishly allowed myself to love Sloan so freely and so openly. I should have known better. The universe had shown me all of his arrogance and chaos, yet I still allowed myself to fall. My instincts had been wrong. I should have listened to the gypsy. I should have listened when Sloan said racing was his first and only love. Those were my mistakes. Now all I felt was a hollow emptiness.

"So that's it then?" I asked. My eyes burned with more tears, but I refused to let them fall anymore. "Either stick by your side and watch you destroy yourself or get the hell out? Those are my choices?"

He shrugged.

"If that's how you want to look at it."

He acted as if he didn't care—as if I didn't matter to him one little bit. There was no going back now—no undoing what he'd said. The hard truth was just something I'd have to swallow.

"I can't believe you would be so callous. After everything…" I whispered, unable to say more without losing all sense of composure.

"Kallie…" he began and reached for me.

"No. Don't. Just leave me the hell alone. I have to go."

Turning on my heel, I tossed the bag of pills on the kitchen table, grabbed my keys, and rushed to the front door.

"Kallie, wait!" I heard Sloan call out as I yanked it open.

I didn't look back.

# Chapter Twenty-Four

*Sloan*

I tried calling Kallie for the rest of the day but she wouldn't pick up. Instead of fighting with her, I should have told her the truth. And the fact was, I didn't take a single one of the damn pills Milo had given to me. Before I could swallow it, all I could picture was Kallie's face, and I ended up spitting it out into the toilet at the last minute. I should have flushed the whole bag—which is exactly what I did after she stormed out.

Later that night, all I wanted was Kallie. I wanted to see her, smell her, and feel her. It was as if I was going through withdrawals. Instead of alcohol and pills, Kallie was my drug of choice. I craved her as if my life depended on it.

I'd tossed and turned all night long, and when my alarm went off at seven the following day, I knew I had to go to her and make things right. I was supposed to be at the track by eleven to help load the totors for the road trip. We were scheduled to leave for Texas tomorrow morning, needing to get there early for weigh-in and heat races, but I had no intention of doing anything until I fixed this mess with Kallie.

After a quick shower, I made it to her house by eight-thirty. Her car wasn't parked in its usual spot in the driveway, and I wondered where she would be this early in the morning. It was too early for her to have left for the track. Worry for her whereabouts gnawed at me as I made my way to her front door and rang the bell, hoping she'd just decided to break with habit and park her car in the garage.

When she didn't answer, I rang it a second time and tried the door handle. It was locked. Peeking through the sidelight window next to the door, I saw suitcases lined up in the hallway. I sucked in a surprised breath when I saw how many there were. A pit in my stomach began to grow. I had a sinking suspicion the bags were not packed for Texas. She didn't need to pack that much for a week-long road trip.

Pulling my cell from my back pocket, I dialed her number. Again, there was no answer. Shoving a frustrated hand through my hair, I dialed Cooper. I knew he would be at the track soon, assuming he wasn't there already. With any luck, maybe Kallie was there too.

"Cooper," I said after my friend answered.

"Hey, man. What's up?"

"Are you at the track by any chance?"

"I just got here."

"Is Kallie there?" I asked, trying to keep the anxiousness out of my voice.

"I haven't seen her. Why?"

"Ah, I fucked up. We had a stupid argument yesterday. She basically told me to go to hell—which is exactly where I went. Last night was one long, miserable night. Now I can't find her."

"Shit, man. You definitely have a way of stepping in it," Cooper said with a slight chuckle. "Can I do anything?"

"Not really. If you see her, can you just let me know and ask her to call me?"

"Will do."

"Thanks."

I ended the call and began to walk back to my car. I racked my brain, trying to think of who else I could call. I'd spent almost every day with Kallie over the past three months, making me all but certain she didn't have any friends around here outside of my inner circle. I thought about calling Gabby to see if she'd heard from her, but quickly scratched the idea when I remembered I didn't have her number.

Just as I reached for the door of my car, Kallie's red BMW pulled into the driveway. I breathed a sigh of relief. Her gorgeous eyes were wide and steely when she saw me. She looked at me like she didn't even know me as a civil war battled across her face.

When she climbed out of the car, I stared at her. She looked hot as hell in a red halter top and those cut-off jean shorts I loved. I could tell she was braless, reminding me so much of the first night we had sex in her backyard when all I had to do was yank at the ties on her neck to free those glorious tits.

With her arms folded across her chest, she stared back at me, hurt dimming her normally bright emerald depths. Deep blue and siren red flowed through her golden blonde ponytail, and I could tell she was angry. She had every right to be. I should have been straight with her—I shouldn't have been so cruel. In her eyes, I was probably nothing more than a liar. The only defense I had was the truth. But first, I needed to feel her in my arms.

Quickly crossing the distance between us, I wrapped my arms around her. She stiffened and didn't hug me back. I didn't care. All that mattered was that she was here.

"I was worried when I didn't know where you were," I murmured as I fingered the red and blue streaks in her hair. I pulled back to look at her. "Do I dare ask what the red means?"

"Red is the color of the devil. It's what I wear when I'm flaming mad."

I chuckled at her no-nonsense tone even though I knew I shouldn't, considering the seriousness of the moment. My only excuse was that I was giddy with relief, knowing she hadn't run off somewhere.

"I'm sorry, Kallie," I earnestly said as I stroked my hands up and down her arms.

"I don't want to hear your apology," she said stiffly. "You've already said enough."

"No, actually, I haven't. All I did was say all the wrong things. I came here today to tell you what I should have right from the get-go yesterday. I didn't take those pills."

She blinked, seeming confused.

"You didn't?"

"Not a single one. After you left, I flushed them."

"Why didn't you just say so yesterday instead of leading me to believe you did?"

"I don't know. I was sore and irritable, but that's really no excuse. I guess I went into defense mode when you accused me, and I immediately turned into an asshole. Milo gave me those things a month ago. I'll admit—I thought about taking them, but…" I trailed off, trying to find the words to explain how she was the one who ultimately stopped me. Wrapping an arm around her shoulder, I turned her toward the house. "Let's go inside, and I'll try to explain."

"No," she said, stepping back and shrugging my arm away. "Sloan, I'm happy you didn't take the pills and decided to get rid of them. But for me, it's more than that. We've been spending a lot of time together, and I think we need to pump the breaks."

"What are you talking about?" I asked, my suspicion about the suitcases coming to the forefront of my mind. "The suitcases in the hallway… those aren't packed for Texas, are they?"

She slowly shook her head, confirming what I already thought I knew.

"I decided not to go to San Antonio with you. I'm going home for a while instead. I've booked a flight home for the day after tomorrow. It's not about the pills and whether or not you took them—it's about me not being able to stand seeing you in so much pain. You love racing so much that you'll kill yourself to make it happen. I can't sit by and watch you follow this path, especially knowing what you could lose. You have everything right in front of you, but you can't see it—you can't see *me*. All you see is a checkered flag."

"Of course I see you, Kallie."

"No, you don't. If you did, you would know…" She hesitated, biting her lower lip as her eyes glossed over with unshed tears.

"I would know what?" I prompted.

"You would know I was a fool who fell in love with a man who will never love me back."

Anguish ripped through my soul at her words. She began to rub her arms as if she were warding off a chill even though the day was shaping up to be a hot one. She looked so distraught, I knew better than to reach for her again—to touch her or try to kiss her sorrows away. Her eyes bore into mine, her expression a mix of confusion, hurt, and sadness. I looked down at the ground, unable to meet her gaze.

*She loves me.*

When I brought my eyes back up to meet hers, I saw the unshed tears begin to fall from her emerald greens. Knowing I was the cause for those tears shattered me.

"Kallie, I—"

She shook her head again and held up a hand to stop me from speaking.

"I wish you good luck on the race. If all goes well, I'll be back in a couple of weeks to finish our contract. As for us… I don't see how there can be an us. The gypsy tried to warn me," she said with a bitter laugh. "We've both made ourselves perfectly clear from the beginning. I told you I couldn't separate my emotions from sex, and for you, racing is and always will be your first love. Despite what I said, I can't settle for second place. Racing takes the cup. I hope she treats you well in San Antonio."

"Kallie, no. I need you there with me."

I saw the storm roll through her eyes. Grief clutched me in its fiery hold, incinerating and blistering. At that moment, everything became clear. I was going to lose her. But I couldn't lose her because…

*I love her, too.*

I tried to push the thought away, only for it to come roaring back with a vengeance. This was a first for me, and I could barely even think, let alone process it. But one thing was absolutely certain—it wasn't racing I needed. It was her—only her. Kallie was more than a pit stop—she was my checkered flag.

However, in her eyes, I loved racing more. It was why she was leaving. It had nothing to do with whether I took oxy or not and everything to do with her trying to run away from a broken heart. I reached out to try to pull her to me again, needing to tell her how I felt, but I wasn't fast enough. In a flash, she turned and ran toward the house.

"Kallie, hang on. Don't run from me again. Let's talk about this!" I called out as I charged a few steps behind her.

It took her less than two seconds to turn the key to unlock the front door before she disappeared into the house. I didn't chase her inside, but only because I needed to process my thoughts. I couldn't run in there half-cocked, professing my love. She wouldn't believe it—at least not right now. Kallie deserved the stars, the moon, and all the rainbows under the sun—and I'd be back later to make damn sure she got them.

# Chapter Twenty-Five

*Kallie*

I peered around the edge of the dining room curtains and watched Sloan pull out of the driveway. A part of me couldn't believe he was leaving without denying what I'd said—that racing was more important to him than I was. But another part of me knew it was all my fault. I'd stood too close to the fire. I'd allowed myself to get lost in him, falling hard and fast, and let the hurricane of emotions break my soul. I'd been warned of this—whether it was a misguided gypsy hoax or a hard truth—and I only had myself to blame.

Even though I was glad to hear he didn't swallow the pills, finding them opened my eyes to the day I would eventually become second to a motorsport. I'd just been in denial. It was evident that racing was his true love—his life's passion. While I'd once thought I'd be okay with that, I wasn't anymore. I couldn't settle for second place.

I let the curtains fall back into place and walked back through the living room to the back yard. My gaze flitted between the patio lounge chair and the pool, causing memories from the first night I'd been with Sloan to flash in my mind. I closed my eyes, picturing our moments together. It was almost too much to bear. I felt empty without him, lost in a black hole of misery.

I'd told him I'd come back after the race to finish out the contract, but who was I kidding? I could barely look at the back yard without missing him. Coming back and facing a man I loved with all of my heart but who would never love me in return would be more than just torture—it would destroy me. It was better if I left now while there was still hope of fixing the pieces of my shattered heart.

Going back into the house, I retrieved my cell phone from my purse and glanced at the time. It was still early on the East Coast, but I was fairly certain my mother would be awake. Sinking into the cushions of the couch, I punched her number into the keypad.

"Hewow?" answered the cutest voice I'd ever heard.

I smiled. My little sister was always an instant mood booster, no matter how bleak I might be feeling.

"Why, hello there, Miss Emma."

"I knew it was you!"

"You did, huh? You're up early today."

"I was hungwy."

"Hungry, huh? Did you have anything good for breakfast?"

"Mommy cut up some owanges and stwawbewies, and I had some ceweal. It was vewy good!"

I had to laugh. It had been a couple of weeks since I'd last spoken to Emma, and she still clearly hadn't mastered her pronunciations during that time.

"That sounds delicious! Now you're making me hungry too. I'll have to find out what mommy's secret is. Can you put her on the phone for me?"

"Sure."

"Kallie?" my mother said.

"I'm here. God, I miss her little face. I hear she's still struggling with the Rs and Ls."

"Yeah. I've been in touch with the school about it. They've assured me it's common, but they are going to start speech therapy with her next month."

"She'll get those pesky consonants down soon enough. Don't worry."

"Oh, I'm not too worried. Your father is another story, though," she added with a laugh. "He's already lined up a speech therapist to work with her next week when we're at Camp Riley."

"Oh, I didn't realize you were heading there! I haven't visited the camp in ages!" I thought back to the few summers I'd spent helping my parents and my Aunt Joy refurbish the property in Abington, Virginia. I could almost smell the tall pines and envision the rays of light that would streak through their branches as they arched over the quaint little pathways throughout the camp like a living canopy. It had once been a performing arts camp run by my grandparents, but after they died, the camp fell to ruin because my mother didn't have the funds to keep it running. After she reunited with my father, they worked together to turn what was left of the property into a literacy youth camp for low-income families.

"Yeah, it was a last-minute thing," my mother explained. "Aunt Joy decided to convert one of the unused cabins into a guest house and asked for your father's help with some of the renovations."

"That sounds like fun. Speaking of dad, is he within earshot?"

"No. He just jumped in the shower. Why?"

"I wanted to talk to you about something, and I didn't want him to freak out."

"What's wrong?" my mother hurriedly asked, the concern evident in her voice. I took a deep breath and steeled myself to tell her the true reason for my call.

"I'm coming home. Sloan, the race car driver I've been representing… Well, I don't think I can be his PR agent anymore. The problem is that there's still just shy of three months left on the contract Quinn & Wilkshire agreed to."

"Kallie, it's unlike you to not see a contract through."

"I know what's at stake. Financially, this is going to hurt me. I was counting on the bonus and possibly making partner so much, but it's not about that anymore."

"Your father definitely won't be happy. Why do you need to break the contract early?"

"I just can't be around Sloan anymore, but you can't tell dad the reasons. At least not yet. I'll have to come up with something—say we just weren't compatible or something. I don't know."

"Kallie, I don't know what you're trying to get at. Just spit it out. What the hell happened out there? Why can't you be around Sloan?"

I hesitated, unsure if I should tell her how far across the line I went with Sloan. I took another deep breath, then exhaled slowly. My mother had always been there for me no matter what, and I knew this would be no different.

"Because I fell in love with him, Mom."

She fell deathly silent and didn't speak for a long moment.

"Is he the reason you broke it off with Dean?" she eventually asked.

"Yes and no. And honestly, it doesn't matter now. I've already booked a flight home for the day after tomorrow, but after we hang up, I'm going to see about bumping it up." I paused and looked around the room. "I just can't be here anymore. The sooner I leave, the better."

"I don't know what happened between you and this guy Sloan, but running is never the answer. Unless, of course—" She stopped short, then gasped. "He didn't hurt you, did he?"

"Of course not. It's nothing like that, Mom. It's just that…" I let my words hang in the air, afraid to voice them out loud. "It's just that he'll never love me back. What can I say? I always pick the wrong guy."

"Don't say that. And how do you know he'll never love you back? I mean, look at your father and me. I thought that too, and we wasted seventeen years because of it. Does he know how you feel?"

"Sort of."

"Kallie…" she said in a warning tone.

"Okay, fine. I did tell him, but not in so many words. I didn't actually say I love you because I already know where he stands. He told me as much. Please don't push me on this. Just trust me. I need to come home."

"Alright. I'll think of something to tell your father for now. Like you said—you weren't compatible with the client. It's not a lie, per se. Just know that you're probably going to have to tell him eventually."

I breathed a sigh of relief.

"Thank you. If I can move my flight, I'll let you know and text you the flight itinerary. Can you pick me up from the airport, or should I plan on calling an Uber?"

"I haven't seen you in three months—of course I'll pick you up!"

"Perfect. Thanks again. I'll talk to you soon. Oh, and is Austin back from Japan?" I asked as an afterthought.

"Yeah. He got back a couple of days ago. He's home for a week, and then he has to go back."

"Good. That will be enough time for me to pin him down. I have a bone to pick with Austin," I added.

"What has he done now?" she inquired with a laugh.

"Not now—it's what he did years ago with a gypsy fortuneteller."

"You mean the one he paid off?"

My eyes widened in shock, feeling like the entire universe had been conspiring against me for years.

"You knew about it too! What the hell, Mom! Why didn't you tell me?"

"I don't know. I guess I didn't think much about it. Why are you so upset about it now? It was a long time ago."

I sighed, not having the energy to get into the entire tale.

"I'll explain it to you when I get home. Right now, I need to run so I can see about moving my flight. Love you, Mom."

"Love you too, baby girl. See you soon."

After I ended the call, I looked around the room once more and felt tears begin to prick the corners of my eyes. I felt foolish, heartbroken, and everything else in between. But one thing remained unchanged—I was really doing this. I was leaving Santa Monica.

Unless I could miraculously get over my feelings for Sloan, leaving meant I would probably never see him again. I wanted to tell myself I'd be okay, but I didn't think I'd ever really be okay again. Over the past three months, Sloan had irrevocably changed me. Our time together had taught me so much about myself. I finally knew what I wanted in a relationship and knew what it meant to give my whole body, heart, and soul to someone. I only wished Sloan could have been the one to give that to me in return.

Wiping the tears from my eyes, I grabbed my laptop from the kitchen table and went to sit down on the couch in the living room. Opening my music playlist, I put a song that seemed to fit my mood, then opened my inbox. As I listened to "Last One to Know" by Leah Nobel, I pulled up my flight itinerary and compared it with other available flights leaving later today or early tomorrow. Within a few minutes, I was able to find a flight that left at five o'clock that very evening for only sixty dollars more than my original ticket price.

"Do I want to leave that soon?" I said aloud to myself. I glanced at the clock on the top corner of the computer screen. If I left my house by two, I should be able to return the rental car and make it through airport security with time to spare.

I tapped my fingernail on the edge of the computer and contemplated my options. The chakra bracelet Sloan had bought for me was around my wrist and clicked against the side of the computer as I tapped. Staring at it, images of our time together washed over me, provoking another lone tear to slide down my cheek. Then there was this ache. It was an ache I knew I'd feel but never imagined it would be this bad. I hadn't even left yet, but I already missed Sloan so much.

Moving the mouse, I clicked 'modify booking' before giving myself another moment to reconsider. After I thought more about it, I hastily brushed my tears away. No good would come from them now. I'd made my decision.

# Chapter Twenty-Six

*Sloan*

I didn't know what compelled me to do it, but two hours after leaving Kallie's house, I found myself pulling through the tall black wrought-iron gates of Oakwood Hills Cemetery. I drove through the narrow winding roads toward the back, heading to the gravesite I'd visited only once before.

When I arrived at my destination, I turned off the car engine and stepped out into the bright sunlight. A sense of serenity surrounded me as I looked around. A few groundskeepers milled about, and I could see a family of mourners off in the distance as they bid a final farewell to their loved one. Everyone was quiet, respecting this place of soulful reflection with calm tranquility.

Walking over the gravel path, I passed gravestone after gravestone. Some had sunk into the soil, their engraved words weathered over time. Others boasted fresh flowers or small American flags, symbols of the connection people had with those who had passed on.

Coming to the end of the path, I moved across the grass and stopped to read a small headstone engraved with the name of the person I'd spent a year trying not to think about.

Charlotte Marie Atwood
September 7, 1962 – March 30, 2020

"Hi, Mom," I said to the stone slab, a symbol of the end to her life's story. I kneeled and pressed my hand over her name.

I sat there for a long while, not sure what else I should say as memories of my childhood flashed before my eyes. After my father's passing, it was almost as if my mother felt she had to make up for what I'd lost—for what we'd lost. My father had left behind a sizable chunk of change, and she had invested wisely. She'd budgeted, and we'd lived modestly, allowing her to devote her time solely to me as a single stay-at-home mom.

I could still hear her laughter on Christmas morning. It had been her favorite holiday, and she always went over the top with presents. Her eyes would light up with delight as I opened my gifts, more excited to see my pleasure than to experience her own. I also remembered her disappointment when I'd acted out, and she would have to tan my hide. Looking back, I wasn't sure who suffered more from my punishments—me or her.

I recalled her encouraging words as she taught me how to ride a bike. Those words weren't all so different from when I'd decided I wanted to race just like my father had. And when I became of age and entered the racing circuit, she was there every step of the way. She never missed a race and rarely missed a practice, her unwavering support making me believe I could be anything I wanted to be.

"Take it to the moon, my boy! Don't let the sky be your limit!" she would say.

However, the thing I remembered most about growing up was hearing her tears late into the night. She had missed my father something fierce. He had been her soulmate, her world—her checkered flag. By day, she had tried to hide her sadness from me, her sole focus being a single mother doing her best to raise a man. She had never known how many nights I had lain awake listening to her cry through the thin walls of our apartment.

I buried my face in my hands, shocked to discover wetness on my cheeks. I blinked back the tears, trying to remember the last time I'd cried—like actually fucking cried. Sure, I had cried when my dad died but I hadn't cried when I learned about my mother's death. I'd been too angry. The last time I shed real tears had to have been back when I was about ten years old and fell off the swing set and skinned my knee.

My mother had been there for that too.

Keeping my face in my hands, I let the tears fall freely, realizing that I'd been too hard on her.

"I understand now, Mom. Really, I do. I know why you couldn't stay, and I forgive you. You showed me what it means to love, and I know you loved Dad with your whole heart. After he was gone, you gave all that love to me, and when you thought I wouldn't make it…" I trailed off, taking a moment to wipe my tear-stained cheeks. I glanced over to my left to where my father's headstone sat alongside my mother's. "I met someone, Mom. I think you would like her. Her name is Kallie, and she's amazing. Because of her, I now know what it means not to be able to live without somebody. It might sound crazy, but I can't imagine my life without her. This girl is the real deal. I want forever with her. The problem is, I screwed up, and now I don't know if she'll have me."

Rising to my feet, I scanned the row of headstones. Fresh cut flowers adorned most of them, but my father's and mother's graves were bare. A pang of guilt tore at my heart, and I made a silent promise to do better. My mother didn't deserve to be among the forgotten—she deserved to be remembered for the strong woman I knew she had been. For too many years, she'd played the part of Wonder Woman, giving all of herself and never asking for anything in return. She had coped with loss and balanced the strains of being a single parent without complaint. She was stronger than she'd realized. My only regret was not telling her that before it was too late—before she thought she couldn't endure the burden of her sorrows any longer.

I began to wonder if she would approve of me trying to race again. She knew how important racing was to me, and I had to believe she had been looking down on me as I worked to overcome the injuries from my crash. Hard work and perseverance were how I got through it—all lessons I'd learned from her.

But this was different.

The pain in my hip had steadily gotten worse with each passing day, and the recovery time was becoming longer. Instead of spending an hour alternating cold and heat, the pain remedy was now continuing well after the sun had gone down. I was beginning to think that what I was doing now had nothing to do with perseverance but more with foolish determination to see it through. After all the agony I went through during my recovery, the last thing I wanted to do was cause more damage.

I thought back to what Kallie had said to me about my attempt to push through the current pain.

*"I just hope you don't kill yourself in the process."*

I knew her words were rhetorical, but they gave me a reason to pause. I couldn't help but think that was exactly what I was doing. Causing myself permanent damage was not the way to honor my mother's memory. She would never approve of that—just like she would never approve of me putting my love for racing ahead of my love for Kallie.

I looked over at my father's grave once more, realizing why I'd come to the cemetery in the first place. Before I could move forward, I needed my parents' approval.

"I'm sorry, Dad. I have to give it up. It's not just about my hip injury—it's about what would happen to Kallie if I got hurt again. She's too important to me. She deserves a whole man, not a broken one. If that means I have to give up racing and find a new path, so be it. I can honestly say, though, I don't think I'll ever be far from the track. I just can't be behind the wheel anymore. I don't know... What do you think about me consulting? Or maybe I could try my hand at being a crew chief?"

As if he were sending me a message from the heavens, the California sycamore trees began to sway. The slight breeze seemed to inject a sense of balance, giving me the courage I needed to embark on a new path.

Smiling to myself, I took a few steps to my father's headstone and placed my hand on the top. Giving it a gentle pat, I whispered, "Thanks, Dad. I'll take the wheel from here."

# Chapter Twenty-Seven

*Sloan*

Just after three o'clock, I returned to Kallie's house. I'd stopped at a local florist along the way and tried to do my best to duplicate the same arrangement of flowers I'd sent her a couple of months back—sunflowers mixed with vibrant roses, lilies, and snapdragons—rainbow colors for my Rainbow Brite.

Flowers in hand, I walked up to her front door and raised my fist to knock. However, I paused right before my knuckles connected with the door. The suitcases in the front hall were gone. Spinning around, I looked at the driveway. Her car was gone too.

Panic gripped my chest as I tried to remember when she said she would be flying home. I was sure she'd said the day after tomorrow. Instinctively, I pulled my cell from my pocket and tapped Kallie's name in my contact list, but my call was immediately sent to voicemail.

"Shit!" hissed.

I was pacing back and forth on the front walkway, trying to decide my next course of action, when a white van pulled into the driveaway. The words Tidy Maids were painted across the side in bright blue lettering. My brow furrowed in confusion when the female driver exited the vehicle and slid open the side door to allow two other women to file out.

"Can I help you?" I asked.

The driver looked up in surprise as if seeing me for the first time.

"Oh! I'm sorry, sir. We were told nobody would be home. We're here to clean."

"Obviously," I said, gesturing to the logo on the van. "But why are you here to clean?"

She looked past me at the house with a confused expression, then looked down at a notebook she was holding.

"This is the right address, right? Number eighty-seven?" she asked.

"Yes, that's the right house number," I confirmed. "Who told you nobody would be home?"

"It was the nice lady who contacted us from Quinn & Wilkshire. She said a tenant recently vacated the property, and it needed to be cleaned top to bottom. She gave us a code to get in through the side door. Is that okay?"

*Vacated the property? Had Kallie left the house for good? Did she go to a hotel?*

My eyes widened, suddenly realizing how I might be able to find out where Kallie was.

"I'm sure everything is fine. You can go on ahead and do what you need to do. Thank you for your help," I said and rushed past the cleaning crew toward my car. Once inside, I pulled up my email on my phone and searched for the contract from Quinn & Wilkshire that Milo had forwarded to me three months earlier. After locating the PDF file, I found the logo, address, and telephone number for the PR firm typed across the top. Dialing the phone number, I impatiently tapped my thumb on the steering wheel as I waited for someone to pick up. After the third ring, a pleasant voice greeted me.

"Thank you for calling Quinn & Wilkshire. How may I direct your call?" she asked.

"Hello. My name is Sloan Atwood. I'm trying to reach Kalliope Benton Riley."

"I'm sorry, Mr. Atwood. Ms. Riley is currently out of the office on assignment. Would you like her voicemail?"

"I know she's on an assignment—I *am* the assignment. Unfortunately, I'm unable to get in touch with her at the moment."

"Oh, I see. Please hold for one moment." It seemed like I'd caught her off guard, so I waited patiently and listened to what sounded like clicking on a keyboard. A moment later, she returned. "Mr. Fitzgerald Quinn, the owner and senior partner, is available to speak with you. If you'd like, I can put you through to him."

*Kallie's father. Fuck.*

I had hoped to get some low-level employee to tell me where Kallie was. I didn't plan on having to talk to her father of all people. He didn't know me from Adam, and I didn't know how to explain what I wanted without sounding like a psychopath.

"That's fine. Put me through," I told the receptionist. I was placed on hold for only a few seconds before Kallie's father's voice came through the line.

"Mr. Atwood. Fitz Quinn here. How can I help you?"

"Hello, Mr. Quinn," I replied as respectfully as possible, then dove right in. No sense in beating around the bush. "I'm actually trying to locate Kallie. Have you heard from her by any chance?"

"Kallie? Um, yes. I'd heard there was a little problem regarding your compatibility. I can assure you, Mr. Atwood. My partner, Devon, and I are on it. We'll have a replacement agent out to you within a few days."

"No, sir. I don't want a replacement. I'm perfectly fine with Kallie representing me. That's why I'm trying to reach her. I need to tell her that I want her to stay," I said, hoping beyond hope that I was able to keep any signs of pleading out of my voice.

"I'm not sure what the confusion is. I haven't spoken to Kallie directly. I just received a message stating that she would be on a plane to return today. I believe her flight leaves at five."

A knot formed in my throat, so big I could barely breathe around it. She was really going to leave. She was giving up on me—on *us*. I couldn't let that happen. Pulling the phone away from my ear, I looked at the time. It was going on three-thirty. The chances of me getting to her before the plane took off were slim to none, but I had to try.

"Thank you, Mr. Quinn. That's all I needed to know. And sir?"

"Yes?"

"I just wanted to say that you have one spectacular daughter."

Without another word, I ended the call, threw the car in reverse, and backed out of the driveway.

I raced through the streets to the nearest on-ramp for the I-405, then headed south toward the Los Angeles International Airport. Traffic wasn't too terribly bad for once. The fifteen-minute drive only ended up being thirty-five minutes. It could have been much worse, but I was still running out of time. I glanced at the clock on the dash as I pulled into a parking space in the short-term parking lot at the airport. It was after four. Most likely, Kallie's plane would begin boarding within the next thirty minutes.

Hurrying out of the car, I hit the button on the key fob to lock the doors. As I ran across the lot toward the airport entrance, I realized I'd forgotten to grab the flowers I had purchased for Kallie but didn't want to waste time going back for them. Getting to her was more important right now.

I couldn't get past security without a plane ticket, so once inside, I went straight to the ticket counter. The line was four people deep, leaving me no choice but to wait. The seconds and minutes ticked by painfully slowly as I stared at the clock on the wall behind the counter.

It reminded me of the old saying about a watched pot that would never boil. I shoved an impatient hand through my hair, wishing the line would move faster.

"Can I help you, sir?" said the attendant behind the counter when it was finally my turn. I glanced at her red and blue name tag with the heart logo. Her name was Judy, and she'd been with the airline company for sixteen years.

"Hello, Judy. I need to get on the next flight to Washington D.C."

"You don't have a ticket?"

"No."

"Let me see what we have available," she said and began typing on her keyboard. "It looks like there are still a few seats available on the five o'clock flight to Reagan National Airport, but I'm not sure if you'll make it to the gate in time. I can get you on the seven-ten flight tomorrow morn—"

"I'll take today's five o'clock flight. I'll run to the gate if I have to."

"Um, okay. Well, I'll need to see some identification," she eventually said. She eyed me strangely, almost as if she were sizing me up, while I pulled my license from my wallet. She took it from me, scrutinizing it carefully. I tapped an impatient foot, wanting to scream that I wasn't on the terrorist watch list. I was simply a man who needed to get to his girl.

"Oh my gosh! You're Sloan Atwood—as in *the* Sloan Atwood!" Judy said.

*Dammit! I don't have time for this.*

"That's me," I responded with a shrug, hoping the people standing nearby hadn't heard her.

"My husband is a huge fan of yours—well, he was. What happened to you was terrible," she prattled on. "We were all praying for you after your accident. I'm glad to see you looking so well."

"I appreciate that," I replied, desperately trying to keep the impatience out of my voice. "Look, I know I seem like I'm in a hurry—I am. You see, the woman who I'm supposed to spend my life with is getting on that plane. I need to get to her."

Her head snapped back, and her eyes were alight with excitement.

"Oh! You said you're supposed to spend your life with her—are you proposing to her here at the airport?" she asked, seeming giddy at the prospect. At this point, I would tell her anything she wanted to hear if it meant she would move faster.

"Yes, ma'am. That's the plan."

"Well, then we'll just have to make sure you make it to the gate in time." Without another word, Judy moved at lightning speed. In a matter of minutes, she began printing my boarding passes. As we waited for my required documents and receipt to spit out from the archaic dot matrix printing machine, she smiled and said, "I'll call the gate to let them know you're coming and ask them to give you a few extra minutes."

"You don't have to do that," I told her, but she waved me off and picked up the phone next to the computer. A few seconds later, she spoke into the receiver.

"Hi, Celia. This is Judy from ticketing. I just wanted to let you know that you'll have a passenger arriving a few minutes late to the gate. It's Sloan Atwood. I'm sure you've heard of him. He's the race car driver who had that awful accident last year." She paused, nodding her head rapidly, while the person on the other end of the line spoke. "Oh, perfect! That works out then, doesn't it? He'll be there shortly. Oh, and I should tell you, he's going to propose to someone when he gets there! Can you believe it?"

She was practically squealing like a schoolgirl.

*Shit.*

The tickets finished printing, and she handed them over to me.

"Thank you," I said, eager to get away from the woman who had nothing but hearts in her eyes.

"Don't worry about rushing. The flight is delayed slightly due to a hazmat issue, so you should make it to the gate in plenty of time."

Not bothering to ask more specifics about the hazmat delay, I thanked her again and rushed to security, where I had to wait in yet another line. As I slowly made my way through the snaking rows of retractable belt stanchions, I had a minute to absorb what had just happened at the ticket counter and found myself chuckling over the irony.

*Married? Right.*

However, the more I toyed with the idea of marrying Kallie, the better it sounded. Hadn't I just been thinking about spending forever with her? That's what marriage meant after all. Perhaps this was fate's way of giving me a nudge. The rational part of me erred on the side of caution. A lifetime was a long time. There were so many things Kallie and I had yet to learn about each other. Still, despite the unknowns, a lifetime with her felt right—like it was just the way things were meant to be.

After I got through security, I followed the signs to my assigned gate number. When I reached it, I didn't even have to search for Kallie. Just like the first day I saw her on the beach, she stood out among the ordinary, and I felt her gravity pulling me like an invisible magnet.

Slowly, I put one foot in front of the other and studied her. Her golden hair was pulled back into a ponytail, the red and blue extensions still in place. She was looking down at a magazine on her lap, her beautiful face focused on whatever text she was reading. My breath caught in my throat. The idea that I might have lost her—that I might lose her still—caused all the air to steal from my lungs.

As if she felt the pull, too, she slowly turned to face me. I couldn't tell if she was sad or happy to see me. She shook her head as if to stop me from coming any further, but I didn't stop walking until I reached the end of the row of chairs on which she sat. Only then did I pause. She stared at me with stormy green eyes for a long while, her expression distant and untouchable, as if she were trying to hide the feelings she was trying to sort out.

Emotion welled up inside me, erupting from a place I didn't know existed. My words—everything I'd practiced in my head during the drive to the airport—got caught in my throat as I stared at her. Instead of trying to say everything I was feeling, I said the only thing that seemed to matter.

"I love you, Kallie. Please don't go."

# Chapter Twenty-Eight

*Kallie*

I gasped. It felt like the ground had quite literally fallen out from beneath my feet. I couldn't speak. A shiver raced down my spine, and energy crashed through the air like a thunderbolt. I knew I had to say something one way or the other, but fear of getting the words wrong rendered me speechless.

Sloan stood only a few feet away from me, his eyes searching mine. His blue gaze was piercing and devastating, just as it was on the day we first met. He was a force of nature, and he was here—for me. Something profound twisted in my heart. My love for him was bigger than anything else I'd ever felt. It was intense and potent—just like he was. As I stared into his expressive eyes, I wanted nothing more than to leap into his arms. However, before I did that, I had to be sure his declaration of love wasn't just in response to mine.

"Sloan, what are you doing here?" I asked once I could find my voice.

"I'm here because I couldn't handle the thought of you leaving."

"But you should be on your way to San Antonio."

Moving over to sit in the empty seat beside me, he took my hand.

"I'm not going to San Antonio, Kallie."

I had to fight every bone in my body to stop myself from reaching up to touch his face. Whenever he was around, I was unable to resist being close to him. But after the emotional and physical strain of the past few weeks, I hesitated. Although he was right next to me, he seemed so far out of reach.

"What do you mean you aren't going?"

"I mean, I quit. I'm giving up racing. You were right—the risk to my body is too great. But it's more than that. It's about you, too. I feel like every turn I've made since before my accident has sent me the wrong direction on a one-way road. I kept trying to dodge the oncoming traffic instead of going the way everyone else was. But then you came along, and you made me realize there was more than one way to travel. I—"

Whatever else he was about to say was interrupted by a loud voice coming over the gate's intercom system.

"Ladies and gentlemen, we apologize for the delay. The captain just informed us that we should be able to begin boarding in about fifteen minutes. As a reminder, those with disabilities and people with small children will be allowed to board first."

"It's a good thing for the flight delay," Sloan said. "I wouldn't have made it here in time if not for that. The lady at the ticket counter said it was a hazmat issue. I wonder what that's all about."

"Poop on the tarmac," I replied, only to receive the most bewildered expression I'd ever seen on Sloan's face.

"I'm sorry?"

"Apparently, when the service guys were emptying the waste tanks from the previous flight, the hose outside the plane broke. So, that means poop on the tarmac—literally. They had to call hazmat to clean it up before we could board. Shit happens, you know?" I said with an ironic smile to try and lighten the somber mood. I felt uncharacteristically nervous because I didn't know why Sloan was here. I wanted to know, yet I didn't at the same time.

Sloan returned my smile, but it didn't quite meet his eyes. He looked out through the floor-to-ceiling glass windows at the plane. When he spoke, his voice was quiet, and I had to strain to hear him.

"You were really going to leave."

Overcome with sadness, I dropped my head and pulled my hand from his.

"Yes. And I still am, Sloan. I just think it's for the best. I can't come between you and racing. I know how much you love it. It would be wrong for me to make you choose. Please don't quit because of me."

"That's just it—I *am* quitting because of you, but it's not because of anything you did or said. It's because of how I feel about you. Kallie, I—" Once again, his words were cut off when his cellphone began to ring. Reaching around to pull it from his back pocket, he glanced at the screen and frowned. "Shit. It's Milo. Kallie, I'm sorry. I need to answer this."

I pursed my lips, trying to hide my irritation over Milo's interruption. I was on pins and needles. I wanted to finish hearing what Sloan had to say. However, this just further proved why I needed to leave—racing would always come first.

"It's fine. Do what you need to do," I waved off as casually as I could to mask the sting.

"Just give me two minutes. I have to do something I should've done a long time ago." Turning back to his phone, he slid his finger across the screen and brought the phone to his ear. "This is Atwood."

"Where the hell are you? You were supposed to leave hours ago," Milo barked. Despite the busy airport, I could hear him loud and clear. He was yelling, and he sounded furious.

"I'm not going to San Antonio, Milo," Sloan told him.

"What do you mean you're not going? The whole crew is packed and waiting—"

"I quit. I'm sorry it's so last minute, but it is what it is. I'll call Tyler and explain."

I stared at Sloan with incredulity. He truly was going to quit. It wasn't just a line he was giving to appease me. Still, guilt clawed at my chest. I had meant what I said—I didn't want him to give up what he loved on account of me.

"Explain? You'll have to do more than explain! The reps at Kapton are going to lose their goddamn minds!" I heard Milo booming, forcing Sloan to pull the phone slightly away from his ear. "Do you know how much money has gone into this? I haven't been busting my ass to get you here for nothing. Do you think I work for free?"

"Well, it looks like you did this time. But don't worry about your precious money. If you have anything out of pocket, I'll reimburse you. I would say I'm sorry that you'll miss your payout for this race, but I'm not. There will be others. I just won't be the driver. You're fired, Milo."

"You can't fire me!"

"I just did," Sloan stated matter-of-factly.

"Does this have anything to do with the blonde bitch?"

"Man, you really are a dick. Don't call me again. And if you even think about smearing my name or Kallie's, I'll have to inform the International Racing Association about the little baggie of pills you gave me. I don't think they'll look favorably on an agent handing out illegally-obtained oxy like it's candy."

"You wouldn't dare. Nobody would believe you, and it would be your word against mine."

"You sure about that? Your fingerprints are all over the bag," Sloan pointed out, then angled his head to toss me a wink. "Your clients will start dropping like flies once word gets out."

"Why, you son of a—"

"Goodbye, Milo." Sloan ended the call with a satisfied smirk and turned back to me. "God, that felt good. I should have cut him loose years ago. He's such an asshole."

"You know, my fingerprints are on the bag, too," I reminded him.

"I know, but Milo doesn't know that," he said with a shrug before giving me a sexy, lopsided grin. "So, where were we?"

"You were talking about giving up racing, and I said I didn't want you to do it for the wrong reasons."

"Kallie, you aren't the wrong reason."

"What about Tyler? I mean, there's so much at stake. If you want to pull out of racing in the MILL because of your hip, that's one thing. But I can't be the reason Tyler's wife doesn't get the treatment she needs."

"I've thought about that. A while back, I briefly spoke to Cooper about doing a fundraiser. I know Rochele was looking into it, but I don't know how far she got. The more I think about doing a benefit, the more I think we'd be able to pull in a ton of cash if we got all of the top drivers involved—maybe do a silent auction or something like that. Serious fans would pay a mint for a signed helmet worn during a prominent race. We might even be able to raise more money than I'd be able to win in the MILL. I won't just leave Tyler high and dry. I know he was counting on me, and I won't let him down."

"That might solve the problem with Tyler, but that still leaves one huge unanswered question. Are you really going to be able to give up racing for good? You're forgetting that I saw you on the track. The way your spirit came alive was like magic—like seeing a caged bird set free to fly. What are you going to do without it?"

"I thought about that, too," he told me and then paused. A faraway look spread across his face for a moment before he focused on me once more. "I went to the cemetery after I left your house earlier today."

"The cemetery?" I asked with surprise.

"Yeah… I felt the need to visit my parents' gravesites. I didn't realize how much soul-searching one can do in a place like that. If I did, I might have gone there long before today."

"What prompted you to go there?"

"I needed to make amends. I've finally come to understand why my mom did what she did. She really loved my father. After he was gone, she gave all that love to me. When she thought she would lose me too, it was just too much for her to handle. I know that with certainty now. I never really comprehended the depths of that love until I met you. When I thought I might lose you, I finally understood what it meant to feel like I couldn't live without somebody. Everything just seemed to make sense after that, and I realized I'd been too hard on my mom."

"Sloan, I—"

"Wait. Let me finish," he said and held up a hand to silence me. "I also talked to her and my dad about life without racing. Neither of them would have approved of what I was doing. You were right about that, too—I was killing myself. I'd blurred the line between perseverance and foolishness. So, I asked my dad what he thought about me possibly getting into consulting or coaching, and the strangest thing happened. Your universe, the one you love to talk about, spoke to me. I *can* go on without racing. I thought about working with Wings Halfway House like you suggested, possibly starting my own racing school, looking for a job as a crew chief, and everything else in between—but I don't want to do any of those things if you aren't with me."

My heart began pounding rapidly. I loved Sloan, but I was terrified to hope. I studied his face, desperately trying to read his expression. I couldn't tell if he was happy, sad, or relieved to have shared all of that with me.

"What are you trying to say, Sloan?"

"I'm saying you made me a believer in romance—and I believe in us. It isn't racing I need. It's you and only you."

I squeezed my eyes closed, trying to sort the multiple emotions that ravaged my thoughts. When I opened them again, I noticed a bunch of people with their focus trained on Sloan and me.

"Why does it seem like everyone is staring at us?"

Sloan's gaze scanned the small crowd waiting at the gate.

"I don't think everyone is, but I'm pretty sure the airline employees behind the desk are. There's kind of a funny story behind that."

I raised my eyebrows.

"Oh?"

He grinned sheepishly and shrugged.

"Yeah… So, when I was rushing to get a plane ticket so I could catch you in time, the woman who was taking care of me was moving at a snail's pace. I tried to hurry her along by telling her I needed to get to the woman I wanted to spend my life with. She got all excited and sort of assumed that meant I was going to propose."

My eyes widened in surprise.

"Sort of assumed? And you didn't correct her?"

"As I said, she was moving too slow, and I had to speed her along. How was I supposed to know she was going to call the gate and tell them I was going to propose to you?"

"Wait, are you telling me the reason people are staring is that they're waiting for a marriage proposal?"

"Maybe. What do you say, Rainbow Brite? Want to get hitched?"

I would have laughed at the idea, but there was nothing humorous about his expression.

"You're serious right now?"

"I can be if you want me to be. But I will say, I thought if I were going to propose to you, it would be someplace better. We're in an airport, for crying out loud—I can do better than this. I just want you to know how serious I am about you—about us. I love you so damn much it hurts. I was a fool not to realize it before today," he admitted, his voice raw with emotion. "I know you have a life in D.C., and I'm not asking you to give that up. The reality is, there's nothing for me here. I can pack up and go wherever you are if that's what it takes. Did you really mean what you said? Do you love me?"

"I meant every word. I do love you, Sloan—but I wasn't thinking marriage. It was more like… I don't know. Take me slow dancing on the beach, make love to me under the stars, and discover each other over time. I never want to get divorced, and I don't think this sort of thing should be rushed."

"I didn't come here to propose to you, so don't feel rushed. But once I started thinking about it, I couldn't shake the feeling that it just seemed right," he explained. "I didn't plan on falling in love with you, just as I don't think you planned on falling for me. But once we met, the gravitational pull was undeniable. I've never felt anything like it before. What we have is rare and beautiful."

He sat a foot away from me, his eyes searching mine. I understood what he was saying. I felt the same way. As I processed the emotion swirling in his endless blues, I saw something in our future that would go on forever. It was all I could do not to reach into my carry-on bag and pull out my tarot deck. Official proposal or not, I just needed a sign—anything that would allow me to leap into his arms and tell him I would be his partner in life forever.

"Now boarding Group C," said a woman's voice through the overhead speaker.

"That's me," I said, wishing I could buy more time.

"It's me too."

I looked around. There was only a smattering of people nearby since two-thirds of the passengers were already on the plane, but it seemed as if every single person in the immediate area had their eyes trained on Sloan and me.

"Should we board?" I asked, more to myself than to him. I was so flustered, and I felt as if every thought in my head was given a voice before I could think it through. "I mean, you could come home with me and meet my parents. Maybe we could talk more about his then—when we don't have so many people looking at us."

I watched him curiously as he shifted from his seat to kneel on the floor in front of me. I didn't panic because he wasn't on one knee. He just seemed to want to be in my direct line of sight so he could have my undivided attention. He reached up and took my chin in between his fingers.

"Kallie?" The questioning tone of his voice was low and husky. Goosebumps pebbled over my skin.

"Yes?" I whispered.

"I know we have a lot to learn about each other. I have no doubt that I want to marry you one day. You're my checkered flag, baby. I want to wake up to rainbow hair spread across the pillow next to me every single damn day for the rest of my life—but I also don't want to skip the steps in between. I want to meet your family and see your home in D.C. I want to learn your favorite songs, favorite foods, and maybe even try Tofurky one day—no promises on that, though," he added with a wink before turning serious again. "But I do promise to give you the sun, the moon, and every one of the millions of stars in the sky. Will you give me the chance to make good on that promise?"

Tears began to well hot in my eyes and threatened to fall. He could be all mine if I allowed it. He could be mine forever. I reached up to trace the lines of his face with my finger, moving over his strong jaw and chiseled cheekbones, pausing only to cup the side of his head. The potent way he was looking at me made my words catch in my throat, and that's when I saw it—my Don Lockwood. Sloan gazed at me just like Don Lockwood had beheld Kathy Seldon in *Singin' In The Rain.* Maybe life could be like it was in the movies, after all. There was no doubt I wanted to spend my life with him—but he was right about the steps in between, and I didn't want to miss a single one.

"Sloan, I don't need you to promise me the moon and the stars—I just want you to promise to watch them with me. Always."

"What do you say we start by jumping on that plane? I bet the sunset will be beautiful above the clouds."

I grinned. "I think that's the perfect place to start."

Sloan got to his feet, gripped the sides of my shoulders, and pulled me up so he could wrap his strong arms tight around me. He rained kisses on my cheeks, forehead, and nose. Tears leaked down my face as I fiercely clung to him. My heart wanted to explode with love. The past three months had been a complete whirlwind, with our relationship moving at breakneck speed. We'd been living in the fast lane, and I didn't know how we'd gotten to this point. All I knew was that I was looking forward to finally slowing down to enjoy the road ahead.

The gypsy had been wrong when she said my eagerness to express my emotions would be my downfall. Yes, I was a Gemini, but she failed to predict I would partner with a Taurus. While the two paired together might look like total opposites at first, Geminis and Tauruses were a dynamic match when the planets aligned in their favor—and that was precisely what had happened. What I shared with Sloan was more than just a fierce physical attraction. We had so much to offer one another as long as we never stopped believing in *us*.

I pulled back to share my thoughts with Sloan, but paused when I heard clapping coming from somewhere behind me. Blinking my tears away, I slowly turned my head to see three airline employees looking at us with wide smiles. When the other bystanders turned to see what they were clapping at, Sloan shrugged sheepishly.

"Should we tell them we aren't really engaged?" he whispered.

"Nah. No need to tell them. I have a feeling we will be soon enough."

Sloan beamed, then stepped back to pick up my carry-on bag. Taking my hand, he looked down at me with eyes brighter than the clearest blue sky.

"Come on, Rainbow Brite. We've got a sunset to watch."

THE END

## MUSIC PLAYLIST

**Thank you to the musical talents who influenced and inspired *Endurance*. Their creativity helped me bring this story to life.**

"Leaving on a Jetplane" by Peter, Paul & Mary
"Ventura Highway" by America
"Marry Me" by Train
"Luminous" by Alice & the Glass Lake
"I Want You to Want Me" by Cheap Trick
"Don't Stop Believin'" by Journey
"The Distance" by Cake
"Boys of Summer" by The Ataris
"Fade Into You" by Mazzy Star
"Highway to Hell" by AC/DC
"Exodus" by Ruelle
"21 Guns" by Green Day
"Last One to Know" by Leah Noble
"Drive" by Halsey

LISTEN ON SPOTIFY

**SUBSCRIBE TO DAKOTA'S NEWSLETTER!**

This email goes out twice a month (sometimes less). It's packed with new content, sales on signed paperbacks, bookish goodies from the Angel Shop, and giveaways. Don't miss out!

Your email address is valued and you will NEVER be spammed. Subscribe here: https://dakotawillink.com/subscribe

**BOOKS & BOXED WINE CONFESSIONS**

Want fun stuff and sneak peek excerpts?
Join Books & Boxed Wine Confessions and get the inside scoop! Fans in this interactive reader Facebook group are the first to know the latest news!

Join here: https://www.facebook.com/groups/1635080436793794

**OFFICIAL WEBSITE**

www.dakotawillink.com

## ABOUT THE AUTHOR

Dakota Willink is an award-winning *USA Today* Bestselling Author from New York. She loves writing about damaged heroes who fall in love with sassy and independent females. Her books are character-driven, emotional, and sexy, yet written with a flare that keeps them real. With a wide range of publications, Dakota's imagination is constantly spinning new ideas. Her work has been translated into five languages and she has sold over 1 million books worldwide.

Dakota often says she survived her first publishing with coffee and wine. She's an unabashed *Star Wars* fanatic and still dreams of getting her letter from Hogwarts one day. Her daily routines usually include rocking Lululemon yoga pants, putting on lipstick, and obsessing over Excel spreadsheets. Two spoiled Cavaliers are her furry writing companions who bring her regular smiles. She enjoys traveling with her husband and debating social and economic issues with her politically savvy Generation Z son and daughter.

Dakota's favorite book genres include contemporary or dark romance, political & psychological thrillers, and autobiographies.

## AWARDS, ACCOLADES, AND OTHER PROJECTS

*The Stone Saga* is Dakota's first published book series. It has been recognized for various awards and bestseller lists, including *USA Today* and the *Readers' Favorite* 2017 Gold Medal in Romance, and has since been translated into multiple languages internationally.

The *Fade Into You* series (formally known as the *Cadence* duet) was a finalist in the *HEAR Now Festival Independent Audiobook Awards*.

In addition, Dakota has written under the alternate pen name, Marie Christy. Under this name, she has written and published a children's book for charity titled, *And I Smile*.

Also writing as Marie Christy, she was a contributor to the Blunder Woman Productions project, *Nevertheless We Persisted: Me Too*, a 2019 *Audie Award Finalist* and *Earphones Awards Winner*. This project inspired

Dakota to write *The Sound of Silence*, a dark romantic suspense novel that tackles the realities of domestic abuse.

Dakota Willink is the founder of Dragonfly Ink Publishing, whose mission is to promote a common passion for reading by partnering with like-minded authors and industry professionals. Through this company, Dakota created the *Love & Lace Inkorporated* Magazine and the *Leave Me Breathless World*, hosted ALLURE Audiobook Con, and sponsored various charity anthologies.

Made in United States
Cleveland, OH
31 March 2026

35205103R00365